A TASTE OF FREEDOM

Liz Ryan

Hodder & Stoughton

Copyright © 1997 Liz Ryan

First published in Great Britain in 1997 by Hodder and Stoughton
A division of Hodder Headline PLC
Published simultaneously in trade paperback form by
Hodder and Stoughton
A Hodder and Stoughton Paperback

10 9 8 7 6 5 4 3 2 1

A CIP catalogue record for this book is
available from the British Library

ISBN 0 340 67210 2 (hardcover)
ISBN 0 340 71698 3 (trade paperback)

Typeset by Palimpsest Book Production Limited,
Polmont, Stirlingshire
Printed and bound in Great Britain by
Mackays of Chatham PLC, Chatham, Kent

Hodder and Stoughton
A division of Hodder Headline PLC
338 Euston Road
London NW1 3BH

A Taste of Freedom

Acknowledgements

How anyone puts up with a writer working on a novel is a mystery. Family life suffers, friends become either slaves or strangers while, at the end, only the author's work is visible. Yet many loyal people have somehow stuck with me through this third book, and I thank them all with the deepest and most affectionate gratitude.

At home, 'Mama' Jeannette kept body and soul together, with Greg and Ciara and lots of laughter even after we lost Rusty on Christmas Eve. Anne, Helen, Sarah, Gerry and Brendan-next-door were supportive to the point of inspirational, while in London my agent Richard and my editor Carolyn once again amazed me with their faith and vision.

At the *Evening Herald*, my editors David Robbins and Paul Drury worked miracles with juggled schedules, while Philip Nolan put every crisis into comic perspective. Without them, not a word could have been written.

Last but not least, this is for everyone in the family who continues to encourage and understand, as well as the many friends and colleagues who never cease to surprise and delight.

Part I

Chapter One

Mary Jameson stretched herself face down on the wooden slatted bench and announced her intention of dying. It wouldn't take long, she promised; in fact it was to be more or less immediate, so perhaps her dear friend Keeley Butler would be good enough to remain with her until the end?

'Of course I will,' Keeley agreed reassuringly, perching on the end of the bench, reaching foward to rub Mary's back comfortingly. Thus they remained in silence, for several minutes. Nothing happened.

And then Mary heaved herself up on one elbow with the most terrible groan, a groan that would not have discredited an Elizabethan traitor stretched on the rack, and dropped her head in the direction of the deck. Her mouth opened like a fissure in an ice floe; but nothing came out.

'Oh God,' she whimpered, 'I have nothing left to give.'

'Of course you have,' Keeley assured her cheerfully, and then bit her lip with a grin. Perhaps that was not the most encouraging thing to say to someone who had already given her all – certainly everything she had eaten in the past twenty-four hours, if not the past week. She tried to think of something more positive.

'I'll go and get you a Coke. Cold and fizzy. That might help.'

'Aaah.' Mary sighed and replaced her head limply across her forearm, her long hair dangling loose as if it were a damp towel she did not quite know what to do with.

Getting up, Keeley strode briskly in the direction of the ship's cafeteria. Well, perhaps 'strode' was too strong a word for it, but she staggered with purpose, picking her way callously between the other inert bodies on the deck and on the floor inside. The trip from Rosslare to Le Havre normally took twenty-one hours, she had been told, but they had aleady been at sea for nineteen and there was as yet no sight or mention of land. There were perhaps three or four hundred people on the ferry, and it surprised her that she was one of the half-dozen apparently impervious to the huge pitch and swell, the waves towering higher than Liberty Hall. Having never been on a boat of any description before in her life, she put it down to beginner's luck.

In the cafeteria she had no difficulty in getting a Coke. She simply picked up one of the abandoned ones which, because its owner had taken the precaution of securing it in one of the metal rings supplied for the purpose, had not spilled over. Just recently abandoned, it was still quite fresh, with little creamy bubbles on top. Picking it up she grasped it firmly to her chest and returned to her dying friend.

'Here we are. Nice and cold. Take a sip.'

Mary turned her head just far enough to get the red and white paper cup into her line of vision, shuddered, and whispered something inaudible. Kneeling on the deck, Keeley inclined her ear closer.

'What? What did you say?'

'I said I – I want to go home. I want to die at home. I want my mother.'

Keeley giggled. If Mary really was going to die, which she doubted, then she was going to have to do it without the ministrations of Mrs Jameson. Mary was a grown-up now, off to France with only the dubious Keeley Butler for chaperone. In fact that was one of the several purposes of this excursion, to get away from their families and prove they were grown women, well able to make their way in the world.

Never in a thousand years would Keeley have thought of going to France. People like her simply didn't. If they went anywhere, it was to the Canaries or the Costa Brava, where they spent two weeks consuming a couple of hundred tequila slammers while wearing stuffed donkeys on their heads. Then, roaring red and violently ill, they returned dutifully to their jobs in factories, canteens and hairdressing salons, and the women amongst them spent the next six months sobbing for Juan who, she suspected, did not sob for even six seconds.

But even this level of ambition had never occurred to Keeley. She was so grateful for the job she'd found two years ago, having left school at sixteen with virtually nothing to recommend her, that she clung to it like a lifebelt, rarely even taking off the time that was due to her. Officially she was entitled to a fortnight in the summer, but someone always seemed to be out sick or missing in action, giving her the chance to notch up a few stars in her copybook by agreeing to work overtime. It meant a bit more money, too, not to be sneezed at when you considered what hairdressing apprentices were paid. Keeley worked it out at exactly 21p for every head she washed.

That was before tax of course, which brought it down to 12p. On average she washed a hundred and thirty heads a week, which left her with £13.26p a week and not a lot of time for browsing through travel brochures. But on Friday nights she went to the pub to meet her friends, including Mary Jameson who had first started coming to The Lantern as a friend of someone else. One evening Mary had arrived with an armful of stuff about France and said she was thinking of going there in the summer, on a working holiday to pick grapes . . . would anyone be interested?

She'd hoped to gather a group, maybe four or six of them, but Keeley was the only one whose ears pricked up. Why, she didn't know, except that the idea of working outdoors appealed to her. It would be heaven to get away from the salon for a while, with its smell of shampoo and chemicals, the smoke that the women emitted like locomotives while they were getting their hair done. What the grapes were picked for, she didn't even know at the time; she assumed it must be for sale in shops and the connection with wine never entered her head. Everyone else said Mary was cracked – why would she want to go on a trip like that, *working* for God's sake? – but apparently Mary had accidentally seen a film called *Claire's Knee* and had got a bee into her bonnet about France.

Keeley had volunteered on the spur of the moment, idly raised her hand and said yes, she might be interested. And the plan had developed from there; every Saturday night thereafter the two of them met to pool and count their minuscule savings. Of course they'd be paid for picking the grapes, but not much; it was essential to bring a bit to get you on your feet, and then there was the ferry fare to be paid. So Keeley worked all the hours God sent, washing scalps vigorously while Mary worked in the supermarket delicatessen, filling carton after carton with vast quantities of coleslaw.

The trip would require a lot of time, a whole month, so

they'd both worked right through Christmas, weekends, bank holidays, amassing enough time credits. Mary had ended up three days short, but the deli manager said she could have them, provided she made them up when she came back.

And now here they were on their way at last, and here was Mary dying, after only nineteen hours. Keeley felt she wasn't showing much fighting spirit.

'Come on, Mary. The worst is over. We're nearly there.'

Mary raised her head just enough to look at her, about an inch.

'This is awful. I've never felt so sick in my life. I thought it would be . . . ooh.'

The boat pitched again and the head clunked back down on the forearm. Well, Keeley thought, I expected it to be different too. I thought this would be a proper sea voyage, that we'd sleep on deck under the stars, one of the other backpackers might even strum a guitar or something. Then we'd wake up to see the sun rising, the water all blue and glossy, the coast of France all foreign and romantic. How was I to know I'd end up nursing a corpse, skating on a pool of vomit?

Cathal Sullivan will laugh himself silly when he hears about it. He'll say he told us so and serves us right, all that stuff, no sympathy. I don't know what the hell Mary sees in him. He nearly scuppered this trip altogether, did everything he could to put her off. She'd have dropped out only I wouldn't let her, reminded her it was her idea and she couldn't let me down after getting me so excited about it. But I suppose we'll be having Cathal Sullivan for breakfast dinner and tea, she'll be talking about him the whole time and writing to him every day. She needs her head examined.

But Mary was pretty keen on him, for someone she'd only met three months ago. Fortunately the grape-picking plan was well under way by then, the tickets were paid for, it was too late to back out for the charms of the barman at The Lantern. Not just the barman, of course; the owner's son, who was merely serving his time before becoming manager and, some day, inheriting the entire gold mine lock, stock and barrel.

Cathal Sullivan was what you'd call a good catch. No great oil painting, but fit and muscular as might be expected of a GAA football player, with grey eyes, short dark hair and a father on the county council. His pub was in west Dublin, in a suburb where Mary lived in the 'better' half and Keeley lived in the other. But the Sullivan family lived forty minutes away from it in the midlands, where they owned a second pub in a small town – another gold mine, that Cathal would also inherit if he played his cards right. And Cathal seemed very good at playing his cards right. He'd persuaded his father to get him a second-hand car so he could commute to the pub in west Dublin, and he'd charmed Mary Jameson into his clutches like a bird off a bush. It had come as a shock to him to hear of her plans to go to France in September, and he had tried everything to put her off. But Keeley had fought back, and won. Thinking of it now, she was somewhat surprised; the pair were going very steady, with Sunday drives to Dun Laoghaire or the Phoenix Park in Cathal's Fiat, the mothers pleased as punch. Of course, Mary was very attractive, with those blue eyes and that chestnut hair swinging merrily in its ponytail, it was hardly much wonder she'd found a boyfriend. But Cathal Sullivan would not have been Keeley's first choice, even if he did have what everyone called a 'future'; she thought there was something a bit smug and bossy about him. Getting Mary out of his clutches, if only for a month, had privately pleased her. Maybe they'd meet some other lads and have some adventures for themselves, and Cathal would be put on the back burner for the duration. Well, she could hope so anyway, and do her best to make it happen, even if it was a long shot.

As Keeley sat there thinking, on the end of the bench where Mary remained prone, she became conscious that the heaving and rolling had stopped. Well, not entirely, but the waves were receding a bit, the water was becoming calmer. Mary's face was still the colour of skimmed milk, but that awful greenish tinge was going, the groaning and whimpering had subsided.

'Feeling better?'

'A – little bit.'

'Right then. Sit up and take a few deep breaths.'

Obediently Mary swung herself into a more or less vertical position, cautiously gripping the bench as she lifted her head and glanced nervously at the ocean.

'Oh, thank God, it's getting quieter.'

'Yes. I suppose when they've cleaned up the bathrooms there'll be a rush on them, but I think you should find one even if you have to queue, have a good wash and brush your teeth. We want to be first off as soon as we dock.'

'Do we?'

'Yes, of course! Every backpacker on the boat will be lining up when the cars start coming off, looking to hitch a lift.'

'Oh Christ, Keeley, I can't get into a car. I'd be sick as a parrot. Why don't we find a hostel in Le Havre and—'

'And waste a night's money? Miss a car that might be going all the way to Aix?'

Mary smiled wanly. Keeley certainly knew how to save money. Not in the sense of being tight-fisted, but in the sense of knowing all the short cuts. It had been her idea to hitch instead of taking trains – perfectly safe, she'd said airily, when there were two of them – and she'd even thought of taking provisions for the journey, sandwiches from the deli where, sure enough, Mary's boss had let her make them up for nothing. Her stomach heaved as she thought of them.

'We'd have to be right geniuses to spot the car that'd be going to Aix.'

'Well, you never know! Look, tell you what. You go get cleaned up and I'll have a bit of a scout around. Ask a few people . . . I'd say their resistance might be low at the moment.'

That was for sure. Everyone must be dying to get off this bloody boat, even if it meant taking two filthy hitchhikers with them.

'OK. I'll meet you back here in twenty minutes. Keep your eye on the rucksacks.' Feebly, Mary got to her feet and tottered away. God, the boat was destroyed, there was going to be a huge queue for the loos. If only they'd booked a cabin, they'd have a bathroom of their own, with even a shower in it . . . at this moment she would sell her grandmother for a shower. But she'd have to make do with a tap, a toothbrush and her face flannel.

It was half an hour before she returned to the bench on the deck, but when she got there Keeley was sitting on it grinning, brown eyes all eager and pleased.

'Look! You can see France! We're coming in at last!'

Mary looked, and thought she'd never been so glad to see anything in her life.

'And I've got us a lift! Only to Paris, but it's a start . . . a couple in a blue Renault, we're to meet them on B deck in an hour.'

'An *hour*?'

'Yes, apparently we're still quite a bit out, a little pilot boat has to come out to guide us in, but – oh, Mary, this is so exciting!

I'd never have gone anywhere if it weren't for you! Get out the map, there, and show me again where Aix is.'

Pulling it out of her rucksack, Mary unfolded it on her knees and they squinted at it together, sea-sickness forgotten as she was suddenly infected by Keeley's excitement. This really was a big adventure, and maybe the only one she would ever have: after all, married women didn't go picking grapes in Provence, and by this time next year she would be Mrs Cathal Sullivan.

It took seven lifts and two days to get down to Aix-en-Provence, but it was a fascinating, fabulous journey – apart, that was, from Keeley Butler's incredible lack of discretion.

Incurably chatty, indifferent to whether or not her audience spoke English, she told them every single thing there was to know about herself and her friend Mary Jameson, curled up on people's back seats with her spiky dark hair sticking out in all directions, her mouth going a mile a minute.

'Hi. I'm Keeley and this is my friend Mary. Thanks for picking us up. We're going to Aix – can you imagine, two young wans like us, from Dublin west, going to a place like that? It was all Mary's idea. She's from a better home, you see. I'm from Pearse Gardens, an awful kip, but she's from Pearse Avenue, much nicer altogether, they're semi-detached there, got nice gardens, no graffiti or anything. Mary works in a posh deli and I'm a hairdresser – well, not a stylist or anything, just an apprentice, but still, it's a job. My father hasn't got a job at all. Just sits in an armchair watching the telly, ever since the brewery changed from wooden kegs to aluminium and he was made redundant. Only ever gets up on Fridays, to go and collect his dole. I keep telling him there's loads of things he could do, carpentry, handyman stuff, get a ladder and wash people's windows for them, but he won't. Been unemployed for six years now, my oul fella. Of course Mam could work, if it wasn't for Poor Tony.'

Poor Tony?

'Yes, he's my brother. Had a motorbike, got a great job as a courier, he loved it, only he was a bit – well, he thought he was Mr Easy Rider, like in the movies. Clipped this woman's car one day and turned round to give her a mouthful . . . well, you should be looking where you're going, shouldn't you, on a motorbike? Only he wasn't, he was busy effing and blinding and next thing there was this lorry, a big one full of fridges and

washing machines being delivered to a warehouse, weighed a
ton. Poor Tony never stood a chance. But he's coming on, now.
He's in the rehab centre. They're teaching him to type, with a
stick he grips in his teeth. Mam goes to visit him every day.'

At this point there would be gasps and exclamations, nudges
from Mary, but Keeley always kept right on.

'In a wheelchair for life. Paralysed from the neck down.
Poor Tony. No compensation money or anything, because
the woman he was shouting at told the police it was all his
own fault, and there weren't any other witnesses. The lorry
driver came out all right though, not a scratch. My family's a
walking disaster – you can tell by my name, can't you? Keeley.
My Mam called me after some film star she saw on the telly.
Said she hoped I'd bring a bit of colour into her life. But I'd
rather have been called something ordinary. Like Mary. Now
there's a nice name, you can't go wrong with that. Mary's got
a boyfriend back in Dublin, Cathal, his oul fella owns two pubs
and he's got a car. Thinks the sun shines out of his ass, if you
ask me, but Mary's mad about him, aren't you, Mare?'

Scarlet, Mary would nod and mumble, point to some distracting object on the landscape, praying for delivery. She was
very fond of her friend, who was always so cheerful and good
for a laugh, but this was a bit thick.

'She asked Cathal to come with us, but he wouldn't. Too busy
working in pub numero uno, the one in Dublin, they couldn't
manage without him for five minutes. He didn't want us to go.
But Mary had seen this film called *Claire's Knee*, she didn't
know it was French at the time but then she really got into it,
followed all the subtitles, came out of the cinema singing the
praises of France. Then she found out about the grape-picking,
that you could just turn up and get work at harvest time, you
didn't need to speak French or anything. Just as well. We haven't
a word between us.'

Some of the drivers offered to teach them a few phrases at
this point, if only to get a word into the conversation; others
decided it was time to pull in for a cup of coffee.

'Oh, right – well, we haven't much money ourselves, we'll
just wait for you in the car, if that's all right?'

And so the hapless drivers usually ended up buying them
coffee, sometimes chips or sandwiches as well, at which Mary
stared mesmerised.

'Look at them, Keeley! They're the size of a baby's leg!

Totally different to Irish sandwiches . . . and what are these things?'

They were gherkins, served on the side. Neither girl had ever seen them before, nor tasted the things in the sandwiches – brie, salami, rillettes. Keeley pulled a face, but Mary was entranced.

'This is fantastic! Go on, Keeley, try another bite.'

'Do I have to?'

'Yes! We're in France, you have to try everything. Besides, this food is being bought for you, it's a present, you can't just say *yuk* and leave it.'

This was whispered in an aside, and the girls lived in terror that when the bill came the drivers would turn to them and demand a contribution, but nobody ever did. Apart from the price of two nights in hostels, the thousand-mile trip cost them nothing.

And then they were in Provence. They smelled it long before they reached it, a mixture of scents they were informed were pine, lavender, olives, herbs. And then the scenery, the landscape fading from green to mauve, from mauve to gold, stippled with peach, cherry, lemon, all kinds of trees growing in the rust-red earth.

'Oh, wow! This is gorgeous!'

Tumbling out of the last car, which let them off two miles short of the village of Rognes, they stood for a moment clutching their rucksacks, blinking in the white light, savouring the hot sun pouring down on their faces, arms, shoulders and legs. Neither of them had ever felt anything so intense in their lives, imagined that it could really get as hot as this. Already their teeshirts were damp with perspiration, their shorts stuck to the backs of their legs.

Around them stood several low stone houses, farmhouses they supposed, grey chunky buildings from whose direction they could hear a distant clinking noise.

'What's that?'

'I don't know . . . cows, d'you think? Or goats? I've heard they put bells on them down here.'

'Oh . . . and that other noise? The sort of whizzing?'

It was closer than the bells, and with a shriek they soon found out what it was – huge insects, like crickets, rubbing their wings together in the coarse yellow grass. Thousands of them, all rubbing furiously.

'M-Mary, let's get going. Let's find the vineyard.'

It had to be somewhere quite near, according to the map and the directions Mary had got from the youth travel agency that specialised in finding summer work for people their age. Hoisting their rucksacks on their backs, they set off, a little overwhelmed by the settling, gathering silence.

'It's very quiet.'

Keeley was half-nervous, half-pleased as she said it; where she lived it was never quiet, the street permanently filled with yelling kids, barking dogs, revving cars, slamming doors.

'Yes . . . listen to it, Keeley. It's quiet as a prayer. So still.'

'They must all be at lunch. They have long lunches in these parts, don't they?'

'Yes. It's probably the worst time of day to arrive. We won't get another lift, unless maybe on a tractor or something. But we're in the right place. Ten miles north of Aix, two miles south of Rognes . . . let's just keep walking and see what happens.'

'I'm thirsty. I wish we had some Coke or something.'

'No. They drink water here, haven't you noticed? Out of little plastic bottles. That's what we need.'

'Huh. As if anyone would pay good money for plain water. There must be something in it.'

'No, I don't think there is. They just seem to prefer it to sweet drinks.'

'Well, I'd settle for anything right now. How do you recognise a vineyard anyway, Mary? What does it look like?'

'I'm not sure. But I suppose we'll know it when we see it.'

Forty-five minutes later, dusty and sweltering, they were forced to concede that maybe they wouldn't. Maybe they'd better go to one of these farmhouses, actually, and ask before they got well and truly lost.

The woman who opened the door did not seem particularly pleased to see them, and then there was terrible difficulty with the language; neither party could understand one syllable the other was saying. It took a good ten minutes and much pantomime before she eventually stabbed her finger to the right.

'Chez Lazouin. Là-bas, à droite.'

Thanking her as best they could, they trudged back to the road, turned right and kept walking.

'Jaysus Mary, I'm short enough already, my legs will be worn to stumps.' Mary smiled, checking her stride so that her friend did not have to trot. Despite her big mouth Keeley was quite small, petite as the French would say, and the rucksacks were heavy. Of course they'd packed like a pair of idiots, bringing everything bar the kitchen sink just in case.

'There! There it is!'

And so it was, miles of dark green vines suddenly stretching away in front of them, dotted with bending, moving figures. The grape pickers: dozens and dozens of them, their arms going like pistons under the unmerciful sun. Working their way methodically along the straight, regular rows, they looked like soldier ants.

Suddenly nervous, they made their way up the long rough avenue in silence, eyeing each other as they caught sight of a large, grey stone house surrounded by geraniums, fingers of some creamy-green creeper twining their way up its walls. Compared to the other houses they had seen, it was extremely well-tended and, they suspected, very ritzy inside.

'Cripes. We're not going to be staying here, surely? I'd have brought my pearls.'

But no. It quickly emerged that they were not. A well-dressed woman came out and directed them, with some distaste, to a wide low barn well away from the house.

'God. You'd think we were knackers, the way she looked at us.'

'Well, I suppose we're not looking our glamorous best. Let's find someone and ask where we can have a shower.'

The barn was in fact a dormitory, filled with bunks and lockers, but there was nobody in it. As they looked around they heard a shout, and jumped.

A man stood in the doorway, beckoning to them.

'Eh! Vous deux! Venez ici!'

Hastily they followed his accusing finger out and round to what looked like a lean-to shed, but turned out to be an office inside. Taking a folder from the desk, the man frowned at them.

'English? American? Dutch?'

'Irish. We're looking for work. We were told you'd have some, if we just turned up, there wasn't any need to—'

'Yes. Two francs a kilo. Meals included. One day off a week. Take two bunks in the dormitory, leave your luggage in the lockers, I will give you a key. Follow me.'

They followed, were given keys from a numbered rack, led back to the dormitory barn and watched while they stowed their rucksacks in two empty lockers.

'Phew, that's a weight off! Now, we're dying for a shower. Where's the—?'

'Tonight, you may shower. Now, you start work.'

'*Now?*'

'Yes, of course. You are just in time after the lunchtime siesta.'

Without further ado the man thrust deep baskets into their hands, pointed in the direction of the vines and left them.

'Keeley, I'm dying.'

Under the brutal sun Keeley straightened slowly up, feeling her spine open out like an accordion, and turned to look at her friend.

Mary was crouched on the ground, gazing despairingly into her basket full of fat purple grapes, clipping shears clenched in her juice-stained hand. Heat blisters peppered her shoulders and neck, sweat ran down her temples, round the backs of her ears and dripped from her gypsy-hoop earrings. The mass of her hair was tied back in a blue scarf, but a cluster of wispy curls stuck to her forehead, also running with sweat which fell and clung onto her eyelashes, making her blink with a puzzled air.

'Jaysus Mary, you didn't die on the boat and you're not going to die here. Would you ever give over!'

'But this is a killer!'

'Mary, look around you. What do you see?'

Vaguely Mary looked, and saw a vast field full of workers like themselves: young Danes, Belgians, Americans, many nationalities as well as perhaps twenty or thirty local people. The foreigners were young but the locals were mixed in age, some of them fifty or even sixty, men and women, all crouching, snipping industriously.

'Yeah, well, they're used to it—'

'And we'll get used to it! We've only been here three days.'

Mentally Mary calculated. Another twenty-seven days to go. Christ almighty.

'So stop whingeing. I know it's hard, but we're having fun, aren't we? I am, anyway.'

Keeley smiled as she spoke, thinking of all the good things about this exhausting job. Nobody could say the work was anything other than a crucifixion, but they were out in the open air – lovely scented warm air at that, not a drop of rain – they were meeting all sorts of people, earning money and being housed and fed while they were at it. Each evening they gathered with the others round big wooden tables set up in front of the barn and were handed hot food they didn't have to cook for themselves – very odd food admittedly, but Mary liked it – and there were big jugs of wine for everyone to help themselves. She'd never have ordered wine in a month of Sundays back at The Lantern, but she'd tried it here since there was nothing else, and somehow it tasted good, out in the open shared with everyone, smelling of fruit and honey and sunshine. Despite the language problem they seemed to manage to talk to lots of people, and slept a deep sleep that filled her, Keeley Butler, with the most robust sense of health she'd ever known. She never came home from the hairdressing salon feeling the way she felt at the end of her day's work here.

'Think of dinner, Mary. Only an hour to go.'

Mary did smile then. She could hardly name a single one of the things they ate, had to be told what every item was, but she couldn't get enough of the extraordinary food. Maybe it was just sheer hunger, they were all ravenous, filling up their plates twice or sometimes even three times – but no. It wasn't just quantity. It was quality. Everything tasted so *fresh*. Despite all the jokes everyone had made back home about snails and frogs' legs they hadn't come across those – not as far as they could make out, anyway – but the other things were amazing.

The Dutch and the Danes assured them that there was nothing exceptional about the food, or *cuisine*, as they called it; said it was just simple peasant stuff. And indeed there wasn't anything unusual about the method of cooking, in normal pots and pans except that they were on a grand scale, rather black and old-fashioned at that. But that wonderful oil, made from olives, made everything taste so different! And the vegetables: tomatoes the size of fists, potatoes cooked in cream and cheese, a kaleidoscope of things Mary had never seen before. Corn cobs streaming with scalding juice and melting butter, green peppers full of crunchy sweetness, smooth nutty artichokes you dipped in the oil and ate with your fingers, big thick slices of something called *aubergine* made into something called *ratatouille*. People laughed when she asked the name of every little thing, asked her what on earth she lived on in Ireland, but she didn't care.

But what was she going to do, when she got back to the deli in Dublin? The manager Mr O'Rourke was very nice, very proud of his 'produce'. But now, after only three days, she knew what it really was. Crap. All that coleslaw arriving in big industrial plastic tubs, that pale slimy ham, cardboard pizza with a few miserable bits of soggy broccoli on it, gooey cheesecake with tinned mandarins . . . yet the customers regarded these things as luxuries, and bought only small cautious quantities on weekends or for party treats. It all came in tubs, tins, packets or cartons – while here, everything tasted as if it had jumped straight out of the sunwarmed soil. She'd starve when she went home, never be able to eat fishfingers or Batchelor's beans again.

And the wine! Only snobs drank wine in Ireland, but now she wondered why; there was nothing remotely pretentious about the earthenware pitchers set out on the wooden tables in the evenings, filled with red, white and rosé wine made right here on the spot. In fact a Belgian girl had told her that Provençal wines weren't even very good, not France's best by a long shot, but what she'd tasted so far made her usual drink at The Lantern – Harp lager – seem like detergent by comparison.

Were there even any pubs in France? So far there was no mention of any. At home she and Keeley would have gone out after work, to drink what suddenly seemed like an awful lot, five or six Harps for herself and three or four vodkas for Keeley, with white lemonade in them. Admittedly they hadn't gone out so often since they'd been trying to save money, but Cathal worked at The Lantern, their friends congregated there, the attraction was constant. Here, they were too tired at night to even venture as far as Rognes, which might have a pub, but it was extraordinary how none of the other, more hardened workers ever seemed to suggest it. The other Europeans, and indeed Americans, simply sat around the tables after dinner, chatting or playing cards, sipping just a little wine, or coffee or even water. Water! They'd think you'd lost your marbles at home if you drank water. Out of a bottle, too! Keeley couldn't get over it.

Mary smiled to herself as she carried on with her work. Keeley wasn't nearly as nuts about the French food as she was, but she seemed to be having a great time, talking to everyone, tanning already, laughing off the heat and strain and rough dirty work. Hardly anyone understood her Dublin accent or expressions, but everyone liked her. Keeley never complained, not just here but at home either, now that Mary thought about it.

Yet Keeley's life was tough enough. She had that surly lazy

father, the 'oul fella' who was in fact only thirty-nine. Christy. Keeley wasn't ashamed of her home, she invited Mary to come to it quite matter-of-factly, but it really was depressing. Christy in his vest slouched in front of the telly, Ma Butler all depressed about Poor Tony, and very accident-prone; she often seemed to have bruises, black eyes, constant little accidents. That peeling wallpaper, lumpy furniture, back yard overgrown and full of rusty scrap. You could hear the neighbours roaring at each other on both sides, the front gate hung off its hinges and the wall was the local art gallery, sprayed and crayoned with the colourful thoughts of kids as young as four, as old as twenty. Dogs overturned dustbins, cats mewled all night, ramps had had to be put in to slow down the constant parade of speeding motorbikes. On Friday nights Keeley handed over half her wages to her mother, Mary knew, but somehow the oul fella always seemed to be in possession of the money by Saturday, sprawling among the empty cans or going out for his only 'exercise', a walk as far as the bookie's shop.

No wonder Keeley had been so keen to come to France. She'd probably have gone to Mongolia, anywhere, to get away. And yet she was so chirpy, joking about the horrors of her home life if she mentioned them at all, not a bit envious of Mary's much luckier lot.

Not that Pearse Avenue was a paradise. But it was a sight better than Pearse Gardens. The houses were sturdier, better kept, built in blocks of two instead of rows of dozens. There was even the odd cypress tree, tub of pansies, mown lawn. The neighbours didn't screech and the cars were neither wrecked nor stolen. You didn't cringe when you looked at the place.

Her parents were OK, too. They both worked, Dad as a mechanic in a big garage over in Walkinstown, Mam as a shop assistant in a bakery where the bread was completely different to the bread here. The cakes, too . . . so far there hadn't been any cakes here, people didn't seem to go for sweet things so much. Instead they liked cheese, said France had a different kind for every day of the year. Well, Ireland had cheese: cheddar and Calvita. Only you didn't eat them after meals, or with wine.

Oh, Jesus. This holiday was going to be the ruination of them both. Even before they'd left there'd been sniggers, sarcastic little jokes about people trying to 'better themselves', and who did they think they were, what was wrong with Tenerife if they had to go foreign?

Fuck Tenerife, Mary thought suddenly. I like it here. I bet
Cathal would like it, too. Well ... not the food maybe, but
the wine, the way everyone works so hard, like he does. Maybe
we could come here for our honeymoon, when, if ... what do I
mean, *if*? Everyone knows we're going steady, are going to get
engaged and then married. Mam and Dad are delighted, saving
for the wedding already. It'll have to be a big white one what
with me marrying a pub. Two pubs. And then we'll ... we'll
have kids, I suppose. In fact we'd have one by Christmas, before
any wedding, if I'd let him carry on that night in the car. Or that
other night, in the car. I bet he's glad now though, because if I
wouldn't do it with him then I won't do it with anyone here,
will I? His mates all said I would, but they were just winding
him up. Anyway there's no chance; even though Keeley says
she'd like to meet a nice bloke, they're not a bit interested in
us, what with all these gorgeous blonde Danish girls and sexy
French ones ... but who could bonk in a bunk, anyway? With
forty other people around?

I must write to Cathal. I would have on the first day, only
that man made us start work on the spot. They sure don't take
any prisoners here. I'll write tonight, after dinner. I can smell
it cooking already. Jesus, I'm starving.

'Why don't you write home too, Keeley?'

'Oh, I'm not much of a one for writing. I'll leave it another
week or two, until they notice I've gone.' Keeley said it with a
grin, an uplift of her chin and snub nose, but Mary thought she
sensed a note of truth in it.

'Then what are you going to do?'

'Chat up that bloke. The Swedish one in the navy shorts. You
know what they say about Swedes.'

With another grin she wandered off, and Mary started writing
on the paper she'd had to ask for in the office, and been given
with a look that said she was a nuisance.

'Dear Cathal,
How are you? Well, I hope, and behaving yourself and
missing me like mad. We're having a great time. It's very
hot and hard work, but there are loads of people our age,
from everywhere, the place is beautiful, the people who own
the vineyard live in a castle. There was a fabulous house when
we arrived, but it turns out that's only the manager's house,

*the owners live in a huge place so far away we can only just
see it, we hear it's got a swimming pool and everything. All
the houses here have shutters, for the sun, and red roofs and
there are shady trees all around them, sort of bluey-green,
it's really gorgeous.*

*But the best thing is the food. Keeley says her tongue is
hanging out for a burger, but I love it. I can't tell you the
names of the things because I don't know how to spell them,
but you should have seen what we had for dinner this evening
(not tea, they have dinner at night) – an enormous salad with
three kinds of lettuce in it, green beans and little sardine
things, kind of salty, plus a fish stew full of just about
everything, and then four kinds of cheese, hard and soft,
some are stronger than others and you drink wine with them.
Most of the wine here is called rosy, but I think the red tastes
better with the cheese.*

*I suppose you think I'm getting fat as a pig! But we work
so hard and picking grapes is very sweaty, we think we might
even be losing weight. We all sleep in a barn at night,* mixed,
*we could hardly believe it, boys and girls all together. Some
of them snore like steam engines. But nobody gets up to
anything, we're all too tired. I wouldn't anyway, I miss you
and I lo—'*

'Writing home?'

A bit annoyed to be interrupted, Mary looked up. It was a
man who was speaking to her, not a boy, a genuine antique in
fact; he must be about twenty-two or twenty-three.

'Yes. To my boyfriend.'

'Ah.'

She decided she'd written enough to Cathal anyway. She
didn't want to bore him with all her talk about food. He
was a meat and three veg man, and he liked what he called a
'liquid lunch', on Saturdays. Besides, she still had her parents
to write to, and an individual postcard for each of her two small
brothers. Where would she get postcards, she wondered?

She turned to the man, a fair-haired tallish chap with a beard,
who had seated himself a little way down the long trestle table.

'Excuse me. Do you know if there's a post office or a shop
in Rognes?'

'Yes. Both. But they close early. You'll have to wait till
Saturday.'

'Oh.'

A bit put out, she signed Cathal's letter: 'Lots of love, Mary.' She'd have to wait two days to post it, now. Still, he'd be pleased when he got it.

'Where are you from?' The bearded one was looking at her enquiringly, with eyes even bluer than her own.

'Ireland. And you?'

'Sweden.'

'You speak good English.'

'Everyone does, in Sweden.'

'Are you – are you on your own?'

'I am now. Your friend has gone off with my friend.'

Keeley had gone *off* with someone? Where? She looked at him in alarm, but he smiled.

'Don't worry. My friend Erik is quite the gentleman.'

Yes, she thought, but Keeley is no lady. God knows what—

'Oh, relax. They've just gone for a walk in the fields. Would you like to go for one too?'

'No, thank you.'

Did she sound a bit prim? Well, she'd told him she was writing to her boyfriend, hadn't she? Was he thick or what, that he didn't get the message?

Reaching his brown arm across the table, he picked up the leftover pitcher of wine and gestured to her.

'Like a glass?'

'No . . . I'll have some water.' She helped herself, and he tucked a hank of blond hair behind his left ear, regarding her with what seemed to be amusement.

'So. What's your name, Irish girl?'

'Mary.'

'*Mary, Mary, long before the fashion grew . . .*'

She was amazed that he knew the song, the same one her kid brothers sang when they wanted to annoy her, or knew a line of anyway.

'My name is Lars. I am a student of mathematics at Gothenburg University. Erik studies engineering.'

Oh, no. Brainy types. Intellectuals. Immediately she felt out of her depth, a little hostile, anxious for escape. But he kept talking.

'What brought you to Provence?'

A ferry and seven cars, she was tempted to say, but decided not to. If Keeley was trying to get off with his friend she wouldn't thank her for messing.

'I – I saw a French film last winter. By mistake. It was called *Claire's Knee* and I went with a bunch of my pals. We thought it was going to be – well, something else. It turned out to have subtitles and it was a bit, you know, slow. But I liked it. I don't know why. I just did.'

'I see. And now? Do you like France?'

'Yes. What I've seen of it, at any rate, which isn't much. The people don't seem very friendly, but I like the sun and the food.'

'If you want to see a bit more, you and your friend could come with Erik and me into Aix on Saturday. It's much bigger than Rognes, you'd get your postcards and stamps there. There's a big market in the mornings.'

'A market?'

'Yes. Food, clothes, houseware, hardware . . . very colourful, we hear. We'd take you on our motorbikes.'

She was filled with interest and dismay in equal parts. A market sounded great, any kind of sightseeing, and Keeley would love the idea of a motorbike, despite the cruel fate of Poor Tony. But students. Men. Older, foreign men, and Cathal fifteen hundred miles away.

'I – I'll have to ask my friend.'

Abruptly, he stood up.

'Of course. Just let us know if you wish to come.'

'Jaysus, Mary, I nearly died.'

'Why? What did he do?'

'He said he was an engin*eer*! Well, studying to be one, anyway. Can you imagine, me going walkies with an engineer?'

'His friend studies maths. They're very old.'

'Bullshit. We're eighteen, they can't be more than three or four years older than us. Anyhow, I don't care. Erik is gorgeous. What was the other one like?'

'Blond. Tanned. Blue eyes. A beard. Grey shorts and a yellow T-shirt.'

'Yum. They're tall too. At least Erik is. I felt like a midget.'

'Was it a nice walk?'

'Yeah. He slowed down so I didn't have to run to keep up. He was a bit serious. Talked about the scenery a lot. Called it the landscape. Seemed to recognise all the flowers and trees – kind of like Mickser Sweeney, really.'

Mary laughed. Keeley's only previous boyfriend, Mickser Sweeney, had had just one subject of conversation: Manchester Bleedin' United.

'So were you bored?'

'Oh, no. It was . . . different. I hadn't much of a clue what he was on about most of the time, but he was kind of – nice. Lifted a branch out of my way, helped me across a stream, real polite. And me in my scruffs, too. I wish I'd brought a few glad rags with me.'

'You did. What about your black skirt and—'

'No, I don't mean that, I mean something – sort of – not glam. Something, you know. Pretty. Floaty. Anyway, I didn't score. He didn't say a word about another walk.'

'Well then, today's your lucky day. Or Saturday is. His friend Lars asked me if we wanted to go into Aix with them on Saturday. They have motorbikes.'

'Oh, Mary, I hope you said yes! Tell me you did or I'll crease you!'

'I said the ladies would discuss the matter.'

'Oh, yes! Consider it discussed, lads, consider it discussed!'

Saturday morning dawned bright as silver, sleek with heat. Mary was surprised to find herself dressing at seven, unable to sleep late as she had yearned to do. Keeley was hopping in anticipation, showered, brushed, perky in a strappy red T-shirt and white shorts, peering round the door of the barn until finally she heard the rumble of engines.

'Here they are! Mary, wait till you see their motorbikes, they're as big as cars!'

It was very nearly true, and both girls felt a thrill as the Swedish lads greeted them with smiley waves, beckoned them to hop on the back and revved away. There was no time for breakfast, Lars said; the market was already under way and early morning was the best time to see it.

But they drove slowly, giving their passengers a chance to enjoy the scenery, hills and fields in shades of terracotta and pistachio, steamy with fast-evaporating dew, gently clunking with the sound of goat bells. The breeze blew Mary's hair free of its moorings and she left it to billow out behind her, relaxing into the deep leather saddle, her lungs filling with dawn-fresh air. She hadn't been sure about this excursion, agreeing to it mostly for Keeley's sake and for the chance to see the market, but almost immediately she began to enjoy it. How could I not, she thought. How could anyone not?

Aix was a very old town, and she was amazed when she saw it; it looked like something rising out of another age, pewter-coloured, rambly, ancient. Yet it was busy, there were lots of men already drinking some cloudy potion at the pavement cafés, where they pulled in twice to ask directions.

'It's a Roman town,' Lars told her, 'but the newer part is only about two hundred years old. That's where the market is.'

Dimly she recalled the efforts of some history teacher to tell her about Roman times, biting her lip as she thought of her bored indifference, the wriggly resistance of the whole class. It had all seemed dry as dust. And now here she was, plonked down in the middle of it.

The market was vast and Erik called a little conference as to where they should start. Lace, linens, ceramics, food . . . ?

'Food,' she said immediately. Keeley grinned.

'Our Mary is mad for it. You wouldn't think it to look at her, would you?' Both men looked, surveying with candid appreciation Mary's slim tallish figure, the sudden sparkle in her pale freckled face and wide blue eyes.

'Then let's find the food.'

It was a whole section to itself, a panorama that even Keeley found astonishing. One stall, protected from the sun by a white awning, sold nothing but big brown eggs, laid only two hours earlier Erik said, translating; his French was very good. Everyone smiled as Mary picked up an egg, gently, turning it in her hands to inspect it although she didn't know why; there was no need to buy anything even if she had money to spare. Damnation, that she couldn't speak French, couldn't ask the vendor about his chickens, his hens, if omelettes were made the same way in this part of the world! But then there were the sausages, at the next stall, straight thick ones swinging in rows from hooks overhead, ten times the size of Irish ones, netted with red string: little curly ones like pigtails, black and white, piled on a wooden tray with a sign that said '*Boudin, 3f la pièce.*' And lots of others besides, wrapped in leaves or encrusted with white beads she was told were peppercorns, smelling so strong her head swam. Keeley held her nose, but Lars was very helpful, explaining about boudin, salami, all the different varieties. Gratefully she smiled at him, and nudged Keeley in the ribs.

'Stop it! You'll offend the man!'

Indeed the vendor did look offended as they moved on in some embarrassment to the next stall, glittering with glass. Oil this time; thick green olive oil, a yellow one made from sunflowers, an almost clear one distilled from rapeseed (Mary made a note to look it up), others filled with sprigs of herbs – thyme, Erik said, rosemary, mint. Some were for frying in, some for salads, others to be drizzled over parmesan or asparagus. Mary opened another page in her mental notebook.

She couldn't believe it when Lars said more than an hour had passed, and would the girls like some coffee?

Keeley said yes, and they were heading for a kind of makeshift café when suddenly Mary realised she couldn't bear it. Couldn't bear to interrupt this magical tour of Aladdin's cave, miss one single thing.

'You go on. I'll catch you up in a minute.'

Sprinting away, she plunged back in among the awnings, breathing deeply as her nose led her first to the cheeses and then to the vegetables. Oh, the smell of them, the colours, the shapes and sizes! With a kind of desperation she fought to understand what the sellers were crying, what the handwritten signs meant, pleading with her eyes to be allowed to touch, to pick things up, to examine.

At home Mr McNamara the grocer would mutter if anyone looked crooked at his tomatoes or onions, but incredibly these grocers smiled and nodded, actually encouraging inspection, offering tiny samples. In ten minutes Mary had tasted twelve kinds of cheese, soft gooey ones, hard nutty ones, salty yellow, creamy white, overpowering orange . . . when she thought her welcome was running out at one stall she moved on to the next, and the next, lifting, stroking, holding whole bunches of carrots up to her nose to inhale their earthy smell, gripping the big velvety peaches and yellow melons from Cavaillon, tracing the knobbly countours of avocado pears, the smooth regal sheen of aubergines, purple and glossy as royalty.

'Mary! Come on! We're going to the clothes section, and then Erik wants to look at records . . .'

Feeling driven from paradise, she rejoined her friends. But fair was fair, it was their turn to see things that interested them. Lars and Erik were being so nice, too, explaining, interpreting, elbowing a path through the crowds. Lars smiled at her.

'You missed your coffee.'

'It doesn't matter. I'll never forget what I saw this morning . . . thanks for bringing us here, Lars. We'd never even have known there was a market.'

'A pleasure' he said simply, and smiled again. She seemed to have forgotten about posting her letters home.

Mary's mind could not have been further from home as she followed the others deeper into the market, discovering the delights of a first trip abroad. Mere chance had brought them all here, really, and both girls were still acclimatising to the weather, the language, the unknown rhythm of the place. But if they were a little bemused by it they were intrigued too, youthfully eager to see as much as they could. Mary had been in the countryside before; she could remember childhood outings with her parents, and later the baby boys, to places like Glendalough, Donabate, the Strawberry Beds. They'd gone on the bus, taken an unvarying picnic of egg sandwiches and Swiss roll, sheltered under trees or bushes from the inevitable showers. But in her memory the days were sunny, she could smell the fresh grass, hear the water, feel the nettle and bee stings, the lovely tired happy glow as they wended their way back through the dunes and hillocks in warm sunburnt evenings. As she'd grown into her teens the Sunday jaunts had gradually been abandoned, the boys preferring to play football with their pals while she went through moody adolescence, no longer wanting to be seen with her parents as if she were a child. Then, one day not long after meeting Keeley at The Lantern, she'd asked her new friend whether she felt like going off somewhere for the day, and been surprised when Keeley said yes, she'd love to, she'd never gone anywhere unless you counted shopping in town.

What, never? No, Keeley asserted, never. So they'd got a bus timetable and picked out the longest journey in it, the number 44 bus that went to Enniskerry in Wicklow. From there they walked all the say to Powerscourt waterfall, chatting, getting to know each other better. Keeley had been wearing tight jeans that day, she remembered, and silly shoes with heels on them; she kept stumbling and cursing, the jeans remained damp all day after it rained on them. But, despite a cold that kept her sneezing for a week afterwards, she'd loved it.

In fact her enthusiasm had been such that she'd nearly got killed trying to climb the wet rocks up the sides of the waterfall, slipping and giggling until she twisted her ankle and came crashing down with a yell. There'd been trouble, too, when she threw a chocolate wrapper on the grass and had it returned to her by some irate man, with a lecture about not littering beauty spots. But her grin had never faded, she'd talked about that day for ages afterwards, and it was the first inkling Mary had had of Keeley's home life. She couldn't imagine never going *any*where, even before Dad had got a car they'd always gone somewhere on summer Sundays, but Keeley wasn't joking when she said she'd never been further than Henry Street, for tights and divilment on Saturdays. The oul fella would no more take his family to the beach or park than he would take them to the moon, she said, and her Ma . . . well, her Ma wasn't very good at organising things. Weekends in the Butler house were for watching the match, when she was a child, for tinkering with broken household equipment of one kind or another, for sleeping late and fighting over who was going to wash the dishes. Tony refused to do it, refused to do anything as he grew up, while Christy created blue murder if his dinner wasn't hot and ready when he rolled back from the pub after Mass on Sundays. Mary's tale of picnics and Swiss rolls had made her eyes widen in the most incredulous way, as if the Jamesons were an exotic species grown as some kind of social experiment. Mary thought Keeley Butler must be the only girl in Dublin who'd never even been to the Zoo, to Dollymount strand or to the Pigeon House, where you could see the *Lady Miranda* and the other Guinness ships rounding the mouth of the harbour, chugging home from places rumoured to be as farflung as Spain and north Africa.

But she's enjoying herself today, Mary thought as they wandered from stall to stall, looking at her friend examining things, her brown eyes wide and disbelieving as the two Swedish chaps dispensed information like tour guides, authoritatively if a bit clinically. Erik and Lars had only arrived in Provence a few days before they had themselves, but they seemed to know everything, must have read up a few books before they came . . . it had never occurred to either girl to do that, and Mary frowned in annoyance; their local library would surely have had something and they wouldn't look such dimwits now. Neither Lars nor Erik made any comment, but she sensed they were smiling inside, catching each other's eye as Keeley's voice rang out again and again: 'What the ruddy hell is that? Ah no lads, you're not serious, pull the other one . . .'

They saw an awful lot by the time the vendors started dismantling their stalls at noon, and then Lars made a suggestion. A quick sandwich, and then a walk round Aix? Would the girls like that, or would they be bored? It was a historic town, but if they didn't mind that . . . ? Mary noticed the way Keeley's head jerked up, her sharp tone as she said of course they didn't mind, they might be green as the grass but they weren't complete eejits. Erik looked at her warily and Mary realised he was taken aback by Keeley's retort, maybe even realised that he and his friend were being a bit patronising. Apparently anxious to make up for it, he bought everyone's sandwiches, and was rewarded with a smile from Keeley which he returned eagerly, looking a little abashed although it was Lars who'd done the damage. But Lars made up for it in turn, buying them all a glass of wine, which restored good humour and made Mary wonder. These guys seemed to have plenty of pocket money, what kind of homes were they from? Or did all Swedes have lots, of money and information and good manners? She'd never met such a polite pair in her life.

But they were trying to be nice, she thought as she ate her sandwich with just a quick peep inside it, and really they *were* nice. Kind of serious, but they meant well, and were generous for two guys they'd only just met. Cathal wouldn't buy wine or propose walking tours – well, there was Dun Laoghaire pier of course, where he took her to walk most Sundays, but he talked so much about himself . . . still, there was a lot he needed to discuss about his exciting future, and the goals he'd usually scored in the match the day before. His team depended on him he said, he had a lot on his mind. These guys were on holiday, it wasn't fair to compare.

Cathal faded from her mind as they got up and followed Erik, who was talking about boulevards and fountains, Keeley nodding at him trying to look as if she knew what a boulevard was. Clueless but valiant, she trotted at his side and Mary followed, with Lars, keen to see the 'old town' which sounded most romantic.

It took some time to find, but then suddenly they were in it, and Mary drew in her breath. Now here was France, as she'd imagined it! Strangely quiet, green-shuttered, the walls the colour of old gold. Every window had a black wrought-iron box

of geraniums, the very pavements seemed to smell of garlic, the
streets were narrow, cobbled, wendy-bendy. Few people were
about, most of them taking their siesta Lars said, but here and
there she caught sight of old women leaning over their tiny
balconies with watering cans, a couple of young men playing
dominoes at a corner café, a sturdy ancient bicycle vanishing
down an alleyway.

There was the strangest atmosphere about it, as if it didn't
belong to the twentieth century at all, as if nobody could
possibly own anything like a television or a fridge, though she
supposed they must. Although each house was a different colour
it blended into the next, creamy, buttery, the shades of tea and
coffee and the yellow wine so curiously called white. Each tiny
window had a lace curtain, aged by the sun and drawn against it,
a long curly handle inside, a glimpse of dark mysterious recesses.
There were no gardens, but lots and lots of flowers in pots and
tubs, ivy dangling in great massed bunches over doorways, thick
wooden doors with no knockers but a row of bells, with names
handwritten in black ink. There was a sense of something off
kilter, too, something she couldn't identify until Keeley looked
up and shrieked.

'They're all crooked! Christ, Erik, these houses look as if
they're going to fall down!'

Erik laughed, for the first time, and Mary noticed his perfect
white teeth, the expensive kind you saw in Hollywood films.

'They've been standing for centuries, Keeley. I don't think
they're going to fall today. They're just crooked because they
were built before spirit levels were invented.'

Spirit levels. Passing lightly over that little conundrum, Keeley
looked up again, squinting against the sun.

'They're dirty, too. The plaster is all falling off. They need a
lick of paint.'

Both men laughed this time, and Keeley looked indignant.

'Well, they do! I mean, this isn't Pearse Gardens, you'd
think—'

Grinning, Erik looked down at her, amused. He really was
tall, Keeley looked childlike beside him, as dark as he was fair,
completely different.

'It's very old plaster, Keeley, part of the architectural
character. It would do terrible damage to these houses to
paint them. But don't worry, they're preserved, taken good
care of.'

'Then why do they look so grotty?'

'Grotty?'

'Yeah. Messy.'

'Because they've been standing for hundreds of years, weathered by the sun and wind – the mistral wind, sometimes it blows in Provence for days on end, full of sand it carries up from Africa. The houses have absorbed it, withstood it, because they are so strong. They weren't built to look pretty, their charm is in their strength and endurance.'

'Oh.'

Keeley looked at Erik as if he were speaking his native Swedish, incomprehensible but challenging, and fell silent while she thought it out. Mary thought about it too, imagined the many people who must have lived here, whole generations; it was as if you could feel them, sense ghosts in the shadows. Pearse Avenue had been built in 1961 her Dad had told her, sixteen years ago ... would it still be standing when her children's children were long dead and gone? She had a hazy memory of the day they had moved there, cardboard boxes as big as herself, Mam putting something on the mantelpiece, a sense of settling in. But she wondered now if it was built to last. It was nice to think of things lasting, of people looking at them with pleasure and wonder as they were looking, now, at these ancient homes.

Lars smiled at her as she stood there, looking up, looking thoughtful.

'History, Mary. See, it's not so dull, is it?'

No. Not half as dull in Aix as it had seemed in the classroom. Not that she wanted to visit any museums or anything, but she liked this area, old and warm and strong; there was something comforting about it.

'No, Lars. It's nice. This place, anyway. I like it.'

He was pleased. She'd seemed a bit funny the first time they met, writing her letter on the table after dinner, but maybe it was just shyness. Her little friend was very talkative, but Mary was quieter, except on the subject of food which seemed to have caught her imagination. He wasn't expecting to have any stimulating conversations with her, certainly not of the kind he had with the students at Gothenberg university, but there was something about her, something stirring slowly to life ... clearly she'd never been abroad before, but she looked as if she was starting to enjoy it. Putting one hand on her shoulder, he pointed with the other down the street.

'See that café?'

'Uh huh?'

'Cézanne painted it.'

Keeley overheard, and grinned.

'So they do paint things! But it's time it was painted again. It's filthy!'

Neither girl could understand why Lars and Erik burst out laughing, but it was a welcome sight. They were very handsome guys, when they laughed.

'No, Keeley. He wasn't that kind of painter. He was an artist. He lived in Provence and painted many street scenes, much of the landscape. There is a museum full of his work—'

'Oh, right. A guy in a smock and a beret.'

Keeley's grin was wicked, but Mary thought she noted something slightly defensive in her tone, something offhand in the way she dismissed the matter because she'd made a mistake. Maybe she thought she'd made a show of herself. But so what, if she had? Everyone had to start somewhere. Not everyone went to college, like Lars and Erik.

'Well, it's too nice a day for museums. Let's just keep walking.'

So they kept walking, and the others kept talking, but Mary lagged behind, looking, thinking, drinking everything in. What must it be like, to live in a city like this? To live in a house hundreds of years old, near boulevards with fountains, in countryside so soft and fresh? It was like her grandmother's old tapestry cushion, faded but cherished, pink and green and brown, telling some kind of story if only you could make out what it was.

I'm glad we came here, she thought. It was an awful journey and we missed an awful lot coming down here in all those speeding cars, but now we can relax. We've got time to see things. Maybe Lars and Erik will take us around, they're quite nice now that we're getting to know them. I hope they will. I feel like a different person in this country, this place. I want to make the most of it, see and do as much as we can. The weather is heaven, the food is seventh heaven, the work is hard but I'm having the time of my life.

Three weeks later, both girls sat together on the lower of their two bunks, sobbing.

'Oh, Mary, what are we going to do?'

'I – I don't know, the only thing I know is that I d-don't want to go h-home . . .'

'Neither do I, I want to go to Sweden and be with Erik.'

Loyally, Mary put her arm round Keeley's heaving shoulders. 'Don't cry, Keeley. You'll get over him.'

'N-no, I won't! He was so gorgeous, so good to me . . . Mary, I'll never find another fella like him! I'd never meet anyone who'd treat me like – like a lady! He didn't mind that I'm pig-ignorant, didn't make fun of me or care that I'm from Pearse Gardens, didn't go on about football all the time or get rat-arsed every night. He took me out and treated me nice, didn't bang on about engineering or anything I wouldn't understand . . . how can he have gone off, just like that? Why didn't he want my address or say anything about coming to see me in Dublin? Why didn't he ask me to go to Sweden with him? After the other night, too. It was so great, I was sure he couldn't live without me after that.'

Mary smiled feebly.

'Well, look on the bright side. At least you've lost your virginity. You'd been saying for ages you wanted to do that.'

Sniffling, Keeley gazed at her.

'Yeah. And so did you. I mean, everyone knows I'm a little tramp – or says I am anyway – but what came over you? What about Cathal? Are you going to tell him?'

'Oh, stuff Cathal! I've lost my virginity to someone else and that's all about it.'

Keeley gaped. Mary sounded so casual, as if her lost virginity was nothing more than an umbrella left on the bus. But she was practically *engaged* to Cathal Sullivan!

'He'll have a canary.'

'Keeley, I don't care. I thought I was in love with him, but now I know I wasn't. My parents loved him, loved the idea of me marrying a bit of money. But in fact he never spent a cent on me. I only realised it the day Lars took me to that beautiful restaurant, the day I tasted champagne and asparagus . . . Cathal only ever took me for walks, the skinflint. He'd never treat me the way Lars did, buy me a dictionary so I could look up the names of everything, take an interest just because I was interested. I didn't fall in love with Lars the same way you did with Erik, but he opened my eyes.'

'Yeah. Erik opened mine, too. This whole holiday has opened

them. I'll never settle down at home again, or go out with anyone like Mickser Sweeney, or be able to stand the cold and rain. It's just so much nicer here.'

'Yes. I wish we could stay. I really do.'

'So do I. If only we spoke the lingo, we could get jobs. Nobody would even notice if I didn't come home, except at work, and they'd find someone else in a flash.'

Hearing her wistful tone, Mary hugged her friend.

'Of course they'd notice. Erik will notice too, when he gets back to Sweden he'll realise what he's . . .'

'Thrown away? That's kind of what I feel he has done, Mary. Thrown me away like a bit of rubbish. He didn't seem like that, but I suppose he must have only wanted the one thing after all . . . a fellow like him would never fall in love with someone like me, not really, he'd want a student like himself, someone educated you could take anywhere. Someone posh.'

'Well, I think you're great. You made him laugh and you make me laugh, you're a real hard little worker and you never minded a bit when I was whingeing in the beginning, getting sick on the ferry and saying the work was too hard. It certainly has been a sight harder than working in the deli – Oh, God, how am I going to go back to that deli? Or to Cathal? I'll have to break it off with him and he'll probably be horrible about it, get up on his high horse and say we had an understanding . . . well, I suppose we did have, but not after Lars. Now that I've tasted champagne it would be like going back to Harp lager.'

They both giggled suddenly as they visualised Cathal in his pub, pumping gallons of it, selling the pints that would make him rich one day, rich!

'But if you're not going to marry him, and don't want to go back to the deli, then what are you going to do?'

'God knows. If I have to go back to Dublin then I think maybe I'd like to see if I could get into the catering college at Cathal Brugha Street. Learn about food. Maybe even open a little restaurant some day.'

'You've really fallen for it, haven't you? The stuff here, I mean?'

'Yes. The food, the way they cook it, the way they eat it, the way it's all part of how they live. I'd much rather learn about it here in the sun than at home, where everyone would say I was getting notions above my station.'

'But – but then—'

'Then what?'

Keeley sat up.

'Then why are we going home, Mary? If neither of us wants to?'

'Because – Jesus, Keeley, we have to! You don't just go off on holidays and never come back.'

'Why not? God, Mary, it'll be freezing and miserable in Ireland now, coming into October, if we could even stay here even for the winter—'

'Doing what?'

Keeley thought. Thought rapidly, desperately.

'I could wash hair, just like I did before. I wouldn't need to speak much French for that, there must be a salon in Aix – and you could get a job as a waitress at that restaurant Lars took you to. You said there were lots of English and Americans at it, they'd probably be delighted to get someone who could talk to the tourists.'

'But – but where would we live?'

'We'd be getting paid, wouldn't we? We could find a little flat.'

A flat. Instantly Mary's mind filled with visions of pots and pans, a cooker, strings of onions and garlic hanging from hooks like in the market, baskets bursting with fruit and vegetables . . . and a job in a restaurant, where she'd be bound to learn something no matter how little French she spoke. Well, none. But she'd pick it up, enough to get by on. Even Keeley would surely rise to 'bonjour' and 'au revoir' and whatever was the French for 'nice day isn't it.'

Poor Keeley. The only one of all her friends who'd wanted to come on holiday with her, and now her heart was breaking over a Swedish chap who'd had his fun and then gone home. It was awful but it was probably true: there was one kind of girl for holidays, another kind for real life. Keeley was the kind who wouldn't count with Erik, any more than she seemed to count with Christy, or with her useless mother who had eyes only for Poor Tony.

As for her own parents . . . they were going to be very let down, about Cathal Sullivan and the two pubs and the car. It would be a lot easier to explain in a letter than in person. She could simply say she was staying on for a few months, until they began to forget about Cathal and he began to forget about her.

She felt little regret or remorse, for Cathal, but she did feel a twinge of guilt. He'd often said he was mad about her, that she was a great girl, pretty as a picture. Even surrounded in The Lantern by lots of other girls, he'd had eyes only for her. He had picked her, and the whole thing had somehow moved very fast, all been 'settled' without ever actually being discussed.

Not that she'd objected. It was nice to feel wanted, unlike Keeley who seemed to have so little luck with men, and Cathal was handsome enough even if he didn't have Lars's seductive style about him, that aura of really knowing what made a woman tick. If he wasn't adventurous, he was steady, and if he didn't spend much money on their dates it was probably only because he was saving up for when they were married. He worked, he was ambitious, and lots of girls would give their right arm for him. If she hadn't seen that silly film, hadn't come to France, the idea of marrying him probably wouldn't have gone flat at all.

But it had. She knew it well before she crept out of the barn that night, out into the fields where Lars was waiting for her, waiting to take the only thing she had to offer. If she had been truly in love with Cathal she would have wanted to give it to him, could never have given it to Lars – Lars What? With something of a shock she realised she didn't even know his second name. He had told her, but it was Swedish, she couldn't remember. Oh, well. It didn't matter. She'd only slept with him because sex was a new experience she wanted to try, and because it would put the seal on her break with Cathal. He'd never marry a girl who behaved like a slut.

Had she? She must have, she supposed, because there'd been no passion in it, no excuse. It bore no resemblance to what Keeley had done with Erik, a deed of sizzling emotion and dazzling delight by all accounts, leaving her demolished with lust and love. Mary felt no love for either Lars or Cathal, no desperate longing, no heartbreak, just a kind of gratitude that it was all over and done with. Lars certainly wasn't pining, and Cathal would get over it in time.

She would write and break it off herself, gently but firmly, to save him the embarrassment of having to explain that he didn't want to marry That Kind of girl. There were plenty of those, but he'd said she was different, she was special . . . she was, she realised now, too young to get married. The world was full of men, all different kinds like there were all different kinds of food and drink. You didn't know that until you discovered them, and tried the various varieties. She wanted to stay here, try so many things . . . and if she didn't go home, didn't even have a forwarding address at the minute, there would be nothing anyone could do or say. No awkward meetings down at The Lantern, no shrieks from her horrified parents. The whole subject of Cathal Sullivan would simply melt gradually, quietly away.

Bestirring herself, she looked at Keeley's woebegone but half-hopeful little face. Usually Keeley was the one who made the decisions, and sure enough this was her idea, but for once Mary was ready to act with alacrity.

'Do you know, Keeley, we could. We not only could, but *will*. We'll check into the hostel in Aix while we find jobs and somewhere to live. We'll stay for – well, I don't know how long exactly, but the winter at least. Maybe a whole year. We'll see how we get on, and decide later.'

Thrilled, but quite taken aback, Keeley gazed at her. The notion had only been wishful thinking, she hadn't expected Mary to take it seriously or to need so remarkably little persuasion. But that was the curious thing about Mary: sometimes she took things surprisingly seriously. She was the one who'd made up her mind to see France, and now she seemed to be making it up to stay. Feeling both excitement and gratitude, Keeley dried the last of her tears on her sleeve and hugged her friend to her.

'Oh, Mary, you're great. This is great. Let's do it.'

Chapter Two

Félix Peyrolle, manager of the Vieux Moulin, thought not. Definitely not. Never in his life had he employed a waitress who wore denim skirts or gypsy earrings the size of basketball hoops, and he wasn't about to start now. Besides, while she could speak English, she couldn't speak French. She'd be unable to translate the orders in the kitchen.

'I am sorry, mademoiselle. No vacancies.'

It made him feel a tiny bit guilty, the way she looked at him. What was she doing here anyway, at the end of the season instead of the beginning? There wouldn't be many British or Americans over the winter. It all seemed a bit pointless.

Discouraged, Mary mustered a very small smile of thanks and turned away. This was the sixth restaurant she'd tried. Time and money were running out. Maybe she'd better do as Keeley said and see if she, too, could get a job washing hair. Keeley had got one straight away, no problem at all, the manager at *Eliane* had simply asked her to do a demo on one of the other assistants and hired her on the spot. What a muddle, if Keeley had work and she hadn't—

'Espèce de salaud! J'en ai marre, je m'en vais—'

Crash! Mary jumped as a stack of crockery went flying and a man shot past her, whipping an apron over his head and dumping it in the lap of an extremely surprised male diner as he rushed out of the door.

He looked so aghast she was tempted to laugh, but thought she'd better get out first. As she followed the cursing employee, who seemed to be having a fit of some kind, she heard another flurry, and then a cry.

'Mademoiselle!'

She turned back. Mr Peyrolle came rushing up to her.

'Ah, mademoiselle . . . perhaps . . . one moment . . .'

Leading her back through the restaurant, he took her into a corner and spoke urgently.

'Would you be prepared to wash dishes?'

Yes. Oh, yes. Anything.

'And perhaps prepare some vegetables?' He made chop-chopping motions with his hand.

Vegetables? Oh, definitely!

Pushing her through the kitchen's swing door, he left her standing in the middle of a vision from hell. It was a vast kitchen, roasting, steaming, bedecked with evil-looking knives, full of scurrying people in white, all looking as if some invisible monster was chasing their tails. Moments later Mr Peyrolle returned, looking flustered, and handed her the retrieved apron.

'A little large, but it will do for now. Start with these plates, please.'

With alacrity she started, plunging her forearms into a huge sudsy sink, not even daring to look up to see where the vegetables were.

Keeley wanted to splurge, to celebrate. They both had jobs now. They could go to Quick for a burger and Coke. Mary looked at her as if she'd suggested climbing the Matterhorn.

'Are you mad? I'm knackered, I just want to sleep. Anyway they gave me some quiche to eat . . . you don't really want to go to Quick, do you?'

Keeley did. She still hadn't got her head around this weird food that Mary had taken such a shine to.

'All right. You can sleep tonight, if you promise we can eat junk tomorrow.'

Faintly, Mary promised. Tomorrow . . . tonight Keeley could knock something together in the hostel kitchen. It was a horrible kitchen, dark and grimy, something should really be done about it. If she wasn't so tired she'd attack it herself. But they'd soon have a place of their own, now.

'Keeley?'

'Mm?'

'How do you look for a flat, I wonder? I mean, we can't read the ads in the newspapers.'

'Why don't you ask that man at the restaurant? The one who gave you the job? He speaks English, you said. He could translate for us.'

He could, Mary thought, but whether he *would* was another

matter. He wasn't what you'd exactly call a decent old skin. But she'd have to ask him. They didn't know another single soul in Aix. Drifting off to sleep, she thought of home, of the two letters winging their way there, one to Cathal and one to her parents. Was there going to be murder, or what? Keeley had written home too, not that she was going to end up on Interpol's missing person list, she said with a grin.

So now they really were grown-ups. They had jobs, soon they would have a flat of their own, and they had done The Deed. Only once admittedly, the night before the Swedes left, but no way was their virginity going to turn up now in any lost-property office. Keeley was still missing Erik, Mary knew, but she was being very good about it; the occasional furtive tear but no crying jags, no endless natter about her Viking god. In fact she was being unusually quiet, for Keeley. Not mopey, but keeping herself to herself a bit, concentrating on her new work, making Mary smile as she fervently practised the few phrases she needed to get by.

'Bonjour madame, comment alley-voo, au revoir madame, merci, merci, merci, bonjour, au revoir . . .'

Au revoir indeed, to Erik, the sod. Even if he hadn't intended to ever see Keeley again it wouldn't have killed him to let her down gently, ask for her address in Ireland even if he never got in touch. For such a gentleman, with all his talk of flowers and trees, all his perfect French, he was really a bit of a brute. Even one postcard would have meant so much to Keeley, tided her over until she came to see that it was pointless anyway, their native countries were miles apart and they'd just have to be content with their happy memories. Funny, how Keeley had taken the whole thing so seriously. Normally she'd be the first to laugh, *had* laughed when one or two of their lovestruck friends came back from Tenerife in bits, pining for the bloke she always called Juan even if he was Carlos or Felipe. But then it was a different matter when it happened to you, and Erik had seemed like such a prize. As she candidly said, she'd never have met a chap like that in her neck of the woods.

Well, they were in a very different neck of the woods now. They were bound to meet a few Frenchmen, who had such a reputation for romance. Mary wasn't pushed about meeting anyone, was much more interested in the Vieux Moulin where already she'd seen a chef serving up *caviar*. He'd laughed when she peered at the tiny black dots, unable to converse but obviously amazed at her ignorance, and then whipped the plate away lest her dripping arms contaminate it. She'd thought about it for ages afterwards, through twenty or thirty dirty plates at least, wondering how such a few blobs of jelly could be so famously expensive, was there heroin in them or what? God only knew what she'd see tomorrow – and when was she going to be put on the vegetables? Today had been nothing but plates and glasses, hundreds of them, nobody had spoken to her or even noticed her existence. But maybe it was just as well, what if she chopped the wrong way and got sacked? The chopping she'd seen done today was incredibly fast and she'd noticed a pattern to it: carrots lengthways, onions in paper-fine slivers and potatoes in tiny cubes. Plus all those other much more exotic items . . . it might be better to watch for another few days until she got a fix on things. Keeley said things were much the same at the salon, she too had been handed an apron and left to get on with it, nobody talked to her, took tea-breaks or snuck a fag.

Mary felt she might eventually crack the system, liked the French way of doing things even if she didn't understand it. But Keeley didn't care what country she was in, she simply liked the sun and the freedom, the long distance between herself and Pearse Gardens, Christy, Ma Butler and Poor Tony. If she met a nice Frenchman, it would be the icing on the cake, help her to get over Erik who'd treated her 'like a lady' and then like a used Kleenex.

Maybe Cathal would say that she, Mary, had treated *him* like a used Kleenex. But she hadn't used him. She'd simply gone out with him when he asked her, had a nice time but never led him on. He'd taken charge, the way men did even in 1977, and there hadn't been any reason *not* to go out with him. He didn't set her heart on fire but he wasn't repellent either; she'd vaguely supposed they'd date until one or other of them lost interest and had been surprised when his interest had quickened, he'd started talking about their 'future.' If she were truthful she'd have to admit she'd even felt a bit rushed, a bit smothered, especially when he drove up to collect her and her parents asked him in, started making such a fuss of him. Everyone's jaw had dropped like a stone when she said she was going to France.

But it was only one holiday, why on earth not? Cathal could have come if he wanted; it was his own choice to let her go on her own. 'Let' her go – he'd actually said that.

And now she was gone. For good. Smiling to herself, Mary rolled over into a deep sleep, thinking of those beautiful purple aubergines they were going to have to let her at sooner or later.

'Mademoiselle! One moment!'
Mary turned. 'Yes?'
Mr Peyrolle, or Monsieur Peyrolle as he'd told her he preferred to be called, came up to Mary – rather sneakily, she thought – as she was about to leave after the lunchtime shift. With a newspaper rolled under her arm, in which he'd circled and explained all the suitable ads with surprising helpfulness, she was anxious to visit the flats before they were all gone.

Monsieur Peyrolle plucked at her sleeve and led her into the dark hallway where customers' coats were kept. For a split second he hesitated, and then he plunged his hand into his breast pocket, extracted a slim leather wallet and removed five banknotes from it.

Mystified, Mary gazed. Five hundred francs. A vast amount, roughly equal to a month's pay. Did he want her to buy something while she was out, get some new tablecloths or something?

'You – ah – you may find you need this.' Mumbling, he stuffed the notes into her hand and, for the first time, smiled at her. A thin prim man of about forty, in a brown suit and wearing round gold glasses, he'd never smiled before. Mary was bewildered.

'Need it? Me? For what?'
'For a deposit. You will be required to give any landlady this sum to be held against any damage you might do, or any bills you might fail to pay.' He coughed. 'Not that there would be any question of damage or unpaid bills, I'm sure.'

'Oh. Oh! Oh, Monsieur Peyrolle, I – I hadn't even thought of it – how kind of you, but how am I—?'

'Don't worry about it. It is not from your wages. It is a little loan, which I am sure you will be able to return intact whenever you should leave your accommodation. Good luck with your search.'

With that he turned on his heel and walked away, leaving Mary speechless. A month's deposit, that she hadn't even known she'd need, from this man who'd seemed so unfriendly, so distant? She was very touched. So touched she'd have hugged him, if he hadn't made his escape.

Pocketing the banknotes, she set off. For the first time since her arrival it was a cloudy day in Provence; the air held the first hush of autumn, the ancient buildings were not glowing but brooding a little, seeming darker and lower in the changing light. Until now she'd always felt like a tourist, but something was different today, she felt more like a – a normal person, who lived here. Or was going to live here, if she could battle her way through the conversation required to rent a flat. It was a pity Keeley couldn't be with her, but Keeley worked until six every evening while Mary had afternoons off and then went back in the evenings. If she found a flat she liked, she'd just have to trust to luck that Keeley would like it too. Anyway, anything would do, all they needed was a roof over their heads.

The ads circled by Monsieur Peyrolle were all for central places, near both the hairdressing salon and the square on which the restaurant was situated; he'd sensibly said it would be handy to be able to walk to work, not to have to spend money on buses or brave the suburbs – not all of the low-rent areas were entirely safe. They both thought it would be fun to live in the centre anyway, where there were cafés and cinemas and brasseries, France's equivalent of pubs.

'Brasseries,' Keeley had giggled, 'for a pair of brassers.'

But, although Keeley was still a Dub and no mistake about it, still wore a lot of eye make-up and her punky haircut, she'd bought a decent skirt and two blouses out of her wine harvest money, said she couldn't be going to work at a posh salon looking like a slag. Mary wondered: while working Keeley wore a smock type of apron which covered her from neck to knee. But the clothes would be handy for impressing landladies at any rate, for which same reason she was wearing a skirt and shirt herself today. Monsieur Peyrolle didn't allow shorts at the Moulin, not even on kitchen workers, and besides it wasn't quite as warm as it had been.

When she reached the door of the first flat there was a pencilled notice on the door: 'appartement loué.' Not knowing what it meant, she rang the bell. Seconds later a furious fat woman appeared, pointed to the notice and slammed the door.

'Loué', she learned then, meant rented. Gone. The next one was gone too. At the third there was such a queue she didn't even wait. She couldn't find the fourth, which seemed to be in a street nobody had ever heard of. Either that, or they couldn't understand what she was asking. The fifth was in a tall narrow building that didn't look very promising, but at least there was neither a queue nor a 'loué' sign on it. Her knock was answered by a small grey-haired woman in a blue floral pinafore which appeared to have come off second best in a confrontation with some kind of sauce.

After the first 'bonjour' there was an awful pantomime until Mary thought to simply produce the newspaper and point to the ad, whereupon the woman nodded and led her up a flight of stairs, another and another. Then, flinging open a door, she pointed into what appeared to be a prison cell.

Two cells, low and dark, a bedroom and a sort of multi-purpose room with a bathroom off it, hardly big enough to swing a kitten never mind a cat. But the kitchen—! It was just a galley, a sink, fridge and cooker on one side, a fold-up table with two chairs on the other. Mary breathed a sigh of pure bliss.

'Oui. Oh, oui!'

The woman looked at her, inspecting, dubious. Foreigners were notorious for midnight flits, noise, domestic disputes, damage.

'Anglaise?'

'No. Irlandaise.'

'Hmm.'

There was an impasse. And then Mary thought of Monsieur Peyrolle's money, took it out of her pocket and held it within alluring sight.

'Deposit. No damage. Very quiet. Two girls.'

Clearly the woman didn't understand, but the five hundred francs were doing the talking in any language.

'Eh bien.'

With a sigh she took the notes, stuffed them into her pinafore and nodded. Then came a babble of instructions, to all of which Mary agreed without the foggiest notion. And finally, a key.

Keeley whistled. 'Well! It's a kip, but God bless Mister Pay-roll!'

Mary beamed. God bless him indeed, his foresight and his generosity.

'It's not a kip, it's our flat. Our new home! At least it's clean, doesn't have graffiti or screeching traffic outside—'

Keeley sat down at the table, grabbing at it as the chair wobbled under her.

'Or sheets or dishes or hot water.'

'It does have hot water, you just need to light that burner thing. We'll have to stay on at the hostel, I suppose, until we get sheets and plates and stuff, but we won't need much for just the two of us. We could probably get everything at the market.'

Keeley grinned. 'It's the pots and pans you want, isn't it? You can't wait to start feeding me all your French muck, I'm to be your little guinea pig.'

Yes. They would eat like royalty, there'd be no tinned peas or fishfingers in this abode. Well, only once a week anyway, on sufferance, in case Keeley rebelled. But suddenly Keeley looked over the table at her.

'Actually, I don't mind. If you want to cook and experiment on me, I mean. I'm not much of a one to tell the difference between cod or haddock, but I suppose if you're going to open your own restaurant some day you've got to start somewhere. Anything I spit out you can regard as a failure, anything I swallow you can count as a triumph.'

Mary thought it would be some triumph to get Keeley even to tolerate things like garlic, much less like them. But if she could get her to, she could get *any*one to. And it was sweet of Keeley to offer to try, game for anything as usual.

'You're safe for a week anyway, until I get up and running. But honestly Keeley, you don't have to eat it, you can have burgers any time you want.'

'No. The next time I get a date with some toff like Erik, he won't be ashamed of me. He'll be able to take me anywhere . . . why don't you bring home a menu from the restaurant and tell me what all the things are?'

'Because I don't know myself! But I'm learning . . . Monsieur Peyrolle let me chop the cabbage today, it had to be done really fine, it was a lovely white crisp one the chef was making into something called sourkraut.'

'I thought he was an old sourkraut. I can't get over that money he gave you. Has he his eye on you or what?'

Mary blinked. The thought had never entered her head. Surely not. He was too old. At least as old as her own father. And he couldn't possibly fancy someone like her, him with his suits and gold glasses and perfect manicure.

'No. Of course not. I really think he was just being kind, Keeley.'

'Well, if he was then snap!'

'Snap?'

'Yeah. I got a tip today. Ten francs, too. I nearly fainted. Until now they've all been tight as a duck's arse.'

'Well done. That's extra money, pocket money just for you. We'll pool our wages for the rent and to buy stuff, but you're not to put any tips into it, you'd be contributing more than me. Buy a lipstick or something.'

'I will not. We're in this together, aren't we? I'd never have got here without you. Never even have thought of it, much less that I could do it. I can't believe we've been here six weeks already . . . what do you suppose they're doing in Dublin at this minute?'

'Coming in out of the rain, turning on the telly—'

They gazed at each other. Telly. It was the first time either of them had even thought of it. At home it was practically a religion, you wouldn't miss *Coronation Street* for anything, or Friday nights down at The Lantern, or Sunday mass, any of the things that seemed so distant now, so remote. Occasionally Mary thought of her parents and brothers, felt the tiniest pang, but other than that Ireland might as well be on another planet.

'Mary, we're going to the dogs. We haven't been to church or anything. Not even out at night.'

Keeley looked slightly bewildered, but Mary smiled.

'Well, I won't be going out at night, I'll be working. And so will you.'

'Me? At what?'

'Painting this flat, making curtains, going to your French class.'

'My what?'

'I asked Monsieur Peyrolle. He says there's one in the Chamber of Commerce, on Tuesday evenings, for foreigners.'

'Is that a fact? And what do they have for people who barely even speak their own language, never mind anyone else's?'

'Oh, come on! You make yourself out much worse than you are. I bet you could learn French by Easter – enough to ask your way round and do the shopping, at least.'

'What do you bet?'

'A slap-up dinner at Quick.'

'OK. You're on.'

Mary smiled. The surest way to get Keeley Butler to do something was to suggest that she couldn't do it, usually; but something told her that her friend was starting to change, just a little, in some invisible way. Starting to grow up, as she was doing too, what with a flat of her own to run. *Their* own. Looking around at the four blank bare walls, she beamed hugely.

'God, Keeley, this is great. I wasn't sure we could do it, but we have. We've escaped.'

'Yeah. You from Cathal, me from Christy. Do you know what, Mary?'

'What?'

'He hits my Ma. Wallops her. Beats the daylights out of her, sometimes.' Oh, Mary thought. Oh, God. The bruises, the black eyes. What kind of dope was she, that she'd never guessed?

'He doesn't.'

'He does. Hit me a few clatters too, when I tried to stop him.'

'But – but why doesn't your mother just leave him?'

'That's what I said to her. Often. Get out. Go to the Women's Aid shelter, get the social welfare to put you into some kind of housing . . . but she wouldn't.'

'Why not?'

'Because she said she was afraid he'd turn on me if she wasn't there. I told her not to be an eejit, I'd hit him right back and then get the hell out of it, leave him to stew on his own. She should have given him a knee in the nuts, years ago.'

Mary was horrified. Not only to hear that Keeley's mother was being beaten, but to hear that she put up with it. After all Keeley wasn't a kid any more, she didn't have to stay, Poor Tony was in the rehab centre . . . why would anyone stay with someone who abused her? But some women did. Many of them. Her own mother, Leesha, sometimes told her bits of local gossip, shady complicated stories about people being bogged down, the courts, the system, the drink, the poor kids.

'I wouldn't stay.'

'Neither would I. That's why I wanted out. I feel really bad about leaving Ma on her own with him, but there wasn't anything more I could do. It was almost as if she *wanted* to stay, in spite of everything.'

'That's garbage. It must be.'

'No. Really. It was like talking to a brick wall. But I tell you, Mary, if I ever marry anyone it won't be a fella like my oul fella.'

'It's a wonder you haven't gone off the whole idea of marriage, altogether.'

'No. There are some good ones. Some decent blokes.'

Mary was surprised she could say it at the minute, so recently after Erik, still so visibly raw. But Keeley had always been a little scrapper, a bouncer-back.

'Besides,' Keeley added, almost as an afterthought, 'I'd like to have kids.'

'Would you?'

'Yeah. Kids and a nice home. Nothing fancy, but something decent. I reckon if I learn French I might move up a notch. Imagine me, Keeley Butler, being able to answer when the customers say comment alley voo! That'd sure knock 'em dead in Pearse Gardens. Not that I ever intend to go back.'

And suddenly something fell into place with Mary. Neither did she. Not that there were any dreadful secrets in her house, any violence, but there just wasn't any excitement in it, any more than there had been in Cathal. The idea of marrying him didn't hold a candle to the idea of running her very own restaurant – and that was an idea both he and her parents would laugh themselves silly at. She'd never even been *in* a restaurant. Except the one Lars had taken her to, and the one she now worked in as a scrubber of dishes and carrots.

A place of her own. That really was a very long way off. Maybe it wouldn't come to much, but she was going to make it come to *some*thing. Here, in France, where the ingredients were fabulous and everyone loved eating out. She hadn't fallen in love with Lars despite the glass of champagne he'd bought her, but she'd fallen in love with the food on first sight. Imagine owning, or even running, somewhere like the Vieux Moulin! Working out the menu, choosing the food at the market, cooking with all those herbs and oils, watching everyone enjoying themselves. It wasn't just food for the body, it was food for the soul. Seeing the regulars come back would be like seeing your own family, nourishing it.

'Well, I don't think I want to have kids, or get married. Definitely not to a Cathal or a Christy. And I don't want to go back either, Keeley. This is our home now.'

They looked around it, and beamed. No furnishings, no utensils; only potential.

There were some complications after that, about putting bills into their names, registering with the tax authorities, massively knotted red tape. But Eliane helped Keeley and Monsieur

Peyrolle helped Mary, infected by their babbling enthusiasm. Both girls were good workers and Keeley was starting to get a fair few tips, making the customers laugh with her chirpy muddled efforts to communicate. Mary's fingers were covered in BandAid and she lived in dread that one of them would turn up one day in a customer's ratatouille, neatly severed, sliced and tasting delicious. The more the chefs shouted at her the more harassed she got, but at least she only had to contend with the really ferocious one at night, the lunchtime chap was much calmer. What was more, he'd spent some time at a hotel in Oxford and was able to talk to her in English.

'Julienne means in thin strips. Flambé means flamed, in alcohol. Haché means minced. Gratiné is with cheese, grated like this . . . I have some cookery books in English if you'd like to borrow them.'

With gratitude Mary did borrow them, staggered home with a whole stack to read between shifts while Keeley was out at work. But there was evidence of her presence: two sheets knotted over a pole at the window one day, dyed yellow and serving as curtains, an idea Keeley said she'd got from a shop window display. The walls changed from murky beige to bright white, there was a table made from an orange crate, draped in fabric acquired the day the salon staff were getting new smocks, and there was a constant stack of blue dishes on the draining board, washed by Keeley because, she said, Mary washed enough of them at work. And one day her stack of cookery books was joined by a French reader for beginners: Keeley actually had joined the language class for foreigners.

'Pain in the arse,' was her verdict, 'but I can keep up OK.'

Mary thought Keeley was more than keeping up. She was diving in head first, providing great entertainment with her perpetual tales of adventure. There was the day she struggled to tell her colleagues she'd been bitten by a mosquito, got mixed up between two similar words and told them she'd been bitten by a musketeer; the day she told a customer to go fuck herself after one of her colleagues had mischievously taught her that the phrase was what you said as thanks for a big tip; the famous day she got arrested. A policeman had arrived at the salon demanding to see the 'illegal immigrant' and marched her off to the police station despite the protests of her boss, Eliane. There she had been harangued for hours until she'd finally demanded her right to one phone call and had rung the Irish embassy in Paris, shrieking that she must speak to the ambassador. Lo and behold, she'd got him, and he had briskly explained the difference between Iceland and Ireland to the cowed policeman, who drove her back to work in a red-faced fury.

Life was never dull with Keeley around, and Mary was delighted with her new flatmate, the new life they'd carved out for themselves. They got on great together, and began to make progress at work. Eliane started teaching Keeley to cut and style, a promotion she'd long wanted but never got at home, while Mary was furnished with a set of knives and let loose on the vegetables, then on the joints of meat, and the fish that had to be boned so carefully. As she chopped and sliced she chatted with Luc, the chef who'd worked in Oxford, soaking up information like a sponge, repeating the names of the dishes like prayers in church. Of course there were other types of cuisine, he conceded with a snort – Italian, huh! Mexican, pah! – but France's was the finest. By far. Gradually she edged nearer to him in the kitchen, sneaked quick glances into his saucepans, began to hover as he prepared a dressing or a sauce, marvelling at the way he twisted lemon skins into curls, worked radishes into the shape of flowers, manufactured a swan from ice. Flattered by the look in her young eager eyes, he tossed her tips like tidbits to a puppy, let her taste his roux, his stock, his famous raspberry vinaigrette. Her mental notebook turned into a real one, filling with details as if she were a detective trying to crack a murder.

She was rarely free at the same time as Keeley, and neither of them had much money, but sometimes in the evenings they had a drink at a brasserie on the square, loving it that you could still sometimes sit outdoors, in the lavender air that was scented now with autumn, with apples and spices and nuts. One evening Keeley even screwed up her eyes, took a deep breath and ordered her beer in French.

'Une blonde à la pression, s'il vous plait.'

Mary laughed, but the waiter didn't, he simply went off to get it.

'Cripes, Keeley, he understood!'

'Yeah. The classes must be working.'

Mary was amazed. The classes were working, they were working, everything was working. They were surviving, they were adults, runaways who actually had found freedom. She felt wonderful and thought Keeley looked wonderful, so lively and cheerful, her dark complexion almost Mediterranean after all the sun. In appearance she'd nearly be taken for a native, and in spirit she'd never seemed happier.

'Do you ever miss home?'

Letters had come for them both, now that they had an address; a sad pained one from Mary's parents, Leesha and Kevin, and a short baffled one from Keeley's mother whose name, Mary discovered, was Gertie. Nobody could understand what they had done or why they had done it, the general message seemed to be that they'd soon tire of such nonsense and come home looking for their jobs, which would be gone, and then what?

'No. Do you?'

Keeley lit a cigarette and looked at her rather keenly, thoughtfully, exhaling with a raised eyebrow.

'No. Well – I miss Mam and Dad, a bit, and the boys. I feel bad about just sort of – disappearing. But I'm so busy, learning so much, I don't have time to think much. They seem so far away.'

Keeley nodded.

'Yeah. Can't be far enough for me. But your lot are OK. Did they say anything about Cathal?'

'Oh yes. Lots. They think I'm a fool.'

'And what do you think?'

'I think – I think I had a narrow escape. He hasn't even written back.'

'Well, you did throw him over.'

'I suppose so. Jilted him, Mam said, for no good reason. Maybe he will write, when he calms down. But I don't really care whether he does or not.'

'He'll probably get someone else, right away to show you don't matter.'

Yes. It was odd, because she'd thought she did matter, but still she couldn't imagine Cathal heartbroken, shattered, his life in ruins. He was the kind of person who got on with life; if his feelings or pride were injured he'd just sort of stick a bandage on them and carry on. He must feel something, she supposed, but it would soon mend.

'What about Erik? Do you miss him, still?'

It was hard to tell, because Keeley had given up talking about him, turned some little key in a lock.

'He's history.'

Stubbing out her cigarette, Keeley blew out a thin stream of blue smoke, picked up her glass and took a deep gulp of beer. 'Well, it did hurt. You know it did, there's no point in pretending. But I've decided to forget what's past and look to the future. You know, Mary, I really think I might be able to make one here.'

'Do you?'

'Yeah. I have a flat of my own, I'm getting on well at the salon, I'm even learning a bit of French. Nobody in my family ever did anything like that before – worked, I mean, got up on their own two feet. I was so sick of it all back home, the – the laziness, the sort of despair, that hopeless feeling. Even when Tony got a job he couldn't keep it two months, he had to go and blow his whole life to kingdom come.'

'But don't you feel sorry for him?'

'My Ma does most of the feeling sorry for him. I suppose I do sometimes, but it doesn't change anything, does it? And that's what I want to do, Mary. Change things.'

'Well, you have!'

'No. I mean really change them. I've been thinking about it. If I stick at things here, the work and the language and everything, I could have a whole new life. Nobody knows anything about me or where I come from. I could get to be – well, the kind of person who – you know. A woman called me mademoiselle in the salon today and I nearly dropped down dead.'

'But that's what they call all unmarried women here.'

'Yeah, I know. But it sounded so – respectful. As if I wasn't just a pair of hands scrubbing her scalp. She smiled and looked right at me, not just through me.'

Mary smiled, thinking of the night chef who constantly looked through her, unlike Luc; to him she was just a pair of hands, as Keeley said. But it didn't bother her the way it seemed to bother Keeley.

'So what do you have in mind?'

'Well, Eliane is teaching me to cut and style. If I make a good job of it she says I'll get promoted at Christmas. That made me think . . . there's no reason why I shouldn't *be* an Eliane some day. Just like you want to get your own restaurant. I could get my own salon.'

For a few moments they were silent, trying to think of all the arguments they'd hear back home, the laughs. But the voices were very distant. Mutually amazed, they looked at each other.

'I can't see why not, Keeley. You never worked at school but you're working here, really hard, I've noticed it myself.'

'Have you?'

Mary had. Noticed not just that, but the way Keeley got up early, enthusiastically, in the mornings, toned down her hair and clothes to suit what was required at work, came home full of stories that showed she was getting on with her colleagues and customers. She was adapting to France, too, making a real effort to get used to the strange customs, didn't grimace at the food any more.

'But I thought you said you wanted to get married, and have kids?'

'Yeah. Some time. I could do that as well, after I got my salon going. Right now what I want – need – to do is polish myself up a bit so I can talk to people. Get a kind of shine, like Eliane has. Since I'm learning French from scratch I can learn it properly, not make mistakes like I do in English. I can – I can do anything I want, if I set my mind to it!'

God, Mary thought, she can. So can I. There's nothing to stop us.

Life settled into a busy routine, purposeful, sometimes exhausting, but there were laughs, late-night chats, visits to the market for food, crockery, things for the flat that began to feel more and more like home. Keeley had a great eye for bargains, pictures and vases started to spring up, a second-hand radio so they could listen to talk programmes, she said, and practise their French. Mostly they listened to music, but now and then they turned on the news, trying to understand it even though they didn't give a fiddler's what President Valéry Giscard d'Estaing was doing. Mary went into the salon and Keeley cut her hair for her, said she needed a quota of guinea pigs and it was only fair that Mary volunteer, since it worked other way round at meal times. Mary quaked as her long auburn hair fell to the floor in chunks, but the result was a triumph; short, snappy, 'gamine' as Eliane admiringly called it, perfect for showing off her beloved earrings and long neck.

'You look great. Much more French.'

Not that anyone would ever take them for French in a million years, but they felt they were starting to fit in, make

real progress. One evening, Keeley came home in a panic, calling
for Mary as she ran up the stairs.

'What is it?'

'It's Sylvie!'

Sylvie was one of the girls who worked at Eliane's, a pretty
blonde who, after a properly cool French interlude, had warmed
to Keeley and become friendly.

'What's she done?'

Keeley flung off her jacket, dumped her bag on the floor and
looked stricken as she kicked off her shoes.

'She's asked me to dinner! At her house, you know, the
way the French do, no pub or anything first. Christ, Mary,
what'll I do?'

'You'll go, of course! Why not?'

'But she lives at home, her family will be there, I won't know
any of the food or wine or what fork to use, I'll make a holy
show – Mary, you've got to teach me what to do, quick! It's
tomorrow night!'

Laughing, Mary said she couldn't anticipate what kind of
food Sylvie might be planning to serve, but all Keeley had to
do was work from the outside of the cutlery in, as guests did
at the restaurant, put her napkin on her lap and watch what
everyone else did.

'Just mimic them. They'll serve you, you won't have to decide
which wine goes with what or whether the dessert comes before
or after the cheese – it'll come after, by the way, so leave
room for it.'

'Oh God. How am I going to talk to them, in French,
all night?'

'Well, Sylvie has a few words of English, she'll help you. Don't
worry, Keeley, you'll muddle along.'

'Dinner, if you don't mind. Me, Keeley Butler. It was far from
dinners I was reared.'

She made a funny face, but Mary saw that she was pleased,
even excited: here was the very first step on the long road she
wanted to travel. Even if the evening was a disaster, it was still
a start. And it was nice to be making friends.

The following night Keeley set off, petrified, gingerly carrying
a cake in a box the way they'd discovered you did when invited
to a French person's home, dangling it between your fingers by
its ribbon. Mary wished she could have baked it herself, but
had to be content with the one recipe Luc had let her try,

which unfortunately was for soup. French onion soup though, a favourite dish which he said would be in great demand now that they were coming into winter. It was very tricky, but oh, those beautiful powerful onions, those crusty chunks of bread, that smooth melting cheese like velvet . . .

'Mary!'

'Sorry! What?'

Keeley turned back in the doorway, looking lovely in a short black dress she'd got at the market, her brown eyes round as plates.

'Wish me luck.'

'Good luck, Keeley. Have a great time.'

Mary wondered how it would go as she went off to work at the restaurant, where the night chef still frostily called her mademoiselle if he deigned to speak to her at all. Luc was Luc but this one was Monsieur, and she thought even Monsieur Peyrolle was a bit afraid of him. Well, you would be, with all those cleavers to hand.

Her own evening didn't start well at all. First she sliced the peppers too thick for Monsieur's liking, then she dropped a tray of basted chickens, slipping on a patch of hot grease and skating across the floor. Monsieur screamed for Félix, Félix came flying in and there was an agitated conference, much stabbing in her direction with a skewer. Mary, her leg throbbing painfully where she'd hit the tiled floor, suddenly felt tears spring to her eyes. Frantically, she tried to fight them back as Félix came over to her.

'Monsieur Peyrolle, I'm so sorry, I fell on the grease, I didn't see it because the tray was so big . . .'

He pulled her out of Monsieur's line of vision.

'Don't worry, Mary. Accidents happen. I'm going to put you back on washing dishes tonight, because he wants me to and there might be a scene if I don't. But he'll have forgotten by tomorrow and you can go back on the vegetables then. In fact, I've been thinking . . . you seem so interested . . . would you like to start some formal training?'

'Formal – training? As what?'

'As a commis chef. With Luc. You could work the morning shift instead of nights, he says he thinks you're worth teaching.'

'Oh! Félix!'

Before he could skip out of the way she grabbed him to her

and smacked a huge kiss on his cheek, springing backwards again like a startled deer.

'Oh my God, I'm sorry, Monsieur Peyrolle, I didn't mean to do that, to call you Félix . . .'

Solemnly, he dusted himself off and adjusted his tie.

'Well, now that you have, you may as well continue. But Mary, please don't upset Monsieur again tonight, I have fifty-six customers out there.'

'No. I won't. I promise.'

Desperately she returned to work, delirious at the prospect of what Félix had just offered, terrified lest she slip again and Monsieur demand that she be sacked on the spot. It was well after midnight and every bone in her body was aching by the time she finished, but she floated home in a dream, gasping as she staggered up the stairs.

A chef! She was going to learn to be a chef!

Showering off the heat, fatigue and smell of cooking, she slipped on a long teeshirt and filled the cafetière with water, thinking that only two months ago she'd thought coffee came in jars and was made in mugs. Now she spent half an hour in the market every Saturday morning, dithering over the week's supply of beans that she ground herself, noting that prices had risen in Costa Rica and that supplies seemed to be slipping in Kenya. Keeley had howled at the price of the grinder and filter, but they were well worth it; once she'd tasted real coffee at the Vieux Moulin Mary had known she could never go back to Nescafé again. Resolutely, she ignored the jar of it that Keeley kept in the cupboard.

Where was Keeley? It was late, by French standards, the streets were very dark and quiet, Sylvie lived a good twenty minutes' walk away . . . anxiously, she went to the window and peered down.

So dark, so silent! In Ireland they'd all be at the pub now, laughing and having a great night – but it was a night she'd had once too often, so predictable that she'd have given up going to The Lantern if it wasn't for Cathal working there, and Keeley always turning up. Now it seemed like a clip from an old film, fixed in its own time, its own era. It was part of the past.

As she peered down she heard Keeley's shoes tapping on the pavement, and opened the window to throw down the keys. Keeley was always forgetting them.

'Hi!'

Keeley waved, but didn't shout up; if anyone complained about noise they might be evicted. Shutting the door quietly behind her, she flew up the stairs and burst into the room.

'How did it go?'

'Oh, Mary! It was wonderful! They were all so nice, Sylvie's father proposed a toast to me – in *champagne*, before we ate – he held my chair ready for me to sit down, I felt like such a lady! And the food was – well, you know me, but it wasn't bad, I didn't have to slip things into my bag or anything. I didn't drop anything or make mistakes – that I know of, nobody laughed at any rate – and somehow we managed to talk in some kind of language, sort of a mixture. And Mary, she has a brother!'

Mary grinned as she took in her friend's flushed face, the brown eyes huge with excited exhaustion, the clearing of a hurdle that really had terrified her. Although their new life was a success it was a struggle too, a never-ending fight to survive, understand, learn, keep up and adjust to new things every day.

'A brother? What kind of brother?'

'A trainee manager kind! He's twenty-one, he works in a department store, you know, that big one, P-P-Pr—'

'Pridoux.'

'Yeah. He's learning to be a big nasty boss. But he's gorgeous. Curly hair, dark, kind of olive skin, a mouth like that guy who was in *Love Story* – Robert, Richard, what's his name—?'

'Ryan? O'Neal?'

'Yeah. And get this, he offered to drive me home!'

'But you walked home.'

'Well, I thought . . . I mean . . . it might be better to—'

'To what?'

'To play a bit hard to get, for one thing. I'm not going to do an Erik this time. And besides, I was afraid he might want to come in for coffee, and, well . . . it's not exactly Buckingham Palace, is it?'

'Oh, Keeley! It's our flat! I thought you loved it.'

'I do love it. I just decided to wait until I got to know him a bit better, find out whether he's the kind who'd be prepared to take what he finds. I think he might be, though. He's really nice, Mary. They all are. I had a ball.'

Delighted, Mary threw in her own tuppenceworth.

'I got into trouble with Monsieur tonight, but Félix took my side. Keeley, he says he's going to let me start training with Luc! To be a chef!'

'A chef? Like a man, you mean? With a big white hat and a moustache and a temper?'

Giggling, they leaned on opposite sides of the tiny kitchen's wall, taking in so many developments in one night, each so pleased for the other. Proud of each other, too; they really could hack it, manage things, get somewhere.

'Well, I'll drink to that! Even your revolting coffee. Pass me a cup.'

Without so much as wrinkling her nose, Keeley drank it, crooking her little finger comically as she took ladylike sips. She'd better get used to it, if Mary was going to be a chef and she was going to fit in, be accepted by people like Sylvie Tourand, the father who held chairs for ladies and the beautiful brother, Vincent.

From the following Monday Mary's schedule changed to mornings, and although it meant getting up at six she fell into it with relief, glad to be off the stressful night shift and even more glad to get away from Monsieur. Keeley had never taken him seriously, said she should just tell him to shag off, but even if Mary had known how to say it she wouldn't have dared. Monsieur was a monster, his reign was one of terror, even Félix paled when he went on the warpath. Luc Bosquet on the other hand, was a joy to work with, to be taken under his wing was both a compliment and a pleasure. Often Mary and Keeley fell over each other in the small cold bathroom, now that they both had to be up early, but they worked out a system and there were no clashes, no friction at all, both of them looking forward to each fruitful new day.

After the first week Luc sat Mary down with a coffee during their mid-morning break, pronounced her progress satisfactory but then looked at her in a way that unnerved her. A short but robust man of about fifty, with dark heavy eyebrows and a slow thoughtful way of speaking, he was an extremely good chef and was actually taken, she suspected, more seriously than Monsieur.

'Mary, tell me – this is your first time away from home, is it not?'

'Yes.'

'What made you choose France?'

'I don't know . . . the sun . . . a film I saw . . .'

'You knew nothing of French cuisine?'

It was more a statement than a question, and she felt able to be honest with him.

'Nothing. Of any cuisine. I don't know what happened. I just got interested the moment I saw it, tasted it. It's so different to what we eat at home.'

'Yes. Well, I think you should learn a little more about it.'

She panicked slightly. Was she not learning as much as she could, as fast as she could? Was he not pleased?

'Your work in the kitchen is excellent. But there is more to food than kitchens.'

'There – there is?'

'Much more. What I want you to do now is start getting to know the region, the specialities, the producers. You must go to see the farms where they grow the vegetables, raise the pigs and the cows. You must visit Marseille and the little fishing villages, talk to the fishermen, go out on some boats if you can persuade them to take you. I want you to tour the vineyards, the orchards, climb the mountains with the goats, see the bees buzzing in their hives.'

She thought quickly. She would have some time, now that her afternoons were free, there were buses to places like Marseille . . . but the farms, orchards, mountains? How was she supposed to get there?

Well, that was her problem, not his. Mr O'Rourke at the deli had often said that; he wanted to hear answers, not questions. 'Just get on with it,' he used to say; he was a busy man – and Luc was even busier, she couldn't expect him to babysit her.

'Then I'd better go, Luc. Where do you think I should start?'

'I will write you a list, make some telephone calls, arrange introductions. And, after Christmas, I will take you to the truffle fair in Rognes myself.'

Before she could confess that this was a new word for her, he got up, crossed the kitchen and came back holding a small white plate, with the reverent look of a priest carrying a chalice. On it was a single tiny piece of something that looked like black cotton.

'Taste it.'

She picked it up and ate it with her fingers, as he evidently expected her to, waiting for the flavour to come welling up.

What you tasted on your tongue, he had taught her, was not the whole story; fine foods carried on down into the throat, spread their flavour into the bloodstream, into the mind and heart. After a few moments, she swallowed, then nodded.

'A type of mushroom? A magic mushroom!'

'Yes. Sheer magic. They are very rare. They grow in winter in the forests, we train pigs to sniff them out, a certain type of pig . . .'

He launched into the whole history of truffles as she smiled to herself, thinking that Keeley would recoil in disgust. But she was fascinated, glancing occasionally at the empty plate with wonder, realising the importance and value of what she had just eaten.

Absorbed in Luc's story, she didn't even notice when Félix came into the kitchen, looked at the two of them with their heads bent over a completely empty plate, and withdrew without a word.

'Oh, please, Keeley, say you'll come with me. I can't go on my own, but I have to go . . . dear God, how am I going to go, where will I find transport?'

Keeley beamed.

'I think I may be able to fix that problem for you.'

'How?'

They were sitting in what now passed for a sitting room in the flat, Mary on the orange crate and Keeley on the floor, cradling bowls of hot chocolate as they luxuriated in Sunday morning, when Keeley didn't have to work at all and Mary didn't start till ten.

'Vincent.'

Keeley had been out with Vincent last night, to a bowling alley where she had beaten his score and, she crowed, impressed him no end with the accuracy of her aim. As a kid, she'd been a whizz with a slingshot.

'Vincent? But he—'

'He wants to take me out. Today. For a drive. Just tell me where you want to go, and I'll tell him that's where I want to go, with my friend Mary, I can hardly leave her on her tod on Sunday afternoon, can I?'

Mary could hardly believe her ears. Keeley must surely want to be alone with Vincent, yet she would offer to do this? And wait for her, until she finished work at two-thirty?

'Oh, Keeley—'

'I know. I'm a gem. Don't mention it. And just don't pick anywhere forty miles away.'

No. It was getting dark much earlier now, they'd only have a few hours . . .

'How about that abbey where they make the calissons?'

'The huh?'

'Calissons, they're a kind of sweet made from fruit, almonds, orange blossom. The abbey is near Simiane, Luc says, not too far from Aix, and you have a sweet tooth – I'll buy you a whole box!'

'OK. Just so long as you promise not to buy me a whole box of cheese when we go to see the ruddy goats, or sardines when we go to Marseille.'

'What? You mean you – you'd—'

Keeley sighed, exaggeratedly, and then smiled.

'Yeah. I'll try to get Vincent to take us to as many of these blasted places as I can. I'll tell him I don't go for drives without a chaperone and he's got to take you with us. Anyway, it'll be out in the country, won't it? I liked the country, that time we went to Powerscourt, and when we were picking the grapes.'

'But Keeley, don't you want to be – I mean – on your own with Vincent?'

'Sure. But we've got nights, haven't we?' Mary looked at her. She sounded so calm, almost confident.

'You're really getting on well with him, then?'

'Yeah. Or more to the point, he's getting on well with me, the lucky man.'

Mary thought about it while she dressed, conscious of a shift in things. After less than two weeks, Keeley seemed to have got the whole question of Vincent Tourand remarkably well in hand, was taking things very slowly and, apparently, calling the shots. There was none of the giddy gossip there'd been about Erik, no sighing or simpering, she wasn't dying to show him off or even to describe him. Only that he was dark, and nice, she was teaching him useful English phrases like 'how is yer oul wan, game ball.' That was the right thing to say to Irish or English ladies when they came shopping at Pridoux, as some occasionally did . . . her eyes sparkled with mischief, determination to tease the French as they teased her. Mary hoped Vincent had a sense of humour. He'd need one, not only to cope with Keeley but to see the funny side of having to drive on Sundays to abbeys and farms and fishing ports, with a gooseberry in the back of the car. What if he hated it, hated her, refused to do it?

But, when she met him that afternoon, she was impressed. Not only did he come to collect her at the Vieux Moulin, with Keeley in the front seat of the Citroen like a trophy, he came right in and asked for her, escorted her out while introducing himself. Far from being resentful, he seemed eager to please, and she thought he was lovely. Dark curly hair, just as Keeley had said, tanned skin and warm hazel eyes, not overly tall but fit and strong-looking in brown cords, a red sweater, the slip-on type of shoes Frenchmen wore. With relief, she saw that his sister Sylvie was in the back of the car too, so there were four of them; it wouldn't be so awkward after all.

Sylvie, who specialised in tints and colours at the salon, was good fun, Keeley said, when you got to know her. But then Keeley was getting to know lots of people, while Mary knew only Félix and Luc. They were kind, but too far out of her age group to become friends . . . this chatty type of friend anyway, that you could go off on jaunts with. Not that Mary minded; she was so busy, often so exhausted, she hadn't time to join the French class where Keeley met people, although she liked it when Keeley brought them back 'to sample our Mary's cooking', now that there were pots and pans to cook in. Félix had been great about that, given her a lot of stuff to take home, saving them the expense of equipping the kitchen. Lately she'd started trying out recipes there, simple things like cassoulet and salads, delighted to have some more appreciative guinea pigs than Keeley. Of course it was a pity about the quiche, the very first experiment, which had turned out so curdled and horrible, Keeley had roared laughing and they'd ended up with a takeaway from Quick. But the coq-au-vin had been better, and just wait until this time next year, she'd be serving whole four-course meals, they would beg for her ratatouille, grovel for her bouillabaisse!

When would Vincent be invited? Keeley had no problem about asking her classmates or colleagues to the flat, but she still hadn't asked him, or Sylvie for that matter. It was as if the Tourand family was out of range in some way, being kept at arm's length . . . and as a strategy it seemed to be working. As they drove off she noticed the way Vincent turned to smile at Keeley, as if to ask whether she was pleased with him, was his behaviour up to scratch so far? Keeley smiled back, but then turned round to talk to the two in the back of the car, lightly, airily.

It was only half an hour to the abbey at Simiane, an easy pleasant drive during which they became acquainted, with a lot of sign language and wonky translation, gesturing and giggling. As soon as they arrived Vincent leapt out of the car, sprinted round and opened the door for Keeley, and Mary was open-mouthed to see her friend demurely step out as if she expected such treatment, with just a small nod of thanks. Mother of God, Mary thought, is this really the same person who used to sit on a wall chewing gum with Mickser Sweeney?

Hardly able to keep a straight face, she approached the abbey with some awe, not just because it was such a magnificent building but because Keeley failed to squint at it dismissively, to say 'Jaysus!' or to light up a cigarette. Usually she did one or other, or all three, when faced with something old, unfamiliar or daunting. Instead, she nodded regally at the monk who stood on the gravel smiling a welcome, and left Vincent to make enquiries about where to start. It turned out that the monk was to guide a tour of the sweet factory, which was in a converted part of the building; they would see all the raw ingredients, the manufacturing process, and then taste the result. Mary thought there would surely be a rebellion at the first two parts of this proposal, but before she could say anything Vincent had got four tickets. It was a pleasure, he said, to find two foreigners so interested in the culinary arts of his country. Keeley caught Mary's eye, turned scarlet and grinned from ear to ear. After some other visitors had joined the group, they set solemnly off.

Mary was the only one remotely interested, and maybe Vincent a bit she thought, but Sylvie and Keeley seemed prepared to behave themselves, their attention wandering but not loudly enough to cause a distraction. Leaving them to tag along behind she followed the monk, noting everything, glad to have Vincent interpreting into pidgin English, helping her as best he could. Almonds, apricots, melons, tangerines . . . the sunny climate of Provence provided them all, and she was enchanted by the colours, the rich heavy scents, the huge white mountains of sugar like miniature Alps. How odd, that monks should run such an enterprise, quite professionally, as if they were businessmen! She'd never known they did anything other than pray. But the one guiding the tour was full of chat, and she wished she could question him, that the tour would last longer. When it ended she kept her promise, bought the biggest box of calissons in the little shop and handed it to Keeley. Back outside in the November sunshine, they leaned against a honey-coloured stone wall, passing it between them, munching, murmuring, enjoying the many flowers still in brilliant bloom. It was one of the nicest Sundays she could remember ever having spent, and the look on Keeley's face was radiant as Vincent looked at her, as if wondering what he could do to please her next.

In the weeks that followed Vincent found many ways of making Keeley happy, and the budding relationship blossomed slowly but surely, until there began to be a note of security about it, a warm bond that brought a great bloom to Keeley's cheeks. Mary saw that she was falling in love, and was greatly pleased when, at last, she invited Vincent to their home. The invitation sounded casual, extended one Sunday evening as they drove back from a visit to an apiary that produced great quantities of honey. Sylvie wasn't with them, and Mary was quick to pick up on her role in the romance, the one small thing she could do to help.

'I'm not a great chef yet, Vincent' she said, 'but do come in, please. I'd love you to try my cooking and tell me what you think.'

Eagerly he came in, and was given a glass of white wine while she set about making supper; nothing too ambitious, just some pasta, but she watched it like a hawk, timed it to perfection and served it drenched in a roquefort sauce. Hot, creamy, light but satisfying . . . he ate every bite of it, and couldn't compliment her enough. Even Keeley ate it, looking blissful.

'You knocked him out!' she said later, after he had reluctantly departed.

'He loved it, I'd say he'll be back for more . . . thanks, Mary. You were great.'

Mary felt it was the least she could do, and began to cook with growing confidence as Vincent returned, and their Sunday supper turned into a regular event. As winter drew in, their talk turned one night to Christmas, to the tree that had gone up in the town centre, the lights that were sparkling in the shops.

'What,' Vincent wondered, 'are you two going to do for Christmas?'

'Work!' they chorused in unison. Both the salon and the restaurant were extra busy already, there were office parties, they knew that Christmas Eve would be frantic.

'Yes, but on the day?'

They looked at each other blankly, not having given it a thought until this moment. What were they going to do? Breaking into the momentary silence, Vincent looked a little apprehensive.

'If you don't have any plans, I was wondering – I mean, we were all wondering, Sylvie and my parents – whether you'd like to spend it at our house, with us? Both of you, we'd love you to come.'

Keeley flushed crimson, looked so happy that Mary understood immediately; Vincent was asking her to join his family. It was a kind of formal acceptance, recognition that she belonged with them on Christmas Day. And she, Mary, was to be included, as Keeley's friend, permitted to see how a French family celebrated, what they ate and what they did. But it was up to Keeley to accept, which she did, looking as if she'd been handed the Christmas present of a lifetime.

'We'd love to, Vincent. Thank you so much.'

Leaning over, she kissed his cheek, and he took her hand, squeezed it tightly and did not let it go. Feeling the emotion between them, something new and vulnerable, Mary made herself as scarce as was possible in the tiny flat.

The letter arrived ten days before Christmas, and Mary stuffed it into the pocket of her jeans as she let herself in, carrying a wicker basket filled with eggs, cream, mushrooms and a bundle of asparagus that Luc had slipped to her. This time she'd get the quiche right, treat Keeley to a delicious supper, Vincent too if she brought him home with her. Keeley frequently did that now, but not invariably; one day she had sat down in the kitchen, curling the collar of her sweater up around her chin a bit uneasily, and said she wanted to talk about it. 'What's to discuss?' Mary had said, surprised, but Keeley plunged in, determined to get things clear. She was very glad that everyone was getting on so well together, she said, that Mary liked Vincent and made him so welcome, but she didn't want her to feel crowded. Everyone needed their space, especially when there was so little of it, and Mary wasn't to think that Vincent was virtually moving in with them.

Mary's heart lurched. What was Keeley thinking of – not of moving out, surely, of getting a place of her own, with him? Did they want to live together, was that it? Of course it would be natural if they did, but – but was it very selfish to hope that it mightn't happen just yet? She and Keeley were so dependent on each other, still two foreigners trying to survive together, and such good friends, having such fun.

Yes, Keeley said firmly, they were. And they were going to stay friends, stay flatmates. Wonderful as it was, she didn't intend to rush her relationship with Vincent, there was plenty of time, everything was perfect just as it was. When the couple wanted to be alone together they would do it somewhere else, not impose themselves on Mary or expect her to go out for long walks by herself at nights.

Maybe later, maybe next summer – but not now, it was much too soon to even think of changing the situation they had set up, and were enjoying so much. They both wanted to get on at work, do well, keep their minds on it, and Vincent wasn't going to change that priority. Mary nearly fell off her chair, to hear Keeley talking so sensibly when it was obvious that she adored Vincent, that he was enhancing her whole life. And this the girl who would have run off to Sweden with Erik, overnight! But Keeley said that was just the point, how awful if she had run off with him, she wasn't going to make that kind of mistake again. If Vincent really loved her, she said lowering her eyelashes with a blush, he would understand, he would wait.

And so the matter seemed settled, much to Mary's relief. With her mind at ease now, she thought about Keeley as she climbed the stairs and entered the flat, about all the places they had visited together in Vincent's car, a kind gesture that she found very touching. Keeley had grown into a close, supportive, wonderful friend, a woman who deserved a good man like Vincent, all the joy he was bringing to her.

And what joy, what news was in this letter? Humming to herself, she brewed a pot of coffee and sat down to read the gossip from home, written in her mother's hand. The Irish stamp looked almost foreign as she tore open the envelope and took out what seemed to be a long letter, four thick pages written on both sides. But there must be plenty to say; it was only the second letter Leesha had sent since her daughter's departure to pick grapes nearly three months before. Sipping her coffee, Mary began to read.

The first page was full of snippets, about the bakery being up to its tonsils in orders for Christmas cakes, her dad Kevin trying to find a good place to hide the bikes the boys were getting from Santa, the weather being awful and what was it like in France, did she have a good warm vest? Mary smiled, wondering what it was about mothers and vests, inseparable as lovers.

And then, without warning, the tone changed. Mary drew in her breath, held the pages at arm's length as Leesha suddenly seemed to collapse under some dreadful weight. She missed her daughter terribly, she said, they all did, the boys couldn't understand why their big sister had run off and left them. At first nobody had taken it seriously, they were all sure it was just a whim and she'd be home in a couple of weeks, but almost three months had gone by and it wasn't funny any more, when on earth was Mary coming home?

Home? But I *am* home, Mary thought, glancing around the flat as if for confirmation; I live here now, look, there are my shoes on the floor, there's my toothbrush in the bathroom, there are my cookery books that Luc gave me to take *home*.

It was an awful situation, Leesha continued. Absolutely awful, what with Mr O'Rourke ringing up furious from the deli, saying that Mary owed him three days' work, then Keeley Butler's mother coming round in a tizz, not understanding what had come over the pair of them at all, and then Cathal Sullivan to face.

Cathal had visited the Jameson house no less than three times, asking whether there was any news, saying he'd got a very strange letter from Mary and that she must be on drink or drugs or some such thing, pressed on her by one of those notoriously persuasive Frenchmen. *Was* there a man, was that it? Or was it all the fault of that Keeley one, who hadn't a lick of sense and probably thought it was all a great laugh? Well, it wasn't a laugh, not one bit funny. Mary should see the way her Dad was moping, going off to work miserable every morning, the way her brothers kept asking for her, had stuck her postcards up on their bedroom wall, wanted to know was she coming home for Christmas.

Was she? Leesha assumed she was, because it was simply out of the question that she wasn't. The two of them would come home, they'd had their fun, didn't they have any idea of the pain and hurt they were causing, not to mention the worry? Leesha hadn't slept a wink since getting Mary's first letter, none of them had, her father wasn't eating a bite and of course the neighbours all thought it was very peculiar.

It was peculiar, she'd never heard anything like it – not that she was angry with Mary, there wouldn't be any cloud over her head when she got back or anything, but she must *come* back. Cathal was upset but he would forgive her, everything would be all right, but she mustn't leave it any longer. The ferry tickets were to be booked the moment this letter arrived, with the Christmas rush they'd be lucky to get them in time, bags were to be packed and both girls were to return right away.

Please, Mary, Leesha concluded. You can't simply vanish into thin air like this. You're our only girl and we want you here with us, what kind of Christmas do you think it would be without you? Come on now, be sensible and do as we ask, make Keeley listen to you, her mother is up a wall without her, poor Tony has nobody else to visit him. Write with the ferry time and we'll come down to Rosslare to collect you.

Horrified, Mary read the signature, with love, XXX for hugs and kisses. Oh, God. Oh, no.

Chapter Three

Sitting in the car down in the street, Keeley just could not seem to get out. It was late, Mary would have supper ready, but she simply could not budge. Not as long as Vincent held her face between his hands, as tenderly as if it were something very fragile, precious as the porcelain he said was called Limoges. Over and over again he kissed her eyelids, her nose, her lips, murmuring softly into her ear, his breath warm and gentle on her cheek. With her chin on his shoulder, her arms around him, she felt as if she were drifting in a deep warm ocean, free but anchored, floating slowly towards some safe harbour.

Neither of them understood the other's endearments, but their body language said everything that needed to be said, told them that they were moving in the right direction, united, at peace and at one with each other. It was the most glorious feeling, that Keeley could not get enough of no matter how long she stayed there . . . but we have tomorrow, she reminded herself, and the next day, all our tomorrows.

Reluctantly, she stirred at last, disengaged herself with a smile. He understood why she wasn't asking him in, knew that it was one of the nights she needed to spend with Mary, and let her go with only the smallest sigh. She got out of the car and he watched until she was safely inside before driving away, carefully, because there was frost on the ground.

Mary thought Keeley had never looked more beautiful as she came bounding in, wrapped in a big chenille scarf of forest green, her dark eyes dancing, her spiky hair in delicious disarray. She burst into tears.

'What – oh my God, Mary, what is it? What's wrong?'

Tears streamed down Mary's cheeks as she picked up a letter and held it out to her. Wordlessly, Keeley sank down at the kitchen table and read it. Read it twice, in silence.

'But – but Mary, this is blackmail!'

Mary lifted her head. 'What?'

'It – it's all about *them*! I'm sorry, I know it's from your mother, but it's just one big guilt trip. Nothing about you, about what your flat is like or how you're getting on, about your job or any interest in anything *you're* doing. Only about how sorry they're all feeling for themselves and what a nuisance you're being. It – it's terrible!'

'But Keeley, I feel terrible. I mean, it is Christmas, I do miss them, my little brothers, they're only six and seven, they must think I don't love them or care about them any more . . .'

'Then we'll find a phone. First thing in the morning, you go round to the post office and you ring them. Early, before you go to work or they go to school. You have a good long chat with everyone and tell them that of course you love them. Explain that the only reason you can't come home is that work is so busy, but that you'll send them presents and come to visit as soon as you can. They'll surely understand that you don't have much money and that every restaurant in the world is up to its eyes at Christmas.'

'M-maybe. But even if they do, they'll want to know when am I coming, then.'

Keeley considered.

'Well, when do you think Félix might give you some time off?'

'I don't know. Maybe at Easter . . . we haven't really talked about it yet.'

'Okay. So tell them you'll be home at Easter, and that you'll ring them every week from now on. Make it clear that you're well and happy and that there's nothing for them to be worrying about. Tell them about how Luc is training you to be a chef, what a fabulous opportunity you've got, how proud of you they're going to be. I mean, some day you really will be a chef, Mary, you'll be earning enough that you can send money home. Meanwhile, tell them you want them to take photos on Christmas Day and send them to you. We'll see if we can borrow a camera, too, and send them snaps of the flat so they can see you have a roof over your head.'

'Yes . . . I suppose . . . oh, but still, Keeley, it is Christmas!'

'Mary, get a grip. It's too easy to get weepy at this time of year. Félix would blow a fuse if you disappeared for so much as ten minutes, am I right or am I right?'

'Yes. You are right . . . my mother says you haven't a lick of sense, but you have. But what about you, Keeley? Mam says your mother is worried too.'

'If we had a phone, I'd ring her. Since we don't, I'll simply write to her, tonight, loads of cheerful stuff that will make her feel better. I was going to post her a present tomorrow anyway.'

'And Poor Tony?'

'Mary, you're going to say I'm a hard-hearted bitch. But have you ever thought that it could be someone else who's in that wheelchair – one of your little brothers maybe, some child Tony knocked down? He deliberately rode that bike like a lunatic, he was a danger to everyone and it's the mercy of God that he's the only one who ended up paying the price.'

'But he was very young—'

'He was twenty. Not six, not ten, not even a teenager. A grown man. Old enough to work, to vote, to get married. To be responsible.'

Mary sighed. Keeley did sound hard. But maybe you had to get hard, when your family was so soft, so flabby and hopeless. When your father was in the habit of hitting people clatters by way of a career. She could understand why Keeley wouldn't want to go home, even if she hadn't met Vincent.

'All right. You write to your mother tonight, and I'll phone mine in the morning. We'll make them understand that everything is fine and that there's nothing to worry about.'

Drying her eyes, Mary looked up and forced a smile. But everything was not fine. There was something that had begun to worry her slowly, quietly, more desperately every day. Something she should tell Keeley, but somehow couldn't. Not now, when everything was so good, so fruitful and happy. Not when she was going to be a chef, and Luc was taking her to the truffle fair in Rognes on New Year's Eve.

Parts of Leesha's letter remained on Mary's mind for some time, sinking in, unsettling her. She felt guilty about the work she owed Mr O'Rourke, until Keeley came up with an idea: why not send him the three days' money, in lieu, with a note of explanation and apology? She felt a bit better when she'd done that, but then she began to think about her father – not eating, Mam said – about her brothers' wondering little faces, about Cathal who was upset. He must be, if he'd been three times to visit her parents. But why did he think she'd been influenced by some man? Was she not capable of making her own decision to stay in France? And what did Mam mean about him 'forgiving' her? Was it not better to call off a marriage than marry the wrong person? After all, they weren't even formally engaged, she wasn't wearing any ring when she left . . . and why hadn't he written, if he was so upset? There was no letter asking her to reconsider, to change her mind, even suggesting that he would wait for her if she just needed a break to think things over. No word at all . . . there was something niggling about it, some lingering feeling of things not being finalised. It would be much better if he were angry, if he wrote a real scorcher saying he never wanted to see her again. She didn't want him going round to her parents' house, keeping up contact with them, reminding them of his car and his pub and his prospects.

But at least the phone call helped. Dad came on the line, then Mam and the boys, sounding baffled and unhappy at first, but then relenting a little, inching their way towards what she hoped would be eventual acceptance. Resolutely she kept her voice light and bright, told them colourful details of her work and flat, of Keeley's romance and how great Luc was, the terrific time they were having.

And they really were, loving every single minute of it. There was a Christmas party at the Chamber of Commerce for all the language classes, in the late afternoon when Mary was able to go to it, and she discovered how popular Keeley was, how many immigrants were living in Aix. Invitations to other parties came out of it, then Félix hosted a get-together for his staff and Eliane invited her ten hairdressers round to her flat for a surprisingly uninhibited hooley; the Christmas atmosphere was just as lively as at home. At lunchtime on Christmas Eve there was even a sing-song in the restaurant, customers and staff all joining in carols, Luc puce in the face as he produced his wife Annette and a bottle of champagne, Monsieur scowling as he watched Luc feed Mary first one glass and then another, toasting her future as a great chef. Félix gave her the most beautiful silk scarf, blue to match her eyes, which watered with tears as she draped it round her neck. He was so good to her, everyone was being so kind and thoughtful, it was impossible to feel even the least little bit left out.

By Christmas morning they were, as Keeley said, 'crosseyed'. But they jumped out of their twin beds and rushed to get dressed, deciding that they wanted to go to church, see how Christmas mass was done in France. But first they opened their presents from home, laughing at the sensible things they contained, warm underwear and woollen tights as if the girls were living in Antarctica. They were sorry the post office wasn't open, to phone Mary's family and pass on a message to Keeley's, but they had spoken to them the night before and felt they were doing their best. Only the thought of Mary's small brothers tugged at her, their yells and smiles when they saw their bikes, their breathless tales of having seen Santa's boots go up the chimney, their round chubby faces. She had sent them games and puzzles, but it wasn't the same as giving them hugs and kisses.

It was a crisp sunny walk to church, Keeley talking all the way there, jogging along in the height of good form.

'It really is a happy Christmas, Mary, isn't it? We've settled in, we've made friends, there's Vincent . . . you'll meet someone nice too, wait and see.'

'I – I'm happy as I am, Keeley. I'd rather not think about men for a while. Luc takes up all my attention!'

Keeley didn't pursue the matter, thinking that anyone who'd escaped from the likes of Cathal Sullivan probably would need a breather, right enough. But Vincent – she couldn't believe her luck, the way she felt, the tingling joy of it, it was as if she'd sprouted wings and flown to paradise.

When they reached the church she gave silent thanks for her good fortune, and Mary knelt in prayer too. The mass turned out to be virtually identical to the ritual in Ireland, easy to follow despite being in French, and to their surprise they enjoyed it. Vincent had offered to meet them outside the church, but they'd told him they wanted to walk to his house and work up an appetite for lunch. It was a longish walk, and their cheeks were glowing when they arrived, Mary a bit nervous about meeting his parents for the first time.

But she was brought in and embraced, no less, by both parents, his father Pierre and his mother Francine, a well-dressed couple with an air of stately calm. Mary noted how they embraced Keeley, with real affection, and the way Vincent hugged her to him, as if claiming a lost treasure although the two had been together only the previous evening. Then his sister Sylvie appeared, there were presents, apéritifs, a look around the house and garden which, while not large, were comfortable and appealing.

Mary was dying to get into the kitchen but Francine wouldn't let her help at all, insisted with much miming and laughing that she must be sick of kitchens, she was to sit down and relax. Mary was quite amazed by the extent and warmth of her welcome; Cathal Sullivan's parents had always been off-hand with her, stiff in a way that suggested she might not be quite good enough for their son. And here, she was welcomed whole-heartedly, though she was only a friend; it was Keeley who was the prospective daughter-in-law. Looking at Keeley, standing in front of the Christmas tree in her best pink sweater and new navy trousers, with her arm around Vincent, Mary thought they really did look like a couple, that there was something confirmed between them. Even though Keeley said there was no hurry, wanted to wait and linger and savour, there would certainly be an engagement if not a wedding in 1978. She had to smile, happy for them; Keeley would be Madame, a Frenchwoman, her children would speak French and have outlandish names that would be the talk of Pearse Gardens. Not that she was likely to take them there too often, but they would have to be brought sometimes, to see their grandmother and delightful grandfather.

Lunch wasn't served for nearly two hours, but it was stupendous when it came, a six-course banquet served on white Battenburg linen with real crystal, a whole host of things that made Mary's eyes widen. Paté de foie gras, a great delicacy from Strasbourg, Luc had told her, smoked salmon which was meant to be a tribute to the 'Irish demoiselles' and made them both laugh, neither ever having tasted it in Ireland. Grapefruit sorbet, a gleaming pheasant stuffed with chestnuts and aromatic herbs, huge dishes of green and red vegetables, three kinds of potato . . . they'd never seen such a feast in their lives.

Keeley whispered to Mary while she thought nobody was listening, 'I'm bursting! I'll explode!'

'Just taste little bits of everything,' Mary whispered back, wondering how Madame Tourand had got that stuffing so moist and perfect, there was a faint flavour of apples . . . 'Calvados,' Pierre told her. 'A spirit made in Normandy. Do you know where that is?'

He and his wife were very helpful, had only a little English but made it go a long way, joined laughing in the pantomime of communication. Everyone, even Vincent, had dreaded long silences, a complete breakdown between languages, but the meal went off very well, in an atmosphere of goodwill, good humour, acceptance into the family. Keeley, who had so feared that first meal in this house, was the life and soul of the party, grinning cheekily although Mary saw that she was watching her Ps and Qs, no longer nervous but still anxious to make a good impression. For no apparent reason, she felt a sudden surge of great fondness for her friend.

She loves it here, she thought, and so do I. Coming to France was a great idea, and staying on was an even better one. I feel awful about Mam and Dad and the boys, but apart from that everything is fantastic. I wish we could stay for ever.

God, I wish we could. How can everything be going so wrong, just when it's going so right? What am I going to do, how am I going to tell Keeley? I'll have to work it out, find the best way and the best time, but no matter what I say, she's going to be gutted.

It was hideous but it was essential, Luc said, that Mary be up at five for the truffle fair on New Year's Eve. He would come to collect her at half past, they would drive into Rognes, have a hot breakfast there and meet all the dealers. Would her friend Keeley like to come along too, just for the fun of it?

Mary asked her again as she brushed her teeth, and Keeley rolled over with a groan, pulling the duvet up over her head.

'I would rather,' she said, 'have my fingernails removed with a flaming chisel.'

So Mary set off in the dark with Luc, muffled up in the one warm jacket she possessed, and they drove in easy companionship along the twisting roads. Luc was not a very good driver, the car slewed several times around sharp corners, and she began to feel the same way she had felt on that unspeakable ferry. The moment they reached the café where they were to have their hot breakfast, she dived into the bathroom and was violently sick.

Luc gazed at her, and tut-tutted.

'So pale, like a little ghost! I will get you some plain dry bread . . .'

'Oh no, please . . .'

He all but forced it down her throat, but against her expectations it did make her feel better. Enough that she was eventually able to face the truffles, but only just: wincing inside, she heard the lack of enthusiasm in her voice, the disappointment in Luc's.

Insisting that she was fine she slogged on, whispering greetings
at his friends as he introduced her to what seemed to be dozens,
trying to avert her eyes from the black glistening . . . ughhh.

It was a very lively crowded fair, full of men in thick sweaters
carting tiny weighing scales about in dirty hands, shouting
and arguing, knocking back shots of some strong spirit at
this god-awful hour of the morning, jostling so that Luc had
sometimes to protect her, pluck her out of the path of some
aggressive vendor. He explained the whole procedure, slowly
and patiently, but she hardly heard a word he was saying,
wishing with guilty fervour that it would end, that he would
take her home and let her spend the rest of this one free day
in bed. But then that meant getting back in the car . . . the very
thought made her head spin.

Next thing she knew she was being helped through the door
of her flat, and Luc's distant voice was explaining urgently,
anxiously, to Keeley that she had fainted. Right there in the
middle of the fair, he had had no idea she was in such a
state. He'd been working her too hard, he asserted sorrowfully,
Christmas had been a nightmare, she must take the remaining
two days of the week off and get some rest.

After some further discourse, about a doctor perhaps, he
backed out, embarrassed and worried, his eyes like a spaniel's
as he made Keeley promise to ring him with further news. Mary
sat on the converted orange crate, her head between her knees,
her head whirling.

'Right,' Keeley said briskly, not a bit abashed at having
greeted Luc in her pyjamas, 'I'm going to make you a pot of
tea, and then you're going straight to bed. If you don't feel any
better after a long sleep, I'm getting you a doctor.'

Mary lifted her head, saw the concern in Keeley's face, knew
that her own must be white as chalk.

'Keeley' she whispered, 'I think I'm pregnant.'

Two hours later, Keeley was still storming up and down, flinging
her hands in the air, thundering across the wooden floorboards
in her bare feet.

'A fool! What kind of complete, thick-headed, bubble-brained
fool are you!?'

'The kind who gets pregnant.' Abjectly Mary gazed at the
floor, mortified, distraught, chastised and scared of her suddenly frightening friend.

'Did you not think? Did you not take any precautions? They were Swedish, for God's sake, they had a truckload of condoms!'

'I – I didn't know what he meant.'

'What? What do *you* mean?'

'He – he asked me if I was "all right." I thought he just meant was I – was I comfortable!'

'*Comfortable*?!' Keeley screeched like a banshee. 'Are you insane? He meant were you on the pill, you halfwit!'

'Well, I didn't know that, I'd never done it before—'

Keeley thumped the wall in exasperation.

'Lord preserve us from the ladies who live in Pearse Avenue! The ones who think sex is about getting comfortable, and that it's only trollops from Pearse Gardens get pregnant!'

'Oh, Keeley, I'm sorry, I don't know how I can have been so stupid . . .'

Keeley looked volcanic, ready to gush flames forty feet high.

'Stupid is right! Sorry is right! What in the name of blessed Jesus almighty are we going to do now?'

'We?'

'Yes! We, us, the idiots from Ireland! The ones with the chiseller under their oxter!'

Despite herself Mary laughed nervously; this was a different Keeley from the one who'd thanked Vincent's parents so graciously for their delightful Christmas Day.

'Well, I'm the one who's pregnant—'

Keeley whirled round. 'We'll have to buy a kit. One of those blue-or-clear jobs from the chemist's.'

'I suppose . . . but it's been ten weeks . . .'

'Why didn't you tell me sooner?'

'I – I – oh, God – I kind of thought that if I didn't say anything, it mightn't happen, mightn't be true . . .'

Keeley looked at her with fascination.

'I have never, ever, in my entire life, met such a complete and total birdbrain.'

Mary's lip trembled.

'Please, Keeley, stop it, I don't feel well . . .'

'Huh. I suppose that's what you'll be saying to the midwife when you're – oh, hell on wheels, when is it due, anyway?'

'At the end of June or the beginning of July it must be—'

Keeley paused to think. 'Look. We're in France, Mary. It's

different here. If you wanted, you could – I mean – you don't
even know the father's second name—'

They looked at each other. Then Mary scuffed at the floor,
concentrating on it as if she were trying to sand it with her
shoe.

'No. I couldn't, Keeley. It's still a child. Like my kid brothers.
I couldn't.' She was relieved when Keeley didn't argue.

'All right. That's one thing out of the way. What we've got
to do now is work out our other options. I'll make some
more tea.'

Mary watched in silence while she did it, feeling monumentally
foolish, deserving all the dog's abuse Keeley could throw at her.
In some perverse way she even wanted Keeley to go on shouting
and storming; her presence was a huge comfort, whatever she
felt it wasn't alone.

Keeley poured the tea, handed her a cup with a look like a
bacon slicer, and sat down on the floor with her legs crossed
under her.

'OK. Let's think. First of all, are you really sick? Can you go
on working, or what?'

'I – I'm not too bad. I could, I'm sure – but Keeley, what's
the point?'

'The point? The point is your job. You're training to be a chef,
apart from paying the rent, keeping body and soul together.'

'But I'm going to have to give it up sooner or later anyway,
how could I work with a baby?'

Mary felt like crying as she said it, thinking of Luc and Félix,
the big steaming kitchen she loved, all she had learned and
achieved, all the things she had yet to do. Would have done.

'We could figure out some kind of system. You'd get maternity leave, and then we could take turns, I could mind it at
nights—'

'Oh, Keeley. I can't believe you'd really offer to do that.'

'Of course I'd do it. We're in this together – and a fine fix it
is, I must say.'

Mary was touched to the point of being ashamed. But how
could two working teenagers bring up a child?

'No. I couldn't let you do that. It wouldn't be fair. You've
got your job to think of, and Vincent at nights. It's my child,
my problem.'

'Oh, would you give over! It's *our* problem. What about a
nursery, then? Some of our customers leave their babies in

something called a crèche while they're getting their hair done, they just pay by the hour—'

'But it would cost a fortune, all day every day. Besides, I'd be worried sick, wondering was it all right. It's my baby, if I'm going to have it then I want to look after it.'

'Mary, that's all very well, but you don't really have that luxury. You've got to do whatever is most practical.'

Mary glanced at her, a little apprehensively.

'Keeley, I hate to say it, but—'

'But what?'

'I think the best thing would be to go home. I feel – I need – my mother.'

'Your mother? For what? You're not a kid, you're going to be a mother yourself. Anyway, your mother works, she'd hardly mind it, would she?'

'I don't know. She might. But I want to tell her anyway, see what she thinks, she'll surely have some ideas once she calms down.'

Keeley put down her cup, straightened up and looked at her seriously.

'Mary. Stop. Think about what you're saying. Think really hard.'

'What am I saying?'

'You're saying you want to go back to Ireland. In other words, you want to forget about being a chef, leave the job you love, go back to Pearse Avenue and baked beans, live with your parents and write off your whole life.'

'It would only be for a while.'

'Yeah. Until the kid is the age we are now.'

'I – I – oh, Keeley, how can I have done this? We were having such a great time, I can't stand the idea of leaving you here on your own, if it wasn't for Vincent I—'

'Leaving me here?'

'Yes, well, maybe he could move in with you and share the rent.'

'Mary, I'm not going to live with Vincent! Not yet, certainly not just because you're gone home. If you really want to go, then I'm going with you. But I think you're stark raving mad.'

'But you can't come with me! You've got your life here, you love it, why in God's name would you do that?'

'Because you're my friend. You brought me here so I'll

bring you back. You couldn't possibly do that ferry trip all
on your own.'

No. Mary knew she couldn't, felt nauseous just thinking
about it, but felt even worse when she contemplated the dis-
ruption it would cause, Keeley having to ask for time off, a
week at least, the rent having to be paid up. Her half of the
deposit having to be somehow worked out and returned to
Félix. Vincent's parents scandalised at the news. Oh, Jesus.

For a while they were silent. And then Keeley spoke again,
very quietly.

'I will come with you, Mary. I mean it. Not just on the ferry.
I'll go home with you and stay until the baby is born, until you
get sorted out.'

'What? Oh, no! Keeley, you couldn't, I wouldn't let you.'

'Sorry, but it's all or nothing. We're not splitting up over this,
I'm not dumping you to cope on your own.'

Mary could not articulate what she felt. Never had she known
that a friendship could be like this, that anyone could be so
strong, so loyal, so incredibly generous.

'K – Keeley, please. What about Vincent?'

'If he doesn't understand, then he's not the man I think he
is. It's only for a few months. Maybe he'd even come over for
a visit.'

'But you *can't*! Stay at Pearse Gardens, you said your father
is violent—'

'I'll deal with him. Or get Vincent to break his bloody jaw
for him.'

Mary was astounded. Keeley would not only go home with
her, she would let Vincent meet Christy, see the kind of family
she came from? As if following her thoughts, Keeley smiled.

'He kind of guesses anyway, Mary. I might have put on a bit
of a shine, but you don't have to scratch very deep to see what
kind of person I really am. I'd rather Vincent knew the truth
than ever accuse me of having hidden anything. If he can take
Christy and Poor Tony, then I'll know he really does love me
to the point of insanity.'

At first Mary thought it would be an awful risk, and then she
thought, no, it wouldn't. There was something about Vincent
that simply told her. He had – what was it called? – some kind
of integrity about him. Something you could trust.

Whereas she, Mary Jameson, was the worst kind of person
in the whole world. Stupid, as Keeley said, selfish, the kind of

feeble girl who wanted her mother the moment she got into a mess, couldn't sort anything out for herself. But she did want her mother. She hadn't meant a word of it, that time on the ferry, but she meant it now. Suddenly she was aching for Leesha, who'd written to say she loved and missed her, she wanted her whole family around her. Dad would go ballistic, but even he would come round, help and care for her. If Keeley would just come with her on the ferry, stay for a few days, she'd be all right after that. But she felt a wretched wrench as she thought of Keeley leaving again, returning to France without her, resuming her happy life here and making other friends, gradually forgetting all about her. She was the kind of friend it would be terrible to lose, the friend of a lifetime.

Getting up, she went over to her, sank down on the floor and hugged her.

'Keeley Butler, you are the best person on this planet. You are—'

Keeley flushed. 'Oh, knock it off. I think you're absolutely bonkers, like I said, but if you want your Mum then we'd better get her for you, hadn't we?'

'I know it sounds crazy. But I do need her, Keel, I don't think I could cope with being pregnant here, working in that hot kitchen, bringing up a baby. I'm only eighteen . . .'

She knew she sounded weak, but she felt so sick, so frightened, so overpowered by the huge responsibility she was facing. They would get a kit and do a test, as Keeley said, but she knew it was going to turn out positive. She was going to have a child.

'If – if you could ask Eliane for just a few days off, I could ask Luc to lend us the boat money, Dad would send it back to him—'

Luc. Her teacher, her friend, her idol. He was going to be so disappointed in her. So was Félix. For a split second, she very nearly changed her mind.

'OK. Let's play it by ear. See how your folks react when we get there and share the glad tidings.'

Murder. There was going to be murder. She thought, mortified, of what her parents might even say, that it was the likes of Keeley Butler you'd expect to get pregnant, someone from the Gardens, not the Avenue. But wait till they heard how fabulous Keeley was being, the thanks she deserved . . . Keeley put her hand on hers.

'Cheer up, Mary. It's not the end of the world.'

She felt that it was.

'M-my work, the restaurant, I love it so much . . .'

'Come on. Don't cry. You might get back to it yet.'

But she felt that she would not, and saw that Keeley didn't really think so either, was just trying to make her feel better. Choking down tears, she attempted to smile.

'I'll come back for your wedding anyway, I'll make that if it kills me. Can I be your bridesmaid?'

'No. Sorry. People with kids are called matrons of honour.'

Suddenly they were both in tears.

'Will – will you be its godmother?'

Keeley made some strangled sound.

'What?'

'I said – only if Vincent can be godfather. Oh, God, Mary, you didn't even want kids, I was the one who did . . .'

'And you'll have them! I'll lend you this one, to practise on, send it over by registered express, you can teach it French . . .'

Tears poured down their faces as they clung to each other, their hearts breaking as they contemplated their paths diverging, the parting of their ways.

Vincent rose to the situation like a colossus. First and foremost, would Mary like him to find and kill Lars?

'No. It wasn't like that, Vincent. But thank you for the kind thought.'

Then what could he do, how could he help? Please tell him, so he could do it immediately.

Keeley reached for the dish containing the omelette Mary had made, and helped him to another slice. It was a delicious fluffy omelette, considering that the chef had cooked it with her eyes shut, her face averted as she tried not to puke into it.

'If you could drive us up to the ferry, that would be a great help, love. Mary can't hitch in her condition, and she'd probably be sick on a train.'

Of course he would drive them, buy the ferry tickets too, there was no question of borrowing from Luc or anyone else. He would drive slowly, Mary would be fine, she was not to worry about anything.

Keeley shone with love as she listened to him talk, fight to express himself in franglais, beg to be allowed help in every way he could. How had she met this wonderful man, why had God seen fit to bless her with all the things she had never known in any other man, the things she'd always believed existed even when there was no evidence of them? Normally she made a point of not going all soppy when Mary was around, but tonight she couldn't help it. Moving her chair closer round the table to his, she touched his face with her hand, and kissed him. Instantly he turned to kiss her back, but then they exchanged a little look. It wasn't fair, in front of Mary who was about to become a single mother, had no man to share her life or child.

Mary felt like kissing Vincent herself. He was a Godsend, Keeley was going to be ecstatically happy with him. What a couple they made, sitting there together, radiating love for each other, concern and goodwill for her. Whatever she did she must never lose touch with them, must find some way of seeing them as often as possible even if she couldn't yet think how. But there were so many things she had yet to work out. Starting with Luc and Félix, how to tell them.

She must do it, right away. They deserved as much notice as possible, they would need to set about finding a replacement. The thought killed her.

But next day she braced herself, went to work and sought them both out, together. Would they have time to sit down with her for just a moment, please, both of them, there was something she needed to discuss? Looking baffled, they sat down at an empty table in the front of the restaurant, wondering probably whether she was going to ask for a rise or – God forbid – whether she could cook for the guests now, serve up her coq au vin with a fanfare of trumpets.

She forced herself to start somewhere, blurting out words, her fists clenched with the effort not to weep.

'Luc – Félix – I must – I have – there is—'

Their look made it worse, fatherly, anxious. Felix cleared his throat.

'Is something wrong, Mary? If it is, take your time. It probably isn't as bad as you think.'

'I – I'm not well.'

Luc nodded. Nodded in a way that told her he was guessing, even as she was speaking, drawing conclusions from her fainting fit in Rognes and the pallor she had seen herself, in the mirror this morning.

'I – I'm terribly sorry, but I'm afraid I'm . . . going . . . to have . . . a baby.'

Félix looked as if she had taken up a frying pan and hit him with it.

'What?'

'I'm pregnant.'

'But how?' It was out before he could help it. Deeply insulting, he realised with horror, only Mary had never mentioned a boyfriend, never seemed passionate about anything other than food . . . surely to God she hadn't been – couldn't have—

'It was a Swedish man I met at the vineyard, when we were picking grapes. The baby is due early in July, I think.'

'You think? But – but you must see a doctor! Haven't you seen one? Mary, I will telephone my wife. Were you – was there – any kind of trouble?'

She realised what he meant.

'No. I was simply stupid, that's all, green as the Irish grass.'

'Oh, this is dreadful. Where is this Swedish man now? Are you still in contact with him?'

'No. I don't even know his second name.'

Félix looked faint with horror. Luc said nothing, but patted her hand. For a moment they all gazed at each other. She willed herself to go on.

'I'm going to have to leave. I'm going to go home, to Ireland.'

Even in the midst of her distress she felt their consternation, the way they were so fond of her, did not want to hear this.

'It's the only way. I can't have a baby here, our flat is tiny, it wouldn't be fair to Keeley, or to you, or to it. I need to be with my family, need my mother.'

Félix made some attempt to recover.

'Yes, of course. But you know we would help you, if you wished, try to work out some roster that would—'

'Oh, Félix. Thank you for saying that, for offering. But we all know what kitchen work is like, the stress, the long hours that nobody can really predict, the way babies get sick and have crises. I don't feel I could devote myself a hundred and one per cent both to being a mother and to being a chef.'

Luc's sudden question astonished her.

'Which would you prefer to be?'

A chef. She knew it without even having to think. She would give anything, anything, to become a great chef.

'I think you know the answer to that, Luc. But I won't say it, because the baby already exists. End of story. End of career.'

Luc, she realised with alarm, was beginning to flare up. Beginning to look as fierce as Monsieur.

'Criminal. It is a criminal waste. It is *scandalous*! You are the first woman I have ever trained, and you do this to me!'

Félix signalled him to simmer down, but he was boiling over.

'I have trained dozens of men, dozens, and not one of them had the talent in his whole body that you have in your little finger! You don't just cook, you create, you think, you feel, you understand – you are a fool, Mary, a *fool*!'

Félix gasped. But she inclined her head. He was right.

'I know. That's what Keeley said too. But it is a human being, Luc. I have to put it first.'

To her horror and Félix's he leaped to his feet, pushed the table violently out of his way and stormed off to the kitchen, swearing as he slammed the door behind him. Félix turned to her with a kind of desperation.

'He's upset.'

That was putting it mildly. His initial sympathy seemed to have vanished, collapsed like a failed soufflé. She wanted to run after him and plead for forgiveness. Wanted to put her head down on Félix's immaculate suit and sob on his chest, sob her heart out.

'Oh, Félix, I've let you down, both of you, so badly, after all you've done for me . . . I – I'll get your five hundred francs, give it back to you . . .'

Suddenly he too looked apoplectic.

'My God, Luc is right! You *are* a fool! Do you really think I would take money from a pregnant girl alone in my country?'

His eyes glittered behind his glasses, and she realised that he was insulted, in the awful way the French could be, she had made a complete mess of the whole thing. Of this terrible conversation, of her career, of her entire life from start to finish.

It took Luc and Félix fully twenty-four hours to regain their composure, but it was almost worse when they did. Mary found herself all but smothered in kindness, drowned in a torrent of guilty remorse.

'I deserved everything you said, Luc. I've wasted your time, thrown away the future you offered me.'

'Nature offered it to you. Nature gave you this wonderful talent.'

'Nature gave me a shagging baby.'

They both laughed, the air clearing between them. But Luc was seriously put out, frustrated.

'You could have gone anywhere. Travelled the world as I have done, cooked for presidents and opera singers, film stars, royalty, famous physicians and scientists . . .'

She had a vision of Pearse Avenue.

'Please, Luc. I can't bear to talk about it.'

He stirred his roux with savage fury.

'Hawaii, Mauritius, the Seychelles, the fruit, the flowers, the ocean . . . champagne flown in on private jets . . .'

'I'll get back to it, as soon as the child starts school, I'll only be twenty-four . . .'

'Women. Women and their babies. Women and their mothers. Pah!'

Mary had met his wife Annette, knew he was very happily married and the proud father of three children, but thought she understood what he meant. A man wouldn't let things get on top of him, wouldn't be scared, wouldn't ever put his career on the back burner. A man would never go running home to his mother. But then men didn't have babies, had no idea how it felt to be pregnant.

'And where,' he continued, 'will you get back to it? Who will train you? I have never heard of any Irish chefs. Certainly none as good as myself.'

Luc, she thought, I promise you I will get back to it. I don't know how or where or when or with who, but I will. I will.

That was what she thought. But not aloud. Something held her back from saying it, from making a commitment he would expect her to keep.

It was decided that the two girls should return to Ireland at the end of January, when Félix would have a replacement for Mary and Eliane could spare Keeley. In the three weeks at her disposal, Keeley set her mind to doing everything in her power to changing Mary's mind. It was a last shot and a long one, but she felt she had to try.

'Why don't you ring them first? Tell them over the phone, and see what they say? They might have a fit, not want you back at all.'

'Keeley, they're my parents. Of course they'll want me.'

'I can think of lots who wouldn't. Roisin O'Keeffe's oul fella

threw her out, Dervla Shortall's parents made her have the baby
adopted . . .'

'Well, mine won't. They'll go bonkers all right, but then
they'll be great. I know they will.'

'Then ring them. Tell them now.'

'No. I couldn't do something like that over the phone.'

Keeley thought she could strangle Mary, the way she looked
at her with her eyes so big and innocent, full of trust in her
parents. Well, maybe the Jamesons would rally round. But what
if they didn't?

'They will.'

'OK, let's say they will. But then what? When it's born, I
mean?'

'Keeley, I don't know! That's why I want to go home,
to see what Mam and Dad think, find out what ideas they
might have.'

'Have you none of your own?'

'Not yet. June seems so far away, I can't concentrate, can't
imagine . . .'

'If I were you, I'd stay right here. Tough it out. Take help
from anyone who offered it. I just can't believe you're leaving
Luc, after all he's taught you and done for you.'

Make her feel guilty, Keeley thought. She seems to be good
at feeling guilty.

Mary thought of Luc, of the basket he had put down on a
table in front of her this morning, telling her to close her eyes.
When she did so, he had handed her a fruit or a vegetable one
by one, made her guess what each item was by its smell, weight,
shape and texture. She had got them all right. He too was trying
to work on her, trying to get her to change her mind. Only Félix
seemed to understand. Félix had got his wife to take her to her
gynaecologist, who confirmed the pregnancy and said yes, the
baby was due at the end of June and the best thing for the
young lady was to return to her own country and family.
Mary was grateful that somebody agreed with her, seemed to
see the point.

'Keeley, Luc has trained lots of chefs. He'll soon get interested
in someone else.'

'Yeah. A man, who won't chuck it all in the garbage.'

'Oh, Keeley, please stop giving out to me.'

Seeing tears threaten, Keeley reluctantly stopped. But then
she recruited Sylvie, got her to come round for supper and have

a go. Sylvie pointed out that France had a fine social welfare system, Mary would get all sorts of help, be entitled to this, that and the other . . . Mary nodded and thanked her, said she would think it over. They saw that she wouldn't. 'She wants her Maman,' Sylvie said next day, at the salon. 'She wants her head examined!' Keeley retorted, massaging a customer's scalp with terse vigour.

Only when Mary began packing her things did Keeley accept defeat, and not with much grace.

'Leave your heavy stuff here. There's no need to lug everything home. You'll be back, baby and all.'

'I – I might. I hope so. Some day. But I don't know when, Keeley. It won't be soon. Here, why don't you keep this shirt, I can't get into it – and this – this – Keeley, what are you going to do when you come back? About the flat, I mean?'

'If you're really going to stay in Dublin, then I suppose I'll have to look for somebody else to share with.'

'I'm sorry. I'm making such a mess of things for you, as well as for myself. For Luc and Félix, everyone.'

'If you say sorry once more I will push you down the stairs.'

'I didn't know it was annoying you . . . sorry.'

Gradually the clothes were packed, the rucksack sat bulging on the floor, every trace of Mary began to vanish. Even, Keeley thought, Mary herself. As the last days passed Mary grew quieter and paler, withdrawing into herself, fiddling nervously with her hair in a new mannerism she had developed, avoiding eye contact and even social contact. She would rather not go to say goodbye to Vincent's parents, she said, it was better to just leave things as they were. When Luc and Félix wanted to take her out to a farewell dinner, she told them she couldn't eat, everything gave her heartburn. And then Keeley noticed the stack of cookery books Luc had given her, sitting unpacked on the kitchen shelf.

'Aren't you taking them with you? Or does he want them back?'

'No, he said I could keep them, but they're so heavy—'

Keeley snatched them off the shelf and all but threw them at her.

'Take them! You'll need them, we'll put them in Vincent's car and I'll carry them on the ferry – Mary, what in God's name is wrong with you? You're only having a baby, not going to a prison camp in Siberia!'

Shamefaced, Mary put them in a cardboard box, feeling Keeley's concern, and protection, and fury.

On the day of their departure they awoke to the sound of rain, small insistent drops tapping at the window, gusting on a pine-scented breeze. Getting slowly up, Mary went to the window, opened it wide and put her head out.

'It's good for the crops. They get so little rain, down here . . .'

Her voice shook, and Keeley knew that she was crying. Pulling her pyjamas around her, she went to her, and put her arm around her shoulder.

'It's not too late, Mary. You can change your mind, even now.'

Keeley thought she knew what the response would be, something about how Mary's parents had been thrilled to hear she was coming home, were coming to meet them off the ferry, there was no way to back out now. But Mary was silent.

'You really can, if you want to. Everything I said still stands, about helping you, we'd all help, even Vincent's parents said they—'

Slowly, Mary turned around.

'I know you would. All of you. And if I thought I could live on help alone, I would stay. But I can't, Keeley. You'll soon be married to Vincent, you'll have your own children, Sylvie has her own life, Luc and Félix can't be expected to keep making allowances for a mother every time her baby cries. It's my child and I've got to face the fact that I'm responsible for it, for its life and my own.'

'You're sure you – you're not just—'

'What?'

'Not just chickening out?'

Candidly, Keeley looked at Mary, saw her glance very quickly away before looking back, meeting her eye with equal candour.

'No. It might appear that way, but it's more than just wanting my parents' help, the comforts of home. I want the baby to get a chance, Keeley. And it's more likely to do that in a family, in a proper house, than here in a tiny flat with its single mother. We're three flights up, I couldn't even get a pram up the stairs!'

'We could find another flat.'

'Oh, Keeley, you know what I mean. At home there'll always

be someone around, heating on, lights, hot water, no panic about bills, there's a garden, neighbours to keep an eye – Ireland is geared to kids, everyone has them!'

That was true. France was quite different in that respect; most parents only had one or two children, well spaced in age, they kept to themselves and did not seem to have the same network that operated in Ireland. Keeley knew she was lucky to have been accepted so warmly by Vincent's family, had heard that foreign girlfriends, even native ones, rarely got so far so fast.

'I suppose you're right about that. Still—'

Wearily, Mary shook her head.

'Let's not talk about it any more, Keeley. It's all decided. I'm going home.'

'All right. I just hope you don't live to regret it.'

'I'm regretting it already. But I'm doing it.'

'OK. Just remember that it's your choice, Mary. You did have a choice.'

Even as she said it, Keeley sensed that Mary did not agree. But it seemed to her one of the things that could be chosen, accepted or rejected. Many things *happened* to people, but this was not one of them. It was not illness or bereavement, a random accident, floods or lightning or avalanches crashing down. Everyone talked about Poor Tony's 'accident', but he had chosen to ride his motorbike the way he did, chosen to abuse that driver instead of look where he was going. And now Mary was choosing to go home.

Mary stood in her nightgown, plucking at her hair, her body already beginning to show the first signs of pregnancy. Stood for so long that Keeley thought she could count every freckle on her pale face.

'We – we'd better get started.'

In heavy silence they washed and dressed, gathered up the final odds and ends, unable to speak as they waited to hear the hum of Vincent's car. Eventually, at nine o'clock exactly as promised, they heard it. Stoically Mary stood up and turned to take a last look around the flat, her first brief home of her own.

'Don't do that, Mary. You'll only upset yourself.'

Keeley flew down the stairs to let Vincent in, muttering to him as she led him up. When he walked in, his face was a study of determined good cheer.

'Well, here we are! All set?'

Before she could answer he began gathering up Mary's things, hefting them over his shoulder, staggering and laughing under the box of cookery books.

'Mind that,' Keeley told him, 'it's full of hidden treasure.'

He carted it out and down the stairs, stowed it in the car and returned panting, eyes twinkling.

'Where do women get so much stuff? A man, he travels with one toothbrush, one change of clothes. What else does anyone need?'

Resolutely he kept chatting, ransacking his school English for words, teasing Mary as he steered her out and down the stairs, winking at Keeley over her shoulder.

'Lucky girls, going to beautiful Ireland, when am I to be invited?'

'When the baby is born,' Keeley replied promptly. 'You and I are both going over then, to be godparents. Mary will give a huge party and cook everything for it herself, she'll have read all Luc's books by then, it will be stupendous!'

Somehow they got Mary out and into the car without letting her shed a tear. Luggage was secured, doors were locked and Vincent drove away at such speed that there was no time to turn back, to look or to linger. Sitting in the back, Mary was silent all the way to the Vieux Moulin, where she was to stop off and say her final adieux to Luc and Félix. It was a very short distance away, but to Keeley and Vincent it felt like miles. When they drew up, she motioned to them to stay in the car, got out and went in alone.

What happened inside they could only guess, shuddering as they thought of it. Even in her warm cream-coloured jacket, wearing a long woollen skirt and a rust-coloured scarf that gave some brightness to her face, she looked frozen as she disappeared behind the thick wooden door.

Keeley thought that one or other, or both men, would come out with her, hustle her back into the car with hugs and good wishes. But after ten minutes that seemed to wear on into eternity, she emerged alone, tears pouring down her face.

Keeley jumped out and ran to her. 'Oh, Mary, don't, come on, you've still got us—'

Mary was taller and heavier than Keeley, but she felt as if she were holding a feather as she bundled her friend back into the car, feeling her shoulders fluttering, her heart breaking. Vincent took a handkerchief from his pocket and offered it to her, but she did not even see it as she buried her face in her knuckles and wept like the rain, sobbing for the friends she had made and lost, for the life she might have had.

Once again it was a hideous ferry crossing, even worse than before, and Keeley and Mary were prostrate with gratitude for the cabin Vincent had got them. It was out of the question, he said, for them to sleep on floors or benches at this time of year, even if Mary were not pregnant. His parents had given him money with express instructions that he was to book them a comfortable cabin as far away from the engines as possible, and Keeley marvelled at their generosity as she kissed him goodbye on the quayside. It was a very long kiss, and after she broke away he walked a few paces, turned round suddenly and ran back for another.

Mary stood up on deck watching as they clung together, hugging and murmuring, wondering what they were saying and thinking how very much in love they looked, how young and vulnerable and happy. Vincent had been so mindful of Keeley, so kind to them both, all the way from Aix to Le Havre, paying for all the food and petrol, insisting that they stay at a proper hotel overnight and that the two girls share a room. Mary was sure he must have wanted to be the one to share with Keeley, must have badly wanted to judging by the way his eyes never left Keeley's face and his hand never left her side, but he merely smiled, did nothing to make her feel she was in the way or a nuisance, which she must surely be. He adored Keeley, and Mary felt guilty about separating them, if only for a week. They were going to miss each other terribly.

When the ship sailed they stood up on deck for ages, waving to him, watching his figure recede but not move, waving back at them as vigorously as if they were sailing for Australia. Mary felt as if she was, could hardly bear to look at the French coastline fading away in the mist; for one wild moment she felt an insane urge to jump overboard and swim back. But then she thought of the baby who might die of shock, and then she remembered that she couldn't swim. Gripping the rail, clenching her teeth, she willed herself to stand and watch the little pilot boat guiding them out of the harbour, until it finally spun round and the man in it left them with a last, peculiarly French salute. As it skimmed away she felt as if it were towing her heart in its wake, and turned trembling to Keeley, thinking that she too must be devoured with the pain of parting from Vincent. But Keeley was glowing, her face whipped scarlet by much more than the biting sea breeze.

'Isn't he wonderful? Isn't he gorgeous, a gem, a giant amongst men? See, Mary, I told you there were some good ones. And he's the greatest.'

Muffled in her navy duffle coat, her cheeks red with cold and love, Keeley blew Vincent a last kiss and turned to Mary.

'I love him so much, Mary. I hope you don't mind me saying it, in your condition and all, but I really do. I can't wait to get back to him.'

Mary smiled. 'I know. That's why I couldn't let you come back with me for more than a few days, Keeley. You belong here. In France, with Vincent Tourand.'

'Yeah. I do. Who'd ever have believed it, that I could settle down in such a country, get a job and a chap like him? Even learn a bit of the lingo. They'll never believe it in Pearse Gardens.'

Mary laughed, her first laugh in days, as she thought of it. Keeley's French accent was atrocious, but her vocabulary was incredible, she memorised every new word and repeated it like a parrot, wasn't a bit shy about attempting conversation even if it didn't always come off. No wonder everyone liked her, because she tried, she didn't care about making a fool of herself or jokes at her expense, she just battled on until she conquered. She was a real little fighter, and Mary admired her endlessly for it. Even now, waving goodbye to her cherished new boyfriend, she wasn't sniffling or feeling the least bit sorry for herself, she was full of cheerful chat, able to smile and look to the future. How on earth did she do it, stay in such good spirits, never let anything get her down?

The boat began to pitch and toss after no more than an hour or two, and they went down to their cabin, decided to skip dinner and see if they could sleep through as much of the journey as possible.

But Mary lay on her bunk, wondering what would happen to her when she got home, wondering how Keeley would fare back in France, her mouth dry and her stomach churning as she contemplated the future. Over and over she thought of Luc, of Félix, of the red earth and the green vines, the lavender fields and the tall pines, the landscape that already seemed so far away. As they drove up through France they had felt the temperature dropping, the air starting to cool somewhere south of Paris, becoming chill as they entered the Loire valley. Vincent had given them a commentary all the way up, telling them everything he could remember about France's towns and plains, history and culture, regional customs and specialities. Driving slowly, they saw much more of it than on their trip south, had time to see things and ask questions, take note of the changing scenery. It was hugely varied, each area quite distinct, beautiful in its own way, and Mary had felt as if something were being pulled from her, dragged from her grasp, some intangible thing composed of smells and sounds, light and air, hidden twists and turns. Keeley's wedding, she reminded herself over and over; I will come back to France for Keeley's wedding.

Thinking of it, she raised herself up on her bunk and reached down to her friend.

'Keeley? Are you asleep?'

'No. Just dozing. Thinking about Vincent.'

'When are you going to marry him?'

'Ha! That's what he asked me, down on the dock.'

Mary sat up. 'Did he? He proposed to you?'

'Yes.' Keeley sat up in turn, her eyes gleaming, as close to blushing as she was ever likely to come. 'He asked me, Mary. He actually wants to marry me.'

'Oh, Keeley, already! I – I'm *thrilled* for you! When's it going to be?'

'I don't know. I told him we'd have to wait until your baby is born and you're able to bring it with you – to the wedding, I mean – so maybe it will be at Christmas. Could you come then, do you think? The baby would be old enough, maybe, we could send you the plane fare so you wouldn't have to take this bloody boat.'

Mary felt her face ignite with emotion.

'You mean you'd wait to marry until I can be there? You'd bring me over on a plane, and the baby? You'd do that, for me?'

'Of course I would. We would. We'd never have met if you hadn't taken me to France, how often do I have to tell you that? Anyway, it'll mean a nice long engagement, Vincent will have lots of time to change his mind.'

About to protest, Mary realised that she was joking.

'He'd be a right fool! He's getting one hell of a woman, Keeley Butler, and don't you forget it.'

'Yeah. That's what I told him. Anyway, start thinking about next Christmas, Mary. Start planning. It'll give you something to look forward to – I mean, besides the baby.'

Keeley hesitated, wondering if she had said the wrong thing. How did Mary feel about having her baby? She had talked about her duty to it, about wanting to care properly for it, but she had never said anything about how she actually felt. She looked quizzically up at her, and Mary looked thoughtful.

'Yes. I suppose I am looking forward to it. In a way. I'm just – well, a bit confused, I suppose. It's cost me so much, Keeley. One night in a field with a virtual stranger, and my whole life turns in the opposite direction to the one I wanted it to go in. I'd feel more, you know, enthusiastic if I'd felt something for its father, if he were with me, if we were like you and Vincent. It seems really weird carrying the child of a man whose second name I don't even know.'

Keeley sighed, sympathetically. 'Well, look on the bright side. You've certainly made your break with Cathal Sullivan and no mistake about it! He'll throw forty fits when he sees the state of you.'

'Yes. That's him out the window all right. I just wish I knew what my parents are going to say.'

'Sweet suffering Jesus is what they're going to say, look at the cut of our daughter, isn't that lovely.'

'Oh, Lord . . . I'm glad you're going to be with me when we get to Rosslare.'

'Are you going to tell them right away?'

'I don't know. I thought I would, get it over with, but maybe it would be better to wait till we get home, get comfortable . . . I have been away for five months, against their wishes, it might be a bit tricky at first.'

'Mmm. Still. You're four months pregnant now . . . it's starting to show.'

'Is it?'

'It is. They could well guess the minute they set eyes on you.'

'Oh well, then it'll be over and done with, out of my hands.'

Keeley eyed her, curiously. Would she not prefer things to be *in* her hands, where she could control them?

'Listen, Mary. Listen hard. When we get home, everyone will be saying that to you.'

'Saying what?'

'Saying "listen, here's what I think you should do." If you
listen to me, you won't listen to any of them. You'll make your
own decisions and not let anyone else make them for you. It's
your baby, not theirs. Your life.'

'Yes. It is. I'll be glad to hear any helpful suggestions anyone
can make, but I know I'll have to make my own mind up in the
end. I just hope Mam and Dad don't want me to do anything
that I—'

'Mary! Whether they do or not, you just do whatever feels
right for you. And for the child, of course. I mean, they might
want you to have it adopted or fostered or something.'

'I know. I've been thinking about that. And I don't want it,
Keeley. I don't think I could stand to give away the baby after
I've had it, after leaving France and giving up so much for it.'

'Well, if you did have it adopted, you'd be free to come back
to France.'

'Yes. But I think it would kill me, not knowing where the child
was or who it was with, whether it was happy, safe, doing well
. . . I'd be thinking about it all the time.'

'Would you?'

'Yes, of course, I'm its mother. I know lots of girls do give
their babies up, but I don't think I'm cut out to be one of them.
If I was younger maybe, if I was only sixteen like Dervla Shortall
. . . but I'll be nineteen next month.'

Nineteen. Thinking about it, they both suddenly felt absurdly
young. Far too young to be in a situation like this. It was
kind of ridiculous, and kind of terrifying. For a moment, they
contemplated it.

'Keeley?'

'What?'

'Have you ever slept with Vincent?'

'No.'

'No? Honest to God?'

'I swear it. Not that I don't fancy the socks off him. But
where would we have done it? His parents were at his house,
you were at the flat most of the time. Besides, I didn't want
to. Not until I got to know him better. It's only lately that
I feel I have got to know him, especially since I told him
about you being pregnant. He was so strong about it, so
helpful, I started to feel I could really trust him. I nearly
did the other night, at that hotel we stayed in, but then
we thought no, it would be awful to do that right under

your nose, leave you on your own while we had a good time.'

'You gave up your first chance to sleep with him because of *me*?'

'Well, yeah, but there's no need to make it sound like any big deal. We'll have the flat to ourselves when I get back, until I find someone else to share with at any rate. He says it should be him. But I just said I'd think about it. I don't want him to think I'd live with him just because I need someone to share the rent.'

'You're amazing. You really are.'

'Rubbish. I'm just copping myself on, that's all. I told you I'd never get into another Erik mess and I meant it. Play it cool, that's my motto now. Even when I don't want to!'

Mary nodded, thinking how far they had travelled since the first time they had boarded this boat. This godawful boat, that was swaying and lurching under her like a roller-coaster. Queasily, she clutched at the wall.

'Ooh. How long have we been at sea, Keeley?'

'Now, Mary. Don't start thinking about it. You survived the last time and you'll survive this time. Just lie down and keep still. It's not that bad.'

But it was getting worse. For ten or fifteen minutes she lay obediently still, trying to think about something, anything else. But in the silence she could hear the waves mounting and crashing, the engines chugging slowly and heavily, the wind whistling demonically down the echoing corridors. White and nauseous, she rolled over, and her stomach seemed to roll separately, like a sack of onions dropped and split on Luc's kitchen floor.

'Oh, God, Keeley . . . I'm going to die. I really am, this time.'

'You're right, Mary. You are going to die, at my hands, if you keep groaning and moaning for the next eighteen hours. Here, take one of these pills Vincent gave me, he said they were good for sea-sickness.'

'But it mightn't be good for the baby.'

Oh, Keeley thought, why does she do it? I know she's pregnant, but she knows I'll look after her. We have a cabin this time, it's much better. If only she'd make an effort, show some spirit instead of rolling over and playing dead. She could, a little at least, if she'd only try.

How does she do it, Mary thought, how does she just make

up her mind not to let it bother her? I wish I could be like that. I wish I was her, anyone but me, anywhere but on this awful ship. I want to go home, I don't want to go home, I don't know what to do or what I want.

Chapter Four

In her best Sunday clothes, Leesha Jameson went running up
to claim the tall, milk-white girl who came staggering off the
St Patrick, faint and swaying, clutching her rucksack in front
of her like a babe in arms. A very different girl to the one who
had left for France last September, her long hair cut short, stuck
to her temples, her bright blue eyes dim with exhaustion, her
rolling gait heavy and weary.

'Mary! Mary, love, it's me, it's Mam!'

Mary collapsed into her arms and burst into tears, stuttering
inaudibly, dropping her rucksack as she clung to her mother.
And then her Dad was at her side as well, hugging her, scooping
her into a warm, sturdy embrace. Trooping up behind them,
almost invisible under the carton of books and her own rucksack, Keeley felt a pang of nostalgia herself, looked involuntarily
around in case her own mother Gertie had come to meet her
as well. But there was no sign of her, and Keeley quickly
decided why: there wouldn't be room in Kevin Jameson's car
for everyone on the drive back to Dublin. It was a two-hour
drive, you had to be sensible about these things. Holding the
luggage, she waited for Mary's family to have a good cry and
pull themselves together.

Eventually Mary turned around.

'Where's Keeley?'

Everyone looked up, and she grinned at them.

'Hiya Mrs Jameson, hiya Mr Jameson.'

She was delighted when Leesha gave her a quick hug and
Kevin took the carton from her, said she was far too small a
handful to be carrying a big box like that. As they all composed
themselves and walked to the car, both girls looked around
them, inhaling the Irish air that smelled so familiar and yet
so different, taking in the Wexford fields that stretched away

from Rosslare harbour, deep dark brown at this time of year, the sky steely grey and dotted with shrieking seagulls.

'Home,' said Kevin, echoing their thoughts as he beamed at his daughter. A tall, quite handsome man of forty, with reddish hair, freckles and big capable bones, Keeley thought he looked like the kind of man who was built to last. Strong, upright, brisk as he stowed their gear in the boot . . . briefly, dismally, she envisaged Christy in his vest and his armchair, probably not even sure what day she was due to appear. And Gertie in her apron, looking worried, so totally unlike Mary's mother, who was wearing a nice pair of coffee-coloured trousers with a tan-and-white checked sweater. New shoes, a slim shoulder bag, lipstick, her black hair recently cut and styled. Though not as well styled, Keeley thought, as she would have done it. Brightening, she put Christy and Gertie out of her mind and thought of Eliane, the salon, her recent promotion.

There was no doubt about it. Leesha and Kevin were very glad to have their daughter home. Not a word of recrimination did they utter as the car swung out onto the Dublin road, nothing at all about the one-month holiday that had turned into a five-month escapade, no mention of worry or anger or anything that might sour her return. Instead, there was lots of eager talk about the family.

'The boys are bursting to see you, Mary' Kevin said happily. 'They wanted to come down to Rosslare, only there wasn't room, they're waiting for you with a big banner over the door, "Welcome Home Mary" is written on it in crayons. They've been at it for a week.'

Wan, but starting to recover, Mary smiled at him.

'I can't wait to see them. They must have grown.'

'Oh aye. Two demons, bold as brass. Your granny is minding them. She's dying to see you too. Made a big chocolate cake for you and all. We'll have a right party when we get there.'

Neither Kevin nor Leesha saw the glance the girls exchanged in the back seat, the glance with the hovering question in it: when am I going to tell them, when are you going to tell them? Amidst all the excitement at the ferry, neither parent seemed to have noticed Mary's increased weight and rounded figure, or if they had they had put it down to French food, put the nausea down to sea-sickness even though Keeley was fit as a fiddle. Quietly, imperceptibly, Mary slid her hand across the seat to

Keeley's, and Keeley gave it a little squeeze: don't worry, they love you, everything will be OK.

The journey flew by, full of news of neighbours, cousins, aunts and uncles, the bakery, the garage, the government and taxes and bishops and football matches. So-and-so had said such-and-such on the Late Late Show, Ken Barlow had done this on Coronation Street, Hilda Ogden had done that, a huge bomb in the North, a clogged beer pump at The Lantern, a new car for the Johnsons . . . they began to feel as if they had never been away.

But we have been away, Keeley thought. Things are the same here, but we're different. Mary is very different, as you'll soon discover, and I'm only a visitor now. I'm going back to Aix, to Vincent, to styling hair and learning French, to our flat. My flat, now. Vincent has the keys, he'll have it all warm and ready when I get home. It *is* my home, you know. Whatever happens in Pearse Gardens, it's only temporary, I don't live there any more.

But she felt a shiver of nervousness when finally the countryside melted away, the traffic got busier and they began to approach the city. Mary turned sideways to look out of the window, see if Dublin was the same as they'd left it, but Keeley couldn't concentrate. What if Christy simply slammed the door in her face, said that since she'd gone away she could stay away?

At last they turned into Pearse Avenue, and there was the big white banner, made from a sheet: 'Welcome Home Mary' crayoned on it in every conceivable colour in wobbly childish writing. Even though it wasn't for her – her own brother would never have done such a thing even if he was able to write – Keeley shared Mary's tremor of emotion. And then the little boys, Steve and Sean, came rushing out, hurling themselves at the car.

'Mary, Mary, Mary!'

Attaching themselves like limpets, they climbed up on her, and only Keeley noticed that she had difficulty in lifting them, looked for a moment as if she might be dragged to the ground by their weight. They were hefty boys for six and seven, solid in blue jeans and Aran sweaters, rusty-haired and impish looking.

Then their grandmother hurried to engulf Mary in hugs, a grey-haired but strong-looking woman of about sixty-five, pulling her inside amidst the pandemonium. Everyone trooped into the house which looked so weirdly different, although it was exactly the same as before, half-brick, half-concrete, white front door, white venetian blinds. Ordinary, but warm and welcoming, smelling of baking and laundry and recently-taken baths. Uncertainly, Keeley stood on the threshold.

But then Mary turned back.

'Keeley? Come on, come in!'

She thought maybe she shouldn't. This was Mary's home-coming, not hers, the family would want her to themselves. But then Kevin gave her a nudge as he went past with the luggage.

'Come on, Keeley, nice cup of tea and some chocolate cake . . . or maybe it's wine and snails you'd prefer after all your travels, eh?'

Relieved, she grinned cheekily. 'Oh no, Mr Jameson, it's Mary who'll want those. And a few frogs' legs!'

And maybe she really will, she giggled to herself; pregnant women want all sorts of things, you know, boiled eggs with marmalade, potatoes with custard . . . Jaysus, wait till she tells them. Just wait till she tells them.

But there seemed to be no tension, Mary was even looking better as she sat on the sofa tussling with her brothers, Granny Jameson bustling to make tea in the kitchen, the boys shouting and only Leesha looking the tiniest bit anxious.

'Mary, let me look at you properly, you're so pale, I thought you'd have a lovely tan.'

Instantly Mary coloured. 'Oh no, not at this time of year, it's winter in France too, and I was sick on the ferry . . . I'm fine, Mam, I really am.'

Leesha peered at her intently, and Keeley held her breath.

'H'm. Well, I suppose it's nothing a good night's sleep won't cure. At least you seem to have put on a bit of weight. I'm glad to see you've been eating properly . . . I suppose you got the occasional nourishing thing at that restaurant?'

'Yes. Loads of lovely things.'

'Of course, your job at the deli is gone, Mr O'Rourke gave it to Aine Connolly from Augustus Road . . . but never mind, we'll talk about that later. Boys, get down now and let Mary eat her cake!'

Later, Keeley thought. Later tonight there's going to be ructions. But there's nothing I can do to help Mary with that. She's going to have to tackle her family herself, and sooner or later I'm going to have to go to mine. I suppose I may as well get it over with.

Drinking her tea, eating her cake and Mary's as well, Keeley stayed for half an hour before standing up, catching her reflection in the mirror over the fireplace as she did so, wondering if there was anyone who really wanted to see her. Gertie? Christy? Tony? No. Not really. But she'd better go.

'Thanks very much, everyone, for the lift and the tea and everything . . . I'd better be off now.'

As if remembering her existence, Leesha looked at her.

'Oh, yes, Keeley, your mother is waiting for you. Sorry, I forgot to tell you, she said she'd have come over here only your Dad isn't too well, has a bit of a 'flu, she says. But they're both fine, it's nothing to worry about. Kevin, give Keeley a run round to Pearse Gardens, will you?'

Obligingly Kevin stood up, and Keeley bent down to give Mary a quick, reassuring hug.

'Bye, Mary. I'll call round to see you tomorrow.'

They exchanged a long look, one that not only said how nervous they were, but how strange it was to be separating, staying at different places. Each knew the other was thinking of the flat, the fun they'd had, the freedom and independence, and the secret they now shared. Feeling almost the bond of sisters, they clung briefly together.

'Bye, Keeley. Come early tomorrow.'

'Not too early,' Leesha interjected, 'our Mary is going to have a good lie-in.'

Hastily, Keeley gathered up her things and followed Kevin out to the car.

At nine o'clock that evening, after an enormous meal that Mary had scarcely touched, Leesha Jameson looked at her daughter and spoke firmly. 'Bed. You're worn out. I'll do you up a hot water bottle.' Kevin nodded, thinking that their poor girl realy did seem to be wilting, there was hardly a wag out of her.

'Yes, that's the best thing. A good long sleep and you'll be right as rain.'

They were both taken aback when she stood up, walked over to the kitchen window, walked back again and faced them as if they were a firing squad, bracing herself with a deep breath.

'No, Mam. No, Dad. There's something I've got to talk to you about.'

Automatically Leesha glanced round in case the boys were within earshot, but they seemed to have actually gone to bed as instructed, worn out with the excitement of seeing their sister. Granny Jameson was in the front room, nursing a celebratory whiskey, also safely out of earshot as she watched a film on television.

'It's all right, Mary. We know you mightn't want to see him again just yet.'

Baffled, Mary frowned. 'See who?'

They both gazed at her, as if France had robbed her of her wits.

'Well, Cathal, of course! We told him you were coming home today, but that you'd be tired, he wasn't to call until you rang him yourself to invite him.'

The vehemence of her next words left them astounded.

'I won't ring him! I won't be ringing him at all! I broke off with him months ago!'

'Yes, we know that, but you were in France. You weren't yourself.'

Mary thought that she had never been more 'herself' in her life than during those wonderful days in France. Painfully acute, the memories welled up: the smell of grapes, of peaches, of thyme and honey; the vision of Keeley's yellow sheets, billowing down the long window; the sound of Luc's slow deep voice, of steel knives on white marble, the calm dark dining room and the bright frenzied kitchen; the taste of cheese and asparagus and vinaigrette, that single truffle, as sacred as a sacrifice. Things she had never seen or known before, that felt now like some essential part of her.

'I was myself. I knew exactly what I was doing.'

'Oh, Mary.' It was Leesha who spoke, softly, as if soothing an invalid. 'Of course you didn't. Not really. It was just the kind of moody thing girls do when they're away from home for the first time, trying to assert themselves.'

'How do you know? You've never been away from home, and I never had been before.'

Her tone was deliberately quiet, but Leesha paled, and Kevin looked up rather sharply.

'Mary. Don't speak to your mother like that. I don't want to hear any cheek out of you, just because you've been to France.'

Cheek? Did they think she was still a child? After she'd

worked and lived and survived abroad for five months? And yet . . . she'd come home because she needed them. Not just loved and missed them, but needed them. Until her own child was born, at least, she was going to have to try to see things from their point of view – which, hopefully, would be that she needed looking after and caring for. Yes. To all intents and purposes, she was still a child in this house. Biting her lip, she sank down on a chair.

'Sorry. I didn't mean it. I just meant that – that I have definitely broken off with Cathal, for good, and don't want to see him any more.'

'But why, Mary? He's such a nice chap. He's been worried sick about you.'

'Has he? He never wrote.'

'He just didn't know what to say. Men aren't very good at writing letters – are they, Kevin?'

Kevin confirmed that they were not. He'd sooner wrestle Muhammad Ali than write one himself.

Oh, God. Feeling somehow that this was going to be a huge struggle, Mary forced herself to go on.

'Well, whatever the reason, it's broken off and I'm not seeing him any more. But that's not what I want to talk to you about.'

Both Kevin and Leesha moved their chairs in closer to the table, ignoring the debris of the meal that would usually be cleared up immediately, and sat looking at her, looking uneasily at each other.

'Then what is it, Mary? If it's about your job, you're not to worry. We'll keep you while you look for something else.'

'Thanks, Dad. But that's not it either.'

'Then what? For heaven's sake, child, tell us . . . you . . . you're not in any kind of trouble, are you?'

A patina of horror spread across Kevin's ruddy face even as he said it, and Mary saw that he was guessing. Guessing, at last, thank God, it was nearly over. Just two more words to go.

'I'm pregnant.'

She waited for as long as it took for the shock to sink in, let them gape and clutch at their chests, at each other, understanding that it was natural, all parents would react the same way.

Eventually, Kevin spoke. 'You are going to have a child? Have I got that right, Mary? A child, a baby?'

'Yes.'

His voice was low and steady, but she quailed from what she knew was coming next.

'Who did this to you, Mary? Who, and where, is the father?'

'He's in Sweden.'

'*Sweden*?' Both parents chorused together, bewildered as well they might be, no longer quite sure what language she was speaking. 'But – but we thought you were in France – you *were* in France—'

'Yes. I was. I met him in the vineyard where we were picking grapes.' Lifting up a fork, she twirled it in her fingers, looking at them half pleading, half defiant.

'I – I did it of my own free will, there wasn't any – anything for you to be angry about. I don't know what came over me, but when I got to France I felt somehow different, I realised that I didn't really love Cathal at all, that I was too young to get married. I wanted to break away from him. Completely away. So I slept with Lars.'

'Lars?' Kevin looked like a drowning man in a mountainous ocean, grasping at a log. 'Lars what? What's his second name, where in Sweden does he live?'

'He lives somewhere called Gothenburg. At least, he studies there. I don't know if he's actually from there. He studies maths. And – I'm afraid I can't remember his second name.'

'Can't *remember* it?' Kevin sounded as if he'd been bitten by a Rottweiler. 'You mean to say you do not know what your child is called, what its father is called?'

'No. I'm sorry, I racked my brains for weeks, but I couldn't remember.'

'So – so this person – doesn't even know he's left you pregnant? He just had his way and went sailing back to Sweden, is that it?'

'Yes. That's more or less it. I only slept with him once, the night before he and Erik went home.'

'Who's Erik?'

'His friend.'

'His friend. I see. And can you even remember the friend's second name, is there any way we can trace them?'

'No. The only thing I know is that they're students in Gothenburg.'

'Well, that's a start. I'm going to call Barry O'Neill. He's a guard. He'll be able to find out down at the police station –

how you – there's Interpol, they track people down in cases like this—'

Mary sighed. 'Oh, Dad. There's no point. Really.'

'What do you mean?' It was Leesha who spoke suddenly, finding her voice. 'There's every point! This man is the father of our – our grandchild! Dear God, we're going to be *grand*parents!'

Beseechingly, Leesha turned to Kevin as if urging him to do something, immediately, and Mary felt terrible for what she was doing to both her parents.

'Mam, he was just a student, we only did it for fun, he's a thousand miles away now. Let it go. Please.'

'But we can't just let it go! What about child support, maintenance?'

'I told you, he's only a student.' Wretchedly, Mary thought of the plentiful pocket money Lars and Erik had seemed to have, the well-off families they were obviously from. But Lars had asked her if she was 'all right', he had thought about contraception and it wasn't his fault that she hadn't understood. In fact, it was Leesha's fault, if fault lay anywhere. Her own mother, who'd never explained these things clearly, not even when her daughter was setting off abroad.

'Look, Mam. Dad. Lars is long gone, and a wild goose chase would take ages, probably cost a lot of money. Even then, if he was found, what would there be to stop him from simply denying the whole thing?'

Kevin frowned, with more than a little anger she thought. 'Was he the type who'd deny it?'

Privately, Mary didn't think he was. He mightn't be very interested, but he'd probably cough up if he had to. But she didn't want money from some indifferent stranger in Gothenburg.

'Dad, I don't even know what type he was. Not really. He and Erik were only around for a few days, they left shortly after we arrived.'

'Well, I still think—'

'No, Dad. Please. Let's forget about what's past and try to just come to terms with things as they are now. I – I've been hoping that you and Mam might . . . not be too angry . . . I'd be very grateful if you could help in any way, or had any suggestions . . .'

'Suggestions! What I'd suggest is that I go over there to Sweden, find that young fella and break his bloody neck for him!'

But Leesha put her hand on her husband's arm. 'Oh, Kevin. Let it be. It wouldn't change anything. Mary is pregnant and what we've got to figure out now is what to do about it, if she really doesn't think this – person – is worth chasing after.'

'No, Mam. I don't think he is.'

'All right, then.' Suddenly Leesha looked at her, not just her face but her body, recognising, accepting. 'When is it due?'

'At the end of June. I saw a doctor in France, Félix's wife took me to him, he said June 27 or thereabouts.'

'June 27. So that gives us five months. Well, I don't know what's to be done, Mary. I really don't. But I suppose we're going to have to figure out something.'

'Yes. I tried to figure it out in France, but I couldn't. All I knew was that you probably wouldn't want me to have a baby on my own over there and bring it up by myself, miles away from you.'

Leesha's face softened. And her voice. 'No. We wouldn't want that at all. Would we, Kevin?'

'H'mph. No. We would not. Tell me, Mary – had Keeley Butler anything to do with this? Did she put you up to it, encourage you?'

'No. She didn't. I know you think she's a bit of a brat, but she was great. I'd never have got this far without her. She did everything she could to help, her boyfriend even gave us a lift to the ferry and got us a cabin on it.'

Leesha had been gazing at Mary's stomach, but her head jerked up.

'Her boyfriend? Keeley Butler has a boyfriend?'

'Yes. A really nice one, his name is Vincent, he's a trainee manager at a department store. In fact he's her fiancé now. He asked her to marry him just before the ferry sailed.'

'Fiancé? You mean to say that Keeley Butler is getting married? To a trainee manager? Keeley *Butler*?'

Oh, no. In a flash, a flash too late, Mary saw that she had made a mistake. Her rough-diamond friend from Pearse Gardens was making a good marriage, while she was the one pregnant, by a Swede whose name she couldn't remember. It was not the kind of thing Leesha and Kevin were likely to appreciate.

In silence, they sat around the table for some minutes. Then, wearily, Leesha got up.

'I'll make you that hot water bottle, Mary, and then you'd

better go to bed. You need to rest, and your father and I need to talk.'

Suddenly exhausted, and flooded with relief that the worst was over, she nodded meekly and attempted a smile. After all, she was home. She had done what they wanted, and come home. Not without a little excess baggage, but she was here, where they said she belonged.

Late next morning, Mary sat on the sofa reading a story to Sean, watching Steve building a moon station, whatever that was, with his Lego bricks. Steve was always the busier of the two little boys, but she knew he was listening to the story too, and she felt a surge of affection as she looked at them, half-dressed in their sweaters and pyjama legs, faces sticky with the remains of a jammy breakfast. Steve lay on the floor, but Sean snuggled up to her, still little more than a baby at six, his eyes never leaving her face. It was he who had woken her up that morning; despite being forbidden to, he had crept into her bedroom and put his hand on her face.

'I missed you, Mary' he said, 'I don't want you to go away again.'

And at this moment she felt she couldn't, hardly even wanted to as she felt her own pleasure in them, their smiles and affection and funny chatter. If her own child was a boy, it would be great to have one like Steve or Sean, chubby, happy, so full of life and energy. For the first time, she thought of it, not as a blob but as a person, with arms and legs and a face . . . Sean and Steve were going to be uncles. For some reason she felt that the baby would be a boy, and that they would love it. Love him.

Leesha came in, rumpled in a pink dressing gown, carrying a cup of coffee. It was a Sunday, and everything was running late, almost in slow motion, nobody would dress before noon, when there would be a flurry to make the last Mass at twelve-thirty. Mary was surprised when Leesha told the boys to get up, go and wash and get ready for church. They pleaded for the last of the story, but it was almost finished anyway, and then they were left with no choice but to scamper away. Leesha sat down on an armchair, but did not sink into it, remained seated on its edge, studying her coffee.

'Mary.'

'Yes, Mam?'

'Your father and I have been talking.'

Mary could see that they had. Her father had yet to appear,
and her mother looked tired, older than the night before, the
skin puffy around her eyes. It occurred to her that Leesha
would be forty soon, in May. Forty. It sounded like a vast age,
weighty and sort of serious. And Leesha was looking serious,
in a way that made her nervous. What had her parents said to
each other?

'About me?'

'What else? Half the night, it was nearly four when we got to
sleep.' She paused, drank some coffee, and sighed. 'Mary, have
you any plans? Any idea what you want to do, when the baby
is born?'

Relieved to be asked, Mary leaned forward. She was afraid
that maybe they would try to tell her what to do, give her no
choices.

'Well – it will be born at the end of June, so I'll have the
summer with it. I suppose it'll take me that long to get to know
it, to learn about feeding and changing and how to look after
it. But then – I thought – maybe – if I could only work out some
way – I'd like to go to Cathal Brugha Street in September. If I
could get in. I'd have to apply now, find out if they take people
who left school more than a year ago.'

'Cathal Brugha Street? The catering college?'

'Yes. I loved working in that restaurant, Mam. I really did.
Luc was training me to be a chef. I'd give anything to go on
with it.'

'But chefs are men!'

'I know. Usually they are. But Luc said there was no reason
why a woman couldn't be.'

'There's a very good reason, already. You're going to have
a baby. How on earth could you go to college? You couldn't
bring it with you, and who'd mind it? I'm out at work all day,
so is your father.'

Feeling guilty, hating herself for the sense of disappointment
she felt, Mary gazed at the floor. It was unreasonable, and
unfair, but for a few brief moments she had allowed herself
to hope . . . her mother had sometimes said she was worn out
working in the bakery, tired of having to get up so early, wait
for buses on cold dark winter mornings. If only Leesha would
mind the baby, it would be the answer to a prayer.

She said nothing, and Leesha was silent in turn, looking at
her.

'I don't know whether you thought I might offer, Mary. I suppose it must have crossed your mind. But the fact is that I can't afford to give up work, whether I'd want to or not. Your Dad doesn't earn a huge amount and my wages make a big difference in this house. We have the two boys still to think of, they'll get more expensive as they get older . . . we haven't had a holiday in years, the car is seven years old, the bills keep coming in . . . I'm sorry, Mary, but I can't. It's out of the question.'

Mary nodded. She could understand, she had to accept.

'Maybe you could get a job in some kind of restaurant here, since you learned a bit in France. But then you'd still have the same problem. You'd spend all your money on a minder, have nothing left . . . we're willing to keep you, Mary, we'll be delighted if you want to live at home with the child. But you'll still need something for yourself. And for it, when it starts school, costing money.'

'Yes. I suppose so.'

'If only the father – oh, look, it's not that we're angry with you, but really, Mary, it was a very stupid thing you did. Not to even know his name! But we'll stand by you. You needn't worry that we'd be hiding you away, be ashamed of you or your child at all. We're only worried about – about the practical things. That's why we think – your father says—'

'Says what?'

'Says that adoption would be the best thing. For you, for the baby, for everyone.'

'But it's mine! I want to keep it!'

'Do you? Why?'

'Because – *because*, that's why! It's my baby. That's all. My baby, and my job to do the best I can for it.'

'Yes, but what is the best? Mary, there are couples who have no children of their own, no money worries, lovely homes . . . women who don't have to work, who want to stay home with a child and can afford to. They'd give it much more than you can.'

She thought of the face, the small face like her brothers', and suddenly she thought of Keeley. 'Don't let anyone tell you what to do,' Keeley had said. 'Don't let anyone decide for you.'

'They couldn't love it the way I would.'

'Oh, Mary. They'd love it very much. It would grow up very happy and well cared for.'

'But I'd never be sure of that! I'd never see it again, I wouldn't know!'

'The social welfare people would know, they check all the couples and keep a watch for a long time, make sure the child is fine. In fact, it's very hard to adopt, you have to really prove you're able to be a proper parent.'

'I don't care. I'm not giving my baby away to anyone.'

'But—'

'How would you feel if someone wanted you to give Sean away, or Steve?'

'Mary, please, don't be silly, it's not the same thing—'

'It is! You couldn't give them away and I can't give mine away!'

Leesha sighed, sat cradling her coffee mug, feeling the resistance in her daughter.

'Well, you said you wanted to hear our suggestions. And that's what we suggest. If you don't want to do it, we can't make you. But then what are you going to do?'

'I don't know.'

Something told Leesha that it might be best to say no more for now. Something in Mary's expression, lost and worried, that might well bring her round to the idea of adoption, in time. There really didn't seem to be any other workable solution . . . unless . . . but they had five months to think things out, to make Mary see sense. Slowly, heavily, she stood up.

'All right. Why don't you just think a little bit about it, anyway? You don't have to do it, it's only an idea. There are so many other things to be thought out yet, anyway. Who's going to tell your grandmother, and explain it to the boys? What will we say to the neighbours? If you are going to keep it, what school will it go to? You have to put their names down early these days, you know—'

For a wild moment Mary thought of her grandmother, the only surviving one. But Granny Jameson was sixty-six, she lived way over in Ringsend, miles away – no, it wouldn't work. Or even be fair, to ask her.

'Mary? Are you going to get dressed, come to church with us?'

'No, Mam. I don't think so. I don't feel up to it.'

She really didn't. She needed to be alone for a little while, to think. And she felt – well, not as bad as she had some mornings, but not great. The smell of breakfast was making her slightly faint, the rashers and eggs Leesha had fried specially for her, and been so disappointed when she couldn't eat them. Out in the kitchen, they sat cold and congealed, and she wondered how she would ever eat again. All she could face was fresh light things, fruit or maybe a plain croissant – but croissants were unheard of here.

'Didn't you go to church in France?'

'I – well, no, we didn't. Only at Christmas.'

'Only at Christmas? Why? Was that Keeley Butler's doing?'

'No. It was just that – we didn't understand in French, and anyway I had to work on Sundays.'

'Well, as long as you're living in this house, you'll be expected to go here. You can't let your religion slide – oh, I knew I should never have let you go! Your father said it, and he was right.'

Gathering her robe around her, Leesha shook her head as she left the room, took her empty mug to the kitchen and went upstairs to tell Kevin. The first effort had not succeeded. But there would be others, there was no need to panic yet.

Mary remained on the sofa, willing Keeley to come soon.

But the day crawled by, and there was no sign of Keeley. The rest of the family went to mass, drove Granny Jameson back to Ringsend and then came home for a late lunch of chicken, roast potatoes and marrowfat peas, the same lunch they'd had every Sunday since Mary could remember. Sometimes it was beef instead of chicken, but otherwise it never varied, and Mary was already recoiling at the thought of the jelly and custard to be faced afterwards. Kevin turned to her, looking worried.

'Mary, you've got to eat.'

'I had some chicken.'

'That's not enough, for a—'

Glancing at Sean and Steve, he stopped in mid-sentence, but decided to pursue the subject later. The church thing, too. It would be a very bad example for the boys if Mary didn't even go to mass. And – well, he'd say nothing this time, but if she was going to live in this house she'd have to give her mother a hand with the cooking. She'd worked in a restaurant, was well able to peel potatoes and give Leesha a break, on Leesha's day off too, when she should be resting. Pregnant or not pregnant, she'd have to make some effort.

But it was only her first day home. He didn't want a row. For the sake of peace he opened his newspaper when the meal was over, and smiled at her. 'Just give your mother a hand with the washing-up, Mary, and then there's a good film on television. Tell us, was the telly any good in France?'

'I don't know, Dad. We didn't have one.'

'What, no telly for five months? You must have been bored stiff. Bet you're glad to be back to the comforts of home now, eh?'

His grin was warm and friendly and she knew he meant well, sensed that he and Mam were deliberately avoiding any further mention of her 'condition', for now.

'Yes. It's great to be home. But I think I might go out for a walk when the dishes are done, just to see if everything's the same as I left it.'

He grinned again over his newspaper. 'Oh, it is, don't worry! Nothing's changed.'

No. Nothing except me, she thought. Nothing else. The film will be a detective or a western or an old musical. The boys will get bored and go over to play with the Dempsey kids, or the Dempsey kids will come here. Dad will fall asleep and have a snooze, when he wakes up Mam will make tea, there'll be a jam sponge cake and – I've got to see Keeley. She said she'd come here, but it's three o'clock, I can't wait. I need some fresh air, anyway, before Dad gets stuck in about having the baby adopted. I know he's going to talk about it, later tonight when the boys are in bed.

Putting on her coat, she slipped away as soon as she could. Keeley's house was a fifteen-minute walk away, and the cold January air was reviving, refreshing. As she walked she looked for signs of change, scanned the familiar houses for – for what, really? The occasional pair of new curtains, a puppy she hadn't seen before, a garage door patched up where a football, probably, had gone through the old timber. Nothing that proclaimed any drama, any new activity, anything exciting at all. And yet, all kinds of things must be happening, behind these Sunday-silent doors.

Keeley's house, when she reached it, looked exactly the same. A mess. Tiny overgrown garden that would take all of an hour to mow, if Christy ever fixed the lawnmower which had been broken for longer than she could remember. Gate hanging loose, paint peeling, litter and graffiti. No sign of life, inside or out. Of course it was Sunday, Mrs Butler would be at the rehab centre with Tony, a trip that involved two long bus journeys. Poor Mrs Butler. Poor Tony.

As Mary knocked and stood waiting, she wondered what Keeley would say when she heard she had been right, about Leesha and Kevin wanting the baby adopted. It was the sensible thing, if you looked at it sensibly, but – where was Keeley? Why was there no answer, no sign of anyone being at home? She knocked again, harder.

After another long interval, the door inched open. Just a fraction, enough to reveal a glimpse of dark spiky hair, one startled brown eye.

'Keeley, hi, let me in, I couldn't wait any longer, you were right, they do want—'

But the door opened no further, Keeley didn't speak.

'Keeley, it's me, Mary! Let me in!'

Still nothing, only a look so strange that suddenly she caught her breath, caught some whiff of something. Of fear. Almost of terror, in what little of Keeley's face she could see. In a flash, she knew what it was.

'No!' Pushing open the door, letting the daylight pour in, she grabbed her friend and looked at her: at the swollen jaw, the purple bruises, the eye that had been hidden, livid, completely closed.

'Did he do this? Did Christy do this?'

Dumbly, Keeley nodded, tried to speak and failed. Mary felt the purest rush of fury she had ever known, an electric surge of adrenalin.

'Where is he?'

Keeley recoiled, motioned to her to be quiet, her mouth so swollen it was almost unrecognisable. But her eyes flew to the kitchen door, and Mary followed them.

'In there? Is he in there?'

Not waiting for an answer, she released her grasp and reached the kitchen in two strides. Keeley's father was sitting at the table, in trousers tied up with some length of something, a stained vest revealing the thick red neck and barrel chest, the muscle gone to flab, arms thick as table legs. As she burst in he whirled round, knocking over his can in shock, his glazed bloodshot eyes fighting to make sense of the sudden apparition. Before he could speak she was on him, hooking her hands into the straps of the vest, yanking him to his feet. Shorter than her, he stared up as if at an avenging angel fallen from the skies.

'Did you do that to Keeley? *Did* you?'

'Wh – what – who the fuck are you?'

She tightened her grip. 'I'm Mary Jameson. Keeley's friend. And you are a pig. A disgusting, filthy pig, a brute, a prize shit and a miserable little bully. That's all you are, Christy Butler, just a lazy stupid little bully who thinks no woman would ever dare stand up to him. Well, I'm standing up to you. I'm calling the police and getting you charged with assault.'

He gasped as she flung him down, so hard the chair shot up against the sink, his back thudding into its dowels as she stormed back out and seized Keeley.

'Come on. We're leaving.'

Propelling Keeley onto the path, not even bothering to find her a coat, she slammed the door all but off its hinges behind them, pushing and dragging, hauling her friend until they were far enough away from the house to pause for breath, and the winter sunlight revealed the horrific extent of the damage. Keeley's face was like an aubergine, in both colour and shape.

'Jesus Christ. You need a doctor. How long ago did he do it?'

Tears came to Keeley's eyes with the effort of speech, her voice mangled and barely audible.

'A-about two hours ago.'

'*Why?*'

But Keeley shook her head, unable to answer. Mary's breath came in bursts as she marched on, drove them both on, down the street past the shocked stare of what few people they passed by, until finally they reached Pearse Avenue and the Jameson house came in sight.

'I'm going to send my Dad round to kill him.'

Keeley tried to protest, but so feebly that Mary realised her fight was all used up. In her haste she hadn't registered it at the time, but now she recalled noticing something wrong with Christy's own face, red streaks on it. Fingernails. At least Keeley had fought back. Always a fighter, only not strong enough this time, against a father who'd had so much practice at the physical kind.

As they went in Kevin and Leesha came running out to them, alarmed by the sudden noise, the slamming door. And then they stopped dead, frozen in horror.

'My God – Keeley Butler – what—'

'Her father did it. He beat her up. Dad, call Barry O'Neill and get him round here.'

To his credit, Kevin didn't even wait to ask a single question, embarked on no debate at all. Instead he went to the phone and dialled, breathing rapidly as he waited for an answer. Twittering and gasping, Leesha led the two of them into the sitting room, where Mary was relieved to see no sign of her brothers.

'But her own father – he can't have – Keeley, did he really do this to you?'

Keeley nodded as she sank onto the sofa, her head bent as if trying to hide the evidence. One side of her face was much worse than the other, the left side – because, Mary realised, Christy was right-handed. She winced as she thought of it, almost able to feel each blow herself. With an effort, she made herself sound calm, as comforting as her anger would allow.

'Keeley, just sit down now and get your breath. I'm going to get some ice from the fridge – Mam, have we any TCP, Savlon, stuff like that?'

Leesha still looked disbelieving.

'Yes, in the bathroom, I'll get them.'

Leesha went off, and Mary could hear her in the hall, talking to Kevin as he put down the phone after what had apparently been a very brief conversation. As fast as she could, she went to the kitchen, whacked the frozen ice-cubes out of their tray and brought them back in a bowl. Kneeling down beside Keeley, she put the first one gently to her cheek.

'Sorry, I know it hurts, but it'll help.'

It stuck to her fingers, burned them as she held it in place, replaced it with another when it began to melt. What she needed was a whole bag of them, she thought, she would have to wrap them in a towel . . . Kevin came into the room, and knelt down beside her.

'Keeley. Can you look up? Look at me?'

It was agonising to watch her try to do it, with the eye that wasn't closed, but almost black under the lower lashes. Kevin took her hand.

'Don't try to talk. Just listen to me. Mary and Mrs Jameson are going to look after you until Barry gets here. He's a friend of mine. A policeman. He's going to ask you some questions, just a few, and then we'll take you to hospital. Barry says Blanchardstown is on casualty duty today, it's not far. Will you be all right till then?'

Keeley murmured yes, and Kevin stood up, took Mary aside while Leesha took his place, unscrewing a tube of Savlon.

'Mary. Are you sure it was Christy? Absolutely sure?'

'Absolutely sure. He's done it before, she told me. He beats her mother as well.'

'Right. That's all I wanted to know.'

Mary was grateful to him as he went to make tea, not that Keeley would be able to drink it, but for his reaction, the way there was no doubt or accusation in his face, no suggestion that Keeley Butler was the kind of girl who got herself into trouble. By the time the tea was made Barry had arrived, not in a police car but in his own; he'd been off duty at home when Kevin called him. Not particularly tall, but stocky and robust, he had very short, very red hair, a friendly face that Mary could remember since her childhood. He and Kevin had been great buddies for years. He didn't look very official today, in old corduroys and a sweater with Donald Duck absurdly knitted into it, but he had an air of quiet authority about him. After some conference in the hall with Kevin, he came into the front room and looked at Keeley for a moment before approaching her.

'Keeley? I'm Barry O'Neill. I'm a policeman. Mary's father rang me because he says your father – your father did this to you. Is that right?'

Yes, Keeley whispered, that was right. And why, Barry continued, sitting down beside her, had he done it? What had happened to start a row? Mary clenched with pain as she watched Keeley try to answer, and she wondered where Barry's notebook was, why wasn't he taking any notes?

'France,' Keeley mumbled, her voice thick, her mouth the size of a beef tomato.

France?

But that was all. Keeley couldn't articulate another word, and under the bruises she was turning very pale.

'All right. We'll talk about it later. Let's get you checked out first.'

Barry patted her hand, and between them they lifted her to her feet, helped her towards the door until Kevin suddenly stooped down and lifted her up, carried her out to his car in his arms. Mary was touched by the way he did it; whatever he thought of Keeley Butler, he was being very helpful now, she felt she could rely on him. When Keeley was settled everyone got into the car except Leesha, who said someone had better stay home for the boys, but she too put her arm on Keeley's shoulder, comforting and sympathetic. Then she told them to

wait, and ran back to get a cardigan, because Keeley was starting
to shiver.

Mary sat in the back beside her friend, holding her hand,
alternately grieving and ranting aloud all the way to the hospital,
urging Barry to bring all the force of the law thudding down on
Christy Butler's head. He didn't respond with the vehemence she
wanted, but simply said that yes, something would be done.

Casualty was crowded and they had a long wait, but after a
couple of hours a nurse finally took Keeley to be examined while
Mary supplied details for files: name, age, address and what
exactly had happened. She wanted no cover-up, no protection
of the little Hitler in Pearse Gardens.

The nurse advised them to go home. Keeley's jaw needed to
be X-rayed, an oculist would have to look at her eye; they'd be
better off going home and telephoning later to see whether she
was to be kept in overnight for observation. Barry said he was
on night duty and had better go, but Mary made up her mind
to stay, and was pleased when her father said he would too. He
was being really great about this.

So they sat, watching the hideous parade of accidents, drunks
and disasters, and Mary wondered how many of them actually
were accidents, would be written off as such. Well, this one
wouldn't. Kevin wanted to know why she hadn't told him
before that her friend's father was violent.

'She only told me in France. I never knew before, but it's been
going on for a long time. I don't think it was ever as bad as this,
though.'

And the mother was being beaten too?

'Yes. Keeley wanted her to leave, to go to the Women's Aid
place or tell the cops or do something, but she wouldn't.'

Kevin said little more, but she saw that he was thinking about
it, turning it round in his mind. Eventually, after nearly three
hours, the nurse returned, leading a stitched and bandaged
Keeley by the arm.

'Nothing broken, so she can go home – that is – you'll be
able to look after her, will you?'

To Mary's relief, Kevin nodded. 'Yes. She'll be staying with
us.'

Keeley's jaw was badly distended, the nurse said, here were
some painkillers and a prescription for more. Her lower gum
was stitched so she would have to drink through a straw, eat
nothing solid. She was to come back tomorrow to have the

dressing on her eye changed. In a brisk way that said she had seen it all before, she handed her charge over to them.

In a relieved but grim silence they drove home, Keeley drowsy and confused with whatever drug she had been given, and Mary was very glad to see her house when they arrived, looking cosy and cheerful after the antiseptic hospital. Kevin had phoned to say they were on their way, and Leesha had a warm fire burning, lights on, a bed made up.

'It's only the fold-out one in Mary's room, Keeley, but Granny Jameson slept on it the other night and says it's very comfortable . . . come on, it's all ready for you.'

Without a word Keeley let herself be put to bed, in Mary's pyjamas with a hot water bottle, and after a cup of tea with her parents Mary went up to bed herself, suddenly worn out. As she undressed she thought again of how good they were being, what a comfort it was to have proper parents and a proper home at a time like this. Where would Keeley have gone, what would she have done, without this refuge to come to?

It was three days before Keeley was able to speak properly, the swelling went down enough that she was at least recognisable and functional. Mary wondered that her mother, Gertie, didn't come looking for her, until Kevin said he'd been round to the Butler house, told them where their daughter was and suggested they stay away until further notice.

'Well, Christy would hardly come, but didn't her mother want to?'

'What her mother wants,' Kevin replied, 'is beside the point.'

Mary realised then that he was including Gertie Butler somehow, blaming her almost as much as Christy although she had not even been in the house when the episode happened. She thought about it until Barry O'Neill came back, questioned Keeley some more and then delivered an infuriating verdict.

'There's nothing can be done. Not from a legal point of view.'

'What? But why?'

'To begin with, there were no witnesses. It's only the daughter's word against the father's.'

'But how could there be witnesses? It happened in their house, not out on the street!'

'Exactly. That's one of the many reasons why police intervention is rarely possible in domestic disputes. Plus, the complications are impossible in court . . . wives can't testify against husbands, family members come under enormous pressure, lawyers hate handling these cases because they're so messy and there's no money in them ... the best thing is to just leave it go.'

Keeley managed a twisted smile.

'At least you gave him a good fright when you showed up.'

But Mary was furious. 'That wasn't enough. I want something done – Barry, there must be something.'

Barry glanced at Kevin, and then nodded at her, maddeningly calm.

'I'll go round in uniform and put the frighteners on him. Don't worry, Mary. Just take care of Keeley until she's well enough to go back to France.'

Yes. Already she'd had to ring France twice, on her parents' phone at their expense, first to tell Eliane that Keeley was ill, and then to tell Vincent. Against her will, at Keeley's insistence, she told him that it was just a stomach bug. Even that was enough to worry him, his voice became very anxious, but it was Keeley's choice. Anyway, her French wasn't up to explaining the truth, and there was nothing Vincent could do from where he was. After Barry left, Mary turned to Keeley, who sat in front of the fire looking pale and lost in borrowed clothes that were much too big for her.

'How are you feeling?'

'Better, thanks. How are you feeling?'

Surprised, Mary blinked. In all the fuss, she'd almost forgotten she was pregnant. 'I'm fine. But I'd feel a lot better if only there was something could be done about that man.'

With her good eye, Keeley studied her. 'You were amazing. I never knew you had a temper like that, when you were really riled.'

'Neither did I. I wanted to kill him.'

'Well, even if you didn't, it made me feel great. Not just to see him go flying, but to see that you cared so much.'

'Of course I care! You're my best friend.'

'Yes, but you ... you got so angry, for my sake. I've never seen you get angry for your own sake. You were upset about having to leave France, but you didn't seem angry.'

'Well – it's my own fault I had to leave. That was different.'

'Maybe. But hang on to that temper of yours, Mary. It's worth keeping – and losing, when need be.'

'I just wish I could have done more. I can't believe he

did what he did, all because you said one word, by accident.'

One word. Christy had asked Keeley was she going back to
France, and she had answered 'oui' by mistake, instead of 'yes.'
It had simply slipped out, because she'd been concentrating so
hard on learning French. And then he had gone berserk.

He would teach her, he had roared, to come home – bam!
– talking all uppity – bam! – to her father – bam! – with her
nose – bam! – in the air. He would teach her a lesson and no
mistake. Keeley had fought back, tried as hard as she could to
disable him. But she was eight stone, he was twelve, and he had
the advantage of lots of practice, on Gertie.

'I think he's mad, Keeley. He should be locked up.'

'Well, you heard Barry. There's nothing can be done. I'm just
glad to be away from him, out of it. Anyway, tell me about your
parents. How did they take the news?'

Mary sat down in the armchair facing Keeley, and thought
about it before answering.

'They were pretty good. Very good, actually. They want me
to have it adopted, but there was no lecture, nothing about sin
or shame or any of that stuff. When I said I didn't want to have
it adopted, they didn't argue, they only asked what I do want
to do, then. At least Mam asked, she did most of the talking,
but she and Dad seem to be agreed about it. I can make my own
decision – just as long as they're not left holding the baby! Mam
said she won't be able to mind it, that she can't afford to give up
work, which is fair enough. But it means Cathal Brugha Street is
out of the question. I'll have to find some kind of job that will
give me enough to support the child and contribute something
to the house, if I'm going to be living here.'

'Are you? Going to be living here?'

'I can't see where else. Besides, that was the point of coming
home. It is a home, Keeley. A proper home.'

Yes. Keeley could see that it was. And that there was a lot to
be said for it. She was very grateful to the Jamesons, not just to
Mary for looking after her, but to Kevin and Leesha for fussing
over her while her own mother, Gertie, did as she was told and
stayed away. Of course there could be many reasons for that –
guilt, fear of incurring Christy's wrath herself, refusal to face the
truth – but still it was Mary who had taken everything in hand,
and it was Mary's parents who were dealing with the situation,
supplying shelter and comfort and everything she needed. She

was very grateful to them all. The pain she felt now was more mental than physical; Gertie's cowardly absence, the fact of not being able to visit Tony. She couldn't go to the rehab centre with her face in the state it was, they would think she had come for treatment herself, and Tony would be alarmed, maybe upset. Did he know that their father beat their mother? She'd never known him to mention it, if he did, while he lived at home, and there had been no question of raising the subject since his accident. The nurses said he mustn't be distressed, burdened with any family problems which, in any event, he could do nothing about. To visit him in these circumstances would do more harm than good, and it dawned on her that Christy was destroying their whole family. For all Tony's faults, he was her brother, she would have liked to see him.

At least Mary had a normal home, a normal family. One that welcomed her, wanted her and even accepted, apparently, her pregnancy. There was no recrimination in the air, and Mary seemed content, relieved that there were no scenes, no hysterics. Like a missing piece of a jigsaw, she had simply slotted back into place.

'Still . . . won't it be hard to stay here now, after you've had your own place? I mean, your parents are terrific, but . . . it could be for eighteen years or so. You'll be nearly forty.'

Forty! The shock of it hit her like a juggernaut. Oh, God. Well, not quite forty, but not far off it.

'I – I can't think about that, Keel. I'll just have to take one day at a time.'

'Yeah. Well, there are certainly worse places you could be. Pearse Gardens for instance, chez Christy.'

Keeley grinned lopsidedly, and Mary smiled in turn, glad to see her friend able to laugh off her horrific experience. Or appear to laugh. Inside, she must be in little pieces.

'Keel, when you get back to France, are you going to tell Vincent what happened?'

'I won't have to tell him. One look will tell him.'

'What do you think he'll do?'

Keeley turned to look down into the fire, the sleeves of Mary's sweater dangling to her knees, making her look almost childlike.

'I hope he'll take me in his arms and hug me to death and set a date for the wedding. I never want to come back here again.'

No. And the only reason she had come in the first place,

Mary thought guiltily, was for her. She came here for me, this happened because of me. And now – I have to tell her what Barry O'Neill said. I have to.

'Keel?'

'Mm?'

'When – when you were in the hospital – we got talking. Me and Dad and Barry.'

'Yeah? About what?'

'Barry asked me a lot of questions. About you. I told him you were engaged.'

'Oh?'

'And he said – he said he hoped – you weren't going – from the frying pan into the fire.'

'What? What does that mean?'

'He said it means that the daughters of violent men often marry violent men. He said it was a psychological pattern, whatever that is, that it was very common. The only reason I'm telling you is – oh, God, I know Vincent is the best in the world, but – I just want you to be sure, that's all. Really sure. I mean, you've never had any kind of argument with him, have you? You don't know what he might be like when he's angry.'

'No. I don't. That's one reason why I wanted a long engagement, Mary. To find out all those things. And I still want it to be long, although I'm as sure as anyone ever can be about another person, about Vincent.'

'Are you?'

'Yes. But he'll have a whole year to prove me right. I'm still thinking of a Christmas wedding. I'm just keen to set the date now, that's all, to be sure that it's really happening.'

They were both silent, for a moment, thinking about Vincent. Keeley's bruised face seemed to soften, to relax for the first time since her father's attack; her fiancé was completely different, kind, reliable, good-natured and loving. But she understood why Mary had had to say what she had, was only doing it out of concern for her.

'You will be at the wedding, Mary, won't you? Promise?'

'I promise. I don't know how, but I will be, baby and all.'

Again they sat thinking, quietly, not needing any words, about the same thing. About how different life was going to be, for them both, from now on.

After ten days Keeley was well enough to travel, and it could be put off no longer. She hated leaving Mary, hated leaving Ireland without seeing her mother again, but her mother sent word that she was to go. Keeley was not to visit Pearse Gardens again.

'But why doesn't she come here, to say goodbye to you?' Mary asked.

'I think – I think she's too ashamed, Mary. She doesn't want to see my face, see what Christy did. Maybe she feels bad that she was with Tony when it happened, wasn't there to protect me even though she couldn't have. She can pretend it doesn't happen to her, but she can't pretend it didn't happen to me.'

Mary smiled, grimly. 'Well, I don't think it will be happening again for a while. To her or to anyone.'

It was unlikely. Kevin had come home late from work one evening and casually told them that he'd heard word of another little incident at Pearse Gardens. Someone had waylaid Christy Butler as he rolled from the dole office to the pub, in an alleyway in the dark February evening. Beat him up and broke his arm, he said offhandedly. Must have been after his dole money. Barry O'Neill was investigating.

Both girls gazed at him, astonished. But Kevin simply opened his newspaper and looked up the weather forecast.

'Should be better for your trip tomorrow, Keeley, than it was on the way over. Nice and calm.'

In bed that night they talked about it, hardly able to believe what was in their minds. No, they decided. It must have been a mugger. An accident. Like all those women and kids in the casualty department, victims of endless accidents. Poor Christy.

'I can understand now, Mary, why you wanted to come home. You are better off here, your parents will mind you much better than I could have.'

'But you did everything you possibly could, Keel. I can't stand it that you're going away, I don't know what I'm going to do without you.'

'You're going to have that baby and then I'm going to be its godmother. It'll be my duty to see that you bring it up properly, so I'll be in constant touch, you'll have to bring it to me for regular inspection as well.'

Clinging to that thought, clinging to each other, they put Keeley's few possessions into Kevin's car once more next morning, and then Keeley turned back to say goodbye to Leesha, who was staying at home to mind the boys.

'Bye, Mrs Jameson. Thanks – thank you for looking after me. For everything.'

Leesha hugged her, more warmly than when she'd arrived. 'Goodbye, Keeley. Remember that you have a home here, any time you want to visit. And you'll soon have one of your own, in France.'

That was what kept them going, all the way to Rosslare, past fields filling with white snowdrops and purple crocuses, coming alive with the first signs of spring. Mary had a home, for herself and the baby, and soon Keeley would have one too.

The sea was still and blue, as Kevin had promised, when they reached Rosslare, the sky clear and serene. Only the ship itself looked huge and dark, towering over them as they stood on the dock. Putting the rucksack down beside her, Kevin kissed Keeley and then made himself scarce.

Mary took her in her arms and hugged her fiercely.

'I'm going to miss you – I can't tell you how much I'm going to miss you – but you'll have Vincent . . .'

'And you'll have a child, the next time I see you . . .'

Their tears mingled as they stood locked together, feeling again the closeness of sisters, the pain and the protectiveness. There was no need for words, for promises; they would always be there for each other, for the child they felt belonged to them both. Not once had they visited their old haunts, seen their former friends, because they had each other, a shared future no matter how many miles came between them. A great physical distance, but they would always be together in mind and heart. With a last gasp, Keeley broke away, and ran to the ship without looking back.

And then its engines started, it turned and sailed away.

Chapter Five

Spring, Keeley thought. Spring has definitely sprung. It's the first of April, but it's not a joke. The sun is shining in the street, it's shining in my whole life.

With her wet hair wrapped in a towel, feeling fresh and scented from the shower, she went to the long window and threw it open, stood looking down as she inhaled the air already perfumed with budding window boxes, new leaves on the trees, the coffee and pastis that were once again being taken outdoors. When she leaned out and craned her head to the right she could see all the way down to the corner café, see the round metal tables glinting in the sun that felt warm on her shoulders and face. Voices drifted up, and she smiled when she found herself recognising lots of the words, automatically eavesdropping just to see if she could follow a whole sentence. Often, now, she could.

It was Easter Monday, a holiday that France celebrated, Vincent said, with great enthusiasm. Later in the morning, he would call for her and they would drive down to a village called Sausset les Pins, on the coast. They would walk by the water, maybe even have a swim if it was warm enough, and then have one of those long lunches she thought were so funny, with dozens of little things on dozens of different plates, ages between courses, a whole production as she called it, not just a meal. In five months he had learned a lot of English, saying he would match her word for word, and it was much easier to talk now, to communicate.

She supposed she should be getting dressed, getting ready for the trip, but it was early, there was no rush, and she was enjoying every drop of sunshine, every bird that flew past the window, every wave from the well-dressed women walking by below. Not that she knew all of them, but she knew the ones who got their hair done at the salon, and they knew now that this was where she lived, always waved if they happened to pass by. And didn't they look well, this morning, Madame Didot in a lemon skirt and white blouse, Madame Germain in a blue dress and wide pink hat, Madame Castex in a mint-green suit even though she was only going to the bakery for a couple of baguettes, her shoes tapping purposefully until she spotted Keeley and looked up.

'Bonjour, Mademoiselle Butler!'

'Bonjour, Madame!'

Soon, she would be able to talk to them. Not just enough to ask how they were, tell them how she was, but enough to consult them about what they wanted done to their hair. Once she could do that, Eliane said, she would be unleashed on them as a stylist, and she was working at it like a demon, practising all the phrases on her colleagues, on Sylvie and on Vincent, whose daily job it was to say that he wanted 'something short and wispy, please' or 'a new look, a fringe, nice and full at the back.' Often he laughed so hard he couldn't get the words out and they both ended up speechless with laughter, but it was working, she was nearly there. Every night she sat down for half an hour with a photograph of a model from a magazine and memorised every detail of her hairstyle, not just the cut itself but the shape of the 'tête', the 'cou', the 'oreilles.' Then he quizzed her as if he was a difficult customer, until she got it perfect.

Sometimes she felt that everything was perfect. Not only did she love him, she loved her work, felt accepted now, part of his family and of the team at the salon. She loved the weather that became warm so early, caressed her skin as she walked to work, permitted her to put away trousers and tights in the middle of March. The day flew by, no matter how busy it was she never felt bored, or too tired to meet Vincent afterwards, to go bowling or for a walk or to eat dinner with his parents. Their wedding was fixed for next December 20, and they were all saving money for various things: Vincent for the engagement ring he couldn't afford yet but insisted she must have, would have by June; Pierre and Francine for the meal at a restaurant after the ceremony – since her own family was not – ah – not in a position to pay for it, she would permit them the pleasure and please not say another word about it—, and then her own tiny nest egg was mounting up, for the plane fare that would fly Mary over to be matron of honour. She had rung Air France, and been delighted to discover that babies flew free. She giggled to herself as she thought of it, a little winged cherub whizzing across the clouds to France, wearing its tiny backpack, coming in to land at Nice airport.

Of course there was no question of her parents attending. Vincent had ruled out Christy, amongst a lot of other promises, after he saw and heard what had happened in Dublin at the beginning of February. Gertie would be invited, but there was no point in saving for her fare, she would never make it. Keeley knew that to all intents and purposes she had no family any more, and rejoiced in the thought of joining Vincent's.

Meanwhile, somewhat to her surprise, she was sharing the flat with his sister, Sylvie. Sylvie had jumped at the chance the moment she heard that Keeley was looking for a new flatmate, said it would be great fun to move out of home for a while, even if the flat was only twenty minutes away, it would be a taste of independence. Keeley was afraid that Pierre and Francine might argue, but they'd laughed and said yes, go ahead, why not? Of course, sharing with Sylvie wasn't the same as sharing with Mary, the whole atmosphere was different, maybe less interesting now that there was no experimental cooking, no news of Luc and Félix, no frantic trips to farms or fish merchants. But they got along well, spoke only French so that it would be comfortable for Sylvie and instructive for Keeley. She was in the deep end now, and nearly top of her class at the Chamber of Commerce. Keeley Butler, who'd got a D minus for French in her final school exam.

The sense of progress, of achievement, was incredible. But above all it was the freedom she loved, the whole weight of Pearse Gardens being lifted from her, her miraculous escape into Vincent's outstretched arms. Once or twice she had tested him, in small ways, dropped out of the final match in a bowling tournament they were hoping to win, refused to attend a party one of his friends was having. But although he'd been cross he hadn't been angry, had only shouted a bit after first ascertaining that she wasn't ill, that there was no good reason for her behaviour. But even when she shouted back he wasn't provoked, only exasperated, asking the ceiling what had inspired him to choose such a contrary Irish woman.

There was absolutely nothing nasty, vicious or vengeful about him that she could find, and Mary's disturbing words about maybe going 'from the frying pan into the fire' were beginning to recede in her mind, even if she could not forget them entirely. Gut instinct told her that Vincent was worthy of her love and trust, would never turn into a man like her father, inflict another scar like the one under her left eye. It was just a thin white line now, almost completely covered by her eyelashes, but its effect on her was out of all proportion to its size. It was a warning, a reminder she would carry all her life, of the consequences of being locked into an unhappy relationship. She had not voluntarily entered into her situation as Christy's daughter, but adult relationships were voluntary – miserable if you misjudged them, did not properly assess what you were doing. So far Vincent had given her nothing but happiness, and it grieved her to have to hold back. But she had been deliberately holding back, refusing to let love carry her off on its rainbow wings. It already said much for Vincent that, after all this time, he was putting no pressure on her even when he obviously, desperately wanted to sleep with her.

She wanted to sleep with him, too, and felt very close now to the point at which she could do it. Several times they almost had, but she always pulled away, more reluctantly every time until now, she thought, the moment had almost come. Vincent had proved himself; it was nearly time, and that was why she had been to see a doctor two weeks ago. Her new life felt like an opening flower in her hands, as fragile as it was beautiful, and she would not let it be wrested from her, hijacked as Mary's life had been, by an unborn person of colossal power and importance. A child changed everything, dictated everything, and she was not having one, not for a long time, until she was far more secure.

There was little she could do about her previous life, but so much she could do about this new one, to guard and protect it. In many ways she was still young and impetuous, but the things she had seen and experienced were enough to wise her up in other ways, the ways that mattered. Vincent thrilled her to the bone, but she was wary now, forced against her will to test and think, to be cautious. Erik, Lars, Christy . . . the evidence was all there, like a dossier of photographs, stacked in her mind. Men were dangerous, it was like handling fireworks.

And yet, what a time she was having with Vincent! They did everything together, walking, bowling, eating, sometimes cycling when Sylvie could be persuaded to lend Keeley her bike, and at weekends they kept up the tradition Mary had instituted, of visiting the sea or countryside. For weeks now everything had been in blossom, the air was lush and charged with a kind of confident optimism – the kind that you could only have in a climate like this, where people were able to plan crops and harvests and outdoor events with little fear of disaster. There was something benign in the atmosphere, a serenity that was very soothing, appealing. Whenever they drove to Rognes or Sausset or even nowhere in particular, she marvelled at the fertile landscape, the wealth it engendered, both physical and spiritual. Not only were the houses solid and prosperous-looking, there was such a peaceful aura about them, something that put Pearse Gardens at a very distant remove. No graffiti-sprayed concrete here, no fights or filth or noise; only the tinkle of goat bells, the hum of insects, the rustle of leaves and the scents of earth and ocean.

It was heavenly. Of course, things could go wrong, and Vincent said they sometimes did, but the predominant feeling was one of peace and security. Even the low stone farmhouses looked calm, but there were other houses too, big ones that took her breath away, with blue swimming pools glinting in velvety lawns, people playing tennis on their very own tennis courts, extraordinary cars in the drives. What on earth must it be like to live in such places, how did their owners manage to get so incredibly rich? Either they must be exceptionally lucky, or they must work like blazes. At what? You'd certainly never make that kind of money as a hairdresser, not if you worked round the clock till you were ninety. Yet there was a way. Demonstrably, there was a way, if you could only figure out what it was you too could live like this, under the sun with plenty of space and quiet and privacy, far removed from the reach of things – people – like Christy Butler. It was another world.

Where was the key to it, what shape was the key? Every time they drove through this landscape she wondered how you got in, through the glass wall that screened off the rest of humanity. Vincent wondered too, and they laughed as they speculated, compared their modest abodes with these grand residences. Not that many flaunted grandeur – Vincent said you had to go to Nice or Cannes for that – but they were so well kept, so quietly confident, even the rustic ones in keeping with the landscape. Flowers bloomed on schedule, creamy labradors patrolled immaculate grounds, you could practically eat your dinner off the gleaming white terraces. Even the children played in harmony, you simply couldn't imagine them burning a car or wrecking a garden for fun, swearing or littering or torturing a cat for kicks. It was a completely different way of life, eye-opening, hauntingly attractive.

But they were young, Vincent reminded her; the people who owned these houses were mostly older, had worked their way up to such prosperity over twenty years or more. Maybe they too had started in small jobs, been glad of any salary at all, of simply being young and healthy the way they were now. If he ever got rich he would gladly give her the sun, moon and stars, but for the moment – well, had they not a lot to be thankful for? She had kissed his neck and said yes, they certainly had. But she stored the images away in her mind, another file to be taken out and flicked through from time to time, a reminder of just what life could be like.

At length, she pulled reluctantly away from the window and her reverie, but left it open as she dressed, thinking of Vincent's impending arrival and their plans for the day. In the bedroom she could hear Sylvie waking up, mumbling, the bed creaking as she got out of it. Sylvie was a heavy sleeper for such a delicate-looking blonde – sometimes she even snored – and always had trouble getting up in time for work. But today she was going cycling, like half of France, Keeley thought; they were mad keen on bikes and races and forest trails. Eventually the door opened, and Sylvie sauntered out yawning, running her hands through her rumpled hair.

'Uhh . . . bonjour, Keeley. Quelle heure est-il?'

Glancing at the clock, Keeley told her it was neuf heures et le quart and that there were croissants sur la table, but she'd have to make her own café. There were many things she tried to do to fit in in France, but the mysterious process of grinding and filtering coffee was beyond her. Sylvie grinned.

'At what heure is my brother coming pour toi in his voiture?'

At ten, Keeley said with a sudden flutter of pleasure; God, she couldn't wait to see Vincent! All in a rush she flew off to dry her hair, find some clothes, get her game together. Not that he ever minded if he arrived to find her in what he called 'déshabille', but she enjoyed dolling herself up for him, the way he always whistled and teased. Anyway, she wanted to look good today; she had a little favour to ask him. Just a small favour, but still, one worth making an effort for.

It seemed like no time before he arrived; she still hadn't found her sandals, but her lipstick and eyeshadow were on, she felt she looked well even in her bare feet by the time she heard his car and ran to the window to throw down the keys. He came bounding up, two steps at a time, looking very summery and energetic in shorts and a light blue sweater. Kisses for her, kisses for Sylvie, coffee for him. Across the table, she smiled fondly at him.

'Vincent. About the wedding . . . I've been thinking.'

Eagerly, he looked up. He was always thinking about it himself, also thinking sometimes that he'd been a fool that night in January, not to seduce Keeley into bed when he'd had the chance. Not that he was going to rush her, because he understood why she needed time, but there were times when the mere sight of her . . . and now Sylvie seemed to be round the flat even more than Mary had been, it was driving him crazy.

'What have you been thinking, ma petite?'

'Well, I was just wondering . . . how would you feel about having the reception at the Vieux Moulin?'

'The Moulin? Where Mary used to work?'

'Yes. I know it's a bit expensive, obviously we'd have to ask your parents, but since we'll only be having a small gathering . . . ?'

'Well, yes, it's a lovely restaurant, I can't see why not. But Aix has many good restaurants, you haven't seen any of the others yet.'

'I know. But it would be such a thrill for Mary, if she could see Luc and Félix again, show them her baby – it would mean such a lot to her.'

He sat back with a mock sigh.

'Then it is decided. Who am I to come between such dear friends and a baby? Especially when I am to be godfather to that baby – I am a prisoner of duty, already!'

Keeley laughed, but then decided to plunge on; she might as well get everything off her chest.

'And – there's something else, as well.'

He looked curiously at her, noting the way she didn't simper or flutter when she wanted something, or go the long way round at it. Sometimes with his two previous girlfriends he had felt unsure quite where he was with them, but he knew with Keeley, and liked knowing.

'You want a baby of your own?'

'No! That's the very last thing I want. All I want is to be

there when Mary's is christened, for us both to be there, as I promised her.'

'Alors?'

'Alors . . . well . . .' She hesitated, looked round to make sure Sylvie was still in the bathroom, not listening to what might be a difficult question for her brother. 'If we're going to the christening, we need to think about how to get there. The ferry takes too long, and planes cost money. Then we'll have to pay for a bed and breakfast, because we can't both stay with Mary's parents.'

'No. I suppose we can't. I hadn't really given it much thought yet.'

'So – the thing is – I know you're saving up to get me an engagement ring, chéri. But I don't really need one. What I need is to be at that christening. For both of us to be at it.'

Anxiously she watched his face, wondering how he would take it. For a moment, he looked merely puzzled. But then he realised what she was asking.

'Ah. Ah ha. You want me to buy plane tickets with the ring money.'

'Yes. Please. It's not that I don't want – don't appreciate – it's just that the christening will be in a few months, we could get a ring later—? Please, Vincent. Say we can.'

For a moment he sat thinking, surprised. He had thought an engagement ring would mean much to her, not only as a symbol of his love, but as the first valuable gift she had ever been given. She did not need to tell him that nobody had ever given her anything much before, not even for birthdays or Christmas, and this ring had been invested with importance for him, for that reason. He wanted – he wanted, he suddenly realised, whatever she wanted. Whatever would make her happy.

'Yes. We can, Keeley. If that is what matters to you. We will go to Ireland and leave the diamond for another day – for our first wedding anniversary, maybe?'

'Oh, Vincent.' Stretching her hand across the table, she touched it to his face, looking at him in a way that knotted something in his heart. 'You are wonderful. Just wonderful.'

He rather thought he was himself, at that moment. Already he had been to several jewellery shops, had started searching . . . he couldn't deny a twinge of disappointment. But that look made up for it, a look full of love as well as gratitude. She did appreciate the significance of the ring, he saw, was not just assuming he could get one whenever she wanted one.

'Our first anniversary, our second, our fiftieth. We are going to have many anniversaries, you and I.'

He started to say something, something about how much he loved her and would always try to do as she wanted, even if it was not always easy. But Sylvie came back into the room, all sporty in biking gear, chatting blithely.

'The club is meeting at eleven, I have to go, we're doing the run by the Lac de Bimont and up Mont Sainte Victoire – have a great day in Sausset, you two, and don't wait dinner for me tonight, we're all eating at Alexandre's place afterwards. If you're asleep when I get home, Keeley, I'll see you in the morning. 'Bye!'

Jauntily she went out and sprinted down the stairs to the bike she kept in the hall. Then the front door closed behind her, and a few seconds later they heard her whizz by the window, zipping off to meet her friends for what sounded like a long arduous cycle. The Sainte Victoire mountains were not the Alps, but they were no doddle either, she would be worn out . . . she would be gone, they suddenly both realised, all day and half the night.

For a charged split second their gaze locked, and for that second Vincent allowed himself to hope – to wish – but no. Keeley had made it gently clear that sex was not a priority for her, told him her reasons, warned him it would be a long wait. It felt endlessly long, already; but to push her would be to lose her. Forcing himself to remain seated, he looked down into his empty coffee cup.

'We'd better get going too, before the whole day is gone.'

'Yes.'

With slow deliberation she got up, took the coffee things to the sink and washed them, dried them, put them away. Then she went into the bedroom, saying something about getting her bag, glancing back at him as she went.

What was taking her so long? Frustration made him impatient.

'Come on, Keeley, let's get moving!'

But several more minutes elapsed before she came back into the room, not carrying her bag, not carrying anything.

Instead she walked up to him, almost in slow motion it seemed, and put both arms around him, put her lips to his, reached up on tip-toe to whisper in his ear.

'Let's not go, Vincent. Let's not go to Sausset. Let's go to bed.'

It wasn't working, Mary thought as she fried the steak to a cinder, the way Leesha and Kevin liked it. It hadn't worked, wasn't working and wasn't going to work. She was willing to make many compromises for her parents as long as she was obliged to live under their roof, she was even willing to cook this bloody steak in a way that made her want to hurl it, pan and all, through the kitchen window. It would kill Luc to see what she was doing, it was killing her, but she would grit her teeth and do it. The only thing she would not do was have her baby adopted. They could work on her round the clock, try everything from bribery to corruption, but there was nothing they could say or do to change her mind. When would they see that, give up this wretched battle of wits?

As the steak spattered and sizzled she could hear water running upstairs, Kevin taking a bath after his dirty day's work, Leesha chivvying the boys out in the garden where they were engrossed in something involving insects. Both parents had a lot more leisure time now that she was more or less running the house, but she wished they wouldn't put so much of it into this fruitless campaign. She was going to keep and care for her baby, somehow, even if she still hadn't worked out exactly how. After it was born she would see if she could find some kind of job that could be fitted around it, something part-time for the first few years at least, until the child started school. There must be some local café that needed a lunchtime cook or waitress or dishwasher . . . if it meant her life was going backwards instead of forwards, well, she'd just have to put up with it. For now the baby was more important, in a few years she would try again, start over somehow.

When the steak was done to the consistency of a handbag, she called everyone to table. Hungry, the boys came galloping in, Kevin ran whistling down the stairs, Leesha arrived in time to serve the potatoes and be helpful. It was such a luxury not to have to cook any more, she said, but she couldn't get used to it, Mary should take a break sometimes and get out a bit, see her old friends. But Mary had lost interest in her old friends, didn't want to go drinking or nightclubbing when she was pregnant as a barrage balloon. Didn't know what she wanted, if she couldn't have what she really wanted, which was Luc and Félix and rare juicy steaks seared for sixty seconds. As she served these ones, they thudded onto the plates, and everyone began to eat enthusiastically except herself.

She knew that her parents worried about her loss of appetite. Yet there had been ructions the day she cooked coq-au-vin; the moment they heard its name they recoiled in horror.

'What, with wine in it? Oh no, Mary, we couldn't eat that . . . and so expensive . . . just a plain stew next time, please . . .'

She fumed, but she gave up; even if everyone was willing to eat the things she wanted to cook, hardly any of the ingredients could be got. Noses were wrinkled when she even mentioned them, Steve and Sean looked aghast when she described cheeses, herbs, dishes she had cooked in Aix.

'Fish? Yuk! We hate fish!'

But Ireland was an island, she told them, the sea was teeming with beautiful blue mackerel, the rivers were alive with golden trout and pink salmon, you could grow fennel in the garden probably, it didn't need a hot climate . . . Kevin had glanced out the window at his garden as if she'd suggested planting dead bodies in it.

'Gardens are for little boys to play football in, that right, Steve, Sean?'

'Yeah!' they chorused. 'You get food in the shops, Mary!'

It wasn't food, she thought, it was just fuel. But it was what they wanted, and she could see that they found her talk of France irritating. Also that it made Leesha uneasy, as if the family's diet was somehow being called into question, her lifelong methods of cooking challenged. When Mary had her own home, she said, she could cook what she liked, but meanwhile why not just stick with what they all knew and were happy with? In the end Mary stuck with it, said no more, and was the only one not happy with it.

It gave her no pleasure to watch them wolfing down every bite on their plates this evening, but it did make her think: what would it take to get Irish people interested in real food? There was a handful of good restaurants in the city centre, she knew, so there must be some people who were interested. But they were formal expensive restaurants, for people with enough money to travel a lot, learn about foreign cuisine and assess the value of their own. Ireland had no gastronomic tradition, but it did have fertile land, unpolluted fields and rivers, you could do wonders with the native produce with just a bit of imagination.

So when was anyone ever going to have any imagination? And if she couldn't interest her own family, who could she interest?

Distracted, she became aware that Leesha was talking to her. 'Have you any plans this evening, Mary?'

No. She didn't have any plans. Somehow she couldn't seem to plan anything until after this baby was born.

'Then why don't you have a nice hot bath – a bubble bath? You look a bit tired.'

Why not? Hot baths were very appealing these days, they took the weight off her limbs, gave her a brief but pleasant floaty feeling.

'And then, I tell you what, get dressed and put on something nice, a bit of make-up. You can't be sitting round in your tracksuit all the time.'

Was she? Well, it was comfortable in the mornings, and in the evenings too, watching television. But maybe they were tired of looking at her in it, she supposed she could brighten up a bit even if she wasn't going out anywhere.

'OK. I get the message, I look a fright!'

'No, of course you don't, I just thought it might cheer you up a bit, that's all. I tell you what, Kevin will get some beer from the off-licence, one glass won't do you any harm, we'll have a chat about the baby and the christening.'

The christening? God, could it be? Were they finally coming round to the idea that she was keeping the baby? After three months of getting nowhere, she was getting somewhere? Well then, she would bath and change and freshen up, maybe this evening they could all talk like adults.

She felt a bit silly when she came back downstairs, an hour later, wearing a new maternity dress that Leesha had got for her, a bit of lipstick, her hair washed and blow-dried. But she did feel better, and Leesha smiled.

'That's better. You can't let yourself go altogether just because you're pregnant, you know. Now, what about names? Have you thought of any? Let's see if we can decide on one before your father comes back from the off-licence, and surprise him.'

Surprised, but pleased, she turned her mind to names. After all she was seven months pregnant now, and if a name was decided the baby might become more real to her parents, more personal, harder to reject.

'If it's a girl I'd like to call her Keeley, only Keeley hates the name herself.'

'I'm not surprised. Let's make an alphabetical list and see what we can come up with.'

Leesha fetched a paper and pen while Mary noted that Sean and Steve had gone upstairs to get ready for bed; although her increasing girth had finally had to be explained to them, the subject was never discussed in their presence if Leesha could help it. Dad was a long time gone to the off-licence, too; the house was unusually quiet.

Leesha came back, pulled the sitting-room curtains and sat down with her, apparently not noticing that Kevin must have met someone he knew, and gone off for a pint with them.

'Angela? Anne? Alan? Aidan? Bernadette? Brendan?'

They had got as far as J when Mary thought she heard the doorbell ring, and Leesha jumped to her feet.

'Oh – I'll get it!'

Studying the list, Mary nodded, not paying attention until, after a few minutes, she began to wonder who Leesha could be talking to out in the hall. When the sitting-room door re-opened she turned round in surprise, not having heard the hall door close, no sound of anyone leaving.

'Who was—?'

But it was not her mother standing there. It was Cathal Sullivan.

'Hello, Mary. Long time no see.'

She sat frozen, immobilised. How could this be – be Cathal Sullivan? Cathal Sullivan was only a dim memory, a name from a past that felt like years ago. This dark, ruddy-faced man in the doorway was a virtual stranger, like someone she'd met at a party, or one of her old school teachers. Someone with whom she no longer had any connection.

She could not understand it when he didn't vanish, a mirage, a hallucination. But he did not vanish. He came into the room, all the way in, right up to her. And then he bent down, placed a kiss on her cheek.

'It's good to see you.'

This man was – was saying it was good to see her? This man in a white shirt and grey trousers, with grey eyes that knew her, recognised her? Several seconds elapsed until she realised she was staring, not speaking, not responding. And then the truth jolted into her mind: Leesha. Leesha had done this, arranged it – and now, disappeared. Everyone had disappeared, and she was alone with Cathal Sullivan.

Her voice, when she found it, was faint. 'Hello, Cathal.'

Smiling, he sat down in an armchair without invitation.

'You look well – for a pregnant lady! Your mother told me you were expecting.'

Automatically words of explanation and defence flew into her mind, but she held them back, caught them in time.

'Are you keeping well? Feeling all right?'

She would have to say something, she supposed. Something, to get rid of him, cut this pantomime short. It was absurd. 'Yes, I am, thank you.'

'Good. I've missed you, you know.'

Something in his tone caught at her, something that sounded faintly . . . what? Of course he must have been hurt, a little, when he got her letter breaking off with him. But she'd assumed he would have recovered by now.

'Well, you never wrote.'

'No. I couldn't, Mary. I was too upset.'

'Were you?'

It was a mistake to even ask him, she thought as she said it, but surprise forced it out of her, made her shift a little uncomfortably on the sofa. It was so much easier to write a letter than see the person in the flesh, have to face the reality. He was only twenty-three, but she thought he looked older than she remembered him, a little diminished. All the hard work, of course, at the pub that was his life. At this moment he did not look like a star football player at all, he looked like a man with a lot on his mind. But surely she couldn't be, still?

'I was. Very upset. I loved you, Mary, and I thought you were going to marry me.'

'I – I'm sorry. I thought so too. Until I got to France.'

'And then, you fell in love with somebody else.'

It was more a statement than a question, but it was not accusing. It was not true, either; at least she could spare him that much.

'No. I didn't fall in love with – with the baby's father, if that's who you mean. I just fell in love with France.'

'With France?' He leaned forward, as if trying to under-stand.

'Yes. With the sun and the scenery, with the way of life, with all the new things I was discovering. I was too young to marry you. To marry anyone.' Still dazed, she sat motion-less.

He raised his hand to his forehead, rubbed it as if trying to clear his mind, make room for this information.

'What kind of things? What were you discovering?'

He wanted to know? But nobody wanted to know. Everyone hated it when she blathered on about France. He would hate it too, it would drive him away.

'I was discovering that I could survive on my own, be independent. Keeley and I got a flat, and we were meeting lots of people, having great fun. I got a job in a restaurant, and discovered food.'

'Food?'

'Yes. It's a different thing, over there. You don't just eat and run. Every meal takes ages, everyone talks about what's going into it and how it should be prepared. I was working with a chef called Luc, he taught me about all kinds of things . . . that food is one of life's great pleasures. Have you ever tasted saffron, Cathal? Olives? Anchovies?'

That would do it, she thought. That would surely do it.

'No. What are they?'

She blinked. 'You want to know?'

'Well, yes, if they're so interesting.'

Was he joking, being sarcastic? But he was still leaning forward, looking intently at her, as if he was actually interested.

'Saffron is a yellow spice, very rare and expensive although they use it a lot in Provence, it gives the most wonderful flavour to rice, pasta, fish . . . olives are – well, you must know what they are?'

'Yes, but I've never tasted one. Are they good?'

'Fabulous, salty and bitter, very strong, you can stuff them with almonds or peppers for contrast, or use them with duck, squid, mussels . . .

'What's squid?'

'It's a type of fish, chewy, sort of like an octopus.'

He would get up and go now, surely. Run out of the room gasping at the thought of such disgusting things.

'And anchovies?'

'They – Cathal, what do you care what they are?'

'I'm just trying to learn something, while I have the chance.'

'Why? I mean, they're French things, you don't get them here.'

'No, but you might some day. You never know. Things have changed a bit since we joined the Common Market.'

'Not a lot, that I can see.'

'No, not a lot. Not yet. It takes time. But I can see it coming, slowly but surely.'

'Can you?' She could not grasp this situation, hardly knew what she was saying.

'Yes. I had two customers this week wanting to know if I served wine by the glass.'

'And do you?'

'I do now.'

She was surprised. Wine was almost a four-letter word down at The Lantern, awful stuff drunk by snobs and what his football friends called cissies, at the kind of pub where they put a mat under your glass and expected you to use it.

'Well, I hope you get the demand you expect. It might be just a flash in the pan.'

'No. I don't think so. The suppliers said demand has been increasing this year.'

She was heartened to hear it. Maybe by the time her child was at school and off her hands a bit, there would be a demand for new food too, as well as drinks. But how had Cathal got her onto this subject, why was he here at all?

'Cathal, I'm sorry I broke off our – our relationship, without any warning. You must have been upset. But I had to do it. I wasn't ready to settle down.'

'No. Your mother told me that. She said you were restless. I suppose it can happen.'

'Haven't you ever been restless?'

'Not really. I work off a lot of energy on the football pitch.'

Football. It had taken him all this time to mention it. That certainly was a change. For a moment they looked at each other, wondering.

'But – but football isn't everything, Mary. Maybe I used to talk too much about it.'

'You did.'

'Well – I wouldn't on Sunday, if you'd come out for a walk with me.'

'A walk? With you?'

'Yes. Just a walk, and a talk. You could tell me more about France, and about your baby.'

About her baby? By another man? She thought she must be hearing things.

'But why? What would be the point?'

'Does there have to be a point? We used to be friends, that's all. I'd like to hear about what you've been doing, what you're going to do now. Are your parents giving you a hard time?'

'No. But they want me to have it adopted.'

'Will you?'

'No. I won't.'

His eyes widened a little, not in reproval so much as curiosity. 'Then what will you do?'

'I'm not sure. I've been trying to think of some way to go to catering college, but I can't.'

He considered. 'Perhaps I could help you.'

Sitting up, she leaned forward to him. 'Could you, Cathal? How?'

'Come out with me on Sunday, and I'll tell you.'

Sex, Keeley thought dreamily. So this is what sex is all about. This is why people go crazy for it, spend their lives chasing after it, can't live without it. This is how it's meant to be. Lying in the arms of the person you love, listening to him breathe, watching his eyelids close as he falls asleep, holding you as if he will never let you go, never be a separate person again. This is as far as any human being can go, physically or spiritually, yet I feel as if a door has opened, that my life is about to go further than I ever thought possible. I'm exhausted, but I'm charged with energy, reborn. With this man at my side I feel I could climb the Himalayas, sail round the world, swim to Australia, do anything and everything. Why didn't I feel this way with Erik?

Because I didn't love him, nor he me. Vincent is a completely different person, this is a completely different experience. Mary would say this was lobster and caviar and champagne all rolled into one, a banquet I never expected to taste in my life, because people like me are never invited. But Vincent has invited me, into his heart, his mind, his soul.

Rolling over, she touched his shoulder, put her lips to his cheek. 'I love you.'

Dazed, sated, he said nothing, only wrapped her tighter in his arms, ran his finger down her spine, covering her in kisses. How smooth her skin felt, how delectable it smelt! And how happy she looked, flushed, glowing, her heartbeat only now returning to normal after an Olympic decathlon of love and sex, the months of waiting pouring into hours of ecstasy, hours and hours and hours of it. And yet, above all the things she had done this magic, memorable day, it was that smile that gave him enduring pleasure, that look that told him he had won at last, won her fair and square. Soon she would be his wife, but already she was his life. Burying his face in her hair, he breathed long and deep, locked her into his embrace.

In turn she wrapped herself around him, feeling as if they were lying not in her narrow single bed but in a field of rose petals, not under a duvet but under a drift of clouds. I feel, she thought, like a child of the gods. Me, Keeley Butler, the child of Christy Butler. How did I ever get from there to here?

On the wings of love. I didn't think hairdressers were supposed to have any, only poets and painters and people like that, but that – that's what makes life fair. You might not have much else, but there's always the hope that you can have this. If I got a chance of it everyone has a chance, the impossible can happen even to the most hopeless cases. I've no money or talents or education to speak of, I haven't got the face of a film star or the figure of a model, but I've got Vincent.

God, if we stayed in this bed for a hundred years, I couldn't express how much I love him! He must know how much, now, he looks so stunned, so overwhelmed. He waited so long. He waited, he thought I was worth it. I can't believe he values me that much, but he does.

Will it always be like this? Will his body always feel as beautiful as it does today, will his arms always be a haven to me, will we always want each other this much?

I think we will. I feel that we will, even when we no longer look beautiful to anyone else, we'll always be beautiful to each other. I have no idea why he loves me so much, but he does. He's given me confidence in him, given me everything I could ask of him. He'll never leave me, hit me or hurt me. Nobody could be so tender, so caring, and then do that.

Yet he's so passionate too. I thought I'd unleashed a demon, it was like letting a tiger out of a cage, I can't even remember getting to the bed. But I'll remember this day for ever, this first day, he has given me a memory that will last a lifetime. At last, I've got something of my own, something worthwhile, something to cherish.

And I've got something else too, lately. I didn't realise I was searching for it, much less finding it, but I've got self-respect. I like who I am now, I've stopped putting myself down all the time. Not only because Vincent loves me, but because I'm good at my work and Eliane tells me so, because I've learned to speak French, made friends in a foreign language, made a life in it. If anyone had told me that could happen a year ago, I'd have died laughing. But I have done it. Mary should be here, to pay her debt and buy me that dinner she bet me. Only I've gone off burgers these days. She was right about there being better things.

Vincent is one of the better things, the best thing that's ever happened to me or that ever could happen. Whatever I do from now on will be for him, through him, with him. I think he knows I've been testing him, but it's only with my head, not my heart. Every instinct tells me I can relax, I can trust him, ours will never be a marriage like my parents'. Even today, when he was practically pawing the ground like a racehorse at the starting gate, he took time, he took care, he was ready to be patient or considerate if I'd needed him to be. I suppose some people will think he's too good for me, but I don't feel that way at all, I feel equal with him, that we're partners. I'm his woman now, but I'm my own woman too. Funny how the French have the same word for it, woman and wife. It's not the same thing. I want to be a great wife to him, but I want to be the kind of woman he'd be proud of too, the kind I'll be proud of myself. The kind my mother never was and never will be – confident, able to decide things and do them. How can she live the life she does, how did she ever get into it? What makes a woman marry a man like my father? And what makes a man like my father, was he always the way he is, even before I was born? I don't remember him being violent when I was a child. But I don't remember much love either.

Love changes everything. Even if you're poor or sick – especially if you're poor or sick – it feels wonderful to be loved. And I feel wonderful. Absolutely wonderful.

'I just can't understand why you did it, Mam. I still do not understand. It's a complete waste of time.'

'Mary, would you stop making a mountain out of a molehill! We did it because we thought you were hanging round too much at home, it would do you good to see someone your own age and get out a bit, that's all. I mean, you never had any row with him, did you? It's not as if you hate him, is it?'

'No, I don't hate him, I just—'

'Well, then. It's only a walk, for God's sake, he's not asking you to elope to Gretna Green with him, is he?'

No. Cathal was not asking much, was not making any demands at all. He had had a cheek to come to see her, but if things had been the other way round, she supposed, she might well have gone to see him. A letter wasn't satisfactory, you'd want to talk to the person who'd let you down, discuss why they'd done it, try to change their mind. Not that Cathal stood a snowball's chance in hell of changing hers, but at least he hadn't been accusing or tried to start a row. Instead he had taken an interest in what she said, made an effort to listen if not understand. He seemed to have improved, a bit, on the old Cathal. Maybe the shock had done him good, been just the jolt he needed.

But she had lost interest in him, wouldn't have agreed to go for any walk if it wasn't for the bit about his maybe being able to help her. It would be some stupid scheme starring himself, no doubt, but in her present situation she had to admit she needed all the help she could get. Needed it enough to listen to whatever it was he had to say.

But her arms felt leaden as she lifted them to brush her hair, got ready without enthusiasm. He would drive up in his red Fiat, her parents would be delighted, the boys would be excited because they thought him glamorous, a barman in a pub, had caught their parents' note of approval. For a moment she sat looking at her reflection in the bedroom mirror, feeling like a puppet, manipulated by others, crushed by the sense of anticipation in the house and the knowledge that her performance was not going to be satisfactory. But she had warned them, they had brought disappointment upon themselves, as she had brought her present predicament upon herself the night she slept with Lars. Thinking she was breaking free, she had shut herself into prison, taken a completely wrong turn into a dead end.

Dressed, looking presentable if not fabulous, she went downstairs and sat down to wait with her father, who put down his newspaper to survey her. His face registered no more than she deserved, but he raised a smile.

'You look very well. And it's a nice day for a walk. I hope you'll enjoy it.'

'Thanks, Dad.'

Thanks a lot, she thought, for getting me into this, plotting it with Mam, telling my ex to call round without even consulting me. But she knew her parents meant well, and in most respects they were being so supportive, trying to do their best for her even if it wasn't what she wanted. They had even helped Keeley, not because they liked her but because she was Mary's friend, had taken her to the hospital, put her up in their own home, and then Dad had sorted Christy Butler out, with his friend Barry O'Neill. At least, she was pretty sure he had, although something warned her not to ask him outright. She owed them one, the least she could do was humour them by going for a walk with Cathal Sullivan.

There he was. She recognised the sound of the Fiat despite not having heard it for so long, and saw the way Leesha flushed instantly, eagerly but a little apprehensively.

'Don't worry, Mam. There won't be any kissing or making up, but I'll try to be civil to him.'

Leesha nodded, like a mother hen pecking at a dish of corn.

'Yes, anyone can manage that much, it would be nice if you could just be friends with him. Everyone needs friends, especially—'

'Yes. All right.'

Before he could come in she went out to him, cheating Leesha of the chance to serve tea in her best china. She was steeled to this encounter, but there was a limit to what she could bear.

He seemed slightly more real today, still unwelcome but marginally less bizarre, less foreign to her.

'Hello, Cathal. How are you?'

He stood on the path for a moment, surveying her with a smile.

'I'm great. This is just like old times.'

Oh no, she thought, it is not. Nor will it be. Let's just get it over with, Cathal. Get it over with, and go our separate ways.

'Come on, then.'

Opening the gate he ushered her out, and she could feel her parents' eyes following her from the window, behind the blinds, investing the moment with all the significance it did not have. Quickly, she got into the car.

'Where are we going?'

'Where would you like to go?'

Well, that was a turn-up for the books. He'd always chosen the destination before. Evidently things were to be different today, he was determined to please. For a fleeting instant she almost felt sorry for him.

'How about Howth? I haven't had a breath of sea air for ages.'

She liked the sea, when she was not actually on or in it, and Howth was popular on Sundays, would be full of walkers on the pier and cliffs, with no chance of their being alone.

'Right. Let's take the coast road.'

As they set off she inspected him, frankly if not very politely, noting how his narrow face had filled out a little, his large capable hands were still so confident on the wheel and gearstick, his trouser cuffs rode up as he accelerated, revealing colourful check socks. For some reason he had always worn jazzy socks, at odds with his otherwise conventional clothing. A navy sweater, today, white open-necked shirt, navy gaberdine trousers.

'Are you comfortable?'

She was not at all comfortable, but realised he was alluding to her pregnancy, wondering if she wanted to tilt the seat back.

'I'm fine, thanks.'

And then, to her complete astonishment, she burst out laughing. It was almost an exact replica of the fateful conversation she'd had with Lars, the night he'd asked her if she was 'all right.'

His face lit up. 'Well, I don't know what's so funny, but it's great to see you in such good form.'

'Oh – I just remembered something, that's all. It wasn't really all that funny.'

You can say that again, she thought grimly. But her mouth twitched again as she thought of Keeley, storming up and down the flat, demanding to know what in the name of blessed Jesus almighty they were going to do now. She still didn't know, but she knew what she wasn't going to do. Poor Cathal, wasting his time.

'So – what's all the news? I haven't seen anyone or heard a thing since I came home.'

'I know. I kept expecting to see you come into The Lantern, but your friends said they hadn't seen you, that you'd dropped out of their crowd altogether.'

'Yes. I was bored with the same old faces and same old routine before I even left. In fact that was one reason I did leave. I didn't want to be still sitting in the same pub with the same people having the same conversation every Friday night for the rest of my life.'

'Well, they're all getting on great. Grainne is engaged to Liam, and Colm has got a hot new job with Bord Báinne.'

'Bord Báinne? The Milk Board?'

'Yes. They're marketing Kerrygold in Britain, and he's in charge of the lorries that bring it over. A whole fleet of trucks, he says, quite a step up from being a driver.'

'Mm . . . still, I thought he liked being a driver.'

'Sure, but if you get a chance to earn more, you've got to take it, haven't you?'

She supposed you had. Not that she'd ever thought much about what chefs could earn, but certainly you had to take whatever opportunities came your way. What a fantastic opportunity Luc had been.

'And Paul's father died, Enda won a hundred quid on the dogs, Marian says she's thinking of opening a boutique . . .'

One thing she would say for Cathal, he could talk the hind legs off a donkey. There was no danger of awkward silences, being a barman he knew all the gossip, would supply an endless stream of it all the way to Howth. Unless he turned to the wretched subject of him, and her.

But he didn't. When they reached Howth he found the one parking space available on the entire seafront, eased into it and turned enquiringly, almost eagerly, to her.

'Like an ice-cream?'

She thought of the white glutinous stream pumping from a machine, full of sugar and chemicals, topped with a chocolate flake.

'No, thanks.'

'Oh. Well. Never mind. Cliffs or pier?'

She looked at the pier, teeming with people, far more than she'd expected, almost black like a colony of ants. But she couldn't climb up to Balscadden cliffs, at seven months.

'Maybe we could just walk along the front and up the hill, as far as the village?'

'Sure. You set the pace, just tell me if you get tired, we'll have a drink in the hotel if you do.'

He held open the car door while she heaved herself out with as much grace as she could muster, and for a wretched moment she thought he was going to take her hand, as he used to do. But he thought better of it, and put his hands in his pockets as they strolled slowly over the grass to the water. The sun and sea air, she had to admit, were refreshing, made her realise how very shut up she had become at home.

The breeze blew her hair back from her face, and he nodded at it.

'I like the new hairstyle.'

'Thanks. Keeley did it.'

'Ah, yes, the lovely Keeley Butler. Did I hear something about her father—'

'I hope you didn't. She has enough problems with him without people talking about them.'

'Uh, yes. Anyway, she's living in France now? For good?'

'Yes. I would be too, if it wasn't for this baby. But look, Cathal, let's not talk about all that. Let's talk about this idea of yours, whatever it is?'

He looked down for a moment, then up and out to sea, considering.

'Well. That's the thing. It's all tied up, in a way, with you having been to France, with having a baby.'

'I don't follow.'

'The pub. The Lantern. You know my father is making me manager next September?'

'Is he? But you're only twenty three. I thought managers were older, that you'd have to wait ages.'

'That's what I thought. But there was an incident a few months ago. Two of the barmen were caught with their hands in the till. Not by Joe. By me.'

Mary remembered Joe Foley, the current manager, with some affection. An affable man in his late fifties, he had been running The Lantern for years.

'Surely your father didn't – sack him?'

'No. He was going to, but then he thought it might look bad, because he's been there for so long and everyone's so fond of him. So he's offered Joe early retirement, when he turns sixty, an offer that has been not surprisingly accepted. It was Joe's job to keep a close eye on the staff, and he didn't do it.'

'Oh. But still, he had been doing it, for ages, maybe he just had a bad day.'

'No, Mary. The guys had a racket going, for weeks, and he didn't cop it. So, bye-bye Joe. Oh, don't worry, he'll get his golden handshake and all that, even a farewell party. But after that, I'll be manager. Dad reckons I've got my eye on the ball.'

Oh, God, Mary thought. If he starts on about his father, I will scream. Dear Daddy Donal, who thinks the sun shines out of his son's left ear.

'So, naturally, when I take over, I want to make some changes.'

'Such as?'

'Such as – well, that's where you come into the picture.'

Reaching the end of the promenade, she looked at him as they turned away from the sea and headed up the hill.

'Me?'

'Yes. Tell me, Mary, did you learn much about food in France?'

'As much as I could in five months. Luc was a brilliant teacher. I was only hired to wash dishes, but in no time he had me working on the vegetables, visiting farms and orchards and vineyards, making stews and salads – well, helping him make them, under supervision. He gave me bundles of books to read, told me all about ordering supplies, how you always have to watch out for waste in a kitchen – it's not all tossing and flaming and flourishes.'

'Do you think you'd know enough to set up a small kitchen at The Lantern?'

She stopped dead. 'What?'

'A kitchen. Bar food. There already is a kitchen, as you know, for soup and sandwiches. But I can see demand ahead for full meals. Nothing fancy, but a bit more than what we're doing at the moment. Starters, main courses, desserts.'

She didn't know what to say. She couldn't believe she was hearing this.

'I – Cathal, I – oh, my God.'

'Does that mean yes, or no?'

'It means I – I would absolutely love to do such a thing. I'd adore it! But I'm only nineteen, I have no experience—'

'Have you confidence? Do you think you could do it?'

Shutting her eyes, she thought of Luc.

'Yes. I think I could.'

'Then let's give it a try.'

'But – but why me? Don't you want a professional, someone older? Besides, I'm going to have a baby. It would be a fulltime job, if you want to serve food in the evenings as well as at lunchtime; how could I manage with a baby?'

He put his hand on her shoulder, and steered her in the direction of the hotel.

'Let's go have a drink, and I'll tell you how.'

*　　*　　*

I will strangle her, Keeley thought, if she says one more word. One more complaint, one more cheep out of her, and Madame Bonnard is going to be handed back to Monsieur Bonnard in a plastic bag with her name tied on a label round it. She is an old bag. Why doesn't she get a nice new hairstyle anyway, instead of this horrible tight perm she's had for years? I could take ten years off her, if she'd let me. She's stuck in a rut. Do all middle-aged women get stuck in one, get so cranky and snappy? Crikey, if I ever turn into someone like this, Vincent has my permission to feed me arsenic and tell the police it was suicide. I'd rather . . . what's wrong with her, anyway? Going to the hairdresser's is supposed to be fun, you're supposed to enjoy it.

But some of them don't seem to enjoy it at all. My mother would love it, if there was ever any money for going to salons, if she was let go to one. She'd think all her birthdays had come together. These women don't know how lucky they are. And they're at an age where they can afford it, don't have to scrape every penny together, if their clothes are anything to go by. I wonder why so many of them are so old? Well, Madame Bonnard isn't exactly ancient, only about forty, but we don't get many of twenty. Why is that? Have they no money, or is it something else? If I was a nurse or a shop assistant or something, would I want to come here?

Well, I'd want to get my hair done if I could, because it makes you feel so good. But . . . Eliane could do the place up a bit. Those beige tiles are so boring, the magazines are months out of date. And there's no music. We had music at the salon in Dublin, why doesn't Eliane have any here? We could have a kettle too, make tea for any customer who wanted it, some of them look as if they'd love one when they come in after their shopping. Would Eliane think I was being cheeky if I made a few suggestions?

I suppose she would. It's her salon. Maybe doing it up would cost a fortune, tiles might be really expensive in France. But the other things wouldn't cost much. I'd get music and new magazines if I was the boss. And get someone to paint designs on the tiles or something, if they'd be too dear to replace. Jazz things up. The French don't chat the way the Irish do, but they might if – if the atmosphere was more sociable. Madame Bonnard might not whinge so much, or maybe she'd whinge at other people as well as me, spread her misery round more equally! I bet these women would gossip just like Irish women, if things weren't so formal, so stiff.

That was one of the good things about Ireland. Everyone nattered and had a laugh. Some of the women at the salon there were miseries too, and no wonder when you heard some of the things they'd tell you, but they usually cheered up by the time their hair was done, went off with a smile on their faces. There was always a bit of craic. They're not very big on craic in France.

I wonder what it'd take to put a smile on Madame Bonnard? I'd nearly ask her what's bugging her, if Eliane didn't discourage chit-chat with clients. The client is always right, she says, just give them what they want and don't argue, even if it's the wrong thing. That's silly. Madame Bonnard should go blonde and get a feather cut, off her face, she could look like Jane Fonda if she wanted. If I was let talk her into it. I'm only half her age, but I reckon I know my stuff when it comes to hairstyles.

I wonder has she any daughters? We hardly ever seem to get their daughters, only the mothers. Maybe there's some other salon they prefer, somewhere that'll do their hair pink and punk if they want it. I haven't heard of anywhere, though. And the younger women who do come in here don't seem very adventurous, it's usually just a wash and trim – a 'brushing' as they call it – when they have a hot date. How hot can dates be, with women who look like their mothers? Maybe that's one of the things Vincent likes about me – I'm not a replica of Francine, I don't wear perms or pearls or sensible shoes.

Eliane doesn't seem to worry much about getting in the daughters. But I would. I'd want to get them as young as possible, from about sixteen or seventeen. What would attract them? A Ziggy Stardust theme, disco music, smocks with slogans printed on? That would jazz things up all right, only then it might put the mothers off. Still, there must be some way of doing it. Something better than rows of dryers lined up like lamp-posts, magazines that everyone's read already, one potted rubber plant that makes you feel like you're at the dentist's. If I was Eliane I'd get a major make-over here.

But I'm not Eliane. I'm just Keeley Butler who's damn lucky to have a job, and if I want to keep it I'd better keep my big mouth shut.

'*Dear Keeley,*

How are you? I'm sorry I haven't written for ages, but things have been busy all of a sudden, there's been a lot to think and talk about. Are you busy too, getting on well at the salon? I'm thrilled Eliane is letting you cut and style now, it must be loads more fun than just washing.

How's your French coming on, and how's Vincent? I often think of you both, wonder what you're doing at the same moment I'm sitting here writing to you. Do you ever run into Luc, or Félix? Please say hello to them for me, if you do. Tell them I'll call in to see them when I come over for your wedding.

I think of your wedding all the time, and hope you and Vincent are really happy together. But – Keeley, that's why I'm writing to you. Are you sitting down? I hope you are, because I've got something important to tell you. Pay attention, because I want you to understand. No, it isn't that I'm going to have the baby adopted after all. It's just the opposite. I hope you'll think I'm doing the right thing. The great news is that I'm going to be running a restaurant! Starting in September, and the even better news is that I can be with the baby while I'm working, not have to get anyone to mind it or worry about anything.

Well, it's not a restaurant, exactly. It's the kitchen in The Lantern. No, I didn't go back drinking there! Instead, it came to me. Or Cathal did, to be exact. Cathal Sullivan, out of the blue, arrived at my house one night. I'm nearly sure my parents set it up, but anyway it's all turned out for the best.

The Lantern is going to start serving pub food, and Cathal wants me to be in charge of everything. I thought he'd be furious with me for breaking off with him, but he wasn't. Instead he asked me about France and the stuff I'd been learning from Luc, and then he came up with this idea. I'm really glad you made me bring Luc's books back with me, because I'm stuck into them now I can tell you, learning all sorts of stuff even though most of it is much more complicated than bar food. Mam hated me cooking French food and nobody would eat it, but nobody minds me practising a bit now, they know I have to learn in a hurry and anyway these recipes are only for very simple things. Cathal says to start simple, but I'm hoping to do some nice things later on, get customers used to them gradually. We had a bit of a row over curry and lasagne – Cathal wanted me to stick with boiled bacon and cabbage – but I won, because other pubs are starting to do them. If things go well, I might just end up with my own restaurant after all, because Cathal says he'd extend if they did, either build a dining room on to The Lantern or think about turning the other pub (you know his father has another one down the country, it's called Fursey's) into a full-time restaurant. Apparently there isn't any for miles around.

I can't tell you how pleased I am, and relieved. I was worried sick about what I'd do after the baby was born, but this solves everything and gives me another crack at cooking after all, as well. I bet Luc would be impressed – my own kitchen, and not twenty yet! I can hardly wait to start. Can hardly wait for the baby to be born, either, I'm big as a house and it all seems to be going on for ever.

Which brings me to my other news. Are you ready for it? You might be a bit surprised at first, but I hope you'll see I'm doing the right thing, and understand and be encouraging about it.

Keeley, I'm getting married. To Cathal. He asked me, the same night we were talking about Fursey's and all the things we could do with it if we turned it into a proper restaurant. Assuming things go well at The Lantern, first. I suppose you're nearly falling off your chair, after all the things I said about not being in love with him any more.

Well, I won't pretend I suddenly am, in the starry-eyed way at any rate. But he's being so good to me, offering me such a future, one I thought I'd lost . . . the first time he suggested we get married, at a hotel in Howth, I turned him down flat. But now I can see the sense of it. There's room for us to live over the Lantern, when the current manager moves out (Joe Foley, you remember? He got into a bit of trouble) Cathal will be moving in and taking everything over, running the pub and the accommodation that goes with it.

And the best thing is, he's willing to take on the baby, treat it like his own child he says. In fact we've decided to tell everyone it's his, that I got pregnant just before going to France and that that's why I came back. So it won't look like too much of a shotgun. I can tell you my parents are delighted about that!

I just wish you could come over for the wedding, with Vincent. But I know you won't be able to, because we've decided to get married right away before I have to be wheeled down the aisle. We had a bit of a job persuading the priest, in my 'condition', but finally everything is sorted out and we're tying the knot on May 12. Can you imagine?

Well, maybe you can't. I know it's a bolt from the blue. But please try to be happy for me. I'd love it if you could be bridesmaid, but I don't expect you to come over twice in one year, and I'm still relying on you to come for the christening. You are going to be godparents, aren't you, you and Vincent?

I'm relying on you to write, too, and be supportive even though I know you didn't like Cathal much, before. But he's changed, Keeley. He's much nicer now. I think it did him good that I left, it made him appreciate me. He doesn't go on nearly so much about football or his other interests – well, except the pubs, which is understandable since he's being made manager of one of them so young. It's a big responsibility, he says, like my child is a big responsibility. He'll have a lot on his plate, so please try to forget the person you thought he was before and see what a great help he is now, what a go of things we can make between us. Of the future, and of our family as well. I can't believe my luck, that the baby is going to have a home and a father and maybe even a brother or sister some day. And I'm going to have a kitchen to call my own. Isn't it great?

Sorry about the shock, but it all happened so fast. Pick yourself up off the floor now – please! – and wish me buckets more luck, OK?

Lots and lots of love,

                                                          Mary.'

Chapter Six

'No! I won't do it, Vincent! I can't!'

'Keeley, you can. You must. She's your friend. Your best friend, that you never stop talking about, care so much about – God almighty, you even sacrificed your engagement ring for her! So why won't you do this for her, try to see things her way?'

'I'll tell you why.' Furiously Keeley snatched a blouse off its hanger, looked at it and flung it on the floor before grabbing another one. They were going out, to an art exhibition of all the deathly things, tonight's opening sponsored by the company Vincent worked for. Art was important in Aix, he said, because of Cézanne having lived there, and the fact that he had been invited to attend this event was a good career sign. It didn't matter whether or not he liked art or knew the first thing about it, which he didn't; the point was that he was expected to show up, with his fiancée. Wearing a new suit, he looked very neat and sleek, smelling of aftershave, his curly hair tamed and slicked down. Keeley longed to plunge her hands into it and ruffle every curl back out, had a wicked desire to spray her own into punk spikes, paint her nails black and slap on a mouthful of blue lipstick. She simply wasn't cut out for what he called 'corporate events', and was terrified of getting everything wrong – the wrong blouse, wrong earrings, wrong word. What if she said the wrong thing, got her French muddled and made a holy show of him? It was all very scary, and what with Mary's letter as well, she was wound up like a spring, ready to leap every which way.

'So tell me, then.'

Whisking up the letter from the orange crate where it lay – God, she must get a proper table some day – she slapped it under his nose.

'Look at it. Read it.'

'I can't. It's all in English.'

'Right then, let me quote you the main points. First, she's going to run a kitchen, do bar food. Hurray, whoopee, that's great. The heat is off her to have the baby adopted, hurray again. But second – not first, but second – she's getting married. To Cathal Sullivan. Vincent, she doesn't love him! She says herself she doesn't. Not really, not the way we do.'

'So maybe it is a marriage of convenience – partly, anyway. But Keeley, everyone is different. Even arranged Indian and African marriages sometimes work. Mary is simply giving this man a chance, that's all. And herself, and the child.'

'She'd never marry him if it wasn't for that child. And that bloody pub and the carrot he's held under her nose, the second pub that could be turned into a restaurant if she makes a good job of the first.'

'Maybe she wouldn't. But it is a great opportunity, for someone you said yourself was stuck at home with her parents, in a blind alley.'

'Her parents. That's another thing. They set her up. They don't want that baby, nor Mary mooching round unemployed, a bad example to her kid brothers.'

'I thought you liked her parents. They were very good to you.'

'Yes. They were. Very good, in a crisis. I think that's why Mary's let them win . . . she seems to feel obligated to them, in some way I don't understand.'

'Win?'

'Yes . . . they always liked Cathal, liked his prospects, wanted her to stay with him. And she's been living with them for months, got used to the comforts of home – Vincent, this isn't a relationship, it's a – a transaction! She's been brainwashed!'

'But maybe she'll grow to love him. He must love her, if he wants to marry her.'

'He loves the fact she's learned to cook and can run his damn kitchen for him.'

'It must be more than that. He's taking on a child, as well. Someone else's child.'

'Yes. She says he's "willing" to take it on. Like he was doing her a big favour – and sure enough she's very grateful, babbling about how lucky she is. But she – she's getting into debt. She'll spend years paying it off, being grateful and thankful.'

'How can you know that?'

'Because I know Cathal. He's a creep. She says he's changed, but I – I don't think she has her wits about her at all, at the moment. She's let herself be talked into this because it means she can cook, and be with the baby, have a home and income of her own and not be a burden to her parents.'

'Well, if those are her reasons you must try to respect them, Keeley. And you must congratulate her. Otherwise she might think it was sour grapes, because you were the one getting married and now she's beaten you to it. It would look mean and petty.'

Keeley threw herself down on the bed and began to struggle with the stiff new pair of high heels she'd had to get for 'this gig', as she called it.

'Do you really think so? You don't think I'd be a bad friend to encourage something I'm against, and a worse one if I didn't tell her all the reasons why?'

'I – I'm not sure. I think the Irish are different from the French, maybe, in their friendships. More honest, less polite. Here in France—'

'In France what?'

Biting his lip, he looked uncomfortable. 'In France people simply say congratulations when you get engaged, regardless of what they think.'

She eyed him for a moment, before the penny dropped. 'You mean everyone has congratulated you, even though they think you're making a mistake?'

'I – I – yes, well, you may as well know the truth, Keeley, since you're so keen on it. I don't mean my family. They really do like you. It's only – some people – nobody close—'

She was hurt. Deeply hurt, as if she had been stabbed. If she was as honest with herself as she wanted to be with Mary, she knew that many of Vincent's friends and colleagues must indeed be wondering what he was doing with her. She neither looked nor sounded like proper 'wife material.' But she was trying her best, working like a demon at everything she felt was expected of her, and she thought she'd been succeeding, enough that Vincent would never be ashamed of her, or feel let down in any way. The thought of letting him down was even worse than the thought that he would ever let *her* down, be influenced by his friends' opinions or actually give in to them, call his marriage off.

Yet she expected Mary to act differently? Call her marriage off because friend Keeley didn't like friend Cathal? For some seconds she sat immobile, her shoe in her hand, thinking.

'Keeley?'

'Mm?'

'Are you all right? I'm sorry if I upset you, I didn't mean to, I just thought maybe it's better if you . . . you know the truth. You can't win the battle if you don't even know you're fighting it.'

'The battle . . . and there was me, thinking it was an art exhibition.'

'Yes. There will be some people there who – well, you might feel under the microscope a bit. But don't worry. I'll help you, and look after you.'

She knew he would. As she was helping him, or trying to, by going to this damn gig, in an outfit that made her feel like her granny, in shoes that would lift her high enough to see the paintings she knew nothing about, in a stupid fluster of nerves in case she made a hash of the whole thing. She wasn't just Vincent's fiancée, she was his partner, they were a team and they would work at it together . . . but she was scared, throbbing with hurt as the truth sank in. Most people, tonight, would probably think she was a mistake, think that Vincent Tourand should know better – just as she thought Cathal Sullivan was a mistake, and that Mary should know better. She turned the situation round in her mind before speaking again.

'Vincent . . . are you sure about me? Really sure?'

He came and sat beside her, put his arm around her and pulled her to him.

It was torture. Keeley's face ached with smiling, her feet begged for mercy, her hand was mangled from shaking others, her brain sagged with the huge effort of remembering all the names, saying appropriate things, getting her verbs straight. To her horror Vincent was wrested from her side, pinned in conversation with some older man, and she was left to sink or swim alone. Drawing on every resource she possessed, she pushed Mary's letter to the back of her mind, and concentrated with ferocious determination. After half a glass of wine she realised it was going to her head, because she hadn't eaten, but she couldn't eat, because the tiny snacks were so fiddly she was afraid of dropping them, that one might break in her hand. If she got rid of her wine, tried to put the glass down quietly somewhere, would someone notice, take offence that she was rejecting their hospitality? Had anyone heard her tummy rumbling? Oh, God. This was a nightmare.

Several times she caught Vincent's eye, and he shot her anxious looks of support, but could not shake off the persistent man who, she realised, must be someone important. Meanwhile people kept accosting her, asking what she thought of the pictures, murmuring that she must be Mademoiselle . . . ?

'Butler,' she smiled again and again, thanking her stars that she had finally selected the black dress she'd worn the first time she went to dinner at Vincent's house. Many of the women were wearing black, and she made a mental note not to consider blouses or skirts for this kind of 'soirée' again. Little black dresses, that was the key to this particular situation. And gradually she realised there was a key to the picture situation, too.

'The light,' she heard people repeating enthusiastically, regardless of which picture they were looking at, 'isn't the light just marvellous?'

So she started to say it too, and by jiminy it worked. Not only was it the right thing, apparently, but it put them in the position of having to respond, be the ones to do all the talking. Half the time she didn't understand their replies, but there was a solution to that, too; you simply nodded and murmured 'yes, absolutely.' Very gradually, she began to relax a fraction, was even tempted to giggle as she realised it was possible to spend an entire evening talking about nothing whatsoever; the more you went round in circles the more they were impressed. Enough to nod at you, at any rate, and remark on your charming accent, how good your French was for a foreigner.

But she was very thankful when Vincent finally returned to her side, even though the persistent man was pitching up alongside him.

'Keeley, I'd like you to meet my boss, Alain Jou. M Jou, this is my fiancée Keeley Butler.'

Alain was short and dapper, about thirty-five, balding and thin-lipped. He surveyed her a moment before extending his hand.

'Ah yes, the young Irish lady. Enchanté, mademoiselle.'

Rigid with resolve, she dropped her eyelashes and her voice, did not shake his hand but merely placed hers in it, limply and briefly as the other women did when introduced.

'Enchantée, monsieur.'

'Are you a fan of Cézanne?'

Oh, Jesus.

'I – am. I particularly like his painting of the café – and isn't it wonderful, the café can still be seen in Aix today.'

Lars, she thought with dizzy gratitude; Lars wrecked Mary's life, but he's just saved mine.

Alain gazed at her as if she'd said she entirely endorsed Einstein's theory of relativity.

'Ah yes. An early work, of course. But hardly to be compared with the *Mont*?'

She felt as if she was clinging to a cliff edge with her fingernails. The *Mont*, the *Mont*, what *Mont* – not the one Sylvie had cycled up?

But it was near, Cézanne had lived here . . . go for it, Keeley. Go for broke.

'Oh, no, what could compare with such a beautiful mountain? Especially at this time of year, the light . . .'

She'd done it. She saw immediately she had, not just by Alain's startled gaze but by Vincent's face, a study of dazzled astonishment, so thrilled and terrified she had to wrench her eyes away. But he needn't worry. Sylvie had told her lots about the Mont Sainte Victoire.

Alain turned to Vincent. 'Well, Vincent, it seems you are engaged to quite an art lover! Please allow me to show her some more of the paintings.'

Firmly, he took her arm, leaving Vincent behind as he steered her to the far wall, the one covered in pictures of – yes! – the Mont. Indicating the first of them with his arm, he looked at it reverently.

'Paul loved it. He painted it in every possible light, in every season.'

Paul. She filed the name away as he talked, warming to a subject that clearly interested him a lot.

'The autumn studies are my own favourites . . . so warm, don't you think?'

Yes. That was all she had to say, just agree with him.

'Of course, these works don't quite capture . . . but we must try, to produce another Cézanne in Aix. There is so much talent, worthy of our sponsorship . . .'

Double quick, she copped on, peering to look at the signatures she hadn't noticed before. These weren't real Cézannes, they were copies by local people.

'And if it were your choice, Mademoiselle, to whom would you award the scholarship?'

Ah. The department store was sponsoring a scholarship. Now she had it – it was like the Texaco kiddies' painting competition at home! The winner got money and the sponsor got free advertising in the newspapers. Every school in Ireland entered the Texaco contest, even her own – God, Vincent might have clued her in a bit about this. In future she'd make him tell her all the facts, the background, before they went anywhere like this.

Quickly, she scanned the wall, wondering which was the right one, the one Alain wanted her to pick. The dozens of Monts were just a blur to her, varying only in colour – and that was why she stopped, suddenly, at a painting that wasn't of the Mont at all. It looked much lighter and paler than the others. Different.

'This one.'

He turned to regard her with some surprise.

'But this is not an oil. It is a watercolour – unfinished, like Paul's original. Why do you choose it?'

She hardly knew why, except that it stood out. What could she say, what clues could she use?

'I like it because, as you say, it is unfinished. It makes me want to finish it.'

He smiled, apparently satisfied. 'Ah, yes. It invites, it draws the viewer in. As does the house itself. Women always want to see inside other people's houses.'

Only as he said it did she realise that the shape was a house, behind some trees. Now the lines and blobs made sense, she could see that . . . that it *was* inviting, as he said, drawing her in. It was a lovely house. All by itself, protected by those trees . . . she would love to be able to see inside it, as she always wanted to see inside the gorgeous houses they passed on their Sunday drives. Who lived in them, in this one?

'Mademoiselle?'

Guiltily she jumped, realising she'd forgotten him, let herself get distracted for a moment.

'I'm sorry, I was just thinking . . .'

'Indeed. I see you really are quite a fan of Cézanne. Have you seen the original?'

She felt she'd better be honest, not push the bluff too far.

'No. I haven't.'

'Then Vincent must take you. Sadly it looks quite different now, but it is still inhabited.'

Oh – the original house, he meant, not the original painting? It was still standing? In Aix, or near Aix? Amazing. She'd love to see it, find out if it was still so – so peaceful, so pretty.

As he led her away, back to Vincent, she was still thinking about it. Why, she couldn't say. But apparently she wasn't required to talk any more. She had passed the test.

'Sadly, the house on the hill is not the winner the committee has chosen. But it is all a question of taste, of course. You seem to have quite original taste, Mademoiselle Butler.'

Suddenly she felt exhausted, too drained to even laugh at the stunt she had somehow pulled. But she had pulled it, and glowed with satisfaction as Alain delivered her back to Vincent.

'Quite charming, Vincent, your young lady is quite charming. We have had a most interesting conversation. I do hope we will meet again soon, mademoiselle.'

With a little bow he left them, and Vincent seized her hand.

'Keeley, you're magic! A genius! How did you do it?'

'I don't know, Vincent. All I know is that you're taking me for a double king-size cheeseburger, with chips and a chocolate milkshake, the moment we get out of here we are hitting Quick like a ton of bricks.'

'Chips! Quick! I will take you to the Vieux Moulin, for this, give you caviar and champagne.'

'No way. I've done my caviar bit. I need comfort food, before I collapse.'

'Dear Mary,

Thank Christ it's Sunday at last and I can grab a few minutes to myself. Vincent and I went to an art exhibition on Friday night, and I'm knackered. It was full of people he works with, boss and all, and I felt like I was doing some sort of exam. As you know, I never passed an exam in my life. But I passed this one. Vincent was thrilled – the only reason we had to go to the bloody thing in the first place was that his company was giving the prizes. I was petrified I'd make a bags of it, but I got lucky, it went great – and guess what, I actually saw a picture I liked! Of a house. Don't ask me why I liked it, it was only a few lines and blobs, not even finished, a copy of one by that guy Lars talked about, remember, Cézanne? Anyway it was a dreamy house, it must be bliss to live somewhere like that. But that's all I'm going to say about me (apart from that the flat is still great, Sylvie's mother gave us a pair of old curtains so the yellow sheet is gone) because I want to talk about you.

I can't believe it. I just can't believe you're getting married. To Cathal, and going to run his kitchen for him! Well, for both of you I suppose, since you'll be Mr and Mrs Sullivan now. You must be so excited! I'm really glad he's changed, you say, and is being good to you. What church are you getting married in, where are you going for your honeymoon? I bet he can afford to take you somewhere lovely and hot and sunny, now he's going to be a manager you'll have lots of money. And a flat to live in, over the pub – that sounds great, you can nip up to see the baby every time it burps!

I'm raging I can't get over for the wedding. But Vincent and I will definitely make the christening, he sends his congratulations and buckets of best wishes. Mary, I'm so much in love with him . . . even if you don't feel quite the same about Cathal yet I'm sure you will soon, it's going to be wonderful, and just wait till you hit the sack with him! I finally have, with Vincent, it's like we both died and went to heaven, you won't believe it when you do it with Cathal – after the baby is born naturally, it must be a bit in the way at the moment. How are you feeling? I hope you're taking care of yourself and letting your mother organise the wedding – Cathal's, too. What's she like?

I'm going to go round to the Vieux Moulin to tell Luc about your pub food, he'll be thrilled, especially the bit about the other pub that you might be going to turn into a real restaurant. You'll have to learn to drive Cathal's famous red Fiat, so you can get to it – Vincent is teaching me to drive, I tell you these French are bloody lunatics on the road, on the wrong side as well! But it's a blast, it makes you feel sort of, you know, independent.

I hope you get to finish the cookery books before the baby is born. What are you going to cook, apart from the curry and lasagne? Will you have a written menu, and send me a copy? I think you should do your famous quiche, Vincent still talks about it, and your chicken stew with the wine in it and those

*salads with all sorts in them – can you get the stuff over there?
Let me know if you have any problems, I'll ask Luc for his
advice. I just wish Vincent and I could be there on your first
day, to be your first customers and tell everyone how great
the new food is at The Lantern. It'll be brilliant experience
for you, before you tackle Fursey's – that's a fun name for a
restaurant, are you going to keep it?*

*Anyway, whatever you do, I wish you masses of luck with
it. I can't wait for the christening so we can see each other and
talk about everything, a letter isn't the same. I saw beautiful
sugared almonds in a bakery the other day, Vincent says the
French bring them to christenings, there are silver ones mixed
in as well and I'm going to bring a whole sack over to you
– pink for a girl, blue for a boy.*

*Will you have time to write again, before the wedding? It's
so soon, I nearly fainted! Please try. I want to hear all about
everything, and most of all about you and the baby. As I
won't be having any for years yet, it'll be like a game, being
a godmother! But I'll make a proper job of it, I promise.*

*Oh, Mary. I wish I could be there with you. I really do.
This is such a big busy year for you, so much is happening
all at once, you must hardly know whether you're coming
or going. At least you have your parents to help – and what
about your brothers, are they going to be pageboys? I feel
awful I can't be bridesmaid, but at least you're going to be
mine. Vincent and I have a little surprise for you, when you
come over in December – Cathal will be coming with you
now of course, I'd better add him to the guest list! Only thirty
guests – how many are you having?*

*So, the next time we meet you'll be a married lady, and
a mum. Tell Cathal he's a very lucky man. Meanwhile, I'm
thinking of you every day, wishing everything that's good for
you and the baby. Do try to write once more before it comes
and you get too busy to bother with your old friend in France!*

Millions of hugs and kisses,

Keeley.'

Well, Mary conceded, it was a long letter. For Keeley, the
postcard queen, it was a real blockbuster job. And it did
sound enthusiastic, about everything. Quite enthusiastic. Only
– only what?

Congratulations, that was what. The word 'congratulations'
was nowhere in it. And neither was the very first sentence she'd

expected to see: 'Are you mad, Mary, are you off your trolley?' That was more Keeley's style, and knowing Keeley's opinion of Cathal she had been braced for it, ready for an argument, a good old slanging match. But this – you couldn't argue with this, it was full of good wishes and best-of-lucks and – and something that just didn't add up.

What was it? Why didn't it add up? Why wasn't Keeley ranting and raving and saying don't do it, you'll regret it, you halfwit? Easing herself down onto the sofa with a cup of tea, she began to read it again, slowly and attentively.

But no. Even second time round, there still wasn't a hint of criticism, or scepticism, or anything negative. Either Keeley was being too polite to say anything, or she approved, had no objections.

It must be the latter, that she unexpectedly but simply approved, had seen the point about marrying Cathal, because Keeley could no more be polite than she could be Princess Anne. If she had any objections, she'd spit them right out. Besides, there was no reason for her to zip her lip. They were friends, best friends, who could argue the toss without taking it personally. Keeley must know that she, Mary, would want to hear her honest thoughts on the matter, on something as important as getting married.

Not that she would change her mind, because it was made up about Cathal. It was just that a few cheeps out of Keeley would have given her something to get a grip on. If she'd had to convince Keeley she was doing the right thing she'd have been able to convince herself – what? What did she mean by that? Of course she was convinced. Otherwise she wouldn't be doing it. Cathal Sullivan was a good, hard-working, respectable man and their marriage was going to be a great success; love would soon put stars in her eyes the same as it was putting them in Keeley's, and meanwhile everything else was perfect. Absolutely perfect, unless you counted Cathal's parents Donal and Carmel, which she didn't. If they didn't thaw, that was their problem. Meanwhile she was growing fonder of their son every day, couldn't wait to marry him and have the baby and set up the kitchen, set up home.

A home, of her own. That was what she needed. And that was what she wanted. Keeley simply understood, that was all. That was why she was raising no objections. She could see that marriage to Cathal was the best thing, for her and for the baby, for everyone, just as her parents said it was, with no doubt at all.

Putting down the letter, she sat staring into the fire for a few moments. And then she got up, raced into the kitchen and began ransacking the cupboards, tearing things out of them. Flour. Sugar. Butter. At the top of her lungs she shouted for the boys, took the pound notes that Leesha left her every day for emergencies, and sent them out for eggs and dried fruit. For what, they asked; what are you doing, Mary?

I'm making my wedding cake, she told them. I'm going to make my own wedding cake, and it's going to be sensational, just wait till you taste it! Enthused, they ran off to the shops, and she stood shaking, measuring her ingredients with trembling hands, until they returned.

'Tell me again, Vincent. Tell me I did the right thing.'

Vincent sighed. He'd told her twenty times already, but convincing Keeley was proving a very uphill task. Patiently, he repeated exactly what he had said before.

'Keeley, you did. You encouraged Mary and supported her, as she asked you to do. You wished her well, you asked for all the details, said everything a friend should say.'

'Yeah. Everything except—'

'Can you imagine how she'd feel if you'd said anything else? If you'd said no, don't marry him, stay at home with your parents, with no work and no money, nothing to look forward to except bringing up a fatherless child alone? Give up the chance of running a restaurant, the thing you want to do more than anything? Sit on your backside and mope, wondering how it might have turned out, if only you'd taken the chance? She wouldn't have thanked you for that, Keeley.'

'Maybe not now. But maybe—'

'Maybe some day? Keeley, it is only a maybe. You don't know for sure. In fact you have no idea how their marriage is going to turn out. And if you threw cold water on it you'd probably never find out, because Mary might never write to you again, if she thought you disapproved, weren't being encouraging. She's in a sticky situation and she needs all the help she can get. I bet your letter cheered her up and made her feel much better.'

'I hope it did. I really hope so, Vincent.'

Vincent was a patient man, and he loved Keeley dearly. But they couldn't go on having this conversation every single day.

'Well, let's assume it did, until you hear to the contrary. Tell you what, let's go out somewhere, get a breath of air. Borrow Sylvie's bike and we'll go for a spin.'

'Where?'

'Where would be fun? I know . . . how about that house you saw in the painting? I asked Alain, he said it's only about fifteen kilometres, out on the road to Puyloubier.'

'Oh. OK. But he said it's changed a lot. D'you think we'll know it when we see it?'

'We'll ask around, if we don't. Come on, let's go!'

Keeley had no memory of ever having had a bicycle, as a child, but she remembered having learned to ride Tony's, remembered a hand on her back steering her as she wobbled along some path near her house . . . whose hand? Hardly Tony's, or Christy's . . . it must have been her mother's. Gertie, trying to do something, trying to make some small brief effort, in the early days before it had all got to be too much. But that effort had paid dividends; the very first time she got up on Sylvie's bike the memory had come flooding back, and as she wobbled down the street she had known it was only a matter of regaining her balance, that she'd soon be whizzing along. Now she went cycling with Vincent as often as Sylvie would lend her the bike, and wished she could afford one of her own.

The bike was in the hall, along with Vincent's, and as they set off she felt her spirits rising immediately, felt the same surge of anticipation she felt when learning to drive Vincent's car, a feeling of going somewhere, getting somewhere. She'd mastered the mechanics of driving, and applied for the test which was notoriously tough in France, but again money was a problem; even if she passed, she couldn't afford insurance.

Damn, she thought as they pedalled out onto the D17, I wish I had a bit of money. Just a bit. I suppose I should be glad I have enough to eat and pay the rent – I *am* glad – but it would be great to be able to buy a bike and get driving insurance. It's out of the question this year, because of going to Ireland and getting married, then next year I suppose we'll be furnishing a flat, but some day I'll do it. There's no point in doing a driving test if I can't bloody drive.

The wind was against them, and after the first five kilometres the road began to wind upwards, but they pedalled on, enjoying the sun and scenery, the pearly spring air that felt so pure and fresh in their lungs; it was a Sunday morning, with little traffic about. But there was no time to stop or linger, look at things, because Sylvie said she wanted her bike back by two o'clock.

Eventually they reached a fork in the road, just before Puyloubier, and pulled in. Left or right? There was nobody around to ask, so they tossed a coin. Left.

The road narrowed and rose more steeply, but that was a good sign, because Alain had said the house was on a hill. The backs of Keeley's legs began to ache as they pushed higher, and she was thankful that it was a racing bike, light, with gears. Even at that, sweat was starting to trickle down her face and neck, and the leather saddle felt like a brick. Were French kilometres like Irish miles, she wondered, when people said fifteen did they mean twenty, or twenty-five, or what?

'There! There it is!' Vincent was pointing and shouting, and sure enough she could see a building of some kind, quite possibly a house, up ahead. But even before they got close enough to see any kind of detail between the trees she knew it wasn't it, wasn't the right one; it had two storeys, but the house in the painting had only had one.

'No. That's not it.'

Disappointed, Vincent got off his bike and flung it up against a tree trunk. 'You're sure?'

'Yes.'

'All right then. I'll knock at this one, and ask.'

A big black dog came bounding out, barking and snapping at his ankles, as he opened the gate; she was surprised to see him aim his foot at it and shout something, something that subdued it. Then there was something of a flurry, the door opened suddenly and an elderly man came out, looking rather aggressive. But when Vincent spoke to him, he lifted his stick and shook it, twice, in the opposite direction to where they were facing. Thanking him, Vincent trudged rather glumly out.

'We went wrong at the fork. Should have continued on right, towards Puyloubier.'

So they freewheeled back down, and Keeley almost came off her bike as they rounded the corner at sharp speed and immediately shot down another hill. 'No, Vincent! It's on a hill, we should be going up, not down!' But even as she said it he pulled off to the left, onto what seemed to be a forest track, beckoning to her to follow him.

And there it was. Even though it had been little more than a sketch in the picture, she knew it instantly, recognised the shape and the angle; they were coming at it from exactly where Cézanne must have painted it, facing the side and back, with the trees on the left. A huge cypress, much taller than in the picture, and a smaller one beside, but still higher than the roof. Of course, they had grown, in the eighty years since Cézanne saw them. Grown huge.

'Oh, my God.'

Getting off her bike, she dropped it on the needle-strewn earth and walked a few paces, as close as she dared. There might be another dog, or owners who didn't welcome trespassers. But Vincent dismounted too, and came up to her, took her hand with a satisfied smile.

'This is it? The right one? The man said—'

'Yes. This is it. I can't believe it really is here. It looks so – so exactly the same!'

'But it can't. Look at the roof, those tiles can't have gone on more than ten years ago. And the brick has been repointed, there are sliding glass doors, they didn't have those in Cézanne's time!'

Looking closely, Keeley saw several twentieth-century innovations, things that had been repaired or introduced. But it didn't matter. This was the same house, and she felt the same sense of – of something she couldn't identify.

'It's gorgeous. Isn't it just gorgeous?'

It wasn't a palatial house, by any means, not half as beautiful as some they had seen on the roads to Marseille or Aubagne; but she was entranced. To see the very house that someone had painted years and years ago, someone long dead . . . it was like seeing a house in a fairytale come alive. She could hardly believe her eyes.

Vincent was looking slightly baffled. 'Well, it's very nice, but I don't see—'

'Is there anyone at home, d'you think?'

He squinted through the greenery. 'Doesn't look like it. Just as well. They're probably fed up with people coming to gawp.'

But there was a stillness, a sense of quiet that made Keeley think that not many people did. Alain had said the painting was only an early, unfinished one, not very popular or well known.

'Come on. Let's take a closer look.'

Shushing his protests, she went on ahead of him, crouching under the trees, wary in case a dog should come flying out of nowhere. But none did, and eventually she reached the garden that had been carved out of the forest, neat and trim with colourful spring flowers, clearly new and nurtured. What must it be like to have such a garden, to live in a house with—

Instinctively, she whirled round. And there behind, below her, was exactly what she knew she was going to see: a panorama of the whole valley, filled with silver and pink and palest green, a view like nothing she had ever seen in her life before. For a time that felt like infinity, she stood looking at it.

'Oh, Vincent. It must be like living in paradise, living here.'

The view, when he turned to look with her, was certainly stunning.

And there was something about the house . . . not any particular feature, just an atmosphere, some kind of aura that had something to do, he supposed, with history, with the fact of Cézanne having chosen it, seen something in it worth immortalising.

'Well – yes, it is nice. But don't start getting any notions, Keeley, please! Much as I love you, and hard as I will work to give you whatever you want, we are never going to have a house like this! This is the kind of house people either inherit, or need a lot of money to buy – not millions, but more than we're ever likely to have.'

He looked sidelong at her, slightly anxiously, feeling that she had led him somewhere he didn't belong. Feeling uneasy, too, that they were in somebody's private garden, and might be caught at any moment. But her smile was almost nonchalant.

'It's not all that ritzy. It doesn't have a swimming pool or tennis court, like some of the big ones down near the coast.'

'No, but it's – it's way out of our league.'

Instead of answering she turned away from him, away from the view and back to the house. For a second she stood staring at it, and then, without a word, she sprinted across the grass. His heart pounded as he ran after her, waited for a door to be flung open and a furious proprietor to emerge. There was no car in the drive, no sign of life, but that didn't mean there was nobody at home.

'Keeley—!'

Ignoring him, she reached the gable wall, grasped a windowsill with her fingers and raised herself up on tiptoe, pressing her nose almost to the glass as she peered in.

'Look! You can see right in, it's got tiled floors, those old tiles

like in the Vieux Moulin, and whatchamacallits in the ceiling –
beams – there are lots of metal things hanging from them.'

'Copper' he said, peering over her shoulder in spite of himself.
'It's quite common in Provence, everyone hangs copper from
their beams.'

She laughed. 'Then tell Sylvie we want a copper something
for our wedding present!'

Vincent thought this had gone far enough. Firmly, he turned
round and headed for his bike.

'Come on, Keeley. Let's get out of here before we get into
trouble.'

Reluctant, but still grinning, she let go of the thick windowsill.
'OK. In a sec.'

With the speed of a sprite she darted round to the front of the
house, out of his sight, leaving him muttering as he guessed what
she was doing – snooping, peering in the front windows. When
she came back, she was grinning with triumphant satisfaction.

'I just wanted to see.'

'Well, now you have. Let's get going.'

Demurely she mounted her bike and followed him away. But
her mind stayed behind, exploring the house, touching the walls
and the furniture, tasting the fruit she had seen in a basket,
listening to the trees creak in a winter gale, building up a fire
in the wide open fireplace; even now, in spring, there was a
pile of logs for the purpose. As she sped down the hill, her
imagination fanned the flames into a merry blaze.

Let me get married, Mary thought. Let me just get married, and
get it over with, because I can't stand much more of this.

But the fuss continued, growing like her baby by the day. First
Leesha and Kevin, twittering like sparrows in spring, chirping
with joy; then Granny Jameson, aunts and cousins and people
she'd forgotten existed, neighbours, former friends from The
Lantern, even Mr O'Rourke from the deli; the house seemed
to be permanently filled with chattering people, cards, parcels,
fabric and flowers.

She didn't want a fuss, and Cathal said neither did he. But
the rapidly approaching event had gathered its own momentum,
seemed to be sweeping her up like a huge terrifying ocean wave,
carrying her high in the air before flinging her down, dazed, on
a shore she could not yet see. The only consolation was that
she knew there must be a shore, eventually, that the noise and

activity could not go on like this for ever. If the phone rang just once more, she thought she would lose her mind.

But it rang, and rang and rang. Auntie Rita, to say she was giving her a duvet set, and what colour would she like? It was as well to ask, 'better than getting the wrong one'; then the hotel, wondering about the place cards, then the florist, something about tulips being prone to droop, would she not consider—? Then the singer from the band, did she want Elvis or Beatles? Then Mrs Quinn who was making the dress, what about some nice beading on the wrists, it would make all the—

'Difference' said Leesha. 'It's the little details make all the difference, you know.'

'What difference, to a bride nearly eight months pregnant, getting married in a tent?'

Leesha's face fell, and then Mary felt guilty, as well as everything else – flustered, nervous, muddled and exhausted. Only Cathal kept her going, kept her sane.

'Don't worry' he said one night as they walked on Sandymount Strand, watching the mail boat chug out to Holyhead. 'It'll all be over soon, and we'll have lots of peace and quiet on our honeymoon.'

Well, yes. At least there was that to look forward to. Considerately he had said that flying to some hot noisy tourist resort would be too much for her, in her condition, and what did she think of just driving down to Courtown, which in May would be nice and warm, but not too crowded or hectic? It wasn't much more than an hour away, although of course they could go further if she felt up to it, to Lahinch or even up to Bundoran – no, she said, Courtown would be lovely. She'd never been there, but it was a popular place in summertime, her parents had fond memories of it. So he had booked them into a hotel, she hadn't had to lift a finger, the honeymoon was the one part of the whole thing she didn't have to think or worry about.

And the cake was a success. Despite the fevered rush in which she had suddenly baked it, it had turned out spectacularly well, everyone who was let see it commented on the unusual icing, the trail of greenery and flowers winding its way from one tier up to the next, little buds strewn here and there along the way. Leesha thought it was a bit odd, had wondered whether a few red roses, in marzipan, mightn't brighten it up? And where was the traditional silver horseshoe, for luck, on top?

'Gone' she replied, 'old Dobbin finally popped his clogs. This is 1978, Mam. I want something a bit different.'

Well, Leesha conceded dubiously, it was different, all right. But a great achievement, for somebody who'd never made a wedding cake before in her life. In fact Fiona Taylor was wondering—

'Oh, no. I'm going to run a restaurant, not a bakery.'

Delighted as she was to discover how well she could bake, and ice a cake too, it was not what she wanted to do professionally. Not a patch on the delicacy of fish, the airiness of an omelette, the earthy crunch of a leaf salad brimming with all sorts of surprises – anchovies, radishes, cashew nuts, Gorgonzola?

Now there was a challenge, and endless fun. Whereas wedding cakes – God, the tensions of weddings, the expectations, the stress, the grannies' recipes, handed down for generations – she'd go bonkers if she got caught up in it all, ever again. No wonder marriage was for life. Nobody could possibly go through it twice.

If only Keeley was here. If only. Keeley would laugh and make her laugh, say it was all a lot of cobbler's and why didn't she just run off with Cathal to Gretna Green or somewhere, get married on the quiet with nobody getting hysterical about tulips or duvets or beads? Several times she sat down to write to Keeley, explain to her how friends and family took over in Ireland, the whole thing turned into a nightmare . . . not that getting married was a nightmare, not at all, only the excitement that went with it. But every time she started a letter somebody interrupted her, one query after another, until finally she managed only a brief page about how she wished Keeley could come, but they would make up for it in August, when the baby was christened. Meanwhile Marian Hayes was going to be her bridesmaid, did Keeley remember her, from The Lantern? Marian was to wear salmon pink, to set off her dark hair and make up for the dress being empire line, which of course was the only option open to the bride, at nearly eight months.

Eight months. Sometimes she put her hand to her stomach, reassuring herself that the baby was still there, that it hadn't disappeared amidst all the fuss and confusion. But no, it was kicking, very much there, the only one safe from the phone calls and questions and list of things to be done. Of course Leesha was a great help, even Kevin was doing his best – but as for Cathal's parents, all she could say was that she had tried.

Tried several times, in vain. Once or twice Donal, the father, had looked at her with a flicker of interest, when she talked about her plans for the food at The Lantern, but as for Carmel, the mother – Carmel had swallowed the news of her son's engagement as she might have swallowed rat poison, gazing with such naked horror at Mary's stomach that it was all she could do to keep a civil tongue in her head. But for Cathal's sake, she did. The last thing she wanted was to start married life with an out-and-out row, with any grounds for recrimination. It wasn't Cathal's fault, he wasn't responsible for his bitch of a mother. Anyway, Donal and Carmel lived in the flat over Fursey's, forty miles away in the midlands, for now she wouldn't have to worry about them very much. Cathal also had two younger brothers, one of whom was to be his best man, and a sister, but they were all right, quite excited about the first wedding in the family, and about Cathal's rakish secret. A love child, no less! Between the two of them they had told the tale so often that they had almost come to believe it themselves, that the baby actually was Cathal's. But it wasn't too awful a lie – after all, Cathal would be its father now, in every real sense. That was a very comforting thought.

In fact the whole scenario was very comforting, when Mary thought about it calmly, late at night in bed. Once the wedding circus was over, they would have two restful weeks in Courtown, and then the baby would be born a few weeks later, and she would have the whole summer to get to know it while working out menus for The Lantern. A breather, Cathal said, before she started work – in fact it would even be all right with him if they didn't, well . . . if she wanted to wait until after the birth, to consummate the marriage. He would understand, in the circumstances, she wasn't to worry about it. That was another very comforting thought.

See, Keeley. He isn't so bad, at all. I told you he'd changed, and he has. He's being really good and nice and considerate. Working like blazes, as usual, but still finding time to take an interest in the wedding, give a hand and not leave me to do everything. He worked out the seating plan for the hotel and he booked the hotel for the honeymoon, organised all the church stuff and went out to buy his suit himself, didn't even drag me into town with him because he knows I can't stand crowded places at the moment. And he isn't having a stag night, which I'm delighted about because I don't want him turning up drunk in the church the way some bride-grooms do.

He's done lots of things. He went to the jeweller's shop while he was in town getting his suit, and got our wedding rings so I wouldn't have to worry about that either. He went to a furniture shop too, and ordered all the basic stuff to be delivered to our flat, so I don't have to go shopping – he even ordered a pram and a playpen! It's bliss not to have to do all those things when you're at the stage I'm at; as far as the baby's concerned all I need to think about is nappies and snuggle suits. And the birth! I pray everything will be all right, but the doctor says I'm fine, everything should be normal.

So things could be a lot worse, Keeley. But they're not. In fact the best thing about this wedding is Cathal, he's being so good, you never know, I could end up with stars in my eyes yet, just like you and Vincent.

Only one more letter came from Keeley before the wedding, shorter than the last but still bubbling with life, as if Keeley were cramming in everything she had missed before. She was thrilled to hear that Cathal was turning out so well, she said, it just went to show that you should never judge a sausage by its skin; she'd been talking to Vincent and he had said everyone deserved to be given a chance, and wasn't it a good thing Mary was giving Cathal one, who knew what might have happened otherwise. The wedding cake sounded fabulous and Mary was to send a photo of it, send piles of photos of everything, have a wonderful wedding and not worry about a thing.

As for herself, she hadn't even started to plan her own wedding, but Sylvie and Francine were starting to do it for her – however it would only be a small affair, as she didn't have any really close friends in France, certainly none like Mary. Besides Vincent's parents were going to pay for practically everything, so they didn't want to push them too far. Soon, however, they were going to start looking round for somewhere to live – in fact she wished she could live properly with Vincent now that they were sleeping together, but since that wasn't what she'd wanted in the beginning, she just had to put up with the consequences. Anyway, Sylvie was very nice, and did her best to make herself scarce so they could have time alone – time they made the most of, sometimes they were in bed almost before Sylvie closed the hall door behind her, and was it dynamite or what! Mary laughed as she read all about Vincent's skin like honey, eyes like emeralds, body like 'that Spitz swimmer guy who won all the Olympic medals.' If Vincent had any fault whatsoever, it was only that he could take things a bit seriously now and then, but she supposed somebody had to, and it wasn't likely to be her.

Right now he was worrying a bit about his job, how long it would take to get promoted and make any sort of decent money, but probably that was just because they were getting married, he was starting to think about furniture and bills and stuff. He looked so cute when he was worrying about all this, she said, but she always laughed and told him she'd still love him even if they had to live in a cardboard box, and then he laughed at himself. Of course there were lots of things they could do if they were earning more – she'd love a bike and to get driving insurance – but no matter how tight their budget was things were still one hundred per cent better than at Pearse Gardens, and Vincent didn't tackle the problem by drowning himself in drink. He couldn't even understand about Cathal not having a stag night, she'd had to explain to him what that was and he said it sounded revolting. But she was glad for Mary that Cathal wasn't having one.

Once again the letter ended in oodles of hugs and kisses, and Mary tucked it into the box of things she was taking with her to The Lantern, where her new life would start but the old one, she hoped, would never be forgotten.

And then it was Saturday, May 12 1978, and Mary was getting married. Really getting married, she thought with wonder as she woke up, pledging to share her life and her child with Cathal Sullivan. For one single second she felt absolute terror flash through her like lightning; and then she smiled. Every bride in the world must feel it – did feel it, Leesha assured her – but only for that first overwhelming moment.

Sitting up, she realised that the house was already buzzing like a beehive, everyone else was awake and starting preparations, she could hear Dad's electric razor, the bath running upstairs and the kettle whistling downstairs. Then, before she could move, the door opened and Sean came in, solemnly carrying a cup of tea – not a mug, but a china cup on a saucer – in both hands.

'Mam said I was to bring this up to you.'

He looked at her with a kind of wonder, as if sensing that today was a day that would change his sister, she would not be the old Mary ever again. She felt tears rise in her eyes as she took the tea and put it on her bedside table.

'Come here, little brother. Come give me a big hug.'

He climbed up on the bed and snuggled into her arms, allowing her to embrace him although he was reaching the age for shying away. For a moment they cuddled in silence, and then Steve came flying in too, hurling himself at her, all smiles and shouts.

'Getting married, Mary! Big party today!'

'Yes, a lovely big party, wait till you see all the flowers and food, you two are going to have a great time.'

'Yep, Dad says he'll give us 50p each if we're good. But we're always good, aren't we, Mary?'

'The best. The two best little boys I know. That's why I'm getting you a new uncle today.'

'Yeah! Uncle Cathal!'

'And a little nephew as well, in a few weeks, to play with.'

'We know. He's in your tummy.'

'That's right. But not for much longer.'

Fascinated, Steve gazed at the bump under the blankets. 'How's he going to get out, Mary?'

'Oh – well, that's a long complicated story, I'll tell you when you're older. But it might not be a he, you know. It might be a she.'

'No! We don't want a girl! We want a boy! Girls are stupid!'

'Is that so, now?'

'Yeah – well, except you, and Mam.'

'H'm. I think you might change your minds about that, in a few years. But whether it's a boy or a girl, I promise you it'll be lovely, and I'll bring it for you to play with—' All the time, she realised suddenly, because there was no garden at The Lantern. Funny, she hadn't thought about that before. But she could bring the baby over here, strapped into the back of Cathal's red Fiesta; wouldn't Mam enjoy that! Sunny family Sundays, out on the lawn, children running about and growing tall as the hollyhocks.

Kissing both boys on the tops of their heads, she picked them up and set them down. 'Right, time to get dressed. You're going to be in all the photographs so I want you to look beautiful.'

With something of a swagger, they ran off, and she drank her tea quickly, looking at the wedding dress hanging from the top of the wardrobe in its plastic sheath, snow white and majestic. She wasn't sure that white was appropriate, in the circumstances, but Leesha had insisted that of course it was, her daughter was going to look the part, be a beautiful bride and no mistake about it. Since Leesha and Kevin were footing the bill, she'd felt it would be churlish to argue.

Anyway, what matter, the main thing was that the dress draped her in a flattering way, didn't make her look nearly as elephantine as she felt. And she really did like her going-away outfit, a dress and jacket in raw raspberry silk with dark blue shoes, bag and wide hat. Even Carmel would have to admit it was elegant.

Getting up, she found the bathroom left sparkling and waiting for her, and then after her bath Leesha called her to come downstairs before she started dressing, there was something she and Kevin wanted to talk to her about. When she went down, she found them beaming in the kitchen, Leesha clutching a small box and Kevin urging her to give it to Mary 'now, before she's gone'. Mary opened it, and found a gold chain coiled inside.

'We – we thought you might like a nice necklace to wear with your dress.'

There were tears, then, as they all hugged and mumbled, Kevin looking unprecedentedly emotional. But then the phone started to ring, a neighbour knocked with a giftwrapped parcel, and Leesha regained command. 'We'll deal with all this. You go up and get dressed in peace.' Slowly, she went, determined not to get into a flap. Sitting at her dressing table, she hung the chain about her neck, and looked at her reflection. I look a bit pale, she thought, but in an hour I'll look beautiful. They'll all be proud of me, nobody will ever be able to say I let my family down in any way. Or myself.

Leesha came up at the end, to help with her hair, a simple matter of fixing the wreath in place as the hair had been cut, styled and glossed the day before. Mary had found herself thinking of Keeley as the hairdresser worked.

And then, almost by telepathy it seemed, the phone rang and Kevin called up the stairs. 'Mary! It's Keeley, from France!'

Abandoning Leesha, she ran down and seized the receiver. 'Keeley!'

'Hiya, Mary! I just wanted to wish the bride luck – how's everything going? Are you all right?'

'I'm fine, nearly ready to leave for the church – you should see me, Keel, all in white, I look like a cake!'

'I'm sure you look good enough to eat. Remember, I want photos – and I want you to be happy, Mary. That's what I really want . . . just for you to be happy. That's all that matters.'

She tried to answer. But she couldn't. No words would come, as she visualised Keeley standing in some coinbox, another world away, on some street in France.

'Mary? Are you there?'

'Y-yes, I'm here. And you're there. So far away. Oh, Keeley, I miss you like hell, I wish you were here.'

'I am there, in spirit. I'll be thinking about nothing else all day – you're to have a great day, Mary, promise me?'

'I promise. I—'

But the line beeped, and abruptly went dead. Half laughing, half crying, she imagined Keeley cursing and rummaging for more coins despite already having used them all up. But in August Keeley would be here for real, with Vincent, and the wedding present she said was too heavy to post, and a sackful of sugared almonds. Pink or blue, they'd know which by then.

As she stood by the phone, still holding the receiver, Kevin came up beside her, looking astonishingly handsome in his grey formal suit, and put his arm around her. 'Is my little girl all right, on her big day?'

Before she knew what was happening she was sobbing in his arms, shuddering, rivers of tears running into his white shirt.

'Nerves,' he said soothingly, and took out his handkerchief, held it up so she could blow her nose in it, as he used to do when she was a child.

The church ceremony seemed incredibly long, the rest of the day seemed bewilderingly brief, and afterwards Mary was horrified by how little of it all she could remember. A whisk of white fabric as she got into a long white car, a blur of multicoloured guests in the church pews, first sight of Cathal kneeling at the altar, waiting for her. Music . . . a gold cross on the priest's robes, a maroon leather bible with another gold cross on it; for some reason that bible fixed itself more clearly in her mind than almost anything else, years and years later she could still see its gold-leafed pages, hear the priest's voice as he read aloud from the New Testament, a passage from St Paul and then the gospel according to Matthew, the silken red page marker dangling all the while, hypnotic. More music, people filing up to receive communion, and then the register office behind the altar, singing names in a book. Only when they came out from there did Cathal solidify in the memories, taking her hand, turning to kiss her cheek as he led her down the aisle, out into a shower of confetti.

It was a sunny day, she remembered, but chilly for May, there was talk of hot toddies and eagerness to get to the hotel. Photographs must have been taken first, but she had no recollection of that, was amazed when she saw them later, her own face and Cathal's at the centre of them, so young, so much younger than she'd realised.

The rest was like a speeded-up film, waiters rushing about in fast-forward, Steve and Sean giggling and grinning, Leesha all glam in yellow and not a bit tearful, Donal's cool kiss, Carmel hatchet-faced. Her bridesmaid Marian caught the thrown bouquet, and indeed did marry herself a year later, but Mary had no memory of having thrown it or who caught it. Instead she remembered the food she couldn't eat, the traditional lukewarm turkey and ham everyone said was delicious, the whole menu she'd wanted to change, but been overruled by both Leesha and Cathal, who said weddings were no time to experiment. But the cake tasted magnificent, after they cut it together and the top tier was taken away for the christening amidst ribald laughter.

Then dancing, hectic dancing that made her dizzy, Cathal bringing a glass of water and patting at her by an open window. Tears, over a telegram from Luc and Félix, but everyone laughing because it was in French, defeating the best man's attempt to read it out. More music, a carousel of noise and colour, and then suddenly a raspberry-red suit, a car, a departure.

Only at this point did Mary's memories crystallise, lock into place with startling clarity. She could see every stripe in the grosgrain white ribbon as it blew on the front of the car, hear each tin can clanking along behind, all the way to Courtown, Cathal at the wheel with his trouser cuffs riding up over bright green socks with black spots on them.

She could see the receptionist's face, knowing and smug, as she checked them into the hotel, inviting Mary to sign for the first time: 'Mary Sullivan', written with a cheap, smooth, black hotel biro attached to a chain. She could see a porter, freighted with luggage, leading them down a dark corridor, unlocking a door, waiting to be tipped. Cathal, rummaging red-faced for small change, the porter gazing down disappointed into his palm, banging the door as he went away.

And she could see the bedroom, where her married life began. See the view, over roofs and outhouses to a distant ocean, the tide out, the beach dark and deserted. A stuck sash window that wouldn't open; a dark wardrobe that wouldn't stay shut, a low wide bed with a blue dralon headboard and matching candlewick bedspread. It creaked under her as she sat down on it, removed her hat and her earrings, eased off her shoes, looked up at Cathal and smiled.

He smiled back, and said she must be tired, she should rest now. He was tired himself, and a bit jittery if the truth be known, what he needed was a good stiff whiskey to steady him after all the excitement. He was just going to nip down to the bar to get one, and would have a cup of tea sent up to her on a tray.

No, she said, I'll come down with you, have it in the lounge, maybe we'll have a sandwich as well, we didn't eat much today.

No, no, he said, you stay here. Just relax and stay here, there's a good girl.

Chapter Seven

Three months later, on a warm windy day in August, Keeley unbuckled her seat belt and left the plane grinning from ear to ear.

'Wow! That was a blast.'

It was Vincent's first time to fly too, and he had to admit he'd enjoyed it as much as Keeley had. For the entire two hours she'd never stopped talking, although her face was turned away from him to the window, exclaiming over the speed and excitement of it all. Only two hours, compared to a whole day and night on the ferry! This, she said, was the life, imagine what it must be like to be one of those people who flew all the time, went on holiday to places like Barbados and Hawaii, led a right old high life.

However, their brief taste of the high life was quickly quenched as they waited for a bus at the airport and were eventually driven into a city which, on first sight, made Vincent wince. Keeley told him the name of those streets she knew – Dorset, Gardiner, Talbot – as the bus made its way through them, but all he could see was a collapsing muddle of dirty decrepit buildings, and so much litter that Dublin appeared to be one vast dustbin, packed solid with drink cans, food wrappers and filth of all descriptions. Excited by the experience of flying, and the prospect of seeing Mary, Keeley turned to him perkily.

'What do you think?'

He searched for words. After all, France wasn't squeaky clean either; Keeley often remarked on the disgusting loos in the cafés, and the way men spat in the streets; it was enough, she said, to put a dog right off its dinner. But the streets of Aix were wide and airy, lined with trees and beautiful buildings, plastic bags did not flap from wires or branches, the fountains were not used as trash cans. Vincent could only hope that he was seeing the worst of Dublin, that things would get better – cleaner, at any rate.

But hope dwindled as they got off the bus and carted their luggage to another bus stop some distance away, picking their way through chewing gum and burger boxes, crisp bags and – Vincent gasped – a baby's discarded nappy. The next bus, when it finally arrived after forty minutes, was relatively clean, but as it set off for the western suburbs he sat rigid with horror, staring out at yet more litter, graffiti, everything from beer bottles to old tyres strewn along the way. Was this really where Keeley came from?

After half an hour they reached the terminus in an anonymous suburb full of identical rows of houses, and Keeley took a piece of paper from her pocket.

'Only five minutes walk, Mary says, the B & B is called St Angela's, we take two lefts and a right.'

Unenthusiastically, he shouldered his rucksack and wondered aloud why nobody had come to collect them from the airport, why they were being put through a journey that was nearly as long as the flight.

'I told you, Cathal is busy working and Mary can't drive – anyway, she's up to her ears getting all the food ready for tomorrow.'

Keeley smiled, thinking of the christening that was, by the sound of it, going to be a very grand affair. Mary had written that Cathal was insisting on the very best for his new daughter, she was making a mountain of canapês and salads and there would even be champagne; Cathal was so besotted with the child it would be a wonder if he didn't put some in her bottle and get the poor thing pie-eyed. But then Mary was mad about the baby too, had written of virtually nothing else since giving birth at the Coombe hospital six weeks ago, on the first day of July.

Keeley could hardly wait to see them both, and was even prepared to be nice to Cathal since it seemed he was turning out to be such a success, shaping up much better than expected. Even though she hadn't liked him before, she had to concede that he had never actually done anything that could be held against him, apart from not having wanted Mary to go to France. But maybe that had only been natural, he simply hadn't wanted to be parted from her. Anyway, he was Mary's husband now, and the child's father in every real sense. Mary's most recent letter had contained instructions that Keeley was not, under any circumstances or influence of any quantity of alcohol, to ever breathe Lars's name again. Instead she was to bring her very best outfit, because this christening was going to be a swish affair, Cathal had even insisted that the lace gown be bought at Switzers, no less. Keeley had to admit that it all sounded very impressive.

The B & B was less impressive, when they found it, but the landlady welcomed them with a pot of tea and took them up to a room that was literally dazzling.

Vincent blinked as he confronted a brown carpet patterned with red and yellow leaves, blue wallpaper twined with green branches and purple flowers, orange nylon curtains and matching quilted bedspread, and a picture of some tortured man having what appeared to be open-heart surgery. Beaming, the landlady then led them into a bathroom bedecked with a plastic wall unit in olive green, black lino, pink shower curtain and a knitted tea-cosy – or was it a child's hat? – with a navy and yellow pompom on top. He dreaded finding out what it contained, but the woman lifted it up with a flourish, to reveal a roll of sky-blue toilet paper. And plenty of towels, she added, indicating two red-and-white handkerchiefs on a rail.

He was very glad when Keeley said they'd better hurry, it was nearly seven and they were due at The Lantern at eight. As soon as the landlady left them, they unpacked and began to change at speed. All the while, Keeley kept chatting, until suddenly she paused with her lipstick halfway to her mouth.

'Vincent?'

'Mm?'

'You – you don't think Mary will be offended, do you, that we haven't got the baby a silver mug or anything very expensive? I mean, the godparents are supposed to give something good.'

'I'm sure she'll understand, Keeley. I mean, just coming over here is cleaning us out.'

It really was, and Keeley bit her lip as she thought of the engagement ring that had been sacrificed for their air fares – dear God, please don't let Mary ask Vincent when is he ever going to produce the sparkler. It wasn't Mary's style, but even as a joke Vincent might take it the wrong way.

She wasn't sure what to expect when they got to The Lantern, but it didn't sound as if there was any shortage of money there. Mary had gone up in the world – apart from her odd honeymoon in Courtown, instead of Majorca or somewhere fancy. She'd been a bit vague about it, written only that they'd had a nice time, but then she'd been very pregnant, exhausted after the fussy wedding, maybe too tired to notice the details much less describe them. Or too distracted with romance, carried away on a tide of love and kisses … but no doubt she'd tell them all about it tonight, over the dinner she was cooking specially for them. Cathal wouldn't be able to come up and join them until closing time, but Keeley was just as glad of that, it would give her time to chat with Mary and get to know the baby.

Baby Imelda, or baby Lucy? Even now, right up to the eve of the christening, the name was still not decided. Mary wanted to call her daughter Lucy, after Luc, but Cathal wanted to name her Imelda, and there'd been lengthy debate about it. Keeley was hoping it would be Lucy, especially since she'd brought a present from Luc, who'd been thrilled when she'd dropped into the Vieux Moulin to tell him of Mary's safe, relatively painless delivery. Besides, Mary was the child's natural mother, whereas Cathal … well, she supposed she'd have to stop thinking that way, but she couldn't help feeling that this was one matter on which Cathal should give in without argument.

Eventually they were ready, and set off hand-in-hand for the pub, which was only ten minutes' walk away, feeling slightly silly with Luc's pink parcel and the promised sack of sugared almonds, which Mary intended to scatter on the buffet table tomorrow.

As they walked she felt nervousness rising in her, as well as anticipation; it was seven months now, nearly eight, since she and Mary had seen each other. Would they find each other changed? Maybe a little, at first … but not much, not really, she hoped. When they rounded a corner and The Lantern came in sight, her voice was a little hoarse.

'There it is.'

Vincent looked, and was very surprised. His idea of pubs was gleaned from tourist magazines, mostly British, containing pictures of cosy old buildings with thatched roofs and tall flowers outside, chintz and beamed ceilings inside. But this was a big, commercial-looking building with its name lit up in green neon and – holy God – an alsatian lying on the path outside the front door. Very gingerly, he picked his way around the dog, which inspected him warily with its unnerving red eyes. But Keeley didn't even notice it as she pushed open the door and hauled him inside, scanning the dim interior for—

'Mary!'

Dropping his hand with a shriek, she rushed forward, into the arms of the tall woman who engulfed her in turn, hugging and kissing and looking, Vincent thought, several years older than the girl he remembered. She must barely be twenty, he calculated, but how changed she looks, how *married*. Even if you didn't know anything about her, if she wasn't wearing a wedding ring and holding a baby in her arms, you'd guess that Mary was a wife and mother, a matron.

Yet Mary looked well, as she reached out to embrace him in turn, clutching him to her on top of Keeley and the infant. Her auburn hair was glossy, pinned back behind her ears to reveal the long neck that curved gracefully into a pale cream blouse, neatly tucked into a long, full skirt patterned with daisies. Her clothes were in complete contrast to Keeley's white shirt and black mini-skirt, but it was not so much her appearance which made an impression on Vincent as her aura, a sense of calm even in the midst of their excitement. There was something serene about her, he thought, something almost detached; and yet she was clearly thrilled to see them. He kissed her on both cheeks, and she responded warmly.

'At last, here you are . . . come on, follow me.'

With the baby in one arm she took Keeley by the other, leading them through the crowded, noisy pub to a door at the back, which opened into a hallway with stairs rising from it. At the top was another door, which gave into the flat where the Sullivan family now lived.

'Come in, come in.'

It was much brighter here, and once inside they all stood looking at each other for a moment, inspecting, assessing, laughing.

'Keeley Butler, let me look at you . . . is this really you?'

'It certainly is. What do you mean?'

'I mean – you look – so French!'

'French? Moi?' Keeley grinned, but Vincent saw that she was pleased, was taking it as a compliment.

And it was true, he realised for the first time: Keeley did look different from the way she'd looked when he first met her. After a year in France she had changed in some subtle way, seemed to wear things at a different angle or in different combinations, even to move and speak at a different pace. He'd never noticed it until here and now, but beside Mary she looked crisp, definite, somehow clear and bright, whereas Mary was softer, more rounded, gentler. When she giggled it occurred to him that she no longer giggled as much as she used to, was less squealy and nervy, and that he preferred the new laugh she had developed, confident and happy. Clearly Mary was seeing a difference in her too, after so much time apart they must both be registering the things you didn't see when you were with someone every day.

But then Keeley's gaze switched from Mary to the baby – a beautiful baby, with hair so blonde it was almost silver, lips soft and rosy as furled petals, skin and eyelids all but translucent in sleep.

'Oh, my God, she's gorgeous. Come on Mary, I'm her godmother, let me hold her.'

With a smile, Mary handed over the child, who stirred and opened her eyes, and looked at Keeley from their azure depths.

'Oh, she's waking up . . . her eyes are blue, just like yours . . . look, Vincent, isn't she beautiful?'

Resigned to a bout of baby talk, and thinking that the infant really was exquisite, he nodded as he reached out to touch her incredibly soft cheek with his finger.

'Hello, little girl. I'm Vincent, and this is Keeley. We're going to be your godparents. And what's your name?'

There was the briefest silence before Mary replied, quietly, 'Her name is Imelda. Imelda Lucy.'

Surprised, Keeley looked at her over the baby's shoulder. 'Not the other way round? Not Lucy Imelda?'

'No. We – we decided just this morning. Cathal has an aunt called Imelda, he – we thought it would be nice to call her after someone in the family.'

'Oh.' Keeley couldn't think why she felt disappointed, but she did. Because Luc would be, maybe? But no, she hadn't said anything to him about it, just in case. Just as well, now. Thoughtfully, she studied the little girl, falling in love with her in those first few moments, caressing the soft fat roll at the nape of her neck.

'So you're Imelda. Well, Auntie Keeley is going to call you Mel. What do you think about that? Do you like it?'

They were all amazed when the baby smiled, as best she could at six weeks, a kind of funny grimace that made them all laugh.

'Yes, Mary, see, she likes it!'

'Ha – I think she likes you. Who'd ever have thought Keeley Butler could hold a baby and not drop it – even make it smile! I suppose you and Vincent will be making one of your own, next.'

Vincent looked slightly alarmed, and Keeley shook her head. 'Oh, no. Not for years yet. Not until we're grown-ups!'

'That's funny. I was just thinking how grown-up you look. You really have changed, Keel.'

She flushed. 'Have I?'

'Yes. I can't quite put my finger on it, but you have. It must be Vincent's good influence.'

Mary said it jokingly, but then she saw the look that flashed between them, a look of such mutual love that she realised she was right. Vincent had done wonders for Keeley, something that was giving her confidence, making her shine and sparkle. She really did look great.

'Well, let me put the baby down, and then we'll have a chat and a drink before we eat. Cathal is down in the pub, but if we start late he'll catch up with us later, I'll keep his dinner hot for him.'

Again Keeley and Vincent looked at each other briefly, wondering. Why had Mary led them straight through the pub and out of it, without pausing for them to say hello to Cathal? But then it was Saturday evening, the place was busy, maybe she didn't want to interrupt his work.

'Ah, no, Mary, don't take her away yet. She'll be grand here on my lap – won't you, Mel?'

'OK. But Keeley, you won't call her Mel in front of Cathal, will you? He really likes the name he – we picked.'

'Does he? OK. But what about you, Mary? What do you like?'

Mary bit her lip, thinking a moment. 'Well – I must admit, Mel does sound kind of cute! But it's usually a boy's name, no?'

'Well, you thought you were going to have a boy.'

'Yes. My little brothers are disgusted with me, for getting it wrong.' Keeley grinned, thinking of Steve and Sean, who'd probably spoil Mel rotten when they were old enough to.

Judging from the number of soft toys around the place, Leesha and Kevin were at it already.

Mary poured drinks, white wine for Keeley and a Guinness for Vincent to try, then a vodka for herself with white lemonade. Keeley grimaced. 'God, that's what I used to drink, by the gallon! I'd forgotten ... I'd say I'd be sick as a parrot if I had one now. We hardly drink anything, only a glass of wine sometimes with meals.'

Sitting back with Mel in the crook of her arm, with Vincent beside her, she relaxed into what she suddenly realised was a very comfortable sofa. In fact the whole room, now that she looked around it, was furnished, muted and plush, a cut above the normal newly-wed standard. Following her gaze, Mary nodded.

'We've been very lucky, Cathal's parents gave us the suite for a wedding present, and of course he got a rise in salary when he took over as manager.'

'Oh. But I thought he wasn't taking over until September?'

'He wasn't meant to, but then Joe left early, vacated the flat so we could move in when we came back from Courtown.'

'Uh huh. And how was Courtown? You hardly wrote anything about your honeymoon – come on, Mary, don't be coy!'

'Oh, it's a lovely place, we stayed in a very nice hotel with a view of the sea ... just a sec, I must go check on my soup.'

Getting up, Mary went into the kitchen, which smelled of something delicious, and called out to them as she stirred.

'I'm doing you a lovely carrot soup, I hope you'll like it, and then a rack of lamb – Vincent, do you like lamb?'

'Aren't I going to marry one?' he replied, laughing and winking at Keeley, relieved that he could more or less follow the conversation in English. And that it wasn't exclusively about babies.

'But Mary, you shouldn't have gone to any trouble, you have enough cooking to do what with forty people coming to the christening tomorrow.'

'It's a pleasure. My cooking has come on quite a bit, you know, you can tell Luc I'm remembering everything he taught me, although I can't get all the ingredients here – I wish to God I had a garden, then I could grow the vegetables myself. But anyway, the Vieux Moulin wasn't wasted on me. How is Luc, anyway? And Félix?'

Remembering the present from Luc, Keeley asked Vincent to bring it into Mary in the kitchen. It turned out to be a tiny lemon romper suit, with a motif of a rabbit holding a wooden spoon, wearing a chef's hat and an apron with a query in French: 'Quand est-ce qu'on mange?'

'When do we eat? Oh, Luc must have gone to such trouble to find this – and we eat now as a matter of fact, you can tell him it was very well timed! Come on, bring your drinks in, let me take Imelda away to her cot.'

Imelda was bedded down, and they seated themselves around the kitchen table, since the flat had no dining room. But it was a sizeable kitchen, fully equipped, with a row of pots on the windowsill in which Mary said she was growing herbs.

'Of course the pub kitchen is much bigger, downstairs – it's being renovated at the moment, you can imagine all the stuff I'll need to cook on a grand scale.'

Keeley thought of her tiny kitchen in Aix, and thought also how confident Mary looked as she served up the soup, completely at home in the room where she most belonged. As they tasted it, she looked at them expectantly.

'Well? What do you think?'

They thought it was wonderful – light, creamy, unusual. Vincent wanted to know whether he could detect fruit, and mint.

'Yes, I blended in an orange and some mint leaves . . . if you like it, then I'll put it on the pub menu. Anything Keeley Butler eats, my customers will eat.'

Vincent grinned. 'Keeley will eat anything now, she's turning into a proper Frenchwoman.'

'I am not.'

Keeley made a face at him, but Mary thought he was right. Never before had she seen her friend dressed so well, looking so assured at table, not a bit worried about trying something new or recoiling, as she used to do, with a look of distaste.

It got dark outside as the meal continued, and Mary lit some candles as well as a lamp, asking all about France as she carved the lamb, which was pink and tender, Keeley commented, 'as baby Mel's bottom.' Mary laughed and looked delighted, but then got up with a slight frown.

'I'll just put Cathal's back in the oven to cook a bit more, he likes it well done.'

'But it's perfect!' Vincent looked aghast as she put it back, and turned the heat up a little. Ignoring his protests, she poured him another glass of the claret which, she said, she'd pinched from the pub. Nobody ever bought the good stuff, but they had to keep it in stock, just in case.

'So tell us about the christening. What do we have to say, and do?'

'Not much, only promise to see that Imelda is brought up a good Catholic and that you'll look after her immortal soul . . . oh, I shouldn't make fun, when you've come all the way from France to do it. I'm absolutely thrilled that you did, you kept your promise. It means a lot to me . . . and it's so good just to see you, for your own sakes.'

Was there a little tremor, suddenly, in her voice? Keeley thought that there was, but couldn't see her face as her hair swung forward over it.

'But Mary, of course we came, I told you we would . . . and you're coming to France in December, for our wedding.'

'Yes, I – I hope I am.'

'You hope? What do you mean? Mary, you're going to be my matron of honour, I'm counting on you!'

'Yes, I – of course I am.'

There was a silence, in which Keeley sat baffled. They'd settled this ages ago, and Mary didn't seem to have any money worries, it would be much easier for her than it had been for them.

'And you'll bring Mel with you, and Cathal.'

'Yes – oh, Keeley, do stop calling her Mel, please!' Mary's tone was so sharp, suddenly, that Keeley inadvertently leaned back out of the way as if Mary was going to hit her.

'I – oh, Keel, I'm sorry, it's just that I really don't think Cathal is going to like that name.'

'Oh, for heaven's sake, it's only a pet name, and anyway, he isn't even here.'

'No, but he will be in a few minutes . . . he's had a long day, he might be a bit tired, you know . . .'

What? Was that supposed to be a warning of some kind? It sounded as if it was. But everyone had had a long day, Mary had prepared tomorrow's meal for forty people, as well as this one, they had travelled from the south of France . . . surely Cathal would simply be glad to get upstairs to his delicious hot meal, sit down with a glass of wine or beer or whatever he drank, and unwind with them? After all, he was only twenty-four, not a crusty old codger of fifty. But even as Keeley gazed at her, Mary's look of calm command seemed to be changing into something flustered.

'Mary, relax! I know you're newly married, trying to be a good wife and all that, but—'

'Yes. Sorry. I suppose maybe I overdo it at times.'

Abruptly, she smiled at them both apologetically. 'Let's have some cheese. I got French for you, specially.'

She was slicing into a block of gruyère when they heard footsteps, and looked up in unison; Cathal running up the stairs, not unduly exhausted at all to judge by the spring in his step. The door opened, and they heard him heading straight for the baby's bedroom, evidently eager to see Imelda. Then, after a few moments, he came into the kitchen.

'Hello! Sorry I'm late – Keeley Butler, it's great to see you! And this must be Vincent?'

He thrust out his hand to shake Vincent's, and then Keeley nearly fell off the chair as he planted a smacker on her cheek, looking and sounding far friendlier than she'd ever remembered him. Looking well and healthy, too, with a bit more weight on him now that he wasn't playing football so much.

'Have you all got drinks? Great stuff – God, I'm starving, I'll bet my Mary has cooked something great, eh, Mary?'

Kissing Mary with a flourish, he pulled out a chair and sat down with them just as Mary got up, and went to ladle some soup into a bowl for him.

'What's this, tomato?'

'No, I thought I'd try something a bit different for Keeley and Vincent, it's carrot soup.'

'Oh, right, terrific.'

He was a noisy but evidently enthusiastic eater, breaking bits of bread into the soup and mopping it up as he talked and ate simultaneously, wanting to know how Keeley was – 'my God, you were only a little scut of a thing, the last time I saw you! You look very different now – this man here has put a right pair of roses in your cheeks, eh?!'

Vincent looked blank, finding his accent and rapid speech hard to follow, but Keeley agreed that yes, life was marvellous, Vincent was a gem.

'You look great too, Cathal. Fatherhood must agree with you.'

'Oh aye, have you seen her? Mary, bring Imelda—'

'Oh, no, don't wake her! We have seen her. And we think she's just beautiful.'

'That's the word for it. Beautiful, beautiful. Wait till you see her tomorrow, in her lace christening gown – and little Keeley to be godmother, eh? You'd better make a right good job of it, Miss Butler.'

'Don't worry, I will, and so will Vincent. We haven't got much money yet I'm afraid, not enough for a silver mug at any rate, but we'll give M – Imelda a proper present as soon as we can.'

'Ah, don't worry, silver mugs will do later. The child isn't drinking beer yet! Well, Mary, I must say this lamb is first class . . . aren't I the lucky man, married to a chef!'

On he went, talking a mile a minute as he wolfed his food, seeming to take over the conversation where Mary had left off. If anything his hospitality was excessive, he kept wanting to refill their glasses, insisted they have Bailey's with their coffee, lamented the fact that there was no spare room for them to stay in, was the B & B comfortable? No need to rush for the bus, he would drive them back to it himself, sure wasn't it only around the corner?

Keeley's misgivings melted away as he talked, telling them all about the great wedding they had missed, the great food Mary was going to serve in the pub, the great wife and mother she was. Having braced herself to be nice to him, she found it was no effort at all, a much easier evening than she had expected. Vincent, who'd been poured a very large Bailey's, looked slightly dazed, but blissfully comfortable.

'And tell us, Vincent, do you play any football at all, over there in France?'

Vincent replied that he persh – personally didn't, but that he did a lot of biking, had a ten-shpeed Raleigh.

'Vincent' said Keeley crossly, 'you're getting jarred.'

Cathal laughed. 'Ah, that's the French for you, can't hold their drink, not in training at all. But sure leave him be, Keeley, isn't he harmless.'

Harmless? It wasn't a word Keeley would pick to describe Vincent, not when she thought of how Vincent had offered to 'find and kill' Mel's real father Lars. But Cathal knew nothing of that, couldn't judge on the basis of such brief acquaintance, so for Mary's sake she was about to let it go when suddenly, provocatively, Cathal winked at her.

It was a patronising wink, she thought, complicit and yet belittling, reminding her of how he used to wink at people in the pub when he was serving more drink than was good for them, as a favour after hours. Appearing to bestow largesse, he was in fact profiting from their greed . . . or even their need, in some cases. It was a knowing wink, yet Mary had found it sexy, it was one of the things that had attracted her to go out with him.

Determined not to be provoked, particularly not on the eve of the baby's christening, Keeley merely stared at him. Stared long and hard, until finally he was forced to look away, turn to his wife with a nonchalant grin.

'So Keeley and Vincent are to be our daughter's godparents. Isn't Imelda the lucky little girl, Mary! She'll be drowned in goodies for the rest of her natural.'

Was that a dig, a jibe at their lack of funds? A hint that she and Vincent would henceforth be expected to rise to certain standards? Taking a deep breath, Keeley thought before replying.

'Vincent and I will take good care of the child, Cathal. Very good care. You can be sure of that.'

He didn't answer, respond to her tone in any way, but she was gratified to see a flicker of something – what? – from Mary. Just some tiny twitch, that told her she had said the right thing.

For what seemed like half an hour or so more they sat talking round the table, Cathal refusing to let Mary clear any dishes away while Keeley talked about her work, in which he sounded interested.

'Not much money in it though, is there? Hairdressing, I mean?'

'No. But I enjoy it. And I'm a stylist now . . . some of the customers tip well.'

'When they're in the mood! Ah well, if you enjoy it, sure that's the main thing. And what about himself here?'

'Vincent's a trainee manager at a department store. Once he's made permanent, we'll be able to afford a proper present for Mel.'

'Mel?'

Oh, Jesus. It wouldn't have slipped out, Keeley thought, if only Mary hadn't made such a thing about it – but, while Mary was looking horrified, Cathal merely looked puzzled.

'I mean, Imelda.'

'Ah. Yes. Imelda. Did you ever see a baby as beautiful?'

For the tenth time Keeley replied that she hadn't, glancing at her watch to avoid Mary's eye. A quarter to three . . . ? But it couldn't be.

'God almighty, I had no idea of the time – we'd better go – we can call a taxi, Cathal, if it's a pain for you to drive.'

'No trouble at all. No, no, leave the dishes, I'll send one of the barmaids up in the morning. Mary, where did you put their coats?'

They'd only brought light summer jackets, but Cathal helped Keeley on with hers, couldn't seem to do enough to be friendly to her. Before she knew it they were sitting in the car, the evening was over, and the only thing she could fault was the speed at which it had passed. It would have been nice to talk to Mary alone for a few minutes, but never mind, she'd get another chance tomorrow.

Cathal delivered them to their door, and sat with the engine running until they found the key they'd been given, waved them goodnight as they let themselves in. Vincent stumbled going up the stairs, grabbing at the bannisters in a way that made Keeley realise she wasn't going to get much sense out of him when she asked his opinion of the man Mary had married.

'Very nice,' he mumbled, and fell into bed with his shirt and socks still on, asleep almost before he hit it.

Yes. Very nice. Friendly, talkative, hospitable. Mad about the baby, wouldn't let his wife wash a dish, kissed her, ate everything put in front of him, said what a lucky man he was.

As she peeled off Vincent's socks and then snuggled down beside him, Keeley could not for the life of her think why Cathal's arrival had made Mary so jittery. And then so quiet, leaving him to take charge. There had hardly been another word out of her.

It didn't make sense. She'd said herself that Cathal had changed, was much improved, and he was. Most definitely. There'd been hardly any talk of football, no blather about his well-heeled parents or his own bright future, nothing off-putting at all. All the evidence was in his favour, pointing to a decent, even likeable husband. One who didn't even seem to drink excessively, or swear, or give any cause for worry about anything.

It must be me, she thought drowsily. I must be imagining things. There's absolutely no logical reason why I wanted to take Mary in my arms and tell her to have a good cry, that everything is going to be all right. Why would I want to do that, when everything *is* all right?

*   *   *

At the christening next day, things were even better. Keeley and Vincent arrived at the church to find Mary and Cathal already there, with a large gathering of friends and family that included both sets of parents, Mary's young brothers and Cathal's older ones, as well as his sister, assorted other relatives and several people Keeley recognised from the old crowd at The Lantern. Hoisting the baby over his head in the grounds outside the church, Cathal was in great form, apparently showing her off so everyone could get a good look, and baby Mel gurgled with glee, wide awake and seeming to understand that she was the star of the show. Mary looked beautiful, Keeley thought, as she stood talking to Leesha, wearing a rose-coloured silk dress that was a far cry from the denim skirts of – of less than a year ago?

That dress, Keeley thought intuitively, cost a fortune. I don't know the first thing about fashion, but I know I've never seen Mary looking like this before. She's wearing make-up too – not just the little bit of mascara she used to whack on, but foundation, powder, lipstick, eyeshadow, perfume, the works. Up close it's a bit much, a bit ageing, but maybe it's for the photographs, she's certainly going to look well in those. Her hair, her shoes, her earrings . . . my God, everything looks so expensive. Cathal must have sent her shopping with a blank cheque. I don't think we're ever going to see those gypsy-hoop earrings again – not even on Mel, when she's a teenager! That christening dress is like something you'd put on a princess, she's going to grow up spoiled rotten. And why not . . . it's better than Christy Butler's method of child-rearing, anyway. Cathal has really taken to this baby in a big way, just look at him, toting her round like a trophy, you'd think he won her in a competition. It's great to see everyone looking so happy.

Everyone trooped into the church, where Cathal arranged the baptismal party with army precision, instructing Keeley to stand *here* and Vincent to stand *there* – no, no, over to the right another six inches, we don't want to block anyone's view! Only when everyone was arranged to his satisfaction did he turn to the priest with a lordly smile, and permit the ceremony to begin.

As she held Mel in her arms, reciting the prayers along with the priest, Keeley glanced sidelong at Vincent and thought what a gesture of faith Mary was making in them as a couple; even though they were not yet married, she was entrusting them with her child's spiritual welfare, demonstrating her friendship and her confidence in them. But she needn't worry, she thought, even though we live so far away we're going to be very good godparents, the best anyone can be. Not that we'll ever be called on, I hope, to do anything more than give presents and make sure Mel has lots of fun, but if – if anything terrible ever did happen to Mary and Cathal, it would be up to us to take this job seriously. Maybe even have Mel to live with us, if nobody else was able to – but that's a very remote possibility; why am I thinking such dark thoughts on such a bright happy day? Maybe because this is the first serious thing anyone has ever asked me to do. Or maybe because Mel is real now, a person instead of a bump, a gorgeous little girl. How good she's being, not even crying when the water is poured on her head – ooh, I spoke too soon!

Briefly, but loudly and indignantly, Mel squealed at just that moment, but Keeley rocked her soothingly, hearing the muffled laughter among the congregation, thinking that anyone would yelp if a pint of cold water were flung suddenly over them. But then she settled down again, snuggling back into Keeley's arms so trustingly that Keeley felt a stab of the most acute tenderness for her, and was glad that Mary did not reach to take her away.

Vincent acquitted himself very well, repeating his lines word perfect, and soon the ceremony was over, everyone was crowding around and Cathal plucked Mel into his grasp, tickling her before passing her to his mother Carmel, who had the aura of a woman about to take charge. It was such a nice day that Keeley thought she'd like to walk the short distance back to The Lantern with Vincent, but she was overruled and they found themselves put into Kevin and Leesha's car, driven away amidst great excitement to the festive buffet Mary had prepared. Again Keeley felt a small pang, wondering when she was ever going to get to talk to Mary on her own – certainly not now, but if no other opportunity arose then she'd create one later in the evening, maybe when there was lots of washing-up to be done. It would be ridiculous, and very annoying, to leave tomorrow without even having had a proper chat.

The flat above the pub was already full of people by the time they arrived, and it took her a few moments to locate Mary, now wearing an apron over her silk dress, passing around plates with an air of calm professionalism while Cathal uncorked champagne loudly, ceremoniously. But as he pulled the corks he looked across the room repeatedly at his wife, and Keeley realised that he was watching her, supervising and assessing as if Mary were auditioning for some kind of role, a part in a play.

Well, she supposed, this is the first time Mary has ever cooked for a big gathering. Maybe he's a bit nervous – crikey, what if everyone got food poisoning, a fortnight before The Lantern starts serving hot meals! But of course they won't. Mary might not have much experience, but she knows today is important, she'll have done her very best. The table looks fabulous, almost like a garden with all those flowers and – what has she done with the sugared almonds?

As she looked more closely at the long table in the centre of the room, Keeley realised that Mary had, in fact, devised a garden made of food. The almonds were strewn like tiny cobblestones in the shape of a path, winding through beds of greenery, red roses carved from radishes, trees of leafy celery, pools of ice, a patio and tiny deckchairs made of marzipan. Each section of the garden contained a different delicacy: salmon studded with lemons beside the ponds of ice, a hollowed-out swan filled with cream cheese, a summerhouse made of paté, walls ingeniously built of bread, sausages and cheese straws. Astonished, Keeley gazed at it, unable to believe that Mary had done all this and still found time to cook dinner the night before, without the slightest hint of the panic it must surely have involved. And there were other things too, on the sideboard – savoury pies and canapés, sweet cakes and fruit, all dressed with flowers and leaves, looking far too good to eat.

But within minutes everyone was eating, exclaiming over the spectacular buffet even as they proceeded to demolish it, wading in with heartless vigour. Such was the crush around the table that Keeley decided to wait, along with Vincent, and they stood sipping champagne instead, wondering where their new godchild was.

'In her cot,' Cathal told them as he filled their glasses, 'there's far too much fuss and noise in here for her.'

It was very noisy, and Keeley had to shout at the people who came up to her, mouthing things she could hardly hear about France, and Vincent, and how much changed she was. They all wanted to know whether she was living permanently abroad now, but didn't seem at all impressed when she said she was, didn't believe it was possible not to be homesick.

You would believe it, she thought, if you could see the home

I grew up in. Anyone in their right mind would bolt from it, as far and as fast as they could. Please don't start the speeches about there being no place like home, because if I live till I'm ninety I never want to see mine again. I'm a thousand times happier where I am now, in the sun, with a job I love, with this man I love.

Candidly, she said so aloud, but still they shook their heads; that weird food you got over there, snails and frogs – euh, horrible! And the French people, so unfriendly . . . Keeley glanced at Vincent, and thought of his sister, his parents, Luc and Félix and Eliane, all the French people who'd been so good to her and Mary. Everyone presumed Vincent spoke no English, and was caught off guard when she introduced him.

'Well, this is my boyfriend Vincent, I hope you won't think he's too unfriendly.'

Vincent smiled at them all as he shook hands, said ingratiating things for her sake, but she could see he was baffled, and insulted. Not by the men, who didn't seem to care much where he came from, but by the many women who still wondered that Keeley would want to live in such an awful country. The more they said it, the more she began to look forward to going back to it.

But the party continued in full swing for more than two hours, hectic and deafening, the buffet reduced to a shambles as trays of pints were brought up from the pub below and everyone got down to the business of serious drinking. After a while Keeley thought she heard the baby crying, and made her way to tell Mary. But Mary was busy, slicing the wedding cake that was now a christening cake, handing plates around the room.

'Oh, God, Keeley, she probably needs to be changed . . . you wouldn't do it, would you? You'll find all the stuff you need beside her cot.'

'Sure – nobody ever said being a godmother would be a picnic!'

Glad to get away from the throng, but without a clue how you changed a baby, she made her way to the infant's bedroom and went in. Newly decorated, filled with toys, it looked like the kind of dream nursery illustrated in catalogues, and again she wondered at the amount of money Cathal and Mary seemed to be spending with such abandon. But Mel was crying her head off. Gingerly, she picked her up.

'Hey, don't cry, it's me, your godmother . . . Auntie Keeley is going to change you, if she can figure out how.'

It was something of a struggle, and a messy one at that, but eventually Mel was wrestled into a nappy that seemed to be on right way round, with the sticky tapes in more or less the right places.

'Now! Isn't that better?'

Mel stopped screaming, and blinked up from the cloud of powder that Keeley had sprinkled all over the changing mat. And then they smiled at each other.

'There, see, I wasn't trying to kill you! Come up and give Auntie Keeley a kiss!'

Lifting the child up, she took her in her arms and began to walk round the room with her, introducing herself to all the toys like an idiot.

'So this is teddy, and this is dolly, and this is gollywolly . . . what a lot of toys you have, little girl.'

The chest and wardrobe were piled high with them, the bed was smothered in them, and only gradually did Keeley realise that virtually everyone who drank at The Lantern must have given Cathal something for his new daughter – but then he knew them all personally, made it his business to know every customer by name. No wonder he had invited so many of them today, and was pouring such quantities of drink into them.

'But you're not his—' she said suddenly, and then stopped in mid-sentence, gazing at Mel. What made me say that, she wondered, especially after Cathal was so friendly last night, is throwing such a ritzy party today? If he hadn't come on the scene, God only knows where this bambino and her mother would be today – certainly not at any party, but struggling along on social welfare somewhere, or having a very small quiet christening at Leesha and Kevin's house. He's being great, and Mary is—

But Mary wasn't. Only as she said it did it dawn on her that Mary was not looking happy, not laughing or radiant at all. She looked well, she was dressed well, she was smiling – but it was a professional smile, the smile Félix gave customers at the Vieux Moulin.

Pacing up and down, cuddling Mel close to her, she thought about it, about the church and the party and the meal last night, until she was sure. But no. She could not remember having seen the old Mary, the real Mary, at all. She had seen a wife, a mother, a cook, a hostess . . . everything except the old friend she had so looked forward to seeing.

I am not imagining it, she told herself. Something is missing, something is wrong. I have to get her on her own, and find out what it is.

It was nearly eight in the evening when the last guests departed, down to the pub where Cathal had decided the party should continue, and Keeley got her chance. Putting her hand on Vincent's shoulder when no-one was looking, she whispered into his ear.

'Vincent, I know you don't know any of them, but I want you to go down with them, just for a little while. I need to talk to Mary by herself.'

'Why? What's the matter?'

'Nothing – just girl talk while we do the dishes. Please go, just for an hour.'

Reluctantly he went, saying something to the effect that the alcohol was endless in Ireland and it would be her fault if he got drunk again and snored . . . hustling him out, Keeley prayed that Cathal wouldn't send anyone up to help; but nobody came, it was a case of all hands on deck down in the crowded pub. The moment they were alone, Mary began to stack dishes and carry them into the kitchen, until Keeley blocked her path.

'Mary, stop.'

'What? But Keeley, there's a mountain of work to be done, it'll take me all night—'

'I'll help you. But first I want you to sit down. Just sit down for a few minutes, you've been working all day.'

Her look and tone were so resolute that Mary paused, eyeing the armchair she was indicating with a kind of panic.

'I can't, Keel, I—'

'Mary, sit. And take this.'

Without bothering to give her a choice, Keeley poured her a stiff whiskey from the nearest bottle on the sideboard and handed it to her. Then, assembling a couple of cheese sandwiches from the debris, she stacked them on a plate and put it in front of Mary.

'Drink that and eat those. You've had nothing all day.'

Abruptly, Mary seemed to sag. Pushing her hair off her face, kicking off her shoes, she sank back into the armchair.

'God, you're right. I am tired. And hungry.'

Sitting down opposite her with a drink in her own hand, Keeley took out and lit one of the cigarettes she still occasionally smoked.

'You must be knackered. That was one hell of a knees-up. I can't wait to tell Luc about that fabulous buffet.'

'I got it out of one of his books . . . was it all right?'

'It was fantastic. I never saw the like, never knew you could do such things with food.'

'Well, it had to be good – I mean, you know, I wanted it to be good, it's not every day your first daughter is christened.'

For a moment Keeley studied her without replying, noting the miraculous way Mary's make-up seemed to have stayed perfect all day, but how drawn she looked under it . . . far more drawn than most young women would look even after a whole night at a disco, the wildest partying through to dawn. Curling her legs up under her, she was visibly deflating like a pricked balloon, looking both younger and older than she was, her face paling as the room lost some of its intense warmth.

'No, it isn't. I hope you enjoyed your own party.'

'I – I did, of course I did, I hope everyone did. Didn't you?'

Thoughtfully, Keeley exhaled a stream of smoke and considered. 'Yes. Being godmother is a real blast, Mary. Vincent and I are really touched that you wanted us, especially now you're back in Ireland and must be making other friends.'

'Oh, but you're my oldest friend, my best friend, and Vincent was so kind to me when I was pregnant, I never wanted anyone else—'

'Did Cathal?'

'What?'

Leaning forward, Keeley looked her in the eye, so intently that Mary glanced away.

'Did Cathal ever want anyone else to be Mel's godparents, Mary?'

'What on earth makes you think that?'

'Never mind what. Just tell me. Did he or didn't he?'

For a few seconds there was silence, in which Keeley prayed that the whiskey would work soon on Mary's empty stomach. If need be she was going to pour her another, even larger one. But then Mary looked down into it, thinking before answering.

'Well – only for a moment – he did suggest – that since you and Vincent live so far away, it might be better if he asked his sister and one of his brothers. But I said no, that I'd asked you and you'd promised, I—' She broke off, and Keeley heard the catch in her voice, knew she'd hit a nerve.

'You what?'

'I told him it was important, I – had – a – a bit of a row with him, over it.'

'But you won?'

'Yes. I won.'

But she doesn't sound like a winner, Keeley thought. She sounds like a loser. What did she lose?

Bracing herself, she sat forward with her glass gripped in both hands. 'Mary. I am your best friend, as you say. That's why you've got to trust me, and tell me what's wrong.'

Like a rabbit caught in oncoming headlights, Mary stared at her, wide-eyed, with a small gasp. 'Nothing is wrong! What do you mean, Keeley, I don't understand what you mean!'

'Yes, you do. You know why Cathal is being so nice to me, when he never used to. You know why he chose Mel's name instead of letting you call her Lucy. You know why he's putting on such a show of being the proud father. You know where all the expensive clothes and furniture are coming from. You know something is wrong, Mary, and so do I.'

'No, Keeley! He is a proud father, and he's proud of me too, he wants me to look nice and for us to have a nice home, he earns good money and his parents are very generous – you're imagining things!'

'Am I, Mary?'

'Yes, you – you are, just as he said you would, you're jealous, that's all!'

It was Keeley's turn to gasp. 'I'm what?'

But Mary dropped her glass, got up and almost ran to her, with a look somewhere between terror and the sheerest remorse as she knelt beside her, put her hand on her arm.

'Oh, Keeley, I'm so sorry, I didn't mean that – it's just that he said – he keeps saying—'

'He keeps saying what?'

But Mary's eyes were filling with tears, her hand clenching as she put it to her mouth and backed away. 'Nothing, it's just me, it's the whiskey . . . Keeley, why are you saying these things? Why are you doing this to me?'

'Mary, I'm not doing anything to you, only trying to find out why you're not happy. You haven't smiled once since I've been here, not properly, you haven't laughed or cracked a joke, you shut up the minute Cathal came into the room last night, you were petrified when I called Imelda Mel . . . you're not you, at all! What in God's name is wrong?'

'Nothing! I told you, *nothing* is wrong!'

Her voice was so resolute, suddenly, so high-pitched and adamant, that Keeley recognised defeat. Mary was not going to tell her.

'All right. If you say so. I'm sorry if I've upset you . . . I won't say anything more if you don't want me to. Except that you can write to me, or ring me at the salon, any time you need a friend. Especially if it's anything to do with Mel, she's my god-daughter now, Mary, and she's a defenceless baby—'

'I know she is! That's why I—'

Whirling around, away from her, Mary stopped speaking as suddenly as if a blade had severed her tongue, went to the table and began stacking dishes at furious speed.

In silence, Keeley got up and helped her, until everything was in the kitchen ready for washing. And then Mary turned back to her, calmly, almost sociably.

'I'll get through these much quicker on my own. Why don't you go on down to the pub and have a nightcap with Vincent?'

Her look left Keeley no choice but to obey.

It was going to take more than one short visit to Ireland, Vincent thought, to figure out the sudden mood swings that seemed to go with the territory. Barely half an hour ago he'd been having a drink with Keeley, who'd apparently decided not to wash dishes after all, and she had been chatting and laughing amiably with him, with two old acquaintances from The Lantern, who were making all sorts of jokes and merriment. Everything had seemed fun, seemed fine. And now, here he was lying in bed with Keeley sobbing into his chest, hiccuping unintelligibly as he stroked her hair and told her to take her time, explain in English if it would be easier.

She stuttered a few words, and then began to cry with even greater vigour, as if something altogether calamitous had happened. Vincent, who'd never seen her cry before, decided she'd either had too much to drink or she was simply emotional, the way women incomprehensibly were, about the christening which had meant so much to her.

Eventually, after gushing a torrent of tears that put him in mind of Niagara Falls, she looked up, into his face, stricken and waterlogged.

'Vincent, do you think I'm mad?'

He couldn't stifle his laugh in time, but her expression warned him he'd better stifle the next one. 'No, of course not! What are you talking about?'

'Mary thinks I am. She says I'm imagining things.'

'What things?'

'The – the whole thing.'

He sighed to himself. This was evidently going to be one of those roundabout conversations, one of those verbal mazes women sometimes wandered into, leaving men lost in their wake, silently shouting for help.

Shifting into a more comfortable position, he tightened his arm around her and kissed the damp end of her nose.

'What thing? What did Mary say? Did you have some kind of disagreement with her?'

There was a considerable silence before she replied. 'Vincent, what did you think of Mary today?'

'Think of her?'

'Yes – how she looked, what she wore, what she said. What did you make of her?'

'I – well, I thought she looked lovely. Very pretty, very well dressed. I don't remember her saying much . . . just the usual things, nothing extraordinary . . .'

'You didn't think she was distant? Remote, not herself?'

'Not that I noticed – but she was very busy, Keeley, there were a lot of people there. I did think last night, when I first saw her, that she looked a bit older – a bit motherly. But in a positive way. There was something sort of serene about her.'

'I see. And what about Cathal? What did you make of him?'

'I liked him. Thought he was very friendly, much more than you'd led me to expect. He seemed crazy about the baby too.'

'And their flat?'

'I – well, I didn't really notice much about it. Except that it was comfortable. Much more comfortable than the flat in Aix!'

'Uh huh. And the conversation about the honeymoon?'

'What conversation about it? I don't remember having one.'

'Ah hah.' Sounding like a cross-examining barrister resting

her case, Keeley looked at him with satisfaction. 'No. You don't remember it, because we never had it.'

It was late, he was tired, and he began to heartily wish she'd come to the point. But something told him he'd better not say so.

Wriggling free of him, she sat up, and leaned her chin on her knees. 'Mary says I'm jealous.'

'Jealous?' He was more baffled than ever. Keeley was not without faults, she could be impetuous, scatter-brained, overly talkative, but jealousy was something he thought completely foreign to her nature. Although she came from very little and had very little, he'd never once heard her envy anyone – on the contrary, she was remarkably happy with the new life she had made for herself, and always delighted for anyone else who got or achieved anything.

'But what would you be jealous of?'

'I don't know. Her expensive clothes, maybe? Her fully-furnished flat? Her baby in its christening gown from Switzers? Her husband being made a manager, when you're still a trainee? Her chances of getting her own restaurant, when I'm a million miles from getting my own salon?'

The list amazed him. He'd never noticed, much less thought, about any of those things. But they were the kind of thing women noticed, and thought about. The kind of thing that could cause friction, if a friendship was not strong. But Keeley and Mary were such close friends – almost like sisters, he'd sometimes thought.

'But – but Keeley, you're not, are you? Jealous, I mean, of any of those things? I know we don't have much yet, and Mary has suddenly got a lot, but it just doesn't sound like you at all. Jealousy's not your style.'

Her voice wavered. 'No. You're right, Vincent. It's not my style, at all. That's why I don't understand why Mary should say it.'

Sitting up in turn, he ran a finger under her wet eyelashes. 'Come on. Don't start crying again. She was probably just tired. You'll kiss and make up in the morning, be the best of friends again.'

She didn't answer, sitting there in the dark, hoping he was right and wondering if Mary was. Maybe she really had imag-ined all the things she had confronted Mary with . . . maybe she'd been the one who was tired, overwrought. And if she was, what had she done? Terrible damage, she felt . . . it was as if their friendship had abruptly been disconnected, unplugged at the mains.

Vincent would probably say it didn't matter, that they'd merely outgrown each other and that she had lots of new friends in France anyway, at the salon and at the Chamber of Commerce. But it did matter. The Mary she had seen today was not the real Mary, the one who'd taken her to France and found a flat and shared everything and hit Christy Butler a box. That Mary had waited hours at the hospital, had her to stay with her parents, insisted she be godmother to her child . . . whereas today's Mary was cool and distant and accusing. Even if women did change when they had babies, as she'd heard, they didn't turn into completely different people.

It was something to do with Cathal. She knew it was. He had changed mysteriously too – admittedly for the better, it seemed, but it was odd, out of character.

What should she do? Go to sleep, try to forget about it, pretend nothing had happened? Return to France and let Mary quietly melt out of her life? But she was Mel's godmother. She wanted to stay in contact, stay friends. Despite all the people at the christening, she hadn't noticed any to whom Mary seemed particularly close, anyone she laughed and joked with or introduced with special warmth. If anything it was Cathal who seemed to be the popular one, while his wife was somehow shadowy, isolated even amid such a big gathering . . .

'Damn!' she shouted suddenly. Vincent jumped.

'Damn what?'

'Damn it. I shouldn't have let her do it. I knew I should never have let her marry Cathal Sullivan. I should have written that time, and said so, at the top of my voice.'

Soothingly, he stroked her back. 'Keeley, Cathal is a very nice man and, as far as I can see, Mary is perfectly happy. The baby is well cared for, they have a roof over their heads, work to do, lots of friends. What's wrong with any of that?'

'I don't know' she muttered vehemently, 'but something is wrong with it. Very wrong, Vincent. You just mark my words.'

Next morning, early while they were having breakfast, the landlady came in to tell Keeley there was a phone call for her. Apprehensively, she got up and went out to the telephone in the hall, wondering whether Mary had rung to apologise, or to spill out her sorrows, now while there was time. The plane was not leaving until late this afternoon.

But it was Cathal.

'Howya, Keeley! Lovely day, eh?'

She nearly dropped the phone, until she realised Mary must have said nothing to him about the row they'd had, not disclosed any news of friction at all.

'Yes. Lovely.'

'So what are your plans?'

'I – well, I want to go and see my brother. You know, Tony, he's in the rehab centre. I've arranged to meet my mother there as well.'

In fact she had no idea whether Gertie would turn up, or had even received her letter suggesting it. She could only hope so, because she missed her mother, couldn't bear to leave without seeing her.

'Oh, right. Well then, tell you what, why don't you let me drive you there? And to the airport, afterwards?'

'To the centre, and the airport? But they're both miles away, and besides what would you do while I was with Tony? You'd have to hang around for – well, for an hour, while I visit him.'

'Ah, sure, what matter? Mary and Imelda will come too, we can have a walk in the grounds or go for a coffee while you see Tony – how is he, anyway?'

She could hardly believe her ears. Tony had been in the rehab centre for two years, but Cathal had never asked about him before.

'I don't know how he is. That's what I want to find out.'

'Well, then, that's settled so. We'll call to pick you up in about an hour, take you to him, and then if there's time we'll all have a bite of lunch before your plane leaves. That OK?'

She thought it sounded wonderful, much better than having to tote luggage on endless buses and – oh, God! Only at that moment did she remember the belated wedding present she and Vincent had brought for Mary and Cathal, a heavy set of wooden salad bowls they'd bought from an African street vendor in Aix. In all the excitement of the christening, she'd forgotten them – and now, would Mary still want them, want anything? Well, there was only one way to find out.

'That would be great, Cathal. See you in an hour, then.'

Bemused, she went back to her breakfast.

The rehab building was a cheerful enough place on the outside, even attractive, with its landscaped grounds, resolutely colourful flowers and big trees with benches under them on which weary bones could rest. Some patients were walking around almost normally, but Keeley felt something shrink inside her as she looked at the ones hobbling on crutches, or steering wheelchairs with their arms, or simply sitting still under the warm August sun. Scanning their faces, she looked for Tony, but he was not amongst them.

At the desk inside, a nurse said he was in his room, with his mother, they were expecting her. She turned to Vincent.

'Do you want to do this? If you don't, if you'd rather wait outside with Mary and Cathal, there's no problem.'

She had no wish to impose it on him, make him face a trauma that had little or nothing to do with him. And she didn't know how Tony would react to seeing her, never mind a strange Frenchman; on her few previous visits he had been mostly morose, sometimes hostile and bitter.

But Vincent nodded. 'Yes. Of course I do. He's going to be my brother-in-law, isn't he? I'll come and say hello, at least, and then play it by ear. If he doesn't like my being there, I'll leave.'

And so they set off, leaving Mary, Cathal and Mel walking in the opposite direction, back out into the grounds where they said they would wait. For a moment Keeley hesitated, watching them, looking at their air of normality, of family solidarity. Mary had turned up smiling, as if nothing had happened, and made a great fuss of the salad bowls, exclaiming out of all proportion to the scale of the gift.

The bowls had seemed like a good idea on the day they were bought, with much laughing and haggling, but now Keeley thought they were a mistake. In Mary's present circumstances, bone china would be more appropriate than ethnic wood, or something a little more refined at least. In Mary's manicured, nail-polished hands they looked all wrong, rough and ready, not funny or exotic at all. If Mary had laughed, she'd have laughed too, been reassured, but instead Mary had said they were magnificent, which they surely weren't.

But at least Mary was speaking to her, glossing over their row, going out of her way to be cordial. Watching her depart, carrying Mel in one arm and taking Cathal's arm in the other, Keeley was glad; she didn't want to leave on a sour note.

Finally she turned and followed the nurse, down several corridors until they reached a long bright room with four beds in it. Tony's was the one in the corner, and she quailed when she saw a curtain drawn around it. But the nurse smiled brightly, drew it back a little, and left them.

Tony was sitting upright, with some kind of support around his neck and torso, and she was vastly relieved when he smiled.

'Hi, Keeley!'

And there was Gertie as well, looking tiny, and very nervous. Keeley flew to her, and to her brother, embracing them as she fought back tears. There were only two ways of dealing with the situation; one was to weep and lament and talk about the awfulness of it all, the other was to smile and be positive.

'Oh, Tony . . . you look much better!'

He did, too, although it still grieved her to see him immobile, unable even to return her hug. But Gertie returned it, with a look that told Keeley she was asking her forgiveness, for what had happened with Christy eight months before. But it wasn't Gertie's fault.

'And you, Ma, you look great too.' She didn't, but Keeley prattled on. 'I've brought someone to meet you both. This is Vincent, my boyfriend.'

Lopsidedly, Tony grinned, and she saw a flash of what he had been before his accident – handsome, dare-devil, full of misplaced energy. But he could speak normally, his thin face had even regained its colour, his dark eyes had far more life in them than the last time she'd seen him.

'Howya, Vincent. I hear you're going to make an honest woman of my sister.'

Uncertainly, Vincent laughed. 'I'm going to marry her in December.'

'Yeah, well, don't count on me for the dancing!'

They sat down, and Keeley took Tony's hand. 'How are you? Any progress?'

'A bit – they can get me into a wheelchair sometimes now, and I can type to beat the band. You know, with the stick. I can even paint a bit, by the same original method.'

'Paint? With a paintbrush?'

'Yeah. Michelangelo, that's me. I'm booked in to do the chapel ceiling next week.'

She grinned. 'That's great. I can't believe anyone can really manage a brush in – in their mouth.'

'Well, I can. No fancy portraits or anything, just daubs of colour, but the nurses like them. Call them abstracts.'

'Have you any I can see?'

'Yeah. Heaps. Over there, by the wall.'

Sure enough, there was a stack of quite big white cardboards, and she got up to look at them, Vincent dutifully following her. As she took up one and then another, her heart clenched; they were like something baby Mel might do if let loose with a box of paints. But Vincent was loudly enthusiastic.

'Oh, yes! The blue, and the grey – I like these colours.'

Tony snorted. 'Well, it keeps me off the streets at any rate. The streets are perfectly safe now from Tony Butler.'

His tone was wry, but Keeley was surprised to hear him make such an allusion at all, almost as if he were acknowledging that he had, indeed, once been a dangerous menace. But he had had a lot of time to think, she supposed, in two years. Two years. Thank God the State was paying for it all, at least nobody had to worry about that. Even Cathal Sullivan was paying, through his taxes.

'These are great, Tony. You should keep at it.'

'Yeah. That's what the physio says. I've told her over and over that I'd rather do a spot of mountaineering, but she won't listen.'

Keeley was glad that he was able to joke, seemed to have cheered up a bit even if she detected some bitterness, wasn't fighting his fate but was being realistic instead. Accepting. The doctors had said it might take a long time to get him to do that.

'Would you do us a picture for our wedding?'

It was Vincent who asked, surprising them all, and Keeley was grateful to him. It was an idea, might give Tony some small goal to aim at.

'Sure I would. But how would I get it over to France?'

She thought. 'Mary is coming over to be my bridesmaid. She could bring it with her.'

She felt a little tremor as she said it, wondering if Mary still wanted to be her bridesmaid. But Tony grinned. 'Mary Jameson? The one you eloped to France with?'

She laughed. 'Yes. She's Mary Sullivan now. She married Cathal, from The Lantern.'

She was surprised when he frowned. 'Yeah. I heard that. Weird.
I wouldn't have thought Cathal Sullivan was the marrying type.'

'What?'

'Ah, you know – football, the pub, the lads. Not what you'd
call a ladies' man – and I hear they have a child now, and all.'

'Uh, yes. Baby Mel. Short for Imelda. I'm her godmother, and
Vincent is her godfather.'

Abruptly, Tony's face seemed to crumple, twist and sag in
some way. It took her a moment to realise why, to visualise
the children he would never have, the grandchildren Gertie
had lost, the nieces and nephews she had lost. Funny, she'd
never thought about that before. But there was no question
that Tony would ever father children; at most, he would be
well enough to live at home with his parents, sit in a wheelchair
and type if he could get any kind of work, otherwise subsist on
disability benefit. Thinking of the bleak vista, she turned to their
mother.

'And what about you, Ma? How are you?'

'I'm grand. It's nice to meet young Vincent. He seems like a
good lad, Keeley.'

Gertie didn't look grand, she looked tired and dejected and
somehow trapped, like a mouse with her little eyes and fuzzy
coat. Keeley caught the drift of what she was saying.

'He is good. He's the best. Aren't you, Vincent?'

Knowing the family history, Vincent nodded. 'I am very lucky
to have met your daughter, Mrs Butler. I will take great care
of her.'

There was a silence, in which Keeley wondered whether she
should ask her mother about coming to France for the wedding.
Now that Mary could afford her own plane fare, she could
spend the money on Gertie – if Gertie would come. But she
didn't think she would, and besides this was the wrong moment,
in front of Tony who certainly couldn't travel. She would write
to her later, and ask then . . . if she did miraculously say yes,
Vincent's parents would surely accommodate her. But she felt
that the effort of going to a foreign country would defeat Gertie,
as well as the mysterious tie that bound her to Christy. And
Christy was definitely not coming, not being invited under any
circumstances.

For some time they talked, about trivial things in which
Tony seemed to take unusual interest. His world has shrunk,
she thought, once he would have wanted to dominate, dictate

the conversation. Now, he must live for television and the radio and visitors, not that he gets many – I should start writing to him. I will start.

'Is there any word on when they're letting you out, Tony?'

'Sometimes . . . they think maybe in six or eight months. But sure what's the rush, where would I be going?'

Where, indeed? Only home to Pearse Gardens, and Gertie having to nurse him then as if her life were not miserable enough already . . . at least she didn't seem to have any bruises or black eyes today. That hiding Kevin Jameson had given Christy must have done him good.

Eventually, it was time to go. Bending forward, she kissed her brother.

'Bye, Tony. I'm sorry it's been such a long time . . . I'll keep in better touch from now on, write to you if you'd like.'

'Yeah. That would be good – only don't tell any dirty stories about Vincent here, because the nurses will be reading the letters to me and they have filthy minds enough already, I can tell you.'

'Hah! I'm glad you warned me. Meanwhile, don't forget that painting. Vincent and I are looking forward to it.'

If he saw that she was trying to humour him, he gave no sign of it. 'I won't. You'll have it by Christmas.'

Bending again, she kissed her mother, wishing there was something she could say or do, some way of making her smile, or even look a bit more animated.

'Cathal and Mary are driving us to the airport, Ma. Would you like to come? We're going to lunch, too—'

'Ah, no. You go on now, the two of you. I'll stay here for a while with Tony.'

And so Keeley took Vincent's hand and they left, feeling sad, and guilty and helpless.

Lunch was splendid, and only Keeley found it strange. When they arrived at the airport Cathal found parking instantly, by dint of sheer assurance it seemed, and slung the car across two spaces. Then, lifting Mel out of her baby seat, he led the way up to the restaurant on the top floor of the terminal, and insisted on the best of everything; his treat, he said, nobody was to insult him by attempting to put their hand in their pocket. Vincent tried to argue, but Cathal shot him down, and Keeley saw that he was embarrassed, would have preferred to at least share the bill after all the hospitality he had had from the Sullivans. But it really would have left him broke, by the time everything was paid for: vegetable soup to start, then steaks all round, then sweet sticky desserts, plus two bottles of wine and coffee afterwards. Keeley had enjoyed the landlady's substantial hot breakfast that morning, but this next big meal only five hours later left her feeling full and fat as a Buddha.

Mary was very animated, talking about the success of the christening and turning often to her for confirmation that it had actually gone as well as she thought it had. If anyone had any criticisms of the food, she said, now was the moment to air them, because soon she would be cooking some of the dishes professionally . . . at first Keeley wondered, thinking how unlike Mary it was to fish for compliments, but then she sensed the anxiety in her friend, the nervousness.

'Mary, it was fantastic, and your food at The Lantern will be fantastic. Unless you get into a panic and mix up your fish with your flans! Why don't you try to relax?'

Mary nodded and smiled rather distractedly before turning to fuss over Mel, who was contentedly sucking a bottle on her lap.

'Tilt it up, Mary,' Cathal said, 'the poor child is getting more fresh air than milk, she'll have wind.'

At that very moment Mel burped like a drunken sailor, as if to prove Cathal right, and he leaned forward to take both baby and bottle. 'Oh, here, let me do it, if you want something done right you always end up having to do it yourself.'

Keeley thought that wasn't a very nice or encouraging thing to say to a new mother, but Mary passed him the child agreeably, looking apologetic.

'Sorry, I am making a bit of a bags of it . . . there, Imelda, go to Daddy, he's going to feed you properly.'

And Cathal did, keeping the child with him for the remainder of the meal while they talked about the people who'd been at the party, the clothes they'd worn and the things they'd said – all very flattering – about the beautiful baby and the excellent food, not to mention the champagne that had flowed like water. Once or twice Keeley tried to bring Luc and Félix into the conversation, and Vincent mentioned activities in France, but it was like throwing a grappling hook that kept falling short of its target, neither of them could get a firm purchase on the terrain. It was as if, Keeley thought, Mary's former life in France was now firmly behind her, belonged to someone else who had been somewhere else . . . and yet Mary had asked about Luc and Félix at dinner the night before last, seemed thrilled with Luc's present and wanted all the news of both men.

But she was getting tired of talking so much about the Sullivans, and decided to take one last shot at changing the subject.

'Tony is learning to paint, Mary. With a brush in his mouth.'

'Really? That's great.'

'So Vincent asked him to do us a painting for a wedding present – you know, to encourage him. We were wondering if you'd bring it over with you when you come to the wedding.'

Cathal sat up. 'Your wedding, you mean? In France?'

'Yes, in December, I'm sure Mary told you she's going to be my bridesmaid . . . we'd better start thinking about a dress for you to wear, Mary.'

'Yes – I'll write to you about it, Keeley.'

Write to her? Keeley couldn't see why they couldn't talk about it now.

'Well, why don't you just tell me what colour you'd like – something warm for winter, maybe red velvet? Then I could have a look round the shops when I get back. Or would you prefer to pick it out yourself? I really don't mind, it won't be a very fancy do—'

Cathal cocked his head sideways.

'Sshh . . . is that your flight I hear being called?'

They listened, and sure enough it was. Vincent said there was no hurry, the outward flight had been called ages before it departed and they'd ended up twiddling their thumbs in the departure lounge. But Cathal stood up.

'Still, we'd hate to be the ones to blame if you missed it. Come on, let's get moving.'

All smiles, he hustled everyone out and led the way to the departure gates, carrying Mel, Mary beside him wearing the smile that had never left her face all day. As they walked, she turned to Keeley.

'It was great to see you, Keel, you and Vincent, we were really pleased you could make it.'

'I was dying to see you, Mary, and baby Mel, and Cathal, of course – I just wish we could have had more time together. I wanted to have a proper chat with you.'

'I know, but didn't the time fly! We will next time.'

Brightly, she walked on, her heels tapping briskly, purpose-fully – almost, Keeley thought, as if she were the one hurrying to the plane. Hanging back, she put her hand on Mary's arm and waited for her to slow down, fall behind the two men. Then, uneasily but candidly, she looked at her.

'Mary, what's the rush, anyone would think you were trying to get rid of me! Look, I just wanted to say – to ask you – is everything all right? I know I put my foot in it the other night, but I don't know why. If anything is wrong, I wish to God you'd tell me.'

For a split second, Mary hesitated, slowed down a fraction. And then her smile widened.

'Keeley, things couldn't be better. I'm sorry I was a bit strung up that night, but I had a lot to do, I'd been work-ing all day and I suppose I'm a bit anxious about this new venture, I have Imelda to mind as well. But I'm fine. Really.'

'You're sure?'

'Of course I'm sure. Haven't I a great new life, new baby, new husband, new home, new job?'

'Yes, but you – you were so upset about leaving your old job, with Luc and Félix. About leaving our flat too—'

'Well, life moves on. We had a great time, but it was just for laughs, not – not real. What I've got now is real.'

It was, Keeley supposed. Real, adult, solid. Mary was cer-tainly leaving her teens behind, joining the serious grown-up world.

'Still, we had a great time, didn't we?'

'Yes. While it lasted. But you'll soon be married now as well, Keeley, you'll see that things change, you have to—'

'Have to what?'

'Have to hurry, or you'll miss your plane! Come on, the guys have gone way ahead, I can't even see them, can you?'

Quickening her step, she hastened on, and before she knew it Keeley was arriving breathless at the gates where Vincent was looking round for her. Cathal beamed.

'So here we are already, the two lovebirds are flying back to France!' Easily, jauntily, he bent to kiss Keeley's cheek. 'It was lovely to see you. Have a good trip home – take care of her, Vincent, you're a lucky man, like me!'

Then he proffered baby Mel to be kissed, but kept her in his arms so that Keeley was unable to hug and cuddle her god-daughter as she wanted to, longed to. But she wasn't leaving without that.

'Come on, hand her over for a proper kiss!'

He had to then, and she snuggled Mel close to her, savouring the baby fragrance, the sweet softness.

'Bye bye baby . . . oh, you're so gorgeous! I tell you what, why don't I put you in my bag and take you home to France with me? Would Mel like to come and live with Auntie Keeley?'

It was the kind of silly thing people said at airports, but Cathal was having none of it. Reaching out, he took the child back.

'Now Keeley, you should at least know your god-daughter's name. Mel is a boy's name.'

She opened her mouth to say she was only joking, there was no need to be so stiff, but before she could draw breath Mary was kissing her instead, enveloping her in a tight but brief hug.

'Goodbye, Keel . . . write to me soon. And you too, Vincent.'

Now that *was* silly, Keeley thought, Mary hardly expected Vincent to write to her. But Mary was clearly treating them as a couple, they were all saying goodbye as one couple to another.

Vincent produced the boarding passes, and they parted with final smiles all round, without a single tear being shed between them.

Keeley was much quieter on the flight home than on the outward one, and Vincent knew she was mulling over whatever she imagined was wrong between herself and Mary. He thought Mary had been perfectly pleasant and happy, Cathal too for that matter, but if Keeley thought otherwise then he would listen to whatever she had to say. She was not in the habit of imagining or exaggerating problems, and he was sorry to see her in such unusually low spirits.

'Penny for them?'

'Oh . . . I was just thinking what a pity it was we didn't get to talk more about our wedding. There are a few details I'd have liked to have talked about to Mary.'

Well, that was true. The visit had centred almost exclusively around the Sullivans. But then it was their christening, their weekend. He patted her hand.

'Never mind. At least you got to see her, and the baby.'

'Yes.'

Then, thinking that she might be a bit more enthusiastic about a trip that had cost Vincent the money he'd wanted to spend on her engagement ring, Keeley made herself smile.

'It was a great party, I did enjoy it – and so did you, didn't you?'

'Yes. Very much. I was glad to meet your mother and brother, too.'

'Were you? Even thought they're – well, a bit depressing?'

'I didn't think they were. Tony was much more cheerful than I expected.'

'Yes, he was, wasn't he? He seems to be improving. I'm going to start writing to him . . . you know, I used to be so angry with him for getting into such a stupid mess, for the other people he could have got into it too. But if he can make an effort then so can I, start looking forwards instead of back.'

'Mm. Imagine trying to paint with your mouth. I can't imagine how he does it. But I liked his paintings.'

That made her laugh. 'Oh, come on, you don't have to pretend to me!'

'But I did. Well – not all, obviously the first ones were pretty awful. But they seemed to get better as we went through them . . . I thought that blue and grey one had something about it, I don't know what . . . it made me want to keep looking at it.'

'You must be a real glutton for punishment. I thought it was like something a cat would do.'

'Well, at least he's trying.'

'Yes. That's why I wanted to encourage him, and was so delighted you asked him to do us one. We don't have to hang it up when it comes, but we'll tell him we did. It's the first time I've ever known him to make an effort at anything.'

'Better late than never.'

'Mm.' Keeley had to agree with that, but still she found herself thinking about Tony's empty, frustrated future. The future that Mary had chosen, too, that seemed so full and busy and bright by comparison. Nothing dark, nothing grey in hers, as she said herself, some people might even say she had it all. Cathal thought so, Mary's parents clearly thought so judging by the smiles they'd had on their faces all day yesterday, lots of the guests had even remarked on how well she was looking, how devoted Cathal was to her and the baby, what a lovely flat they had, what a fine couple they made.

But as the plane began its descent into Nice airport, Keeley was conscious of some weight lifting from her, an inexplicable feeling of escape and relief, gratitude for Vincent and for her carefree home in Aix-en-Provence, for the sun that was shining and the life that was waiting. Turning to Vincent, she gave him a little hug.

Chapter Eight

The summer weeks that followed were warm and light as gossamer, and despite the long shadow she sometimes felt stretching over them all the way from Ireland, Keeley revelled in the days that were not only hot and bright but free; Eliane had closed the salon for the annual August holiday and the rest of the month was her own. Vincent had time off too, and they spent every possible moment together, sweating as they cycled several times to see the haunting house near Puyloubier again. Keeley couldn't explain why it had so caught her imagination, nor could Vincent say why it was beginning to catch his, and so they puffed their way up the hill in silence to stand looking at it, sometimes circling it cautiously, sometimes held at bay by the sound of voices, not daring to go close enough to see the people who lived there. Other times they cycled into Rognes or one of the other villages instead, sweating, dropping their bikes at pavement cafés to sit for hours slowly sipping beer, watching the world go by, planning the walks they took when Sylvie wanted her bike for cycles of her own.

On those days they wandered up into the parched silvery hills, hand in hand, following the shade of olive groves, listening to the crickets whirring in the dusty silence. Chatty as she normally was, Keeley felt the silence falling on her, and was quiet on these walks, discovering for the first time that she didn't need to keep talking to Vincent to communicate with him. Often they brought a picnic in their rucksacks, and simply lay on the grass under a tree, savouring the still peace, eating slowly, brushing lazily at the murmuring insects. More than once she found herself thinking of the first excursion she had ever made to the countryside, with Mary to Powerscourt waterfall, and then she thought of their hot happy days picking grapes at Château Lazouin . . . a whole year ago, now. So much had happened since then that it seemed even longer, a view seen from a distance.

Occasionally they took evening meals with Vincent's parents in their garden, which glowed and drowsed with the accumulated warmth of the day. It was a small but very pretty garden, enclosed behind stone walls thick with clematis and honeysuckle, and gradually Keeley grew to love it. Not that she knew the first thing about gardens or gardening – she could barely tell a rose from a lavender bush – but she thought Pierre and Francine's little oasis incredibly luxurious. The greenery was so thick it was like a secret hideaway, scented with flowers and herbs, drenched in cascading geraniums. Near the house there was a wooden table and chairs, with a white parasol tilted over them, where they sat for hours picking at salads and cheeses, vaguely planning the winter wedding that felt a long way off, sipping at glasses of cold white wine. Never having had a garden in which to sit in Ireland, and having none at the flat either, she savoured this one like a child tasting chocolate for the first time. Sensing her pleasure, Francine took her on little tours of it, explaining a corner here and a corner there, how some things needed shade while others flourished in the sun, thinking that Keeley was like a cutting taking root herself. One day she gave her a present of some pots and compost and a trowel, together with a bundle of green knobbly shoots to plant and some iron hooks from which to hang the pots, on the rail that ran across the flat's long window. Vincent laughed, certain that Keeley would forget to water them and they would die, but she hosed them down with the vigour of a fireman every night, and within weeks the window was a riot of pink blossom. It was then that she began to think of the home she and Vincent would share some day, and to hope that it would have a garden. Just a little one, enough for peace and privacy, colour and quiet, the sense of serenity she had never known before.

Meanwhile there was her driving test to think of, and she used the holiday time to practise with fierce concentration, unable to believe that she had already passed her French test at the Chamber of Commerce and might soon pass this one also. Two tests, in one year! They would die laughing in Pearse Gardens, where the sight of Keeley Butler driving a car would be akin to the sight of a monkey steering an elephant down the street. But her modest success at the Chamber of Commerce encouraged her, even though she knew the simple exam only verified that she could speak French as well as an average five-year old. Still, that was enough for everyday conversation, and she had signed up for a more advanced course starting in September. But her driving licence was one piece of paper she couldn't wait to get, and so she went for long spins with Vincent, down as far as Marseille or Sausset-les-Pins where they could swim, as a reward, in the warm blue Mediterranean. Not that she could swim, in the beginning, but she splashed and floundered, clinging to Vincent until, one day, she realised that he had taken his hands from under her, and she was afloat.

Neither of them wanted to return to work, but gradually August faded into September, and they had to, taking leave of the happiest summer of their lives. The salon was busy after the holidays, with customers lamenting the state of their sun and salt-ravaged hair, and Keeley couldn't believe how cranky they were as they told their tales of fabulous foreign travel. Many had been to French outposts she had never heard of – Guadeloupe and Corsica were especially popular – while others had visited Algeria, Tunisia, all sorts of exotic destinations.

She nodded and smiled as she repaired their hair, but often she thought she'd like to smack them; had they no idea how lucky they were? The idea of going to such places amazed her, but they complained of heat fatigue, insects and inedible food. Crikey, she thought, you'd want to try Christy Butler's junkyard, with its tyres and tin cans, for your summer siesta. The one foreign holiday I ever took in my life, I picked grapes until my muscles were like a girl guide's plaits. I worked till I dropped, but I loved every minute of it. Cheer up and stop whinging before I take a razor to your thick skulls and shave you bald. Then you'll have something to whinge about.

It was a good thing, she thought, that she had her evenings with Vincent to look forward to. At least he was cheerful, always arrived with a smile on his face, didn't go on about his problems although she knew he was having some. After eighteen months as a trainee, there was still no word of a permanent job, a store of his own to run or even a post as assistant manager somewhere. He didn't expect it to be in Aix, he said, where Alain had long run the store, but he had made it clear that he was willing to travel if anything came up remotely within commuting distance. Failing that – well, if he got sent to somewhere on the other side of the country, would Keeley mind very much? It would mean having to leave Eliane and find work in a new city, maybe even somewhere cold and glum like Calais or Le Havre, but it was a prospect they'd have to think about.

Keeley hated the thought of leaving Eliane's salon, and hated the thought of leaving the lovely city of Aix, where she had made friends and put down roots, basked in the warm climate. But she didn't say that.

Instead she smiled and said yes, he wasn't to worry, she'd happily go with him to Antarctica or wherever they wanted to send him. He smiled and kissed her, his relief so visible it was worth it, but she knew he didn't want to leave Aix any more than she did, and wondered whether they would learn to love somewhere cold and ugly. Now that she had had a taste of sunshine and gardens and beaches, wide bright boulevards and sun-baked countryside, it would be an awful wrench to leave. Besides there were his parents, of whom she'd become very fond, and Sylvie his sister, the friends she'd made at the Chamber of Commerce, Luc and Félix whom she often visited to say hello, bring news of Mary and discuss the wedding meal. Lots of ties, some loose and fragile, some already stronger than she realised, binding her to Aix as Vincent was bound. It was his home, he had close friends, deep roots, a warm family here.

He said he would talk to Alain, push his case a bit and explain that, since he was getting married, he needed to know where he was going to be working and living. There was no point in them looking for a flat to rent together if they were going to have to leave it almost as soon as they found it. Listening to him, Keeley realised that he was beginning to worry about the problem, had maybe been secretly worrying it for a while, and embraced him tenderly. Don't panic, she said, the main thing is that we're together and we'll have work somewhere, isn't it a lucky thing there are so many stores to be managed and that hair stylists can style anywhere? If we do get sent somewhere horrible, well, it won't be forever, you can always apply for a transfer later. As for me, all I need is a pair of scissors.

That cheered him up for a while, and they lived in hope through September, October and early November, until the day he finally came home with some news.

'Good or bad?' she said, reaching for a bottle of wine. They'd either want to celebrate, or drown their sorrows . . . but her heart lurched a little as she opened it. He really didn't want to move, and neither did she.

'Well' he said slowly, 'that depends how you look at it.'

'We'll look on the bright side.'

He smiled as she gave him a glass and sat down beside him, pausing to put her arm briefly around his shoulder, to let him know she was with him come what may. Running his hand through his hair, he looked at her with his hazel eyes full of apprehension.

'The good news is that Alain says a vacancy may come up at the end of next year – not here in Aix, but in Marseille, near enough that I could commute. The manager there is due to retire.'

'Oh – well, that's good news! Even if it does mean waiting a year, it's something to look forward to.'

'Yes. But the bad news is that they want me to travel in the meantime, to do a series of *stages* in different branches in different cities.'

'*Stages*? What are they?'

'They're short courses. The idea is that I should get an overview of how the whole company operates by visiting as many of its outlets as possible, spending six weeks in each. Alain wants me to start with Grenoble in January, then Lyon, Orléans, Paris, Rouen . . . I'll be away nearly all the time, Keeley.'

She felt her stomach curl and clench, start to fight it instantly. She couldn't bear to be separated from him for six weeks at a time, constantly, for a whole year. She loved him, wanted desperately to be with him, would rather chuck her job and go with him than be parted from him . . . but then, how would they live? Until he was secure in a permanent post he would continue, he said, to earn very little.

'Would it mean extra money, to compensate for being away?'

'No. They'd pay for my accommodation and travel expenses, but it doesn't mean any rise in take-home pay. Oh, Keeley . . . I don't want to go, don't want to leave you here on your own. But there doesn't seem to be any choice.'

She thought for a few moments, twirling her glass, looking at him in a way she hoped he found supportive.

'No . . . there doesn't seem to be, love. If I left Eliane and went with you, I wouldn't be sure of finding work for such short periods everywhere we went, and hotel expenses would eat up every penny anyway.'

'Yes. There's a chain of hotels the company uses, where I'll be expected to stay, but the allowance doesn't cover spouses.'

For a little while they sat together in silence, thinking about it, trying to come up with alternatives. Then, to his surprise, she smiled. 'Look. I presume you've made whatever arguments you could to Alain, explained about my job, about wanting to stay in Provence and all that?'

'Yes. He said he was sorry, it wasn't his decision, it was head office in Paris. They call the shots, not local managers.'

'OK. Then we've got six weeks, to try to come up with an alternative.'

'Such as?'

'Search me. Maybe you could change companies?'

'I would, if I could find another job, here in Aix or nearby, I'd take it. I've already done my military service, I'm sick of being shunted around, it's not fair to expect someone to spend a year wandering all over France when they've only just got married. I love you so much, Keeley . . . it would kill me to think of you here by yourself when we should be together, you're entitled to enjoy being a newly-wed and setting up home. Just when we're on the verge of getting one and having a double bed and all, at last!'

She laughed. 'We will have one, if you set your mind to it and I set mine, we can figure out something. You start looking for other jobs, and I'll start thinking. I'll even enjoy it. It will be a novelty.'

He had to laugh in turn, and love her all the more for the way she was taking it, being cheerful and optimistic when that was what he needed her to be. Next year looked like being bleak, work-wise, but marriage looked like being wonderful.

'Dear Keeley,

I'm sorry I haven't written for ages, you must have been wondering what kind of awful person I've turned into, but I hope you'll forgive me because I feel terrible about it, it's just that I've been so busy.

Thank you a million times for the card you and Vincent sent on the day the pub started serving hot meals, it was so sweet of you to remember the date. Things got off to a good start and we're really busy already, after only two months . . . of course not everything was perfect at first, the customers didn't like everything I'd put on the menu, so now I've changed a few things and they're much happier. Cathal is too, he said it was silly not to be giving people spuds and bacon when that was what they wanted, so now the quiche and salads are gone, a few other things too, we're serving what he calls "a good feed"! I keep forgetting that the climate is different here and a lot of the French things don't really work – anyway, the ingredients were sometimes hard to get, so as Cathal says things are easier all round now, for me and the customers. I don't even have to make sauces, which are tricky and time-consuming, everyone says they prefer ketchup or brown out of a bottle so that's another thing out of the way.

I've been thinking about you a lot. I really hope you didn't take offence when I gave out to you that time, it was only that I was tired and had a new baby and everything . . . Mel is beautiful now, I wish you could see her, all the wrinkles are ironed out and she's all smiles. Of course I'm up a lot at night with her, but as Cathal says that won't last for ever, I'll soon be able to get a proper night's sleep.

You and Vincent must be all excited, looking forward to your wedding. That's what I'm writing about, actually . . . Keeley, I hope you're going to understand and not be too angry, but I have something awful to tell you. I'm afraid I'm not going to be able to be your bridesmaid. In fact none of us will be able to come. It's just that Cathal is so busy and I am too, you can imagine, a pub is a seven-day-a-week business and we simply can't take the time off. Please don't be too upset? I know it's a let-down and now you'll have to ask someone else at short notice, but maybe Sylvie would do it – I feel terrible about it, I really do, but Cathal says there's no choice if we want to keep our customers, we just have to be here all the time.

Isn't it unbelievable, each of us missing the other's wedding!

But I'll be thinking about you all day on December 20, wishing you so much luck and happiness, Vincent too. You should have heard the way everyone was talking about him after you left, saying how gorgeous he was. Anyway, at least you got over here and were able to be godparents to Mel, that meant an awful lot to me. To us both. I'm enclosing some of the photos that were taken that day, doesn't everyone look great? We're getting them framed, Cathal says we should have a proper album for Mel when she grows up. You should hear him, he dotes on her, is always telling people what a gorgeous daughter he has.

Keeley, I have another favour to ask you. I feel terrible

about it, but – I'm sorry, I can't explain, not yet anyway. Some day I will. For now, I was just wondering if if you'd mind not writing to me for a while? I don't mean postcards, I'd love you to send lots of those like you used to, I just mean anything personal.

You must think that sounds very peculiar, and I suppose it is in a way, but the truth is that – that Cathal is always first up in the mornings, he goes through all the post and I wouldn't like him to come across any, you know, girl talk. I know you'd never say anything dreadful anyway, but you did ask some strange questions when you were here and I don't want him to think you – oh, God, Keeley. I can't explain. I just can't. Will you take my word for it that it's best for the moment, and that I'll sort it out as soon as I can? The last thing I want is for you to stop writing, you can't imagine how much I look forward to it and I want you to keep it up, please don't let's lose touch, sometimes I think you're the only person who knows, who remembers . . .

I'm sorry, Keeley, I'm talking garbage and don't really know what I'm saying. The main thing is that I hope Sylvie can be your bridesmaid and that I haven't messed things up too much. That's all I ever seem to do these days, Cathal says I should go to Mount Argus to get myself blessed.

Have a fabulous wedding and a long happy life together. Mel sends you thousands of kisses and says she's very sorry she can't come to see her Auntie Keeley and Uncle Vincent geting married. She loves you and I love you and we both hug you to pieces.

XXX, Mary.'

'In a nutshell?'

'Yes, please. In a nutshell, Keeley. Leave out everything you're reading between the lines and simply tell me the facts as Mary states them.'

Keeley wiped her face with the back of her sleeve and stood leaning against the kitchen sink, facing Vincent with 'the facts' in her hand.

'She's not going to be my bridesmaid. None of them is coming to our wedding. She's taken her favourite things off the menu and is now serving spuds with brown sauce and not a word of protest. She's working round the clock and Cathal isn't even helping with Mel's night feeds. She's calling the baby Mel in her letter, even though she calls her Imelda when Cathal's listening.

She's making such a mess of everything that Cathal says she should get herself blessed. Cathal says this, that and the other. It's like she – she's being brainwashed! She doesn't even want me to write to her in case he reads my letters – apparently he reads everything. Vincent, Mary is absolutely, totally, utterly miserable. She is married to some kind of weirdo and if you ask me she's starting to lose her marbles, her letter is all rambling blather as if—'

'As if what?'

'I don't know. As if Cathal were dictating it or something, though admittedly he can't have been. But it feels as if he's reading over her shoulder, she sounds like a puppet on a string and – and I'm not having this! I'm just not letting him control her like this! She promised a whole year ago to be my bridesmaid, even if bloody Cathal won't come she could come by herself, or with Mel, fly over one day and back the next, it's only two days. I'm going to ring and make her.'

'But Keeley—'

'No, Vincent! You persuaded me not to warn her against marrying Cathal, said I shouldn't judge him the way people judge me. But I should have done, should have written and said what I thought. I shut up then, but I'm not shutting up now. I'm going to call her this minute – in fact, even better, I'm going to call him. Would you mind emptying your pockets and giving me all your change, because it might be a long call.'

Bewildered and incredulous, Vincent stared at her, and she stared him down until he found himself emptying his pockets as requested, handing her a fistful of coins. Without another word, she found her coat, put it on and went out into the night, banging the door behind her, not even suggesting that he should come with her.

Out in the street Keeley didn't even notice the cold or dark as she strode to the coinbox on the square, opposite the Vieux Moulin. Yanking open the door, she stood thinking and resolving for a moment, then inserted her mountain of money and dialled the number.

There was a long interval before the ringing phone was answered, by a barman she guessed, shouting over what sounded like a rowdy evening at The Lantern. Shouting back, she asked him to find Mr Sullivan.

'Yeah, just a moment, I'm not sure if he's here—'

But he's always there, she thought, he's married to that pub, never leaves its side for a second. Just get him and be quick about it.'

Eventually there was some banging and thumping as the dangling phone was picked up.

'Hello?'

'Cathal?'

'Yes? Who is this?'

'It's Keeley. Keeley Butler, in France. I'm ringing because I've just had a letter from Mary, saying she's too busy to come to my wedding. As you can imagine I'm pretty upset, Cathal, about losing my bridesmaid, not to mention a chance to see my god-daughter. So I decided to ring you, because I know you'll be able to change her mind, to make her understand that it's only a very short break and that she'll burn herself out if she works too hard.'

'What?'

'Make her come, Cathal, to my wedding! I know she'll listen to you. I mean you've got plenty of money and everything, I'm sure it's not a question of the fare being too dear, is it?'

'N-no. Certainly not.'

'Well then. Besides, she's to bring Tony's painting with her. He's doing it specially for our wedding, he'll be so disappointed, I'm sure his physiotherapist will think it's terrible—'

'Dear me, Keeley. I can't imagine what put such a thing into Mary's head. You're right, she must be working too hard. I'm sorry I can't get away myself, you know how busy The Lantern is at Christmas, but I'll see to it that Mary does. Consider it done.'

'That's great. I know you'll make her see sense. And you will make sure she brings the baby too, won't you?'

'Well, Imelda is a little young—'

'Cathal, I want her at my wedding. Besides, you'll be far too busy to mind her while Mary's away. It will be much easier for you this way.'

There was a pause before he replied, in a voice soft and warm as honey. 'Yes, of course, Keeley, you're quite right. I'll book their flight tomorrow, myself. You must forgive Mary for upsetting you, she's not herself at all at the moment – these new mums, so fussy about every little thing! But sure you'll understand when you have a child yourself.'

'I'm sure I will. Meanwhile, thank you very much, and please tell Mary I'm looking forward to seeing her on the 20th, Vincent or I will meet her at the airport – did I tell you I've just passed my driving test?'

'Have you now? Well, isn't that great. Congratulations.'

'Thank you. I'm sorry I have to go now, the coins are running out, but it's great to hear that Mary is going to be my bridesmaid after all. Goodbye, Cathal.'

'G-goodbye, Keeley. Regards to Vincent.'

Yeah, right, she muttered as she hung up. Regards to Vincent, regards to me and your customers and the whole human race, you charming smarmy little shit. I hope that put the wind up you, Cathal Sullivan, now you know there's one person who'll stand up for herself and stand up for Mary too. I don't know what you're playing at, but whatever it is I don't like it, and what's more I know your weak point. You don't ever want anyone to talk ill of you, to say you're a mean miserable bully, you want the whole world to think the sun shines out of your ass. You're covering up for something, with your charm and your champagne, and even if I don't know yet what it is, you know now that I'm on to you. You're trying to control Mary somehow, but you're not going to. No way, buster. We're not having a second Christy in this family.

Everyone kept asking her whether she was nervous as the last weeks before her marriage elapsed, and Keeley was surprised to find herself saying no, she wasn't. Sometimes she thought she should be, thought briefly of asking Sylvie whether there were any terrible childhood secrets she should know about her brother, but the thought went as quickly as it came. It would look as if she didn't trust Vincent; but she did trust him, and trusted her own instincts. In all her life she had never felt so happy or so secure, so much in tune with another human being. In many ways she and Vincent were very different – certainly he was quieter, calmer, more patient than she was – but when she was with him she felt they slotted together like the two halves of a puzzle, felt somehow complete, and serene. Unlike other brides-to-be she wasn't keyed up about her wedding day, thought far more about what life would be like afterwards than she thought about clothes or guests or food or music. After their trip to Ireland they couldn't afford a honeymoon, but it didn't seem to matter. They lived in a beautiful place anyway, and there would be the thrill of moving in properly together, living together as husband and wife. Agreeably, Sylvie had offered to move out and simply leave them to share the flat; she was going to move back in with her parents, she said, because then she could save for the cycling trip she wanted to make in a year's time, a big adventure with some friends who were going to bike down through Europe to Greece and across to Turkey, on into Syria, Jordan, North Africa . . . Keeley was very impressed by this exciting agenda, but not at all envious. Maybe some day, if they were lucky and worked their butts off, she and Vincent would get to see a bit of the world; but for now their own private world was wonder enough.

The only thing that stood between them and complete happiness was the prospect of Vincent's *stages*, of being constantly separated for a whole year – the first year, that they so badly wanted to spend together. Neither of them had yet been able to think of any way round or out of it, and sometimes it was a struggle not to let Vincent see how unhappy it made her. But she thought he sensed it despite her determined efforts to stay cheerful; one evening he had come to pick her up from work and brought her a little present, a book of Paul Cézanne's paintings. In it she found the sketch of the house near Puyloubier, as well as many other places that came alive as she looked at them, not only because of their vivid colour but because they were near, real places in the area. He had to translate the notes on each picture for her, because she didn't yet read French nearly as well as she spoke it, but the book made her smile. Paintings, no less! That really would be the end, in Pearse Gardens, they'd say Keeley Butler had gone completely round the bend.

But soon, she would be Keeley Tourand. One day, she popped out during her lunch hour and bought the wedding outfit she'd seen weeks before, delighted to find it hadn't been sold while she saved for it. Not that it was expensive, by other women's standards, but what it lacked in elegance it made up in pzazz. A long white jacket with a short white skirt, both shot with a flash of amber round the hem and – the best bit – an outrageous hat in crushed amber velvet, tall, with a cheeky brim. Eliane laughed when she brought it back and showed it to her.

'Ah, if only I were young and starting out, like you!'

Keeley grinned. 'Oh, Eliane, you're not old.'

'I am forty-nine, Keeley. Sometimes I feel a hundred and forty nine. I have been working since I was seventeen, on my own without any help, and although my salon has served me well it has also made me very tired. Thirty-two years of hairdressing, I tell you, it takes its toll.'

'Well, you're not to be tired at my wedding. You're to have lots of fun and dance all day.'

'I will have fun. But I don't know about the dancing. Roger has very bad angina, you know, he has to take it easy and I have to look after him.'

One of the girls had told Keeley this before, that Eliane's husband wasn't well and that she worried about him. His health had forced him to take early retirement from his job as a tile fitter, and for nearly six years Eliane had been the sole breadwinner. It must, she thought, be hard going sometimes, and a worry right enough.

'OK. We won't make Roger dance. But we'll make you. I'll teach you the Walls of Limerick!'

They laughed again as Keeley pirouetted round in the hat, but after the lunch break the salon got busy, and Keeley found herself thinking about Eliane and Roger as she worked. Eliane must have been a blushing bride once, must have had a happy wedding day as she hoped she and Vincent would have, but now she was keeping the promise she had made that day, to cherish her husband 'in sickness or in health.' It was a weighty undertaking, one that made Keeley think seriously about the vows that she was about to make, the life that could evolve after the rose petals had faded and the music had stopped.

Of course that was the whole point of getting married; that you would take care of your partner, and they of you, come hell or high water. That was what her own mother Gertie did, despite the hellish life Christy led her she stuck with him, for better or for worse. For the first time she began to see her mother's commitment in a new light, wondered if there was more to it than mere dogged martyrdom, or lack of any alternative. But then, if Gertie was honouring her wedding vows, so should Christy. So should bloody Christy.

And Mary? What mess had Mary got into, why would she not talk about it, only keep smiling that glazed smile? Well, it was early days for Mary, she'd only been married six months, but still . . . she was going to *make* her talk, this time, when she got her hands on her. Cathal wouldn't be there, the pressure would be off, she'd find some tactful way to go about it. God, she thought, what if Vincent turned out to be strange like Cathal, or a pig like Christy, or got sick like Roger!

Well, you couldn't blame anyone for being ill. That was a different thing, involuntary. She was even starting to feel some sympathy for Tony. If anything ever did happen to Vincent – horror – she would love him just the same. But if the marriage went wrong, turned sour . . . ? She couldn't imagine how anyone could stand being shackled for life to someone who treated them badly, didn't love, didn't care, didn't try.

It's a risk, she conceded. It is a risk. But I absolutely do love Vincent and feel sure he loves me – not just in bed where any fool can say it, or on the beach, out on the bikes when we're having fun – but in a real way. A strong way, that will carry us through our whole life together.

And finally the day dawned. Keeley woke up with a burst of absolute joy, thinking of Vincent, hardly able to wait to see him, touch him, marry him. Leaping out of bed, she bounded to the window and looked out on a bright clear morning, faintly twinkling with frost, white and blue and pure. Oh yes, she thought, yes, I do take this man to be my lawfully wedded husband, he is the only man, this is the only life for me!

Flinging on a robe, she went into the kitchen where Sylvie was already brewing coffee, up early for the first time ever. There was much giggling as they talked of Vincent, the ceremony, the newly-wedded life, and only intermittently did she feel a little pang. There was no denying that it was sad to get married without a single member of your own family being there; but Gertie had written to say she couldn't leave Tony, implied that the notion of flying to France and coping with so many foreigners was too much for her. Keeley tried to accept it, but still she thought of her mother, of her brother and even of her father, wishing it could all be different.

But there was no time to brood. The ceremony was at two o'clock, and before she started to dress and prepare for it she had to get to the airport to collect Mary and Mel. Vincent was coming with the car, but she was going to drive, dying to prove that she could. Vincent's father had insured her, temporarily, on the plan that also covered Vincent, and she was very grateful to him. As future in-laws, Pierre and Francine were fantastic, doing everything they could to help, and so was Sylvie, insisting now that she should at least eat a croissant.

'Oh, Sylvie, I can't, I'm too excited!'

Breathlessly she showered and dressed, leaving Sylvie to take

charge of the clothes they would both change into later, and
hopped with impatience until she heard the car, flung open the
window and shouted to Vincent not to bother coming up, she
was on her way down. When she got there she yanked open the
door, and they exchanged passionate kisses before she made him
get out and go round to the passenger side, leaving the engine
running for her to take over.

'Check your mirror!' he screeched as she shot out into the
traffic, narrowly missing a bus. That gave her such a fright she
calmed down until they were safely out onto the autoroute, and
her speed crept up again; she loved the feeling of confidence and
ability that driving gave her, and she was dying to see Mary.

The flight's arrival was announced on time, and she stood
clutching Vincent until the familiar face appeared amongst the
throng of incoming passengers: Mary, carrying Mel in her arms,
smiling a real smile this time. A huge smile, full of the old
affection, and delight.

'Keeley! Vincent!' Falling into each other's arms, they all
kissed and hugged, passing Mel between them for inspection
and admiration, exclaiming over her weight, her sunny smile,
her amazing growth.

'Oh, Mary, I'm so thrilled you made it after all – I was afraid
you wouldn't, right up to the last moment.'

Mary grimaced as they piled into the car, with just a flicker
of embarrassment.

'Oh, it was a dead cert after you rang Cathal. He insisted I
come, that I bring Mel and the painting, get a gorgeous outfit
and enjoy myself. He chose your wedding present himself, too
– wait till you see what it is.'

Vincent still maintained that Keeley had been very rash to
ring Cathal, but she was glad she had, because now here was
someone from home after all, the friend who was next best to
family, the person she most wanted to be with her today. And
what a comfort it was, to see Mary looking so animated this
time, as if – as if she had escaped from whatever had held her
back at Mel's christening. Full of pleasure in each other, they
talked non-stop all the way back to Aix, and Mary drew in her
breath when they pulled up outside the flat.

'Oh, my God, I can hardly believe it . . . is this really our old
place, where I used to live?'

'It sure is, come on, come in, here, give Mel to me, Vincent
will take your luggage.'

Up the stairs they went, into the tiny apartment that had been Mary's first home. In wonder she stood staring around her, drinking in every detail, unconscious of the contrast she made. The flat had hardly changed, was no bigger or grander than it had ever been, but she was – was dressed to impress, Keeley thought, elegant, co-ordinated, her camel hair coat not even creased after the flight. Mary was a woman these days, not a girl, not remotely like the person who'd washed dishes and flung ruined quiches in bins, fainted and panicked and been pregnant. Now, there was a note of control about her, something sleek and shiny, something that made Keeley realise for the first time how small and spartan the flat was.

'As you can see, there's still no sofa, and the kitchen chairs are still rickety! But we're going to stay here for the time being, until Vincent's more sure about his job. Mary, you remember his sister Sylvie?'

Sylvie was her friendly self, all airy smiles as she offered Mary coffee and cooed, in fractured English, over Mel. Vincent had a quick coffee with them, but then stood up.

'I'd better go home and start getting organised.' He headed for the door, but stopped to whirl round and grab Keeley, crush her to him in a vast hug. 'In two hours, we will be married, you will be my wife! I cannot believe it!'

Mary watched as they embraced, and gathered Mel to her. 'Look at that, cherub! See how your godparents love each other!'

Keeley flushed as she gave Vincent a final squeeze and let him go. 'Well, we do, what's wrong with showing it . . . I'm absolutely mad about him, Mary. Stone mad.'

'Yes. I know you are. You're made for each other. It's been a long engagement, but now . . . I want you to be really happy with him, Keeley. Insanely happy.'

'We already are. We—'

But she bit her lip, and stopped. Something in Mary's face held her back from saying any more about Vincent's many merits, about how besotted they were with each other.

'Come on. I don't mean to rush you, but we have a wedding to go to. Let's get ready for it, and talk later.'

And what a wedding it was, Keeley thought several hours later, as she stood up at the Vieux Moulin's top table and her new husband clasped her hand, kissing her as they plunged the knife into the cake that Luc had made with such care and thought and talent. Mary had wept when she saw him; there had been an extremely emotional reunion, cries of joy when the secret venue was discovered. Félix was waiting at the door to welcome the wedding party, and Mary sobbed over him too, grasping him so tight that his glasses fogged up. Keeley grinned as he turned desperately to his wife Lise, whose hair she often styled, to plead that contrary to appearances no, he had not been having a steamy affair with this Irishwoman.

Now, Félix was sitting between Lise and Mary, cheering as the cake was cut and Luc emerged from the kitchen, still in his whites, to nod satisfied over the success of the meal. For Mary's friend Keeley he had pulled out all the stops, thrown in all the extras to magic up a banquet far in excess of anything that had been requested or expected. Keeley herself was at a loss to identify half of the delectable dishes, giggling as she confessed her ignorance in a whisper; Vincent's boss Alain was further down the table and doubtless thought that, as an expert on Paul Cézanne, she was an expert on Provençal food too. Like Luc, she felt a need to mop her face, which was blazing like a furnace.

But then Vincent's father stood up to make a speech, a lovely warm speech welcoming her to the family. To her amazement she understood every word of it, and was even able to joke in return about not needing that big dictionary her in-laws had produced for a wedding present. Everyone laughed, having seen the real present, an envelope containing a voucher for a weekend at the criminally luxurious hotel George V in Paris. A honeymoon, after all. Deeply touched, Keeley laughed through her tears; God only knew what they'd make of her at the George V.

But the honeymoon was to be deferred until after Christmas, and secretly she was glad, not wanting to dash away until after she'd recovered from today's excitement, and had a chance to talk to Mary. As the music started and Vincent led her up to dance, she beamed at him, immensely enjoying the party, so deeply in love she felt almost unworthy. Never, in a million years, had she expected her life to turn out like this.

Mary turned to Félix.

'Doesn't she look beautiful?'

'Exquisite. Never have I seen such a radiant bride. Luc and I were greatly honoured that she decided to hold her reception here.'

'Yes . . . you know, Félix, she did it for me. She wanted to surprise me, bring me back to see all my old friends. I've missed you terribly, you and Luc.'

Surprised, he looked at her. 'Have you, Mary? But what of your own new husband, and child, and restaurant?'

'Oh, it's not a real restaurant. It's a pub that serves hot food, that's all. Nothing like the Vieux Moulin.'

'But it is going well, it is a start?'

'Oh yes, it's a – Luc, come over here and sit down with us!'

Turning from him, she busied herself with the chair Keeley had occupied beside her, pushing it forward as Luc made his way to where they sat, removing his toque to let his bushy white hair spring free. Puffing and sweating, he collapsed onto it.

'Phew. Now I can relax. I didn't dare until the meal was over.'

'Oh, Luc! Don't fib, I know you always have everything under control!'

'Still, you never know . . . those dolts in the kitchen, Mary, it's a wonder none of them has burned the place to the ground. I never found a replacement who could hold a candle to you.'

She felt her face prickle, heard the twinge in her voice. 'I was just saying to Félix how much I've missed you. You have no idea how much.'

Pleased and flattered, he smiled at her. 'Oh, we know you never think of us any more, now you are a chef with a kitchen of your own—'

Reaching for a glass of champagne, he was so stunned by the sudden vehemence of her next words that he knocked it over.

'No! I am not a chef! I am a cook, a galley slave, a jobbing servant, anything but a chef!'

Félix gasped, Luc gazed at her flummoxed.

'What?'

'I said—,' pausing, she reached for a bottle as icy cold as her voice, refilled Luc's glass and then her own, '—that I am a servant, a slave. A slinger of hash. Everything you two ever taught me, about cooking and running a restaurant, has been completely wasted.'

Slugging back the contents of her glass in a single gulp, she thumped it down on the table as they gazed at each other, horrified. After a long frozen pause, Félix adjusted his silk tie.

'But Mary – we thought – Keeley said—'

She turned to look at Keeley, dancing with her arms around Vincent on the other side of the room, a distant study of happiness.

'Keeley said I was a chef? Well, *mes amis*, much as I love Keeley, I have to tell you that she wouldn't know the difference between a chef and a ditch-digger. To her, anyone who cooks is a chef. And I certainly do cook. I cook burgers, and frozen peas, and chips for people to dip into their ketchup. That, Luc, is what I do these days. So much for truffles and vinaigrettes and noisettes.'

Such was the sudden harshness in her voice, the metallic gleam in her eyes, they leaned back as if she had flung scalding oil at them. Stretching across, she grabbed the champagne bottle again and poured by the neck, spilling froth on the tablecloth as she stared at them, her face hectic with colour.

'Perhaps Keeley thought it better not to tell you. Perhaps she didn't fully grasp the situation. But the reality is that – that – I—'

Breathless, they waited for her to tell them what it was. Instead, she raised her glass, gazed into it for a moment, and then flung it with all her force on the floor. Bursting into tears, she hurled back her chair and stormed away.

Keeley thought she heard a small crash somewhere over the music, and shrugged; someone must have dropped a glass. In Ireland, the first broken glass always raised a laugh, signalled that the fun was beginning in earnest. Paying no attention, she snuggled into Vincent, her cheek on his chest, dancing on air until she felt a tug at her sleeve. Opening her eyes, she found Félix.

'Keeley. I am so sorry to disturb you, but—'

Manfully, Vincent intervened. 'What is it, Félix? Can I help?'

'No, Monsieur Vincent, I think it would be better if – Keeley – ah – her matron of honour would like to see her for a moment.'

That, Félix thought, was the most polite way of putting it. Less alarming than the truth, which was that Keeley's matron of honour was sitting on the floor of the ladies' room howling like a lunatic, rocking back and forth with her hands clasped round her knees, telling everyone who came near her to fuck off. Instead of quietening down the howls were getting louder, and he was at his wits' end.

Keeley frowned. Where was Mary? She'd been sitting with Luc and Félix only a few minutes ago, getting happily reac-quainted over a bottle of champagne by the looks of it, but now there was no sign of her. Reluctantly directing Vincent to dance with his mother, she left him, her fingers trailing a moment in his.

'Where is she, Félix?'

He cleared his throat. 'In the – ahem – in the ladies' room.'

As she neared it she frowned again; it sounded as if someone was slaying a live pig in there. Pushing open the door, she stopped dead, grabbing at the wall as she tripped over a bundle on the floor.

The bundle beat its fists at her.

'Go away! Leave me *alone*!'

Mesmerised, she gaped at it, and it hiccuped violently.

Jesus God almighty, she thought, what's happened? Is this muddle of velvet and hair and tears *Mary*? Kneeling down, she touched it cautiously.

'Mary? Dear Lord, what's going on? What's wrong?'

Mary's head jerked up, revealing a face ravaged with pain and rage, streaked make-up all askew, eyelids swollen, nose running.

'Cathal!' she bellowed. 'Cathal is wrong! My life is wrong! My life is *ruined*! I hate him, I hate it, I want to die!'

Ah. Keeley looked at her for a moment, watching it all come spurting out, every drop of poison that had been bottled up for months. Mary looked *flooded*, drowned in tears. Oh, wow, she thought, great timing, pal. But she reached forward and took Mary's face in her hands, kissed her head and then wriggled down to sit beside her, on the tiles, sliding her arm around her shoulders as she looked at her candidly.

'So. It is Cathal. Is it very bad, Mary?'

Hugging her with one arm, she chafed her fingers with the other hand, and suddenly all the fight seemed to gust away, leaving not a woman but a child, a frightened helpless child barely able to whisper.

'It – it's a nightmare. I – I thought it would get better, that we were just off to a bad start, but – oh, Keeley!'

Feeling the chill of the tiles under her, Keeley crouched closer and held Mary to her, murmuring all the comfort she could muster even as the words echoed in her mind: 'I want to die.' That was what Mary had said on the ferry that first seasick

day, and in the vineyard when picking grapes had turned out
to be such gruelling work.

But she was glad the dam had burst, at last.

'Go on. Have a good cry. Let it all out, and then we'll try to
think what we're going to do.'

Mary whimpered. 'But it's not us, it's me! I'm the one who
married him, I'm the one who had the child, I'm the one in
this mess.'

'I know. You're his wife and Mel's mother. But you're my
friend, too. We'll figure something out. It's my fault too, you
know. I wanted to warn you, but I – I didn't. I was a fool, and
now I'm to blame, it's up to me to help.'

The door opened, and one side of Félix's face appeared, a
fearful eye behind half of his gold-rimmed glasses.

'Is – is she all right?'

Keeley turned to him, wondering what kind of spectacle they
must present, slumped on the floor in the midst of her wedding,
mercifully informal as it was.

'No, Félix, she isn't. She – she's a bit overwrought. Do you
think Luc could rustle up some tea?'

Nodding, he dashed away, and Keeley pulled Mary to her
feet.

'Come on. Let's get you out of here, people will think you're
drunk. We'll go to Luc's kitchen.'

As they dusted themselves off and staggered to it she wondered if she might be right, whether Mary actually had had a
lot to drink. But perhaps it had been a good idea to uncork this
particular bottle.

Mary looked around her dazed as they went into the kitchen,
gazing slowly round the familiar array of copper pans and steel
knives, at Luc bustling towards her with a teapot, and began
to cry again. 'This is where I want to be! This is home, where
I belong!'

They both jumped as Luc whacked the teapot down, indicated
chairs and all but flung cups in front of them. 'I told you so! I
said it at the time, why wouldn't you listen!' Mary sobbed all
the louder as he poured camomile tea and recruited Félix for
support. 'Did I not, Félix? Did I not tell her so?'

'Yes, yes . . . but Mary, what exactly is the problem? What
has upset you so much?'

She shook her head, and they all watched in solemn silence
as tears flew down into the tea. 'Everything! Every little thing

I do is a problem, I can get nothing right, he's the boss, I'm an idiot – he and his precious customers know everything, I know nothing, only pie-in-the-sky from France! They don't want pie-in-the-sky, they want steak and kidney pie!'

It took them a moment to figure this out.

'You mean you are cooking what the local people want, not what you want?'

'Y-yes! Everything out of a tin or packet or freezer, nothing fresh, nothing new, nothing interesting. Some day I'll mix wallpaper paste into the soup, and they'll say hey, Mary is coming on!'

Luc sat back, stroking his moustache, considering. 'Well, there is always some local question of adapting—'

She looked up, her face flaming. 'To sliced pans and tinned peaches? Jesus Christ, when I think of the bread here, the hot baguettes plaited with garlic, the peaches warm from the trees . . . if it wasn't for Mel I'd lose my marbles. I swear I'd kill him stone dead with a cast-iron frying pan, he – he – he's a savage!'

Luc and Félix eyed each other, and Keeley saw what they were thinking: Mary's marriage was in trouble, it was more than just the food, it was women's stuff, personal. Out of their arena. With a sigh, she turned to Félix.

'I think Mary and I need to talk – and she needs to rest, first. Félix, would you call a taxi?'

With alacrity, he bolted away, but Luc looked concerned. 'Keeley, you can't leave your own wedding, you have friends and family out there—'

'I know. I'm going to ask Sylvie if she'd mind taking Mary back to Pierre and Francine's house and putting her to bed. There's a babysitter there already, minding Mel. She can just sleep it off, and we'll have a chat later. Thanks for the tea, Luc. And for caring. For everything.'

He stroked his moustache, looking irate.

'Perhaps it is none of my business, Keeley. All I can say is that Mary is welcome in my kitchen any time, if ever she should choose to come back.'

He spoke as if Mary wasn't there, which to all intents and purposes she wasn't. Her colour was toning down, but her face was becoming vacant, distant. Keeley glanced over his shoulder.

'Is there a back door, Luc? I don't want to drag her out the front, Vincent's parents would worry—'

'Yes. Follow me.'

Mary's coat was found, the taxi duly arrived, and they led her to it. As she was put into it she struggled free, stood up uncertainly and, without warning, gravely placed a kiss on Luc's cheek. Then one on Félix, and on Keeley.

'My friends. My best friends, that I've let down. I've let you all down, and ruined the wedding.'

Firmly, Keeley pushed her back into the taxi, and shut the door. They stood watching as it drove away, and then hastened in out of the cold, both men looking sad and perplexed. But Keeley smiled at them.

'Don't mind her. That's Mary. Never happy until she's feeling guilty.'

The festivities continued merrily until nearly midnight, and then a dozen of the thirty guests came back to the flat, including someone brandishing a guitar, who played it half the night. It was a great party, and Vincent and Keeley laughed aloud as they finally pushed the twin beds together, alone for the first time in what was now officially their home.

'What a circus!'

She meant the fun, but he gazed at the beds.

'Yes. We'll have to get a proper bed, now.'

She supposed they would. But the makeshift one served them very well, that first night of their marriage, and the sun was rising by the time they fell asleep in each other's arms, exhausted and entwined, each thinking the other the best, most beautiful person on the planet.

It was very late next day when the newly-married M and Mme Tourand made their way to Vincent's parents' home, which Pierre and Francine immediately told Keeley she must now regard as hers also. Ushering them in, they offered a late lunch, and dodged away to the kitchen adding that their guest was to be found in the sitting room.

Pale and dishevelled in a dressing-gown that Keeley recognised as Francine's, Mary sat on the sofa cradling Mel, looking shamefaced. Sylvie was there too, but with a wink she took her brother's arm and led him away, and the moment they were alone Mary threw herself on Keeley.

'I'm sorry! I'm so sorry!'

Scooping Mel up, Keeley sat down and tucked the child into her arm.

'No need. Nobody even noticed.'

'But Sylvie – your in-laws—'

'They think the Irish are all bonkers anyway. Would I be right in thinking you have a hangover the size of Texas?'

'Uh – well – let's say Kansas.'

Uncertainly, Mary eyed her, but Keeley laughed. 'Serves you right. My matron of honour, fluthered. I must say, my oul fella would be proud of you.'

'I – I didn't mean it, I didn't realise I was drinking so much—'

'H'm. Yesterday, or lately?'

'Yesterday! Keeley, I swear it! I've thought of it a thousand times, but that was the first time I did it. I can't at home, not with Mel, and so much work to be done.'

'OK, I'll take your word for that – but if I ever hear of Mel having any kind of accident, Mary, I'll know what caused it.'

But she saw the way Mary looked at her daughter, and thought that no, Mary would not risk the child's safety. Sitting back, she studied her.

'So. Let me have it, chapter and verse. Is he the one drinking? Beating you? What?'

'No. He never drinks, or lifts a finger to me.'

'So what does he do, that has you wanting to brain him with a frying pan?'

'He – he – oh, Keeley, I'm only telling you this because you live here, in France, I'd never breathe a word to anyone at home . . .' Glancing at Mel, glancing away, she finally fixed her gaze on the bottom of the garden that was visible through the French windows. 'He – he *controls* me.'

It was the very word Keeley had used to Vincent, had suspected from the start. But she couldn't envisage how Cathal actually did it.

'Go on.'

'He – it – it started right away, as soon as we were married. In fact it started before that, if only I'd realised. I thought he was being so helpful, with the wedding and honeymoon and all our plans, but he was taking over. Taking charge, the way his mother takes charge too . . . pointing out all my mistakes, telling me I'm hopeless, wearing me down.'

'But you're not hopeless! You're running his bloody restaurant for him.'

'Yes – on his terms. Keeley, he didn't want a wife, he only

wanted a cook. A slave. I work sixteen or eighteen hours a day but he never lets me have a penny of my own, he hands me an allowance and I have to account for every penny of it, write down everything I spend in a notebook he checks – he ate the face off me one day because I bought double-strength kitchen paper, when the other kind is cheaper!'

'But Mary, I have to say it . . . you're so well dressed, your flat is furnished, you look as if you have the best of everything.'

'That's just it. That's what he wants people to think. Clothes, furniture, anything people will see, be impressed by. You'll see when you open your wedding present, it's Waterford crystal, the very best for you – especially for you, because he's scared of you.'

'Is he? Good.'

'I wish I could stand up to him – but when I tried, he reminded me that he'd taken me out of the gutter, given me and my child a roof over our heads, said we'd be on welfare if it wasn't for him and I'd better not forget it. He – I – Keeley, I think he married me as a kind of revenge, because I'd chucked him for France!'

'That seems like a lot of trouble to go to, for revenge.'

'Yes, but . . . there are other reasons. He got a ready-made family. Me and a baby.'

'What do you mean?'

'I mean—' Biting her lip, she twisted the sash of her robe, forcing herself to speak. 'I mean that – he – we – our marriage hasn't been consummated.'

'What! After six months? But – but why?'

'I don't know why. All I know is that on our first night together he left me in our hotel room, had supper on his own and when he got back upstairs he simply went to bed, rolled over and fell asleep.'

'Jaysus.'

'Yes. I can't understand it, Keeley, because when I first met him he seemed quite, you know – eager. But that's the thing about Cathal. Nothing is what it seems.'

'But Mary – well, I can't begin to understand the bit about . . . about your sex life, or lack of it. But what about the money? Where is it all coming from, does Cathal's father pay him a fortune or what?'

'No. Donal doesn't *pay* him a fortune, as such. Just a normal bar manager's salary. But – but – a lot of money seems to change hands. I saw Donal handing Cathal a whole roll of it once, slipping it to him behind the bar, I don't know where it went after that . . . but I think it has something to do with the county council.'

Keeley was bewildered. 'The council?'

'Yes. Donal is on it, and some of his councillor pals drink at The Lantern, sometimes they all huddle into a corner talking – I don't know about what, only that the talk stops any time I come near them. In fact Cathal has told me to stay away from them, leave them to drink their pints in peace.'

'I don't get it. I don't get this at all.'

'Neither do I. Maybe I'm wrong, imagining things . . . but I get the feeling there might be some kind of racket going on.'

A *racket*? What kind of racket? Keeley's mind flew through all kinds of scenarios, one worse than the other – illicit poitín brewing, smuggling of untaxed alcohol, drug peddling? No. Surely not drugs. The Lantern would be closed down, lose its licence in a flash if its owner was caught at anything like that. And, when she and Mary used to drink there, there had never been any hint of such activities. Nor did Cathal or his father strike her as hardened criminals – a bit *glic*, the both of them, smug and smarmy, but too smart for the kind of blatant activity that would land them in jail.

Feeling that the conversation was turning into some kind of very unsavoury detective story, Keeley clutched Mel to her.

'This is hideous. I thought it was only the restaurant bit, that you told me already, about not being let cook what you want.'

'No. That's the least of it, the only part I could tell Luc and Félix. But it's driving me crazy, as well. I wanted to cook all sorts of lovely things, but he says no, the customers want what they're used to. And he's right about that – horrible boiled stodge. Every time I try to do anything else he says to save my fancy ideas for the other restaurant – you know, Fursey's, in the country. It's still a pub, but he says if I play my cards right I can have it some day to do what I like with. When – when we split up, I think he means.'

'Jesus, why don't you split now! He sounds *sick*, to me!'

'Yes, I think maybe he is. But Keeley, I can't leave him, where would I go? If I stick it out there's some hope I'll end up turning Fursey's into a proper restaurant, and meanwhile Mel has a home . . . he spoils her rotten, it's as if he's trying to brainwash her, get her on his side so he'll have a weapon against me later on. But if I left—'

'You could come back here. Luc said only yesterday that you could.'

'But then I'd have to bring Mel up alone, in some miserable flat, she wouldn't have any of the things she has now. He's even talking about putting her name down for a good school, elocution lessons, music lessons – meanwhile, I'm not even allowed to take driving lessons.'

'Why not?'

'The money – and the freedom. If I could drive, I could get away sometimes. As it is, I even have to ask permission to visit my mother, be home exactly on time, let him know my whereabouts at all times.'

'Why don't you tell him to get stuffed?'

'Because – oh, Keeley, you don't understand! It's not like a fight, a screaming row that I could get a grip on, it's all sort of . . . quiet, menacing, weird stuff I don't know how to handle. Anyone looking at us would think he was a model husband, that we hadn't a care in the world.'

Yes. Everyone had thought that, at Mel's christening. Or almost everyone. Silenced, Keeley sat looking at her friend, noting how hard she was fighting the tears.

'Well . . . I don't know what to say, Mary. I knew something was wrong, but it'll take me a while to figure out all this. Maybe the first thing I should do is ring him and say you're not well, that you won't be home for a few days.'

Briefly, Mary brightened. But then her defeated look returned. 'But where would we stay, Mel and I? We can't stay here with Vincent's parents, and there isn't any room at your flat, I've no money for a hotel.'

'You could stay here. I'm sure Pierre and Francine wouldn't mind for a day or two. Or what about Luc, or Félix? They'd put you up.'

'I – I suppose they would. But Keeley, I'm so ashamed . . . I never would have said anything to them yesterday, only I got drunk. I don't want you to tell Vincent or his parents or anyone, it's too – it's too humiliating!'

Shifting Mel on her lap, Keeley considered.

'But you can't keep this a secret from everyone for ever. Do your parents know?'

'No! They're so pleased for me, so thrilled with Mel, I couldn't do it to them . . . Dad would make me move back home, and then where would I be? Even before I was married I couldn't think of any answer to that.'

'Well, all the more reason for you to stay here while

we try to work something out. If you ask me, you should stay here, full stop. Take back your job with Luc at the restaurant, find a flat, put Mel in a crèche, and start all over again.'

'But I've already told you why I can't do that. It wouldn't be fair to her. She's only a baby, Keeley. I have to go back. And if I don't go on time, there'll be trouble. He only let me go because you insisted, didn't want you to get suspicious. You mustn't ever write, let on you know anything . . . please, Keel, promise me?'

'Yes. I promise, Mary, don't look so petrified. But you'll have to find some address I can write to you at. Could I ring you in the evenings maybe, when he's down in the pub?'

'No! The phone upstairs is only an extension of the one downstairs, he can listen in . . . does listen, even when it's only my mother. He has her charmed, brings her presents, gives goodies to the boys – even if I did ever tell her, I don't think she'd believe me. I feel so trapped, as if no-one would believe me!'

'Mary, don't panic. I believe you.'

Slowly, Mary slid off the sofa to the carpet, her legs curling under her, looking away for a long time before she looked up. 'Thank God somebody does. I can't tell you how glad I was when you rang him, and he had to let me go. I was dying to talk to you, that time at the christening, but he was there, I was afraid you'd let something slip—'

'I'd have kneed him in the nuts and asked him what the hell he thought he was playing at. And that's what you should do! I told you once before, you have a terrific temper when you lose it. You put the wits across my oul fella, I don't think he's laid a hand on my mother since.'

'Hasn't he? Well, that's something. But then my Dad – and Barry O'Neill – maybe they were the ones who scared him.'

'H'm. Well, whoever. The point is that these bullies can be sorted out.'

'That's what I keep telling myself. But it's different when you're living with one, when he has a hold over you – sometimes I see him looking at Mel and I wonder what he might ever do to her if I caused trouble.'

'Oh, Mary! He wouldn't hurt a six-month-old baby, surely? Apart from anything else, he'd have the police after him for that.'

'I don't mean physically hurt her. I mean . . . I don't know exactly what I mean. All I know is that he's a very strange man. And that I feel awful, telling you this stuff the very day after you've got married yourself.'

'Oh, saints almighty, here we go, the guilt again! Mary, you've got to stop feeling awful!'

'Well, I do. For causing a scene at your wedding, as well. But – but thanks for listening, Keel. And for the way you coped yesterday, never said a cross word to me. I hope I didn't mess up your wedding too much.'

'You didn't mess it up. It was great, which is why it's taken me so long to get back to you. We partied all night, I didn't have a moment to myself.'

'Vincent – Vincent is all right, isn't he? Everything he seems, unlike Cathal?'

Keeley couldn't help her blissful smile.

'Vincent is wonderful. Loving and caring and honest and strong. I'm going to miss him like hell when he goes off – did I tell you that he's being sent to work in different branches around the country, for a year?'

'Oh, no.'

'Oh, yes. We've only got ten days together, before he goes to the first one in Grenoble . . . but that's not as big a problem as yours. Jesus, Mary, I don't know what we're going to do about that. I'll really have to think about it. I *wish* I'd warned you off, in time!'

Wanly, Mary smiled. 'I probably wouldn't have listened if you had. Cathal looked like the perfect solution to all my problems – even though I didn't love him, I convinced myself I'd learn to. I tried to. Now, it makes me sick the way he kisses me in public, the way everyone else loves him.'

Keeley started to say something, but at that moment Francine came into the room.

'Are you two girls having a nice long chat? I'm sorry to interrupt if you are, only lunch is nearly ready.'

Instantly Mary leapt to her feet. 'Oh, Mme Tourand, and here I am still in my dressing-gown, your dressing-gown, not even dressed, or helping you! I'll get changed right away, I'm so sorry.'

She rushed away, and Keeley peered at Mel, who was dozing peacefully.

'I suppose that'll be your first word. Sorry, sorry, sorry.'

Chapter Nine

Keeley was unable to persuade Mary to stay, and she returned to Dublin that same evening. They found it very hard to say goodbye, with Christmas so near and one of them so sad, the other so happy. Both of them cried at the airport, and Keeley turned to Vincent for comfort afterwards, confiding to him everything that Mary had told her. Mary had asked her not to, but there was no way she could keep such a distressing thing to herself, and Vincent was so reliable, so trustworthy, the kind of husband you could talk to. His impression of Cathal had been so good he could hardly believe the truth, but when it sank in he was disgusted. If there was any way he could help, Keeley was to let him know immediately.

With Pierre, Francine and Sylvie they spent a lovely Christmas together, and Keeley tried not to think too much what it must be like for Mary, wonder how she was getting through it. But the question stayed at the back of her mind, as well as thoughts of Mel, an innocent child she did not want tainted by the unhappy atmosphere that even a baby could sense. Maybe, for the infant's sake, Cathal would make an effort during the season of goodwill? Even for his own sake, because it must be a terrible thing to be so isolated, so alienated from your own wife at Christmas, loathed instead of loved. Vincent was horrified when he heard the part about the marriage not being consummated, said that Cathal must need treatment, some kind of counselling.

Their own sex life continued even more ecstatically than before; there was something about being married that changed it, took it onto an even higher level of love and security. Blooming, Keeley could hardly bear to think about their separation, but it came soon enough, and they had to face it.

Taking her in his arms, Vincent said every encouraging thing he could think of; he'd be back from Grenoble in six weeks, he was going to get a phone in the flat so he could talk to her, he was furious with himself for not finding any way out of this. In April, to dovetail with his *stage* in Paris, they would have their belated honeymoon at the George V. Meanwhile, Sylvie and his parents would look after her, she was to treat them as her family.

Steeling herself, she kissed him au revoir with smiles hacked out of her heart, and sat on the floor weeping when he had gone, forlorn in the empty flat. The Sullivans' wedding present of a crystal lamp looked both ironic and ridiculous in it, and Tony's gruesome painting leaned against the wall, a tragic chaos of blurs and streaks that she'd written to say was fabulous. Eyeing it, she wanted to hide it, shove it out of sight, but it wouldn't let her, the very thought made her feel like a murderer. Poor Tony, who'd spent four months working at nothing else, because there *was* nothing else.

For a few days she felt mopey, and then she made a decision. If Vincent was to be away for long stretches, if they were only going to see each other one weekend in six, then she was going to have to tackle her time alone, do something constructive with it or something distracting at least.

Since he had taken the car she couldn't drive, and anyway she couldn't expect his father to pay her insurance forever. But she could and did borrow Sylvie's bike to go cycling, and began to ask friends from her language class to go with her. Mostly Arabs, Africans and bewildered Slavs who'd ended up in France through no choice of their own, not many had bikes themselves, but they borrowed in turn, and sometimes asked her to their own tiny apartments. Sitting cross-legged on wooden floors, she discovered exotica she'd never suspected: mint tea, cous-cous, merguez sausages and – memorably – harissa sauce. Crikey, she thought, Mary should dish up some of this stuff at The Lantern, it would give her ingrate customers something to really cry about.

Mary wrote soon after Vincent's departure, trying to sound cheerful, apologising for having denied any problem originally, because she'd still been hoping then that things might work out. But they were no better, and now she was also regretting her outburst to Luc and Félix, ruining a reunion that should have been a joy to one and all. Would Keeley drop in to the Vieux Moulin some time and say hello to them for her, something – well, apologetic?

Keeley snorted. But she did go to the Vieux Moulin, because she wanted to thank both men anyway for making her little wedding so wonderful. Picking a moment that wouldn't be busy, she arrived to find Luc off duty, and Félix wandering among the tables, inspecting everything for the meals that would be ordered later. She squinted as she went in, thinking how dark and deserted the place looked between meals, like a bus station after the bus had left.

'*Salut*, Félix!'

He whirled round and beamed at her, evidently delighted with some company. '*Salut*, Keeley! Have you time for a coffee? Sit down, and I will make us a pot.'

She grinned as he went to brew it himself; apparently nobody was on duty at this time of afternoon. As ever he was dapper and immaculate, even intimidating if you didn't know him, but she thought what a good heart he had under that forbidding pinstriped suit.

He brought the coffee with some delicious little fruit tartlets, and they chatted companionably over it, although Keeley was careful to keep Mary's miserable marriage to herself and give him to understand that Mary was only upset about the cooking part of it, because her husband and his customers were so set in their ways. Thoughtfully, Félix nodded.

'Yes. But it is a pity. Mary has such talent, you know, I had even thought—'

Thought what?

'Oh – it is just a little idea I have had, for a long time now. Luc will tell you it is my hobbyhorse! But, well, I have been the manager here for so many years, the restaurant belongs to a wealthy *patron* in Nice, we scarcely ever see him . . . I am left to run the Vieux Moulin as I see fit, so long as it makes a profit. And it does. A good one, because if I say so myself I am a businesslike person, I know what I am doing.'

She wasn't sure what he was getting at, but she agreed that yes, he was first-rate at his job, Mary had often said so.

'Did she? Well, she was first-rate also. That is why I had thought – well, it was only a notion you understand, but it had occurred to me that she might be a good investment. I am a frugal man, Keeley, you see, I do not drink or gamble, and Lise and I have no children.'

She began to wonder if her French was as good as she thought it was, because Félix wasn't making much sense. But, looking at his thin ascetic face, it wasn't hard to believe the bit about not drinking or gambling. She wondered what luxuries he did indulge in, because he must earn quite a bit, managing the top restaurant in Aix.

'Luc does all the living, for both of us! He has three children, he likes his claret . . . me, I only take a holiday once a year because Lise insists. Over the years, I have inevitably saved a little money. When Mary came along, and started telling me how she would like to open her own restaurant some day – well, I thought that when the time came perhaps I would take a chance for once in my life. Gamble, if you wish, before I die! If she had been interested, it was my plan to propose a partnership to her. She would cook, and I would become a *patron* myself. Rent or buy a premises, and back her.'

Oh, no. Oh, hell. That would be the last straw, if Mary ever found out she would throw herself into the Liffey. A real restaurant of her own, with Félix's funds, and friendship! Keeley grimaced, and he shrugged.

'*Mais c'est la vie*. It was not to be.'

'No. What a pity. You would have made a great team.'

'Thank you. Not that it would have happened for some time, not until she was fully trained and Luc was ready to retire from this place. Another few years, he says, before he heads for his farmhouse in the hills . . . he has done well too, financially, but a chef's life is very stressful. Mary was young and strong, so full of energy . . . it is a great pity.'

He looked so disappointed, so unusually downcast, that she felt sorry for him.

'It's a shame, Félix. But maybe you'll find somebody else.'

'That's what my wife says. You know Lise, don't you?'

'Yes. Pageboy trim and blonde highlights, every six weeks, keep the fringe nice and short.'

'Ha! Yes, that's her. I am amazed you remember her personal details, when you style so many women's hair.'

'Jaysus Félix, I have to remember, because Eliane doesn't keep any files and every customer assumes she's my only customer. Client, I should say. Forget the details and you can forget the tips, some of them are right battleaxes – ooh, sorry, I don't mean Lise!'

Nor did she; Lise Peyrolle was a nice lady, albeit a lady of leisure. Not having any children, she did some charity work but quite a bit of shopping too, often laughing as she arrived with her parcels, saying that Félix was going to kill her. Keeley suspected that he adored her, and that theirs was a very happy relationship. At her wedding, the pair had danced in an old-fashioned way, looking courtly and romantic.

'Well, anyway, Lise says I should keep my ear to the ground, that perhaps one of the other restaurants has a bright new chef worth investing in. But I don't hear of any – if there was one, Luc would know. He can smell out talent a hundred kilometres away.'

Keeley smiled wryly. 'Well, Mary is two thousand kilometres away now. There's no point in holding your breath, Félix, because she's not coming back. She has made her – commitments.'

He sighed as she got up and prepared to leave.

'Yes. We were very disappointed, Luc and I, by what she told us. She did not seem happy, Keeley. And it must have been a wrench for you, to lose your friend. I hope you will keep in touch with her?'

'Oh yes,' she said, 'I certainly will.'

You bet your boots, she thought as she pulled on her hat and mittens, even if Cathal Sullivan reads every bloody word I write he can't pass a law against writing them. But I'm not going to write a word about this, say anything about what Félix wanted to do for her. The ferry didn't kill her and the grape-picking didn't kill her, but that really would finish her off altogether.

The first crocuses had long come and gone, and Aix was dotted with primroses by the time Vincent returned from Grenoble, raced home to claim his wife and do nothing at all with their first weekend together, because they spent it entirely in bed. It was incredibly exciting and reviving, and it was gone in a flash.

'And now,' he said grimly, 'for Lyon. I wish I could do what you wanted to do with baby Mel, pack you in my bag and take you with me.'

'Are you even learning anything?' she asked, hoping his absence might at least be worthwhile.

'Not so far. Grenoble was much the same as Aix. And I suppose Lyon will be much the same as Grenoble. These big companies are streamlined, Keeley, everything is decided in Paris and filtered down exactly to order everywhere else. One store is a carbon copy of the next. And at the end of this ghastly year, I'm not even guaranteed a permanent position anywhere! If this all turns out to be a waste of time, I – I'll—'

But he didn't know what he could do, for now, only kiss her and leave her. Once again she felt like crying, but this time she didn't. This time she swore and raged and worked overtime, because Eliane's husband Roger had got worse and Eliane was away from the salon frequently, fretting about it, terrified that he might be going to need surgery. It meant extra money, and kept Keeley's mind occupied, but at night she missed Vincent horribly.

And then, one milky day at the end of February when she was already discarding winter woollens, a letter came.

'Dear Keeley—

Dearest *Keeley! What a great thing it is to have you to write and talk to, I think I'd go mad without it. But this time I have some good news. The first bit is that I've found somewhere for you to write to me. Write properly I mean, without watching every word. As you know it's been a problem because anyone I asked would have had to be taken into my confidence and Cathal is so damn popular, I was never sure that word wouldn't get back to him, with God knows what results. But now I've found the perfect person, somebody who loathes him as much as I do myself.*

You remember Joe Foley, the old guy who used to manage The Lantern, he was head bartender until they sacked him? Well, I ran into him one day, and we got talking. He's started up a little business, selling vegetables he grows on some land his son has near Lusk. I met him when he was delivering to McNamara's grocery, I'd gone in there for some carrots and shagging spuds. And suddenly I had a brainwave. The upshot of it is that he's going to supply me with vegetables for both our personal use and for the pub, which his son will deliver every Monday and Thursday. Cathal has never met his son, so I'll simply make the cheque out to their company's name and Mr Know-It-All won't know a thing. I think there's a certain justice in that, don't you? Joe and I had quite a talk about it. When I realised how he felt, how shabbily he'd been treated, I decided to take a chance and – well, not tell him everything, but tell him that I had a small favour to ask in return for giving him The Lantern's business.

Joe said certainly, no problem, he would let me give you his address in Lusk and that he'll deliver your letters to me along with the veggies, via his son. He even laughed! Of course it means he'll have to keep a low profile round here from now on so that Cathal can never put two and two together, but that suits him fine, he'd rather be out in his fields than driving the van anyway. His company hasn't got a name yet, but he's going to buy one – apparently you can, off the peg from a place in town, a "Ltd." name that has something to do with limiting your financial liability if you go bankrupt. But he knows he won't go bankrupt now, what with such a big order. The Lantern is doing over five hundred lunches a week and I've had to get an assistant, her name is Bridget. It seems so funny and sort of sad, teaching her to do the things Luc taught me.

Anyhow, you can write freely now, Joe's son's name is Eddie and I'm enclosing their address on a separate page.

The second thing is more serious, and I think it's good, but I hope you're sitting down. Keeley, after nine months, my marriage has finally been – well, made valid you might say. I won't pretend there was any great joy in it, in fact even dull old Lars could teach Cathal a few tricks, but it happened, not long after I got back from Aix. I think it was because of Carmel actually, my mother-in-law. She'd been dropping a few hints about a brother or sister for Mel – the cheek of her! But I sometimes wonder if she suspects about Cathal not being Mel's father, she sometimes looks at her as if she were trying to see signs of him in her, which as you know there aren't.

She was here when I got back that night, cooking supper for her poor abandoned son, and when she was leaving she made some remark about how she hoped the new year would bring us "no troubles, or only little ones." That made me furious, and when she'd gone I said to Cathal that she needn't worry, we weren't likely to have any. He lost the head altogether, Keeley. Went berserk. Next thing I knew, he was dragging me off to bed – at first I tried to fight him off, but then I thought no, I wouldn't because if by any miracle he managed to make me pregnant, I'd have a weapon against him. A son and heir, with any luck, to inherit some day and keep the blasted Sullivan name up in lights.

And now, I am pregnant. Since I hadn't seen any need to go on the pill it's just been confirmed, a new baby is due in late September. I haven't even told him, but when I do I'm going to make it clear he'll have to treat me better from now on if he wants his child born healthy and raised properly.

Maybe you'll think I sound callous, thinking of a child that way. But it will be a little companion for Mel and I've made up my mind to love it as best I can, be a good mother to it – judges always side with mothers, should things ever come to court. But I hope they won't. I don't want my children to end up with a broken home and I don't want them growing up in an unhappy one, any more than I want an unhappy one myself. So I've decided to make one last effort and try to make things work, try to talk to him and make him see that it would be much better for everyone that way. I still don't know what his problem is, but if he can't tell me maybe he could tell a counsellor, we could get some kind of help.

So that's my news. I hope you'll understand and not be too shocked, I know it must all look very strange to everyone on the outside. Meanwhile, your little god-daughter has got three teeth and is eating like the Queen of Sheba, I make her special little things in the hope she'll develop a palate for proper food, Joe is even going to slip me some asparagus to make up in her feed! For free of course, because Cathal would certainly query that extravagance. She's crawling everywhere too, I have to put her in a playpen while I work, but it's great I can at least be with her. She said "Mama" for the first time last week – right in front of Cathal, bless her, which was one in the eye for him, no attempt at "Dada" at all.

How are Luc and Félix, and how is Vincent getting on on his travels? He's such a good guy, you must miss him like crazy. I miss you like crazy, but at least now we'll be able to communicate properly – and who knows, maybe things will even work out with Cathal yet, if not perfectly then at least passably. It's ridiculous that my best friend can't even write in comfort to my own home. I have to admit I did envy you, just a tiny bit, watching you get married to someone who loves you so much, your wedding was so much more romantic than mine despite being smaller and in winter. It just goes to show . . . I never even see half of the people who were at mine, but I bet you do. Sometimes I think the hell with it, I should go out and have a blazing affair with someone, that'd show Cathal, I'm only twenty and why should he make me feel forty? But then Mel might be the one to pay for it. Anyway, now I'm pregnant I suppose even Mickser Sweeney wouldn't look twice at me!

I'd better go. The only time I get to write is late at night, but the pub will be closing soon and Monsieur will be coming up looking for his dinner. If he doesn't shape up when he

*hears about the baby, I might just put powdered glass in it
some fine evening, and you'll be writing to me at Mountjoy
or wherever they put the women prisoners.*

Lots of love,
Mary.'

Keeley was still pondering this letter a few evenings later,
thinking that maybe Mary was one of the women prisoners
already, when she heard the doorbell ring. As she went down
she recalled the day Mary, on hearing about Gertie, had said
that she would never stay in a bad marriage. And now here
she was, shaping up just like Gertie, finding ways to justify
it, to make it bearable if not brilliant. To Keeley it sounded
as if she were somehow colluding in her own predicament,
and she wasn't sure she liked the idea of a baby being used
as ammunition in a battle between its parents. If the decision
was hers she would advise Mary to hightail it out of there,
come back to France and snap up the chance Félix could offer
her to start over. Perhaps there would be difficulties, with Mel
to care for, but they were not insurmountable . . . since Mary
wouldn't do it, she was at least going to write to her and set out
some kind of plan of action, with a time frame on it. Trying to
salvage a marriage was all very worthy, but you couldn't keep
trying for a whole lifetime. What a waste if Mary tried for years
and years, only to find herself in the same mess twenty or thirty
years later, even worse off in fact, because she would be tired
by then, bitter and frustrated, her youth and her looks probably
gone, with nothing to show for it. Gertie had nothing to show
for her efforts, only bruises and wrinkles.

Distractedly, she went to open the door. Spring had brought a
stretch in the evenings, and when she pulled it back there stood
Vincent's boss Alain Jou, framed in the golden sunset.

'Bonsoir, Keeley. May I come in?'

'Yes, of course, Alain, it's nice to see you. How are you?'

A little uneasily, she led him upstairs, wondering what had
brought him. Was it bad news, some kind of problem? French
bosses were very formal and Alain was no exception, so it
seemed strange that he would call on a social visit, even though
he had seemed to warm to her the night of the art exhibition.
If he was going to talk about art now – oh, no. She couldn't
keep up the pretence again, she'd have to simply confess the
truth . . . would she go down in his estimation then, and take

Vincent with her? But she'd probably go down in it anyway, when he saw all the junk and clutter, the state of the flat that didn't even have a proper wardrobe, no room to store things out of sight. Oh, well. There was nothing she could do about it now.

'Sit down, Alain – if you can find somewhere! Would you like something to drink?'

She prayed he wouldn't say coffee, and hit the roof when he got Nescafé. But he asked for beer, and sat down at the kitchen table while she poured it.

'I just dropped in to say hello, really, and see how you were getting along. I know it's difficult for the wives, when the husbands are away.'

She wasn't going to mince her words about that. 'It's awful. But I'm sure it will be worth it, when Vincent becomes manager of the branch in Marseille.'

'Mm. Ah. Yes. Well, I hope he will. I'll certainly recommend that he does. But you know final decision lies with head office. He's a good worker, though . . . and what about you? How is your work going?'

It was going very well, now that she thought about it; she had built up quite a collection of clients who asked for her by name and wouldn't let any of the other stylists near their hair, even if it meant booking a week or more in advance. Even the ones who arrived scowling always left smiling, and tipped generously. Alain's wife was one of them, although neither of his daughters came to Eliane's, preferring to get their hair done at a trendy salon near the university. That made Sylvie mad, because the younger one Yvette dyed hers purple, a colour nobody ever requested at Eliane's. No doubt it made Alain mad too, she thought with a smile. Like Félix, he was a neat formal man – but then Félix was not as prim as he looked, so maybe Alain wasn't either. As Mary knew to her cost, appearances could be deceptive.

'I hope you're getting out and about, Keeley, while Vincent's away? There's nothing to be gained by moping at home, you know. In fact I was just thinking that I must see you're invited to a couple of art exhibitions that are coming up . . . a few friends of mine own galleries, and I know you're a great art lover.'

Hysterically, she tried to fight back the laughter, but she couldn't; it got all mixed up with the fizzing beer and came choking out, to her horror, in an explosion that made her eyes water. Gasping, turning puce, coughing, she had to get up and run herself a glass of water.

'Oh, God . . . excuse me, Alain, I have a terrible cold.'

He nodded sympathetically while she composed herself, and she realised he was almost more embarrassed then she, his eyes roving the room as he searched for something distracting to say.

'I must remark, Keeley, on your original taste. This flat is not large, but it is most – MON DIEU!'

Screeching, he leaped up as if electrified, and dashed from the kitchen through to the other room where he threw himself, to her total bewilderment, to his knees on the floor. Appalled, she ran after him, wondering whether he was having some kind of attack.

'Alain – Alain, what is it? Are you all right?'

He looked as if he was praying, kneeling reverently, with an expression of the purest ecstasy, in front of the wall.

'Alain, what *is* it? What's the matter, do you want me to call a—?'

Briefly he turned to her, his eyes full of some kind of devout fervour, before turning back to reach out and seize, with all his force, Tony's painting. Tony's blob, that had been propped against the wall for so long she never saw it any more. Holding it rigid, he stared at it breathless.

'No. Oh, no. It cannot be.'

Blinking, she stood waiting for him to explain, say something that would prove he was not a raving maniac. He looked so agitated she would not have been in the least surprised to see him whip a pistol from his pocket.

'K-K-Keeley. Who did this? Where did you get it?'

'From Ireland. From my brother.'

'Your brother? He – he too is a connoisseur? He owns a gallery?'

'Oh, Alain. If only. He's a paraplegic. And he wouldn't know an art gallery from a shooting gallery. He only painted this to pass the time.'

'He *painted* it?'

'Yes. As you can see it's not framed or anything, my friend Mary brought it over rolled up in her luggage, but he did it on canvas for that very reason, it's easier to roll up than cardboard. Vincent found those bits of wood to stretch it on because he was afraid Tony might ask us some day what we'd done with it, and he didn't want to have to say it was all creased. But frankly even Vincent—'

Very slowly, Alain got to his feet, still holding the object and breathing heavily, surveying it at arm's length.

'At last. At last I have done it. At last I have discovered one.'

'One what?'

One lulu, she thought. *I* have discovered a lunatic. Vincent's boss is barking.

'A painter, Keeley. A real painter. After all these years.'

'But Alain – I'm sorry, I don't think you can have heard me. I said Tony is a paraplegic. He paints with a brush in his mouth!'

Had she said he painted with a garden rake in his ear, she didn't think Alain could have looked more dumbstruck.

'A brush . . . in his mouth . . . Keeley, you are making fun of me.'

'I swear to God. But Alain, you've only to look at it for crying out loud, to see it can't have been painted by anyone normal!'

'No. This person is abnormal. Completely extraordinary. Unique, gifted with utter genius. Just look at this depth, this perspective, this layering . . . chiaroscuro . . .'

She hadn't a clue what chiaro-whatsit was, but she followed Alain's pointing finger to what he called layering, and saw that Tony had indeed painted some parts over others. Well, no wonder, canvas was probably too dear to waste, and besides you'd want a saintly patience to start over again every time you made a mistake, with a brush in your mouth.

'Alain—'

Solemnly he put down the work, as delicately as if it were a newborn baby, took her face between his hands and kissed it on either cheek.

'My dearest Keeley. I knew it. I always knew you had a wonderful eye, I sensed it the moment we met and you chose the only worthwhile entry in the Cézanne competition. But of course now I know why, coming from a family like this. It is in the blood.'

She thought of Christy, and was afraid to speak.

'Tell me – may I—' he paused to glance once more at the picture – 'would you mind very much if I took this to my friend Serge – no. On second thoughts, it is not insured. Or is it?'

'N-no.'

'Oh, Keeley, just because he is your brother, you must not assume – take him for granted, that he can do another – this must be insured, immediately. Would you mind very much if I asked my friend Serge to come over here, to take a look at it?'

'Who – who is Serge?'

'Serge Rolland. He has a gallery in the Rue de l'Opéra, he specialises in – in new works. Tell me, how long has your brother been painting?'

'Since last summer.'

She thought he was going to faint. Putting his hand to his forehead, he held it there looking dizzy. 'Last summer. And how old is he?'

'Twenty-two, nearly twenty-three.' With what seemed to be enormous effort, Alain steadied himself. 'Keeley, forgive me, but I must go now. Right away. Will you be here in the morning?'

'No, Saturday is our busiest day, I won't be home until around seven.'

'You will be out all day?'

'Yes.'

He paled again. 'Then please – Keeley, lock this flat before you leave. Every door, every window – I cannot believe – I will be back tomorrow evening, at seven sharp, with Serge.'

'OK. I suppose I'd better hoover and clear up a bit, if you're bringing a friend.'

Agonised, he looked at her beseechingly. 'No, please do not touch anything. Do not raise dust, do not mop or wash or go near anything that might damage this masterpiece.'

'Masterpiece?'

'Yes. I will see you tomorrow, if I do not expire of joy overnight.' Kissing her again, he tottered away.

'*Dear Mary,*

I wish you could be here at this time of year. The days are getting warm already, the tubs and baskets of flowers are back out on the balconies, even my little geraniums that Francine gave me are starting to bud. Sometimes I talk to them as I water, what kind of fool am I turning into! But I suppose I miss Vincent and anyway it seems to be doing them good, they've got lots of lovely fuzzy leaves coming out and I enjoy waking up to see a bit of greenery. Francine says I should start feeding them, what a pity you're not here to cook them something nice! I can cook now myself, sort of, but I'll never be in your class, I just bung a few things in a pan and hope for the best. If I ever learn to do anything properly in that line, I'd prefer it to be gardening – I often go to Francine's garden just to sit looking at it, or help her with a bit of weeding, I don't know why but I really enjoy it. It's so peaceful there, sometimes we hardly even talk.

But I want to talk to you, about loads of things. First of all, your new baby – congratulations! – and what you told me about trying to make a go of things with Cathal.

As you well know, I don't like him – never did, and probably never will. But since you're stuck with him and feel you have to make the best of it, there are a few things I think you should do. First, you have to find out where all that money is coming from, that his father gives him and you think is fishy. Suppose they were drug dealers or something, they could both end up in jail and then where would you be! If he won't tell you outright, that'll prove there is something wrong. Is there any way you can listen in on his phone calls the way he listens in on yours, and try to find out more? If you could, you'd at least have what you call a "weapon" against him – a better one than the new baby, in my opinion.

Also, on the subject of money, is there any way you could stash away a little bit of what he gives you? I know you said he makes you keep a list and checks everything you spend, but maybe Joe would give you a few fake receipts or something? The reason I say this is that if you ever did decide to leave him, it would be very handy to have a few bob to tide you over till you got on your feet. If you can manage it, put it in the post office or somewhere and keep it safe. After all you're working damn hard, you have a right to something of your own, even if it's only a few quid, it'll make you feel better . . . think about it, anyway, and try to do it. Vincent and I pool most of our money now that we're married, but I always hang onto a tiny bit just because it makes me feel independent and good about myself, if I run over budget some weeks I don't have to go to him looking for the price of a pair of tights. And then he's not mean like Cathal, he'd never make me explain what I wanted money for – not that I would, if he did! But you're up against it and you have to fight fire with fire.

The next thing is, what about fixing a definite time on your effort to make things work? I hope he's behaving better already now that you're expecting his child. But if he isn't then I think you should give it say a year, or even two years, max. If he doesn't shape up by then he never will. Then what? I know it's hard to know what to do, but you have to try to think of something, some plan you can put into action by the time the kids start school at the latest. Maybe you could quit cooking at The Lantern then, get a job somewhere else and leave him to sort himself out – I bet he'd be nicer to you if he thought you were going to do that.

Please think about it. As it happens, I'm hatching a little plan myself at the moment. I'm not going to tell you yet what it is in case I jinx it, but I've had an idea, and wait till you hear what inspired it.

I don't know whether you met a man called Alain Jou at my wedding? Well, he's Vincent's boss, and he dropped in one evening to see how I was while Vincent's away. We were talking, and next thing he happened to see Tony's painting, the one you brought over – well, I tell you, he nearly lost his reason! Don't ask me why, because it still looks like a blodge of nothing to me, but he went crazy over it. Started asking me all about Tony and couldn't believe he'd done it . . . then he brought some guy called Serge Rolland to see it, and they spent ages discussing it, inspecting it, asking me all sorts of questions. To cut a long story short, Serge asked me if I'd sell it to him. He owns a gallery and I think he wanted to sell it on there. But I said no. Even now I don't really know why, except that it was a wedding present and (bad as it is!) I didn't feel right about giving it to anyone else.

So then Serge asked me whether Tony would consider doing some more pictures, whereupon Alain said he'd like to act as his agent, if he would. Tony's agent! Don't ask me how I kept a straight face. But I did. I said I'd write to ask Tony, which I did, and I've just had a letter back from him. He's so thrilled you can't imagine, he's going to do as many paintings as he can and Serge is going to hang them in his gallery to sell. In return for forty per cent of whatever price they fetch, Alain is going to organise the shipping and whatever else needs organising, insurance and stuff, it all got so complicated I could hardly follow half of what he was saying.

I still can't believe it. People must be nuts, that they'd pay good money for Tony's daubs, but Serge is sure they will. He kept blathering on with Alain about having found a genius! I think they're both bonkers, but it's great for Tony. I really thought it was funny, and sort of sad, when I got his letter written by a nurse, and thought of him painting with the brush in his mouth . . . but he's going to get decent canvas and give it his best shot. He's all excited.

And that's what got me excited. I began to think, if this kind of thing can really happen, if even Poor Tony can get a new career going and make something of his life, then so can I. Not that there's anything wrong with mine, I have none of the problems he has and I already feel very pleased with the way things have worked out since I came to France (thank you, thank you Mary!) but I found myself sort of – starting to aim even higher, shift up a gear you might say. With Vincent away, I have plenty of time to think, and get things worked out before I say anything to him.

Or to you, yet! But I've taken the first steps and they've been very encouraging. So when I go to meet Vincent in Paris next week for our belated little honeymoon at the George V, I'm going to put it to him and see what he thinks. It's a joint project, that will involve us both, and I'm praying he'll be interested. If not, I won't hold it against him, because it is risky – but if a paraplegic in a wheelchair can paint, and make people think he's a genius, then anyone can do anything. At least I think – hope – they can!

So wish me luck. And I wish you lots of luck too, with Cathal and with your pregnancy. I'm glad for Mel's sake that she's not going to be an only child. And I hope for your sake that everything goes well. But you must think about what you're going to do if they don't, do you hear me? I don't want you still slaving for Cathal and trying to please him when you're fifty! God, imagine us being fifty . . . it sounds like another planet, but I suppose we'll get there some day. Our parents are well on their way to it already – I know yours are one reason why you're sticking with Cathal, you don't want to scandalise them or your kid brothers with a broken marriage. But you have to think of yourself too. They're not the ones have to live with Cathal.

Sorry it took me so long to write, but as you can see I've been busy with Tony's new project and my own, I'll tell you all about it after I tell Vincent. Meanwhile, Luc and Félix send their best and say you're to take good care of yourself.

Give Mel a big kiss from me!

Love,
Keeley.'

It was a soft sunny day in April, the air creamy with the scent of cherry blossom, and Mary willed the morning on until lunchtime came and went, the last customer was fed, and she could get out for some fresh air. Out to read and enjoy Keeley's letter too, that was stuffed into her apron pocket since Eddie's van had arrived with Joe's vegetables at eight o'clock, the time at which she started work with Bridget in the kitchen. Tucking it away safe, she had been dying to read it since, but there was no joy to be had from reading it here, when Cathal might walk in and demand to see it.

But there was always a lull in the afternoons, in which she often took Mel out for a walk in her buggy, sometimes as far as her parents' house to see Leesha who, because she started work early, was usually home by three. Stashing the last plate in the dishwasher, she turned to her husband, putting her hand on her back with an exaggerated twinge.

'Oh, I'm tired, this new baby is getting heavy already . . . I think I'll go out for a bit of air, Cathal.'

'OK. Round to your mother's, is it?'

'No, not today – I need to get my hair cut, if you could mind Imelda for an hour, and give me the few pounds?'

She knew he would, because he wanted her to look well, look as if she worked far less than she did.

'All right. Five pounds fifty pence, isn't it?'

'That's right.'

Taking the notes and coins from the till, he counted them out to her.

'Here you are. You'll be back by five, I presume?'

'Yes. Thank you, Cathal.'

Feck you, Cathal, she thought. I should have a bank account and money of my own. I should be able to tip the girl who washes and the girl who cuts, I should be able to go for a coffee afterwards and buy a newspaper and sit reading it for an hour if I want to. I am going to find some way of hiving off a few pounds here and there, that I can call my own . . . if I could only think how to do it. There must be a way. But she smiled sweetly at him as she put the money in her pocket and went to get her coat, covertly transferring Keeley's letter to it. At least he was a bit more agreeable these days, still chuffed with himself that he was to be a father – the genuine article this time, as he put it, as if reminding her what a favour he had done her by 'taking' Mel. Pausing only

to check on the child and kiss her goodbye, she went while the
going was good.

It was a refreshing walk to the hairdressing salon, and
she enjoyed it, enjoyed the warm soothing water and the
invigorating scalp massage, thinking of Keeley and her letter
that she would read when left alone under the drier. Keeley
didn't wash hair nowadays, only cut it, but she knew she'd
been good at it, had always made a point of giving her clients
a really good scalp massage, the kind that made a person feel
relaxed and pampered, all the way down to the neck where
tensions accumulated. As the girl worked she felt hers melting
away, letting her mind drift off on a pleasant daydream . . . this
is how good food should make you feel, she thought, indulged
and sensual, special. I wonder if anyone ever feels like that
after lunch at The Lantern? After a big dollop of shepherd's
pie and then apple pie they probably feel more like a barrel of
concrete.

If only he'd let me give them soufflés, salads, lighter things, if
only they'd try them . . . he'd have a fit if he knew half the things
I make for Mel, but that's one good thing about him leaving
me to do all the feeds, at least she'll grow up with some kind
of a decent palate, she won't bolt down heaps of starch or get
clogged arteries or go into a huff at the sight of herbs. Maybe
she'll even take a real interest, grow up to be a real chef and do
all the things I could have done – would have done, if I hadn't
had her.

But I did have her, and now I'm going to have another. I
actually will be the mother of Cathal's child, this time, and
maybe he'll treat me as such. Things are a bit better already,
and maybe they'll continue to improve. It's not great, but it's
not unbearable, and meanwhile Mel is happy at least. That was
my priority to start with, and I have to keep it in sight.

Eventually she was moved under the drier, and took out
Keeley's letter, slitting it open with her finger as she looked
with pleasure at the familiar handwriting. Keeley no longer
dashed off breathless postcards, she took the time and trouble
to write proper letters that were somehow nourishing, always
cheery and supportive, understanding even when she didn't
understand, thought her friend was behaving like a dolt. It
was a great relief to have told her the truth, Mary thought,
like a pressure cooker letting off steam, I'd have exploded if
I didn't tell someone. It's great that she can write freely now

that Joe and Eddie are playing postman, I wonder what she has to say?

Quite a lot, judging by the fat satisfying bundle of pages . . . oh, isn't that odd, she says I should try to get my hands on some money of my own, just when I was thinking the same thing this very day. I will try, now, let her see that I am making an effort, not as helpless as she thinks I am. And she wants me to put a time limit on how long I'm going to work at my marriage . . . well, that's a harder one, because of the children, but I can see what she means about being fifty some day – Jesus, that *is* a scary thought. I'll be suicidal, if things are no better then. But at least the children will be grown up, my life will be my own. Is fifty too late, I wonder, to find love and romance and all the things I'm missing now? Who would want me, if ever I left Cathal?

I have to make this marriage go right. I *have* to. I'm just going to have to butter him up like a parsnip, keep him sweet as pie . . . God, here's Keeley going off for her weekend in Paris with Vincent, I bet that will be a romantic reunion – and at the George V, they'll have a ball! Why did Cathal take me to that crummy hotel for our honeymoon, when he could have afforded somewhere really nice? He's so tight, you wouldn't get into his pockets with a hammer and chisel. Keeley and Vincent haven't a penny, but you can sense the love even in the letters . . . I can't imagine what this new project of hers is, but I know Vincent will say yes to it. He'd give her the planet Mars, if she asked for it.

And Poor Tony isn't going to be poor any more, he's going to paint. Wow. Who'd ever have thought that would come to anything! It just goes to show . . . I suppose it goes to show, as Keeley says, that anything is possible. If a paralysed basket case can make something of his life, then surely the rest of us can.

She says she can, and I suppose that means I can, too. If only I had her – her *attitude*. She's so positive, hardly even mentions missing Vincent although she's been virtually alone since January. Her letters are like a shot in the arm, they make me feel so much better.

If only she was here in person, and could make me feel that way all the time. If only I could make myself feel that way, more of the time.

The George V was a stupendous hotel, and Keeley gasped when

she saw it. Clutching her weekend bag to her, she stood outside for several minutes before working up the courage to actually go in, surveying it as if a hand might reach out and grab her by the scruff of the neck, fling her back out on the street where she belonged. She'd managed everything else with no problem – the train from Aix, the right bus from the station to here – but this really was daunting. She'd known it was a good hotel, and worn her Sunday best, but now she thought even the doorman looked better than she did, certainly far more impressive and assured. Taking a deep breath, she finally confronted what was clearly a *great* hotel, and strode up to it.

Should she thank the doorman, for holding open the door, should she maybe tip him? – no, nobody else was paying any attention, evidently you weren't meant to. You were meant to take everything for granted, as if you were used to it. As her shoes sank into the deep carpet, she glanced down to check whether she'd polished them, and was very thankful to see that she had. And worn her wedding hat, too, the amber crushed velvet one; it was a bit wacky, but hats were definitely in vogue around here, she could see several women wearing them.

The receptionist greeted her as if she were Dior's top model, and she nearly fainted to find that he apparently intended to let her in.

'Mme Tourand – ah yes – I hope you have had a pleasant journey?' Yep; second class, with a baguette sandwich and a bottle of mineral water, to save the inflated price of them on the train.

'Delightful, thank you' she squeaked, and he smiled encouragingly.

'Your husband has already arrived, and is waiting for you in room 208, I hope you will be comfortable. Please let us know if there is anything we can do for you.'

There is, she thought. You can tell me why Pierre and Francine picked such an incredible hotel. I had no idea, even when Vincent got all excited I didn't realise we were going to a place as grand as *this*. Even for a weekend, it must cost a fortune – no wonder they said they were going to give us a honeymoon to remember. Two nights here would probably get you two weeks anywhere else – and dinner thrown in, as well! Mme Tourand is going to be comfortable all right, so comfortable you'll have to drag her out by the hair . . . look at that furniture, that chandelier! Am I allowed to swing from it, I wonder, shouting 'Geronimo!'?

While the receptionist telephoned Vincent to announce his wife's arrival, a porter materialised to insist on taking her bag, small as it was. But it could be worse, she thought, at least I didn't bring my rucksack – I would have, only Francine loaned me this. It's not Gucci, but it seems to be cutting the mustard, he doesn't look as if he's going to throw it in the bin.

Demurely she followed the porter to a sleek, silent lift, out of it and down a corridor so plush it felt somehow padded. When they reached the room, she was devoutly glad to see Vincent with a tip ready in his hand, and hurled herself on him the instant the porter left them.

'Oh – you're the best bit of all! Give me an *enormous* kiss!'

He obliged without need of further encouragement, holding her as if they had been separated for six years instead of six weeks, kissing her so hard she thought her spine would snap. It was some time before they managed to disentangle themselves, and gaze around at the lovely room.

'Oh, this is the bee's knees! I had no idea it was going to be so swanky – Vincent, I've never seen anything like it in my life! You're going to have to tell me what to say and do so I don't make a show of you.'

'Don't be silly. All you have to do is relax and enjoy it. Look, there are flowers and everything – wait till you see the bathroom.'

It was full of thick snowy towels and gleaming tiles, dishes full of little bath goodies, crested robes for Monsieur and Madame to wrap themselves in when they emerged from the vast sparkling bath. Giggling, she drank in every detail, feeling like a burglar.

'Dear God. I though we'd see a bit of Paris, go exploring, but now I just want to stay here, lie on that bed eating chocolate and drinking champagne, pretending I'm Elizabeth Taylor.'

Grinning, he went to a table where she saw there actually was a bottle of champagne, chilling in a silver bucket, with two glasses beside it.

'Ooh! Where did that come from?'

'From me. It's been so long since we were together, Keeley, I've missed you so much, and you've been so good about it . . . this is a very late honeymoon, and a very short one, but I want you to enjoy every single minute of it.'

'I'm enjoying it already. I was petrified down in the lobby, but they were really nice, treated me like a lady even though I'm sure they know I'm not.'

'Yes, you are. You're my lady.' Taking the champagne from the ice, he poured two glasses and handed one to her, raising the other as she peered at the frothing bubbles, excited as a child on Christmas morning. 'Here's to my wife, the most special lady in the world.'

His face was a little flushed, his eyes full of tenderness as he looked at her, and for the first time she almost believed it herself, that she was a lady, as good as the real ones whose hair she cut, the even fancier ones you saw in magazines. Certainly Vincent believed it, if his expression was anything to go by . . . but then, Vincent had always believed in her. Fleetingly, she thought of telling him about the idea she had, that had been fermenting in her mind for so long she was ready to pop like a cork, but then she decided to wait just a little while longer. If he was against it, their weekend might be spoiled. Better to keep her secret to herself for just two more days, until Sunday evening before she returned to Aix and he departed for Rouen.

Plucking off her hat, she threw it on the bed, kicked off her shoes and sat down in one of the blissfully comfortable armchairs, sipping happily at her champagne.

'What's Paris like, Vincent? Have you seen much of it?'

'Very little. It's been all work and no play – but tomorrow we'll get up early and go for a long walk. What would you like to see first?'

'I don't know. The Eiffel Tower? The Arc de Triomphe? Montmartre?'

'OK, we'll try to get to them all – but it hardly matters if we don't, because the whole city is beautiful, we'll have a great time just wandering. Paris is paradise for lovers.'

She had heard that, and could hardly believe she was going to see it with the man she loved so much; it was as if all her birthdays had come together. Paris, *and* Vincent, *and* the George V! She must remember to get some little present for Mary, and send Tony a postcard from Montmartre, where all the peculiar painters were said to live.

'Oh, I can hardly wait. And what about this evening? We've only got forty-eight hours, let's not waste a—'

'This evening' he said with a flourish, 'Madame has a choice. I can take her for a stroll on the quais, perhaps to see Notre

Dame, and for dinner afterwards. Or if she prefers, she can have room service.'

'What?'

Putting down his glass, he looked at her earnestly, almost shyly, and came to perch on the chair beside her, taking her hand.

'I thought you might like to stay here. That bath is so big, it would fit both of us plus a million bubbles . . . then we could have a candlelight supper sent up . . . and then . . .'

She smiled as she snuggled into him. 'And then we could go to bed early, like good kiddies?'

'Yes . . . it's a double bed, Keeley . . .'

A double, at last! In fact it looked more like a triple, and she laughed as she thought of the twin beds in the flat, that they still pushed together whenever he came home, sometimes coming adrift and falling out during the night. Whereas this one looked as if it would swallow you whole, and you'd have to be winched out of it.

'I think that's a very good idea, Vincent. Please take Madame's champagne into the bathroom while she undresses, and run her a bubble bath the height of Mount Everest – one million bubbles exactly, mind you count them all.'

It was a weekend made in heaven, and they savoured every second of it. Getting out of the vast bed was indeed a challenge next morning, but finally they untwined their arms from around each other, showered under what felt like Niagara Falls and went down to a breakfast fit for royalty. Eating her creamy scrambled eggs with sorrel and smoked salmon, drinking freshly-squeezed orange juice, Keeley thought of Mary and wondered whether she should tell her about it. It was a very un-French breakfast, but the waiter had not only taken her request for scrambled eggs without a blink, he had suggested the addition of the salmon and the sorrel. Mary would want to hear every detail – but would it be fair to tell this tale of gastronomic delight to someone slaving over mountains of shepherd's pie, whose chances of ever sampling the joys of the George V seemed less than zero? Twirling her fork, she pondered it, but then found Vincent looking at her in a way that focused her attention exclusively on him.

'I haven't got egg on my chin, have I?'

'No. You look beautiful this morning, Keeley. Absolutely radiant.'

Radiant was exactly what she felt as they set off after breakfast, out through the tapestried marble lobby into the Avenue George V, away from the Champs Elysées in the direction of the river Seine. Agog, she sensed immediately the scale and majesty of Paris; it felt much busier and noisier than Aix, bustling with crowds and traffic, richly sophisticated.

'And yet the air is so clear, there are so many trees . . .'

Vincent was delighted he could identify them as chestnuts, in lush spring bloom expressly to order. Since coming to France Keeley had developed an interest in trees and flowers, seemed to love greenery of any kind, which didn't surprise him now that he had seen where she came from. The irony of the name made him both wince and smile: Pearse Gardens.

'Would you like to go to the Tuileries?'

'What are they?'

'They're flower gardens, at the Louvre, they should be full of tulips at this time of year.'

'Oh, yes!'

Hand in hand, they wandered down to the river, where the Saturday morning markets were in full flow, and she was thrilled with it all: multicoloured exotic birds in gigantic bamboo cages, piles of ceramic pots and plates from Africa, fish, flowers, wicker baskets and woodwork, vendors hawking every conceivable thing. But he was keenly aware that she never once asked to buy anything, as if to let him know that last night's champagne had been treat enough.

But he wanted to give her some little thing, something she could keep and enjoy after he left for Rouen, to remind her of their honeymoon.

'What are those?'

She was gazing at the series of bottle-green boxes on stilts, with raised lids, standing vertical to the walls of the river.

'Bookstalls. But they sell other things too . . . maps, coins, cards . . .'

At leisure, but with interest, she made her way from one to the next, frowning as she tried to decipher labels and titles; she could read fairly well in French now, but some of this stuff was very obscure.

'Look, theatre posters! I've never been to a theatre, have you?'

He had, as a child, with his parents or in school groups, but not in recent years. It didn't bother him that he had never taken

Keeley, since following the plot would probably be a chore for her, but it did bother him to think that tickets would be an extravagance. He wished he could offer her the sun, moon and stars.

'Oh, and look, art books! Oh, Vincent . . . I've got to get one, for Tony. They're all in French, but he'd love the pictures now that he's painting himself . . . which one do you think would be best?'

Somewhat stunned by Tony's success, and the reverent tones in which Alain Jou now spoke of his brother-in-law, Vincent took some time to look at them, and chose carefully.

'Monet – no – Degas – no – Chagall, hmm – Kandinsky, maybe . . . Picasso – yes, Picasso. Let's get him this one.'

Keeley insisted on paying for it out of her own money, and he felt a stab of love and pride as he watched her, so small, so independent.

'I can't get over this business of your brother, Keeley.'

'Neither can I. Serge Rolland says that painting of ours is worth a lot of money, and could be worth a fortune some day! I think he and Alain are off their rockers. But the main thing is that Tony's painting away like blazes, going to send over a whole batch to them by the time he leaves the hospital – did I tell you he's going home in July?'

'Mm. Will he be able to paint there?'

'I don't know. Probably not as well as he can at the hospital, where he has decent facilities and his physio encourages him – I can't see my oul fella encouraging him at all. But I suppose my mother will help as much as she can, get his paints and canvases for him if only they can figure out where the money's to come from. Serge did suggest an advance, but I – didn't like to—' Her voice trailed off and she bit her lip, uncertainly.

Grasping what she was getting at, he hugged her. 'You didn't like to say your family is broke and Tony hasn't a penny of his own, is that it? Oh, Keeley – Alain and Serge probably know that. Nearly all artists are broke, for one reason or another, when they're starting out. I think you should tell Serge that an advance would be very welcome.'

'Do you?'

'Yes. Definitely.'

She looked relieved. 'OK. Then I will.'

They were ready to move on when a second art book caught her attention. 'Cézanne – look, Vincent, it's like the one you gave me before, only different . . .' Flicking through the pages, she smiled with pleasure. 'The house on the hill is in this one too, but so are lots more, I didn't realise he'd done so many. Aren't they beautiful . . . imagine if Tony could paint like this some day.'

Without hesitation he reached into his pocket for some money, and paid the vendor for it, exchanging some conversation too rapid for her to catch.

'Oh, thank you! I'd finished the other one, now I can go on to this – what did you say to the man?'

He smiled. 'I said it was a present for my wife, the well-known Irish art critic.'

She cracked up laughing. 'The well-known Irish chancer! I wish I could explain what it is I like so much about Cézanne's paintings. But all I can tell you is that I think the colours are gorgeous, and I love the way he sort of leaves – leaves little bits to your imagination. It's like doing one of those puzzles where you have to join up the dots. And the scenery, too – nearly everything he painted was in the countryside. I love it when we go cycling through the very places he must have walked through – or maybe he even had a bike, like us! Sometimes it seems like he's still alive.'

'Well, his spirit certainly is. On our very doorstep, at that.'

'Yes – oh, Vincent. It's just not fair that you're away from Aix so much. It's your home, and mine now as well, it's where we belong!'

Her tone was merely indignant, not complaining, but in those few simple words he heard how frustrated she was, and wished he could say something strong and comforting. Wished he could get on the train and go back with her tomorrow, forget about Rouen and all the other places on his lengthy itinerary. Even Paris, lovely as it was, did not have the soft golden glow of Provence, no haze of lavender, no scent of honey or thyme or sun-warmed fruit. But he had been thinking about the predicament, as she suggested, and would tell her tomorrow about what little progress he had made. Tomorrow, before they parted again.

Walking on and on, they spent the whole day browsing and sightseeing, pausing at occasional cafés, enchanted by all the tantalising nooks and crannies and 'gobsmacked', as Keeley elegantly put it, by the city's grandeur, its gilded monuments and great cathedrals. Eventually they slogged up the hundreds of steps to Montmartre, which was jammed with tourists having their portraits sketched or painted. Tickled, she laughed at the artists in their berets and striped jerseys.

'Ha – they're fakes! Like cartoons of artists!'

'How can you tell?'

'Oh, there used to be plenty of lads like that in Dublin – con artists, who'd haul their stuff into town fresh off the back of a lorry and flog it to all the fools with more money than sense. Made a fortune, some of them did, in between accepting free holidays from the government. If our Tony hadn't banjaxed himself some judge would probably have given him one too – telly, sports facilities, hot meals, the works. And now he's ended up a real con artist!'

'Oh, Keeley, how can you say that? I like his work. I think it's really good – some of it, anyway.'

'Vincent, get real. It's a bunch of stabs and sloshes, that's all. If Alain or Serge can sell it, good luck to them, and to him. But don't try to tell me he's the new Picasso. Hey, did Picasso hang out up here?'

'No. He was Spanish. I don't think anyone rated him very highly either, in the beginning.'

But if it was ersatz nowadays, Montmartre was lively and amusing too, and there was still some genuine talent in it; as they shared a shockingly expensive Perrier they listened to a young man and woman, of about their own age, playing a cello and violin on a corner.

'They're good, aren't they? Not that I know the first thing about classical music, but I can tell they are.'

'Yes . . . look at all the coins people are giving them, everyone likes them.'

'H'mm. So if everyone likes what you do, Vincent, d'you reckon that makes it good?'

'Not always! I mean, lots of people liked what Hitler did, at the time, but did that make it good?'

'No way! But I don't know very much about him either, only that he killed millions of people . . . how could anyone have thought that was good? I suppose I'd know if I'd paid more attention at school . . . I wish now that I had. To history and art and everything. I'm fed up feeling like such a total ignoramus.'

'You're not ignorant. Only curious.'

'I am, Vincent. Pig ignorant. OK, I've learned a bit since I came to France, but it's only a drop in the ocean. I'm going to have to spend the rest of my life knee deep in books. There's just so much . . . and some of it is so interesting, too.'

This was something Vincent liked very much about Keeley; when she knew nothing she admitted to it, but never rejected anything new. In the beginning she had, a little, it had been a battle to get her favourably disposed to French food, but after that the floodgates had opened, and it pleasantly surprised him that now she would listen to music, look at a painting, try virtually anything without turning a hair. Even his mother's small garden was a source of joy to her, and in the Tuileries she had been not only rapturous over the tulips but able to name one or two species, her cheeks as pink as their petals. Without explanation, he suddenly turned to her and kissed her.

'Oh! What was that for?'

'For you. For being you.'

It was evening before they began to think of returning to their hotel, and wended their way back slowly, watching the lights come on the whole length of the distant Eiffel Tower, all over the city they could see below them as they walked down the hill from the Place du Tertre.

'It's fabulous. Like fairyland.'

'Yes. But Aix is home . . . tell me something, Keeley?'

She turned to look into his face. 'What?'

'Do you really think of France as your home, now? Or do you harbour secret plans to spirit me away to Ireland, some day?'

'No, Vincent. I don't. I started to put down roots here as soon as I arrived, and they went deeper when I married you . . . maybe if I'd been older when I left Ireland I'd have more memories, more things to miss. But I was only eighteen, hardly knew who I was or what I was – now, I'm the person I created when I got here. I have a husband and a job and a home, a life. I love it, and I love you.'

He squeezed her hand. 'I know it's not much, for now. But it will get better, Keeley. I promise you it will.'

'Vincent, wouldja give over! It's great, a thousand times better than I ever expected. Anyone would think we were starving in a mud hut, to hear you talk.'

'Still . . . when we were walking in the Rue du Rivoli, past all those jewellers' windows, I couldn't help thinking about the engagement ring you still haven't got.'

'But I've got you! Who cares about a silly old diamond?'

He laughed. 'Oh, come on now, admit it – you're enjoying your taste of luxury at the George V.'

Well, yes. She was loving it, to be honest, studying the other guests and wondering what it was they did that they could afford to stay there. Presumably they weren't all on weekend honeymoons, courtesy of their in-laws. They must have tremendous jobs, and work tremendously hard at them . . . either that or they were funny fish like Cathal Sullivan and his father, able to magic money up out of fresh air. A lot of money. But at least these people spent it freely, weren't mean to their spouses – or were they? She knew, now, about appearances being deceptive.

'Yes, of course I'm enjoying it. But most of all I'm enjoying you. I'm only thinking about the luxury in between times.'

'Oh? And what are you thinking, about it?'

She grinned rather coyly. 'I'll tell you tomorrow.'

'Oh, come on, tell me now.'

'No.'

He persisted, but he couldn't get it out of her. For such a little handful, she could be remarkably strong-willed. However, he brightened as they neared the hotel and he thought of the wonderful evening in store, the exquisite dinner they would eat in the restaurant, the fine wine that every true Frenchman appreciated, and the lovely lady that every true Frenchman appreciated even more.

After their second star-spangled night they were ready to come and live permanently at the George V, and it was no fun to have to pack their bags. But they left them stored at reception, and consoled themselves that they still had almost a whole day in Paris.

'Where to, madame?'

'Are there more gardens somewhere, or a park?'

'Lots. We could go to the Jardin du Luxembourg, there are fountains there, or the Parc Monceau has Roman ruins, and a Chinese bridge over a river, the guidebook says—'

'Oh yes, that sounds good.'

Walking off another memorable breakfast, which this time included the most amazing hot chocolate and croissants either of them had ever tasted, they eventually reached the Parc Monceau to find it alive with dozens of extremely glossy toddlers accompanied by their freshly-starched nannies. Lots of kids, but no graffiti here, no vandals, no fights or broken glass; it was a long way from Keeley's own childhood.

'Crikey, they're so well behaved you'd think they were on Valium or something.'

Sitting down on a bench, they watched them for a while, and once again Vincent took her hand.

'I suppose ours will be savages, when we have them, whooping little Tourands, the terror of Aix-en-Provence. You know, Keeley, if it would help – if a child would be a comfort to you, when I'm away—'

She sighed, but quite contentedly. 'No, Vincent. We have too much to do first, before we have children.'

'Have we?'

'Yes.' She turned to him at the same moment he turned to her, and they both started to speak at once.

'No, ladies first!'

She liked this teasing, that he'd been doing all weekend, about her being a lady. After her sojourn at the sumptuous hotel she was even starting to feel like one, watching her language in case anyone thought Vincent was married to a tramp, eating her food slowly because it tasted so delectable, pampering her face and body in the furnished lotions and potions that felt so luxurious – and that she'd packed a few samples of, surreptitiously until Vincent said to go ahead, hotels expected you to.

'No, you first. What I want to say will probably take ages to explain, so you might as well get your speech out of the way.'

'Well . . . you might think I haven't been looking for any way out of this situation, Keeley. But I have. I've thought of quite a few possibilities. Only I don't know what you'll make of the one I think is our best option.'

'Try me.'

'OK. Look, you love your hairdressing, don't you?'

'Yes.'

'And you're really good at it?'

'Yes. So Eliane says, and frankly I agree with her.'

'And you want to have your own salon?'

She gaped at him. It was as if they'd been coming from opposite directions – literally, her from Aix and he from Paris – and they'd miraculously met at a crossroads.

'Yes.'

'That's what I thought. And the more I thought, the more I became convinced that that's our best hope, Keeley. If you were to open a salon of your own, I could manage it for you. You don't know anything about stock control or paying salaries or taxes, marketing or any of that stuff, but I do. We could both specialise in what we're best at.'

'But – but Vincent—'

'What?'

'Sorry. Nothing. Go on.'

'Well, I know you're young and I'm not much older, but I reckon we could still do well, work well together. It wouldn't cost me a thought to leave the company I work for now. It's just a job, not a career I really love, and I could spend the rest of my life being shunted around, a little cog in a big wheel. I don't know what you think about taking a risk like this, but if you—'

'Oh, Vincent!' To his consternation she burst out laughing, leaving him bemused.

'Is it that funny? Well, maybe it does sound a little far-fetched. But I really thought – in fact, I was so sure you'd be interested, I even took it a bit further.'

'How far? To where?'

'To the bank manager. To several banks, actually, because I'm sorry to say they all turned me down. Nobody seemed to think two youngsters with no collateral would be a good risk. That's where my plan sort of ran into a wall. We'd need quite a lot of venture capital, to equip a salon and get us off the ground.'

She couldn't stop laughing, and gasping with disbelief. Somewhat offended, he tried again.

'Well, you can't say I haven't been working on any ideas. Do you really think this one is a dodo, yes?'

Sobering up, she gazed at him with something close to hero-worship. 'I think it's a gem. An absolute winner, because it is exactly the same as my own. Vincent, this is exactly what I was going to talk to you about! Only I decided to leave it until now, because I didn't want it to come between us on our honeymoon, if you didn't like it.'

It was his turn to disbelieve. 'You're joking. Keeley, you can't have been thinking the very same thing as me.'

She nodded. 'Yes. I have. The only difference is that I've gone even further with it. I hope you won't take it the wrong way that I didn't consult you, but you weren't there, and besides I didn't want you to be disappointed if he said no.'

'If who said no, to what?'

'If Félix said no, to lending us the money. Investing in us.'

'Félix? Félix Peyrolle? But he—'

'Yes, I know, he runs the Vieux Moulin. But he wants something of his own. He told me one day that he'd saved some money, and had been thinking of backing Mary if she ever set up a restaurant – only then she left, and he couldn't find anyone else of her calibre in catering. It was only later – when Tony got so lucky and I saw how eager Alain and Serge were to invest in him – that I suddenly thought, bingo, that's it! If I can convince Félix to put his money into a first-rate salon instead of a first-rate restaurant, we're in business!'

'And – and are we? Did you see him, what did he say?'

'He said yes! His wife Lise is one of my clients and she's always telling him how good I am, in fact he only has to look at her hair to see for himself. So we had a long talk. I explained to him that it was no use my trying to sound businesslike because that was your department, but that I was mad keen to have my own salon and certain I could make a good job of it, if only I had someone to run the business end. Someone like you.'

'But he hardly knows me.'

'No. But I said you were a trainee manager and knew about all the things you've just mentioned – stock control and all that. So he said it sounded full of potential to him, that he'd back me if he could convince Lise and I could convince you. He wants to talk to you the next time you're back in Aix, to both of us together.'

'Oh, my God. Keeley, I can't believe this.'

'You'd better believe it. We've even discussed the theme – the concept, he called it. He thinks it should be a young, lively salon – and what's more, I think Eliane might sell hers to us.'

'Why? Why on earth would she do that?'

'Because her husband is ill and she wants to spend more time with him. She could do that if she got a good lump sum . . . it would need complete redecoration, but all the equipment is there, and in good condition. We'd probably get premises and equipment as a going concern for not much more than brand-new equipment would cost. So Félix says, anyway. He's really keen, Vincent! He talked a lot about how we'd attract new young clients, said all the service industries have a lot in common and that there wasn't a huge difference between a restaurant and a salon, the important thing is to send every client out with a smile on their face. He – uh – he said I smile so much, it would surely be contagious.'

Stopping to draw breath, and blush a bit, she looked at him eagerly. 'And now here you are, telling me you do want to run the place, it's the very same thing you'd thought of yourself! That was the only thing holding me back, the thought that you might not want to leave your job . . . but somehow I felt that you might.'

Yes. Oh, yes. Gazing into her eyes, he felt indeed that he might. Felt that he'd only ever had one better idea than this in his entire life, and that was the day he married her.

Keeley returned to Aix that evening, but Vincent did not leave for Rouen. Instead he found a telephone, called Alain Jou and politely, cheerfully, offered his resignation. Astonished, Alain implored him to reconsider, to think of his future, but he replied that he had thought of it. That was why, with his beautiful brilliant wife Keeley, he now intended to open a hairdressing salon, and furthermore the Jou family would be the very first to be invited to the launch, because Keeley expected Alain's daughter Yvette to be her first enthusiastic new customer – no, client, actually.

Bemused, and not a little annoyed when he thought of the effort he had made to help Vincent's career, Alain snorted and made a long speech about self-employment being extremely risky. Vincent couldn't possibly know anything about the long hours, the endless worry and responsibility; had he thought of all the overheads – salaries, insurance, rates, taxes, equipment, advertising? They wouldn't turn a penny profit for at least a year if not two, and what would they live on in the meantime?

Love, said Vincent grandly – oh, and they had a backer. A private investor with lots of money, a friend of his wife's. Alain snorted again, and had to fight back laughter as Vincent rattled on, exploding with enthusiasm as only a young man of his age could. But he was very curious to know who the backer might be.

Vincent replied that all would be revealed in due course. Meanwhile, would Alain get the personnel department to put his affairs in order, and tell Yvette that Keeley recommended a particularly fetching shade of plum? Alain said he would do no such thing – but finally he laughed and wished them both good luck, if they really were determined to do it.

Yes, Vincent said, they were determined. In fact, he went on in a flurry of euphoria, Alain might even consider resigning from his own post some day to become Tony Butler's full-time manager, since brother and sister were both so very talented. This was a bit cheeky, and Alain was surprised to find himself not remonstrating, just in case Vincent might be right.

The conversation concluded with mutual goodwill, and Vincent returned in high spirits to the car where he had left Keeley waiting for him, to find that she had changed places into the driver's seat. Horrified, he told her there was no question of her driving them back to Aix, she'd never manage the Periphérique – but she insisted she would, because he was not the only manager in the Tourand family, she could go places too and would he please get in beside her.

Quaking, he got in, but after a few unnerving miles he began to relax, and accept that Keeley had learned the skill of driving just as she had learned the skill of hairdressing, with total efficiency. All the long road back they talked about the salon, and the future, and the spectacular success they were going to make of it. Some day they would return to the George V, and pay their own bill, and it wouldn't cost them a thought.

Chapter Ten

As he made his way hand in hand with Keeley to the Vieux Moulin, Vincent was briefly unnerved. What if Keeley had over-estimated Félix's interest in this costly, risky venture? What if Félix didn't take a shine to him, decided against backing two youngsters with more optimism than anything else? He had quit his job, he'd be high and dry, Alain would never let him hear the end of it . . .

'Vincent,' Keeley said firmly. 'Felix is going to love you. He's going to see all the potential in you that I see, and he is going to insist that you run our salon. Have you got that clear, or do I have to say it again?'

'I've got it clear,' he mumbled, wishing he'd arranged this meeting before resigning – and realising, suddenly, that it was a lesson. Get your facts lined up first, ascertain your position, and then act. He'd never do it the wrong way round again.

It was mid-afternoon, again in the lull between lunch and dinner, and Félix sat waiting for them looking even more primly forbidding than usual, peering over his glasses at a pile of handwritten notes and figures. But he jumped to his feet when they came in, and shook hands cordially before kissing Keeley, with warm familiarity, on both cheeks. Vincent was both impressed and outraged.

'And here's your husband, Keeley, the man who had the luck and sense to marry you!'

'Yes – how are you, Félix? It's good to see you,' he replied in what he hoped was a manful tone, thinking that his marriage to Keeley had indeed been a farsighted thing. Urging them to sit down, Félix produced coffee and indicated the pile of papers.

'It might be a long conversation. I have been doing some projections . . . very boring for you, Keeley, I'm afraid! But I'd like Vincent to take a look at them and tell me what he thinks.'

Keeley nudged him as Félix poured the coffee, and Vincent caught on; Félix wanted to see whether he even knew what projections were. But he was able to smile as he squeezed her hand reassuringly under the table; he had not only studied them but loved them, found them absolutely fascinating. Gazing at the mass of figures, he looked at Félix.

'May I?'

Felix nodded, and he picked up the first page, running his eye slowly down it before picking up the next, and then another. It took him a few minutes to tune into Félix's style of calculation, but when he did he felt a wave of relief: this was the work of a very competent man, but if anything Félix was thinking small. After years of managing a restaurant for someone else he was clearly in the habit of caution, was neither a visionary nor a gambler. As he studied the figures in silence Vincent could see ways of expanding their parameters, making the sums of money work even harder than Félix imagined. Several times he paused to ask questions, and Félix responded in the restrained tone of someone who had never before been let off his financial leash. His projections were almost touchingly modest, solid and somehow earnest.

Of course they were only projections, based on cursory research; neither of them had yet investigated real costs in detail. Still, Félix clearly hadn't been letting the grass grow under his feet since Keeley first approached him.

'These look sound as a bell to me, Félix, as blueprints. But may I ask you a bit more about them?'

Certainly he could, Félix said, looking like a father addressing a son, prepared to be indulgent. But the first question took him by surprise, and the next one caught him totally off guard. Vincent Tourand might be young, but he seemed to know his maths. Spreading the papers over the table, they were soon immersed in them, and for the first time ever Keeley witnessed the amazing spectacle of Félix Peyrolle taking off his jacket and rolling up his sleeves.

Sipping her coffee, she tried to feign comprehension and disguise her impatience – as yet, the word 'hair' hadn't even been mentioned. It all seemed to have to do with margins and grosses and balances, stretching her French to its limits until finally she gave up, thinking that it was all so clinical they might as well be talking about opening a hospital or college department. But she was conscious of seeing a new Vincent emerging, something in him she had never seen before as he sat engrossed and efficient and, apparently, very knowledgeable. Of course he must have learned all this stuff when he was training for his original career, but he'd never talked about it, all she knew for sure was that he was a good hard worker. Now, he looked to her like Einstein, and she felt a tingle of pride in him. She also felt redundant, acutely conscious of her inferior education.

'Excuse me,' she eventually murmured, 'I think I'll just go out for a breath of air.'

They both nodded absently, not hearing or noticing when she slipped away. Blinking in the light that was almost pure white after the dark of the restaurant, she went for a walk, window shopping and wandering for half an hour, but when she came back they were still at it, sitting there oblivious of all else. As she stood looking at them, she knew that the deal was sealed. She was going to get her salon, Vincent was going to run it and Felix was going to back it. They were partners.

'But weren't you nervous? Didn't you think I might blow it?'

Vincent sat on the rickety chair at the kitchen table, with a photocopied stack of the figures in front of him, while Keeley wrestled with the cafetière because this, he had insisted, was no time for instant.

'I did not. Not for a moment. Why would you?'

'Because I'm young and inexperienced and I've never managed anything before.'

'No, but you've been trained to. It's what you do. It never even crossed my mind that Félix might change his.'

He beamed at her, and touched her hand as she put the cafetière down on the table. 'My God. Talk about blind faith. But you needn't worry, Keeley. It's not misplaced. I'll do all the purchasing and accounting, the taxes, hire the staff and run the rosters, place the advertising, deal with things you probably haven't even thought of – we're going to need a back-up water supply, because Aix sometimes runs a bit dry in summer. And commercial water rates, of course – I'm sure Eliane has those already?'

'Search me. I suppose she does. But Vincent, what if she won't sell?'

'Then we'll have to find somewhere else. But let's arrange a meeting with her next, and see what happens. If she turns our offer down, Félix says he knows of a vacant premises on the rue Manuel, but I think that's a bit off the beaten track. We want to be as central as possible.'

'Yes. A lot of Eliane's customers come in before or after they go shopping, it would be a pity to lose them when they're so reliable and regular.'

'They're reliable because you are! Lots of them book you specifically, don't they?'

'Yes. And they've got enough money to get their hair done frequently, although they won't let me experiment with new styles . . . I don't want to lose them, but I'd like to get a few new clients too – you know, younger, more adventurous.'

'Well, Aix is a university town. But the students are away during the summer, and broke as often as not. I think the safest thing is to stick with the regular customers at first, and maybe go after their daughters later . . . who knows, if things go well we could even consider expanding in time, open a second salon with a younger theme?'

'Wow, wouldn't that be something! But let's concentrate on the first, and do as you say. There's no point in having a manager if I'm not going to listen to him. Still, if we get Eliane's place I want to decorate and jazz it up, make it fresher and more attractive to everyone.'

He thought for a moment, looking intently at her, and suddenly kissed her nose.

'Right. We will do it up and put your stamp on it. Give it a new name, too – have you thought of anything?'

'Oh, I've been thinking about it for ages! And I think we should simply call it *Cut!*'

'*Cut!* But why? That's an English word.'

'I know. But that's why it'll stand out. Besides, it's short and easy to pronounce, and even French women will know it's got something to do with Hollywood, it'll make them feel like film stars!'

He was dubious, but she looked so eager he decided to go along with this one thing. After all, most of the other decisions would be his, while she was doing the cutting.

'OK. We'll try the name out on my mother and sister. If they like it, we'll use it.'

Suddenly she felt so excited she could hardly contain herself. With a name on the salon, she could actually see it taking shape, like a perfect cut.

'Oh, Vincent, this is going to be magic! I can't wait to get going, get my hands on it!'

'Well, even if Eliane does agree to sell, Félix reckons it'll take two or three months to set up shop. There's a lot of work to be done first.'

'Oh . . . as long as that? But you have no income now, in the meantime . . . we'll starve on mine alone.'

'No, we won't. Félix has offered me a temporary job until then. A very humble one, but a job just the same.'

'Has he? Doing what?'

'Waiting tables, at nights. I won't earn much, but it'll keep the roof over our heads, and I'll be free during the day to get this project off the ground.'

'Isn't Félix a doll! But you'll be exhausted, and we'll hardly ever see each other.'

'I know. But Keeley, that's part of starting a business. You have to make sacrifices and put in long hours.'

'I suppose . . . oh, God, Vincent, it's so good to have you home. I can't believe you're sitting right here at this table and not dashing off again. I didn't want to tell you, but I missed you no end when you were away.'

Glad of the excuse to put down the revolting coffee, he put his arms around her, and held her to him.

'I know. I nearly went mad without you, too. I love you more and more every day I spend with you . . . tell you what, why don't we celebrate our new venture with dinner and a bottle of wine, right here at home?'

'Uh . . . because there isn't a bite of food in the fridge! I'll never get the hang of this housekeeping lark. If Mary was here she'd whip up a feast out of two carrots and an onion. We should have taken Félix up on his invitation to stay and eat at the Moulin.'

'No. I think it's better to stay off his turf, especially since I'll be a waiter there as of Monday. Oh well . . . I guess I'll just have to take Madame to Quick, if she doesn't mind footing the bill.'

'No problem, if sir doesn't mind sharing one plate of pasta between us. I lost out on tips today, because of having to go and meet Félix, and I had to beg Eliane for the hour off. I'm very fond of her, but I must say she can be a right battleaxe during working hours.'

'H'mm. I suppose that's what your employees will be saying about you this time next year.'

They both laughed. The notion of either of them being anybody's boss seemed hilarious . . . and it was a long way

from fillet steak at the George V back to pasta at Quick.
But what great fun they were going to have, living together
properly at last, even if they did have to do it on fresh air for
the foreseeable future.

At the end of an unexpected but delicious lunch at the Vieux
Moulin, Eliane was mystified when the manager of the restaurant
came to the table she was sharing with Keeley and Vincent,
offered everyone a digestif and then sat down with them.
Baffled, she turned to Keeley.

'All right. I give up. Why have you taken me to lunch, and
why is Monsieur Peyrolle joining us with a bottle of Cointreau
in his hand?'

Nervous and excited in equal proportion, Keeley laughed.
'Because you'll need a drink when you hear what we want to
ask you!'

'Will I?'

'Yes – go on, Félix, you do the talking.'

But Félix shook his head. 'Oh no. This is your idea, Keeley,
you do it. You could talk your way through a brick wall.'

'Oh – well – all right, I will! Eliane, you're going to think we're
mad, but the three of us, Vincent, Félix and me, would like to
make you an offer for your salon. Buy it from you, I mean.'

Eliane's hand flew to her throat.

'Buy my salon? The three of *you*?'

'Yes. If you'd be interested in selling it, for a fair price, Félix
would like to pay for it, Vincent would like to run it, and I
would like to – to become the new Eliane! We want to go into
partnership, and you say you want to spend more time with
your husband . . . if we offered you a lump sum, in cash, would
you consider it?'

'I – I – my goodness, Keeley, I don't know what to say. This
is such a surprise, and you – you are so young.'

'Yes. I know I am, and so is Vincent, but Félix is old enough
to know what he's doing. We've been discussing it and planning
it and we thought we'd give you first crack at an offer from us.
We won't be offended or anything if you turn us down, but
I hope you won't be offended either when I tell you that I'm
going to have to leave your employment, because I really want
to start up a place of my own.'

For a moment there was silence all round, and Keeley prayed
she had put things the right way. The French could be so touchy

about what they called etiquette, and she'd never put a business proposal to anyone in her life. Still, there was no point in beating about the bush. Either Eliane was going to sell, or she was going to have a rival salon to contend with.

In slow motion, Eliane put down her glass and stared at her.

'Well . . . I must say, Keeley, I never expected my most junior stylist to sneak up on me like this! But if you are serious, and can make me a serious offer . . . well, yes, I would consider selling. Much as I enjoy my work, my husband is very ill, and he is more important than it. But I would need quite a lot of money to enable me to retire, at my relatively young age. Also, the premises are valuable, the equipment is in good order and the client list is solid as a rock.'

'Yes. We know that. But Félix here is the one with the money. He'll talk to you about it – go on, Félix, break open your piggy bank.'

She held her breath as Felix made his offer, and Eliane sat back thinking, making mental calculations. Vincent said nothing, but looked a lot calmer than he could possibly be.

'No.'

Eliane looked apologetic as she finally reached her decision, and Keeley groaned.

'*No*? Oh, Eliane! Félix isn't a millionaire, but he's making you a good—'

Vincent kicked her shin and she shut up abruptly as Elaine sighed sadly.

'Yes, it's a good offer, but it's not good enough. I have extra expenses, you see, because Roger is ill, his medication is so expensive, his medical care – the insurance is not adequate – I would need at least another hundred thousand francs to be able to support us properly.'

Keeley suppressed a gasp. A hundred thousand francs was a huge sum, she could live on it for years. But Félix spoke up, sounding less daunted than he surely felt.

'I am afraid that is beyond my resources, madame. The most I could raise is another fifty thousand.'

There was another prolonged silence, in which Keeley wondered how Félix might raise even that much. And then, suddenly, Eliane smiled.

'Let us say sixty thousand. Monsieur Peyrolle, and we have a deal.'

Felix never wavered. 'Very well, madame. My final offer. Sixty thousand on top of the original sum.'

Beaming, Eliane extended her right hand. 'Agreed. I will sell you my salon, and you have my best wishes for its success.'

It was all over so suddenly, so amicably, that Keeley felt dizzy with relief as Vincent grabbed and hugged her and then, to his consternation, they both jumped up and hugged Félix. God only knew where he was going to get the extra money, but they were going to make it worth every penny.

The days and weeks that followed were so busy, so demanding and absorbing, that Keeley found time to scribble only a post-card to Mary, telling her that her project had borne fruit, she was opening a salon and further details would follow. It felt as if she had barely fallen into bed when it was time to get up again, and there were days when she and Vincent saw no more of each other than a passing kiss on the stairs; but they had never felt happier despite the dire speech Félix made to them one evening, warning them of all the pitfalls they now faced.

It was extremely difficult, he said, for married couples to work together. They must be prepared for many arguments which, if they had any sense, they would patch up every night before going to sleep. The salon would exert many pressures which should never be taken home; shout and scream all you like, he went on, but don't sulk, don't take it personally, keep your relationship separate from your work. Solemnly they nodded and said they would try.

Then there would be the teething problems everyone ran into at the start: builders not renovating on time, suppliers trying to rip them off, staff finding it difficult to work for such young bosses, clients not turning up for appointments . . . he had encountered endless hassle in his first few years at the Vieux Moulin, similar to those Vincent and Keeley now faced, but everything would work out eventually – probably – hopefully – if they were patient. He wouldn't interefere, but they could ask his advice whenever they felt they needed to, and *must* ask if it was anything serious. Keeley appreciated everything he said, but her impatience to get started made her fidgety, and half of it went in one ear and out the other.

Vincent, on the other hand, drank it all in, thinking, considering, pursuing things whenever he wasn't sure what Félix meant. Every night he waited tables at the restaurant, but every day he went to the salon to talk to Eliane, question her endlessly, and finally to supervise when the decorators arrived. Keeley wanted the place to look bright and fresh, but she didn't have the first idea how to achieve that look when it came to choosing paints, fabrics, new flooring and windows, so Félix and Vincent worked it out between them while she busied herself with a music system, a coffee dispenser, plants and all the bric-à-brac that would make her clients feel warm, relaxed and comfortable. Previously all staff and clients had addressed each other as 'madame' in the formal French manner, but she resolved to dispense with that; everyone would simply call her Keeley and regular clients, at least, would be called by their first names unless they strongly objected. One day she and Vincent had their first row, as Félix predicted, a furious shouting match over the position of a hair dryer, and she was ready to hit him over the head with it until he stood back and started to laugh.

'We don't need to plug it in anywhere' he said, 'you're generating such electricity it'll work by itself.'

She was amazed to find herself laughing back; in the house she had grown up in no argument had ever been defused by a smile or a joke. Finally they tossed a coin to decide, and although she was satisfied to win she was even more pleased that Vincent didn't say another word about it. After all, she was the one who would have to work with the equipment, and in turn she tried to leave what he called 'administrative decisions' to him even when some of them sounded quite crazy.

When it came to interviewing staff they did it together, with Félix, because she felt sure she would get a fit of the giggles halfway through, it was such a ludicrous position for her to be in. But Félix and Vincent took it seriously, and insisted on six-month contracts for everyone they hired, so that both parties could be sure they would get on together before making any long-term commitment. Sternly, Vincent even warned his sister Sylvie that she would be treated like anyone else, but Keeley grinned at that and told Sylvie not to mind him, she was a brilliant colourist and would be treated royally – until she departed on her cycling tour at any rate, and they had to find a replacement. That worried Keeley a bit, but Vincent simply said it was months off, they would cross that bridge when they came to it.

It wasn't until she sat down, one evening in April, to write a list of people to invite to the opening that she realised she had not heard from Mary for some time . . . quite a long time,

six or eight weeks now that she thought about it. When the
list was finished she dashed off a short letter, inviting her and
wondering how she was. Was Cathal behaving himself, was
Mel walkie-talkie, how was the pregnancy progressing? For a
moment she considered telling Mary that Félix was putting up
the money for the venture, but then decided to say only that a
local businessman was putting it up. If Mary ever found out the
truth, that she might have had her own restaurant in Aix if she
had stayed, it would upset and grieve her terribly. Might even
unhinge her altogether, if things were no better with Cathal or
The Lantern. As she sealed the letter Keeley felt a stab of guilt,
and sadness in the midst of her joy. If Mary did manage to come
to the launch, she would warn Félix to say nothing.

But weeks after the letter had been posted there was still no
response, and she had time to worry only intermittently as the
day of the opening, June 1, drew near. One sunny morning, as
she stood knee-deep in the rubble the decorators said would
soon look palatial, Luc drove up in his Citröen and came in,
all smiles.

'Bonjour, Keeley! I have come to discuss the menu!'

Devouring her in a hug, he produced a list from his pocket
and asked her to choose: did she want beef or chicken salad
for the launch, prawn quiche or bacon quiche, cheese canapés
or fish, or both, or the whole lot, or what? And the wines – he
recommended an Alsace, but if she preferred a Burgundy or a
Chablis . . . ?

She grinned wryly. 'I want whatever Félix says I want, Luc!
He's the one who's paying for it, and it would be nice if he
doesn't have to sell his house when he gets the bill.'

'Oh, Keeley, such nonsense, the buffet is my good-luck gift
to you all, I will cook it personally, there will be no bill – now,
I was thinking of some olives with the charcuterie, but if you
have other ideas, this is the time to say so . . .'

Simmering with enthusiasm, he sat her down and insisted she
choose, with absolutely no regard for cost. Greatly touched by
his generosity, she went through the proposed menu with him,
feeling some bittersweet sensation; he was a wonderful friend
and she couldn't think how to express her gratitude to him – but
what a shame that Mary was not here with them, that they were
not all planning this buffet together. Mary would have loved it,
and she would have loved her to do it, to show off her culinary
talents to all of Aix.

It seemed as if all of Aix was coming to the event, Luc remarked when she showed him the guest list; Félix had invited many wealthy people who dined regularly at the Moulin, and Alain Jou had contributed people who shopped in his store, bought paintings at Serge Rolland's gallery . . . with any luck the invited journalists would turn up, and *Cut!* would open in a blaze of publicity. Keeley smiled.

'I don't mind telling you, Luc, I'm petrified. A hundred people, and I know about six of them! Bigshots, too, all coming to my little salon . . . I feel like a right chancer.'

Surprisingly he didn't laugh, but looked at her quite seriously.

'Keeley, let me tell you something I have learned as a top chef at a top restaurant. You will agree that I am a superb cook, non?'

She grinned. Modesty was not one of Luc's many virtues.

'Yes, brill! I can still taste that fabulous meal you cooked for my wedding.'

'OK. You are in no doubt about that, and I am in no doubt that you are a superb hair stylist. Félix has told me, his wife has told me, my own wife has told me. So, that is not the question. The question is, how to let everybody know that you exist. In the beginning, you must not be shy. You must make a lot of noise, provide a spectacle, lots of colour and excitement for people to talk about. That is why this launch is so important. Aix is a big city, there are plenty of other parties every night of the week, but we must make sure this one stands out.'

Interested, she looked at him quizzically. 'Right. And how do we do that?'

'Well, you rely on me for the food and drink, of course. I assure you it will be most dramatic. But you must make an enormous effort too. You must forget that you are young, that you are a foreigner whose French, if I may say so, is sometimes rather peculiar. Forget your origins, forget your inhibitions, and go for broke. On the night this salon opens, I do not want to see you in any little black dress, I do not want to see you holding your husband's hand, I do not want to see you wavering or wondering about anything. You will wear something very sexy, you will talk and smile and greet people with every ounce of your forceful little personality. You will drink no alcohol but you will sparkle like champagne. And of course you will do

something startling with your hair, to remind people why they
are here.'

She grasped his drift instantly, eagerly.

'Right! I've spent nearly two years learning how to behave
like a lady, but for one night I'm to let my hair down – or put
it up in lights, or something!'

'Yes. In restaurants, people love to eat good food, but they
also want to feel they have had a night out. They adore watching
food being *flambé*, hearing tantrums in the kitchen, even scenes
between quarrelling couples. Anything colourful, provided they
still have a good meal – so, your launch must be colourful, and
so must you.'

'Crikey, Luc, you've saved me just in time. I was going to get
out my little black number and concentrate on being a good girl,
getting all my verbs right.'

'Damn your verbs! Buy an outrageous dress and lots of fake
jewellery, wear your highest heels and your most vivid make-up.
When you shine, your salon will shine too.'

His tone was very definite, and suddenly so was hers.

'OK! Leave it to me, Luc, I know how to be a tart! I'll wear
a miniskirt up to my armpits and dance on the tables!'

'Yes. Something like that, anyway. Vincent will try to tone
you down, but you mustn't listen to him.'

'Oh, don't worry, he has a sense of humour under all that
quiet good sense. Anyone who married me has to have.'

He sat back on the worktop he was using for a chair, and
considered her from under his deceptively fearsome eyebrows.

'I don't think there's any joke about it at all, Keeley. Since
first making your acquaintance I have got to know a remarkable
little woman – one with far more stamina and resilience than, I
am sorry to say, her friend Mary displayed when the chips were
down. Tell me, how is Mary? Is she coming to this party?'

'I – I don't know, Luc. I'd love her to, but I haven't heard from
her for ages. You know she's pregnant, and very busy with—'

'With that mistake of a child, that worse mistake of a
husband, that *total* mistake of a miserable restaurant! My
God, Keeley, it makes my blood boil!'

Taken aback that he knew, or guessed, so much, she groped
for words that would not sound disloyal.

'Oh, Luc, she did what she thought right at the time, and
now she's trying to make the best of it. It's not all as bad as
that – baby Mel isn't, anyway. She's gorgeous.'

'Ha. I've said it before and I'll say it again – women, women and their babies! Look, Keeley, this might sound very indiscreet and I hope you won't take offence, because I'm only trying to give you some good advice – which is, don't have any children if you want to get this business of yours off the ground. Don't even think of it, for ten years at least.'

She bit her lip, thinking that he was being a bit personal, but also thinking that he was right.

'No, Luc. I don't plan to. Not for a very long time – maybe even twelve or fifteen years, if I can put Vincent off for that long.'

'H'm. Does he want children?'

'Not now. But in the long run, I'm sure he does. Most men – most people – oh, sorry. I forgot Félix doesn't have any. But I'd better not ask you whether that was by choice or accident.'

'It was by accident. He and Lise married late, and then it simply didn't happen. Perhaps that is why he has adopted you, in a manner of speaking! But they are a very happy couple, always have been.'

'Yes. I can see that. And so are Vincent and I . . . we don't feel any need to become parents, but even if we did we'll have no time and no money for a long while yet. If I ever do have a child I want it to have everything I never had – lots of love and security and the kind of home it won't have to apologise for or run away from.'

He looked at her keenly, but then laughed. 'When my children were young, I wished they would run away! All of them! Teenagers are a curse invented by Satan!'

'The cheek of you. I was one myself until recently.'

'Yes. You were young and lost, and hurting and angry, I think, when you first came to France. But you have made such progress, and now you have a wonderful opportunity to make more. Much more, if you have the wit I think you have.'

He grimaced at her, as if to say she'd better have, and stood up to take his leave of her with another of his all-consuming hugs. Walking him to the door, she thought how she would never have had such a conversation with the reserved, formal Félix, but what great friends both men had bizarrely become.

And meanwhile there was Mary, her oldest and closest friend, not even writing to say whether she was coming to the opening of her new venture. Chillingly, unwillingly, she felt a little pang of hurt, wondering whether Mary had miraculously salvaged her marriage to Cathal, and no longer needed her. No longer even wanted her, perhaps, because she knew too much.

The month of May was mellow and balmy, and despite their heavy workload Vincent insisted they go cycling one Sunday, for air and exercise and a break from the whole thing. Packing a rucksack of bread, gruyère, cherries and mineral water, he suggested they head for Puyloubier and visit Cézanne's house, where they had not been for months.

But Keeley shook her head. 'No ... let's go somewhere else.'

'All right. But why? Have you gone off it?'

'No. I still love it. But that's just the problem.'

'What is? What do you mean?'

'Oh – I just mean – that – well, you'll probably think this is absurd, but I – I'm haunted by it! Every time I look at it I can see myself living in it, sleeping in it, eating out in the garden in summer, lighting fires in winter ... when I think of the house I grew up in, and my chances of ever living in that one, or somewhere like it, I feel ridiculous. I mean, here we are in a tiny flat, starting out on a venture that will take years to break even, never mind turn a profit – I'd just rather not torture myself with visions of lovely houses or Cézanne paintings or anything else way out of my reach.'

He squinted at her. 'You're getting nervous, aren't you? About the salon, now that it's so close to opening?'

She flushed, a little defensively; she didn't want anyone, even him, to see the nerves behind the breezy bravado. 'Don't be silly! The salon has nothing to do with it! Anyway it's going to be a great success – it's just going to take a long time, that's all.'

'Yes,' he said thoughtfully, as they mounted the bikes and set off towards Ventabren instead. 'It is. We might eventually be able to move into a better flat, even get a house some day, but it would probably be better not to think in terms of houses like that. One salon would never yield that kind of return. We'll have to wait until we have several.'

She whirled round to him, nearly falling off her bike, that she had borrowed yet again from Sylvie.

'What did you say?'

He shouted over the breeze and traffic. 'I said we'll have to wait until we have a whole chain of salons before we buy the house at Puyloubier!'

She could hardly believe her ears. This was steady, sensible Vincent, talking about owning a whole chain of salons? And that house? When all she could think of was Felix's investment, and the terrifying prospect of what would happen if they lost every penny of it?

'Vincent, you're mad! You're barking!'

'Yeah!' he called over his shoulder. 'I am. Barking mad, about you.'

Mary's letter, when it came two days before *Cut!* was launched on the unsuspecting citizens of Aix, hit Keeley with such force she felt as if the floor had been yanked from under her. Vincent had left early for the salon where the final touches were being put frantically in place, and she was about to follow him there when she ran into the postman. As he put the envelope into her hand she felt a sudden stab, as if its edges were saw-toothed, and returned upstairs to read what she sensed intuitively was going to be bad news. Travelling over a thousand miles from Ireland, the letter felt as if it had not flown but crawled, its bulk leaden in her hand.

Sitting down at the kitchen table, she looked at the familiar yet somehow strange handwriting, and sliced it open with fingers cold as knives.

'Dear Keeley, I lost my baby. And now I think I'm losing my mind.

It was a boy. I miscarried him in the third week of April. I was carrying a crate of vegetables into the kitchen and suddenly there was blood everywhere, such pain I thought I was going to die. Bridget called the doctor and I was taken to the Coombe, but it was too late, my child was dead.

I don't remember much about the next few days, except that Cathal was there all the time, the nurses said they'd never seen so many flowers or a husband so distraught. For once it wasn't an act, he really was distraught. But not about me.

When I came home he told me our marriage was over. We would continue to live together, he said, under his roof; my daughter would continue to be his daughter and I would continue to run his home and kitchen for him. But he had no use for a wife so stupid, so useless that she couldn't even carry his son to full term, do the one thing that any woman, any proper wife, could do.

You're going to tell me I should have said all the things

I've thought of myself since then – that it was no marriage anyway, how could it be over when it never properly started, that he's a brute who needs therapy and so on – but I felt so sick, so stunned that I couldn't think straight, didn't answer him at all.

And then he took something out of his pocket and started waving it at me, shouting and ranting, saying I was a deceitful bitch as well as a useless wife. At first I couldn't see what it was, but then I realised, it was my post office book.

I'd done what you said and started to save a little money – very little, but I'd found a few ways to get a pound here and a pound there and put it into an account, I thought of it as my running-away money even if I wasn't going to have enough, or be able to leave, for years. It gave me hope. But while I was in hospital he went through my things and found it. I won't tell you the things he said, the language he used, but even though he didn't lay a finger on me I felt as if I'd been beaten up. Now he's checking every penny every day, sometimes he even cross-questions Bridget in front of me about how much meat the butcher delivered and how much was used per meal, and how much is left. Not only is my money gone, I feel as if every shred of dignity is gone, so humiliated that sometimes I can hardly face the staff never mind the customers. And they're all being so nice to me, asking me how I feel the way you talk to an invalid, saying not to worry, I'll soon have another child. It's all I can do not to cry right in front of them. I never will have another child and I can't stop thinking about my little boy . . . he never even had a funeral, there isn't any grave to visit.

I'm sorry about writing such a depressing letter, I feel so guilty when you must be over the moon, so excited about your new salon. But I have to tell you, you're the only person I've ever trusted or would ever dare trust. I don't have any friends here because my working hours are so long and because Cathal discourages visitors – even though one of the nurses at the hospital said wasn't I lucky to have a husband who kept bringing so many flowers, he must be my best friend. I think if I told anyone the truth, they'd think I was raving mad. I feel as if I am going mad.

I'd give anything to come to your party but of course it's out of the question. I don't even have the money to send you a good-luck bunch of flowers. All I can send is my best wishes, and kisses from your god-daughter – Mel is

*the only thing keeping me from either killing Cathal or
killing myself.*

*Keeley, please write to me the minute you get this. I never
needed to hear your voice as much as I need to now.*

Love,
Mary.'

Stricken, frozen, Keeley read the letter a second time, in full,
without moving. Then, oblivious of Vincent and the many other
people waiting for her, she went to the phone that had been
installed so Vincent could call her when he was away on his
travels. Dialling Ireland, she sat like a statue until somebody
at The Lantern answered.

'Get me Mrs Sullivan.'

Her tone was so curt her request was fulfilled without
query, and in less than a minute she heard Mary's voice,
faint, whispery.

'Hello?'

'Mary, it's me. I've just got your letter. I'm not going to say
anything now, only one thing, and I want you to listen carefully,
do exactly as I say.'

'K – Keeley, I—'

'You're to go to your parents, right now today, and ask them
for two hundred pounds. Then you're to book yourself and Mel
onto a flight, pack your things and come straight over here.
You're not to think about it or argue about it, you're just to
do it. Have you got that?'

'Keeley, you don't understand – I can't – I—'

'Mary, if I understand your letter correctly, you are suicidal.
And I am on my way this minute to see Félix, to tell him to get
a couple of spare beds ready. Also to Luc, to tell him you're
coming back to work. Phone from the airport and one of us
will pick you up.'

'Keeley – no!—'

There was some sort of noise, a kind of gasp, and Keeley drew
breath to quell whatever protest Mary was about to make. But
then she realised that Mary was not talking to her. She was
talking to someone else. Seconds later, Cathal's voice came on
the line.

'Is that Keeley Butler?'

'Yes, Cathal, it is. I'm talking to Mary, please give the phone
back to her.'

Without another word, it went dead.

It took all day, and four more calls, for the message to sink in.
Each time Keeley rang back, a voice told her that it was sorry,
but Mrs Sullivan was not available. At first, she had visions
of the row that must have ensued, Cathal shouting and Mary
pleading, but she determined to wait it out; Cathal could not
stand guard over his wife all day. Only hours later did she
remember that the phone in the flat was an extension of the
one in the pub, and realise that the barmen must have been
instructed not to put any calls through to their boss's wife.

'But won't they think that's very odd?' Vincent asked, as
worried as herself when he heard. Furious, frustrated and
desperately anxious, she flung open the window and drew a
deep breath before turning back to him.

'No! That's the worst of it, Vincent. He has a perfect excuse.
He'l have said that Mrs Sullivan isn't well and mustn't be disturbed. He'll have them all thinking what a concerned protective
husband he is. Oh, God . . . what am I going to do?'

Vincent thought, carefully and at lenght, before replying.

'Well – there are two options, as I see it. The first is that
you go over there in person. I'll borrow the money for your
fare from Alain or Luc, if that's what you want to do.'

'Oh, Vincent . . . it is. It's exactly what I want to do! But he
won't let me see her. If I turn up at The Lantern, Cathal will
tell the barmen I'm a problem customer who's barred, and get
them to throw me out.'

Yes. If Cathal had cut the telephone communication, he
would probably block Keeley in person as well.

'Then – if Mary is as wretched as you say she is, Keeley, why
don't you phone her parents? Tell them everything Mary refuses
to tell them and get them to take things in hand?'

She considered. Kevin Jameson was the kind of man who,
if he thought his daughter was in trouble, would certainly go
round to Cathal and sort him out. Mary didn't want him to
know, but whatever the consequences they could hardly be
worse than the situation she was in now. Even if Mary was
furious with her for doing it, as she probably would be, it was
better than risking the alternative.

Over and again Mary's voice echoed in her mind, sounding so
stressed, so scared . . . either Cathal had unluckily been within
earshot when the call came through, or he had listened in on

it. He was a weird, sick man. There was no knowing what he might do next – or what Mary might do. Abruptly, Keeley made up her mind.

'You're right, Vincent. That's a good idea. I'm going to phone her parents.'

Not allowing herself to debate it further, she got the number from international directory enquiries, steeled herself and dialled it. On the third ring, Leesha Jameson answered.

'Hello Mrs Jameson, this is Keeley Butler.'

'K – Keeley, in France? My goodness, this is a surprise! How are you?'

'I'm very well, thanks. But . . . Mrs Jameson . . . I hope you won't think I'm interfering, but Mary isn't well. She's not well at all.'

'Oh, I know! The doctor says she's over her miscarriage and she says it herself, but she's pale as a ghost, still very weak. Cathal is beside himself with worry, looking after her round the clock.'

'No! No, Mrs Jameson, I know you think he is, but he isn't.'

There was a startled silence. 'What? What on earth do you mean?'

'Mrs Jameson, Mary doesn't want you to know this, but she's in terrible trouble. With Cathal, I mean. I had a letter from her today, I'll send you a copy of it if you want – he's treating her like a slave, a chattel! She's very depressed and I'm very worried about her.'

Another silence, longer this time. Keeley felt her hands clammy on the receiver, and saw clearly the price of this call: Mary might never speak to her again. But on the table the letter urged her on: *I think I'm losing my mind . . . a wife so stupid, so useless . . . a brute who needs therapy . . . Mel is the only thing keeping me from either killing Cathal or killing myself . . .*

Eventually Leesha found her voice. 'Well, Keeley, I always knew you didn't like Cathal, and suspected you were a bit jealous of Mary when she married him. But I never thought you'd go as far as this. I simply cannot believe you are saying such poisonous things about my daughter and son-in-law.'

Stunned, Keeley felt as if Leesha was in the room and had stabbed her. But she kept going. 'Mrs Jameson, I'm not! You must listen, please! I told you, I'll send you her letter, I'll send you the other ones I've kept—'

'And I will put them in the fire and burn them unopened, if you go to the trouble of forging them. I always knew you were bad news, Keeley Butler, the same as your father and brother, but never in a million years would I have expected this of you. After all we did for you . . . no wonder your father hit you that time, you must have had his heart scalded. Well, you won't scald mine. My daughter is happily married to a wonderful man and I'll thank you never to contact me or her again.'

The phone was slammed down. It reverberated so loudly in Keeley's head that she didn't hear her own sob, didn't realise she was crying until she was in Vincent's arms and her tears were soaking his shirt.

'V – Vincent, she didn't believe me! She said I was bad news and jealous and – and a liar!'

Clinging to him, she wept uncontrollably, not only for the hurt that Leesha had inflicted on her but for the harm that had been done to Mary: if Leesha didn't act now, tell Kevin or do something, Mary would be well and truly alone. Alone with Cathal Sullivan, who was smart enough never to hit or bruise her, but who was maiming her slowly, stealthily, invisibly.

Vincent held her tight, stroking her back, trying to contain the anger he felt on behalf of the wife who had only tried to help.

'I don't think she heard you, Keeley.'

'What? But she – she heard every word!'

'No. She heard nothing, of what she didn't want to hear.'

With less than twenty-four hours to go to the opening of her new salon, Keeley felt as if her feet were made of lead as she walked round Aix looking for the dress that Luc had insisted she get, something sparkly and shimmery – all the things she did not feel. By noon she had found nothing, and decided to call in on him although he would be busy. Even if he could only spare her a minute or two, she somehow felt it might cheer her up to see him.

The Vieux Moulin was crowded, Félix so distracted with customers that she merely waved at him, and made her own way through to Luc's kitchen. He was up to his eyes, but beamed when he saw her.

'Eh, ma petite! Wait there, and I will be with you in a moment!'

She waited while he arranged some things on plates, went to stir something and shout at a sous chef who was sweating over a steaming cauldron. Then, wiping his hands on his apron, he came over to her.

'No panic, Keeley! Everything is in good order for tonight, the food is prepared, the wine is chilling . . . have you got your outfit, are you all ready?'

'No . . . I've been shopping for a dress, but I can't find anything.'

'But, mon dieu, Keeley, why have you left it so late?'

'I – I was busy, and then I got distracted with – with something personal.'

He looked at her woebegone face. 'Oh, not a row? Not with Vincent?'

She smiled in spite of herself. 'No. Not a row with Vincent. Just something – something in Ireland.'

She didn't want to tell him, say anything about Mary's difficulties, but as usual he guessed. She had never known anyone like him for simply guessing things.

'I see. Well, Keeley, I don't have time to talk now, so let me be brief. If you want to make your friend Mary happy, you will go back out right now and find the most magnificent outfit in Aix. She will be with you in spirit tonight, and she will want you to look your best. There is a boutique on the rue Mazarine, where my daughter buys the most scandalous – go there quickly, and get something. Tell them to send me the bill.'

'Luc! I'll go there, but I certainly won't—'

He sighed exaggeratedly. 'Please. Just tell them. They are so used to it, they know my address.'

His martyred stance made her laugh, and he laughed in turn. 'Go on, now, something outrageous, something *fast*! I will see you tonight, but I will not recognise you!'

He chased her out, and she did feel better as she headed for the rue Mazarine. In the shop she felt even better, when the assistant showed her a short, tight-fitting party dress in jade velvet, with a low-cut collar of gold lamé. Sleeveless, sexy and daring, it fitted perfectly, and although she did not charge it to Luc she did not care, either, about the wanton extravagance. If she and Vincent had to live on yoghurt for a month, what the hell. This was their big night.

Her spirits rose further as she carried on to other shops, one she had never dared enter before, and added shoes, glossy tights, a fake gold necklet to her booty. Half of the women coming to the launch would doubtless be wearing the real 22-carat

McCoy, but so what – this would gleam and glitter just as brightly even if it fell apart tomorrow. When her funds were exhausted she spent her last ten francs on a deliciously frothy, reviving café-crème and then, dying to show it all to Vincent, dashed home to the flat.

He arrived just as she did, covered in dust from the salon where one of the new recessed lights had fallen out and pulled a chunk of plaster with it. She giggled.

'Thank God it only fell on you, and not on a client!'

'Huh. The workmen are repairing it, but they promise it will be fixed and they will be gone by five . . . Luc called to say he will deliver the food at half past . . . Félix says he has invited the *mayor*, Keeley, what will we do if he shows up?'

'Ask him whether he'd like a body wave,' she grinned, thinking of the man's head, pink and bare as a balloon. 'Oh! Did the balloons come?'

'Yes, yes, there's a man there now pumping them up, four dozen, green and gold . . . oh God, if everything's not ready on time I'll shoot myself!'

'It will be. Look, just let me wash my hair and then you can have the bathroom to yourself.'

When it was washed she sat down in her bathrobe in front of an arsenal of weapons, and got to work. Tonight, her hair absolutely *had* to look a million dollars. Rubbing it towel-dry, she sprayed it with a gel she knew would take hold like cement, twisted twenty pipe-cleaners into it and laced each one into the next, piling it all high except for a few wisps round her ears and neck. Then, after she had blow-dried the whole construction hot and hard as concrete, and given it a punch to make sure there was no danger whatsoever of collapse, she took out a can of gold spray, the kind normally used on Christmas trees. Vincent came out of the bathroom just as she raised it, and yelped.

'No – stop – you're not going to spray it *gold*!'

'I am,' she replied calmly, and proceeded to. He stood gasping until the awful deed was done, and she turned to him smirking like Madame de Pompadour.

'Well – what do you think?'

He surveyed the mound of gold loops, and burst out laughing.

'Exquisite. Especially with your bathrobe.'

'Ah. Wait till you see the dress.'

It just looked like a mound of fabric in its box, but when

she was washed, changed, made up and standing in it, he was dazzled.

'Jesus Christ, Keeley, I never knew you could look like this.'

'Neither did I.'

He kissed her so hard she thought that if she didn't stop him the launch would be over by the time they got to it, and peeled him off laughing, reluctant.

'This is no time for fun and games. This is serious stuff.'

'You're telling me.'

The new shoes and spectacular hairstyle added at least four inches to her height, and by the time he was standing ready beside her in his suit she was glowing with excitement.

'Now, look in the mirror! Don't we look fabulous!'

'You certainly do. All I want to look is respectable and businesslike.'

As ever he sounded calm, even assured. But she thought she sensed apprehension in him.

'Oh, Vincent. I know you're nervous. We both are. But who ever heard of a business built on nerves? We've *got* to be confident, think positive – for Félix's sake as well as our own. If he can give us all this money then the least we can do is look as if we deserve it. Behave tonight as if the salon already *is* a success.'

He kissed her again, tenderly this time, lovingly.

'If it's half as successful as our marriage, Félix Peyrolle will be a millionaire by Monday. But whether it is or not, I will love you till the day I die, and long after that. You are the most wonderful woman on this planet, Keeley Butler.'

She smiled at him, a little wistfully.

'Yeah. That's what my oul fella always used to say. I'm a treasure.'

Even as she said it she made light of it, her eyes twinkling, but he caught her sardonic note, some fleeting sadness as he held her tightly, protectively to him.

'If this party goes on like this,' Felix muttered to his wife Lise, 'we'll have to call the police. Tomorrow, *Cut!* will be *Shut!*'

Lise didn't hear him, but Félix permitted himself a smile. It was a wild party, eclipsing even the rowdiest he'd ever had to subdue at the restaurant, but it was going like a house on fire. Luc's astonishing buffet, speared with sparklers, studded with flowers and strewn with edible ribbons, had got things off to a spectacular start, while the Irish musicians Keeley had found put everyone in good form. Even better – and unusual in Aix – was the mixture of people, everyone from glamorous society women to Polish and Moroccan immigrants, mixing with increasing vivacity as the wine flowed and the music pulsated. Never having been to a 'proper' party in France, Keeley had simply done things the Irish way and invited everyone – Jaysus, she'd said, if any of my pals from the Chamber of Commerce ever starts a business, I'd throw a fit if they didn't invite me. Now, she was circling among them all, looking like a Martian in Félix's opinion, but chatting, laughing, bubbling with delight at everything.

And it wasn't a fake smile, he thought, recalling the thousands he'd seen, that he'd often had to fake himself. It was real, it was happy, and it was a great relief to him.

Earlier that day, she'd come into the Moulin looking so downcast that he'd shuddered at the forlorn sight of her, looking as if she'd been hit with a shovel. But whatever the problem was, she was showing no sign of it now; no sign of nerves either, although some of these ritzy guests must be intimidating to a – a kid.

That's all she is, really, he thought. A kid who has somehow persuaded me to invest my life savings in her. I have no idea how she did it . . . in fact I seem to remember feeling as if it was *my* idea. But if we fail, it won't be for lack of trying. I'll regret losing the money, but I won't regret putting it into her and her husband. They've no experience, but they have ability and energy, they'll work and they'll try with every breath in their bodies. I feel rejuvenated just looking at them. What a pity Mary . . . but Mary isn't here. Mary has made her life elsewhere and I can only hope she has half the courage, the vision that this girl has.

Not a girl. A woman. She looks extraordinary tonight, but she also looks like someone coming of age. Her jewellery is junk but there's something real, something solid about her. Vincent knew what he was doing, the day he married her.

Félix jumped out of his reverie as an Algerian girl in a saffron robe touched his arm, her own jangling with silver bracelets.

'Salut. Like to dance?'

Dance? In this crowded space? But other people were, and with a sudden burst of reckless vitality he thought yes, he'd love to dance, the Algerian version of a rhumba or whatever it turned out to be. With his life savings invested, he might as well go the whole hog.

From across the room, Keeley caught sight of him as he was led away and smiled as Lise Peyrolle came up to her.

'I hope you're having a good time, Lise? Félix certainly seems to be.'

Thoughtfully, Lise looked at him as the tall, dark Algerian draped her jangling arms around his pin-striped shoulders.

'Who'd ever have thought it? My prim and proper husband. He's a new man since he got involved with you – involved in the business sense, I mean!'

'Yep. He's in great form. I just hope he'll still be in great form this time next year when the first annual returns come in.'

'Keeley, you mustn't worry. Félix still has his job, if it comes to the worst, we won't starve . . . I was a little dubious when I heard what he wanted to do, admittedly. But when I saw the new animation in him, heard it, I thought – yes, this is buying him a new lease of life. I will permit and encourage him to do it.'

'Thank God you did. We tried to borrow from a bank, you know, but they didn't want to know us. We'd have been sunk without Félix.'

And without all these other people too, she thought. Luc with his warm wonderful friendship, Alain Jou's support, Vincent's parents, Eliane who taught me to cut and style. It's great that everyone is able to be here tonight.

Everyone except Mary, who first brought me to France. I wish – but what's the point in wishing? That's what she does, and where does it get her?

Wishing achieves nothing. You have to act, make things happen. Christ almighty, why doesn't she get her butt and her child on a plane and scarper out of that ghastly marriage! I'd have helped her, the way everyone helps me, but she just doesn't seem to believe she could manage on her own. It's like any man is better than none.

But half of them are a waste of time. Waste of energy, waste of life. My mother's life is wasted on Christy. Mine might have been wasted on Erik. I'm thrilled with Vincent, but if he ever treated me the way Cathal treats Mary, even for one day, you wouldn't see my heels for dust. Vincent says you have to cut your losses if things aren't working, and that's what I'd do.

Jesus Christ, this business had better work. Here I am dolled up like a film star, and not tuppence to my name. There's Alain

Jou, trying to flog someone one of Tony's unspeakable paintings
. . . I couldn't say no when he asked me to hang a few up tonight,
but I hope he's not going to make a habit of it.

Still, if Tony can succeed, I can succeed. He's only got Alain
and Gertie to help him, but I've got Vincent and Félix. For them,
I'm going to give it my best shot.

And Mary? Who's she got? Not even her mother, not even
me any more, maybe, after what I did . . .

I can not, must not think any more about Mary tonight.
Tonight is too important. Where's Vincent?

Locating him on the other side of the room, she went over
to him.

'Hey, sailor! Like to dance, give a girl a good time?'

Drawing her to him, he put his arm around her and kissed
her cheek.

'Yeah. I'll give you a good time right now, and a great
time when we get home. But you know what I really want to
give you?'

'No. What?'

'A good life, Keeley. A really good life. That's what I want
you to have.'

It wasn't the time or place for intimacy, but she didn't care,
and rested her face against his chest.

'I have that already. No matter what happens next, Vincent,
I have that already.'

His lips brushed her hair, her skin, as his arm tightened
around her. 'So have I. We have nothing else, but we have each
other . . . and for me that will always be the most important
thing, Keeley. Your health, your happiness and your love.'

She nodded, holding him close as she realised the truth of it;
important as this night, this venture was, it would never matter
more to her than this man, this love she had found when least
expecting it and most in need of it.

Part II

Chapter Eleven

'Mel! I'm going to start the spring cleaning! Come on up here and give me a hand, would you?'

The blithe, careless sound of Mel Sullivan's voice floated up from the hall. 'Get lost, Ma! I'm going round to the tennis club, it's junior singles this morning, then a bunch of us are having lunch in the pub, Dad said to bring as many as I like. I'll see you tonight, before the disco – hey, if you find my red shirt, iron it, will you?'

Mary went out onto the landing, and was just in time to see a blonde ponytail swishing out the front door, a glimpse of racquets and white trainers disappearing into the early summer sunshine. Leaning on the bannisters for a moment, she sighed, and went back to her stack of dusters and detergents. But then the front door clicked open again, and her daughter's voice called up some afterthought, some command disguised as a request.

'Oh, and Ma – I've told you before, I'm fourteen now! It's not Mel, it's Imelda, if anyone calls looking for me!'

The door snapped shut, and Mary sat down on the edge of the bed she was about to pull out, dust and hoover under – Mel's bed, unmade, strewn with clothes, surrounded with posters of rock stars, tapes for the ghetto-blaster, videos for the television in the corner. The bedroom, she thought wearily, of an extremely pretty, popular, spoiled, selfish little brat.

Well, no. That wasn't altogether true. 'Little' was the wrong word. Mel was tall, like her father, with his Swedish good looks, her sapphire eyes, her arctic teeth. She would not, in fact, be fourteen for another five weeks, but she was almost frighteningly well-developed in mind and body. Not in the sense of shining at school, where her teachers said she was bright but lazy, but in the sense that she was streetwise, clued-in, 'on the

ball', as Cathal put it. Physically she would pass for at least
sixteen, and Mary suspected she often did pass for it in the local
shops, because navy-blue John Player cartons often turned up
in strange places. Teenage drinkers were not allowed in The
Lantern, or in any other pub officially, but Mel had easily won
the battle about what that meant. It simply meant they weren't
to be served alcohol – but there was no law against them being
on the premises, with Cathal's full blessing, so long as they
stuck to Coke. For the moment they did stick to it, but they
were imbibing the rowdy smoky atmosphere of the place like
mother's milk, and Mary foresaw that – unless closely watched
and discouraged – her daughter would be a heavy drinker by
twenty.

Well, Ireland in general was a heavy drinker. She would be
one herself, in fact she would be a shambling alcoholic, if it
weren't for something that had happened one day when she
was young and Mel was a baby. It was the day after Keeley's
wedding, the wedding she had got drunk at, and Keeley had
spelled it out in no uncertain terms.

'If I ever hear of Mel having any kind of accident, Mary, I'll
know what caused it.'

For some reason that had registered, made a lasting impression,
so much so that she never again drank more than one glass of
anything during the years of Mel's childhood, terrified that if
anything ever did happen to the girl it would be all her fault.
Even now, on the days when she thought she could go to The
Lantern, drink an entire case of gin and then another of whiskey,
she couldn't do it. She wished she could, because oblivion would
be bliss, but she couldn't.

Bliss. That was what everyone thought her life was, looking in
on it from the outside. Strangers, customers, acquaintances . . .
what they saw was a well-dressed woman of thirty-four, living
in a well-tended house in a street full of well-groomed gardens,
with a well-to-do husband and a well-polished car. Nearly ten
years had passed since they moved out of the flat over the pub,
into this detached shiny house, filled with expensive furniture,
nifty gadgets, curtains from Switzers, carpets from Arnotts.
Cathal drove an Audi, Mel went to Loreto, there were birthday
parties, Christmas parties, a pair of pink skis out in the utility
room. When Mel wanted riding lessons, Mel got riding lessons;
when Mel wanted Calvin Klein jeans, Mel got Calvin Klein
jeans; and when Mary wanted bus fare, Mary asked Cathal for

it. Soon, the daughter would be giving the mother lifts in the father's Audi. And nobody would think that strange, because everybody knew Mary Sullivan couldn't drive.

What nobody knew was that Mary Sullivan wasn't let drive. Wasn't taught, wasn't insured, wasn't given the time of day. If she made a phone call she wrote down its destination and duration which Cathal then checked against the bill; if she needed a new deodorant she ticked it off on the itemised supermarket receipt; if she had to go to the dentist she was delivered and collected like a child.

Once, just once, years ago when she was at the end of her tether after the baby died, a dim ray of light had shone briefly through the prison window. Her father Kevin had come round one evening, and managed to get Cathal out of the way for the five minutes his mission required. The moment Cathal left the room, he told her there had been a strange phone call from Keeley Butler in France, which had upset and enraged her mother Leesha very much. The gist of it was that Keeley thought something was wrong between Mary and Cathal, and – well, Leesha said it was preposterous, but was anything?

For an instant, Mary's heart had soared to the skies. And then she thought of her daughter, already enrolled for Loreto, assured of everything Cathal's money could buy. She thought of the pub called Fursey's in the midlands, the carrot that lured her on from day to day, week to week. And she thought of life back at home with her parents and the child they'd wanted adopted, no Loreto, no Fursey's, no future for mother or daughter.

'No Dad,' she'd said brightly, clearly. 'Nothing is wrong. I – I can't imagine why Keeley would say that.'

Satisfied and relieved, he shook his head. 'Neither can I. Jealousy, your mother says, because you and Cathal are doing so well. Put it out of your head and if you'll take my advice you'll drop that friendship, Mary. No real friend would say such a terrible thing about you. Poor Keeley must be eaten alive with envy.'

Trembling, it had taken her days to get over the shock of it, the dizzying sight of escape so near and then so far away. From that day forth she had clung to the vision of Fursey's, the reward, the real restaurant at last, when Mel was safely reared.

But thirteen years later Fursey's was still a pub, Cathal's parents still lived over it. Nothing had changed. Not one thing, in her life, while others went vigorously forward; her brothers

Steve and Sean were men of over twenty now, Steve a cadet pilot, Sean studying architecture at UCD. Her bridesmaid Marion Hayes had emigrated to Australia and met a ranch-hotelier there, left her husband and run off with him. Luc, that most inspiring of chefs and wonderful of men, had quit the Vieux Moulin to buy a vineyard, and nowadays she saw his wines on Quinnsworth's shelves, in Cathal's cellars. Félix Peyrolle had taken early retirement, and Keeley Butler was . . . was too depressing for words.

Once, for nearly a year, there had literally been no words between them. The more she thought about Keeley's phone call to her mother, the angrier Mary had got, until eventually she had convinced herself that all her misfortunes were Keeley's fault. Keeley should never have made her stay in France in the first place, dipped her toe in its waters when she could not swim. Keeley *should* have made her stay in France, for good, refused to take no for an answer. Keeley had said this, done that, called her mother with scandal about her marriage . . . resolutely she wrestled down every doubt, every argument as it arose in her mind, until she all but had a noose around Keeley's neck. When letters came from her she read them, filled with suspicion, investing every line with double meaning, determining not to answer them. And she didn't, until the day of her twenty-first birthday arrived, and a card with it.

'Mary,' it said simply, 'are you alive? Please just let me know whether you're alive and my god-daughter is all right.'

And suddenly she had cracked, burst into tears and let it all come pouring out. The ingratitude, the self-deception, the weakness of trying to blame the friend who had tried everything to help. The friend who'd sent this card, remembered the date, was still out there somewhere. Out there, and needed, and missed. Missed terribly, and not only as a confidante . . . how could she have let Cathal and her parents brainwash her into seeing Keeley as anything other than what she was?

She sat down and wrote a long letter that day, full of apologies and attempts at explanation, begging forgiveness, admitting all guilt. Mel was well, she was coping, everything would be all right if only Keeley would write to her again – abuse, anger, anything, only just write to me, Keeley, please.

Back came a letter, in Joe's vegetable van: 'I'd break your bloody neck for you if I thought I wouldn't swing for it! Were you having some kind of nervous breakdown or what?'

And it dawned on Mary that she was having one, had had one in between rolling pastry and stuffing chickens. She'd never been quite sure what a nervous breakdown was, but now she knew: it was the dark blank space between the death of her baby and the arrival of that birthday card. Some people went into clinics or hospitals when they had them, but she hadn't had time, she had had a hundred meals to prepare every day, a child to raise, a husband to humour and serve, supplies to source, staff to supervise ... like a neglected saucepan, the nervous breakdown had got put on a back burner, and boiled over unnoticed. Afterwards, there was a lot of very messy mopping up to do.

But mopping up was something Mary did well. What she did best, she sometimes thought. She mopped up after Mel who used their home as a hotel, she mopped up after drunken customers who spilled the food she had cooked on the floor, she mopped up the bitter blood between her husband and herself. Often there were long silences, but there were no fights; they shared their roof under a kind of vague armistice, getting through the months and years like warder and prisoner, resigned to each other. Often Cathal was away, at football matches or on trips hosted by breweries, wine companies, pub suppliers; she lived for his absences and never enquired into them. Occasionally, when he was late back, she wondered whether he might have someone else, even hoped that he had found another woman. A mistress, to distract him, put him in good form, prise open his pockets ... she had heard somewhere that a man's guilt often took the form of sudden generosity. But there was no evidence of any woman, and her personal budget remained tight as a vice. Since the day he had found her savings account, she had never again dared to hide another penny from him.

Sometimes Mel was away too. Only three months ago, her school class had gone skiing in Italy, and Mary was horrified to find that she did not miss the daughter for whom her career, her whole life, had been sacrificed. She worried about her, she fretted about injuries and any number of possible disasters, but she did not miss her. The realisation made her feel appalling guilt, and on Mel's return she smothered her in hugs and kisses, but Mel shrugged them off – 'For God's sake, Ma, I'm not a baby! Get a life!' Yet she accepted Cathal's embrace, returned it, even seemed to flirt with him a little as she showed off her tan and her certificate for expertise on the pink skis.

The trip had cost a small fortune, and Cathal had filled the girl's purse with pocket money as well; yet there had never once been a family holiday, nothing more than a day's excursion to the beach or the mountains. Every summer, every Christmas, Keeley implored Mary to come and visit France – shag Cathal, she said, we'll pay your fare and it will cost you nothing to stay with us. But Mary knew the way Keeley and Vincent lived now, and fended each invitation firmly off. Even if it didn't cost much it would cost something, and anyway Cathal would never permit it. Visit the loathed Keeley Butler! She might as well ask permission to visit Myra Hindley or the Kray twins, such were Cathal's views on 'that Butler woman.' To this day she lived in dread that he would discover the system for smuggling letters, and burned each one as soon as she read it. Cathal suspected their existence, she knew, or some form of contact, but he could never prove it.

Sinking down on Mel's bed, the spring cleaning forgotten, she sat with a duster in her hand, thinking. How much longer, until Mel was fully adult, no longer her responsibility? Four years, until she would be eighteen . . . and then, what? More than anything, she wanted a loving relationship with the daughter who had cost her so much, a friendship as Mel grew into a woman. But somehow Cathal had got the girl onto his side from the start, bribed her as a toddler and bought her affections as she got older, wooed her and won her with ease, because Mary could not compete. Until recently, Mel had still been a child, was capable of spontaneous shows of affection to both parents, things that sometimes even raised a laugh and lightened the atmosphere. But since turning into her teens she had become self-conscious, aware how her smiles and hugs were treasured, how her parents competed for them. Now, it was an unspoken contest of sorts, and Cathal was winning it hands down.

Although there was a line over which Mel never stepped, Mary sensed that her daughter was absorbing Cathal's attitude to her, starting to treat her more as a housekeeper than a mother, even to faintly despise her. Advice was ridiculed, help was rejected, there was no question of Mary going shopping or seeing a film or doing anything with her daughter; Mel had her own friends now, and did everything with them. But Mary had no friends, because friends went out for a drink or to dinner, on trips and jaunts that cost money.

Money. There was no shortage of it, even if she personally had none, and she still wondered where it all came from. Of course much of it came from The Lantern, which turned a healthy profit, but she knew there was another source. Something to do with Cathal's father Donal, and his position on the county council.

'Jesus God,' Keeley had screeched in more than one letter. 'It's as plain as the nose on your face, you idiot! His oul fella is taking bribes for planning permission! Every time a new supermarket goes up, he pockets ten grand! And then he slips half to the son, so nobody will get too suspicious . . . they have a racket going, and if you could only get proof you'd have one hell of a stick to beat him with. Try to get proof, Mary – try everything, by fair means or foul.'

She did try, but never succeeded. Just as she got rid of Keeley's letters, Cathal got rid of whatever evidence might incriminate him – and besides, it was this extra money that sent Mel off on skiing trips, paid for all the perks the girl enjoyed. If she dug too deep, Mel might suffer. So she had never dug very deep.

But now, it was becoming slowly clear to her that the money was not benefiting Mel. In fact it was poisoning her, spoiling her and turning her into the kind of person who, in years to come . . . but if she said that, voiced her opinion, both father and daughter would simply laugh at her. Laugh her off, brush her off, not even take her seriously enough to get annoyed. It was becoming slowly established that Mother was a bit dim, given to peculiar ideas which were as absurd as they were harmless. Mary looked around her daughter's room as she pondered this recent development, and was suddenly nauseated.

The wardrobe bulged with clothes. The floor was ankle-deep in them. On the dressing-table there was already a basket of cosmetics, barely visible for the other basket of jewellery, the tapes and cassettes, the mountain of evidence that her daughter was turning into – had very nearly become – a disaster. A failure, a human being as worthless as the man she thought was her father. Mel Sullivan was going to hell in a handcart.

As a rule, Mary clamped down on whatever feelings of anger surged up in her. Experience had taught her that it was easier to put up and shut up, evade things rather than confront them. The Mary Jameson who had belted Christy Butler a box seemed like another person to her; she could hardly even remember the event, the day rage had propelled her to lash out at injustice. But today, at this moment, it came back to her, she had an

almost ungovernable impulse to sweep the dressing-table clear
of every frippery that shone on it, to break everything she could
lay her hands upon – to break not only things, but patterns. The
pattern of Mel's life, that was leading inexorably to catastrophe,
perhaps even tragedy.

Her own life had been wasted, but Mel – Mel was only
fourteen, only a child under the already sparkling surface. For
Mel, she wanted to – was *going* to – to – what?

What, she thought frantically, can I do? What would Keeley
do, if she had a child? What would Keeley do?

Keeley would think of something. Over the years she and
Vincent have had lots of problems, but they've always found
a way out of them or round them. Vincent figures a way out,
but Keeley simply comes up with one off the top of her head.
I'll write to her. I'll ask her, tell her that Mel is growing up too
fast too soon, getting out of hand, she needs—

Keeley! That's it! She needs Keeley. A dose of Keeley Butler,
to sort her out. Keeley could talk more sense into her in a
day than I could in six months. And what's more she might
even listen, because she knows her godmother is everything she
admires . . . wealthy, successful, respected. All those presents,
that Cathal hates but Mel loves, he's never been able to think
of a way to stop Keeley from sending them or Mel from getting
them . . . if I can just think of a way of getting her to France,
I could save her. Save her from Cathal's influence, her bloody
grandparents, maybe even from herself. It's time Mel met her
godmother, face to face.

How? Keeley never comes to Dublin, and Cathal would never
let Mel go to her. Not unless . . . not unless Mel really *wanted* to
go. He'd go bananas, but if Mel kept asking him, he'd give in,
because he always gives her everything she wants. Dear doting
Daddy, that everyone thinks is such a gem. I'll work on Mel,
and Mel will work on him. And in the meantime, I'll write to
Keeley. If I can't get myself out of this miserable mess, I can get
my daughter out of it.

'Vincent, do you happen to know where the camera is?'

Vincent looked up from his Sunday morning newspaper at his
wife, who was sitting on a striped sun lounger in her swimsuit,
looking very pretty apart from the wrinkle in her forehead. But
then she had one of Mary's letters in her hand, and Mary's
letters always produced wrinkles.

'In the top drawer of the bureau I think . . . why?'

'Oh, I just want to take a few snaps.'

He grinned, and put down the newspaper to pose exaggeratedly in Hercules fashion, flexing his biceps.

'Ah yes, of course, Madame wishes to immortalise her Grecian god of a husband.'

Keeley laughed, but shook her head. 'No, sorry, you're not the star of this show. I want to take pictures of the house.'

'Why?'

'To send to our god-daughter. She's coming to visit, if I can entice her with a preview of all our wordly goods.'

Dropping the pose, he sat up, astonished. 'What? Mel is coming here? To us? But what about her father—?'

'Her father will have to agree to it, if she pesters him enough, and Mary reckons she will pester him once she sees our splendid abode.'

It took Vincent several moments to digest what Keeley was saying, and grasp the idea that Mel Sullivan, whom they had not seen since she was a baby, might actually be coming to visit. To their home.

But when he did grasp it, he was conscious of a feeling of great pleasure, even of delight. To have a child around the house would be a new and very welcome experience . . . not that Mel was a child any more, as such, but she was young and – and, amongst all his blessings, a child was the one thing he had never been able to count. Not that he had felt the need of one, in the early years of his marriage to Keeley at any rate, when they had only been kids themselves. It was agreed between them, then, that they needed to give all their time and attention to the struggling young business that had consumed so much energy, so much passion and creativity; for years there had been no question that either of them could afford to take even a weekend off work, never mind the several weeks of maternity leave that would be inevitable if Keeley became pregnant. It was discussed, it was accepted, and that was that.

But now . . . lately . . . the subject always seemed to be somewhere at the back of his mind. Perhaps it was the house, he thought as he looked at it, because this was certainly a house made for children. A garden, a swimming pool, a tennis court, two labradors, trees to climb, bikes to ride; it was only a new house, but somehow it felt as if its soul was old. Old and warm, like the stone from which it was built, yellow-mellow as Keeley

called it. It had taken years to achieve, years of rented flats and
tiny houses they had never had time to take notice of, *live* in,
because they were permanently at one salon and then another.
The first nine years had been a blur of suitcases and removal
vans, until, to their amazement, they found themselves with
both the time to think and the money to build. Not buy, after
all, because the lovely house at Puyloubier was not for sale, but
instead they had engaged an architect and described what they
wanted.

A low stone farmhouse, built on traditional Provençal lines,
with thick walls and lots of little windows, tiled floors, glass
doors opening onto a patio and garden – oh, and beamed
ceilings, Keeley had added, to hang copper thingies from. A
fireplace for winter nights, piled with logs, and four bedrooms,
because you never knew.

The pool and tennis court had come later, after the house
was completed, and then the dogs, Cleo and Zazie. Sometimes
they were both still taken aback by all these things, the lifestyle
that had gradually resulted from the growing chain of salons,
which now numbered seventeen, all over Provence. Each one
had an individual look, to suit the local area and clients; some
were young and jazzy, some were soothing and restful. But all
were very successful, so much so that Keeley no longer styled
much hair at all, but spent an increasing amount of time
at the hairdressing school that had been founded to train
staff. It had not taken much time to discover – the hard
way – that hairdressers were notoriously given to instability,
restless creatures who roved from one salon to another, and
the early years had been a nightmare of crises, uncertainty,
near-calamity. Félix had gone grey with worry – and later,
gone to the Maldives for a whole month, where his wife Lise
had persuaded him that he could afford to retire. The Vieux
Moulin had a new manager now, and they often ate there with
both Félix and Lise, drinking Luc's wines with friendship and
still-surprised pleasure in their own achievements. Sometimes
there were fresh dramas, panics, things that went wrong and
caused many sleepless nights; but they were able to cope with
them now, and enjoy the compensations. This house was their
greatest compensation, and they loved living in it.

But it seemed to Vincent that it cried out for children, and he
wondered when Keeley would hear the cry too. After all they
had been married a long time, they were in their mid-thirties

. . . but every morning Keeley continued to rise at five, gulp her coffee and her pill, and dash off to work. Work that took her to Nice and Nîmes and Montpellier, Apt and Arles, Tarascon and St Remy . . . 'Of course we'll have children some time,' she said airily whenever he brought the subject up, but Vincent was beginning to wonder whether her work had not become her child, such was the love and care and time she put into it.

But he had to admit that he was proud of her. Very proud; on the day she had first addressed a meeting of business entrepreneurs at the Chamber of Commerce, he thought he would explode with love and admiration, could not get over the brisk confident way she made her speech in the voice that still had traces of an Irish accent, and accepted a bouquet from the chairman afterwards. Now, she regularly addressed such gatherings, fitting them in between visits to salons as she zipped around in her navy-blue, metallic BMW. His father Pierre had objected that the car was not French-made, but she had merely smiled and said neither was she.

Perhaps not. Yet in so many ways Keeley was French now; the way she dressed, the way she spoke, often even the way she thought. She loved to entertain, as he did himself, and often Luc came down from his mountain retreat to preside over the cooking of meals for ten or twelve people. There was a maid, and a gardener, but Keeley could frequently be found doing their work herself, ringing Francine in a panic because a petunia had wilted, or hosing the whole garden in summer, dogs included. They had a wonderful life together, but sometimes Vincent wished his wife would slow down long enough to enjoy it, relax just a little.

She did relax when they went on holiday, but never for more than a week. Over the years they had visited, but not really seen, bits of Italy, England, Spain, Greece, Morocco and America, punctuated with phone calls and faxes, things that made him wonder when or whether they would ever truly be alone together. Eventually he made it a rule that she was not allowed to bring her briefcase abroad, or talk about work when they got there. That slowed her down, but only temporarily.

And still she grew dearer to him with every passing day. Watching her as she padded into the house to get the camera, he smiled at her small resolute figure; at thirty-four she was still cute as a button. And on these Sunday mornings, in summer, she was almost always relaxed, laughing as they swam together, stamping her foot with a grin when he beat her at tennis, chatting to the dogs as if they were Christian beings. As she came back out of the house, carrying the camera, he felt a surge of love so strong it seized his heart, and fell silent.

'OK – now, Mary wants the pics to be sunny and seductive, so let's start with the pool . . . jump in there, Vincent, and splash around, make it look like fun!'

He laughed. 'Keeley, this is ridiculous. If Mel wants to come here, then she can simply come. She knows she's welcome, any time.'

'Yes, but she thinks we're doddering old folks, we have to show her that we're not! Mary is going to show her these photographs and persuade her to come on the strength of them – get her hooked before she says a word to Cathal.'

With a sigh and a smile, he got up and dived into the pool, bobbing up to squint at her curiously.

'Why does Mary want her to come, anyway? What's the sudden rush?'

Keeley aimed the camera, and clicked. 'She thinks Mel is getting spoiled and that we might be able to knock a bit of sense into her before it's too late.'

'Why us?'

'Because everyone in Ireland seems to think the sun shines out of Mel's overly-developed backside. Nobody ever tells her off except Mary, and apparently she doesn't listen to Mary. Personally I think she should buy a horsewhip.'

'Or a megaphone! That's always been Mary's trouble, she just wouldn't speak up loud and clear for herself . . . how's she getting on with Cathal, and the pub?'

'Well, it's the same as usual with Cathal – uneasy truce at best, still no money, no control, nothing. As far as the pub goes, I think things are getting worse. She says people in Ireland are getting more interested in food now, some really good restaurants are opening – which, of course, is making her twice as frustrated. She'd love to get her hands on Fursey's, but she can't. I think it's just a carrot Cathal dangled to get her to marry him. She'll never have a place of her own as long as she stays married to him.'

'But in Ireland people have to stay married, don't they? No divorce?'

'Not yet, although I hear there's another referendum coming on that – but Jesus God, Vincent, half the country is separated!

All Mary has to do is leg it out of there and come over here –
which is what I'll be telling her for the rest of my life, the way
things are going.'

'Why do you persist? You must be fed up with the whole
thing.'

'I persist, as you well know, because she's my friend and I
love her. She got me out and some day I'll get her out. Besides,
I'm Mel's godmother, there's family duty to consider.'

'But that's partly what's holding Mary back. Her parents,
that she refuses to scandalise with a broken marriage.'

'Well, I think maybe she'd risk scandalising them now. Her
brother Sean is living with his girlfriend Ruth Keane and they
nearly had hysterics when they heard that . . . until Sean told
them to shut up and say hello to young Ruth or he'd never
visit them again. Now it's all sweet as pie, you'd think Sean
and Ruth were Darby and Joan, Mary says. So if Kevin and
Leesha can swallow that, they can probably swallow anything
else. Mary didn't want to upset them, but she might as well
have just gone ahead and got it over with. Anyway, Leesha
doesn't care about her. She just cares about Cathal's money
and what the neighbours think – as was proven after my famous
phone call.'

Vincent remembered that phone call, and the pain it had
caused, the anger he still felt when he thought of Keeley in
tears. It was one of the very few occasions on which he had
ever seen her cry.

'Well, Mel is Leesha's granddaughter. Maybe money is what
matters most to her, too.'

'I think it is, right now. That's why we're to send these
photos of our ritzy house. To get Mel over here, and then
work on her.'

'Right! But not with kid gloves!'

Keeley laughed, and took another photo as he clambered out
of the pool to tussle with the dogs.

'No. There won't be any kid gloves. When I get my mitts
on that young lady, I'm going to sort her out. Starting with
teaching her a bit of respect for her mother.'

Mother, Vincent thought hopefully. At least the word 'mother'
is in her vocabulary now. And when Mel gets here, when we
start playing parents to her . . . who knows, maybe Keeley will
decide it's time to have a child of our own.

'How long is Mel coming for, if she comes?'

'Oh, I don't know . . . a month, maybe? In August? We could take a bit of time off then, organise some fun for her between beatings.'

Time off? Vincent clutched that phrase to him, and stored it hopefully away. Soon, he was going to talk to Keeley seriously about the whole question of children; but let's start with this child first, he thought, and see whether nature takes its course.

Cathal was livid. Banging down his cup of breakfast tea, he purpled with rage as he turned to his wife.

'France?! Did you hear that, she wants to go to France, to – to stay with her fucking godmother!'

'Cathal, please don't swear in front of her.'

'Swear? I'll swear all I bloody like! You put her up to this, didn't you? This is all your goddamn idea, Mary!'

Wondering how to deny it, Mary faced him with ill-concealed anxiety, even a little fear. She was useless at telling lies, never able to 'manage' her husband in the silky nonchalant way other women did. If you could call a man your husband, when you hadn't shared a bed with him for thirteen years.

'No, I—'

Flushing, Mel jumped to her feet and cut across whatever her mother had been going to say.

'Daddy, don't be stupid! Ma never said a word about France, she probably doesn't even know where it is! Auntie Keeley wrote to *me*!'

Cathal's face darkened yet further. 'Auntie? She's not your shagging aunt, she's only—'

'She's my godmother! I've never even met her, and it's not fair! She sends me loads of presents and now she's sent all these photos. Look, she lives in this amazing house, they've got a pool and tennis and everything – I want to go! It'll be sunny over there, why should I have to spend the whole summer here in the rain – Daddy, please! I *want* to!'

'I don't care what you want, I'm not having this, you're not going near that interfering bloody Butler troublemaker—'

Mel collapsed back onto her seat at the breakfast table, threw her head down on her forearms and burst into tears.

'S-she has a BMW, she says she'll take me shopping in it – to all the boutiques – and now you won't let me go – I hate you! I *hate* you!'

Aghast, Cathal gazed at her, her fists drumming on the table. Never before had he heard anything like it from Imelda, whose voice never rose above the softest wheedle, whose favourite phrase was 'Oh Daddy, thank you, you're the greatest.' After a pause, he cleared his throat.

'Imelda, stop that.'

'B-but you won't let me go – to learn French – I'll be way behind when I go back to school—'

Sob, sob, sob. And the unspoken implication that all the friends would be going to France in the summer, to learn French.

'And they live near the coast – there's a beach, Auntie Keeley says her friend Félix has a yacht – a *yacht*! Ohhh . . .' Gallons of tears, torrents of them. Mary held her breath, saying nothing, trying to look indifferent.

Abruptly, Cathal leaped to his feet and slammed down his newspaper.

'Oh, all right! All *right*, Imelda, I said! Just for God's sake stop that whinging.'

Instantly, Mel stopped. When she looked up, her smile was sunny as summer in Bali, tears twinkling like diamonds on her long lashes. 'Oh, Daddy, thank you – can I really go? Really, truly, promise?' She simpered winningly, and he nodded reluctantly.

'Yes. You can go, since you – oh, bloody hell!'

He stormed to the door as Mary's heart did cartwheels of relief, of a joy she had not known in years. For the first time, she had won. Won, without even letting him know she was fighting. At last, she had managed something.

But then he turned back, and she cringed inwardly as he came over to her, his face a study of fury. Bending down, he whispered something into her ear.

'Bitch,' he spat. 'I'll get you for this, you bloody bitch.'

In shorts and a teeshirt, with secateurs in one hand and a trowel in the other, Keeley knelt on the grass, gazing unseeing at the herbaceous border she was supposedly trimming. Overhead the July sunshine blazed in a pure blue sky, and thoughts flitted around her head like swallows.

Over the years, she had had many good ideas. Settling in France had been a good idea, going into partnership with Félix had been an excellent one, the salons were a smash

hit, the hairdressing school a monument to ingenuity and
determination. And her marriage to Vincent was such a success
she didn't even try to figure out why, in case she unpicked the
seams and unravelled the whole thing. But, now that it was
actually imminent, she was starting to wonder if Mel Sullivan's
visit was such a good idea.

At first, the prospect had thrilled her. She had even written
direct to Mel, bypassing Mary to invite the girl herself, so that
if anything went wrong Mary could not be implicated, accused
or abused by Cathal. And it had worked; Mel was raring to go,
due to arrive next week. A room was ready for her, an itinerary
of fun excursions planned, friends' teenaged children hijacked
for numerous activities. Vincent was looking forward to Mel's
arrival so much he had even arranged to take leave from work,
a sign of real interest and enthusiasm.

But . . . but. Keeley squatted back, resting her weight on the
backs of her legs as she tried to pinpoint some reason for her
sudden doubt, the feeling of apprehension that was growing in
her mind.

It wasn't Mel. Nothing to do with Mel, personally. At
thirty-four she was well able to handle a girl twenty years
her junior, just as she handled new recruits in the salons, with
a warm welcome and a firm approach. No matter how spoiled
or selfish Mel might be, she must have some saving graces,
and anyway the visit would only last four weeks. She would
do everything in her power to make friends with Mel during
that time, to amuse and enjoy her even while working on her,
trying to curb her worst excesses. Inevitably there would be a
few clashes, but it wasn't that; she had long since learned how
to deal with clashes.

So what was it? For a long while Keeley continued to kneel,
absently running an earthy hand through the hair which, in
summer, she wore short and curly with copper lowlights. In
front of her, the lavender glowed in the reflected heat of the
stone wall, hypnotic, normally calming, but not today. In the
distance she could hear the even splash of water as Vincent
swam rhythmic lengths, the sprint and snuffle of the dogs, the
tranquil purr of some neighbour's lawnmower. All the restful
sights and sounds of a summer Sunday in Provence; but she
was restless, uneasy.

No. Not uneasy. Unwilling. That was the truth of it, and at
length she was forced to confront the truth. The prospect of

Mel's visit was making her face up to something she did not want to face: a child. Children. The subject she shied away from every time Vincent brought it up, deflected, laughed off in a way which, she thought, was starting to distress him. Or bother him, at least, disturb him under his calm surface.

Vincent wanted children. He didn't push it, but he didn't deny it either. He wanted to become a father, he was ready for it, his sister Sylvie already had two children with her cyclist husband. He adored his niece and nephew, and now he wanted cousins for them. A son or daughter, to complete his happy marriage, enliven his peaceful home. And why not? As wishes went, it was perfectly reasonable.

But Keeley did not want children. Not yet. Not until the last possible moment, perhaps four or five years from now. In her teens she had briefly thought a baby would be nice, fun to have around; but as time went by her feelings changed. Over and again, she looked at her own mother Gertie, still trapped with Tony who, although a successful painter now, remained handicapped, entirely dependent on her. She looked at Mary, and at the price she had paid, continued to pay, for Mel. And then she looked at her work, so satisfying, so challenging, so *controllable*. Out of chaos she had created order, and she wanted to keep her life in order. Whereas children, demonstrably, were problematic, messy, unpredictable – everything she had escaped, and put firmly behind her. Even Sylvie, who loved her children, admitted that her days of cycling through Turkey and Syria were over, and that furthermore she often longed to throttle one or other of her cheeky, demanding, extremely provocative offspring. Sometimes, when she spent more than an hour with them, Keeley feared that she might even have inherited her own father's short fuse, because she ached to spank them herself, with resounding force. And they were only her niece and nephew, by marriage; what might she not do to her own infants, if she had any?

Nothing, Vincent said, when she confided this thought to him. She wouldn't touch them, do anything to them, because it was different with your own children; unless you were emotionally unbalanced or completely psychotic, nature had a way of keeping you in check, tempering your anger with love and understanding. And Keeley was not, in his experience, psychotic.

Vaguely, she smiled to herself. Until now, conversations

about children had always ended more or less the same way, with a laugh. But now, it didn't feel like a laughing matter any more. Vincent was ready, and she was not. For the first time in her married life she was aware of some disappointment in her husband, in her. It was camouflaged, it was lightly brushed aside, but she sensed it was there.

Was she wrong, to feel this way? Was she self-centered, too enthralled by the rewarding, fulfilling life she led? Too fond of its material prizes? There was no denying that she enjoyed it, loved it; the sense of purpose that had blossomed the day the first salon opened, the sense of achievement as the next salon and then the next multiplied like mushrooms. Even as she worked herself to the bone she was thrilled with the progress she made, the customers' every compliment, the adrenalin and the buzz. It was her creation and Vincent's, and for years they had thought of little else. But then, in latter years, the urgency had relaxed a fraction, been diffused with a feeling of security and stability, so that for the first time they were able to stand back and look around them, give attention to other aspects of their life.

That was when they had started to think about building this house, and gradually build a broader, more normal life as well. Slowly they made a new circle of friends, got out more, went sailing with Félix and attended parties, learned to entertain, found time to enjoy the sun and the long, lush Provençal days.

Even now Keeley couldn't get over the well-being she felt as she stood in her own garden or someone else's, cocktail glass in hand, her bare arms caressed by the warmth and the gleaming light, talking with people she liked or loved, assured, confident, accepted. She had never got an engagement ring, in the end, because it seemed redundant by the time they could afford it, but Vincent had given her a beautiful eternity ring studded with diamonds, later a gold chain and a gold bracelet which she wore all the time, be it with jeans or black velvet. They were not important to her in themselves, but their symbolism was important, she treasured the love and success they represented.

And then, there were the books, the paintings, the music. Ever curious and conscious of her ignorance, she read everything she could lay hands on from Flaubert to Brétécher cartoons, guzzling thirstily, learning, learning, learning. The new house included a library, a wall-to-wall stereo system forever playing Brel or Brahms, and an eclectic collection of paintings bought purely on the basis of personal taste. Nowadays she knew a good deal about art, was great friends with Alain Jou and Serge Rolland, but still she studied, wondered, buried herself in big books that made Vincent laugh. In the salons she hung Tony's paintings, to promote them as Alain asked her to, and was happy to think of both the pleasure and the profit accruing to her brother. Most of his money went into a savings fund, for the inevitable day when he would have to live and cope alone, with professional nursing but no family. There was enough to buy a house too, but Christy refused to move, and Gertie refused to leave without him, so the three continued to live in Pearse Gardens and quite a bit of Tony's funds, Keeley thought, went into the pocket of Christy's publicans – Cathal Sullivan included.

Vaguely she worried about her brother, but Tony seemed happy enough once he could paint, and by way of tribute to his resolve she hung his first painting, the one that had so astonished Alain, in the hall. She still held her original opinion of it, but everybody else exclaimed, admired, and commissioned others on the strength of it. Elsewhere the house was full of local works, by people she encouraged and helped, sometimes became friends with. Original Cézannes were out of her reach, but these, she thought with glee, were the new Cézannes. In her eyes anyway, which was all that mattered in her home.

Life was such fun, so fascinating, she simply could not see how a baby could possibly fit into it. Of course she wouldn't have to give up work entirely, if she had children, but she would have to slow down, adjust, accommodate . . . the mothers who worked for her were always saying how exhausted they were, or trying to conceal it, half-asleep on their feet. Small kids cried all night, bigger ones yelled and rampaged and turned their homes into bomb-sites. Keeley had lived in a virtual bomb-site once, and she didn't want to live in one again.

Vincent would help, naturally. He would share the work, it wouldn't all fall on her, they could have an au-pair as well. But what was the point of having a child if you were hardly ever going to see it? And – and how might her marriage have to be rearranged, to fit around a child? She had never felt truly loved when she was one herself, but she felt truly loved now, and something in her was reluctant to share Vincent with anyone else. For the first time in her life she was the exclusive recipient of someone's affection, and Vincent's was so warm, so precious, she could not bear the thought of diluting it.

If she told Vincent that, he'd say she was crazy, so she didn't tell him, but she thought it and felt it. It was irrational, it was even painful at times, but it was the result of her childhood; she needed and wanted her husband to herself. At night, when she lay naked in his arms and everything else was stripped away – the suits, the briefcase, the BMW – she felt so young, so childlike it terrified her. How could she ever assume the duties, the responsibility of motherhood? At work she was strong and capable, shouldered the responsibility of two hundred employees and the families who depended on the continued success of *Cut*!, but a baby . . . oh, God. Even now, in 1993 when fathers were involved, mothers were responsible. Mothers were the focus of it all, the ones blamed if it went wrong. Nature dictated it, society reinforced it, and there was no point in denying it. Having a child was a major, lifelong undertaking, and she was not ready for it. Not ready to slow down, to share Vincent, to face the risks and the imponderables, the hundred and one things that could go wrong with a child.

And yet . . . sometimes she thought of Mel as a baby, so sweet, so beautiful. But look at Mel now, a monster apparently, a demon daughter. Look at Tony, in his wheelchair, his mother feeding and dressing him at thirty-six years of age. The tender trap, that Vincent now wanted to spring on her.

I wish I wanted it, she thought. I really wish I did, because I love Vincent with all my heart. If I still feel this way in another few years, I'll go ahead and take the plunge regardless, because he wants me to. But not now. Please, not yet. Not just yet.

Mary was silent in the back of the car as they drove to the airport, Cathal and Mel chatting in front as if she were invisible. Having been forced to let Mel go to France, he was acting now as if it was his idea, full of exquisitely-faked enthusiasm. Some day, she thought bitterly, an Oscar will arrive in the post for that man.

At the airport he led the way masterfully, checked Mel in and steered her to the departure gates, where she kissed him, hugged him and then pecked her mother's cheek.

'Bye, Ma.'

'Bye, darling.' In spite of the girl's resistance, Mary held her tight, for the fraction of a second it took. 'Have a lovely time, and say hello to Keeley for me. To Vincent too.'

Briefly, Mel's indigo eyes registered a slight flicker of curiosity, in which Mary saw the sudden question: who exactly is Keeley, how do you know her, how come she's my godmother? But then she whirled round distracted, as Cathal stuffed an envelope into her pocket.

'Just a few bob in case you see any nice clothes – ring me if you run short, sweetheart.'

'Oh, thanks Dad, I will – I'll ring you anyway!'

And then, in a blur of colourful clothes and accessories, she was gone. Mary's mind raced ahead of her, to the duty-free shop where within minutes the first of the money would be spent on cigarettes. Cigarettes which, hopefully, Keeley would confiscate.

As soon as she was out of sight, Cathal stopped waving, turned round and strode away. For a moment Mary thought he was actually leaving without her, such was his body language, and ran to catch up. At a brisk clip they reached the car, got in and drove away, in silence.

The silence continued all the way home, where she went to put on the kettle, longing to fill it with gin. He went upstairs and she heard some rapid movements, sounds of doors and drawers opening as if he was searching for something. But the sounds were coming from his own room, not hers; at least he was not apparently hunting for evidence, hunting her down. By the time the kettle boiled and the tea was made, his footsteps were descending the stairs, and she braced herself. Now. The fight was going to start now.

But he was carrying a suitcase and a holdall, a coat over his arm. Barely glancing at her, he spoke as if to the tea-pot.

'I'm off. Golf trip. No point in staying here till Imelda comes back. Bill will give you thirty pounds a week out of the till. Keep note of everything you spend it on. Here's the number for when she rings, tell her to call me there.'

Throwing down a piece of paper on the table, he was gone before she could even ask, 'What will I tell your parents, if they're looking for you? Where are you going?'

But then she realised: he would have told his parents, his employees, everyone else already. She was the only one who didn't know. Good old Mary, he would have said, holding the fort while I'm away on business. Isn't she a great girl, be lost without her.

For a moment, pain froze in her throat like a stalagmite. It was years since she had cared about the personal hurt, about his coldness or his insults. But the public humiliation, the having to pretend she knew where he was when she didn't, to ask Bill for cash like a child – that stung tears to her eyes, tears she bit back until she heard the sound of his car revving away.

But then, they didn't fall. On the contrary. As she sat down with her cup of tea it hit her like a laser beam, cutting through everything else – he was gone! Mel was gone! She was *alone*!

Alone, totally alone, for the first time in fourteen years. Her hand shook as the shock sank in; apart from her duties at the pub, to which she would now have to walk every day, she could do what she liked. Nothing radical, of course, with barely enough for basics and Bill, his head barman, watching her ('keep an eye on Mary for me, will you, Bill, you know she's a bit nervy when I'm away?') but, here in this house, she was her own boss. The thought was so wildly liberating, so exciting she felt almost faint.

How long was he gone for? 'No point,' he had said, 'in staying here till Imelda comes back.' Four weeks? Could it be? No – that was surely a trap, he would reappear before Mel did, pounce to catch her in whatever misdemeanour it might be. But a couple of weeks, at least, two or even three if she was lucky.

Where was he gone, how far away? She picked up the piece of paper with the phone number on it. It had an 021 prefix. Cork. A hundred miles or more, three hours' drive on Irish roads even in an Audi. And, if he really was playing golf, he would be reluctant to leave for anything less than an emergency. Golf had replaced football as the great love of his life, apart from his fixation with Imelda.

Mel. Mary thought of her daughter, halfway to Aix by now, and of Cathal's relationship with the girl who was not his, the girl he had merely 'taken' out of – not out of charity, certainly not out of charity. Was Mel really just part of the 'deal' whereby he got a cook for his pub and a housekeeper for his home, or . . . many times before had she thought about it, but never had she allowed herself to reach the inevitable conclusion even Keeley never voiced. The conclusion that there was something really wrong with Cathal Sullivan, something so seriously wrong that he needed a child either as proof of something, or as a cover for something. Or both.

Sipping the tea, she thought of the day, twelve years before, that she had miscarried their child. Their only child, their only evidence of 'normality', of their intimacy, his masculinity. He had gone berserk when the little boy died . . . not with grief, but with rage. Every time she wondered why, she clamped down on her wonder, slammed shut the lid of Pandora's box. The thought of what it might contain was too terrible to ever see the light of day.

But now, she was alone. All alone. She had two weeks, at least, to think, to face it, to make herself do what she knew she must do, and find out.

Not for her own sake – it was far too late for that – but for Mel's. Appalling as the girl was, she was her daughter. Her duty. Covertly, she had watched over her from the start, kept tabs on every kiss, every cuddle, every childhood game . . . but there had been nothing. Whatever Cathal Sullivan was, he did not appear to be a paedophile. He worshipped Mel, but did not see her as Lolita. Whatever it was, it wasn't that; she could not in all honesty say that she had ever remotely sensed her daughter to be in danger.

So what *was* it? What did he want Mel, need her *for*? Public proof of something? That fitted . . . the lavish christening, the lie that the child was his. And the boy really *would* have been his. After the miscarriage, they had never had sex again. Mel had grown up believing that her 'father' had a football injury which necessitated sleeping alone, would never even think to query the situation now that she was old enough to.

The tea was growing cold, but Mary kept sipping it, revelling in the silence, the utter stillness of the house. She was going to use this silence, this blissful isolation, to every inch of its advantage. She was going to take time out, and find out. Cathal would have locked his room and everything in it, taken the keys away – but somewhere there was another key, one that would unlock his secret life and maybe even her prison door, if she turned it the right way.

Speeding along the autoroute, with the top down and the wind in her hair, Mel whistled from the depths of the cream leather seat.

'Wow. This is cool! It must be a real blast to live here.'

Keeley smiled into the mirror. 'Yes. It is.'

Brightly, Mel smiled back. 'Ma told me you've been here for fifteen years. Did you always have a BMW?'

'No. I had two feet, when I arrived, and then the loan of Vincent's sister's bike.'

'Really? So how'd you get the great car?'

'I worked for it.'

'Oh, right. The seventeen salons and all that.'

'Not at first. I started off with a bottle of shampoo and a pair of hands.'

'Huh?'

'I washed hair. For about 20p a head, before tax, in Dublin.'

'Yeah? 20p? God, that must have been in the dark ages . . . I get £20 a week pocket money, from my Dad.'

Keeley smiled again, both at Mel in the back seat and at Vincent beside her. 'Good. You'll need that. France is expensive.'

Mel blinked. 'Yeah, right. But you guys are going to look after me, aren't you? Bed and board in that great house you sent the pics of?'

'Bed. Not board.'

Mel sat bolt upright, and then leaned forward. 'What? What do you mean?'

'We mean bed. Not board. You've just said you've got £20 a week. That should cover your food.'

'But – but – you invited me! I'm your guest! Your goddaughter!'

'Oh. OK. So you are. Tell you what, then. We'll throw in the food if you'll throw in a bit of housework. Nothing much. Just make your bed, keep your room clean, give a hand with a bit of cooking and maybe mow the lawn.'

'But you have a maid, and a gardener! You said you had!'

'Yes, we have. But it's August. They're on holidays.'

Mel pouted so fiercely that Keeley laughed outright. But then she relaxed back into the seat, smiling nonchalantly as she examined her nails.

'I don't know how to cook.'

'Really? That's funny. Your mother is a fabulous cook.'

'My mother? She is in her eye. She just does pub grub. Nothing like I bet the restaurants do here.'

'She trained in a restaurant here. A Michelin-starred one. We'll take you to eat in it before you leave, if you're good.'

'If I'm *good*? Hey, I'm not a kid, you know.'

'No? So what are you?'

'I – I'm a *teen*ager.'

'Oh, yes. Like I was the first time I came to France. Clueless, bog-ignorant, didn't know my ass from my elbow.'

For a moment there was silence. Then Mel piped up again. 'Yeah. Everyone was then, weren't they? Not like today. Now, we've got it sussed. I've been to Italy, you know. Skiing.'

'Uh huh.'

From the back seat, Mel glowered at both Keeley and Vincent. Granted, they did not seem to be quite as dull or dreary as her own parents, but neither did they seem to be taking her seriously, grasping how grown-up she was. Reaching into her tote bag, she extracted a duty-free cigarette, and lit it with a perspex lighter stamped Val d'Aosta. No reaction. She peered into the mirror and blew out a cloud of smoke.

'Don't mind if I smoke, do you?'

'Not in the open air.'

Well, this was the open air, and Mel conceded that she was enjoying herself as they whizzed along in the ritzy car, feeling quite film-starrish in fact, glad she'd put on her lipstick at the airport.

'So tell us about this great house of yours.'

'No need. Here we are.'

Without warning Keeley slewed the car around a tight corner, so suddenly and sharply that the cigarette shot out of Mel's mouth and she choked on a cloud of suddenly-swallowed smoke.

'Uh – ugh—!'

'Mind it doesn't burn the leather.'

Picking up the butt between his fingers, Vincent dropped it with a smile and squished it out with his heel on the gravel. 'So. Welcome to our home, Mel. Let me open the boot so you can get your luggage out.'

Both Vincent and Keeley strode forwards, heading for the front door, leaving her to heft the two bursting suitcases crammed with clothes for every possible eventuality. Vincent was a great-looking guy, for his age, but she wasn't much impressed with his manners. Where was all this French chivalry stuff?

And what was Keeley talking about, saying her mother had trained in a Michelin restaurant? Admittedly Ma used to talk a lot about French food, but she didn't any more, and if she'd ever mentioned her training she, Imelda, could remember nothing about it.

Frowning, she followed Keeley down a long wide corridor filled with paintings, round a corner and into a room which had a terrific view out over the pool – and virtually nothing else. It was a large room, but apart from a bed and an unvarnished wooden cupboard that seemed to pass for a wardrobe, it had none of the comforts of home. Instead of a carpet there was only a striped rug on the worn-looking yellow tiles, a pale battered coffee table, and a flimsy curtain in voile or muslin fluttering in the breeze from the open window. The walls were painted some shade of cream or sand, as if the painter had changed his mind and gone over the first layer with a second, there wasn't even any wallpaper; Mel's jaw dropped as she absorbed the unnerving simplicity of it all.

'Where's the tv?'

In that wooden cupboard, she hoped, along with the CD player and stuff. But Keeley grinned, and shrugged. 'There isn't any.'

'What!? No telly?'

'No point. You don't speak much French, do you?'

'No, but—'

'Then you won't be watching television. Whenever you do want to, you're welcome to use the one in the living room, any time before 10 pm so long as you tell us what programme it is . . . the news might be useful for improving your French, the newsreaders speak very clearly. You can read, too, there are plenty of books. D'you like these flowers? I just cut them for you this morning, everything grows like a weed in this climate.'

And looks like it too, Mel thought sulkily; they're not proper flowers, just branches and leaves and that wispy stuff. And would you look at the vase, all rough and cracked! You'd think she could afford Aynsley or Waterford or something decent like we have at home; Granny Sullivan gives us a new one every Christmas.

Briskly, Keeley embarked on a guided tour of the room.

'We don't use curtains in summer, only shutters, they work like this . . . the water is solar-heated so it's a bit cool in the mornings . . . it might take you a while to get used to the bolster, but nobody in Provence uses pillows . . . if insects bother you shut the windows before you turn on the light . . .'

Bolsters? Insects? Dropping her bags on the tiled floor Mel sat down on the bed, which felt low and rather odd.

'I'm starving. When's dinner, Keeley?'

'At eight. Out on the terrace, in this weather – we're having a few friends round this evening, so you can dress up a bit if you like.'

Mel brightened. 'I've brought lots of clothes. Wanna see?'

Snapping open the first suitcase, she pulled out what looked like an entire boutique, and held up one outfit after another.

'Dad gave me money too, to go shopping. Can we go tomorrow?'

'Not tomorrow. Vincent's sister and parents are coming to visit – Sylvie's daughter is about your age, nearly thirteen.'

'Twelve, you mean? Huh, a kid! I was fourteen six weeks ago – uh, thanks for the birthday present. I meant to write.'

'I'm sure you did. Anyway, I'll leave you to get comfortable and have a shower. Let me know if there's anything you need.'

A bloody good spanking, Keeley thought as she left the room, that's what you need, you little monster. Well, you might have broken your mother's heart, but you won't break mine.

When she reached the living room its glass doors were wide open, and she could smell charcoal, see Vincent getting the barbecue ready out on the flagged terrace, pulling herbs and tossing them onto the coals. Thoughtfully, she went up to him and put her arm around his shoulder. 'Hi. I hear you're a guy who mixes a mean martini.'

He straightened up and grinned at her.

'Yeah. Prize brat, isn't she?'

'Prize, award-winning, Grade A. What on earth possessed us?'

'Mary did. Mary wrote and like a fool you agreed . . . but let's give the kid a chance, Keeley. She's only – what – fifteen, sixteen?'

'Fourteen. Going on thirty-five. I'd say she's spraying herself in Chanel even as we speak.'

'Hmm. Jailbait. We're really going to have to watch her, Keeley.'

'Yes, chéri. Two olives, and feel free with the vodka.'

While he went inside to mix their drinks she pottered at the barbecue, wondering what had happened to the gorgeous baby with the gummy smile and the fat neck. Mel was still gorgeous,

but strictly in appearance. Well – it was early days. By the end
of the month, young Ms Sullivan might have other qualities
to recommend her, if she, Keeley, was given a free hand and
Daddy Cathal stayed out of it. Was Cathal still afraid of her, as
Mary had once said? If he was, he might not phone or interfere
too often.

Vincent returned with the drinks, and she thought how
handsome he looked, his olive cheeks flushed with sun, his
dark hair worn short these days, but still so thick and curly.
And his smile . . . most of all she loved that smile, so intimate,
as if for her alone. Handing her a glass, he dropped a kiss on her
cheek and led her to the canvas chairs that stood haphazardly
between terracotta pots of lavender.

'Let's just relax for a few minutes before Luc and Félix arrive
. . . cheers, chérie, here's to our lovely god-daughter, may our
own be twice as nice.'

He raised his glass and she raised hers in turn, squinting at
him against the setting sun.

'Our own what? Daughter, do you mean?'

'Yes, well, we will have one eventually I suppose . . . won't
we?'

'I suppose . . . but Vincent, we have so much already. Let's
not push our luck. I mean, I am thirty-four, maybe—'

'And I'm nearly thirty-seven. We're just the right age, now, I
think. What do you think?'

He turned to look at her, keenly she thought, intently.
It was a loving look, even humorous, but it was searching,
too.

She couldn't lie to him, give him false hope. She couldn't. But
she couldn't tell him the truth either, blurt out all the muddled
feelings that would sound so silly and selfish.

'I think – that we – should maybe see how we get on with this
child, first. By the time she leaves you might have gone right off
the idea!'

'Mm. Maybe. But she's spoiled, Keeley, not typical – why
don't you put her to work washing hair, that might fix her!'

Keeley thought that wasn't a half-bad idea. A bit of work
might be just the job for Mel – only she already had lots of
pocket money, and besides the nearest salon, the first one they'd
opened in Aix, was closed for two weeks' summer holidays.
There was the one near the university, but it wasn't very busy
in August. And driving the girl further afield would be a hassle.

But at least the question seemed to have distracted Vincent. Quickly, she pursued the red herring.

'We'll put her to work at something, that's for sure. Waitressing, maybe, like Mary used to do? Walking the dogs, babysitting for Sylvie, washing the cars – I know, pulling pints in a brasserie, like her oul fella!'

Vincent laughed. 'She'd make a buxom barmaid, that's for sure. I can't believe Mary lets her wear all that make-up.'

'I'm sure Mary doesn't. I'd say she slaps it on as soon as she's out of sight – and slap will be the word, if she wears it around here.'

'Oh, you're a hard woman, Keeley Butler. You'll make a great mother.'

'I – my God, Vincent, look at the time. Twenty past seven, and everyone coming at half past, I'd better put on a bit of lipstick myself.'

As if electrified, Keeley jumped up, put down her glass and raced into the house. Vincent followed her with his eyes until she vanished, and then, reluctantly, he turned his attention to the smoking barbecue.

Standing amidst a cluster of ceramic pots that kept snagging her glossy tights, Mel didn't know whether to be disgusted or delighted.

On the one hand, a poolside barbecue was definitely her idea of fun. As the sun had gone down the lights had come on, illuminating the turquoise water, the flowering trees that smelled heavenly, the rich yellow stone of the house which now glowed magically. The air was so warm, so perfumed with herbs and flowers she could hardly believe it, and to her surprise Vincent was allowing her to have a glass of wine. Just one, he said, but it was a start, she'd soon work on him to give her another. The shellfish grilling on the barbecue smelled absolutely delicious, and this man Félix was talking about the yacht on which, he promised, he would take her sailing.

So far, so good. But the downside was that Keeley had made her take off all her make-up and change out of the dress which, she said, was 'far too tight and bright.' Mel had argued that she was let wear what she liked at home, but Keeley had squashed her by lifting the phone and saying, fine, she'd just call Mary to check. Defeated, Mel had been forced to change into an ordinary summer dress and remove her nail varnish as well; as a result

of all this she felt practically invisible, and was being treated
as such.

The guests, when they arrived, were another disappointment.
Granted there was a couple with a set of teenaged twins, about
sixteen, but the twins didn't speak English unless you counted
'allo' and 'ow do you do', which hardly had the makings of a
rave night. Her own French went no further, and so she was
bored already with the twins, who were a bit supercilious in
any case.

Then there was a big heavy man called Luc, who inexplicably had seized her, kissed her and showered compliments on
'Mary's leetle daughter.' 'Ow was Mary, he kept asking, 'ow
was her kitchen, her business, her wonderful self? He had
trained Mary, taught her everything he knew ... gradually
it dawned on Mel that her mother actually must have been
to France, sometime way back in the dark ages, and learned
to cook here. This guy Luc kept saying she was gifted, he had
seen her talent at once, at *once*; whereupon Mel thought of
Ma's shepherd's pies, and laughed aloud. Since then, Luc had
not addressed another word to her.

And then there were the wives. Félix's super-glamorous wife
Lise, who was sophisticated and stunning and looked at her as
if she were one of the labradors, and Luc's vast wife Annette
who was dressed like a peasant, laughed too loud and talked
too much. The twins' parents were at least forty, spoke no
more English than their offspring, and as the drinks part of the
evening progressed Mel had been forced gradually back into the
company of Keeley and Vincent, who at least did speak English
and suddenly seemed quite young by comparison.

Vincent was standing over his barbecue, brushing some liquid
onto the enormous prawns he said were called langoustines; the
liquid was scented with lemon and thyme and Mel could hardly
wait to taste it. In jeans and a dark red sweatshirt, brandishing
a long fork amidst the aromatic smoke, he looked dashing and
rather hunky. He was talking to her in between jokes with
his guests, but Keeley wasn't paying her any attention at all.
Changed into a cream linen dress, showing off a good tan and
even better gold jewellery, she was a very different person now
to the woman in casual trousers, shirt and sunglasses who'd
driven the BMW with the wind in her hair.

She was – Mel groped for the word – she was elegant.
Elegant in some very low-key way, talking to all her guests

in turn, laughing but not shrieking, making sure everyone was comfortable without appearing to be watching them at all.

Where did I get her, Mel wondered, where did I get this weird godmother? She's not a bit like either of my parents, I can't imagine how they could even know each other. I must find out, the minute I get a chance.

'*Alors!* OK, everyone, *à table!*'

Vincent waved his trident-type fork at the table, and Mel was amazed to see everyone drift over to it, seat themselves within a minute of being summoned. In Ireland everyone would keep right on drinking, ignore the food until they were good and ready for it.

But she was certainly ready for it herself. She was salivating with hunger and the odour of those chargrilled prawns, the colour of that huge salad – not plain green like at home, but filled with reds, yellows, oranges, curly things and crunchy things she didn't recognise. As she gazed at it the large man, Luc, got to his feet, took up a wooden implement and began to stir it vigorously, tossing and twirling like a juggler.

'*Eh voilà, ça va mieux!*'

Everyone laughed, and she joined in as if she understood. Next thing the sizzling prawns arrived on a tray and that was passed around, each person helping himself or herself in turn until finally the twins got their mitts on it and she, Mel, was left with only the smallest four remaining prawns. Hey, she thought, I'm the new guest here, that's not fair!

Outraged, she looked down the table to see whether Keeley had noticed the injustice, whereupon Keeley sent the salad bowl down the table to her, and she was obliged to console herself with that. But, when she tasted it, what a salad! As each new flavour burst on her tongue, she asked Vincent what it was: curly endive he said, pine nuts, water chestnut, anchovy, radish, roast garlic and balsamic vinaigrette. Nodding, she wondered why Mary, her own mother, never served up anything like this. She must call Daddy tomorrow, and tell him about these extraordinary discoveries. If Luc had ever taught Mary stuff like this, maybe Dad would persuade her to dust off her old recipes.

But meanwhile, the French conversation was daunting, and Vincent wouldn't give her any more wine. She pouted, and then tried flirting a little, but nothing worked; the Chablis skipped by her and sailed merrily away down the table.

She smiled winningly. 'Just a beer, then?'

'No. You don't mix wine and beer, Mel.'

And so she was left high and dry until, ages later it seemed, a huge platter of cheeses appeared. What, no dessert? She thought she could kill for a big slice of strawberry cheesecake, or pavlova or even apple pie. Instead, Vincent was pointing out an awful smelly thing called Maroilles to her, urging her to taste it only after the gentler goat's cheese or the nutty-flavoured Emmenthal or the springy stuff he called Chaume.

Hunger drove her to take a piece of each, cursing the twins who'd savaged the prawns. Normally she didn't like cheese, but four prawns, even four fantastic ones, wasn't enough for a growing girl. Why had there been no potatoes? It was all very peculiar.

'*Attends*,' Vincent said, not unkindly. 'I will let you have a tiny drop of Fleurie with the Maroilles, just for experience's sake.'

He made her continue with water first with the other cheeses, but she was forced to admit it was worth the wait; the pungent Maroilles made her eyes sting, but followed by the ruby wine the combination nearly blew her head off. Wow! So this was what people meant by cheese and wine!

Vincent smiled, so did Luc and Keeley. 'A first adult taste, for our little girl . . . how is it, Mel, do you like it?'

Little girl? *Little girl*? Furious, flushing, she looked at them loftily. 'It is,' she said with chilly dignity, 'excellent.'

They all burst out laughing, and she felt like stamping her foot with rage. *Why* would nobody take her seriously, what was the matter with them?

She thought of protesting; and then, she thought not. From the corner of her eye she spotted something . . . could it be . . . oh, God, yes. It was – it looked like – the most blissful chocolate cake ever baked in all creation. The moment she saw it she longed to plunge her fork into it, but then they really would think her a child. Jigging on her chair, she tried to contain herself for the twenty full minutes it took Keeley to get around to cutting it.

But then, at last, the heavenly dark rich chocolate, melting down her throat tasting faintly of almond, the creamy mousse inside it perfumed with vanilla, silky-soft, bubble-light . . . ooh. Mmmm. Who on God's earth had baked this?

'*Moi*,' Luc said. 'In France a guest often brings a cake, Mel.'

She didn't care if he called her Mel all night, so long as he wrote down his recipe and gave it to her, to take home to mother Mary.

Luc replied that he most certainly would not write it down, it was an ancient recipe that Mary already knew perfectly well. If Mel liked the cake, Mary would teach her to make it in a jiffy.

'But I can't cook,' she protested.

'This is not cooking,' he replied, 'this is baking.'

And then abruptly he turned away from her, went back to his conversation with Lise Peyrolle and her mousy-looking husband – the one, inexplicably, with the yacht. How could this prim old guy, who wore round glasses and a starched white shirt even in August, possibly sail a yacht? The longer the evening went on, the more perplexing it got. Baffled and ignored, she accepted Vincent's offer of coffee, reached into her pocket and took out her cigarettes.

Nobody noticed, much less offered to light it for her, not even the male twin who actually wasn't bad-looking, when you got used to his know-all expression. Loudly, she clicked her lighter and lit it herself. Keeley's head jerked up.

'Mel, please put out that cigarette.'

'What? But you said it was OK to smoke outdoors—'

'Not at table, before other people have finished eating. Certainly not at my table, without so much as asking permission.'

'But—'

'*Put it out.*'

Keeley's tone and expression were such that she did put it out, defiantly stubbing and twisting it into an empty prawn shell. Luc gasped aloud, looking apoplectic until Keeley put her hand, lazily, on his arm.

'Never mind, Luc. The poor child has only just arrived from Ireland, it's not her fault.'

Poor? *Child*? And the insinuation that she had somehow disgraced her country, as well as herself? It was too much. Mel got up, flung back her chair and flounced off, into the house and away to her room, before anyone could see the tears welling in her eyes.

Out on the terrace, Luc remained scandalised. 'Keeley, she is Mary's daughter, how can she—?'

Keeley sighed. 'Luc, you forget. She isn't just Mary's daughter. She is—' Just in time, she stopped herself. Of course Luc already knew, as did Félix and their wives, that Mel was the product of Mary's fling with an unknown Swede, fifteen years ago in a field. Mel didn't know, but the conversation was in French, so even if she could hear she wouldn't understand.

That wasn't what stopped her. Nor even what she meant. What she meant was that Mel was Cathal Sullivan's daughter – the daughter of a brute and a bully, who had reduced his wife to a drudge, begging for money for this, permission for that, everything but the right to breathe. Mel was not civilised for the simple reason that her home was not civilised.

Vincent frowned. 'Oh, Keeley. You've upset the poor kid, on her first night with us.'

Grimly, she smiled down the table at him. 'I hope so, Vincent. I hope I've upset everything that Cathal Sullivan has ever taught her – that she's the axis of planet earth, can do what she likes and rely on her looks to charm everyone cross-eyed. She has her parents twisted round her little finger, but' – Keeley's smile widened – 'the beauty of this situation is that we are not her parents, and I for one am not remotely charmed.'

In her room, Mel lay on her bed, sobbing loudly. At first she thought they would hear her, or worry when she did not return, and come looking for her. They would apologise, sympathise, tell her they were sorry and lead her back out for a soothing glass of wine.

But nobody came. After half an hour she sat up, hiccuped, and dried her eyes on the sheet, satisfied to see her mascara streaking it. Mother was always complaining that mascara was impossible to wash out, stained everything permanently. Good.

She wanted her mother, at this moment. Wanted her, and was going to phone her – even better, phone Daddy. Daddy would have a word with Keeley, several words possibly, and sort her out after she told him how horribly she was being treated.

Sniffing, she reached for the phone. The phone that was beside her bed at home, and must surely be here too . . . but, groping, her hand fell on nothing but a low small table with a vase of tiny flowers on it.

Damn and blast. Where was it? Getting up, she scoured the room, looking in corners, behind the bathroom door, among the books and towels, clothes and stuff she hadn't put away yet – but there was no phone.

None. Definitely. Suddenly Mel felt like Robinson Crusoe

marooned on his island, stranded, shrieking aloud into the silence. Daddy, she thought frantically, help! Get me out of here, I hate it!

But Daddy was a thousand miles away. And August, suddenly, looked like being a very wicked month.

Chapter Twelve

Two weeks later, Keeley stood leaning against the frame of the kitchen's open door, cooling her bare feet on the slate floor, cradling a glass of wine in one hand and puffing on a cigarette with the other.

'Well,' Sylvie offered, 'look on the bright side.'

Keely sucked the cigarette down to its dregs and stubbed it out, looking daggers at her sister-in-law. The same age as herself, Sylvie sometimes seemed older these days, because she was the mother of two children and had gained some weight now that she no longer cycled up mountains.

'What bright side?'

'She'll be going home in a fortnight.'

'A fortnight! Jesus Christ almighty, I'll be in the asylum by then!'

Sylvie grinned. Normally Keeley drank very little, and hardly smoked at all, but since Mel's arrival she was almost as bad as the girl herself, sneaking sips and puffs at every chance she got. The atmosphere had a warlike tension about it, as if the entire house might explode at any minute. Even the dogs' hair seemed to be standing on end, and at this moment Keeley looked more like a hedgehog than a hairdresser.

'Well, you've done your best. After all you're not her mother, you're only—'

'I know, I know. That's what she keeps saying. Only her god-mother. But Sylvie, you were around when Mary got pregnant, you remember how involved I was . . . at the time the child felt like a joint project, and somehow I've felt that way ever since.'

'Maybe that's just because you haven't any kids of your own. Vincent says—'

'I know what he says – that poor Mel is sweet and misunder-stood, I'm visiting the sins of the fathers and being too hard on her. But he's not the one who took her shopping, to see the salons or out sailing with Félix . . .'

'What did she do?'

'What didn't she do! She spent more money in one day than my juniors earn in a week, on all this lycra and spandex gear that makes her look like a hooker – then at the salons she had the nerve to filch a whole range of hair products when my back was turned – when we went sailing she threw up all over Félix—'

Sylvie hooted. 'Oh, my God! Over Félix!'

Reluctantly, Keeley grinned. 'Yes. It's a great pity your brother wasn't able to be there that day, because it was not a pretty sight. I know her mother is a bad sailor, but I think this up-chuck had more to do with wine than water. She'd sweet-talked Vincent into letting her have two glasses with her lunch before we left – two glasses, Sylvie, at fourteen, at noon! Vincent is hypnotised by her, thinks she's wonderful – but I'm the one left to mop up the mess.'

Sylvie sighed, and smiled. 'That's what happens when you have kids, be they your own or someone else's. The guys do all the fun stuff and the women do all the work. Thank God my own are getting to the stage where I can think about going back to hairdressing . . . will you have a vacancy for a brilliant colourist, do you think, in about a year?'

Keeley considered, fanning herself with a newspaper as she gazed out over the garden. It was very hot, even the heat-hardy mulberry bushes looked parched, the walls and terrace were baking to the touch, the air dry and stifling.

'Well – I guess we will, for the boss's sister! But Sylvie, colouring techniques have changed a lot – don't take this the wrong way, but I think maybe you should do a refresher course first, at the hairdressing school.'

Sylvie nodded. 'OK. I suppose it is twelve years since I worked . . . but I'll be glad to get back to it. Maybe this time next year I'll be the one working and you'll be the one at home with junior!'

Keeley spun round. 'What?'

'Well, Vincent says you're thinking of starting a family—'

Abruptly, Keeley threw her unfinished wine down the sink and sat down at the table, chafing at its oak surface with her hand.

'Does he?'

'Yes – sorry, I didn't realise it was a sensitive subject.'

Keeley frowned, and then sighed.

'It's not sensitive. It's just not decided. He's much keener than I am . . . of course I will do it eventually, since he wants me to, but the time isn't right yet – I'm up to my eyes in work, Sylvie, even these few weeks off with Mel are going to have to be made up somehow, we're doing all the styling for a big fashion show in Nice next month and the salon in Alès is opening in October—'

'And the biological clock is ticking, Keeley. Don't leave it too late, if you really do intend to get pregnant. It took me nearly a year to conceive Laure after I came off the pill.'

'That's what your mother says. That it took her three years to conceive Vincent and three more to get you! But I'm from Pearse Gardens, Sylvie – everyone there always got pregnant like a shot.'

Sylvie laughed. On the rare occasions that Keeley mentioned the place where she grew up, she had a way of making it sound like the repository of all evil.

'If you say so. It's none of my business really—'

She interrupted herself, and both women looked up as Mel sauntered into the room. Wearing a mauve bikini top and a sarong skirt, lipstick and some coconut-scented sunblock, she strolled to the fridge.

'Hi. Just thought I'd get a Coke. Where's Vincent?'

'He's gone to the office to do some work.'

'Oh. But isn't he on holidays?'

Keeley replied that he was, 'as far as any self-employed person ever can be.'

'But my Dad's self-employed, and he's still on his holidays, down in Cork.'

'While your mother runs the pub.'

'Oh, no, Bill is running it, she just cooks.'

Keeley knew that this was so; as soon as she heard about Cathal's absence she had taken advantage of it to ring Mary every day for luxuriously long conversations, well out of Mel's earshot. Mary was indeed cooking as usual during the day; at night she was down on her hands and knees with a screwdriver, a nail file or a meat skewer, trying to unlock Cathal's room and search it for clues, for evidence. So far, nothing had worked, and Keeley grinned to herself as she thought of what she had suggested next – that Mary lock herself out of the house, break into it and pretend it had been burgled. Smash open Cathal's door and every lock beyond it, go through everything and then call the police sobbing hysterically. Mary was nervous and unconvinced that the ploy would succeed, but she'd urged her to simply go ahead and do it, quick, before Cathal came back. Time was running out. All Mary needed was a pair of gloves and a cool head.

And what, she wondered wryly, would Miss Mel have to say about all that? Thus far, Mel did not even seem to think it odd that Cathal had gone off without Mary; she called him in Cork whenever she was let use the phone and chatted brightly with hardly any reference to her mother. On the other hand, when she called Mary she mentioned Cathal in every second breath. There were times when Keeley longed to rip one of the copper frying pans off the kitchen beams and whack her senseless with it.

Sensing some kind of Mexican stand-off, Sylvie intervened peaceably.

'How are you enjoying Provence, Mel – sorry, Imelda?'

Mel swigged from the Coke can and blew a wisp of hair up off her forehead, pushing out her lower lip into a kind of pout.

'It's OK – I like the food anyway, and the shops. And the pool. But Keeley won't let me go out anywhere by myself.'

'Well, you are only fourteen, you don't know the area or speak the language . . . but if you'd like to go out with Laure, I'm sure Keeley would lend you a bike and you could go cycling with her and her friends.'

Mel grimaced. Sylvie's daughter was far too young for her.

'Thanks, but I'm not really into cycling. I tried it once already, Keeley and Vincent took me to some marsh place to see those flamingo birds . . . God, my butt felt like a brick afterwards.'

Sylvie bit back what she thought, which was that Mel's well-padded posterior would benefit from a couple of hundred-kilometre cycles, and tried again.

'So what would you like to do?'

Mel glanced at Keeley. 'I'd like to go to a disco, if I was let – and I tell you what I'd really like. A spin in the BMW.'

Keeley gaped at her. She'd taken Mel for lots of spins in it, down to the coast, up as far as Avignon, to cafés and markets and numerous quaint villages.

'But you have been in it. We went to the perfume shops in Grasse and to—'

'I don't mean that. I mean, I'd like to drive it.'

Both women stared at her, astonished. 'But you're only fourteen! You can't drive!'

Mel tossed back the last of her Coke and shrugged casually. 'Sure I can. My father taught me during the Easter holidays. He took me to Dollymount beach and gave me lessons in his Audi.'

Keeley burst out laughing. 'Mel, I don't care if he gave you flying lessons in his Spitfire! You're not even old enough to hold a provisional licence and there is absolutely no way you are even going to sit behind the wheel of my car or Vincent's or any other.'

Mel shrugged again, glancing at Sylvie as if to say 'I told you so.'

'Oh, well. Sylvie asked me what I'd like to do and that *is* what I'd like to do. I don't mean on an autoroute or anything, I just mean around here on the little country roads. God knows they're quiet enough.'

'Mel, forget it.'

'Oh, come on, Keeley, please! You'd be with me, I wouldn't go fast, we could just mosey into Aix for lunch or something, that's only ten kilometres . . .'

The whole arsenal of charm was brought out: the wheedling voice, the big blue eyes, the angelic smile. Infuriated, Keeley thought of Mary, unable to drive to this day, at more than twice her daughter's age.

'No. As in no way. End of conversation.'

Braced for argument or sulks, she was relieved to see Mel simply flick her ponytail, untie her sarong and head out to the terrace. 'Oh, all right. It was only a suggestion. I'm going for a swim now, if that's OK with you?'

Keeley didn't bother to answer, but turned grinning to Sylvie, who was preparing to leave.

'Delightful, isn't she?'

'Oh – I presume she was only joking. You shouldn't rise to the bait, Keeley. Kids of that age love to annoy adults.'

'I suppose you're right. I'm just not used to having one around. I guess I'm the L-driver, in that department.'

Wrapping a towel around the brick she held in her right hand, Mary took a deep breath and whispered to herself in the dark of the back garden, hedged and screened by trees from its neighbours.

'Ceviche. Bouillabaisse. Brandade. Confit. Piperade. A la poivrade.'

Each was a word learned from Luc, a culinary term she had not been required or permitted to utter for years, and she savoured it on her tongue, rolled it round her mouth as she gazed at the window and gathered courage.

But her heart was hammering, her knees quivered like jelly. Gripping the brick, she muttered again, a second mantra that brought her blood to the boil.

'Guilbaud's. Dobbin's. L'Ecrivain. Les Frères Jacques.'

They were the names of restaurants, Dublin's temples of gastronomy which, she heard, were weaving magic spells with food these days. Time after time she had implored Cathal to take her to even one of them, give her the money to even eat by herself, to see what was happening to Dublin cuisine these days. The longing to see, to taste, to know was like a physical pain. But he had laughed at her.

'Why would you want to go to those places, can't you rustle up a steak here at home any time! Fancy names and fancy prices, that's all they are.'

'Please, Cathal, just once – for Christmas, for my birthday, for our wedding anniversary? We could bring Imelda with us . . .'

'Give over, and get on with your work.'

Crash! The brick flew through the kitchen window, and with an exultant rush of adrenalin she reached her towelled hand into the hole it had made, stretched her fingers down and raised the hasp inside. It was something of a struggle to climb up on the windowsill, then, and shimmy through the narrow frame, but at the second attempt she managed it, and slid panting into her own kitchen.

Crouching instinctively, as if she really was a burglar, she groped for the mallet she had borrowed from Joe and left ready on the table. It was a remarkably heavy mallet with a steel head, and she gripped it with a surge of joy, the sudden unleashing of a fury she had subdued for years, as she raced up the stairs.

Wham! Bam, wham, bam! Swinging it at the lock on Cathal's door, she blessed the joys of detached houses as it splintered the wood, began to loosen the moorings of the lock. It was noisy, but nobody would hear, and she was conscious of physical pleasure as she hit the door again and again, as violently as if it was Cathal himself. When it finally yielded she stood astonished by her own strength, savouring the wreckage and debris as she peered around the room she had not entered for longer than she could remember.

His bed was in the centre of the room, and as her eyes adjusted she made out the shape of a chest of drawers in one corner, a large wardrobe in the other – mahogany, if she recalled it correctly. Good, she thought; let's start with that.

Three blows of the mallet were enough to make it fly open, little chips of wood springing out in all directions, the lock dangling like a broken limb. Dropping the mallet, she reached in, touched a row of suits and shirts with the plastic gloves usually reserved for filleting meat. If only she could see better, dared to turn on the light – and then it dawned on her that she could, if she pulled the curtains, nobody would think it odd to see a light on in her house, should anyone be awake at four in the morning. Crossing the room she flicked it on, and immediately pulled the heavy drapes.

Now. Let's see. Go through every single pocket, Keeley had said. Every jacket, trousers, shirt, suitcase, holdall, shaving kit – everything. Yanking them all off their racks, she flung them on the bed and got to work, the blood flowing in her veins like lava. Christ, what if he came back, walked in, caught her? A vision of him sneaking stealthily up the stairs urged her to start searching at speed, plunging her sheathed hands into every crevice, tearing out random dockets, receipts, crumpled tissues, business cards, scribbled envelopes . . . frantically she forced herself to read each one, take it in, but nothing made any impact on her consciousness, seemed incriminating or connected with anything.

Sweat poured down her face and neck as she worked her way through it all, paused frustrated, and then turned her attention to the chest of drawers. It had five drawers, each one locked separately, but after a battle she hammered her way into the first one and pulled it out, which gave her easier access to the one below, and the next one in turn. Socks, underwear, boxed handkerchiefs from distant Christmases, a nail kit, a shaving adaptor, a writing set in a leather case . . . a whole drawer full of neatly-rolled ties, another filled with gloves, scarves, new shoelaces, tiepins and cufflinks . . . whatever she might eventually be able to accuse Cathal of, it wouldn't be untidiness. The drawers were arranged with army precision, but they yielded nothing.

Damn, damn, damn! Why had the bastard locked them,

then? Was he paranoid, did he know she'd be driven to this some day, was he even managing to thwart and frustrate her all the way from Cork? Gasping with mixed terror and vigour, she pushed and kicked her way through the mess to the bed. There was no other furniture in the room – so it must be the bed, it had to be.

Hauling off the duvet and sheets she set to work, shunting the heavy mattress off its base, heaving that across the floor until she could see the rectangle of lighter-coloured, unworn carpet underneath – and still there was nothing.

Jesus! What next? Don't forget the top of the wardrobe, Keeley had reminded her, and underneath it; the curtain lining, the pelmet, you'll need scissors. In her agitation she had forgotten that, but she pulled a pair from the nail kit and slashed the curtain hems, shook the fabric until she was sure it was empty. The pillows, the mattress – all slashed as well, then she stood on a chair and ran her hand along the wardrobe top, finding nothing, only dust.

Her heart and her hopes began to sink as she reached further back, almost falling off the chair and bringing the wardrobe down on top of her. If Cathal had anything to hide – and she was sure he had – he had hidden it very well indeed, obliterated every trace of evidence. Taking a deep breath, she paused to think, marshal her mind into the cool order Keeley had insisted was vital. Don't panic, Keeley had said, don't get rushed or flustered . . . but what if Cathal was on his way home even now, driving through the night, swinging his Audi round the last corner, into the drive?

As she thought of it, her nerve snapped. She couldn't go on. He would catch her, he would kill her. It was maddening, heartbreaking, but she had to get out of this room – now, immediately, before his hand wrapped itself round her wrist . . . jumping down off the chair, she ran across the room, and tripped on the rucked carpet under the bed.

Falling headlong, she grabbed at the base of the bed, and it moved with her until one wheel caught tighter in the carpet, stopping it just before she was crushed against the wall. Gasping, soaked in sweat, she heaved herself upright and lunged for the door, her hand automatically groping to switch off the light.

But what burglar would switch off a light? Should she leave it on? Frantically she tried to decide, her gaze sweeping through the chaos like the beam of a lighthouse until it came to rest, suddenly, on the pale brown corner of something on the floor.

An envelope. A big manila envelope, sticking out from under the rucked carpet. Like a coiled spring she leaped on it, yanked it out in a cloud of dust. But she couldn't open it. Not here. Grasping it to her, she ran out, slammed the door and raced for the sanctuary of her own room.

The sight that greeted her in the mirror made her yelp, and then laugh hysterically. Her knotted hair was damp and wild, her face was filthy, the hem of her sweater was unravelling where she had caught it in something. But all she could think of was the envelope. Collapsing onto her bed, she held it in hands that were trembling so violently she couldn't open it, frozen in a mixture of terror and elation.

Yes, she thought, *yes*! I've done it, I've got something! Got something on him, at last . . . whatever is in here is going to set me free, I know it is, why else would he hide it – why can't I stop shaking? I've got to stop, and find out what it is.

One thing Keeley had to say for Mel, she thought, was that the girl had an excellent appetite. No matter what was put in front of her she ate it, never turned up her nose at things she didn't recognise, never mentioned her weight or her figure, never compared Keeley's cooking to her mother's. Up early this morning, because Vincent had challenged her to a game of tennis and was already outside hitting balls, she was wolfing her way through a large brioche, a jar of locally-made peach jam, a couple of *petits suisses* and a bowl of hot chocolate. Keeley grinned.

'The country air seems to agree with you, Mel.'

Her mouth full, Mel didn't answer, but pushed back her chair and headed for the door.

'Hey. What about the dishes?'

Mel waved dismissively. 'Keeley, you've got a dishwasher for God's sake, just bung them in!'

'No. *You* bung them in. They're your dishes.'

Muttering what sounded like a very Mickser Sweeney expression, Mel whirled round, stamped to the table, gathered up the crockery and heaved it anyhow into the dishwasher.

'There. All done.'

Her expression was defiant, and Keeley sighed; after two

weeks she felt she still wasn't connecting properly with Mel, that everything she said slid off the girl's shiny Teflon surface. As yet no conversation had lasted longer than three minutes, nothing registered or was remembered next time. Thank God she wasn't her mother!

But, later today, she was going to talk to her about her mother. Show Mel old photos, copies of the ones Mary had sent home to Leesha all those years before, of the tiny flat where they had started out. Tell her about Mary's training with Luc, her talent, her ambitions . . . anything and everything that might arouse interest, forge some kind of bond between all three of them, force Mel to acknowledge Mary as a person, an individual with interests, a life of her own. Not that Mary had a life of her own any more, but she had had one once, and might have again, when, if . . . if she had done what she was told to do, had promised to do, and dug some dirt on Cathal.

Had she? Left alone, Keeley eyed the phone, and thought of ringing her. At that exact moment, it rang.

Keeley was so absolutely sure it was Mary that she ran to it and picked it up without even bothering to ask. Normally she was the one who did all the calling, but she knew even as she spoke: today, Mary was calling her.

'You've done it! Mary, you've done it, haven't you? You've got something?'

'Yes! I have, Keeley, I have!'

'Wait.'

Putting down the phone, Keeley went to the door and kicked it shut; even though Mel was out on the tennis court, she did not want one word of this conversation to reach her ears.

'OK. Mel's out of range. Now tell me, quick!'

'I – I found an envelope. A big one, under the carpet in his room. It – it's – it's full of—'

Mary's voice broke off, and she nodded impatiently but sympathetically; no doubt it was all very traumatic, it would do Mary good to cry.

But then she realised that Mary was laughing.

'Mary, what *is* it? What did you *find*?'

'I found – money! Piles of it, Keeley, over twenty thousand pounds, in cash!'

'Money? But – is that all?'

'No, it's not all, but – Keeley, you don't understand! I've never even had twenty pounds to call my own, and now I've got twenty thousand! He'll think the burglar stole it, but I've got it – Keel, you've got to think of somewhere I can hide it, I have to ring the police and they might search the place, I don't want them to find it—'

'OK, we'll think of somewhere – but what else did you find?'

Again, to her amazement, Mary laughed, quite hysterically Keeley thought.

'Photographs. Four photographs. Full colour enlargements.'

'Of *what*?'

'One of a judge. I recognised him. He was in the papers a few years ago, to do with a property development, some row over planning permission for a cinema or bowling alley or swimming pool, something like that.'

'But what's that got to do – oh!'

'Oh, yes! And then another photo, of a politician. Then one of the two of them together, at a party. And then one of Cathal himself, standing between them . . . Keeley, they're all wearing women's clothes! Every one of them, they – they're transvestites!'

Mary sounded almost incoherent with laughter, but Keeley froze.

'Trans*vestites*? Your husband is a transvestite?'

'Yes! He's wearing a green dress and make-up and a lovely pair of high-heels, the judge is wearing a red blouse and black skirt, the politician has a *hat* on him . . .'

Again Mary was overcome with laughter, but Keeley was stunned.

'Mary, this is terrible! How can you laugh, your own husband, I mean he is your husband after all – if it was Vincent, I – I'd throw up, I'd die!'

With an effort, Mary calmed herself.

'If this had happened years ago, in the beginning, I would have died. Cried and nearly died, from the shock of it, the horror . . . wondered was it my fault, what was wrong with him, where could he – we – get some kind of help. But now – Keeley, don't you see?'

'No, I don't see. You're married to a weirdo, a real one after all, what on earth are you going to—'

'I'm going to blackmail him, as he is obviously blackmailing these guys! These pictures were taken at a party, they were all drunk by the looks of them, it must have been at a private house or club – and now he's got them in his pocket! They steer the planning applications through the councils and the courts, permission is granted to Cathal's friends and his father's friends, the friends pay up and start building . . . Keeley, I even met the politician once, in Cathal's father's house! It must have been before the photos were taken and the blackmail started – he was very pally with Daddy Donal, must have trusted Cathal enough to pose for these photos when he had drink in him. I don't know whether Donal knows his son is a transvestite, but I doubt it – he's the kind who'd go berserk if he did. Cathal Sullivan will never be able to say boo to me again.'

'But won't he think the burglar swiped the photos, along with the money?'

'No, because I'm going to tell him I found one, that it was lying on the floor when I came out of my room – I was shut in my room, you see, terrified, while the house was being burgled.'

Suddenly, it was Keeley's turn to laugh. It was fully fifteen years, she thought, since she had last heard Mary sound so firm, so confident, so on top of a situation.

'So – Cathal is a transvestite, a blackmailer, a criminal, and you're married to him!'

'Yes. I am, legally. But you know well that it's never been a marriage, Keeley. I feel nothing for him now, not even looking at these pictures here in my hand – no pity, no sympathy, no concern whatsoever. A real wife would. She'd be upset and aghast and wondering how to help, how to save the marriage, protect the child . . . all I feel is high as a kite, delighted! I can't tell you how glad I am you made me do it. In fact I'd leave him, leave him tomorrow, only twenty thousand isn't enough to live on for very long, and Mel is still only fourteen.'

Mel. Keeley had forgotten about her.

'So what are you going to do?'

'I'm going to stash the money away safely somewhere until Mel is eighteen, in an account earning interest, and then when she's old enough I'm going to leave. I'm going to go back to France and start cooking. Cooking properly this time, cooking up a storm.'

'Oh, great! Luc will be thrilled – and so will I, if you come back here.'

'Yes. I want to go back to Provence. I will go. But first we have to think of where to hide the money – if he knew I had it, he might find some way to get it back . . . I don't want him using Mel as a battering ram.'

'He might use her to make you give him the photo.'

'I'd say he'll be too busy wondering what use the alleged burglar is going to make of the other three. Jesus, he'll sweat gallons, night and day, for years! I'll be the least of his worries. But if he does get heavy, I'll say I made a copy, on the photocopier in his office – several copies, in fact. So he might as well just start being Mr Nice Guy right away – I tell you, Keel, my life is about to change radically from the moment he gets back here.'

'He's still in Cork?'

'Yes. I have to ring the police soon and then ring him – it's only six o'clock over here, but I can't delay much longer – Keel, quick! Where is a good place to hide twenty thousand pounds?'

'Jesus – let's think! Could you put it in your mother's house somewhere?'

'Ye-es . . . in Sean's room maybe, since he's been living with his girlfriend Ruth nobody ever goes into it. I could put it under the carpet the same way Cathal put it under his. But I'd be worried that my mother—'

'I know! Take it there today. After the police have gone it'll look normal to want to see your mother, and then the next time Tony is sending a painting to Alain, put it in with it! I'll talk to Alain, and when the canvas arrives I'll take it out, open a bank account for you over here!'

'Brilliant! That's exactly what I'll do. In fact I'd come with it, if I didn't have Mel to think of – how is she, Keel?'

'She's marginally improved, but really Mary, you and Cathal have her ruined – she even wanted to drive my car.'

'What? God almighty, Keeley, don't let her! Cathal gave her a few lessons, but she's far too young, she—'

'Mary, you can rest assured I won't let her. But never mind her for now, you'll have her back in two more weeks, sadder and wiser I hope. And nicer to her mother.'

'She ignores me because Cathal ignores me. But he won't be ignoring me any more, Keeley.'

'No. Not with your photo of him in a green dress, he won't. Jesus, I can't get over this, I can't believe it!'

Mary giggled. 'I'll send you the other photos with the money, so you can keep them safe for me and see for yourself –

Keeley, you don't think customs will go through the package, do you?'

'They never have yet. Tony simply gets Ma to label them as commercial samples. Alain said that was the handiest thing and he's done it ever since. I'll write to Tony today and tell him to expect a visit from you, then next week you can go to him and work things out between you.'

'It'll look a bit odd, me going to see your brother.'

'Why? Just tell my ma you want to see his work or something, she'll probably be pleased, and Christy won't give a damn.'

'OK. Look, I'd better go now, but I'll call you again tomorrow.'

'Right. And – hey, Mary! Well done! I wasn't sure you'd have the guts to do it, but you did, there's hope for you after all.'

She could hear the smile in her friend's voice. 'Thanks, Keel. Thanks for making me do it. I was petrified, but it was worth it.'

They hung up, and Keeley remained in her kitchen, listening to the distant *thwack* of tennis racquets outside, dissecting and absorbing Mary's unexpected extraordinary news. A transvestite! The marriage must be very far gone, way beyond all help, that Mary not only wasn't distraught but actually found it funny. Very funny . . . suddenly Keeley found herself laughing too, laughing so hard that Cleo and Zazie shuffled up to her, snuffling at her legs, wondering what was going on.

In her kitchen, a thousand miles away, Mary picked up the phone again immediately and dialled her local police station.

'H-hello? This is Mrs Sullivan in Forest Crescent. I want to report a burglary.'

'Just a moment, I'll put you on to the duty sergeant.'

She hoped her voice sounded tearful and trembly enough, but as soon as the duty sergeant came on the line she knew she was going to get away with it, knew everything would be all right.

'Mary? What's all this about a burglary? This is Barry O'Neill here . . . is it your own house, are you all right?'

Barry O'Neill. Dad's friend who, fifteen years ago, had helped Kevin to sort out Christy Butler. She smiled down the phone.

'Yes, Barry, I am. It's dreadful, the house is destroyed, but I'm all right.'

Cathal hit the roof. Not only to find that his house had been burgled, but to find the police taking a very lackadaisical attitude to it, all but yawning as they brushed surfaces for fingerprints with a desultory air. Of course burglary was so common in Dublin now that it was impossible to interest them, get them excited about anything less than a murder – in fact even that was almost a daily event. But this was *his* house, dammit, *his* property! If they weren't going to treat this affront, this outrage with the seriousness it deserved, he was bloody well going to bring pressure to bear. He knew a judge, a certain influential judge, who would get on their case, put a rocket under them. He wasn't going to take this lying down . . . and what the hell was the matter with Mary, standing there cool as a breeze only hours after she had been trapped in her bedroom, she said, while some gruesome stranger ransacked their home? If her door hadn't been locked, the police commented, she might have been murdered . . . yet she simply gazed indifferently at him when he arrived after his three-hour dash from Cork, and said yes, you never knew what burglars would do these days.

'Why wasn't the bloody alarm on?' he snapped at her. 'Didn't I tell you to put it on every night?'

'I forgot,' she said, and went to make the police a pot of tea.

Speechless with rage, he went to see the extent of the damage for himself, forcing himself not to race straight up to his room where, he prayed, his worst fears would not be confirmed. First he went into the living room, where all his mother's magnificent china lay in smithereens, the Aynsley vases, the Waterford, the Wedgwood, the mahogany sideboard she had given them for their first wedding anniversary . . . the burglar must have had demonic strength to do all this, with a mallet the police said; they'd found it lying out in the garden.

But the bedroom – the moment he saw it he knew he was gone, the envelope was gone. Virtually the whole room was gone, only the walls left standing, the destruction unbelievable. Clutching at the door frame for support, he steadied himself, forced himself to think clearly, and came back down to the kitchen.

'I want a forensic team in here,' he shouted at the sergeant, who had had the temerity to accept a cup of tea in the midst of it all. 'I want your forensics in here right now!'

One of the police officers paused, held his brush aloft. 'Sir,' he said, 'we *are* the forensic team.'

'Hair!' Cathal roared. 'Hair, sweat, saliva, skin, I want it all! Not just fingerprints!'

Sergeant O'Neill looked up. 'Be bloody lucky to even get fingerprints,' he observed. 'They usually wear gloves you know. Balaclavas. Shoes you can buy ten-a-penny in Dunne's. Jeans, donkey jackets . . . know their stuff, these lads do. Nothing unusual, nothing identifiable, nothing traceable. But don't worry, sir. We'll do what we can.'

'You'd better! And then some! I want my—'

He broke off, and Barry O'Neill gazed at him again. 'You want your what, sir?'

'I – I want – my rights!' he spluttered, subsiding as he felt himself under scrutiny. Belatedly, he went to Mary and put his arm around her.

'My wife has had a terrible shock! What kind of country is it when women aren't even safe in their own homes? It's a wonder she – Mary, tell the sergeant now, don't be afraid – he didn't go near you, did he? He didn't get into your room?'

Evenly, Mary looked at him. 'No, Cathal. I woke up when I heard the crash downstairs, and then all the noise. I got up and locked my door immediately, and stayed in my room until he was gone. It must have been an hour at least – I've already given Sergeant O'Neill all the details.'

Again, the sergeant seemed to inspect him, as if he were the one under suspicion.

'And may I ask, sir, how long had you been away for? Your wife says you were in Cork playing golf – in a hotel, were you?'

'Yes – I – most of the time – I stayed with friends one or two nights—'

'I see.' For a moment it looked as if Sergeant O'Neill was going to pursue this, but then he lifted his cup and idly sipped his tea.

'Ah, yes. I know Cork well, myself. Lot of contacts down there. Nice place. Very nice. Small, though, isn't it? Everybody knows everybody.'

Abruptly, Cathal pulled Mary closer to him. 'Sergeant, if you don't mind, my wife needs me, I'm just going to take her through to the living room – no, the dining room, it doesn't seem to be quite so badly damaged.'

'Of course, sir.' Calmly, Barry drained his cup and left him to it. In the dining room, Cathal steered Mary to a chair and seated her almost forcibly in it.

'Mary. The police haven't asked you – yet – but I want to

know. Why didn't this – this man break into your room? He broke into mine, into everywhere else, yet there isn't a scratch on your door.'

She was aware of his look as she cursed silently, cursed herself for not thinking to give her own door a few whacks of the mallet.

'I have no idea, Cathal. I didn't get a chance to ask him.'

'Well, I think it's very odd.'

'Do you?'

'Yes. I do.'

'Perhaps he didn't have time. It was getting light. Maybe he heard the milkman coming or something.'

'H'm. Maybe.'

They eyed each other. And then Mary reached into her pocket.

'He must have been in a hurry. He dropped this.'

Without a blink, she handed the photograph to him. The photograph of himself, in a green silk dress, lipstick and high-heeled shoes. He whitened, and continued to whiten until his face was all but transparent, she could see the bones and veins under the skin. For what felt like eternity, there was silence between them.

And then he spoke. Spoke in a furious whisper, fighting to camouflage the panic she could see rising in him like a geyser.

'It was a party! A fancy dress party – just a lark, on one of our golf jaunts—'

'I'm sure it was. That's what I said to Sergeant O'Neill when I showed it to him.'

'Y-you – showed – this – to Sergeant O'Neill?'

'Yes, of course I did. It's a clue, isn't it? There might be fingerprints on it. You said you wanted fingerprints—'

As if it were in flames, he dropped it on the table. 'Now it's got everyone's on it! Yours and mine and probably the bloody sergeant's! Why didn't he put it in a plastic bag?'

'I don't know. Why don't you ask him?'

Breathing like an express train, he began to pace the room. Up and down, round the table several times, until abruptly he stopped beside her.

'Has Imelda phoned? Have you spoken to her about this?'

'No. Not yet. I thought I'd wait to see whether you thought it would be a good idea or not. She might find it all a bit frightening.'

He got the message. She saw that he did, and pushed it home.

'Cathal, after the police leave, I think you and I need to have a chat. Quite a long chat, about Imelda, and this photograph and – and other things.'

'What other things?' His face was paper white, his voice splintering like an adolescent boy's.

'About money, for a start.'

'What about it?'

She had to fight back laughter as she thought of the twenty thousand pounds, and saw that he was thinking of it too. Twenty thousand pounds nestling in her handbag, ready to be taken round to Leesha's house, and not a thing he could do about it even if he knew. Because the police would want to know where so much cash had come from, wouldn't they? Why wasn't it safe in the bank, and what was the story with the revenue commissioners? Twenty thousand pounds, that's a lot of money, sir, to keep in notes under your bedroom carpet.

'Cathal, you left me with thirty pounds a week while you were away. It wasn't enough. Not nearly enough.'

'But I pay all the bills! All you needed was a few quid for sundries, thirty pounds was plenty—'

'No. It wasn't. What's more, I didn't like having to ask Bill for it. From now on I want three hundred a week, for myself, in cash, out of which I will buy groceries, and clothes for Imelda. What I do with the rest of it will be entirely my own business. I want it ready for me at the pub every Friday when I finish work.'

'But you can't need three hundred pounds a week!'

'I didn't say I needed it, Cathal. You're not listening. I said I wanted it.'

And you, she thought, can well afford it. That fucking pub is a goldmine. I've slaved in it day in and day out for fifteen years, I know how much you take in – and how much you declare to the taxman too, give or take a few bob. And now, it is my turn to take a few bob.

Suddenly, he leaned down, snatched up the photograph and tore it into pieces.

'Now! If you think you can blackmail me, Miss Mary, you can think again.'

She didn't even raise her voice. 'Are you sure that's the only photograph, Cathal?'

'W – what?"

'I said, are you sure that's the only one?'

She was glad, then, that the police were in the next room. His face darkened, turned so vicious it was almost murderous.

'Have you any others?'

She sat back and thought about it. 'I might have. I might have had time to make a copy of that one on your photocopier, or I might have found some others. Were there others, Cathal?'

He was nailed, caught between the awful thought that she had them, and the even worse thought that some criminal had them. Some criminal who, even if he didn't recognise Cathal Sullivan, would certainly recognise the judge and the very public politician. Venomously, he spat his next words at her.

'All right. Hand them over and you can have your three hundred a week.'

'I don't know what you mean. But I'm glad you understand what I mean. Three hundred pounds every Friday. Oh, and driving lessons, and I'd like to visit Keeley in France, and then I'll be needing a car of my own. Meanwhile, you might have a little chat with Imelda about her manners. I find her quite disrespectful to me at times.'

He was silent.

'And I think it's time we changed the menu at The Lantern. I'll eat at some proper restaurants over the next few weeks, maybe take my Mam and Dad with me or my brothers . . . I hear Dobbins and Les Frères Jacques are excellent. I could learn a lot from them, maybe adapt some recipes for the pub – unless you think it's time to open Fursey's as a restaurant?'

'Damn you! You know Fursey's belongs to my parents, it's not for me to—'

'No. It never was, Cathal, was it? It was just a carrot, to trick me into marrying you. Well, I guess I deserved all I got – or didn't get. I was a fool.'

The door opened, and they were interrupted by a sudden vision of Sergeant O'Neill's red hair and ruddy, sociable-looking face.

'Sorry to disturb you, but we've finished our investigations . . . except for just one thing, sir. When you went upstairs and checked the other rooms, did you find anything missing?'

There was a long silence as the two men looked at each other, and Mary watched Cathal's spine stiffen, his fists clench as he drew a deep breath and forced himself to reply.

'No, sergeant. No, there wasn't, as far as I could see.'

Cheerfully, Barry grinned. 'That's grand so. Since nothing of value seems to have been taken . . . well, we'll be on the lookout for whoever broke in, of course, but at least there was no serious theft. Very wise of you not to keep any money or valuables in the house. We'll be off now, and let you know if we have any further news.'

Calmly, Mary thanked him and went to see him out, and Cathal's mouth tightened with fury as she left the room. There was twenty thousand quid missing, dammit! Twenty thousand green ones, that he couldn't say a word about, because . . . and what did Mary mean, they needed to talk *after* the police left? They'd already talked their heads off, or at least she had, surely there couldn't be more to come?

But when she returned, he saw that there was. Plenty more. It seemed that the conversation was only starting.

Ten days later, Keeley and Vincent sat stretched on adjoining sun loungers out on the terrace, draping sweaters over their shoulders against the cooling twilight as the sky deepened from cobalt to navy and fireflies began to dart about. It was a hushed, still evening, pungent with summer scents, the pool water reflecting the rising stars, small and distant. After dinner, Mel had gone to her room, to read she said, and Vincent smiled as he finished his coffee and linked his fingers into his wife's.

'See, she's not so bad. This visit has done her good after all.'

H'mm . . . Keeley had to concede that Mel had been better this last week, beginning to show some signs of civilisation now that her veneer was being slowly worn away. Not that she particularly felt like talking about her at this moment; she felt like simply sitting in silence with Vincent, holding his hand, savouring the love and peace between them. Even now, fifteen years after first finding them, both qualities were dear to her. But Vincent liked to talk about Mel, and she couldn't deny him what he wanted; to this day she remembered how good he'd been to the distressed, pregnant, panic-stricken Mary.

Speculatively, she sat thinking about Mel, wondering what if anything lay under the shiny surface.

'Yes. I have to admit she's almost bearable now. In fact, there have been odd moments when I've nearly felt sorry for her.'

'Sorry? Why?'

'Oh, I don't know . . . because she's so young, I suppose, and

I can remember how insecure you feel at her age. I think she's inherited her mother's insecurity, too, some lack of confidence that she tries to disguise with all that tarty clobber – I think the demanding and posturing is all a bit of an act, to get attention. Of course, her father is a consummate actor.'

Vincent grimaced. He was still having difficulty digesting the appalling story that Keeley had told him, about what Mary had discovered. It was going to be no easy thing for Mary to pretend that all was normal, when Mel went home – dear God, what a dreadful situation! He simply couldn't laugh, the way Keeley could and Mary evidently could too. Surely Mary must feel very mixed emotions, even if she was choosing to air them selectively; it was a terrible thing for a wife to have to face. Terrible.

'There must be a lot of tension between them – Mary and Cathal, I mean – at the moment. It's a bad time to send Mel back to them.'

'Well, she's got to go some time. Her school re-opens next week.'

'I hope Mary can handle it all.'

Yes. Keeley hoped so too; hammering down the lid on Pandora's box was going to be some struggle for her. Mel liked to convey a worldly, grown-up impression, but she was only a child, far too young to be exposed to adult complexities never mind discover that the man she considered her father was . . . somehow her jaunty, stagey confidence had failed to wash here, in this rural Provençal retreat, and under it Keeley could detect something – what?

Something vulnerable, something lost, searching . . . unexpectedly she had shown interest in the photos Keeley had shown her, of early life with Mary in their flat in Aix. She had laughed at its tiny size, giggled over tales of failed omelettes and quiches flung in bins, but she had returned to the subject several times since, asked questions and seemed to be mulling over the unexpected revelation that her mother had, in fact, once existed as an independent human being. When she wanted to know why Mary had left France, Keeley was ready for the question.

'She went back to marry your father.'

It was close enough to the truth, and Mel seemed pleased by the romance of it. Ma must have been mad about Dad to give up her training with a great chef . . . but she couldn't have learned very much, could she, if she came back to Ireland only able to cook the simplest things?

'She was able to cook some trickier things too, only there wasn't much demand for them.'

Mel looked puzzled. The Ireland she knew was full of restaurants, every supermarket was choc-a-bloc with French, Italian, Indian, Chinese food, Thai, Mexican . . . but boy, it must have been a real drag back in the olden days, with only bacon and cabbage and spuds.

'I thought that was way back, sort of after the Famine.'

'No, it went on right up to about the time you were born, people would look at anything foreign and say yuk, I'm not eating that. Even Irish things like oysters, they wouldn't touch them with a bargepole. I was one of the worst offenders myself, when I came to France my idea of heaven was a hamburger.'

'Yeah, well, I often go to MacDonalds with my friends. But I must say I like the food over here. I wish my Ma would cook it sometimes, since you say she knows how.'

'She would, if you asked her. She'd be delighted.'

Mel said no more, but the next time Luc dropped in to visit Keeley overheard her questioning him – did you teach my Ma to cook, really?

'Yes,' Luc growled, 'for all the damned good it did either of us. She'd have been a genius, a real superchef if only she'd stuck with me instead of running home to her mother.'

'She didn't run home to Granny,' Mel contradicted him. 'She ran home to marry Daddy. She was crazy about him.'

Luc and Keeley exchanged glances, and left it at that. The rest of the story, the truth of it, was up to Mary, if she ever chose to tell it. Her thoughts running both backwards and forwards, Keeley shifted on the wooden slats of her chair, and turned to Vincent.

'It's going to be very hard for Mary, you know, when Mel grows up and she's finally free to start over. Her training is way out of date, and it wasn't even finished – in fact she'd barely started. She'll be very rusty, have to learn everything again virtually from scratch. And Luc is retired now.'

'Well, if she does come back here, we'll help her. She can stay with us and use that accursed money for a course at a good cookery school.'

'M'm. She'll be nearly forty by then . . . still, cooking isn't like athletics or ballet or playing the violin, you can go back to it at any age.'

'I suppose you can. But age does impose some limits, Keeley, on other things. On having children, for instance.'

Tightening his hand in hers, he turned to look at her questioningly, and she flinched away. Oh, no, please don't let him be going to start on that subject.

'Well, in a few years Mary can start cooking and we can start a family! She and I will both have buns in the oven.'

Keeley grinned, hoping to dismiss it lightly. But he persisted.

'Don't you think we're the right age now, Keeley? I mean, I want to be young enough to play with the kids when they come, to kick a ball and take them cycling, have fun with them.'

'Oh, Vincent – you will be able to do all that, you won't be a hundred! I'd just like to wait another four or five years, that's all.'

'I know. And I'm trying to understand. I really am. But you'll be in your late thirties then, I'll be over forty . . . it's cutting it very fine. I mean, there's no guarantee you'll get pregnant the minute you decide you want to, Keeley . . . couldn't we start thinking about it now?'

'*Now*? Right away, you mean?'

He sat up and faced her frankly, his look hopeful, loving as always, but more resolute than she had ever seen it before.

'Yes. This year, Keeley. I'd love to do it. I really would.'

'But Vincent, it's still too soon! I have so much to learn yet, so much to do—'

'You'll always have things to learn and do. But you've learned and done so much already – come on, Keeley, please. Say you'll do it, for me. If we want to have more than one or two children, we have to get started soon.'

'More than one or two? Like, how many?'

'Maybe three . . . even four? This is a big house, we have plenty of money, we'll get an au pair if you like, to share the work.'

'It – it's not that!'

'Then what is it?'

She didn't know what it was, couldn't say. Except it had something to do with her own growth, her own development, catching up on all the things she had missed out on as a child herself. She could never rid herself of the feeling that she still lagged behind, had yet to earn her place in the adult world. She was an impostor in it, a chancer who'd be caught out some day, turfed out unless she was fully equipped to fight back.

'It – it's me, Vincent! It's just me, I'm not mature enough to handle kids, I mean, look at a teenager like Mel, it's all so difficult and complicated—'

She heard every drop of the disappointment in his voice, and saw it as she looked into his hazel eyes.

'Of course it is, Keeley, for everyone! Everyone wants to be a perfect parent, but nobody ever is.'

'You can say that again,' she replied, thinking of Christy Butler.

Vincent's voice was beginning to rise, and for the first time she felt they might be heading for a row. Not a tiff, but a real row of the kind they'd never yet had. And still he fought his corner.

'If everyone waited until conditions were perfect, nobody would have any children, ever – you just have to take the plunge, Keeley!'

Take the plunge. The expression touched some nerve in her, terrified her the way she'd been terrified when he was teaching her to swim years ago – and yet, he had taught her. She hadn't drowned, sunk without trace. But this was different, a bigger and much more serious undertaking. She felt as if he was making her walk the gangplank, prodding at her, forcing her to jump into stormy shark-infested waters.

Abruptly, she felt weepy, panic-stricken, and leaped up, snatching her hand away from him. Without another word, she ran across the dark dewy lawn, round the back of the house to the other side of it, and leaned up against a cool dark wall, panting, fighting tears.

Of course he was right. Everything he said was reasonable and logical, perfectly fair, but for that very reason she felt he was closing in on her, wearing her down. Any minute now, if she hadn't left him, they would have started shouting – not that there was anything fearful about him, he was no Christy Butler, he would never hurt her or get physically aggressive. But he was angry with her, and she was angry with him . . . it was better simply to remove herself from the conflict, and wait until they had both calmed down.

For some time she stood immobile, cooling her heated cheeks on the wall, plucking at a tendril of jasmine, irresolute. Part of her wanted to run back to him, tell him she loved him, would have his children if only he'd give her just a little more time . . . if she gave him time, he would soon come looking for her, contrite and maybe even a little worried because he didn't know where she'd gone. He would take her in his arms and hug her, tell her he hadn't meant to upset her, come on, let's kiss and make up, forget the whole bloody subject for now.

But he did not come. Straining her ears, she listened for his footsteps, but heard nothing, only the gradual slowing of her own racing heart, the whirn of cicadas in the grass, the slow distant drip of some leaky tap.

Where was he? Was he as angry as all that, that he wouldn't come for her, to her? He must be, sitting brooding on that bleached old bench, thinking what a raw deal he'd got after all, what a rotten wife. A wife who worked her butt off, shared every burden of their joint business, was capable and devoted and adored him, great *craic* in the sack as he often teased, laughing as he imitated her Irish accent . . . but a wife who, when the chips were down, wouldn't do what he wanted. Wouldn't do what all the other wives did, even though she was perfectly fit and healthy and able to do it.

Oh, Vincent . . . come on, come and find me, come and talk to me. Let's not quarrel, we have so much going for us – our home, our friends, the salons, the dogs – we have each other. Félix and Lise don't have any children, but they're not fighting over it, are they? They're happy, they—

Suddenly, her train of thought squealed to a stop, slammed on the brakes with such force she gasped as she stared into the dark, made out a space under the vine-draped pergola where there should be no space. Where there should be a car, two cars, hers and Vincent's.

But there was only one, his silver-grey Citroen DS, solid and reliable like himself. Three or four hours earlier, she had parked her navy BMW beside it. But the BMW was not there now. It was gone, and in a sickening flash she knew who had taken it. It had not been stolen, nor broken into, because there was no need; she had left the keys on their usual hook in the front hall.

For a split second, her voice wouldn't work, her feet wouldn't move, but then she was sprinting frantically back through the garden, back to the pool under the pinprick stars, screaming.

'Vincent! Vincent, *quick*, she's gone, she's taken the car!'

She could see him turning, then getting up in dark silhouette as she ran, flew at him.

'Mel – my BMW – I left the keys on the hook – she's—'

Words jerked out of her at such a rate she couldn't breathe, couldn't articulate as he reached out to catch her, caught her wrist in his hand. In the shadows, his eyes were as stunned, as terrified as her own.

'Mel has – Keeley, she can't—'

'She has! Vincent, it's gone, I know she has – oh my God, in the dark, on the wrong side of the road, she'll be killed – we have to go after her, hurry—'

She made to run back to his car, haul him with her, race out immediately, but he held her back, thinking urgently.

'No. Keeley, you stay here. Phone the police, tell them to put an alert out for your car. Describe it exactly, and then stay by the phone. I'll take mine and go after her.'

In seconds he had reached his and started the engine, even before she got to the house and threw herself on the phone, shaking so violently she hit the wrong digit twice, and could barely speak when her call was answered. As she spoke she could see Vincent from the window, reversing and then turning his Citroen at speed, driving away into the night, his face set like granite.

The night was not nearly so warm in Ireland, there was no question of sitting outdoors, yet Cathal was sweating, his sleeves rolled up and his tie hanging loose as Mary went on with her relentless probing, on and on and on like a dog with a bone.

Even now, he hadn't cracked. Not on the matter of the money, which he insisted was an emergency cash fund he'd always kept at home in case The Lantern ever burned down or was burgled – just an emergency fund, which he added to from time to time. Lots of people kept money at home, what was so bloody odd about it?

Elderly people, she retorted, kept money at home. They were frightened of banks, frightened of busybody tax inspectors and civil servants and losing their pensions, their medical cards and bus passes. They kept their money in their tea caddies and wardrobes, under their mattresses, and that was why they were forever being attacked, often murdered for what turned out to be only a few miserable pounds. Nobody else kept money at home, certainly not businessmen who handled large sums of it, so would Cathal please stop stalling and admit the truth, which was that his stolen £20,000 had been dishonestly come by?

No, he shouted, he'd admit no such damn thing, because it wasn't true. The only reason he hadn't been able to tell the police that £20,000 had been taken from his room was that – well, everybody fiddled their taxes a bit, for Christ's sake, there was no big deal about it. Only the revenue commissioners might have made a big deal of it, that was all, if the police had notified them of its existence. Now, some damn thief had made away with it and, he thundered, he was going to swing for that thief when he, or she, was caught.

'She? I don't think there are many lady burglars, Cathal. I never heard of one at any rate, they all seem to be men in the newspaper reports.'

Fuming, he eyed her narrowly. He was totally sceptical of the whole story of the alleged burglar who had all but demolished half the house, found the well-hidden bundle of money and dropped an incriminating photograph which, conveniently, Mary had found and was now using against him. A stupid photo taken at a stupid party, that was all.

Yes, she agreed, a stupid photo. Ridiculous, laughable. His mother would get a great laugh out of it, and his father and his golfing cronies, and Mel of course – they'd all think it was a hoot when they saw the copy she had made. Except that they weren't going to see it, because he was going to give her £300 a week and everything else she wanted, including complete freedom to go where she liked, see and talk to whom she liked, cook what she liked and do what she bloody well liked.

On that, he was forced to grudgingly agree, even as he continued to protest his innocence. Oh, come off it, she retorted, you're wearing a goddamn dress, what kind of complete idiot do you take me for?

He didn't take her for so much of an idiot now as he had before, but neither would he budge, and so she continued to hammer away at him, determined to get at the truth. Once he told the truth, she said, they might even be able to discuss his 'problem' calmly and clearly, arrive at some means of dealing with it. There were counsellors, he could get help—

'I don't need or want any fucking help!' he screeched, and she eyed him sagely, said something about how he must be in denial. But there was no need, she wasn't angry with him, she might even be able to understand if only he would explain . . .

'I'll explain nothing,' he shouted now for at least the nineteenth time, 'because there's nothing *to* explain!'

Sighing, Mary sat down at the kitchen table where he was attempting to eat the meal she had cooked tonight, a *blanquette de veau* that seemed to be all but choking him, whether because it was 'foreign muck' or because he was he was strangled with emotion she couldn't tell.

'Cathal. Look. There's no point in going on with this, pretending nothing has happened. Something has happened, something serious, and our marriage is never going to be the same again. Not that it ever was a marriage, but it was a domestic relationship. Now, that relationship has changed, and we're both going to have to adjust. I don't want Mel upset or worried in any way, I don't want her to sense any kind of atmosphere when she gets home, and I don't think you do either.'

He didn't reply, but she knew he agreed. For some reason Mel's affection and respect, even adulation, mattered to him – because she was the only child he was ever going to have, perhaps? Or because she was the incarnation of feminine beauty, the kind of female he aspired to be? Numerous possibilities flitted through her mind, but she didn't know nearly enough about transvestism to hazard guesses at how a transvestite's mind worked. If only he would come clean, talk about it, seek advice or even let her seek it for him. Perhaps she would seek it whether he let her or not, because she had to find some parameters, some way of coping with what she now knew him to be. Had she ever loved him, she would be desperately upset, bewildered, undermined and frightened by what was going on, sad for him, fearful for their marriage – but she did not love him. Nor, in spite of everything, did she hate him. She felt beyond emotion. Her mind was working clearly but her heart, she realised, had stopped long ago.

Distracted by her thoughts, she belatedly realised that he was looking at her, hostile, defensive and yet somehow pleading, like a school bully suddenly set upon by a bigger bully.

'You – you needn't worry about Imelda. There'll be no problem when she gets home.'

What did that mean? That he would continue to be discreet, confine his bizarre activities to 'away games' as if they were soccer matches? Somehow she didn't think he had ever dressed up as a woman here in their home, there had been no hidden clothing or cosmetics . . . swallowing at the thought of what she might have found, she was very relieved she had not. The photograph was bad enough. And, mercifully, it seemed to indicate that there was some other venue where he must go to meet men of like disposition; somebody else had taken it, and she did not recognise the setting.

Or did he mean that he would treat her properly, now, when Mel was around? She had made it clear that she wanted him to, that he must do it and would do it if he knew what was good for him. Well, Mel was due home on Friday, she would soon find out.

Or perhaps he meant that he was not going to take his anger out on her daughter, Mel would not be used as a weapon or bargaining chip, he would do the decent thing and continue to treat her as if she were his own daughter. That much she would say for him, he always had treated Mel well, even too well at times; there was genuine affection between the two – and that, now, was why she was able to feel a little sorry for him. Mixed up as he was, gratuitously authoritarian, sexually confused, he was not actually evil. Nasty, yes, controlling and domineering and maybe even horribly scared of her at the back of it all, but not violent or physically cruel.

He was, she thought wearily, simply a mess. One or other, or both, of his parents, must have gone wrong somewhere – which, thinking of Carmel and Donal, was hardly surprising. Probably a shrink would say that his masculinity had got muddled at some early point, that everything was all kinked and would have to be straightened out, if he was amenable to straightening out. Or maybe he simply had this tragi-comic streak in him through some quirk of nature, it wasn't anybody's fault. Whatever it was, it wasn't the worst thing that could happen; how much more gruesome to discover that he was a rapist or murderer or had spread Aids all around him, abused small children or conned elderly ladies out of their life savings. The photo of him in the dress was disturbing, but not nearly as disturbing as the money she had found with it, because she was certain that that really was tainted, had criminal associations.

That was why she kept on about it, nagging and probing, endeavouring to find out whether it really was connected to the photos of the judge and the politician as she was almost certain it was. But she had yet to shift him an inch, after more than a week, on the matter of the money. He wasn't, she supposed, going to say or even hint at anything that could actually land him in jail, and although she was endeavouring to sound reasonable she knew he didn't trust her an inch.

Well, why would he, when she had done him out of twenty

thousand pounds and stolen four ruinous photos which, if he stepped out of line, would all make their way to the surface? He wasn't sure she had the other three, but he must be praying she had – praying, also, that her concern for her daughter would come before all else. She might dearly want to land Cathal Sullivan in trouble, but she would not want to land Mel's father in it. Nor did she; as fathers went, he was not the worst, not by a long shot, as Keeley Butler could testify.

But meanwhile, they were at an impasse. His face was bent sullenly over his plate, his expression masked and guarded, his demeanour that of a man determined to get on with his own life regardless. She was not getting through to him, he did not want her understanding or sympathy or support, which in any event were mixed with numerous other emotions. Vividly she recalled his years of scorn for her, his coldness, his vicious attack when she miscarried the child, each episode still a bloody bruise under her skin. Whatever his destiny, she neither wanted nor intended to share it with him; all she wanted was to know where she stood, the truth about the money and the pictures, and a guarantee of decent behaviour for the remainder of the years they would live together. She had more or less got the latter, but hope was fading for the former.

And then, in four or five years when she was free, when Mel was adult – what? With luck it might not be too late to resume her career, her love of food and cooking, but was that to be the only love she would ever know? At forty, would it be too late for anyone else, for some other man, some belatedly happy, fulfilling relationship? Was this wretched man the only one she would ever share any kind of life with, or would she die alone and unloved?

Of course Mel loved her, in her way, but that was different. And, in time, Mel would grow away from her, particularly if Mary went to live and work in France as was her goal. Mel would most likely remain in Ireland, near to her father, until she in turn found work further afield, or married some hopefully good man. Whatever the depth or breadth of Mel's feelings for her – and there were times when little feeling at all was evident – the relationship was filial, not voluntary. Duty came into it – on her side now, on Mel's side later perhaps.

Where would she be when she was sixty, when Mel was forty? Where would Cathal be, where would they all be, as independent people, as a family? As she looked at Cathal's set shoulders, his fixed look of resistance and aura of resentful anger, she could only hope that they might find peace, if not in each other then in their child who gave them some common purpose, united their flimsy family and would lead the way into the next generation. Thus far they had not made a very good job of Mel, she felt, but things would change now, hopefully for the better. There would be more respect, more balance, a degree of freedom and hope. Cathal knew he had been conned and cornered, was morose and bitter tonight, but in time his anger would cool and fade, settle into acceptance.

Acceptance. She had accepted so much, against Keeley's long-running advice. 'Never lose your anger,' Keeley had counselled. 'Keep it hot for the day you'll need it.' But it was all very well for Keeley to talk; she didn't have to compromise in her marriage, fight the small daily struggle for survival, swallow her pride for the sake of her child. If she had a child she'd understand better, if Vincent were not the wonderful husband he was – but Keeley's personal life was close to perfect, she was in love and dearly loved, content to leave children for later. As late as possible, she said, and Mary marvelled at such freedom; she felt as if she'd been a mother for a hundred years. And motherhood put everything into perspective, your priorities no longer included yourself. If it wasn't for Mel she'd have brained Cathal years ago, cleared off and left him; instead she was caught in a web of responsibility that included not only her child, but grandparents, aunts, uncles, the fabric of a whole family. It was hard going, but at least she could say she'd done her best, she wasn't entirely a failure, not where her duty and her daughter were concerned.

Chapter Thirteen

This is what I mean, Keeley thought furiously, this is what I bloody mean about not having children. A situation like this, where a fourteen year old kid has gone off in a sports car in the middle of the night, in a foreign country, thinking she can drive because her stupid father has given her notions, given her everything she ever wanted. I'm going to kill her when I get my hands on her, she'll be despatched home to Cathal in a jamjar. *How* can she have done it, how can she have been such a little fool?

It's Tony all over again. This is how Tony ended up in a wheelchair at twenty years of age . . . oh my God, don't let it happen to her. Don't let her crash, hurt herself, kill some innocent person, somebody's mother or father or child. Maybe she won't be able to drive it; maybe she'll stall and Vincent will find her stuck at the side of the road . . . she can't be able to get very far, somebody will notice her, stop her, the police will pull her in.

I've never seen Vincent look the way he did when he went off after her. So harsh, so angry . . . with Mel, or with me? Which child was he thinking of, the one in our care or the one we don't have? Dammit, I will have one, I'll do anything, dear God, if this one comes back to us safe and sound. How long has it been, already?

Her anxiety rising in unequal proportion to her anger, starting to subsume it, she glanced at the clock. Nine twenty. Less than half an hour, since Vincent went off and she was left here to wear a track in the kitchen floor, chain-smoking for the first time in her life, feeling as if her skin were too tight for her, couldn't contain her conflicting emotions. Over and over the gruesome video ran in her mind: hospitals, doctors, drips, skulls, fractures . . . should she ring Mary? She itched to ring her, but she couldn't, to communicate such worry prematurely would be tortuously cruel. Sylvie, then? Félix, Luc? Pierre and Francine? No. This was her burden to bear, her test of endurance, to share it would not be fair to them. Tomorrow, when it was all over, she'd tell them, laugh it off as a bad joke.

A terrible joke, that was tearing her apart. And Mel was not even her own child. But she didn't think the anguish could be any worse if she was, only now there was guilt in it as well, the agonising prospect of having to break the bad news to Mary if there was bad news. She couldn't do it. But she'd have to do it, if—

God, she screamed silently, where *is* she? On some quiet country road only a hundred metres away, or on a main road, an autoroute full of speeding traffic? Surely she'll have the sense to stay around here at least, she wouldn't dare go into Aix or further. She wouldn't. She couldn't. Not even Mel Sullivan is as stupid as that. What was it she said to Sylvie that time, about not wanting to go far, only a few kilometres – Jesus, what's that?

In the brittle silence, punctuated only by the infinitely slow ticking of the clock, she thought she heard something. Something that sounded like a car, if only she would let herself believe it.

But it was a car. Coming up the drive, scrunching on the gravel and then turning in under the pergola – her car. Her BMW, that she knew the sound of immediately. Mel.

Leaping at the door, she shot out and around to the side of the house, just in time to see it shudder to a stop and then its lights go off. Before Mel was able to open the door, Keeley had wrenched it almost off its hinges, her whole body filling, floating on a tide of relief. Relief so violent it took violent form, grabbed hold of every nerve, every muscle, every bone in her.

'You little *bitch*!'

Her face upturned in the shadows, Mel looked at her almost casually. 'Cripes, Keeley, get a grip. I only went for a little spin. Look, safe and sound, no harm done.' She shrugged as she got out, and handed Keeley the keys. 'Here you are. Great car. I would have loved to really let rip, take it out on the motorway, but the gears and everything are on the wrong side, bit of a pain—'

With all her force, Keeley stood back, lifted her hand and struck her across the face. The sound rang out like a shot, and even in the dark she could immediately see the imprint of her palm on Mel's cheek. Propelling her round by the shoulders, she pushed her into the house, deaf to the howl delayed by shock and followed by tearful sobs.

'Get into that house and out of my sight before I kill you! Stay in your room until I can trust myself to *speak*!'

She felt murderous, all the tension turned to fury as they reached the kitchen, where in the light she saw tears coursing through Mel's make-up, glittering in the blue eyes that looked so suddenly childlike.

'Y – you *hit* me! You hurt me! You had no right! I'm going to phone Daddy—'

Keeley ripped the phone off the hook and all but threw it at her. 'Here! Phone Daddy, and tell him what you've done! Do you realise the police are out looking for you, and Vincent, scouring the countryside? Ring your Daddy, and then ring the police, tell them they can stop searching now for the child driving the blue BMW – go on, ring them!'

Mel's lips quivered as more tears flowed. 'Why are you making such a big deal of it? I only—'

'You only stole the keys, because you knew I'd never give them to you, and why not? Mel, whether you like it or not, you are a *child*! The law won't allow you to drive for years, and why do you think that is? Huh? Why, Mel – answer me!'

'You're horrible! I hate you! I can't wait to go home!'

'You see? You're even talking like a child. I – oh God, look, just go to your room and stay there until I simmer down. Stay there, and think about the damage you might have done. Not just to yourself, but to some other person. Think long and hard about it, Mel.'

'But I didn't do any damage. To anyone. And stop calling me Mel, I'm not a baby, I told you before—'

Keeley had to grip the worktop to steady herself. She simply could not believe that the girl would keep arguing, brazen it out like this, as if she really had no inkling how serious her behaviour was.

'Go. Just go, and don't say another word.'

Sobbing and snuffling piteously, Mel went. Immobile, Keeley waited until she heard her footsteps disappear and her bedroom door slam before sinking onto a chair, trembling as she ran her hands distractedly through her hair and leaned on her elbows, incredulous.

But at least she was home. Home safe, not a scratch on her.

Not even, as far as she knew, on the car. Right now, she hadn't the strength to go out and check it for dents, not that she cared if there were any. So long as the girl was all right, nobody was injured, nothing else mattered. Spotting some wine in a bottle left over from dinner, she reached for it and poured herself a glass, feeling faint. Really she could use a stiff brandy, such was her shock and relief. But in a minute she had better phone the police station, apologise for the alarm, and then wait for Vincent. He too would be furious, and devoutly thankful.

For five minutes she allowed herself the luxury of simply sitting, her mind going numb, her body rallying and reviving as the wine warmed it. Then, feeling steadier, she got up and went to the phone where it lay, thinking of the car phone Vincent had often mentioned getting. If only he had got it, she could contact him now, put him out of his misery. Meanwhile, she'd better speak to the police, who'd been remarkably reassuring when informed of the missing BMW and girl driver. Now that the drama was over, they'd probably be less sympathetic.

But before she could find the number, she heard another car turning into the drive, coming slowly towards the house on the gravel. Vincent. Somehow he had found out, and come home. But it didn't sound like the DS, it sounded like a lighter car. Biting her lip, she went to the window. It was unusual, in France, to have unannounced visitors after nine in the evening. Switching on the porch light, she reached to open the door even as there was a knock on it.

Two uniformed policemen stood together, looking uncertain.

'Mme Tourand?'

'Yes – come in, I was just going to ring you. It's all right. The girl has come back. Incredibly, there doesn't seem to be any damage, but I think it would be a good idea if you spoke to her, made her realise the—'

She broke off, frowning at them. They seemed to be looking through her, past her, not listening to her.

'I – what is it? What's wrong?'

They glanced at each other. 'Mme Tourand. Please. Sit down.'

Cathal had gone to bed, up to the partially restored room in which he was more or less camping until new furniture arrived and the scene of the crime was repaired, but Mary remained

downstairs, ironing. Even with Mel away there was plenty of
housework, and the only time she got to do it was late at night
after her day at The Lantern. But not for much longer. One of
the many things she was planning to do now was get in some
help, the part-time Mrs Mop she had wanted for years.

But ironing pillowcases was somehow soothing; her hand ran
up and down them automatically as she thought of other things,
Mel's homecoming in particular. Part of her would be delighted
to see her daughter, part of her was still enjoying the respite from
endless demands. As an only child, she conceded, Mel was badly
spoilt. Henceforth, she would have to be stricter, as Keeley said
she had been, to some effect at that. The trip to France seemed
to have been a success; Mel had even learned a bit of French,
and sounded quite chirpy when she called home.

At that moment the phone rang, and Mary revelled in her
new freedom as she went to answer it. It was almost certainly
for Cathal, at this hour, his father often rang late or Bill from
the pub, with some closing-time query. But she could answer
it now, at last, without fear of interruption or inquisition. Oh,
the luxury of it!

'Hello?'

'Mary?'

She caught her breath as she heard the French accent, somehow familiar and yet unfamiliar – someone who knew her name
– good Lord, it couldn't be!

'Félix!'

Thrilled, she could hardly believe it. Dear Félix, after all these
years? . . . but it was an hour later in France, what was going
on, why was he calling her? Instantly, her mind flew to Mel.

'Félix – it's not—'

'No' he said softly, apparently reading her thoughts. 'It's not
Mel, Mary. It's Vincent.'

'Vincent? Keeley's Vincent?'

'Yes. He's been in an accident. A traffic accident, in Aix. I am
at their house now, with Lise, we are looking after Mel. Keeley
asked us to come over before she left for the hospital and she
also asked me to telephone you.'

'W-what happened? How bad is it?'

'It's bad, Mary. I won't go into the details of what happened,
for now, but Keeley said . . . she needs you . . . she said you'd
understand. Also, Mel is involved.'

'What?'

'Don't worry. Mel is fine. But – Mary, I think the best thing is for you to come over right away.'

Her mind was out of the starting blocks like an Olympic runner. Cathal's money, that was hidden at Leesha and Kevin's house until Tony could smuggle it out to France – she'd go there, get it, and take the first flight to Nice, or Paris, wherever the first one was going.

'Félix, I'm on my way. Tell Keeley I'll be with her in the morning. And – Félix, should I bring my husband? In what way is Mel involved?'

She heard him sigh, and knew then that he knew. Her wretched marriage, to a wretched man; somehow he had guessed, or Luc had guessed for him. Probably they had known for years.

'No, Mary. That won't be necessary. Just come on your own.'

No, Cathal said firmly. It was out of the question. Mary was going nowhere on her own, certainly not to France, she'd never be able to cope with whatever the situation was. Besides, Imelda was involved. Either he would go or they would both go, to find out what kind of trouble Keeley Butler had got their daughter into.

Mary stood her ground, held onto it in a way that amazed them both. Félix had told her to come alone and that was what she wanted to do. Was going to do.

'I can manage, Cathal.'

'Don't be absurd. You haven't even any money.'

She rejoiced as she thought of the money she did have, wondered whether it was that very knowledge that was driving her on, freeing her to do this. Saying nothing, she packed at speed while he paced around her. 'I'll ring Aer Lingus,' he said at length, 'I'll book us both on the first flight in the morning.'

'Book me on it,' she replied, 'and if there's any need for you to come over, I'll let you know when I get there.'

His colour rose, his face full of scudding emotion as he saw that he was losing control, holding only the tattered skeins of authority, unable to dictate as he had done for years.

'I said we'll both go! Imelda needs me – and so do you, whether you think it or not!'

His tone warned her that he was limbering up for a fight, determined to assert whatever was left of his status, and that if she let herself be drawn in she would lose, because she was so used to losing. He had a way of sucking her in, engulfing her, crushing her in the mill of his mind, deploying all the tactics which, when he played football, always put him on the winning side.

But he was not going to win this time. Whatever had given her the strength to ransack his room was pushing her on again, and she recognised the moment for what it was: definitive. If she let him overpower her, decide for her, she would be a doormat for the rest of her life, a loser not only in his eyes and in her daughter's, but in her own.

With a sudden enormous burst of energy, fuelled equally by the worry of what was happening in France and by the vision, the ignominy of her future, she slammed shut the lid of the suitcase. Racing down the stairs she shot through the house like a tornado, out to the utility room where his golf clubs were stored. Seizing one, she ripped open the side door, ran out into the drive and raised it high over her head, paused for a split second and then brought it down with a reverberating crash onto the windscreen of his Audi.

The glass splintered into a wide cobweb, but did not shatter. With all her force she lifted the club and struck again, smashing the screen to pieces, watching with satisfaction as hundreds of glass globules fell into the interior. From the corner of her eye she could see him, looking down aghast from the bedroom window, and sensed eyes watching from neighbouring windows too, tiny flutters of curtain fabric. Tucking the golf club under her arm, she strode back indoors as he came running down to her.

'Now,' she said, 'your car is all broken. You're not going anywhere. Say one more word about it and I will smash all the other windows in it, smash every window in this house as well.'

He gaped at her, then lifted his hand to do what she knew he had long yearned to do, to hit her with immobilising force. Ducking the blow, she ran back upstairs, grabbed her bag and swung it down into the hall, pausing only to yank a coat off the stand beside the door. Before he could gather his wits she was gone, out into the street, praying that pride would stop him from coming after her, publicly reclaiming her.

He did not come. After a couple of hundred yards her pace and her breathing slowed, and she forced herself to think.

Where could she go, for the night? It was too late to go straight to the airport, there would be no flight at this hour ... as she kept on walking she thought about it, about the friends she should be able to turn to, if he had ever let her have any. But there was no-one, not one soul she could think of who would give her a bed for the night, refuge with no questions asked.

Leesha. Leesha and Kevin, her parents. Leesha had contrived this marriage, now she might as well know the true state of it. The charade was over, she would go there and simply tell both parents the truth, that she had had a row with Cathal and Mel was in trouble in France.

Whatever had got out of her that night she searched Cathal's room had expanded until now there was no longer any containing it; it felt like a parachute billowing out into masses and masses of silk, silk that was infinitely stronger than it looked. Quickening her pace again, she walked on, negotiating the mile and a half to her parents' house without needing to think, without even wanting to.

Her knock was loud, almost forceful, bringing Kevin to the door immediately.

'Mary! Good Lord, what are you – at this hour – why—?'

Bewildered, he gazed at her suitcase, her flushed face, as she walked past him into the hall.

'I need a bed for the night, Dad. There's been an accident in France, Keeley's husband is injured, I'm going over there in the morning.'

'But where's—'

'Cathal? He's at home. We've had a row. He wanted to come with me and I didn't want him to.'

'But why not?'

She turned to him as he led her reluctantly into the sitting room where Leesha was watching television, noting how quiet the house was now that the boys were gone, the boys who were grown men now, free to lead their lives as they wished, without question or interference.

'Because, for the first time in my life, I want to do something on my own. Go to my friend and my daughter and do things my way. Good evening, Mother.'

Leesha looked up at her, as baffled as Kevin, and they exchanged glances as if to say, she's overwrought, needs careful handling. With an air of concern, Leesha got up.

'What's happened, Mary? What's this about an accident, and a row?'

Mary repeated what she had told Kevin, in a tone that sounded icy even to her own ear, and sat down.

'But there's nothing for you to worry about. I can handle it. All I need is to sleep here overnight – oh, and I could use a whiskey, Dad, if you have some.'

Whiskey? Again they glanced at each other, and she could see what they were thinking, that whiskey was a man's drink, our Mary hardly ever even touches a cream sherry. Eventually, reluctantly, Kevin sighed and went to the sideboard, poured her a very small Paddy.

'Thanks,' she said, and downed it in a gulp. Leesha looked alarmed.

'Mary . . . I really think . . . the best thing would be . . . I'll just call Cathal and let him know where you are.'

'No.'

'What?'

'I said, no. Don't.'

Bristling, Leesha began to assume her mother-knows-best tone and stance. Suddenly weary, Mary raised her hand.

'Don't say anything. I don't want to discuss it. If you want to help, Mother, just turn on the heating in Sean's room and give me some fresh towels for the morning. I'll be leaving very early.'

Leesha opened her mouth to reply, shut it again and signalled to Kevin what was already obvious, that she wanted to talk to him out in the kitchen. They left the room, and Mary went to pour herself another whiskey. Assuming that the £20,000 was still safely stashed under Sean's carpet, she would be on her way at first light in the morning.

The journey was long and complicated, involving a change of plane in London, and Mary marvelled at the way money oiled every wheel even as she became conscious that people were staring at her, at the roll of cash which nowadays was an almost unheard-of method of payment. Leaving them to their suspicions, she clutched her passport, thanking the gods and Keeley Butler that she still had the one she'd first used fifteen years earlier, updated on Keeley's insistence 'because you never know when you might want to pay me a visit.' She never had paid another one since Keeley's wedding, but the passport had lain dormant along with her hopes, and she smiled wryly as she looked at the photograph of the woman she had once been. Undoubtedly, she would get a second look from the immigration official when she produced it in France.

As the plane took off for Nice her thoughts returned to Keeley with sharp focus, and to Vincent who had been so good to her all those years before, driven her to the ferry that took her back to Ireland. How badly injured was he, and what role had Mel played in his accident? Keeley must be out of her mind with worry, she loved him so much . . . vividly Mary remembered Keeley's giddy joy on the night they had first met, her small shape kissing him later on the quayside at Le Havre, her mixture of apprehension and delight that he wanted to marry her. Never once afterwards had Keeley said anything to emphasise her luck or her happiness, to draw any comparison between their two contrasting situations, but it was impossible to deny; Keeley Butler had made a wonderful marriage, and Mary Jameson had made a hideous mistake.

Or was it? Any outsider would say that it certainly was. But it had achieved its purpose, it had provided Mel with a home and an education, two parents and a relatively stable background . . . yet now Mel was 'involved', Félix had said, in this disaster. In what way? As the plane flew on down over central France, her mind flew ahead of it, desperate to discover, to know.

Several times Keeley was aware of Luc's arm around her shoulder, of his voice gently persuasive as he put a cup of tea into her hand, urged her to eat whatever it was he had brought to her. She smiled and thanked him, and went on sitting beside Vincent, her fingers linked into his, waiting for some response. As yet there was none, and the doctors said there would be none, but she didn't believe that, because Vincent loved her, would never leave her in this silent, unbearable way. And she loved him, was going to will him better through sheer force of resolution.

Even when the machine stopped its rhythmic bleeping, when the needle on the screen stopped tracing its little Alpine peaks and valleys, she did not believe that Vincent could die. He was young, he was healthy, it was not true what these people were saying, that he was dead. Even Luc was telling lies, whispering them into her ear, cruelly trying to convince her to let go, to come away.

'No,' she said, simply. Vincent had not yet come back, but neither had he gone away. He had not, would not. Not without even saying goodbye.

'Please, Keeley.'

She shook Luc off, and bent to kiss Vincent's bruised face. Surely a kiss would revive him, he would feel her lips on his skin and understand that she was waiting for him, that he must wake up. Someone was trying to make her let go of his hand, but she resisted, held it twice as tightly, fiercely. Around her, there was an anguished silence, but she was impervious to it, concentrating everything on the man she loved with all her heart.

The silence lengthened, then solidified as Luc and the other people left the room, leaving her where she wanted to be, alone with Vincent. From outside, their voices drifted in, but she remained oblivious, holding on, keeping her husband with her.

And then a new voice, very soft, very familiar.

'Keeley, it's me. It's Mary.'

She looked up. 'Hello, Mary.'

Mary's face was wet with tears, but that was only natural, she supposed; Luc had been weeping too, the sight of Vincent was a shock for everyone. But tears were no use, no help at all; she wanted Mary to smile, to be cheerful and supportive and say that everything would be all right. It was Mary's turn to do that, to be supportive.

And indeed Mary was taking her free hand, squeezing and chafing it, warming her a bit. It was a warm day, but she felt oddly cold, shivery despite the summer sunshine.

'Keeley . . . look at me. Please look at me.'

Obediently, she looked, even managed a smile.

'You came, all the way . . . but it's all right, Mary. He's going to be all right.'

'No, Keeley. H – he isn't.'

'Yes, he is. Of course he is.'

'Keeley, Vincent is dead.'

Like a child she stared at her friend, uncomprehending. What did Mary mean? How could Vincent be dead, when he was here in front of her, his hand in hers . . . ?

'Keeley, he isn't breathing. He's gone . . . please, Keeley. You must let go of him.'

Let go of him? Allow Mary to lift her hand, take it away from his, into her own? She tried to resist, but some force in her seemed to be extinguished; she felt pliant as rubber as Mary lifted her to her feet, put her arm around her and led her away from the bedside, away from Vincent.

As they went out into the corridor she was aware of medical staff going into the room, taking her place at Vincent's side as Luc was taking his place at hers, supporting her on one side while Mary supported the other, drawing her into some life she no longer knew.

For years Mary had wanted to return to France, to cook French food, to work with Luc in his kitchen, preparing a meal fit for the gods. But as she stood over the wooden chopping block now her eyes stung with pain, her throat felt seared as the meat Luc was searing savagely over a leaping flame, and she felt his fury even greater than her sorrow.

On his insistence, virtually his orders, they returned from Vincent's funeral in a small cemetery near Aix to Luc's house in the mountains, where everyone else was gathered around Keeley out on the hillside terrace overlooking the valley, caring for her as best they could while a meal was cooked for them. Mary couldn't see Keeley, who was seated, but she could see Félix and Lise, Vincent's parents Pierre and Francine, his sister Sylvie with her family, the art dealer Alain Jou, several friends and colleagues from the salons and Luc's wife Annette, circulating with drinks.

And Mel, standing apart, leaning on the balustrade gazing down into the valley, her face bleached with shock. Mary knew that her daughter was in agony, completely unable to face the enormity of what she had done, that Vincent, her godfather, was dead.

It had taken some time to piece together the puzzle of what had happened, but eventually the picture clarified: after driving around the local area in vain, Vincent had decided to head for a café in Aix which was frequented by teenagers, apparently thinking that Mel might have gone there to buy alcohol and mix with youngsters of her own age. As he went to turn into the parking area outside it, a youth had come out, jumped onto his motorbike and revved away at speed across his car. Swerving to avoid him, Vincent had slammed at full force into the wall alongside the café, and been thrown through the windscreen. His injuries were such that it was better, apparently, that he had not survived.

In the four days since, everyone had speculated endlessly as to why he had not been wearing his seat belt, but the truth of that was, Mary knew, the hardest part for Mel to contemplate; he had forgotten to put it on because he was so desperate to find her, had leaped into his car and simply driven away without thinking of it. His anxiety to save her life had cost him his own. The weight of that knowledge was so crushing, Mary thought, that neither she nor Mel would be able to heave themselves out from under it for the rest of their lives.

And then there was all the other speculation, murmured and whispered in the church, in the cemetery; if only he had had a car phone, Keeley might have been able to contact him in time, if only his car had had an air bag . . . but every 'if only' made it worse, so painful that Mary could hardly breathe as she chopped the vegetables now, and watched beetroot juice stain her hands like blood.

Cathal had nearly lost his mind when informed what had happened, that Vincent had been killed while looking for Mel, who had stolen Keeley's car but returned home unscathed. He was coming over, he insisted, would be there immediately; but almost hysterically Mary had shouted him down over the phone, saying that she was staying with Keeley and that Mel was staying with her until further notice, until she worked out some course of action. Cathal was the one who had taught Mel to drive, and his presence would only make everything worse. Much worse; it was bad enough for Keeley to even have to look at Mel, never mind face her loathsome father.

But Keeley hardly seemed to see Mel, or anyone. Limp as a rag doll, she let Mary and Luc and Félix steer her through the church ceremony and the funeral, not protesting, not weeping, not saying anything at all. Vincent's parents had had to choose the flowers, the music, the site of the grave, because her mind simply wasn't working. Apart from mechanically thanking everyone who offered sympathy, she had said nothing since leaving the hospital. Even her clothes for this morning's funeral, a black linen suit, had had to be chosen by Mary.

Shovelling the vegetables into a dish, Mary looked at Luc, watching him work off as much emotion as he could in his cooking, organising a meal that would stick in the throat of everyone who touched it. Yet she was grateful for this immediate purpose, the task of feeding twenty people, because what came after that she could not begin to imagine. Sooner or later she was going to have to take Keeley home, and Mel too, and address the question of what to do with, for, both of them. Under no circumstances, she thought, could either of them be left unsupervised for a single moment.

If only Keeley's parents . . . but neither of them had come from Ireland for their son-in-law's funeral. Christy, it appeared, couldn't be bothered, while Gertie was unable to leave Tony. Vincent's parents, Pierre and Francine, were doing their best to comfort Keeley, but were clearly shattered by their own grief, the loss of their only son. Dignified, they did not weep at the graveside, but Sylvie had wept like the rain, anguished by what she called her brother's 'stupid, senseless' death.

At length, the meal was ready, and Mary and Luc looked miserably at each other.

'We'll serve it outside,' Luc said, and she nodded at him, thinking how little he had changed in the many years since she had last seen him. His hair and moustache were grey, but his physical energy seemed undiminished, his capacity for the strong emotion which, at this moment, was channelled into violent, barely-subdued fury. Like Félix, he had become very fond of Vincent over the years, treating the young Tourands like part of the family. Félix had wept at the funeral, was white with stunned disbelief, but Mary thought that if Luc got near Mel, he would kill her.

Yet Mel had begged to be allowed to attend the funeral, sobbed that it was the very least she could do even though she knew what everybody thought of her. Mary didn't yet know what to think: on the one hand she was so disgusted with her daughter she could hardly articulate it, on the other, she sensed the depth of trauma in the girl. To be responsible, at fourteen years of age, for a man's death . . . but there was no point in pretending she was not responsible, indirectly at the very least, nor that she would not be haunted by it for many years to come.

They carried the platters out onto the terrace, and immediately Mel left the balustrade, came to her mother's side.

'Is there anything I can do?' she whispered.

'You can get the cutlery and all the rest of it, Annette will tell you where to find everything.'

Silently she vanished, and Mary put the food down on the table, went to seek out Keeley. In the midst of her friends and in-laws, she looked heartbreakingly small and vulnerable, somehow alone. Gently, Mary touched her shoulder.

'Come on, Keel. Time to eat something.'

Obediently, Keeley got up and moved slowly to the table, removing her dark glasses as she went, and Mary was horrified by the vacancy, the speechless grief, in her eyes. Other than pain, there seemed to be nothing in them at all. Looking somehow weightless, she sank onto a chair, and Mary took the one beside her, attempted some word of comfort.

'Don't worry. I know this is an ordeal, but afterwards we'll take you home, you can lie down and rest.'

'Yes. Thank you, Mary.'

Her voice was toneless, and Mary almost winced as Mel came to distribute cutlery, not daring to look at Keeley as she set it before her. How on earth were they all going to face being together, at Keeley's house later? But they would have to go there, there was no question of leaving Keeley alone, and Mel could not continue to stay with Félix and Lise as she had done on the nights since the accident. Félix was forbearing, but she knew he was feeling Vincent's loss acutely, finding it difficult to be civil to Mel much less accommodate her under his roof.

But it was Félix who tapped the side of his glass with a knife when they were all seated, and waited for the murmur of conversation to stop.

'I think we should say grace,' he said, his glasses glittering in the sun so that it was impossible to see what lay behind them, 'and a prayer for the repose of Vincent's soul.'

Without waiting for a response he recited grace, and then a short prayer, in French. Mary did not know the words, but watched as everyone else, even Vincent's parents and sister, pulled together sufficient strength to say it with him, their heads bowed under the shade of a soughing, silvery olive tree.

Everyone except Keeley, who sat like a statue, unseeing, unhearing.

The following day, Mary sat in the gentle morning sun by the pool, absently sipping the creamy coffee that Mel had made unbidden, trying to eat a hot buttery croissant without much success. Keeley had not yet appeared, sleeping like a stone after taking the 'petit comprimé' that Lise Peyrolle had slipped to her. It was not like Keeley to use medication – as a rule she laughed off any minor illness and had never mentioned seeing a doctor in her life – but Mary thought that perhaps this one sleeping pill was not an entirely bad idea. Judging by her appearance, she had not slept on any of the other nights since Vincent's death. Nor had she cried, as far as Mary could tell, nor eaten, nor spoken.

Inevitably, eventually, she must do all of these things. Perhaps there would even be an outburst today, the dam would collapse to allow the grief to come flooding out. Or perhaps it would take time . . . a week? A month, maybe? It couldn't be forced, but it needed to happen.

Meanwhile, life seemed suspended. Wondering what to do, Mary nibbled at the crumbling croissant, brushing the flakes off her blue cotton skirt, feeling her hair starting to curl already in the gathering warmth. As if through a veil she noticed the beauty of her surroundings; wide green swathes of well-watered lawn, exuberant russet vines climbing up the old-gold walls of the house, two labradors lying quiet on the flagstones, trees throwing their shade under the perfect blue of the sky. It was the first time she had been to Keeley's home, and she was taken as much by its unpretentious charm as by its aura of serenity. Clearly she and Vincent had made a remarkable success of their hairdressing business, must have worked like demons to afford all this, yet there was nothing showy, nothing fussy about it. With a small smile she thought of the dozens of figurines she had smashed in her own house to make the 'burglary' look convincing; shiny, sentimental, twee little things – she couldn't imagine now how she had ever let them cross the threshold. But Leesha and Carmel had kept giving them to her, relentlessly imposing their vulgar taste on a house they regarded proprietorially, sensing that she was not truly mistress of it. Whereas here . . . here, Keeley had always been the boss, had never tried or wanted to impress anyone, accept anything. There was an air of contentment about it, of refuge and retreat, that was very soothing.

But Mary's mind was busy, she felt it going up through the gears as she thought, wondered about what to do, a questing sense of mission mingling with her sorrow. Poor Vincent. Although she had not seen him for many years she had loved him like a brother, and mourned his death for more reasons than one. For himself; for Keeley; for the death of the dream he had always embodied in her image of him; the love and tenderness and loyalty that really did exist, as long as he existed, living up to everything her own husband did not. The world had been a happier, more hopeful place with Vincent in it, and she bit back tears as she thought of his bright warm eyes, his dark curls and sun-flushed face, his laughter and enthusiasm as he tackled her first attempts at cooking, all those years ago.

And now, what to do, how to help? For the first time, roles were reversed; Keeley needed her, was stripped of the perky buoyancy and brisk good sense that had sustained her, sustained their friendship, for so long. In a way, she was ill, needed looking after as if she were an invalid. Mary thought that she would recover, because it was simply in her nature to, but it was going to take time. A long time, to judge by the hollow, rigid look of her. She had lost so much: her best friend, her lover, her business partner, the only real family she had. Often, Mary knew, she had invited Gertie and Tony to come and visit, stay for lengthy holidays here with her, but they had never come. And Christy, of course, was a write-off. If she had children, perhaps she would be a tiny bit less emotionally dependent on Vincent, they would occupy and distract her at least. But she did not have any.

And, dear God, what of her own child? Mel's state of shock was almost as great as Keeley's, she was wandering around like a wraith, pale and quiet to an unnerving degree. Today, she had been due to return to Ireland, go back to school on Monday, and Mary was torn as she thought about that. Part of her blamed Mel for what had happened, longed to drive the girl to the airport and put her on the plane, return her to Cathal whose misguided indulgence had been the cause of the whole thing. Another part of her argued that it would be better to keep Mel here with her, pick up the pieces and try to put her daughter back together. At fourteen she was little more than a child, one who had been playing with matches and watched agog as the house burned down. Cathal would comfort her, if she went back to Ireland, but he would not help her to come to terms with what she had done, make her accept the responsibility which was the only way forward. Far from learning from the experience, she might end up denying any hand in it.

One way or the other, she, Mary, was going to stay here. Because of her daughter, Keeley was alone, widowed, in a terrible state. Keeley needed care and support from her, and she was going to get it. Cathal would just have to rely on Bridget to run The Lantern's kitchen, or get in some help. For how long? She had no idea. But that wasn't the main issue; the main issue was what to do with Mel. Could Keeley bear it, to keep Mel here? So far she had shown no interest in the girl, neither abused her nor said any word of forgiveness, as if she had forgotten her god-daughter's existence completely.

But if Mel stayed, she would have to go to school. Would some local school take her, for just a few weeks or one term, until Christmas maybe? And if it did, how would she learn anything through French? Or would Cathal come flying over to reclaim her, insist on taking her back to Dublin, her friends, her grandparents and cousins? What did Mel want to do, herself? Would it be wise to even consult her?

For an indeterminate time she sat mulling over it, until at length she decided she had better speak to the girl, broach the subject of what had happened at least – now, while Keeley was sleeping and would not be disturbed. Getting up, she put her hands in her pockets and wandered slowly into the kitchen.

Mel was sitting at the table, barefoot in shorts and a loose top, her hair tied back from the beautiful face which, for once, was not masked with make-up. Apparently unable to look her mother in the eye, she did not raise her head, but went on pulling at a piece of string, frittering it to pieces. On the table, a snowstorm of crumbs testified that she had eaten something, but the coffee in a bowl had a skin on it, looked cold and grey.

'Mel.'

The eyelashes flickered marginally upwards.

'Yes?'

'Why don't you come out on the terrace with me? I want to talk to you, and we might as well be out in the sun.'

'OK.'

Getting up, she followed Mary out, trotting behind like a puppy, her ponytail swinging as she walked, half-apprehensive, half-defiant. On the terrace, they sat down on the slatted beechwood sun loungers, and Mel gazed into the pool. Mary thought for a minute before speaking.

'First of all, do you want to tell me why you did it?'

Mel's lip trembled. 'I did it for fun, Ma. I only did it for fun.'

'Yes. Well, I suppose teenagers do do stupid things for fun. You could hardly have foreseen that Vincent – but what about yourself, Mel? Didn't you think that you might get killed, or kill someone else?'

'No. I – I didn't really think about anything. I reckoned I'd be safe if I stuck to the back roads, it was late, there was hardly any traffic.'

'I see. But then, why didn't you simply ask Keeley for the keys? Why was it necessary to steal them?'

'Because – because she was so strict! She wouldn't let me do anything, I knew she'd say no even though I'm able to drive.'

Able to drive! For a split second Mary wanted to jump to her feet and hit the girl. But she forced herself to be calm.

'Mel, you're not able to drive until you're seventeen and pass a test. That's the law.'

'I know. I – I just wanted – oh, Ma, what am I going to do?! Vincent's dead, because of me. I killed him—'

Tears started to her eyes, but Mary held up her hand, as if to say they would be wasted.

'Mel, you didn't kill him. It was an accident. If anyone's to blame, it's that stupid biker who shot out and made Vincent swerve. Don't dramatise yourself. You were a contributory factor, that's all.'

'What's a – a contributory factor?'

'It's one of the several things, or people, who make something happen. You set a chain of events in motion, which makes you partly to blame, but you're not wholly to blame.'

'I am! And now Keeley – she won't even look at me – how am I—?'

'How are you going to make it up to her? Mel, you can't. Nothing on God's earth is ever going to make this up to her. All you can do is accept your part in it, and tell her how sorry you are, and learn from it. That's part of growing up, of becoming the adult you think you already are. You have to take at least half of the responsibility, accept that you've done something terrible, and think about the consequences of your actions in future.'

Silently, wretchedly, Mel did seem to think, pulling at her hair, biting her lip.

'Are we going to stay here, with her? I can't stand it – it's so quiet – yesterday nobody even spoke to me—'

'Mel, you can't blame them! Vincent was their friend, their son, their brother! If you hadn't taken Keeley's car, he wouldn't be dead.'

The tears began to flow, with loud sobs and shivering shoulders, and again Mary was torn. Maternal instinct urged her to get up, take Mel into her arms and soothe her like a baby . . . but she was no longer a baby, and had to stop acting like one. To comfort her now would do more harm than good.

'I – I want to go home! When are we going home?'

Mary considered. 'I'm not going home. I'm going to stay here to look after Keeley.'

'W – what? But I have to go back to school! What about Daddy? What about the pub grub?'

'Cathal will have to manage on his own for a few weeks. As for your school . . . that's one of the things I wanted to talk to you about. I'm going to give you a choice. Either you can stay here with me, and we'll try to get you into some local school, assuming that Keeley will agree to let you remain in her house. Alternatively, you can go back to Dublin and live with – with your father, until I get back.'

They looked at each other, Mel's face tear-streaked, Mary's impassive as she waited for the inevitable response. Mel would choose to go back to Cathal.

'W – which do you think I should do?'

'You want my opinion?'

'Yes – Ma, tell me! I'm all mixed up, I don't know what to do!'

'I see.' Again, Mary stopped to consider, with a sigh. There was really no easy answer.

'Well, if you stay here, you'll have to change your attitude. I mean, seriously change it. You'll have to put up with a lot of inconveniences – losing your friends, studying in French, behaving according to my rules and Keeley's – and you'll have to be self-disciplined, because I'm not letting you upset Keeley more than she already is. I'll be busy with her, and I'll expect you to help me with whatever I ask, do things on your own initiative, cause no trouble of any kind.'

'Uh huh. And if I go home?'

'If you go home, I won't be there, so you'll have to look after yourself when Cathal is busy. He – he has problems of his own at the moment.'

'Has he? What's wrong with him?'

'S – something personal. Something that has nothing to do with you. But your two grandmothers will help you out, and you'll probably do better as far as your studies are concerned. You'll have your normal life, a chance to put this tragedy behind you as much as you can. It will be up to you to learn from it, and start behaving with more sense, stick to the rules that are there for your own good.'

Mel didn't answer, and Mary left her to think. After a while, she looked up, her blue eyes clouded with uncertainty. And then, her mind seemed to change direction.

'Ma, is it true that you can cook? Really cook, I mean, the way Luc says he taught you?'

'Yes. He did teach me – or started to, at any rate.'

'Then why don't you cook proper stuff at the pub, or at home?'

'I – because there was no demand for it at the pub, when I started out. And at home, your father didn't want fancy food, as he calls it.'

'Well . . . I think you should. At the pub, anyway. I really like the kind of food they do here – I bet lots of people would like it.'

Surprised, Mary blinked. 'Do you?'

'Yeah. It's fun. Nothing boring about it.'

'Well, if you're interested . . . maybe you could learn a bit about it yourself, while you're here. Or if you decide to go home, you could give Bridget a bit of a hand on weekends, learn something about running a kitchen.'

'Me?'

'Yes, you! I have other things on my mind at the moment, but there's nothing to stop you. In fact there'd be more chance of you persuading Cathal to change The Lantern's menu.'

'Why?'

'Because – because you're the new generation. He'll see that we can't go on serving up the same old stodge if we want to stay competitive, attract new customers.'

'Ma?'

'What?'

'Is it true that you left France to marry Dad? Luc and Keeley say you did.'

God, it was getting very warm. Mary ran a hand through her damp hair, fiddled with a tendril at her neck. 'Yes. In a way, it is true.'

'What do you mean, in a way?'

It was the longest conversation with her daughter that Mary could ever remember having, and she began to feel it as stressful as it was gratifying, even pleasurable despite the sombriety of its catalyst.

'I mean, in a way, Mel. Things are not always as cut and dried as they seem at your age. Let's just say I went back to Ireland for – for family reasons.'

'Like what?'

'Lord, aren't you persistent!'

Mel frowned. 'But I want to know. Were you crazy about Dad or what?'

Now, Mary thought. Now I can tell her the whole story, tell her the truth, if I want to. She's interested, she's open to it, this might be the only chance I'll ever get.

But what if I do? What is to be gained? What might be lost? Should I just tell her part of it, enough to assert myself yet leave her with some respect for Cathal? I stayed with him so that she could have a home, a family environment . . . no. It's not worth destroying that now, nor would it be fair to her.

With an effort, she smiled. 'If you must know, I went home because I was pregnant. With you.'

Mel sat bolt upright. 'Jesus! You were *pregnant*? You slept with my father before you married him?'

'Yes. I'm afraid I did – did have sex before marriage. I wasn't entirely the old fogey you might think – not that that means you should do it!'

'But then, why did you come to France?'

'I came to – to get away from Cathal, for a while. Then, when I discovered I was pregnant, I went home, and he asked me to marry him.'

'Why did you want to get away from him?'

'I just needed a break. Needed to think. Everyone should think long and hard before getting married, Mel.'

'Right. You won't catch me marrying anyone.'

Mary had to smile. 'Won't I?'

'No way. Not till I'm at least twenty five. I want to have loads of fun first.'

'Good. I hope you will have fun. I want you to travel and see some of the world, not settle down with anyone before you're ready. Marriage is much easier to get into than out of.'

'Did you ever want to get out of yours?'

'I – yes, sometimes I did. Everyone does, from time to time. Being married can be very hard work, especially when you're running a business together.'

'Yeah, I s'spose. Except for Keeley and Vincent. They – I think they really loved each other.'

Mel's voice fell, and Mary could not tell what she was thinking. Thinking that her godparents' marriage was happier, perhaps, than that of her parents? Or thinking about the tragedy she had helped to bring about? Sensing some doubt, Mary steered the conversation back to its purpose.

'Well, anyway, that's the situation, Mel. Either you can stay here with me, or you can go back to Cathal. Either way, you'll have to take some new responsibility for yourself. One parent can't mind you round the clock.'

Pausing, she thought about the wisdom of letting Mel return to Cathal, in the light of what she now knew about him. But somehow she knew that Mel would be perfectly safe in that respect, that Cathal would always keep his personal life, his confused sexuality, to himself. In fact he would die, she thought, if Mel ever found out.

'Then – then I think it would be better for me to go home, Ma.'

'Do you? Why?'

She felt a twinge. Always Cathal . . . always winning, in the battle for Mel. But then Mel looked at her, with a variety of emotions.

'Because – for one thing, I don't think Keeley could stand the sight of me. The best way I can help her is by getting out of her face.'

Yes, Mary thought. That might very well be true.

'And for another, it would probably be better for me to go back to school. I'd learn more there than here.'

Yes. Undoubtedly. It sounded as if Mel might be learning something already.

'And – and Dad might give me some extra pocket money, if I helped out in the pub with Bridget.'

She laughed at that, the old Mel bobbing up, with an eye to profit every bit as sharp as Cathal's own. But she liked the idea of Mel helping Bridget in the kitchen . . . if only she would stick at it, not go goofing off the moment someone was having a party.

'All right. Then we'll put you on a flight and send you home. When you get there, don't volunteer to help Bridget unless you mean it, because it's a hard slog. But before you go anywhere, Mel, you're going to have to talk to Keeley. It's going to be very difficult, but you'll have to try to come up with some kind of words, some kind of apology however inadequate.'

Mel nodded. 'I know. Oh, Jesus, Ma . . . what am I going to say?'

'God only knows. There's so little anyone can say . . . she's devastated. Absolutely devastated.'

Mel didn't reply, letting the weight of the word sink in Mary saw, struggling to understand Keeley's feelings as an adult must feel them, without any parent to take charge and make things better. It was the first bereavement Mel had ever been exposed to, quite apart from the guilt of her own role in it.

Sitting together, they said little more, letting the sun seep into their bodies if not their hearts, dreading the moment at which Keeley might finally appear.

But still there was no sign of her. Eventually Mary thought perhaps she should go to her room, make sure that she was all right. With a little anxiety she got up and left Mel by the pool, stroking one of the dogs uneasily, forlornly.

But there were sounds coming from the kitchen, and to her relief she saw Keeley standing in it, looking ghastly in a white towelling robe. Hastening her pace, she went to her and gathered her into a hug.

'You're awake, at last! I was just coming to look for you . . . did that pill help you to sleep?'

'Yes.' Keeley's voice was barely a whisper, the dark circles under her eyes mauve like bruises.

'Then sit down and I'll make you some breakfast – we've had ours, and a bit of a talk. I'm going to stay here to mind you for a while, but Mel is going back to Ireland. She – she has to go to school.'

'Yes.'

Sitting down, looking down, Keeley gazed absently at the floor, while Mary busied herself with bread and coffee and wondered what to say next.

'She – Keeley, there simply isn't anything she can say to you that would sound remotely adequate. She knows that what she did is unforgivable. But she wants to try to say something, if you feel able to listen?'

No answer. Mary turned to look at her, noting the pallor, the unbrushed hair, the awful air of lethargy. Over and over, Keeley kept twisting the two wedding rings on her finger, her own and the one she had taken from Vincent's hand in the mortuary. It was too big for her, but secured behind her own.

'Keeley? How do you feel this morning? Can you eat something?'

'Yes. Of course. Thank you, Mary.'

Mary winced. It was like a doll speaking, programmed, pointless. She put down the coffee pot and went around the table to her, knelt on the floor, put her arms around her.

'Keeley, it's all right. You don't have to be polite to me. Just say whatever you feel, cry if you want . . .'

But Keeley remained stiff, upright, dry-eyed. For an aching interlude neither of them said anything, and Mary could only hope that Keeley felt her support, her concern, was absorbing it somehow. But then, at length, Keeley looked at her, with a flicker of faint animation.

'Mary?'

'Yes, Keel?'

'Will you do something for me?'

'Of course I will. Anything you want.'

'Will you take Mel away?'

Away? Despite herself, she felt a pinch of hurt. What Mel had done was terrible beyond words, she understood how Keeley must feel, but she was still her child, so young, so overwhelmed by what she had done . . .

'Away now, do you mean? But she isn't here, she's out in the garden—'

'Send her home, I mean. Back to Ireland. Today. I don't want to see her. I don't want her in my house.'

'Oh, Keeley—'

'Please, Mary. She was due to go today anyway. Just send her.'

She could see that Keeley meant it, was genuinely distressed by the prospect of having to hear Mel out, listen to her abject, useless apology. Yet Mel needed to make it.

'Are you sure, Keel? She's only fourteen you know, and she—'

'Yes. I'm sure.'

Keeley's eyes were suddenly hard and bright as coal, and Mary flinched as she looked into their darkness.

'All right. If that's what will help you best. I'll tell her to pack her things, ring Cathal to tell him to meet her, and take her to the airport.'

Even though Mel had elected to leave anyway, she felt guilty disloyalty as she said it, her mind battling her heart. Was there no other way? Abruptly, the flame of animation died in Keeley's eyes, and she lowered her lashes over them.

'Thank you, Mary.'

Chapter Fourteen

Mel was silent in the taxi that took them to Nice airport, and Mary was taut with tension as she thought about what she was doing; handing her child over to Cathal Sullivan, in effect, leaving Mel to his exclusive influence. It was the last thing the girl needed, and she could only pray that, if it did her no good, it would do her no harm either. As soon as Keeley was remotely capable of looking after herself, she would have to go back to them both, resume her primary role as a mother and, in the process, resolve some role as a wife. If she and Cathal could not be partners, in any real sense, they were still parents.

'Ma?'

'Yes, Mel?'

'W – when are you coming home?'

'I – I'm not sure. As soon as I can. Whenever Keeley comes out of this trance she's in. But meanwhile I'll ring you every day, and you're to ring me any time you need me – any time, night or day.'

'D – did Keeley say I was to go? Did she want me to leave?'

Mary thought it must surely have been obvious, from the distant way that Keeley had said goodbye to the girl, barely even looking at her as Mel attempted to clumsily kiss her, say some awkward thing she couldn't articulate. But Mel seemed to have put Keeley's coolness down to the general state she was in, and Mary was glad she could save her that much.

'No, I – I told her you'd decided to leave, yourself, and she simply agreed that would be the best thing. Your ticket was booked anyway, there was no point in changing it for the sake of a few days, and anyway you have to go to school.'

Mel nodded, and seemed marginally comforted.

'I – I'll work harder at school, this term. My French is better already.'

'Yes. I want you to work harder.'

Mel lapsed back into silence, but Mary felt the uncertainty in her, the nervousness, as they reached the airport and made their way to the check-in. The flight was already boarding, but en route to the departure gates Mary stopped, put her hand on her daughter's arm.

'Mel. When you get home, you'll find – you may find your father a little preoccupied. As I told you, he has things on his mind at the moment. So try not to rock the boat, OK? Just get on with school and don't make any demands. I'll get your grandparents to keep an eye, and – and try not to think any more about Vincent than you can help. It was an accident, OK? There's nothing you or any of us can do about it.'

Looking surprised by her mother's calm, Mel faced her, and suddenly threw her arms around her neck.

'I wish you were coming home! I want you to come with me!'

'I will come, soon . . . but Mel, Keeley is my oldest, closest friend. My only friend, if you want the truth. She's looked after me for a long time, in ways you will never know about, and now I have to look after her.'

Tears rose in Mel's eyes, but with an abrupt gesture, almost as if she were angry with herself, she brushed them away, hugged her mother tightly and ran through the gates without looking back.

Keeley was dressed when Mary returned, sitting out by the pool, looking wan and vacant. Gingerly, Mary seated herself beside her, feeling bruised by Mel's departure and yet faintly relieved; the atmosphere had been almost unbearably brittle.

'How are you feeling, Keel? Can you – can you talk about it yet, do you think?'

Keeley stared into the water. 'What is there to talk about? Vincent is dead. All the talking in the world won't bring him back.'

No, Mary thought, it won't. And I'm the one who sent Mel here, I'm the one who set this terrible chain of events in motion. But what's to be done, now? Keeley has Vincent's family to think of, and seventeen salons to run, two hundred people – my God, listen to those dogs whining, she hasn't even fed them.

Getting up, she went and got them food and water, patting them as she realised that even they were miserable, sensing

Vincent's absence and Keeley's frozen detachment. When she
returned to Keeley's side they followed her, stretched on the
flagstones and began to nuzzle gently at their mistress's feet.
Absently, Keeley fingered their fur, and Mary wondered what
direction to take.

'Pierre and Francine said they're coming over tonight. And
Félix is coming tomorrow, he wants to—'

'I don't want to see anyone.'

'But—'

'*Any*one! Mary, if you want to help, then please just tell them
I'm not well, not able to handle anything yet.'

'All right. I'll put them off, for a few days anyway.'

But eventually, they would come. Eventually, life was going
to start going on again around Keeley, and she would have to
tackle it at least, if not participate in it. Looking at her, Mary
assessed her pallor, her gaunt, pent-up pain. Never had she seen
anyone looking so demolished, so crippled with grief; but she
felt there was no point in persisting yet. When her baby son
had died, more than twelve years before, she too had ceased to
function in some way, ceased to communicate. But today, her
sense of guilt was not as pressing as her sense of purpose, her
sense of having to *do* something to help.

But then Keeley twisted around in her direction, still not
looking at her, pushing at the two wedding rings on her finger,
and spoke quietly.

'We were having a row.'

'What?' Puzzled, Mary wondered did she mean with Félix,
or with Vincent's parents, or what? Who was having a row?

'Vincent and I. We were having a row over children. He was
telling me how he wanted children, three or even four, and I was
telling him how I didn't, wasn't ready for them. He looked so
angry when he got into the car.'

Keeley's voice trailed off, and Mary quailed as the words sank
in. There had been a row, one that could never be resolved, made
up, forgiven.

'Oh, no. Keeley, I'm sorry, I didn't realise—'

'He just drove away without even looking at me, and that
was the last time I saw him.'

Oh, Jesus. What a burden to have to bear, guilt as well as
loss, fifteen years of happiness ended in dispute, in a conflict for which Keeley was evidently holding herself responsible.

'But you told me a long time ago that neither of you wanted children, felt ready for them – I thought you were agreed—?'

'We were, at the time. But then – he changed – and I didn't.'

Mary didn't know what to say. Only that she'd better weigh every word, watch her step carefully in this emotional minefield.

'It would hardly have been a normal marriage without a few cross words, Keel. Everyone has them. But you know Vincent loved you.'

'Yes. But did he know I still loved him? Because if I did, then I'd have done it, right? I'd have said OK, the time has come, let's get pregnant, fill this fucking house to the brim with whooping kiddies!'

Keeley's voice rose, on a note of anger that Mary thought was not far off hysteria. Anger that Keeley was turning on herself like a gun. But she was glad to hear it, glad to hear something, at last.

'So let's say you had agreed. Let's say you were pregnant now, with a child that would never know its father. That's not the answer either, is it, Keel? Vincent wouldn't have wanted his child left alone, never having a dad, and he wouldn't have wanted you bringing it up alone either.'

'No, but – oh, Christ, why didn't I just do it? Just do the one bloody thing he wanted, months ago or even years ago? *Why*, Mary?'

'Because you felt it wasn't right then! And if it didn't feel right, it wouldn't have worked, you'd have resented it – Keeley, don't start punishing yourself. Please. I've done that for years, and I can tell you it doesn't work. Nothing changes, you just end up hating yourself as well as everyone around you.'

Keeley didn't answer. Instead she suddenly jumped up, walked away, went over to a cypress tree and slammed her fist so violently into its trunk that Mary almost felt the blood spurt from her own knuckles.

Go on, she shouted silently, go *on*! Punch that tree, kick down the walls, hurl rocks through the windows. Do whatever it takes to get the pain out, Keel.

I tore my house asunder, I smashed Cathal's windscreen with a golf club, and I can tell you it feels much better than curling up and dying.

*   *   *

In the weeks that followed Keeley's pain took many forms. There were long wretched silences, punctuated with seemingly irrelevant rages over trivia, and there were the tears that Mary was devoutly relieved to see flowing. Busy with her friend, she put the other worry of Mel on the back burner, because Mel's phone conversations indicated a growing return of confidence. She always asked about Keeley, but gradually other topics crept into her conversation as well; Daddy who had told her not to worry, Daddy who was paying her a fiver an hour to help Bridget in the pub kitchen, Granny Jameson who couldn't understand what the hell was keeping Mary so long in France, Granny Sullivan who'd taken her shopping and let her buy tons of make-up. Sharon Kelly was having a birthday party, Terry Finnegan had asked her to go to a hop with him . . . but yes, she said, she was working at school too, everything was OK, except that the house felt a bit funny without Mary in it.

Mary hoped that it did. In a way, her absence might be doing Mel more good than harm, and it could only be doing Cathal good. And what was equally important, she realised with some surprise, was that it was doing *her* good. As Keeley began to revive very slowly, she felt herself reviving too, Cathal's voice beginning to sound more and more distant whenever he spoke to her on the phone. Cathal, who hadn't even sent Keeley flowers, acknowledged Vincent's death in any shape or form at all. There was something in that that hardened her resolve to stay with Keeley.

One day at the end of September, she made up her mind to do two things. Hoping that the first might lead to the second, she got up early, went in her bathrobe to Keeley's bedroom, and knocked on the door.

'Come in, Mary.'

Even now, after a month, she was taken aback when she saw Keeley without make-up; her friend seemed to have aged ten years. But Keeley sat up and attempted a smile.

'Still here? I keep expecting to wake up and find you gone.'

'Gone? I'm not going anywhere.'

'But your family – Mel, Cathal—'

'Are managing perfectly well without me. Or not quite perfectly, I hope! The longer I stay here, the more they'll appreciate me when I come back.'

Even as she said it, Mary felt a jolt; did she mean *when*, or did she mean *if*? Until that moment she had had every intention of returning to her home, her family, her duty . . . but now . . . suddenly she felt a flash of confusion, and pushed the question down in her mind.

Padding over to Keeley's shuttered window, she threw it open.

'Come on, Keel, get up.'

Keeley's sigh was small, and stifled, but Mary heard the query in it: for what?

'Get up and put on something – I dunno, something nice, or something off the wall. I'm taking you out.'

'Out where?' Keeley sat up as she said it, looking lost and childlike in her wide bed, her hair tangled as a bale of twine.

'Just out. We're getting cooped up in this house.'

There was no denying that. Apart from Luc and Félix, Vincent's family and a handful of friends, Keeley had seen no-one since Vincent's death. The house itself, Mary thought, was beginning to feel like a tomb.

'Mary, I really don't feel – I don't think—'

'Come *on*! It's a beautiful day. Have a shower and get dressed and then we'll go into Aix . . . I want to spend some of Cathal's shagging money. I'll treat you to the best lunch you've had in a month of Sundays, any restaurant you like, the dearer the better.'

Keeley smiled wanly.

'I'd forgotten about that money.'

'Yeah, well, I'd say Cathal hasn't. You made me find it, it's your duty to help me spend it.'

Keeley reflected. And realised, then, that Mary had not left her side, had not been anywhere at all since her arrival, apart from taxi trips to the supermarket for essentials.

'All right. I'll get dressed . . . just give me half an hour to shower and get myself together.'

Satisfied, Mary left her, and was pleased when Keeley appeared eventually in a short brown skirt and white shirt, heavily made up to disguise the nocturnal ravages of grief.

'OK, let's go.'

Not giving Keeley any time to demur or change her mind, she led her out to the BMW that had not moved since Mel brought it back on that terrible night. She wished she could drive it, take charge and take Keeley into Aix herself. I must learn to drive, she thought, I will learn. I'm not going to be a passenger for the rest of my life.

Keeley looked at her as they got in and she started the engine, with a flicker of her old self.

'Where to, madame?'

'Why don't we go into the centre and browse the markets while you decide where you'd like to eat.'

Keeley had barely eaten enough to keep a budgie alive, shown no interest in food since Vincent died, but Mary was determined to make her eat well today. She smiled encouragingly as her friend reversed the car and turned it towards the gates, looking stiff and uncertain.

'Hey, Keel, would you do me a favour?'

'Of course, if I can – what is it?'

'Would you give me a driving lesson some time?'

Keeley hesitated, bit her lip, and Mary saw two things go through her mind: Vincent died at the wheel of a car. And Mary is asking for something she should have had years ago.

'Yes, I – I will, it must be a pain that you can't do it.'

'It's a royal ruddy pain. Cathal would never let me learn. But Cathal isn't here, is he?'

Keeley smiled faintly as they turned out onto the road, and set slowly off for Aix. It was a journey of only twenty minutes' duration, but Mary sat back in her seat and enjoyed it, seeing and smelling all the old things she had once so loved about this corner of France.

'Look, they're starting the harvest in those fields . . . d'you remember the time we picked the grapes, Keel, it was so hot and such hard work, I whinged my way through it from one end to the other? I was such a moan, I don't know how you put up with me.'

'Well, we're quits now. I've been a moan all this month . . . I don't know how you've put up with me, never mind stayed with me. Cathal is going to be furious when you get back – but Mary, I'm glad you stayed. I really am. I think I'd have gone to pieces without you.'

Mary touched her hand on the gear stick, and looked at her quizzically.

'You're not going to, though, are you, Keel? Go to pieces, I mean?'

'No. I thought I would – perhaps I even did at first – but now I feel I've cried so much I'm numb. I miss Vincent every minute of every hour, I can't stop thinking about him, but I know I'm going to have to do something about it. Take the business in hand at least, it can't go on much longer without me.'

No. It couldn't, and it was one of the things Mary wanted to discuss over lunch. Since Vincent's death Félix had been helping out, supervising the management of the salons, but he had privately asked her to have a word with Keeley about it whenever she thought appropriate, because there were some decisions he could not make for her.

'Keeley – does it hurt to talk about Vincent?'

She wouldn't do it, if it was too much for Keeley to bear. Thus far there had been no reminiscences, no allusion to happy memories or things the couple had done together, no photographs displayed or wept over. Keeley felt so many emotions, Mary guessed, that she was afraid to disclose all but the most obvious of them.

'Yes, it does hurt. It hurts like hell. But I'm going to have to do it, aren't I?'

'Yes. I think you should. Otherwise he'll get sort of – you know, enshrined. Too sacred to ever be mentioned.'

'Mary, some things are too sacred to ever be mentioned. Even to you, who knew him from the start. But as far as ordinary conversation is concerned, I won't freak, or collapse or burst into tears.'

'Good. He is still part of your life you know, even if – if he's not here. You have the business you started together, the house you built with him, his parents and sister . . . I think you should visit them soon.'

Pierre, Francine and Sylvie had all been to see Keeley, but she had not yet gone to them, and Mary thought it was time she did. The contact was important, especially in France where neighbours did not drop in casually to cheer you up.

'You're right. I will go. They've lost Vincent the same as I have.'

Glad to hear her taking that attitude, Mary nodded, inhaling the warm perfume of bougainvillea and mimosa, the gritty scent of the ochre earth, goats and grapes that faded from sight as they began to approach the city of Aix. After some searching they found a space and parked the car. Automatically, after all these years, Mary turned in the direction of the market.

'I bet I can still find it – come on.'

The Saturday morning market was as big and busy as ever, shaded by white awnings, studded with price markers thrust into piles of fabric, crockery, and food. Sniffing, Mary followed her nose.

'The vegetables! The fruit, the eggs and cheese . . . God, they're all still here, as if I'd never left! Here, Keeley, have an apple.'

Buying a bag, she handed her a big dark green one, and beamed with pleasure.

'Twenty francs . . . at home I'd have had to write that down in my notebook for Cathal to inspect and complain about. You can't imagine what it's like to be able to just buy something without having to account for it.'

'It must have been terrible . . . but Mary, what are you going to do with all that money, now that you've got it?'

'I haven't decided yet. It's not actually a huge amount, but I want it to at least be a basis for something. It'll keep me until I make up my mind, anyway, I won't have to ask you for pocket money.'

'Oh, Mary. You know I'll give you whatever you need.'

'Yes. I know that. But the great thing is, Keeley, I don't have to ask you. I don't have to ask anyone. I – I'm *free*!'

As she said it Mary suddenly whirled around and grabbed Keeley by the arm, her face lighting up with joy. 'I am! I'm free of him, he'll never control me again, I'm in France and I have a wallet full of money!'

Keeley laughed, a small anxious laugh. 'But what about Mel? How is she getting on with him?'

'Mel is fine. Guilty and pondering her terrible sins, for which I don't expect you ever to forgive her. But in every practical sense she's all right, studying and working in the pub at weekends, doing things she never had to do before – ironing, cleaning, things it'll do her good to learn. Of course Cathal says he's going to hire a home help, which I must say is rich. He'd never let me hire one, even though I was working all day in the pub.'

'Is – is Mel really all right with him, do you think?'

'Yes. If I didn't feel sure about that, Keeley, I'd go home like a flash. But the two of them are getting along fine, the grandparents are taking turns to visit – of course it's a nuisance for Carmel to have to drive up and down to Dublin, but she'd sooner do it than risk her son having to search for his own socks.'

'A lace sock at that, with frills round the cuff!'

To Mary's astonishment Keeley suddenly burst out laughing, and she laughed with her until tears came to her eyes.

'Oh, Keeley, it's so sad, isn't it, and so funny? And so good to see you laughing.'

Keeley flushed, and said nothing. Composing themselves they walked on, touring all the stalls, Mary bending to smell the piles of onions, the courgettes with their bright orange blossoms, the beetroot caked in fresh clay.

'Fresh, fresh, everything so fresh ... but out of season, for me.'

'What do you mean?'

'I mean ... it's too late, Keeley. I'll never be the chef I wanted to be.'

'Oh, Mary. Do you really think not?'

'Yes. Let's be honest, Keel. I'm nearly thirty-five, I've missed out on too much. Cuisine has moved on without me. I could still be good, given the chance, but I'll never be great. Even if I started training again from scratch, if Luc wasn't retired and could help me, I'd always be a step behind.'

'But it's not like running or ice-skating or ballet dancing, is it? You don't peak in your twenties in a kitchen, as far as I know.'

'A lot of people do. And it takes huge energy, it's physically exhausting – you need that spark you only have when you're young, not drained by other things. That's when you have to get a firm grip on the ladder. But I lost my footing.'

Keeley saw what she meant. Even if Mary managed to haul herself back onto the ladder, she'd always be on a lower rung of it now than the people who'd climbed it since. Uninterested as she was in food herself, even she had noticed the progress in the restaurants Vincent had taken her to. Things had moved on.

'But then, what are you going to do, Mary?'

'I told you, I don't know yet. But one thing is sure. I'm not going back to cook mush at The Lantern. If I live to be a hundred I will not defrost one more bag of frozen peas – Christ, Keeley, look at them! Real peas, in their pods ... come on, make up your mind. Where are we going to have lunch?'

The Vieux Moulin came to both their minds, but they both thought not. It wasn't the same place now, with a new chef and manager; it would only sterilise their rich memories of it – and besides, Keeley had danced with Vincent there, on the wedding day when Mary had got drunk. Keeley wrinkled her nose, and thought.

'Luc mentioned a new place in the Rue Espariat, we could try that – he said it's called the Chèvre something-or-other.'

'OK. Let's see if we can find it.'

Leaving the market, they headed in the direction of the Rue Espariat, and after much searching eventually found a narrow doorway with Le Chèvre Qui Saute scripted over it. Mary squinted.

'The Jumping Goat?'

'Weird name. But let's take a look inside.'

Inside was a revelation, a large airy restaurant with bright white linen and flowers on each table, light streaming in from an unexpected patio at the back. Her French more fluent than Mary's, Keeley asked the maitre d' who came up to them whether he had a table for two.

'Yes. This way, ladies.'

Ladies. Suddenly they were both inclined to giggle, but followed him demurely to a rectangular table screened from the patio by open glass doors. With a flourish, he snapped napkins open onto their laps, and handed them each a menu from under his arm.

'An apéritif, perhaps?'

Keeley thought of the car. 'Just some mineral water, please. But Mary, you have whatever you like.'

Feeling somehow elated, Mary ordered a kir. She was thrilled to have persuaded Keeley to have come out with her, and thrilled to think she could afford this ritzy lunch.

'Make that a kir royale, actually.'

He nodded and left them to persue the menu. Without debate Keeley settled on rillettes followed by a mushroom omelette, but Mary took ages to make up her mind, exclaiming and muttering to herself.

'Pork with juniper berries! Now there's a combination I'd never have thought of – monkfish with leeks and garlic – crikey, Keeley, look at that plate they're bringing to that man, I can't see what's on it but the presentation is stunning, did you ever see such colours?'

Finally, with a kind of sigh over all the other things she was rejecting, Mary ordered eiderdown soup, made with onions, milk, eggs, white wine, tomatoes and cinnamon. Keeley gasped at the combination, but was ignored: 'I have to try it', Mary said firmly. And to follow, quail wrapped in bacon, simmered in olive oil, brandy and pepper, with grapes and croutons.

'You'll never manage all that' Keeley pleaded.

'Watch me,' Mary replied, and turned to the waiter. 'With anchovy artichokes on the side, please.'

Sipping their drinks while they waited, they gazed at the fabulous food arriving on the tables of other early lunchers, and Mary all but purred.

'Fifteen years I've waited for this, Keel. Fifteen years, to eat in a sodding restaurant. I begged and pleaded and never once would he take me to one, nor let me go on my own. Never once, in our entire lousy rotten marriage.'

Oh, brilliant, Mary. Well done. Ten zillion subjects under the sun, and you pick marriage to discuss with the widow Tourand. Grimacing, she felt the blood rush up her neck and face.

'Sorry. I guess my marriage is the last thing you want to talk about. Or anyone's.'

Keeley did look pained, but she shook her head. 'No. Never mind, Mary. Talk about it if you want to. I know I was lucky to have had a good marriage. A great marriage . . .'

But it was too much. Keeley's voice trembled, her eyes gleamed with tears she fought to hold back. Reaching across the table, Mary took her hand.

'I know. It was great, wasn't it? It really was. I'd cry fifteen million gallons if I'd lost a man like Vincent – but you know I understand, Keel, don't you? Even if my marriage was nothing like yours, I know how you must feel. Cry if you want, the hell with the waiter.'

Keeley took out a handkerchief and sniffled into it, stifled her sobs and gazed at Mary.

'What did you say?'

'Huh?'

'About your marriage . . . you said it *was* nothing like mine?'

Mary sat back and stared at her. 'Did I say that?'

'Yes. You did. In the past tense. I learned all about tenses at the Chamber of Commerce, and what you said was definitely past tense.'

For a minute Mary said nothing. And then she sighed, a sigh of relief Keeley thought.

'Yes. All right. I may as well admit it. My marriage is over. It was over anyway, for years. But now I – I just don't know how I can ever go back to him. I feel as if I've escaped from prison.'

'But what about Mel?'

'I'll have to think about her. Think how to explain, how to look after her, find out what she wants to do. But it's so complicated, I can't work it out here and now. In fact I don't want to work it out here or now. I brought you here for a nice comforting lunch and that's what I want you to have. Also, there's something I need to ask you about.'

She paused while the waiter arrived with their starters, and Keeley waited for her to pursue whatever immediate thing was on her mind. But then Mary tasted her soup, and seemed to forget whatever she had been going to say.

'Oh, this is exquisite! The milk and the onions just meld together – taste it, Keeley!'

Obediently Keeley tasted, and was surprised. The ominous-sounding dish really was delicious.

'Mmmm – that experiment paid off! I'd never have ordered something that sounded so ghastly.'

'Well, there you go, you're adventurous in other things. But that's just what I wanted to discuss, Keel. You know you haven't set foot in any of your salons since Vincent died, and – well, Félix is wondering what your plans are. I told him I'd talk to you and persuade you that you must start taking some interest again. Apart from anything, it's not fair to leave him saddled with all the work.'

Keeley dipped her head. 'No. It isn't.'

'Well then . . . it's not that anyone is trying to rush you, we know you're very upset and that it will be a long time before you're back to yourself. But if you don't feel up to running things, then maybe you should think about hiring a new manager to – to do Vincent's share. Félix is retired, he's out of practice he says, finding it a chore.'

'It is a chore. It's very hard work, and I've no business letting him do it for so long. I've been thinking about it, and planning to talk to him anyway. It's time I took it off his shoulders.'

'So you will hire a new manager?'

'No, Mary.' Keeley paused for a moment, raised a forkful of rillettes to her lips and put it down again. 'I'm not going to hire anyone. I'm going to sell the business.'

Mary nearly choked. 'Oh, no! Keeley, you can't! You set it up with Vincent, you nursed it along and brought it to maturity – it was your baby, yours and his! It *is* your baby, that's why you never had time for any others.'

'Exactly. And look at the result. Vincent died unfulfilled, and

I'm alone now with no family worth talking about. I loved the project while it lasted, and I made a great deal of money out of it, but my heart has gone completely out of it. There's just no point to it without Vincent. I don't want to work with any new manager, we were a team and now there's no team any more.'

'There are the two hundred people who work for you, and seem to be very fond of you.'

Mary knew they were, because she had spent the past four weeks fielding concerned calls from them. But Keeley went on. 'I'm very fond of them, too. We've had great fun, a lot of laughs and satisfaction and rewards. But I simply cannot go on without Vincent, Mary. I couldn't endure it. It would be torture.'

'Oh, Keeley—'

'Please. Don't try to talk me out of it. I've made up my mind to sell. It's a very valuable business, it will fetch a lot of money and the staff will keep their jobs, only with a new boss.'

In spite of her horror Mary finished her soup, and wiped the plate with a chunk of bread. 'But you're only – what, thirty four? You're too young to sit around doing nothing!'

'Yes, well . . . I won't exactly be doing nothing.'

'No? Well, if you're going to bow out of your business, I can't see what—'

'I'm going to study.'

'*Study?*'

'Yes. I've been thinking of enrolling at Aix university, if I can persuade them to let me in. I think they make allowances for foreigners and mature students. If they will let me in, I'm going to study art and French literature.'

'Good Jesus. You're not.' Mary's eyes widened to the size of the plate the waiter was removing.

'I am. Don't ask me why, because I really don't know except that I'm interested in art and – well, if I learned a bit about French books I'd learn a bit more about France, I'd be able to convince myself maybe that I belong here. Until now I've always felt . . . I don't know, like I was about to be found out any day, kicked out.'

'That's ridiculous. You're perfectly entitled to be here. Ireland is in the EU, has been since 1973, you were married to a French citizen . . .'

'I know. But I've always felt a bit on the edge of things, possibly because I didn't have enough education to fight my corner, or bone up on the things that matter here. If the university won't let me in, I'll find some other kind of classes somewhere.'

Mary was flummoxed. Granted, Keeley had succeeded in learning French, studied with surprising success before; but there had been a purpose to that, she'd needed to do it. The idea of studying just for the sake of it sounded very strange to her, and the notion that Keeley didn't 'belong' in France was nonsense. How could her confident, normally up-beat friend be so insecure, under the skin? Everything in her life was far more successful than in Mary's own.

'Well, if you want my honest opinion, I think you're off your trolley.'

'Mm. I suppose that's what the university will think too, when I apply. Unless maybe they happen to need . . . I don't know, a donation to a new library or research or something.'

Mary laughed aloud, and was heartened by the sudden wicked gleam in Keeley's eye.

'You'd bribe your way in?'

'Yes, if I have to.'

Their main courses arrived, and Mary waded into the quail she'd never tasted before, the very name – *caille* – a distant memory from Luc's cookery books.

'Oh, this is fabulous! This – this is *civilisation*!'

Keeley's omelette looked delicious too, if less spectacular, but she barely touched it. Mary frowned at her.

'Please, Keeley, eat it. For me, if not for yourself. I've never been able to treat anyone before, and I want you to enjoy it now that I can.'

Keeley made some effort then, but paused after a few bites. 'Mary, where exactly is Cathal's money? Did you change it into francs, or what?'

'I changed two thousand of it. The rest is here in my bag, in Irish punts.'

Keeley flinched, and visibly paled. 'Oh, dear God. We'll have to go to a bank, right away – we'll go to mine, open an account immediately. You could be mugged, you fool! Or it could have all been confiscated at customs when you came over, you're not allowed to move that much money between countries.'

Mary's eyes widened innocently. 'Aren't you?'

'No. I don't know how you got it through.'

'I never even thought about it, and nobody asked. I suppose I didn't much look like a smuggler.'

Keeley had to laugh. 'Talk about an innocent abroad! Next thing people will be hiring you to smuggle drugs.'

Mary looked thoughtful. 'D'you think anyone would hire me to do anything, Keel, at my age?'

'Well, you're not exactly ancient. I'm sure you'd get something, though it mightn't be exactly what you want – why do you ask?'

'I ask because . . . I'm only thinking aloud, you understand, as things are coming into my head . . . but Keeley, I really feel like I belong here. It's weird that you don't, after all these years, because I do, after one month in Provence and one hour in this restaurant. I just feel so completely at home – even my French is starting to come back.'

Keeley had to concede that Mary looked very much at home, eating with gusto, savouring the glass of wine that had followed the kir, even starting to gesture with her hands like the people at other tables. For a few minutes, she thought about it.

'Look, Mary. I don't want to influence you, because you really do have responsibilities in Ireland whether you like it or not. But if you want to stay here, and can find some way to do it, I'd be thrilled if you'd stay with me. Long-term, I mean. I can't bear the thought of living alone, in that big house . . . I'd love it if you'd stay. It would be like old days back in our flat!'

Mary's whole face lit up, she even stopped eating for a minute.

'Oh, wow – it would! If you really mean it, Keel, I'd love to stay. If I could only think of some way of getting rid of Cathal and taking care of Mel.'

'H'm. Well, as regards Cathal, why don't you just bloody leave him?'

'He'd go nuts.'

'So let him go nuts. You're in a foreign country, it'd be very difficult for him to pester you.'

Yes. That was true. Mary felt that she was somehow safe here, that Cathal couldn't get at her, wouldn't be able to cope with the hassle of French red tape at all. Although he was very devious . . . but it wasn't his face she saw in her mind's eye, it was Mel's.

'It's the old problem, Keeley. As long as my daughter is under his roof, he's got a hold over me.'

'Then bring Mel here.'

'He'd fight me hammer and tongs on that. And Mel might not want to come. And you might not want to have her. I could well understand that, if you didn't – God, Keeley, I feel so guilty! I never should have sent her to you, it was the stupidest, most selfish thing I ever—'

Keeley sighed. 'Mary. Listen. If you are going to stay with me, then it's on one condition. That you never again utter the word "guilty" in my hearing. You've been guilty about one thing or another for your entire life, and I'm sick of it. Sending Mel here was a perfectly reasonable thing to do. I am her godmother after all, nobody could have foreseen what would happen.'

Mary gazed at her. 'You can't mean that. You were so disgusted with her you asked me to send her away, put her on the next flight, you couldn't stand the sight of her.'

'No. At the time, I couldn't. But I've had time to think since then. She is only a kid, as you pointed out, and I am simply going to have to work on forgiving her. I can't say I have yet, by a long way, but I'm open to the eventual idea of it.'

'Keeley, I don't expect you to do it. I haven't forgiven her myself. I keep thinking of that night over and over . . .'

'We're all going to be thinking of it, for months, maybe for years. We're just going to have to learn to live with it.'

Mary was silent, hardly able to believe Keeley's composure, her calm generosity. It must be costing her a great deal, she thought, to say that. Deeply touched, she put down her fork and took Keeley's hand. 'You are an incredible friend, and I love you like a sister.'

Keeley looked as if her face was held in place with scaffolding, and Mary saw everything that she was striving to hide. She was not surprised when Keeley made no reply.

After a silent pause they resumed their meal, and finished it with coffee. But then, the pleasure of paying for it! Mary requested the bill, and triumphantly took a roll of notes from her bag. Keeley winced.

'I think we'd better go to the bank right now. I know the manager, I'll get him to sort this out.'

'OK.' Mary grinned equably, and Keeley led her out of the Chèvre Qui Saute, down the street in the September sunshine. The bank was some distance away, but she felt like walking, for the first time since Vincent's death. As they made their way along the cobbled streets she set her mind to the question of how to explain her cash-rich Irish friend to the manager, and was grateful for the distraction. It took her mind off Vincent, if only for a short time, and restored some tiny fraction of the sense of purpose she had lost.

Two days later, after visiting Vincent's grieving parents, Keeley invited Félix to come to dinner with his wife Lise. Mary would cook it, she assured him, it would be perfectly edible. Hugely relieved to hear her sounding like herself, to hear her voice at all, he accepted with pleasure.

Mary made a huge production of the meal, anxious to justify herself as much as to use her rusty skills, and they sat down to a veritable banquet that made Lise blink and gaze at Mary in wonder. But it wasn't until the dessert stage, of caramelised figs with Normandy cream, that Keeley came to the point.

'Félix. First of all, I want to thank you with all my heart for running my salons for the past five weeks. I know it's been hell for you and I apologise for not having been able to do it myself.'

Félix frowned, paternally. 'It is the least I could do. You have suffered a terrible shock, and loss.'

'Yes, but that doesn't make it your responsibility. So now, I'm going to take it off your shoulders.'

Neither he nor Lise could hide their relief; it really had been a nightmare trying to figure out Vincent's system after so many years in retirement. Toying with her coffee, Keeley lit a cigarette, and they saw that she was nervous.

'I'm going to sell the salons.'

There was a stunned silence. For a tortured moment, Félix looked as if he was going to burst into tears.

'What?'

'I'm going to sell. Lock, stock and barrel. I can't go on without Vincent.'

'Oh, no – oh, Keeley—'

'Yes. I'm sorry, Félix. I know it must be a disappointment to you, after your investment and all your help. But my mind is made up. I don't want to work with a new manager, I don't want to carry on alone, the burden is simply too great and there would be no joy in it, only reminders . . . I'm going to sell the whole chain as a single entity, if I can find a buyer for the lot.'

Strangled, Félix said it was much too soon to make such an

important decision. Given a few more months, Keeley would feel differently.

'No. I won't, Félix. I – I don't care to discuss it in detail, but please believe me that it's the best course. The only one.'

'But you worked so hard—'

'I worked too hard. I was obsessed. And now, I've used up all my interest in salons, in hairdressing, in work itself.'

Félix sat desolate, unable to reply. Lise lifted an elegant eyebrow enquiringly. 'But Keeley, you are too young to retire. What are you going to do?'

'I'm going to take a few more months off, maybe until Christmas, to try to pull myself together. And then I'm going to study. Art and literature.'

They were aghast, she could see, taken totally aback. Admittedly Keeley loved paintings, and devoured books, but this was taking a hobby too far. Much too far. Desperately, Félix tried to rally.

'Mary, you must speak to her. She doesn't know what she's doing.'

But Mary looked supportively across the table at Keeley, and turned to him calmly. 'I think she does, Félix. We've talked about it, and I can see where she's coming from. It would be desperately painful without Vincent.'

There was another frozen silence, in which Félix and Lise attempted to digest the finality of Keeley's decision. Steeling herself, Keeley spoke again.

'I know, Félix. You financed us, you got us off the ground, the business has always been your baby in a way, as it has been mine. I'm truly sorry to upset you. But I hope we will always be friends.'

He nodded vehemently. 'Yes. I cannot say I am not very shocked, even disappointed. But we will always be friends, Keeley.'

'Thank you,' she said quietly, and extinguished her cigarette, feeling some part of herself extinguished.

Apart from Cathal's hectoring phone calls, demanding to know when Mary was coming home, autumn was serene and subdued, as was Keeley herself. Mary often found her out by the pool, sitting in the cooling sun with a sweater round her shoulders, lost in thought. But she didn't intervene, thinking that Keeley needed some space and privacy, time to adjust.

Meanwhile she monitored Mel by telephone, telling her of

Keeley's decision to sell the business, determined that she should know the ongoing consequences of what she had done. Mel wanted to be let speak to Keeley, to try to dissuade her, but Mary decided against letting her. It was an adult thing, she said, too complex for Mel to meddle in. Mel argued about that, but Mary thought she heard something sinking in.

For several weeks she continued to debate her future and her options, as Keeley was debating hers, and each found the other's company nurturing, sustaining. In the evenings they lingered over long suppers, talking, speculating, trying to repair their emotions and somehow fill the vacuum that Vincent had left.

But it was a huge vacuum for Keeley, and she got into a morbid habit of visiting his grave every day, asking Mary to wait for her in the car at the gates of the cemetery. Her visits were brief, but she was always silent on the way home, and Mary thought sadly of the first car journey they had ever made together, with Keeley chattering nineteen to the dozen all the way from Le Havre to Aix-en-Provence.

To rouse her, she asked Keeley one day to give her her first driving lesson, hoping that she wouldn't find herself referred to a driving school. But Keeley said OK, let's get into the car and I'll explain it to you. Quaking, Mary got in.

It seemed simple enough in theory, and it wasn't until Keeley told her to switch on the engine that Mary stalled.

'Oh God, it'll shoot off with us!'

'Not unless you put it in gear, it won't.'

Gingerly, Mary turned the key, and listened in panic to the engine revving, her hands clamped to the steering wheel.

'Take your foot off the bloody accelerator!'

In a panic Mary looked down, and her foot seemed to freeze to it, making the car rev like a jumbo jet.

'Oh Jesus, this is rocket science!'

Keeley burst out laughing. 'Well if it is, Keeley Butler has a licence to practise it! Come on, Mary, just ease off the juice.'

Frantically she lifted her foot, and was amazed when the furious roaring stopped.

'Phew. I thought we were going to take off for Tokyo.'

'We're not going further than the end of the drive. Now, put it into first.'

That was another matter, and they both winced as the gears ground horribly and the engine cut out. When Mary started it again the car leaped forward, in first after all.

'Keeley, I can't. I can't do this.'

Sweat was running down her temples, down her midriff, her palms were virtually gushing with it. Keeley looked at her grimly.

'Just shut the fuck up and do what I tell you.'

Startled, she set her mind to doing it. After an exhausting hour, they had travelled the length of the drive. Satisfied, Keeley grinned.

'OK. That's enough for today.'

Beaming, Mary jumped out of the car, ran around it and threw herself on her friend. 'I did it, I did it! I can drive, I can drive!'

'You can in your arse,' Keeley retorted. 'But we'll have another go tomorrow.'

At the end of October Mary applied for, and got, a provisional licence. Whooping dementedly when it arrived in the post, she ran into the little study where Keeley was doing paperwork. The sale of the salons was under negotiation.

'Look! Come on, I'm taking you out to lunch again!'

From that day on they got into the habit of going out to lunch, Mary revelling in driving them to the restaurant, in the food they ate, in the ill-gotten means to pay for it.

'Foie gras,' she purred one day, savouring a last mouthful. 'Cathal would have a heart attack if he knew what I was spending his money on. Why don't you have a glass of champagne, Keeley?'

She grinned hugely, and Keeley did have one, the first in a long time. And then, to her own surprise, she had two more. Mary watched astonished as she knocked them back one after the other. Keeley grinned with giddy abandon; and then tears began to pour down her face.

'Oh, my God – Keeley, what is it? Vincent?'

'Y-yes,' Keeley sobbed, brushing the tears away as more fell. 'Vincent and – and Mary, I sold the salons this morning. Signed the last document. They all belong to a man in Nice now.'

Hiccupping, gasping, she put her face down on her forearms and wept her heart out.

Finally, Cathal's howls could be ignored no longer. Mary would have to go back and face the music.

'I'll come for Christmas,' she promised, and hung up with her heart in her mouth. She had still formulated no precise plan, only knew that she wanted to stay in France, and that telling Cathal in person, on his turf, was going to be no easy thing. Putting down the phone, she turned instinctively to look for Keeley, but then stopped herself; Keeley wasn't in great shape today, missing the many employees who had become friends and who had begged her not to sell the business.

But she couldn't have gone on with it, Mary reminded herself. She'll miss it for a while, but then she'll get on her feet, meet new friends when she starts her studies. Maybe she'll even . . . Jesus, how can I be thinking that? She won't meet any new men. Not in that sense. She's going to take years to get over Vincent. He was simply one in a million, all she ever wanted. Right now, I don't think she wants anything or anyone.

How awful to be a widow so young. But at least there's a finality about it, she knows where she stands, whereas I – Christ, what am I going to say to Cathal? What am I going to do about Mel? I'm starting to miss her, I have to see her – but then what? If I stay here, I'll have to find work. But who'd hire me, as what? I'd be lucky to get a kitchen job, which would put me right back where I was at home. Or a waitress, if they're not all nineteen-year-olds these days, most of them seem to be. Cathal's money won't last forever, I have to think of something – anyway, waitressing doesn't pay enough. I need work that would keep me properly, with enough to support Mel if she decides to live here with me. But what if she doesn't want to—? God, what *am* I going to do? I'm not a teenager this time, I'm thirty-four and the mother of my own teenager. I've got to think of her, even if it means . . . even if it means going back to Cathal, after all. Maybe that's what I should do. Go back to him and stick it out, for as long as it takes to finish rearing Mel, make an independent adult of her. It would only be for another four years, or five, six at the most.

I should go back. It's going to kill me, but I'm going to have to think about it. Seriously think about it.

'Mary?'

She jumped out of her reverie, but couldn't shake off her feeling of despondency as she turned to see Keeley coming into the kitchen, looking equally sombre as she went through the morning's post.

'Hi. Anything interesting?'

Keeley held an open envelope between two fingers, as if contemplating dropping it in the bin. She was very pale.

'I don't think that's exactly the word for it. It's a cheque. For Vincent's life insurance.'

She put it down on the table, and stared at it. 'Five million francs. That's what his worth was, in monetary terms.'

Mary felt a frisson, shivered slightly as she too stared at the envelope. There was something ghoulish about it, something distasteful that made her want to sweep it out of sight.

'What can I say, Keeley? It's a comfort to know that you won't starve, but very cold comfort.'

'No. I won't starve. Between that and the sale of the salons, I won't ever have to work again.'

Keeley's voice was toneless, and Mary grimaced as she thought of the irony: Keeley never needing to work again, while she contemplated waitressing or the prostitution of returning to Cathal. After her 'desertion' as he now called it, life with him would be harder to bear than ever. He would think of a hundred and one humiliations to inflict on her – nothing overt, because of the photographs, but small, subtle, endless punishments.

Prostitution. She had never thought of the word before, perhaps never allowed herself to think of it, but that was what it was. Bed and board, material support for herself and her child in return for the charade of being Cathal's wife, the reality of being his slave. She was a kept woman – even now, she was living on his money.

'I – I'm going to make a pot of tea, Keel. You look as if you could use a cup.'

'Thanks, Mary. I could.'

She busied herself with it while Keeley continued through the rest of the post: bills, flyers, condolences still coming in from people who were only now hearing of Vincent's death, or finding time to write. One card was from a very old friend of his, a man Keeley had never met, who had been to school with him twenty five years before. The man now lived in Paris, and she read his folded card twice, moved by it.

'People liked Vincent, didn't they, Mary?'

Yes. She had seen them at the funeral, in large numbers, many holding handkerchiefs to their faces, distraught as Vincent's coffin was blessed and buried. She was thinking continually of him herself, seeing his smile, hearing his boyish laugh, remembering how he had offered to find and kill Lars-from-Gothenburg. Briefly, she thought of Lars, saw his face and heard his voice too: where was he now, who was he? Just for a moment, she allowed herself to wonder.

'Here we are, tea's up.'

Keeley took her cup, and looked at her questioningly.

'Did I hear you on the phone to Mr Right?'

'Yes, you did. Mr Magic Moments in Ireland. I told him I'd go home for Christmas – I have to, Keel – but what are we going to do about you? Will you come with me?'

Keeley hesitated, and considered. She had not been to Ireland for a long time. A very long time. But her mother was getting old, now, in spirit if not body, worn out by life with Christy and the endless care of Tony. Thanks to Tony's painting they had enough to live on in comfort, and Keeley often sent gifts of money, but she had no idea how they really were. Was it time to go and see them? She thought that maybe it was, because under no circumstances was she going to accept any of the well-meant invitations that would be extended to her at Christmas, to stay with Félix or Luc or even Vincent's parents. The exquisite loneliness of that, she thought, would be unendurable.

'I – let me think about it.'

'OK. But I hope you'll come. I'll need you with me for moral support when I confront Cathal.'

'What are you going to say to him?'

Keeley looked at her keenly, suddenly, and Mary realised that her friend had been waiting for a decision, some kind of definite decision, about whether she was going to stay in France and, if so, what she was going to do there. Sitting down facing her, she gazed into her teacup.

'I don't know, Keel. I'd give anything to stay here. But I just don't know how I can earn a living. Cathal's money isn't enough to set up a restaurant, even if I still felt confident I could run a real one, which I don't. It's only since I've been here I've realised how stiff the competition is, how very far I've lagged behind.'

'You've been cooking some great meals here.'

'Yes, by your standards, perhaps, but not by top professional standards. You're too easy to please when it comes to food, you still judge by Irish standards and don't really care anyway. I could give you beans and chips and you'd be delighted.'

Keeley smiled a little. Mary was right about that. In fact she'd often slung beans on toast for Vincent, when he didn't feel like cooking himself or going out . . . beans on toast, here at this table, eaten with such love and laughter. For a split second she wanted to take a sledgehammer and demolish this table, demolish the entire kitchen, tear down the whole house with her bare hands.

Gripping the thick oak, she steadied herself. 'Then what, Mary? You have to face Cathal with some kind of plan. Something solid that he can't argue with, already under way.'

'But I can't do anything until I know what Mel wants to do, wants me to do, even if I knew what to do myself.'

Keeley said nothing, reflecting, putting considerable thought into it for several minutes.

'What do you know?'

'Huh?'

'What do you know how to do, Mary? What have you been doing all your life?'

'I've been slinging hash in a crummy pub. Stuff the French would throw in the bin, barely even deign to feed to their cat.'

'Mm. Bangers and mash, steak and kidney pie, apple crumble, that kind of thing?'

'Yes. Stodge, prepared in industrial batches, frozen and defrosted. Except for the stuff out of packets and tins.'

'The stuff I missed when I came to France?'

'Yes. I suppose.'

'So if I missed it . . . all the Irish immigrants in France must miss it. The English ones too, because their food is much the same. And then there are the tourists, the French people who've been going to Ireland ever since they saw *Barry Lyndon* and *Ryan's Daughter* . . . they miss the pubs, they say, they love those old pubs in Dublin and Dingle and Connemara.'

Mary frowned. 'Keeley, if you think – I told you, I want to cook proper, decent fresh food. It's that or nothing. There's no point in doing my penance twice over.'

Keeley didn't seem to hear. 'Tell me, did you pick up much about running a pub in all your years at The Lantern?'

'Nothing on the business end, because Cathal guarded the money as if he was on sentry duty at Fort Knox. The only thing I picked up was the atmosphere, the way people liked it if there was a match on telly that they could all cheer together, or a darts game going, or a bit of a singsong.'

'H'm. Well, then, you want to hear what I think?'

'What do you think?'

'I think I should invest some money in a pub. An Irish pub, in Aix.'

'A – an Irish pub?'

'Yep. It would have to be in an old building of course, to look like the real McCoy – probably cost a fortune to get one. But then, I have a fortune, instead of having Vincent or my salons.'

'Keeley – oh, no—'

'I'd say Guinness could be interested, if we approached them, and Irish Distillers. They're already supplying an Irish pub in Paris, and one in Brussels I hear. Anyway, the point is, Irish booze, Irish music, Irish food – or a French version of it, fresh as a daisy, cooked by Mrs Sullivan here.'

Mary felt a little faint. Keeley couldn't be serious.

'Why not? You could do traditional dishes, Mary, since you've abandoned hope of joining the nouvelle cuisine brigade, or whatever it is this year. Only the sausages would be made by your own hand, you could bung herbs or spices or whatever you like into them, you could turn potatoes into an art form – I've always fancied them with a bit of bacon chopped into them, myself – you could dig out a few Irish recipes and dickey them up, there must be some.'

'Darina Allen,' Mary sighed softly. 'I could buy all her books, they're like bibles in Ireland these days. She has a programme on telly, forty-nine thousand ways to put fire in your fillets . . . Jesus Christ!'

'Where does He come into it?'

'Keeley, I could use Cathal's money to do one of her courses, in Cork! She has a cookery school at Ballymaloe, it costs the earth by all accounts but a few weeks couldn't cost more than a few thousand, even allowing for air fare and accommodation – oh my God, Keeley, we could! We could open an Irish pub that would actually be a showcase for Irish food. I bet Bord Fáilte would even lend a hand because it would be such a good ad for tourism, during the summer Irish tourists would come to eat with us—'

'Us? I take it you could be interested, then?'

Suddenly Mary's mind swung back fifteen years. Fifteen years, to the day she told Keeley she was pregnant, and Keeley asked, 'What in the name of blessed Jesus almighty are *we* going to do now?'

This was what they were going to do, now. The two of them, together. Keeley would finance it and she would cook in it, cook properly at last, not the fine cuisine she had once envisaged but fresh, first-rate traditional fare, jazzed up with all sorts of innovations. Her own ideas, that she would be free to experiment with.

If Keeley was sure about this, that was, not just talking off the top of her head. Anxiously, Mary eyed her.

'Keeley, this is a fantastic brainwave and I just don't know what to say. I'm *thrilled* with it! But – are you sure? You don't think you might miss the hairdressing, even yet?'

'Well, the hairdressing school has asked me to be a consultant, so I'll still see a bit of it. But it was always the customers I really enjoyed, cranky bags and all as some of them were. I could drop into the pub sometimes and amuse your customers with my rendition of Dicey Reilly.'

Mary had a vision of Keeley singing, leading the troops in full cry, and laughed.

'You'd get free drinks, if you did.'

'Then – do we have a deal?'

Wildly excited, but conscious of Keeley's proposed investment, she hesitated, thinking.

'We do. On two conditions. One, that we employ a very good manager, since I haven't a clue about business stuff and Vincent always did yours. Two, that I talk to Mel first. If she says no, she wants me to come home, then that's what I'll have to do, Keel. It'll choke me, but I'll have to do it.'

Keeley nodded, and bit her lip, also thinking. 'Right. I can understand that, I guess. But I think the first thing we should do is book two tickets to Dublin for Christmas. I'll come with you. I want to see the lovely Cathal, and my mother and brother, and my god-daughter.'

'You want to see Mel?'

'Yes. I think it's time she and I had a little chat.'

Mary quailed. 'Oh, she'll die when she hears that—'

'Yes, well, Vincent really did die, because of her. There are a few things we need to get straight.'

'But you won't – Keeley, promise me you won't try to influence her? She has to be free to—'

'Mary, she will be. She'll be free as a bird. Meanwhile, I suggest you ring Luc and ask him if he has any recipes for bacon and cabbage.'

Luc. Mary's heart pirouetted with pleasure, and pride. At last, she was going to set up her own kitchen, and he was going to be her first guest. If Mel would agree to some mutually satisfactory arrangement, that was, and if Cathal Sullivan didn't find some way of scuppering the whole inspired, wonderful plan.

But whether he did or not, he would never scupper her friendship with Keeley Butler. He never had yet, and he never would. Getting up, she went to the wine rack housed in a brick cavity in the wall, and took out a bottle of champagne. Keeley eyed it askance.

'Are we drinking to our new venture already, at ten o'clock in the morning?'

'You can drink champagne at any time. But no, Keel, it's too soon to toast that. We're drinking to each other. That's all. Just to you and me, to us, to lifelong friendship.'

'Oh. But the champagne isn't chilled.'

'Well, I won't tell anyone if you don't, that we served it the bog-ignorant way this once.'

Keeley laughed as the cork shot across the room upon Mary's words, and a stream of froth fizzed all over the table between them. Mary watched her laugh, listened to the old Keeley in it, and locked the memory away as one of the most bittersweet, satisfying moments of her life. Their joint, entwined life, in spite of the distances and differences between them, in spite of the taut divergent emotions that she knew were still to be negotiated. Like an old rosebush their friendship had been battered by many storms, yet it was still growing, still blossoming.

Chapter Fifteen

Mary's spirits seemed to rise with the plane as it took off from Nice for Dublin, higher than Keeley had seen them for longer than she could remember, but she knew her friend. After a little while they would level off, and by the time the plane began its descent Mary would, she thought, be descending with it.

At first, Mary was all talk, could not stop talking, about the vegetables she would grow herself in Keeley's garden. It was a huge garden, sunny and sheltered, everything would thrive in it. What about the plot of unused lawn at the side, how would Keeley feel about filling that with herbs, lettuces, courgettes, runner beans climbing up their bamboo supports, bell peppers, maybe, under cloches . . . ? She'd have to find out about the micro-climate, she supposed, nutrients and feeds and whatnot, but if Keeley didn't mind giving over the space she would plant every inch of it, grow everything organically, learn all there was to be learned about market gardening.

Keeley smiled and nodded, but her mind was far removed from the project she had conceived to help her friend, to give her some means of staying where she wanted to be, doing what she wanted to do and earning a living independent of Cathal Sullivan. If Mary would commit herself to it, the details would sort themselves out, but she wondered whether Mary was really committed, or merely euphoric. The prospect of escape from Cathal was one thing, a wonderful thing to judge by Mary's flushed, radiant look; the prospect of meeting him, and telling him, was something else again.

All her life Mary had talked about leaving, about escaping. But Keeley knew the bonds of marriage, knew how tightly they bound, how deep they went after fifteen years. Mary would be like a prisoner released from incarceration, she thought, dizzy with delight at first but then disorientated, nervous, unsure of her place in the scary outside world. As she was unsure of her own, lost and terrified for all her talk of studies and pubs and things that were, in effect, no more than occupational therapy. Time and time again, her mind flew to Vincent, groped and ached for him, fell into the endless void of his loss. What was the point of any of it, without him, what was really the point of this dismal flight to Dublin?

As she thought of her mother she knew she should feel happy, feel something about their reunion, their first sight of each other after all these years. Instead she felt leaden, her mind dropping down through the gears until it was in neutral, idling, wondering where they were going. Gertie could have come to France, could have brought Tony to live with them long ago, when she and Vincent were a carefree couple; but Gertie had steadfastly refused, chosen to stay with Christy and devote herself to an existence that was little short of martyrdom. Not a single joy had she ever had, that Keeley knew of, not one heady moment of success or thanks or even acknowledgement from her indifferent husband or self-absorbed son. Reading between the lines of occasional, intermittent letters, Keeley got the impression that maybe Tony was grateful to Gertie in some unformed, unspoken way; but he was unable to express it, not because of his condition but because of his conditioning, the macho climate that Christy had created from the start. Real men didn't say 'thank you' to anyone, least of all their mothers or wives or whoever took care of them.

Keeley wondered whether either man had ever even given Gertie a present, for Christmas or birthdays or any reason at all, but if they had Gertie had never mentioned it. What must life be like, with no presents, no thanks, no love, no outings, no fun at all? Many people would feel sorry for Gertie, if they knew of her miserable drudgery, but Keeley felt a sudden surge of anger, a longing to seize her mother and shake her, make her insist on the fact of her own existence. Why wouldn't Gertie ever *say* something, *do* something, for herself? Why were she and Mary so alike in that respect, still apparently convinced that any man was better than none? At least Mary was young enough that she could yet save herself, and even seemed intent on it at this moment; but Gertie, she felt, was a lost cause. She had chosen to marry Christy, chosen to stay, accepted her lot as if she deserved no better. Now, Keeley thought, maybe she couldn't even conceive of anything better. The thought was infuriating and deadening all at once, but if it was accurate it was, once again, Gertie's choice. Again she would ask Gertie to come and live with her in France, and again, she felt sure, Gertie would refuse.

Keeley's bags were full of presents, but even those would be accepted with little comment, apart from the inevitable 'Oh, you shouldn't have.' Clothes unworn, make-up unused, chocolates gazed at anxiously, uneasily, because they were foreign. To Gertie, Keeley lived on another planet, a businesswoman who had become more alien as she became more successful, an incomprehensible stranger. Christy, she knew, would try to do her for money, but the bastard could try till he turned black in the face; neither his barman nor his bookie was getting a penny out of her. Thank God she had enough money that she had been able to book into a decent hotel, and would not have to sleep one night under his roof.

Mary was booked into the hotel too, but Keeley glanced at her, wondering whether she would stay in it, or be lured home by Cathal. Cathal, using Mel as bait, enticing her back into his clutches. Mary had bursts of resilience, but she also had bouts of extreme self-doubt, the twin torments of guilt and duty that had haunted her all her life. But they were very real to her, and Keeley could understand them, because Mel was only a child. A child, that cruellest and most effective of weapons.

As the plane began its descent somewhere west of London, Keeley felt suddenly exhausted, and realised that Mary too had fallen silent. For ten or even fifteen minutes they sat together, thinking but not speaking, until without warning the plane lurched, jolted them alert. Keeley felt as if she were in a plunging lift, her mind plummeting as her body fought gravity, fought for a grip. Automatically her hand tightened on the seat-rest, and she felt Mary's tighten on top of it, their knuckles whitening in unison.

A soothing voice came on, the pilot over the intercom, apologising for a little turbulence. Just a local storm, nothing to worry about, he promised, as the seat-belt sign flickered on. But everyone felt tension in the aircraft, and fell extraordinarily quiet.

The plane dropped again, a horrible sickening drop that made both women gasp. Glancing at each other, they exchanged reassuring smiles, but Keeley saw that Mary was petrified.

Oh, fuck it, she thought, what does it matter? Who'll cry over us, who'll really miss us if this bloody plane crashes, if we're both killed stone dead? Vincent is already dead, and what's the point without him? Not a lot, that I can see.

Except that he'd kill me for thinking that. He'd wring my neck and say I was going to pieces, he'd be furious with me, and disgusted. Oh, God, why didn't I have his child? Then I'd have something to live for – why didn't I, why have I nothing to hold on to now? Mary hasn't got much, but she has that much.

Mary sat poker-stiff, barely daring to breathe, her thoughts parallel to Keeley's but entirely different.

I don't want to die, she thought. Not this time. I have a daughter and I have a life, whatever it turns out to be. Don't let it be ripped away from me, not now when I'm only just conceiving it. I'm fighting for it and I want it. I won't let go, I will not *let* this plane crash.

Turning to Keeley, she gripped her hand tighter, and etched a smile across her face as the plane bucked and pitched.

'Come on, Keel. Nothing to be scared of, they said there wasn't. We're nearly there.'

Nearly where, Keeley wondered, where the hell am I going, why, for what? But she forced herself to smile back, to accept Mary's reassurance and draw comfort from it, thinking of that first ferry journey when the ship, also, had rolled and pitched and seemed certain to sink. She'd been the mad optimist then, the voice of cheer and comfort – and now, it seemed, Mary was taking turns with her.

Taking her turn at last, after all this time. Well, she thought with the ghost of a smile, better late than never. Better late than bloody never.

Tottering off the plane when it finally landed, they fell weak-kneed into a taxi and directed the driver to the – the what? Such was their residual panic, neither of them could remember the name of the hotel. But then it came to Mary.

'The Westbury,' she said firmly, clearly.

As the car whizzed down a motorway that Keeley didn't know existed and began to weave its way through city centre traffic, Mary's colour began to return, even heighten with nervous anticipation. Cathal had been livid when told about the Westbury, but she was glad Keeley had insisted on it. It was not his turf, he would have less power over her there, whatever it was he might be going to say to her.

But Keeley sat listless, gazing out at a city she barely recognised, apart from the litter that had been the first thing
to catch Vincent's eye. Plastic bags still flew from the trees,
the streets were still full of cans and cartons, but there were
so many new buildings she hardly knew where she was, felt
completely disorientated. When she left her native city it had
been fondly called 'dear old dirty Dublin', but now there seemed
to be nothing old about it. It was full of spiky-haired kids in
leather jackets, bikers in black lycra, 24-hour supermarkets and
an unholy mess of traffic. The six-mile trip to the hotel took
nearly an hour, and she felt drained, bone-weary by the end of
it. But Mary jumped out of the taxi, paid the driver and marched
her into the hotel. For someone who had never checked into a
hotel before in her life, she did it with remarkable efficiency,
and grinned as the porter took their bags. 'Gin,' she said briskly
when they reached their room, and whipped open the door of
the mini-bar. Seconds later, a glass was thrust into Keeley's
hand. 'Here. A double. Knock it back and you'll be oxo.'

Obediently Keeley knocked it back, her colour returning as
she recalled some joke she had once heard about Japanese
Airlines: 'We hope you enjoyed your fright and will fry again
with us soon.' Giddily, she began to laugh, and Mary laughed
with her.

'Ha. Politically incorrect, that's what those jokes are called
now – go on Keel, have a fag, I can see you're gumming
for one.'

Keeley's hand was still shaking as she lit up, but gradually
she did begin to feel better. A hot bath, she thought longingly,
and then sadly, *with a million bubbles in it.*

Mary was unpacking already, all their suitcases, hanging up
clothes and stashing the gifts for their families, whistling at the
luxury of the room.

'If the restaurant's half as good, we're in hog heaven – hey,
pour us another drink, Keel, and turn on the telly, let's see
what's happening.'

Keeley poured, and stabbed at the state-of-the-art television
controls until she finally managed to turn it on. A daytime
re-run of a chat show leapt into life, and she gaped at it
astonished: Gay Byrne chairing a Late Late discussion of the
now imminent divorce referendum. After fifteen years out of
Ireland, if was as if she had barely been away for fifteen
minutes.

'But Mary – my God, they can't *still* be talking about it! I mean, I'd heard Ireland had changed so much—?'

'It has changed, Keel. A lot. On the surface.'

With the weirdest sensation of walking into a time-warp, Keeley sank onto a chair and gazed at Gay, greyer and thinner now, but still hosting the longest-running talk show in the world.

They debated their strategy at length, and eventually agreed on it. While Keeley went to visit Gertie, Tony and the Christy there was no escaping, Mary would tackle Cathal, here at the hotel over dinner. Calmly and clearly – she hoped – she would explain to him that she was going to stay in France, open a pub in partnership with Keeley, and that it was her eventual intention to bring Mel to live there with her. Not immediately, because Mel had her schooling to complete, but she could come for the holidays and then, when she was old enough, come permanently.

That was the plan, and Mary skittered around it like a nervous showjumper as Keeley coached her over all the obstacles.

'What'll you say to Cathal when he explodes?'

'I'll say my mind is made up, so he may as well get used to the idea gracefully.'

Screwing her earrings into place in front of the mirror, Mary sounded firm but looked, Keeley thought, like a schoolgirl rehearsing her lines for the Christmas pantomime – fervent, but fearful, almost frantic.

'And when he says he bloody well won't, that you're not doing it and he's not having it?'

'I'll tell him he has a choice: let me go or I'll send those photographs to every newspaper in the country.'

'So you'll admit you stole them yourself, and the money?'

'Yes. I was afraid to tell him at the time, but I'm not afraid any more.'

'Are you sure, Mary? Are you absolutely sure you won't let him shout and scare you, threaten dire retribution on Mel?'

'I – yes, Keeley. I am sure. If he even mentions her in any threatening way, I'll take out the photos and wave them around the restaurant.'

'What if he won't agree to meet you there? What if he insists you come to the house?'

'I'll simply refuse. I'm not going near our house until this is settled, and then I'll only go to talk to Mel.'

'And what if Mel says no? Come home, Mum, I don't want you to go and live in France?'

'Th – then I'm in trouble, Keel. But let's start with Cathal and clear that hurdle first.'

'OK. Are you sure you don't want me with you?'

'No. It's my marriage, Keel, and I have to end it. All by myself.'

'All right. Then pick up the phone now, and call him. Let me hear you say to him what you've said to me.'

Mary's hand was surprisingly steady as she reached for the phone and dialled the number, and Keeley stood watching, holding Mary's gaze, holding her breath. Planning it was one thing, but doing it was another.

The ringing phone was answered almost immediately, as if Cathal had been waiting to pounce. But then he knew Mary was arriving in Dublin today, would have come to claim her at the airport if he had been given any information. But Mary had not even told him which hotel she was staying at, yet.

'Cathal?' Mary's voice was soft, holding steady. 'It's me. I'm home.'

Keeley couldn't hear the reply until Mary held the phone out to her, and they listened together to Cathal saying how some bloody hotel wasn't home, home was here in Forest Crescent and she was to come straight away.

'No, Cathal. Not yet. I want to meet you first, on neutral ground. I'd like to have dinner with you tonight.'

He expostulated furiously, and the irony of it struck them both: dinner together at last, in a proper restaurant. He sounded as if he was choking already, refusing to have any truck with such a scheme.

Mary drew a deep breath. 'Well, I'm afraid it's that or nothing, Cathal. You can either see me here, or not at all.'

There was a short sharp silence. And then they heard him calling Mel, telling her that her mother was in Dublin, in some hotel, refusing to come home. Would Imelda please get on the line and talk sense to her?

Mel came on, sounding puzzled. 'Hi, Ma! What are you doing? Dad says you—'

'Mel, listen. I can't come home. Not yet. I have to talk to your father first. Don't worry, I'll see you tomorrow, we're going to have a long talk.'

'But why can't you come now? Ma, you've been away for ages! I want you to come home!'

Mary's grip tightened on the receiver, and she glanced at Keeley. 'Mel, I promise you I will. But only after I talk to Cathal, here at the hotel, tonight. It's grown-up stuff, Mel. I'm sorry, but this is the way I've got to do it.'

There was some muffled conversation that they couldn't hear, and then Cathal came back on, gruff and irritable.

'All right. Have it your own way. Tell me where the hell you are and I'll meet you at eight.'

She gave him the details, and he hung up abruptly. But Mary didn't flinch, and Keeley saw that his anger had left her totally unmoved. As beginnings went, it was the best they could have hoped for.

Mary wanted another drink as she dressed to meet Cathal, but Keeley said no. This encounter was best handled stone cold sober, with all Mary's wits about her. As she said it she saw that Mary was getting nervous again, edgy despite her resolve.

'No Dutch courage, Mary. Just courage. Have you got the photographs?'

'Yes. They're in my bag. Oh, Jesus, Keel—'

'Mary! Just *do* it!'

Mary gulped. 'Yes. All right, Keel, I will. I'll do it.'

But Keeley was icily sober now as well, pasting make-up onto her face with a kind of contained fury as she braced herself to meet her own demons. There was a phone at last in Pearse Gardens, but there was no question of Gertie or any of them coming to the Westbury. Keeley knew that she would have to go to them, and had rung to say she would be there at eight.

It was Mary's turn to look encouraging. 'Don't worry, Keel. He won't hit you this time.'

She stiffened visibly. 'I know he won't, Mary. My only worry is how I'm going to stop myself from hitting him.'

Mary thought she would hardly blame her if she did. Christy had not even rung or written to sympathise when Vincent died. But Christy Butler, she thought, must be a spent force by now. Just a little oul fella who didn't matter any more, had no clout literally or otherwise. He wasn't worth the time of day, much less getting into a stew over.

Keeley, when she finished her toilette, looked rather intimidating. As small as ever, but raised up on high heels, squared off somehow in a tailored jacket and crisp dark skirt, hair slicked back and face masked in cosmetics.

'How do I look?'

'Fearsome.'

'Good.'

Bending over the bed where Mary was sitting, she squeezed her shoulder, tightly.

'OK. I'm off to see the wizard . . . I'll take a taxi and be back by midnight. And when I get here, I don't want to hear any sob stories or excuses, have you got that? I want to hear that the separation is amicable, if possible, and final, regardless.'

'Yes. I've got that.' Mary nodded resolutely, like an understudy being pushed on stage, and Keeley smiled at her, grimly.

It was a large, restful restaurant called the Russell Room, bathed in soft light and music, decked with flowers and candles. Despite her anxiety, Mary was conscious of the many factors designed to soothe as the waiter seated her at a corner table. On principle it seemed, Cathal was late.

Steeling herself, she declined the offer of a drink, and was unable to focus on the menu when it was handed to her, her mind a million miles from food for once. Part of her willed Cathal to arrive and get it over with, part of her wished that none of this was happening, had to happen. How, why had it all come to this, her marriage dissolving and ending in this lovely romantic restaurant?

Because I never got my own restaurant, she reminded herself, hearing Keeley's voice in her head. I got hope, and then nothing else. Nothing at all, no love, no respect, no freedom . . . only a home for my child . . . and a baby who died . . . oh, God, was it all my fault? Some of it must have been . . .

He came blustering in, greeting the maitre d' like a long-lost friend, and was ushered to her table. As he bent to kiss her ceremonially, she smelled whiskey, thickly disguised with mouthwash and aftershave.

Suddenly revolted, she was glad their table was a remote one, and that she was facing the wall. Wretchedly, she noted the reflection of a Christmas tree in the window, and at that moment the waiter came to pull the curtains shut. Heavily, Cathal seated himself.

'Mary.' His tone was conciliatory, even sociable. 'How are you? It's great to see you back. We've been worried about you, Imelda and I—'

She raised her hand. 'Cathal. Please don't bring Imelda into any of what we're going to discuss tonight. This is strictly between you and me.'

He blinked, looked injured. 'But she's our daughter—'

'No. She's my daughter.'

That wasn't fair, she knew, and this time his air of injury was not feigned. But how often had he hurt her? She thought of having to ask Bill the head barman for petty cash, for pocket money like a child. As the sommelier arrived with the wine list, she intercepted it between the two men, and flicked it open without glancing at either of them. Running her eye swiftly down the French burgundies, she selected and ordered the most expensive one on offer.

'But we haven't even decided what to eat yet—'

'Never mind. I feel like starting with that one.'

In fact she had no intention of drinking more than a mouthful, since Keeley had so sensibly warned her against it, but she was suddenly determined to run up as big a bill as possible. An enormous bill, that he would have to pay. Pleasantly, she ran her eye over his ruddy, well-padded face, noting a small broken vein, a first touch of grey at his temples.

'You're looking well.'

He frowned, but he was facing the room, and it turned into a kind of grimace.

'H'mph. I can't imagine why I would be, because you've had me worried sick. Nearly four months, Mary! For God's sake, why did you do it? How could you stay away so long, with Imelda to consider?'

'Cathal, I spoke to her every day on the phone. She knew I had Keeley to look after, when Vincent died, and some thinking to do.'

He glanced away, over her shoulder, and she saw that Vincent's death was the last thing he wanted to talk about.

'And have you?' His tone was confrontational.

'Have I thought? Yes. I have.'

Without further elaboration, she picked up her menu and studied it. Let him work at this. Smiling vaguely, she pondered her choices. Some cornets of smoked salmon to start, perhaps, stuffed with fresh crabmeat on a cranberry cream? Or canteloupe melon on parma ham, drizzled with amaretto? Dublin Bay prawn bisque?

He eyed her irritably. 'Well then, what do you want?'

She sighed, and thought about it, and smiled up at the waiter who came with impeccable timing.

'I'd like the bisque, please.'

He ordered the same, brusquely, knowing she was deliberately misunderstanding him. But he did not repeat the question until the waiter was out of earshot.

'All right, Mary. Out with it. I thought we'd already discussed your terms, and agreed them. But it seems I was mistaken. What is it you really want?'

She looked at him frankly. 'I want a divorce, Cathal.'

He sat back, his expression triumphant. 'Mary, there is none. Not in Ireland. As you'd say yourself, it's not on the menu.'

'No. Not yet. That's why I'll have to settle for a separation, until divorce is legalised. I don't think it'll be much longer, do you?'

'Don't be ridiculous. There'll never be divorce in this country. Anyway, what about Imelda – your daughter, as you so helpfully remind me?'

'I told you, leave her out of it. When we've resolved our situation, we'll discuss hers. Not before.'

His nostrils seemed to narrow and tighten as he bent his head abruptly over the menu and then, after no more than ten seconds, clicked his fingers imperiously. Looking startled and not impressed, the waiter came over.

'I've changed my mind. I'll have a prawn cocktail to start, and then the fillet steak, well done, with roast potatoes.'

Wincing, she looked away from him, as far around her as her line of vision would allow. To her right she could see a party of four, well-dressed business people out for what she supposed was a celebratory meal, all four of their mobile phones poised ready for action on the table. Mentally, she made a rule for her pub in Provençe: mobile phones would be banned, business conducted in places of business at times of business.

Further away another couple, also smartly dressed and in their thirties, sat reading their menus in silence. With a small shock she realised that they looked not unlike Cathal and herself – prosperous, glossy, out for a nice relaxing evening. Ireland was renowned for fun in the evenings, for the *craic*, but as she watched the man wade into his first drink, she wondered: why did people drink so much, so constantly, as if they were trying to obliterate something? Was this couple also hiding from the reality of a failed marriage? Or from debt, putting on a show of prosperity? From some unsustainable illusion, an image they had created? Somehow, it was not the impression she got in France, when she watched people eating out in a way that said they had been used to it for centuries, but here she felt a self-consciousness, a kind of brittle bravado that made her feel as if she were not in Europe but in America. Although Ireland's history was very old, it was a young republic, uncertain whether to embrace the old or the new – but leaning more, she thought, to the latter. Television was Americanised, slang impressions were imported from California, fast food flourished, there was as yet little sense of security, dignity or real confidence. The shiny, plastic new Ireland was impressive, in material terms, and a sight better than the drab, po-faced island of previous years, but she was reinforced in her conviction that it was not what she wanted. Whatever Cathal threw at her tonight she was going to refute it, leave him, finish it and have her pub in Provence.

He cleared his throat and started again. 'So where were we?'

'We were talking about separating.'

He grinned at her. 'Separating. After fifteen years, with a pub to run and a child to rear? Mary, don't be pathetic.'

'Call it what you like. But Cathal, I've been thinking, working it out for four months, and I have made my decision. I am not coming back to you.'

He all but laughed aloud. 'But sure what would you do? You have no money, no education worth talking about, you're too old to get a job, your daughter is here with me—'

'I'm going to open a pub of my own.'

This time he did laugh, so loudly that the business group turned slightly in his direction.

'A – what – of your own?! Well, now! Have you been raiding banks at gunpoint or what?'

'Keeley is going to invest in it.'

His face darkened instantly. 'Ah. Of course. Little Miss Butler strikes again. Well, let me tell you, Mary—'

'No. Let me tell you, Cathal. Keeley is a very wealthy woman, and she is going to buy the premises. I am going to cook in it, and we have a list of companies who, we expect, will be interested in investing in it. Very interested.'

'Right. And a flying pig landed at Dublin airport this evening.'

'It makes no difference to me whether you believe it or not. I'm going to do it. I don't care whether we formalise our separation or not, because I want nothing from you. I can, and will, support myself.'

He looked around him, to check whether anyone was listening, and waited while the waiter removed their starter plates. The bisque, Mary noted, had been very good.

'But – but you can't just flit off to France! You are *married* to me!'

She sat back from him. 'Cathal, I'm married to a transvestite.' His eyes darted in all directions, although her voice was low, and he put his hand on hers.

'Mary – I told you, it was only a party, fancy dress – I thought we'd agreed – you can have your £300 a week—'

'I'm sorry, Cathal. But things have changed. Everything did, when I went back to Aix, when Keeley was widowed. It's too late.'

His grip tightened on her fingers. 'No. It's not too late. There's the family to consider. My parents, your parents—'

'Have nothing to do with it. I've pleased them for years, done what they wanted and you wanted, and now I'm going to do what I want.'

His steak had arrived, but he did not touch it, did not even take up his cutlery. Releasing his grip, she sliced into her sole, and savoured the flavour of windswept ocean that flowed from it.

'Mm. This is excellent, Cathal. I wish you'd taken me to a few nice restaurants like this before. It might have helped us, apart from helping my skills in your pub.'

'For God's sake, nobody in their right mind would eat Dover sole at The Lantern.'

'How do you know? You're probably right, but how do you know for sure? H'm? How exactly do you know, Cathal?'

His voice rose a fraction. 'Because it's far from Dover bloody sole they were reared!'

'Well, it's far from Dover sole I was reared too, but I must say I'm enjoying this.'

She cut another piece, and he glared at her.

'Stop throwing red herrings into it, Mary. The fact is that you are my wife and Imelda's mother. End of story.'

She looked up at him. 'Story, did you say? Funny. I was just thinking what a story it would be, if the newspapers ever got hold of those photographs. The ones of the councillor's son and the judge and the political bigshot in their party frocks.'

He whitened to the colour of the fish. 'You bitch. You have them, haven't you? It was you all the time.'

'Yes. It was me, Cathal.'

'I knew it. You thieving, deceitful—'

He jumped as the waiter materialised at his elbow. 'Everything to your satisfaction, sir? Madam?'

'Yes, yes, everything is fine.' Defiantly, he glanced at his untouched food, and the waiter melted away with the faintest of smiles.

'So. All right. You've got the photos. But I have your daughter, Mary.'

Crunch. This was it. She took a breath, and thought of Keeley.

'Yes. You've been a good father to her, Cathal. I'll give you that. And, since I have no wish to disrupt her life, I am going to give her the choice of staying with you, if you and she both want her to.'

He leaned across the table at her, and hissed into her face. 'By God, Imelda will stay with me! I'll see to that, don't you worry!'

She forced herself to sound calm. 'How will you see to it, Cathal?'

'Because I'm the one who pays the bills! You don't really think she'd leave her comfortable home and her expensive school and her fancy friends and her skiing holidays just to go mooching off to some backwater with you, do you?'

'No. I don't think she would, and I don't expect her to. In fact, I want her to stay here, until she's got her exams and is old enough to make her own adult decisions. But I'm going to see her tomorrow, Cathal, and talk to her. I think she sees things in a slightly different light since – since Vincent died.'

'She had nothing to do with it! That man was killed by some lunatic on a motorbike!'

'I didn't say she had, although we could debate it. But I didn't ask you here to debate it. I'm simply telling you that I am going to talk to her, and offer her the option of coming to France whenever she wants to.'

She was more shocked than surprised when he leaped to his feet, knocking over both their glasses of wine, and thumped the table with the flat of his hand regardless of the sudden hush around him.

'Imelda will not go to you, to France! By God, Mary, I'll see to that! I'm going home to see to that right now!'

He started away across the restaurant, but whirled back to her and thrust his face almost into her plate.

'Oh, and the bill, Mary – you can tell the waiter you'll be paying it your fucking self.'

He assumed she had no money, she supposed, and intended to humiliate her, leave Keeley to pick up the tab. But she simply smiled at him.

'Of course, Cathal. It's a pleasure to treat you, especially with your own money. The £20,000 I stole from you, because you never gave me a penny in my life.'

She said it loudly and clearly, and he snorted like a bull as he strode away from her, followed by the fascinated gaze of every diner in the entire restaurant.

'Number seventeen, Forest Crescent, please.'

The taxi driver nodded and turned the car, and Keeley sat into the back of it, wondering how surprised he might be when she asked him to wait there for her and then drive her on to number 28 Pearse Gardens. She looked, she knew, more like a resident of the former than the latter, and more like a resident of the Westbury than either.

For over twenty minutes they drove through dark but lively streets, filled with kids heading for the pubs and the night's quota of booze, pool games and giant-screen *craic*. The route was unfamiliar to her, she felt like a tourist, but her only interest in it was that it should be speedy. At this minute Cathal was out to dinner with Mary, in the very hotel she was leaving, but God knew how long that might last.

Number seventeen, Forest Crescent, when they reached it, was a uniform house in a uniform row of them, separated from its neighbours by approximately twenty inches on either side, blue-painted, net-curtained, a light glowing in the porch. Asking the driver to wait, Keeley jumped out and went in, rang the bell briefly but briskly.

After a pause an interior light was turned on, and Keeley braced herself as she saw the outline of what looked like an elderly woman appearing in the hall. Not old, but someone around sixty, taking her time and walking cautiously.

There was a click of locks, and the door opened on the safety chain.

Gritting her teeth, Keeley smiled. 'Hello, Mrs Jameson.'

Leesha's hand flew to her chest. 'K – Keeley Butler! Good God! What in the name of heaven are you doing here?'

'I'd like to see Mel, please.'

'Mel?'

'Imelda. My god-daughter. I assume you're minding her while Cathal is out?'

Leesha looked as if she'd opened the door to a hooded thug, and went to close it. In the nick of time, Keeley shoved her foot into the gap.

'Please. It won't take long. I just need to speak to her for a few moments.'

'I – I don't care what you need. You're not welcome here.'

'I can see that. But it's important.'

'Maybe it is to you. Not to me, or to my granddaughter. Please take your foot out of this door before I—'

There was the sound of another door opening within, and Mel's face peered around it. 'Nana, who is it, what—?'

Keeley stood on tiptoe and waved furiously. 'Mel, it's me, Keeley! I want to see you! Please let me in!'

Mel came out into the hall, looking bewildered and a little nervous as she approached her grandmother, blinking to ascertain that the woman on the doorstep really was Keeley.

'Nana – it is Keeley, let her in!'

Grudgingly, the safety chain was released, the door swung open, and she was admitted. Smoothing her hair, she grinned at Leesha.

'Thanks very much, Mrs Jameson. Don't worry, I haven't come to kidnap her or deliver drugs or anything. I'd love a cup of tea though, if you're putting on the kettle.'

Muttering, Leesha backed off, glancing sidelong at Mel as she tried to decide what to do.

'Very well. Since Imelda is agreeable, you can have five minutes with her. What you mean by turning up here like this is beyond me – at night, with no warning. Of course the Butlers never did have a telephone, did they.'

Ignoring that, Keeley stood resolute, watching until her back disappeared into the kitchen and Mel took her by the arm, led her into a sitting room where another teenage girl was watching television.

'Jane, this is my godmother Keeley Tourand, she's come from France.'

Greetings were exchanged, and then Mel nudged her friend. 'Give Nana a hand in the kitchen, will you Jane, she's making us a cup of tea.'

Openly wondering, Jane went, and Keeley hugged Mel to her.

'Let me look at you, Mel! How have you been?'

In fact Mel looked very well, in designer jeans and a pink sweatshirt, expensive white trainers that made her appear even taller than she was. But she also looked apprehensive.

'I – I've been fine. How have *you* been?'

Keeley took the indicated seat on the sofa and looked at her frankly.

'I've been surviving, Mel. That's all I can honestly say. Surviving, and working at getting better.'

'It – it must be hard for you. Keeley, I – you – you never let me say I was sorry, but I am. I truly am. Vincent was lovely, he was so good to me, he – I—'

'Yes. I know. But Mel, that's not what I've come to talk about.'

Puzzled, Mel also sat down. 'What have you come about? And where's Mum?'

'She's having dinner with your father. They're discussing something. Something that involves you.'

Mel looked alarmed. 'Me?'

'Yes. You. But it's nothing for you to worry about. She'll be here tomorrow to explain it to you herself. The reason I'm here is – well, look, Mel, I'm not going to beat around the bush, because your grandmother doesn't like me and I suspect she's going to throw me out the first chance she gets. So will you do me a favour and just listen to me now, for two minutes?'

'Y – yes, of course I will.'

'OK. Well, the situation is, your mother is going to have a long talk with you tomorrow, and she's going to ask you a question. A hard question, that involves making a choice.'

'A choice of what?'

'She'll tell you what. The answer will be up to you, and I'm not going to try to influence what you decide. The only reason I'm here is to ask you whether, when you're making your mind up, you'll do me a favour?'

A favour. She saw that Mel was delighted to get the chance

to do her one, to do anything that might absolve in any small way her terrible guilt about Vincent's death.

'Sure I will. What is it?'

'Will you think about your mother, as well as yourself, before you decide?'

'I don't understand.'

Keeley leaned forward to her, her hands clasped on her lap as if trying to contain her conflicting emotions. She was still finding it very difficult to decide how she felt about Mel.

'Well, when you took my car keys that night, Mel, you were only thinking about one person, right? You were thinking about yourself, about what you wanted.'

'Y – yeah. I was.'

'OK. This time, I want you to think about other people, about the consequences of what you're doing. And saying, when Mary talks to you. I want you to try to think of her not only as your mother, but as a person, a human being who has needs and feelings just as you have. She's in a tricky position, and you could help her a lot if you wanted to. If you made up your mind to.'

'But what does she want?'

'You'll find out, from her. All I'm asking is that you give her a fair hearing, and consider what might happen to her if you don't, if you make up your mind too fast, or exclusively in your own favour.'

Mel frowned uneasily, with a hint of the pout Keeley recognised.

'She's going to ask me to do something awful, isn't she?'

'Not at all. In fact, it might be something you'll enjoy. The point is, I want you to be open to it, to her – not shutting the door in her face the way your grandmother tried to shut it in mine, literally, just now. I want you to listen and think and try, for once, to give her a break. That's all. Will you do that for me?'

The door opened, and Leesha came in with a tray, followed by Jane carrying a plate of biscuits. Reluctantly, Leesha put the tray down on the coffee table, and faced Keeley even more reluctantly. But Keeley stood up.

'Thanks, Mrs Jameson, but I won't stay to sample your delightful hospitality. I have another call to make. Mel, will you see me to the door?'

Mel got up and followed her as she walked into the hall.

And then, to Keeley's surprise and pleasure, she threw her arms around her.

'Th – thanks for warning me, Keeley. I will try to think this time, before I do anything rash.'

Keeley beamed from ear to ear. 'That's great. That's all I wanted to ask of you. It's not too much, is it?'

'No. No, it isn't. I'm still not sure what you're talking about, but I'll hear Ma out when she explains it tomorrow – Keeley, she is coming home tomorrow, isn't she?'

Gently, Keeley kissed the girl's perfumed cheek.

'Yes, Mel. She is coming tomorrow. She's dying to see you. She loves you, you know – in fact, she loves you much more than you know.'

Slinging her bag over her shoulder, she sprinted out, down the drive to the taxi, and her next social call, on Christy Butler.

It seemed impossible that the house had not changed at all in fifteen years, but if it had the changes were not visible to the naked eye. The gate still swung off its hinges, weeds and nettles perforated the lawn even in winter, and the window frames flaked with rust and grime over dented, lopsided venetian blinds. As she walked up to the door, Keeley found her fists clenching of their own accord.

It opened, and her mother Gertie stood looking at her; small and round as a pincushion, her face a net of wrinkles, her hair not yet completely grey but not dark or shiny either, pulled back into a kind of bun. But her eyes lit up with what appeared to be genuine pleasure as she beheld the daughter she had not seen since Keeley was a teenager, and gathered her into an uncertain embrace.

'Keeley. Our Keeley. We've been waiting for you . . . come in, come in.'

Keeley hugged her in turn, and they exchanged a long look before Gertie pulled away, and called into the depths of the house.

'Tony, Daddy! She's here, she's here!'

Daddy? Had Gertie always called her husband that? Keeley found that she couldn't remember, and wondered at the irony of it. But she would call him Christy, not Daddy, or Dad, or anything paternal.

Smiling at her mother, holding onto her arm, she let herself be led into the front room: and there sat Christy, solid and squat in his armchair, gazing at a larger, louder television than she remembered. The volume was deafening, but he made no attempt to turn it down. Further back, in the corner, Tony sat beaming in his wheelchair.

She went to him first, with a pang of pleasure as he reached out to her with his eyes, and kissed him on both cheeks. They felt like tissue paper, thin and dry, the skin of a thirty-seven year old man who got no exercise and, she thought, little fresh air. But she felt joy in him nonetheless, vibrant gladness to see her, and hunkered down beside him, her eyes level with his as she put her hand on his sleeve.

'How are you, Tony? How have you been?'

'Game ball,' he replied with a twinkle, and she laughed. His state of mind was anyone's guess, but despite his immobility he seemed the brightest, the most animated of the three.

Patting his hand, she stood up and turned to her father.

'Hello, Christy.'

'Howya,' he replied, not taking his eyes from the screen.

Fleetingly, she thought of putting her foot through it. Instead she sat down on the sofa where Gertie indicated, feeling a dislocated spring poke at her through its fabric. Maternally, Gertie began to bustle.

'Give me your coat, love, and I'll pop out to the kitchen, make a cup of tea. Christy, turn down that telly, there's a good man.'

It dawned on Keeley that Gertie really must be pleased to see her, that she would actually ask Christy to do something he clearly didn't want to do. Grudgingly, he flicked the remote control at it, and turned the volume down a fraction. But he went on watching it.

'Great programme, this,' he said. Forced to look at it, she saw two priests, one older and greasy, with a shambling look about him, the other younger, giggling into a mobile phone. Apparently it was a comedy, similar to one she had watched as a child, and she suppressed a grimace as she realised what a cliché it had been even then, the two Irish priests, battling the bottle and the women and each other. Any moment, she knew, an aproned housekeeper would appear, clucking over them.

Turning away, she edged closer to Tony.

'How's the painting going, Tony?'

It was going well enough, according to Alain Jou; Tony's paintings still sold steadily, although none had ever fully realised

the promise, he said, of the first. Tony only did ten or twelve a
year, but it was a remarkably regular output from someone, as
Alain put it, 'in his position.'

Tony smiled, a little wryly. 'Not bad, considering. I work in
the back room. I'll show you the masterpieces in progress after
you've had your tea. I sleep there, too – easier than having to
run upstairs to bed when I roll in from the disco.'

She grinned, wondering at the amount of work that Gertie
must have to do, wondering whether Christy ever helped lift
Tony in and out of his wheelchair . . . wondering, too, what
inspiration Tony could find in this house. Had he any friends,
did anyone ever take him out anywhere?

Gertie came in with the tea, and she watched as a child's
sealed plastic mug was put on Tony's lap, with a long tube
extruding from its spout. With practised ease, Gertie put the
tube into his mouth, and left him to sip from it. Keeley was
handed a cup and saucer, Christy was given a mug from which
he began to slurp noisily.

Only then did Gertie pour her own tea, and sit down on an
upright chair, looking at her daughter, taking in her hair and
clothes and make-up.

'You look well, love. It's great you could come and see us at
Christmas time – isn't it, Daddy?'

Christy grunted. Raising her voice over the television charac-
ters', Keeley addressed her mother and brother.

'It's great to see you. You've hardly changed at all.'

Nor had they; Gertie had greyed and put on some weight,
Tony was thin and gaunt, Christy looked somehow flattened
down, but they were all recognisable, only slightly blurred by
age. Again, she had the sensation of walking into a time warp,
of something permanently fixed.

Bending down, she put her tea aside and reached for the large
carrier bag she had brought in the taxi.

'I've brought you lots of presents. I hope you'll like them –
these are for Christmas, these are for now . . . here, Tony, will
I open this for you?'

Yes, he said eagerly, open it, Keeley. Removing the twirly
ribbon and chequered paper from a flat package, she took out
a book and held it up so he could see the cover.

'Vasarely.'

He squinted at it. 'Who?'

'Victor Vasarely. He was Hungarian, but he worked in Aix,

built an art foundation there . . . if you'd ever come over and visit me, I'd take you to see it. There are lots of his paintings up on the second floor, I think it's wheelchair-accessible.'

Tony gazed at the book, and then at her. 'Visit you?'

'Yes! I know it would be a bit tricky, but it isn't impossible. I've often told you in my letters that you—'

Gertie got up and began pouring more tea. 'It must be very hot over there, Keeley, I don't know how you stand it – but then everyone is off to the sun these days, the Lavins across the road are going to the Canaries for Christmas, I can't understand it at all. Imagine eating your turkey outside, in the sun! It wouldn't be the same at all, would it, Daddy?'

No answer. Embarrassed to see her mother ignored, Keeley reached again into the bag and handed her a blue parcel with silvery stars on it.

'Here, Ma, one for you too . . . if it doesn't fit you can always come over and change it!'

Cautiously, Gertie took the parcel, opened it and unfolded a blouse of azure silk.

'Ah, Keeley, you shouldn't have! This is much too good.'

Why, Ma, Keeley wondered? Why is it too good? Don't you deserve something nice? But even as she wondered, Gertie put down the blouse, folding it carefully without even holding it up to her, in a way that suggested it would stay folded for a long time.

'It's lovely. I'll keep it for Sunday best. For Christmas.'

'OK – this Christmas, I'll expect to see you wearing it! I was wondering about Christmas, actually – would you all like to come to the hotel where I'm staying and have lunch there? It would be a nice change for you, you wouldn't have to cook . . .'

Christy's head jerked up. 'No. We'll stay here and eat in our own home.'

It sounded like a command, and Keeley frowned at him, leaving his gift in the bag at her feet. He could rummage for it himself – would probably never wear the cashmere sweater anyway; she longed to knot its sleeves around his neck. But he couldn't dictate Christmas to her, to everyone.

'Why? What's wrong with a change of scenery for one year? It would save Mam a lot of work and hassle—'

'We'll stay here,' he replied firmly, 'same as always.'

She persisted. 'I think Mam should decide, since she's the one has to do the work.'

But Gertie shook her head. 'Ah no, love, your Dad is right, we'll be better off at home. You can come here, to us.'

For a moment Keeley thought Gertie was simply appeasing him, but then she saw something else: Gertie really didn't want to go to a hotel, was intimidated by the prospect. Reluctantly, she let it drop.

'All right.' What did it matter, without Vincent? Clearly they wanted to stay here, and she didn't care if she spent Christmas at the bottom of the ocean, on top of a mountain, eating rice with her hands in a mud hut. As yet, nobody had mentioned Vincent. But then she felt Tony looking keenly at her, and wondered if he was remembering him, thinking of the dead brother-in-law he had met only once, but whose encouragement had made such a difference to him. It was Vincent who had first seen the potential in those wild dark hospital daubs. And sure enough, Tony spoke up.

'Christmas is going to be rough for you, Keeley, without Vincent . . . how've you been since – since August?'

She hesitated. He had his own problems.

'I've been a bit down, naturally, but Mary's been a great help. She came over and she's been staying with me.'

Again he looked keenly at her. 'Has she? For long?'

'For four months. And now it looks as if she might be staying permanently. Her marriage is – is falling apart, frankly.'

He seemed to affirm something he knew already. 'No wonder, married to that Sullivan fellow. I'm surprised it's lasted as long as this. But tell us, Keel, have you got room for her? What's your house like?'

Surprised, she blinked. She had described it in a letter when she and Vincent built it.

'It's lovely . . . it's kind of like a farmhouse, only one storey, built of local stone, there's a gorgeous garden and we – I – have a couple of dogs. It's very peaceful, very relaxing . . . maybe even a bit too relaxing, now! I've sold my business, you know, I'm at home a lot at the moment.'

Tony couldn't move, but he looked as if he was trying to lean forward. 'How many bedrooms are there?'

'Four – why?'

'Just wondering.' He said no more, and Gertie took up the conversation, recounting all the local news as if Keeley still knew the neighbours, could still remember the Hickey girl and Jimmy Kavanagh who had the greyhound and poor

Maura Lynch whose husband had walked out on her one fine morning . . . eventually Christy's programme finished, and he got to his feet.

'I'm going out for a pint.'

Keeley rejoiced as he left the room, and the atmosphere relaxed immediately. But Gertie's litany continued: the Brannigans' stolen car and the O'Sheas' leaky roof, Madge Riordan's terrible arthritis, the Mackey boy who'd got five years for burglary . . . eventually, Tony interrupted.

'If you'll push me into the back room, Keel, I'll show you my paintings.'

She got up and turned him round, with the feeling that Gertie was watching Tony somehow possessively, making sure she didn't jolt the wheelchair or bump into anything. The chair only just fitted through the doorway, but she got it out eventually and into the adjoining room, where she remembered a table where she too used to paint, as a child on rainy days.

But the room was changed now, into a cross between a bedroom and a studio, with artist's materials everywhere, canvases stacked around the walls, an easel in the middle of the floor facing the window which looked out on the rubbish-filled garden. The easel looked odd, but then she realised why – it was lower than normal, so that Tony could reach it with the brush in his mouth.

Looking around her, she started to say something. But Tony cut her short, as if fearful that Gertie was following them, glancing anxiously at the door, and then imploringly, at her.

'Keeley, get me out!'

'What?' Bewildered, she thought he meant out of his wheelchair, that he wanted to get up somehow. His tone was beseeching.

'Out! Out of here, before I lose my mind as well as everything else!'

His eyes met hers, dark, intense.

'But I – what do you mean, Tony?'

'I mean I'm going mad! Keeley, you can't imagine what it's like, it's like a prison, the two of them – Ma does her best for me, does everything, but I'm going round the bend! I want to – I have to – Keeley, will you take me to France? Take me to your house and let me live with you? I earn money you know, I could—'

She all but collapsed onto the bed. 'But Tony, I told you ages ago you could come to me! You and Mam both, I don't know how many letters I wrote—'

'She never told me. She never said a word. She reads me your letters, but she never mentioned – but Keeley, she won't go. She'll never leave this house or that bloody oul fella. I'm her reason to stay, but even if I go she won't, you'll see, she'll stay with fucking Christy for the rest of her days. But will you take me, Keeley? Please?'

'You – you mean, for good? You want to come and live with me in Provence?'

'Yes – anywhere, but especially there! I hear the light is perfect for painting, the weather is brilliant, you have a garden you say, you have spare rooms – oh, Jesus, Keeley, say you will!'

It was totally unexpected, and she wondered as she looked at him. He needed constant care, would be a big responsibility, without Gertie. And what would Gertie be, without him?

But he was right. She did have room, it could be done. And she had often asked him – on the assumption, she admitted, that it would never happen.

'I – Tony, I would do it, I will do it, if – if you think you can manage without her. I don't know the first thing about nursing; we'd have to get someone—'

But I could get someone, she thought. I can easily afford to hire a nurse to look after him. Only—

'Yes! We will get someone! Oh God, Keeley, do it now! Take me back with you, don't leave me here. I can't stand it another minute.'

'But I'll have to ask Mam whether she wants to come too.'

'Yeah. OK. You can ask her, but I promise you she'll say no when the chips are down.'

Yes. Keeley thought about it, and acknowledged that her brother was almost certainly right. Gertie would never leave Christy, never move to France; unlike her generation and Mary's, women of Gertie's age did not leave their husbands. Regardless of how badly they were treated, they stayed, stayed on and on until the bitter end. And how bitter could it be, she wondered, thinking of Mary negotiating with Cathal as she sat here, facing her desperate brother. His whole body seemed clenched with anticipation, with hope.

'All right, Tony. Leave it to me. I'll talk to Mam and see whether she'll come, or let you go on your own.'

'Keeley,' he almost shouted, 'I'm thirty-seven! I'm a grown man! Not much of a one maybe, but an adult! I don't have to get permission! All I need is your help!'

Her help. It only hit her then: how much of it he would need, for how long. For the rest of his life. It would be like having a child, a child who could never grow up.

Mary was sitting on her hotel bed when Keeley got back, twining a lock of hair round and round her finger, looking elated in a kind of terrified way. Keeley flung off her coat and all but grabbed her.

'Did you tell him? What did he say? What happened?'

Mary looked up at her with a sort of desperate determination.

'Yes. I did it! I told him I was leaving him, going to live with you and get my own pub. He laughed at first, didn't believe me, but then he – oh God . . .'

'Oh God what?'

'He got up and walked out. Said he was going home to Mel and that I'd never get her, he was going to see to it. Keeley, he – he's probably talking to her as we speak, poisoning her against me, brainwashing her—'

Keeley grinned, and sat down on the opposite bed.

'Mary, don't panic. I know he and Mel are close, but Mel isn't stupid. She'll listen to your side of the story tomorrow, you'll see.'

Mary's eyes were very blue, full of hope, drawing on all the cheerful optimism in Keeley's voice.

'D'you think she will? She won't have hysterics, or say I'm a selfish bitch – I wouldn't blame her, if she does.'

'Well, I don't think she will. I think she might decide it wouldn't be half bad to have a mother in France, to divide her year between being pampered by Daddy and visiting Mum in the sun . . . anyway there's no point in anticipating trouble before it happens. Why don't you just turn in and get a good night's sleep.'

Restlessly, Mary got up and began to pace the room. 'I will in a few minutes . . . what about you, Keel? How did you get on with your lot?'

There was hurt in Keeley's voice, Mary thought, as she began to speak; but she didn't let it show in her face.

'I got a cup of tea and a warm welcome – from Mam and Tony anyway – and all the news. It was like the past fifteen years never happened.'

'What did they say about Vincent?'

'Nothing.'

'Nothing?! But didn't they ask how you are, how you feel—?'

'Tony did. Christy watched telly, and then went out for a pint.'

'I don't believe it.'

'Well, there you are. I'm practically a stranger to them, Mary, just someone who emigrated fifteen years ago. They have their own lives. My parents have, I mean. But Tony has none. He says he's going round the twist.'

Mary considered. 'I can believe that. It must be terrible, being paralysed, having to live at home, rely on your mother to do everything for you.'

'Yes. He's had enough of it. He says he wants – he wants to come and live with me. With us, if you're coming too.'

'What?'

'He wants me to take him home with me, back to France. Apparently he never knew I'd offered years ago, to take him and Gertie both. She never told him.'

'But – but does she want to come too? Both of them?'

'I haven't asked her yet. I'll save it for Christmas lunch, which is to be endured there because they won't eat it here. But Tony says she won't come, and I think he's right. She'll never leave Christy.'

For a moment, Mary was silent.

'Why not? She doesn't have much of a life with him, does she?'

'She doesn't have any, that I can see. None at all. She might as well be married to a bad-tempered cabbage. But who knows, Mary? Who knows what goes on between two married people, what reasons they have for staying together?'

Yes. Keeley was right there, Mary thought. Everyone would be shocked to hear that she wanted to leave what looked like a nice solid marriage to the popular, upstanding Cathal Sullivan; equally, people would wonder why Gertie Butler wanted to stay with a lout like Christy. Who could ever really tell what went on behind closed doors?

'But, Keeley . . . if Tony does come to you, he'll need an awful lot of minding.'

'I know. I'll have to hire a nurse.'

'Yes, but apart from that . . . he'll be around the house all the time, and if things work out with Mel, I'll be there as well

. . . she'll probably be there too, during her holidays . . . it's an awful lot for you to take on.'

Keeley sat back, kicked off her shoes and sighed. 'Yes. It is a lot. For a woman who didn't want any kids, I'm going to be pretty busy playing mother to the whole damn lot of you.' She laughed, but Mary didn't.

'Keel, are you sure about this? That you can cope, I mean, with all of us?'

Keeley dropped her gaze, and studied the carpet.

'Let's put it this way, Mary. I'd rather have my house and my time full of people to worry about than have it empty, with nobody to talk to only Vincent's ghost.'

Vincent. Again Mary heard his laugh in her memory, saw his youthful face, and wondered. How could she, or Tony or Mel, ever fill that vast space in Keeley's heart?

But maybe it was better to fill her house, as she said, and the time which otherwise would stretch into empty eternity. Maybe a houseful of problem people was better than a houseful of silence . . . ?

Maybe. Or maybe not. What would Keeley do if Tony proved too heavy a burden, if Mel's visits were too painful a reminder, if she, Mary, did not get on with her as they had done as youthful flatmates, years ago? In fact it was probably easier to divorce a disastrous spouse than it was to get rid of people who came to stay, and settled in.

I've got to help her, she thought. She's a fantastic friend, and I'd better be one too. Not just because I'm burning my boats and don't ever want to go back to Cathal, but because I'm *only* her friend.

Only her friend, and not the husband she loved, the person she wanted to live with all her life. The person she would be with instead, if my daughter hadn't caused his death.

Keeley awoke next morning to see Mary emerging from the bathroom, already showered, and anxious, apparently, to get going.

'Mary? It's only – uh, what time? – ten to seven.'

'I know, but I couldn't sleep any longer. I have to go to Mel.'

As Keeley struggled fully awake she began to rummage in the wardrobe, dress herself with gestures full of tension, comb her hair jerkily, impatiently.

'Do you mind having breakfast on your own, Keel? I haven't time, I couldn't eat—'

'No. That's OK. But Mary, don't panic. You'll only get confused and say all the wrong things.'

'If he even lets me in! What if he won't, if he won't let me near Mel – Keeley, what'll I do?'

'Mary, it's your house, isn't it? You've got a key to it, I presume. If he gets bolshie you just stand your ground for as long as it takes. I daresay he'd sooner let you in than have his wife standing on the doorstep shouting and banging for all the neighbours to hear.'

'Y – yes, I suppose he would . . . oh, I've never been so nervous in my life!'

'Well, be nervous if you must. Just don't make a bags of it. Do whatever you have to do until you get in, sit Mel down on her own and say everything you've got to say to her.'

'Yes. I will. I – I'll go now, before I lose my nerve.'

'Mary, *don't* lose it! Not unless you want to lose every-thing—'

Mary stood suddenly still, and looked at her.

'I'll tell you the one thing I don't want to lose, Keeley. I don't want to lose my daughter. She might not be perfect, but she's the only one I've got. And I'm the only mother she's got. If, at the end of it all, she wants me to stay with her, then that's what I will do. No matter how hard it is, no matter what it costs, I'll bite the bullet and do it.'

Yes. Keeley knew that she would. Saying nothing, she merely got up, went to Mary in her pyjamas, and touched her hand lightly to her friend's face. Not being a mother herself, she could only guess at how it must feel.

It was barely light when the taxi drew up and Mary got out of it, gazing petrified at her own home. And what a nice, normal home it looked, even attractive with the dew glittering on the neatly clipped lawn, the woodwork painted, the curtains clean and crisp. Cathal had got in a home help and was, clearly, keeping up appearances.

Taking her key from her bag, she put it in the lock and turned it, half expecting it to be blocked, to discover that the lock had been changed or the door bolted. But it turned smoothly, and she entered the silent hall. And then, immediately, there was a noise, a flurry of energy.

'Ma! You're here, you're home!'

Mel came running out of the kitchen, her hair flying loose, a piece of toast in her hand, her face detonating with emotion as she threw herself on her mother and hugged her more tightly than Mary could ever remember her doing since she was a toddler.

Absence, it seemed, really did make the heart grow fonder.

'Oh, I'm so glad to see you! I thought you'd never come!'

Mary hugged her in turn, smoothing her hair, kissing her cheek over and over. 'Of course I was coming. I told you I was.'

And then there was another flurry: Cathal, fully dressed even at this early hour, flushed, fresh and – and smiling. Smiling broadly, as Mary stared at him, and was grasped into his wide, very strong embrace.

'Here she is at last! After four months with her friend, she's home to her family! Come on, Mary, into the kitchen with you, breakfast is on the table.'

She couldn't find one word to say as he led her in, pulled a chair from the kitchen table and held it out for her with the most gallant smile. Amidst the cups and plates, a vase of red roses stood majestically, and he beamed.

'A few flowers, to welcome you home.'

She was mystified. Flowers? How, why? Where had he got them, between last night and this morning, and for what reason? Expecting rage, another row, all she could see was evidence of sweet reason.

'Imelda, put on a fresh pot of coffee there, and fry up a few eggs for your mother while she gets comfortable.'

Mel jumped to it, and Mary sank down on the proffered chair, feeling uncertain, unsteady to the point of weakness. In the taxi she had rehearsed all her speeches, and now it was as if the performance had been cancelled.

Wonderingly, she watched Mel scoop coffee into the perker and fill it with water, heat oil in the frying pan and crack two eggs into it, holding them in one hand while she put bread in the toaster with the other. The kitchen was sparkling clean, floor and tiling scrubbed, cutlery gleaming, everything warm, welcoming, perfect.

And then it hit her. Cathal had decided to change course. Decided to give this encounter his best shot after all, because the alternative was to be deserted by his wife. Deserted, humiliated,

embarrassed in both his private and public life. Until now there
had been an excuse for her absence, and she could almost hear
him reciting it to his parents, his customers, his staff: 'Mary's
visiting a poor widowed friend in France – can't leave her on
her own, you know – but she'll be back by Christmas.' Now,
it was almost Christmas, and he intended to keep her here by
whatever means came to hand. For himself and, above all, for
his image.

But Mel was cooking enthusiastically, and she decided to eat
the meal with the two of them, get a fix on the situation before
saying anything. If Cathal had indeed to spoken to Mel last
night, tried to get the girl on his side, there was no sign of it,
and Mary was very unsure of her ground.

Mel served up the food, hot and delicious, and she smiled
appreciatively as she forced herself to eat it.

'Mmm, this is very good. You must have learned something
about cooking, Mel.'

Mel beamed, not even seeming to notice the use of the pet
name she hated.

'Yes, I have, I do Saturday lunches at The Lantern with
Bridget you know, I've nearly saved up enough for new skis.
Daddy says I can go to Val d'Aosta again in March.'

Mary made a note of it. There were many excellent ski resorts
in France too, a small carrot to dangle if carrots were needed –
as, undoubtedly, they would be.

Mel sat down with them and took up her own breakfast
where she had left it off, talking animatedly. 'Doesn't the
place look great? I spent all day yesterday cleaning it with
Mrs Murphy, we wanted it to be really nice for you when you
came home . . . why did you go to that hotel instead, Ma? Did
Keeley ask you to?'

'No. I just needed – needed to. Mel, you're not going out
anywhere this morning, are you?'

'No. School's on Christmas holidays. Jane asked me round
to her house, but I said I couldn't go because you were coming
home.'

'Good. I – I'd like to have a little talk with you.'

Instantly, she sensed Cathal's alarm, his determination to
resist even now. As if a bunch of flowers changed anything,
after fifteen years!

'Ah, well now Mary, I think you and I are the ones who need
to talk, before you go gossiping with Imelda.'

She braced herself, and smiled pleasantly at him.

'No, no. Mel and I are going to have a good long chat. Girl talk. There's a lot we need to catch up on – Mel, these eggs are really great, the olive oil works much better than lard.'

'Yeah, doesn't it? I found some of your cookery books while you were away and read them – bit out of date, but there were a few interesting tips in them.'

Cookery books? Mary couldn't remember the last time she had bought one – had the money to buy one – but then it came to her; Mel must have unearthed the half-dozen Luc had given her, the ones Keeley had insisted she bring back to Ireland. Keeley had been so firm about it, as she was now going to have to be firm. Swallowing a mouthful of hot strong coffee, she set her mind to it.

'Cathal, I know you have to get to work. Don't let me delay you. I'll come down to The Lantern at lunchtime and—'

'Ah, not at all, I'm in no rush. Sure you've only just arrived.'

'Yes, but I know it gets busy early at this time of year. You go on now, and I'll see you later.'

'Not at all, they can well manage without me for a few hours, I wouldn't dream of leaving you—'

To their mutual surprise, it was Mel who intervened. 'Oh, go on Dad, Mum and I want to have a chat!'

Left with little choice, he looked at them both for a moment, searching for some reason to dally, to stay. But, in unison, they urged him on. 'Go! You've got your paperwork to do and deliveries arriving and Bridget on her own in the kitchen. Tell her to keep us a nice bit of beef for our lunch.'

Mary could see the battle in him as, very reluctantly, he got to his feet.

'All right. We'll have a proper family lunch together, I'll put champagne to chill and we'll toast your mother's return – eh, Mary?'

She nodded, and smiled again. 'Yes. Some champagne would be lovely.' If it wasn't too late, she thought, years and years too late. Silently, she waited for him to put on his jacket, locate his briefcase and his keys, and go. But then he turned back, and came over to her. Stooping, he placed a fat, fulsome kiss on her cheek.

'It's great to have you back, love. I'll see you at noon and we'll have a right royal celebration.'

Yes, she thought. We might, at that, because I hope I'll have something to celebrate by then. If Mel – if only – it all depends on Mel.

When he was gone, they eyed each other. For a moment, they were both silent. Then Mel got up, took the pot of coffee and poured them both a fresh cup. Something in her face, her manner as she did it, told Mary that her daughter knew something, was expecting something. There was something apprehensive about her; but nothing hostile, nothing demanding or accusing.

She took a mouthful of the coffee, and a deep breath.

'Mel. I'm sorry I've been away so long. I truly am. I didn't want to leave you here, but Keeley really—'

'Needed you. I know she did, Ma. And that was my fault.'

'Well, yes, it partly was, although that's not what I want to talk to you about. How much responsibility you take for Vincent's death is up to you, but you needn't worry that I'm going to try to make you feel any worse than you already do.'

'Ma, that's partly what makes me feel so bad. You could have gone berserk, you could have screamed and shouted and punished me, but you didn't. You were really good about it – and so was Dad, he's never made me feel bad at all. Which kind of leaves me with only myself to be angry with.'

'Are you? Angry with yourself?'

'Yeah. I was a stupid prat, and I wrecked Keeley's life. Maybe I didn't kill Vincent, exactly, but I sent him out to his death.'

'Well, if that's how you feel, then that's what you've got to live with. But – Mel, that's what I have to talk to you about. About living with things. Or not living with them, if they become unbearable.'

Mel put down her coffee and frowned, struggling, Mary thought, to look and sound adult. She was not adult, but she was not a child either. Even in these four months she had grown another inch, she had the figure of a woman, and some kind of composure that had not been there before. Also the intuition, Mary thought, to know that they were going to have a serious talk. Clasping her coffee cup, she looked somehow ready for it.

'Go on. Tell me what you mean.'

'What I mean is – oh, Mel! It's so hard to find the right words, to say exactly what needs to be said.'

'Well, try.'

Suddenly, without preamble, Mary took the plunge.

'Mel, I'm going to leave your – your father. Our marriage is in trouble. It's been in trouble for a long time, for reasons I'm not going to tell you because it wouldn't be fair to him. He's a good father to you, and I'm not going to start making accusations against him behind his back. But there are problems – irreconcilable differences, as they say – and we are going to separate. I'm sorry if I sound brutal, but there's no point in beating around the bush. You have to know.'

Mel paled, and did not reply. Desperately, but gathering momentum, Mary continued on down the hard, bleak road.

'I'll stay here for Christmas, but then I'm going back to France. I'm going to live with Keeley and open an Irish pub in Aix. My marriage is finished, and there is no point in trying to save it, or repair it, or pretend about it. I simply married the wrong man, for the wrong reasons.'

'What reasons?' Mel's voice was very low, but attentive.

'I – I can't tell you. Suffice it to say that we're completely incompatible and I have been unhappy ever since my honeymoon. I tried to make it better, but it got worse. Now, it's gone past the point of no return.'

'But – but Daddy is—'

'I know. You adore him and I can understand that, because he has always adored you. He's not a bad man, in the sense that some men are really evil. He's never been violent, he's always worked hard and provided for us, but – he – he has certain characteristics that I can no longer live with.'

'Like what?'

'Things you're a little young to understand. But he doesn't love me, or respect me. I have never been his wife in any real sense. The main reason I've stayed with him is – is you. I wanted you to have two parents and a stable home, and I hoped you'd continue to have those things until you were grown up. I nearly made it. But not quite.'

There was another long silence, and Mel began to pluck at her hair, coiling a long strand of it around her finger in a gesture Mary recognised as one of her own.

'But you – you can't just go away, for good! What will we do? What will I do? Mum, I don't want you to go!'

Mary sat back, and looked at her.

'Yes. I know I'm your mother, Mel, and my first duty is to you. If you absolutely, totally feel unable to live here without me, then I won't do it. I'll drop everything and stay until you're eighteen, or even longer if you go to college. But I was hoping you might agree to another plan.'

Mel pouted, and she saw that tears were threatening. 'What plan? What is it?'

'I was hoping that you might stay here with your father, as you have been doing, studying, working a bit in the pub, talking to me every day on the phone. And that then you might come to me for your school holidays, four months in the summer, two weeks at Christmas and Easter.'

'But I couldn't go to France, to Keeley's house! Not after what I did! She doesn't want me!'

'Mel, I want you, and Keeley understands that. She hasn't forgiven what you did, but she's trying to. If you come to her house she will welcome you and talk to you and continue to be your godmother . . . in fact I think you matter even more to her now, because she had no children with Vincent. She's angry with you, but she still loves you.'

'How can she love me?'

'You'd be surprised how. She loved you the first day she ever set eyes on you. She even let me marry Cathal, when she was against it, because she knew you needed your father, your family.'

'I still need you! Both of you!'

There was fear in the words, a note of panic, and Mary forced herself to stay calm, keep a steady nerve.

'I know you do. That's why I'll stay, if you feel you can't cope any other way. But, Mel, we are never going to be a proper family again, the three of us. I could live here until you're eighteen, until you graduate, until you marry, until you have children . . . I could keep on finding one reason after another to stay here all my life. But I'm only human, Mel, and I desperately want to *have* a life. Now, before it's too late. Not just an existence, but a real life. I can make one, now, but only you can let me have it. Does that make any sense to you?'

She was a little taken aback when Mel nodded, and then looked abruptly out of the window, her mind apparently wandering momentarily.

'All my life, Mel, I've wanted to be a chef. A proper chef, a brilliant chef. I got the chance to be one, but I gave it up when I found I was expecting you. Now, it's too late. I've missed out on too much, lost the moment . . . but in a pub in Aix, I could cook to the best of my current ability. I could be free. And you,

I hope, could be with me some day, maybe achieving the things I never did. You like cooking, don't you?'

'Yeah. Well, I like food. I don't really know much about cooking it yet.'

'No. But you'll learn . . . would you like to start learning now?'

'Now? What do you mean?'

'I mean that, before I start this pub, if I am going to start it, I'm going to do a course with Darina Allen in Cork. Right away, after Christmas. Would you like to come with me, and do one too?'

Mel's face lit up. 'Oh, yes! I'd love to!'

'Then we could go together. If you think it might help you to think, and talk to me, we could spend a week there learning all about good Irish cuisine. And learning about each other. Because I don't expect you to digest what I'm saying to you right now, or make any decision before you're ready. We could just go there and be together and see what happens.'

Mel considered, making a visible effort to control herself, to not burst into tears like a baby.

'But what about Dad?'

'We'll spend Christmas Day with him, New Year as well if you want to be with your friends. I want some time with him anyway, to make my position clear to him. And then we could go to Cork at the beginning of January. I'll pay for your course, it'll be my Christmas present to you.'

'Uh huh . . . but Ma, what if I say no? I mean, if I say no, I don't want you to live in France . . . will you be mad at me?'

'No. I won't be angry, Mel, because you have a right to me. To have your mother here at home. Only it won't ever be a home, really, because I can only be here in body. In spirit, I belong in France. I don't know why, but I do. I need to cook properly, before it's too late, and I need to live apart from Cathal. I can be a housekeeper here, but I can't be a wife to him, I can't be myself, I can only be a – a kind of prisoner.'

Another lengthy silence. Feeling sad, and torn with guilt, pain for her child, Mary sat at the table, watching her.

She was so young, under all the slick clothes and easy assurance, so young and vulnerable. But somewhere, she thought, there was a kind of strength too, a kind of pragmatism. The detached pragmatism that had enabled her father, Lars, to have sex for gratification, sex without love. And then to get onto his

motorbike and go back to Sweden without a backward glance.
Lars had not been an emotional kind of man, and until now Mel
had not been an emotional kind of girl. If they shared anything
apart from their physical features, it was the ability to recognise
and make the most of whatever life was offering to them.

And yet . . . at this moment there seemed to be a tenderness
about Mel, some tinge to her skin that made Mary want to hold
her, hug her as if she were still a baby, taking its first steps and
falling over. Standing up, she went around the table and bent
over her, wrapping her arms around her neck and shoulders,
kissing her hair.

'I know it's terrible for you, Mel. I know everything I'm saying
is a terrible shock, and very hard for you to deal with.'

Mel did not turn around, but she put her hand on her
mother's. 'Yeah. It is terrible. But it's not a shock.'

'What? Why, Mel? Did you sense that something was wrong,
between Cathal and me?'

'No. Not really. But Keeley came here last night and . . .
and told me that you were going to ask me to do something
difficult.'

'Keeley? She came here? She said that?'

'Yes. She said that you wanted to talk to me, and that I was
to think before answering you. So that's what I'm trying to do,
Ma. Trying to think.'

Mary was stunned. Keeley had promised not to influence . . .
and had not influenced. Clearly Mel was trying, as she said,
to think.

'I see. Well, then, take your time. Take all the time you need,
and don't feel guilty if you finally decide your answer has to be
no. If it is no, I'll still be your mother – and your friend, I hope.
We'll work everything out as best we can.'

'OK. And – and Ma?'

'Yes?'

'Will you ring up and book the Darina Allen course? We'll
need to do something about it today, if we're going in January.'

Despite herself, Mary found herself smiling, just a fraction,
as she nodded agreement. Whether Mel had the cool character
of her Irish or her Swedish father she could not tell, but, as
Keeley might say, it wasn't off the ground she had licked it.

And then Mel twisted round to her, looking at her candidly,
earnestly. 'Ma? Do you really mean it?'

'About Darina Allen? Yes, I mean it.'

'No. About Dad. About wanting to leave him. About not wanting to stay married to him any more?'

Mary held onto her daughter, and onto her resolve.

'Yes, Mel. I do mean it. I know you love him and he treats you very well, but I don't love him, nor does he love me. Unless you are very much opposed to it, I am going to leave him. Leave him for good.'

Her voice trembled, cracked, and the tears came at last; first Mel's and then her own, mingling on their joined hands as they fell. It was the first time they had ever shared sorrow, or found comfort in each other, in this house, and although Mary was the cause of her pain Mel did not draw away from her.

Chapter Sixteen

It was the most agonising, depressing Christmas lunch she had ever endured in her life, and Keeley felt like a cardboard cut-out of herself as she sat there at the table trying to eat it, helping Gertie to feed Tony, listening to her father burping and chomping, watching him pick bits of turkey from his teeth with his fingers. Eating steadily, he said little to her; but for Gertie's and Tony's sake she resolved to be cheerful, sociable, slogging away at conversation as if it were the Himalayas to be conquered.

Afterwards, she helped Gertie clear and wash the dishes while Christy collapsed into his armchair and turned on the television, a can of beer on the floor beside him. Tony said nothing, appearing to watch the television also but waiting, she sensed, for her to broach the subject of his departure. Every time she looked at him he looked back hopefully, almost desperately, willing her to make the first move.

Eventually, she sat down with her mother and turned to her, wincing inwardly. Gertie was going to be hurt, and very lonely if she chose to let Tony go to France without her. Again, Keeley reminded herself that Gertie *had* a choice, that she could accompany her son to sunny, fragrant Provence if she wished.

'Mam. I – we – Tony and I – we want to talk to you.'

Gertie blinked curiously, balancing a cup of tea on her lap.

'Oh, aye? About what, love?'

'About – about his future.'

'His future?'

Already Keeley thought she detected a tremor, something flinching in Gertie's face. But she plunged on.

'Mam, you – you're getting on. Tony is worried about you. He feels he's going to become a burden to you, more and more so as time goes by.'

It was the kindest way of putting it, but even so Gertie wrinkled her forehead, and sounded defensive when she replied. 'A burden? To me? Ah, Keeley, don't be silly, love. I'm well able to manage – amn't I, Tony?'

She turned to him for confirmation, and he nodded. 'Yeah. Sure. You are now, Ma. But it's getting harder as you get older . . . a day will come when you won't be able to do it any more.'

'Maybe it will. But sure I'm not even sixty yet. It's a long way off.'

They could debate exactly how long, Keeley thought, but to what purpose? Tony wanted to go now, and was depending on her to help him. She steeled herself.

'Mam, it's not that far off, and Tony doesn't want to wait until it happens. He – he wants to come to live with me. Now. In France.'

Gertie's free hand flew to her bosom.

'Wh-at? To live with you – Tony, you don't! You can't want to leave your home here and – and go all that way, to a foreign place like that! Keeley couldn't mind you the way I do, she's never done it, she doesn't know—'

'No. She doesn't. But we could – can – get a nurse, Mam. I earn enough from my painting, and there's nothing else to spend it on.'

Gertie was beginning to blanch, to quiver like a small round bird on a windswept branch.

'A nurse! But it wouldn't be the same, she wouldn't know you—'

'She'd get to know me. But, Mam, the thing is, we want you to come too. Don't we, Keeley?'

Tony looked hard at her for confirmation, and she nodded.

'Yes. We do. You're not getting any younger, Mam. I could look after you in France, the house is big and comfortable, you'd have a much easier life.'

Gertie's gaze flew to Christy, slouched in his armchair with his back to them, his hand resting on his can as he watched his programme oblivious to them.

'But then who'd look after your father? Do – do you mean you want him to go too? All of us, Keeley?'

'No, Mam. Not all of you. Christy wouldn't budge even if he was invited, but he's not invited. I – I don't want him living with me, in my home.'

'But I couldn't leave him on his own! Keeley, love, I couldn't!'

She leaned forward and put her hand on her mother's knee. 'Why not, Mam? He pays no attention to you anyway, he'd hardly even notice you were gone.'

'But – but who'd cook his meals for him, and do his laundry? Who'd look after *him*?'

Keeley's voice hardened. 'Who cares? Let him shift for himself, Ma!'

Gertie's eyes began to brim with tears. 'Keeley, love, he's your father! I know he's not the best in the world, but he's my husband, thirty-six years we've been married, I couldn't just go off and leave him! He needs me, and besides I – I—'

'What? You what? You want to stay here and let him hit you another few belts, is that it?'

Gertie looked alarmed, glancing at Christy's back with a nervous gulp.

'Keeley, don't say things like that! He hasn't . . . hasn't done anything like that for a long time. For years.'

'Maybe not. But he doesn't give you much of a life either, does he?'

Again Gertie gulped, her voice low and tense.

'Keeley, it's my life. Mine and his. It's not for you to say things like that.'

With a sigh, Keeley supposed it wasn't. Without much hope, she tried once more.

'OK, I won't say them then. But Mam, please say you'll think about it. Think about coming to France with me and Tony – because Tony really wants to come, and I've promised him I'll take him.'

Gertie turned to her son. 'Tony. Have you really asked your sister to do this, without even asking me first?'

Again he nodded, with as much vigour as his limited head movement allowed him. 'Yeah. I have. I'm sorry, Mam, but I do want to go. It's time for a change. It'll be easier for you, whether you stay here or come with me, and I'll be able to paint better over there.'

'Why? What's the difference where you paint, son? Don't I get you everything you need and send your work off to that man for you? Don't I clean the brushes and buy the canvases and—'

'Yes, you do. You're great, Ma. But you can't go on doing it for ever. You need a break. Why don't you just say you'll come, and live with us in the sun?'

But Gertie shook her head, her hand somewhere near her throat, her mouth tight and turning down.

'No. I couldn't go over there. I don't know anyone, I don't speak their language, the sun's too hot – the neighbours – if I left your father—'

'Hang the neighbours! Hang him!'

It was Tony who said it, hissing under his breath, and Gertie recoiled.

'No. Don't say any more about it. I won't go.'

And that, Keeley recognised, was that. They could plead and argue with their mother till Doomsday, but they would not shift her. She was, in every way, wedded to Christy. Welded to him, for life.

'All right. If you're sure, Mam, then we won't talk any more about it. But we'll ring you all the time – won't we, Tony? – and if ever you change your mind just let me know, I'll buy your plane ticket and meet you at the airport, you won't even have to take a bus.'

Gertie looked close to tears, and they were sorry for her as she began to question Tony, to ask him why he so badly wanted to leave her after all she'd done for him . . . but that was just it. His dependency was chafing at him like a rope, and only kindness prevented him from saying so. Forcing themselves to smile, they both tried to console her, until eventually, unexpectedly, Christy looked round.

'What's all this? What's going on?'

Gertie flew to his side. 'Tony wants to go to France to live with Keeley.'

Christy raised one eyebrow a fraction. 'Is that so? Well, there's gratitude for you. We look after him for seventeen years and that's the thanks we get. Lovely.'

A dozen retorts sprang to Keeley's mind, but she stifled them with a grimace; there was no point in having a row, ending it all on a sour or angry note.

'He needs a change of scene. He's going to paint in my garden – it's sunny nearly all year round, it'll be good for him. But he'll keep in touch, don't worry. We both will.'

She put a little menace into the last of this, and saw it register: they would be checking up on their mother, monitoring her health and welfare – not, she thought, that Gertie would report it to them or to anyone if Christy did abuse her, now that she was going to be alone with him.

If only she would! If only she'd get sense, get a life, leave the old sod and come with them! But Gertie stood immobile at her husband's side, stolid as a tree-trunk encased in poison ivy. Christy's grip on her was tight and total, potentially lethal, but after all these years she was engulfed, swallowed up in him.

Looking at them, Keeley bit her lip, and thought of Mary, at home with Cathal and Mel. Mary was fighting for her freedom, struggling up and out of all the ties that were choking her, and showed signs of winning. But even yet she could be devoured and defeated and, at the very least, it was going to be a painful battle, leaving deep, numerous, ugly scars.

But Mary, although she looked tired and anxious, sounded optimistic when next they met, the day before Keeley's departure for France with Tony. In a small, warm café near the hotel she had checked out of, she updated her friend on her progress over copious mugs of hot chocolate.

'Christmas was gruesome. Cathal never stopped fawning over me all day, Mel kept *looking* at me, in a way that . . . oh, I can't describe it, Keel, but it made me feel so guilty. I knew it was going to be our last ever family Christmas, so I did my best, but there was this tension all the time, humming away under the surface.'

'And now?'

'Now, I've talked to Cathal and made my position crystal clear, he's starting to turn nasty again. He rang my mother and got her to come round yesterday, Dad too, it was like a kind of family conference to decide what to do about me.'

'It's not their decision. It's yours.'

'Yes. That's what I kept telling myself. But Mam and Dad had a right old go at me, went on for ages about my duties and responsibilities. I might as well tell you that your name was mentioned too, they think you're putting me up to the whole thing.'

'Oh, for God's sake, when will they ever see and accept that you're a grown woman? I know it was me who persuaded you to stay in France that time when we were kids, but going there in the first place was your idea – don't they ever give you credit for having any initiative of your own, even now?'

'No, I don't think they do! I suppose I was a doormat for so long, they've got used to me that way . . . but in spite of everything I feel much better now that I'm taking my life into my own hands. It's bloody hard work, but I feel stronger, as if I'd been asleep and woken up full of energy. And Mel is being better than I expected her to. There have been a few tears – quite a few, if I'm honest – but she hasn't asked me flat out not to go.'

'Good. I hope she won't do that.'

'She might, even yet. We're going to do a lot of talking, I hope, at the cookery school next week. But so far all she's done is ask a lot of questions abut how things are in France, the kind of food I want to serve in the pub, whether I'd pay her to work in it if she came over in the summer . . . and she's been talking to Cathal, too. I think she's trying to find out what exactly is wrong between us. But all he does is tell her I'm off my rocker, going through some kind of breakdown, that I'll soon get sense and everything will be all right.'

'Has he made any threats, or tried to bully you?'

'No. I think he's beginning to realise that it's not only a waste of time, but will make things worse. His new strategy is to try to reason with me, negotiate . . . at least if Mel does make me stay he might be a bit more bearable.'

'Or he might say, ah hah, I've got her now!'

'Well, it won't wash if he does. If I have to stay I'll still be looking for my £300 a week and plenty of respect, consideration . . . did I tell you that his father is retiring soon from the council in the midlands, and he's going to contest the seat in his place? He seems to think he has a future in local politics. And that he might even move there, commute to The Lantern – I think it's his way of suggesting I'd be a step nearer to getting my hands on Fursey's, if I stayed with him.'

'H'm. I suppose he's trying to think of every tactic he can – but really, Mary, politics! The man couldn't communicate his way out of a wet paper bag.'

'Ha – I know that and you know it, but nobody else seems to know it! I wouldn't be a bit surprised if he gets elected, he's so plausible.'

'Yeah – well, who cares what he does so long as he gets out of your way and stays out of it. Anyway, it'll only be you and Mel next week down in Ballymaloe, and she's the only one you really need to worry about.'

'Yes. I know. And I'm going to work on her like blazes, Keeley. I am going to try absolutely everything I can think of to persuade her to let me go. I think what she needs above all is reassurance that I'll still be Mum, that I'll still be there for her even if I'm not physically present. If I can convince her of that, and paint a really alluring picture of the life she could have with me in France, I think I'll be home and dry.'

'Ha! We should get Tony to paint it for her! He's over the moon, can't wait to leave . . . neither can I, for that matter. It's only now, after this brief return to my old life, that I really appreciate the new one, though I suppose it isn't really new any more. I don't just feel I'm going back to France tomorrow, I feel I'm going home. Even – even if Vincent isn't there.'

Mary put down her mug and took her hand, tightly.

'No, he's not there, but it's still where you belong now, Keeley.'

'Yes. For the first time, that's what I think too. It's only when I look at it from here that I can see the roots I've put down, the way I well and truly am transplanted . . . it's just as well my mother turned me down, Mary, because she never would transplant, settle in. She'd wilt and wither and die.'

'Uh huh. It's funny, that, about plants and people. Some adapt anywhere, some need sun, some want lots of space and others want company . . . I think you're the hardy variety, Keel.'

'I hope so, Mary. I haven't felt very hardy since Vincent died. But I know that's what he'd want me to be – tough and hardy, a survivor in any circumstances.'

'He would. He'd be pleased as punch with you, if he could see the progress you've made already.'

Keeley felt sad, but encouraged. 'Have I? Can you see some?'

'Yes, I can – lots of it! It's going to take time, Keel, a lot more time, but I know you'll make it.'

She smiled. 'Right. And if I can make it, you'll make it. I'll expect you to ring me when you arrive at Nice airport, the week after next.'

Mary smiled in turn, and looked hard at her. 'Yes. I will ring you right away, when – if—'

'No, Mary. Not if. Only when.'

Keeley left for France next day, with her brother and all his equipment, both medical and artistic, in tow. Leaving her mother was an experience she found harrowing, and Gertie did not help by crying like the rain, sobbing pitifully over Tony. But at length she and Tony managed to disentangle themselves, and go. Christy said little, but before getting into the taxi she shot him one long, last, warning look.

And, after a harrowing, silent, accusatory New Year's Eve, Mary left Cathal for her course in Cork, with Mel. When he refused to let her have the car she stunned him by phoning Avis and requesting that one be delivered to her, because she was driving to her destination. His face, as she turned the ignition and backed out of the drive, was a study. In the passenger seat beside her, Mel sat giggling and wondering.

'When did you ever learn to drive?'

'Keeley taught me last autumn, and I passed my test just before I came over.'

'How come you never learned before?'

Mary reflected a moment, and decided to divulge that much.

'Your father discouraged me. He didn't think I'd be able to do it, or needed to.'

Mel shrugged. 'Huh. Bilge. You should have just gone ahead and done it.'

Yes, she thought, I should have. And I would have, if he'd let me have the car, paid for lessons, paid for insurance . . . but I'm not going to tell her about the financial situation, it's too humiliating, and she probably wouldn't believe me anyway. Not that I'd blame her, when her pockets are bursting with cash he gave her this very morning, and her cheeks are still warm from the kiss he gave her with it.

It was over a hundred miles to Cork, the longest drive Mary had ever attempted, and for the first thirty or forty miles of it she concentrated ferociously, nervous about driving on the left, about the unfamiliar car and roads which were a lot trickier than straight, simple French autoroutes. So as not to have to talk, she let Mel put a tape in the deck, shutting out the raucous music as she peered ahead, hands clamped to the wheel and all reflexes primed, anticipating skids on the rain-slick road.

But by the time both sides of the tape were played out, the rain was easing off and she was beginning to relax. The map lay unfolded on Mel's lap, but she consulted it only on request, sprawling on the front seat and looking lost either in thought or in the mindless music. When it ended she reached for another tape, but Mary forestalled her by suggesting a coffee stop.

The choice was not infinite, and after a few fruitless miles they settled for a pub which, on the outside, looked attractive enough. Inside, a fire was burning, and they settled themselves

by it, rubbing their chilled hands over its heat. A girl of about
seventeen came up to them, and waited without enthusiasm to
take their order.

'Some coffee – and maybe a sandwich, Mel?'

'Yeah. Cheese and ham would be good.'

Mary ordered for them both, and after a lengthy interval
the girl came back with a tray, from which she unloaded an
industrial metal coffee-pot, plates, cutlery, milk and sugar in
similar metal containers, and their plastic basket of sandwiches.
Mel wrinkled her nose.

'Ugh. Sliced pan. For God's sake, you'd think they could get
a bit of decent bread, there are probably hundreds of women
around here who bake it.'

'There must be. And look, sliced pre-packed cheese too, and
the ham is greasy.'

Because they were hungry, they bit into the food anyway, and
tasted the coffee which was sharply stewed, metallic from the
pot. Frowning, they looked at each other.

'This is crap, Ma. You should complain.'

Complain? It dawned on Mary that she never had, about
anything, in her life. Apart from her long angry letters to
Keeley, into which she diverted all her rage, she had bottled
everything up – and never had the chance to complain in any
kind of hostelry, because Cathal had never taken her to any
and she'd never had the funds to go with a friend, or alone.
But now, things were different – and were going to be a lot
more different. Turning around, she beckoned to the waitress,
who strolled slowly over.

Pleasantly, Mary smiled at her. 'Sorry to bother you. But
the coffee is stewed and the sandwiches are – well, we were
wondering whether you might have any other kind of bread,
or cheese? Something not out of a packet?'

Baffled, the waitress blinked. 'Well . . . I can get you some
fresh coffee, I suppose. But those are the only sandwiches
we have.'

'All right. Fresh coffee then, and we won't bother with the
sandwiches.'

The girl trudged away, and Mel looked at her mother
approvingly.

'Good. I'm glad you did that. And I hope you're not planning
to pay for them, even though we've taken a bite.'

'No. I'm not going to, Mel. They're inedible. I'm telling you,

you won't ever catch me eating food like that, or paying for it, or serving it in my pub.'

Mel sat back, crossed her legs and reached into her bag for her cigarettes. 'You mean The Lantern, or the one you want to open in France?'

'The one in France. I made many compromises at The Lantern, Mel, for both Cathal and the customers, but my days of compromise are over. And please don't light that cigarette. I can't stop you smoking with your friends, but I won't have it when you're with me. You're too young and it's bad for your lungs at any age.'

Mel made a face of mock-horror. 'What! No fags for a whole week?'

'Not in my company, no.'

'But Keeley—'

'Keeley's not your mother. I am.'

Reluctantly, Mel stashed the packet in her pocket, and eyed her warily.

'You've changed, Ma. Changed a lot. You never used to give out to me about anything.'

'More fool me. I should have flung you over my knee and given you a good spanking when you were young enough to appreciate it.'

Uncertain whether she was joking, Mel gazed at her. 'You used to be such an old softie. Now you sound like Dracula's mother.'

'Good. It's never too late to learn.'

They drank their coffee, entered into a brief dispute about paying for the sandwiches, won it, and returned to the car. On the next leg of the journey, Mel seemed more animated, paying attention to signposts, taking note of the changing scenery, chatting about their cookery course.

'But you did one before, didn't you, Ma? With that guy in France – Luc? He said you'd have made a fantastic chef.'

'I would have, if I'd gone ahead with it.'

'Were you ever sorry you didn't?'

Yes, Mary wanted to shout, I was sorry every single day of my life! But she didn't say it. It was not Mel's fault that she had been conceived; the child, as the saying went, had never asked to be born.

'I had you instead.'

'And did you – did you ever regret having me?'

Fleetingly, Mary took her eyes off the road to smile at her. 'No, Mel. I'm very glad I have you.'

There was a silence after that, in which she saw that Mel was digesting her words, pondering the direction her mother's life might have taken if she had never existed. Crushing the temptation to intervene, to say something soothing, she left her instead to ponder it.

Keeley's nerves were totally frazzled by the time she got home, despite endless help from airline staff, taxi drivers and the numerous other people who helped her get Tony home with her. The journey was a tortuous struggle, and she began to realise how much she had taken on. But Tony was grinning from ear to ear, his spirits rising with every passing mile until, finally, they were delivered to her front door.

'Jaysus! This is a fucking mansion!'

Although she swore herself when provoked, she flinched to hear how much Tony did it, quite naturally after years of living with Christy. But at least he didn't speak French, so nobody would know he was doing it apart from herself. In time, he might even grow out of it.

'Do you like it?'

He gazed around him, looking up at the early clematis already budding over the doorway, down at the saxifrage creeping through the rockery, across to the tennis court and pool which, at this time of year, was still covered.

'It's amazing. I had no idea you were as rich as this.'

'Well, we weren't always. We were poor as church mice in the early years, and then we were so busy . . . poor Vincent never really got much value out of this house, he died just when we were starting to get time to enjoy it.'

'Yeah. That wasn't fair, Keel. That really wasn't fair. You must have worked your butts off for a place like this.'

'We did. But we had fun too . . . would you like me to wheel you round the grounds before we go indoors?'

In fact, Keeley found, she was dying to see the garden herself, had missed it while she was away. In January it was full of cool pale colour, the lemony buds of clematis which in Ireland would not appear for another two or three months, the milky fronds of honeysuckle, silver-green rosemary and baby-pink cyclamen . . . inhaling deeply, she paused to smell the herbs, the fragrance of spring already in the air, and looked up at the high walls cloaked in green. There was something so reassuring about this house, something that made her feel cocooned, protected, comforted. Taking the handles of his chair, she left their luggage stacked in the porch and began to wheel him through it.

'D'you do it all yourself?'

'Yes, in winter it's manageable, the gardener just drops in occasionally in case there's any heavy digging or planting. But I like to do as much as I can myself.'

'It's beautiful. God, Keeley, you can't imagine how much this means to me, to be in a garden, out in the air.'

'Didn't you ever get out, back home?'

'Only in summer, if one of my friends thought of it . . . but I didn't have many friends, as you can probably imagine. Taking me out is like taking a baby in a pram – in winter nobody ever bothered, there were times when I'd have wanted to end it all if it wasn't for the painting. It kept me sane – most of the time, anyway.'

'Well, you'll get out all the time here. You can even paint outdoors if you like.'

'Yeah – hey, Keel, steer me over to that blue flower there, would you?' She wheeled him to it, a variety of ceanothus which, again, flowered much earlier here than in northern climates. It was not yet fully in blossom, but it was a mist of promise. For several minutes he sat looking at it, and then screwed up his face in a mixture of pleasure and disgust.

'I wish I could touch it. Hold it, and smell it and see what it feels like.'

'You can. Here.'

She pulled a branch of it to him, put it close to his face so that it brushed his skin, its blueness making him look even paler than he was. But we can change that, she thought; a few weeks of spring weather will soon put a bloom in his cheeks.

He grinned up at her. 'Well, who'd ever have thought it, Tony Butler stopping to smell the roses, or whatever this is.'

She laughed, thinking how he had held onto a sense of humour, and warming to him for it.

'Wait till you see the garden by Easter. If you're looking for inspiration for new colours, this is the place to be.'

'I'll bet. You know there are some people in wheelchairs who can do quite a bit of gardening – I saw one on telly once – but they're more mobile than me. They can use their hands, and bend a bit.'

'Well, I bet not many of them can paint like you.'

She laughed inwardly as she said it; it was horribly true. But undeniably many people did like his pictures, enough to buy them, and she was thankful that the early one, the wedding present, was one of the first things he would see in the hall. There were a few others too, down in the cellar or somewhere, she'd better hang them tonight before he got to see the whole house.

'I'll be able to paint much better here. I know it already.'

'Yes. I'm sure you will. I'll take you to the Vasarely Foundation and all the places Cézanne painted . . . Vincent and I used to cycle to a house near Puyloubier, up on a hill—'

'*That* house? The one in the book you gave me? Does it really exist?'

'Yes. We modelled this one on it, only it had to be adapted a bit because the site is much lower, flatter.'

'It is flat. Easy to get the chair around.'

She hadn't noticed that, but now she saw he was right, there were no awkward steps or obstacles. Pushing him, she continued on until he had seen everything, and the light began to lower a little into evening. It was eerie how his voice came to her without his head turning, but she supposed she would get used to it.

'So when do we eat? I'm starving!'

'Good. We'll have an early supper.'

Getting him into the house was relatively easy, because of the wide corridors, and the maid Céline came to help with all the equipment. Both women laughed when he winked at Céline, and whistled.

'Whew, there's an eyeful! Hey, Céline, you married?'

Céline didn't understand him, but Keeley thought of the many girlfriends he had had before his accident, and was sorry for him. Under normal circumstances he would probably be married now, with a clutch of kiddies and some long-suffering wife who despaired of him, and was fond of him, in equal proportion. But the Butler clan seemed doomed never to propagate. Musing on it, she took him to what was to be his bedroom, and was touched by his enthusiasm.

'Jaysus, it's enormous, I feel like the king of Siam! And my own bathroom and all!'

'Yes.' Shutting her eyes, Keeley thought about it. 'We'll have to find you a nurse, as soon as possible. I'll see if I can find an agency in the morning.'

'Right – but Keel, I'll pay for it myself, OK? I know you're loaded, but I'm not going to scrounge off you. I'll paint bundles of pictures and Alain will – hey, when do I get to meet Alain?'

'Tomorrow, if I can find him and he's free. He'll be delighted to hear you've moved here.'

He was briefly silent, and then looked candidly at her.

'Don't worry, Keel. You'll be delighted too. Maybe it'll take a while, but I know a lucky break when I get one. I won't be any more of a nuisance than I can help, I won't pester you to take me anywhere or do anything for me. Just being here is miracle enough, it's like I died and woke up in heaven. I – I'll try to be a bit of company for you. Good company, because you must miss Vincent like crazy.'

'Yes. I do miss him like crazy, Tony, even at this minute although you're here beside me and Céline has the house warm, feeling like home. But I'm glad you are here. In a way we don't really know each other, despite being brother and sister, but we'll get to know each other and muddle along somehow. You don't seem to complain much, so I won't either.'

Again he looked at her, reaching out in the curious way he had, with his eyes. 'That's OK, actually. You can complain round the clock if you like, because I'm used to being paralysed whereas you're not used to being widowed. You can whinge morning, noon and night, just so long as you keep me here and don't chuck me out the first time I spill paint on the floor. You can cry on my shoulder all you like, and I won't be able to budge, or do a thing about it.'

He smiled at her, an infectious smile that made her smile back. He wasn't the man she wanted in her house, or even in her life, but as men went there were worse. A lot worse, thousands of Christys and Cathals . . . at least this one wasn't mean or bad-tempered or domineering. As a youth he had had the makings of all those things, but now, what he had lost physically he seemed to have gained spiritually. Mentally, he coped well, he had recovered as much as anyone could from his trauma.

Well. If he could do it, maybe she could too. In time. Eventually. Meanwhile, she could walk around the house, she could go into the kitchen and open the fridge and take out bottles of gin and tonic, without waiting, as he had to wait, to be asked what he'd like, and be helped to drink it.

*　　*　　*

Settling themselves into a guesthouse, Mary and Mel slept early after their long journey, and awoke next morning full of mutual enthusiasm. For winter it was a beautiful day, clear, crackling and full of low sunshine, and the brisk bright air propelled them through an invigorating breakfast. Mel tunnelled her way industriously through a sizzling grill of bacon, tomatoes and mushrooms, devoured a plate of fruit with yogurt, two Danish pastries and three cups of coffee before sloping out onto the patio, in the cold, to smoke one cigarette which she showed every appearance of savouring to the full. When she returned indoors she was smiling, her cheeks glowing.

'Hey, Ma. You look well this morning.'

'So do you,' Mary replied, although her nerves were beginning to twang. What if the course was too difficult, too advanced, too challenging? Mel was only a beginner, while she had long forgotten everything that Luc . . . but there was only one way to find out. They would have to go and see it for themselves. Besides, she had invested a hefty chunk of her rapidly-dwindling resources in it. Keeley would kill her if she simply turned on her heel and said no, forget it, I can't do this.

Ballymaloe was a big country estate that made them whistle when they reached it, surprised by the extensive lands full of sheep and spring lambs, the ancient look of the place although it was purpose-built, had only been a cookery school in recent years. Mel grinned at the lambs, and blew them a kiss.

'Good morning, this morning! Tonight, mint sauce!'

'Oh, Mel!'

'Well, sorry, Ma, but chefs can't be sentimental, can they? Nature produces food for us to eat and it's up to us to make the most of it. Besides, I love roast lamb.'

Again Mary thought of Mel's father, her cool Swedish father with not an ounce of sentiment in his body. It wasn't the kind of person she ever wanted to be – but on the other hand, where had softness ever got her? Not an inch. If she'd continued as she started out, she'd be cooking sludge at The Lantern today, deferring to Cathal and carrying out his instructions to the letter.

'Well, let's check in and see what's what.'

Inside the house perhaps forty people, were chatting, coffee cups in hand. The other students, they were informed amidst introductions, and everyone looked at Mel rather surprised; she was easily the youngest and most glamorous of them. After a tour of the kitchen gardens and other facilities the course finally got under way, and Mary panicked a little to see Mel paired off with someone else, a doughty-looking woman of at least fifty who was, she said, a pillar of the Irish Countrywomen's Association. Dear God, they would hate each other, Mel with her lipstick and jewellery, the pillar with her support tights and sensible shoes! But as they stationed themselves at the tables assigned to them Mel was giggling, and to her curiosity so was the lady from the ICA.

First, an introduction to local produce. As the lecture progressed Mary found herself relaxing, listening with increasing interest; it reminded her of the day she had sat in Luc's kitchen over a plate of truffles, the day she had guessed all of his fruit and vegetables by smell, shape, weight and texture. Absorbed, she listened, and after the first hour was astonished to hear herself asking questions.

Questions! As a schoolgirl she had never asked a single one, reluctant to attract attention, reluctant to challenge authority or embark down unknown paths. But she was thirty-five now, she reminded herself; and besides Mel was asking questions by the dozen with not the slightest sign of shyness. If a teenager could do it, she could certainly do it.

The morning flew by, and a lunch over which they scarcely saw each other, but got acquainted with the other students. There was a very flamboyant restaurateur with a serious moustache and a serious air of authority, a waistcoat and a well-established restaurant, he said, just doing a refresher course; there were two widowed sisters who hoped to open a guesthouse together in the summer; there was a man whose wife had left him with five children to feed and, apparently, a most consoling small, profitable farm; there was a nun who had left her convent and proposed to teach home economics. Most of all, Mary warmed to a small, humorous woman in jeans and a Paco sweatshirt who simply wanted, she explained, to be able to cook for the many guests she liked to entertain.

'I'm always asking friends round,' she said candidly, 'only to end up flinging spaghetti in a pot and then cooking it to mush. I thought it was time I found out how to do it *al dente* – and besides I wanted a break from my husband and kids, they were driving me up a wall. Up the great bloody wall of China, if you want the truth.'

Mary laughed, thinking of Keeley who'd battled through her

daunting French course at the Aix Chamber of Commerce so many years before, and achieved her goal. And then she laughed again, for no particular reason other that she was enjoying herself.

Although she had a serious purpose, and life at The Lantern had always been so deathly serious, she suddenly saw no reason not to enjoy herself. Why not? They could all be struck dead by a bolt of lightning, any number of disasters could happen to any of them, so why not simply make the most of this interesting, care-free day? For the first time in longer than she could remember, she began to relax.

Relax, and stop worrying, stop wondering, stop feeling guilty about anything. Maybe that was why her cheddar fondue, when she finally produced it, tasted so good. It was a simple dish, demanding nothing more than some garlic, parsley and white wine with a bit of chutney, but she was thrilled with the attention it attracted, the compliments.

'You're a professional, aren't you?' demanded the bejeaned woman accusingly. Hugely flattered, Mary replied that – well – yes – she had studied cookery before. Ages ago.

'I thought so. It's like riding a bike. You never forget,' the woman said matter-of-factly, adding that her name was Jackie, she was a librarian with three kids, and she lived in Mayo. If Mary should ever happen to visit Mayo, drop in, Mary, take pot luck.

My God, Mary thought, astonished; I'm making a friend. Is it really this easy to make friends? Is this all there is to it, when you get the chance? During the course of the afternoon she chatted on and off to Jackie as she worked, discovering that Jackie had a daughter around Mel's age: 'Poisonous little wagon,' Jackie said succinctly, kneading the dough for fennel bread with vigour. 'But I suppose she'll be OK when she's about forty.'

So. Other women felt ambivalent about their kids too, did they? Until today Mary had never had a chance to find out, to compare notes with anyone. But she looked over at Mel, who was whacking Tabasco into something as she chatted with the moustached man in the waistcoat, and felt a surge of affection for her. Mel was selfish, ungrateful and disrespectful, she had always treated her mother like a housekeeper, almost a servant; but she was no worse, apparently, than other teenagers. Maybe she too would be fine when she was forty – or sooner, now that she was beginning to learn that her mother could not always be taken for granted.

It was a tiring but enjoyable day, and at the end of it everyone ate together in the house, sharing food and wine and joint observations. Mary was surprised to hear people asking her questions, showing interest when she explained her plans to open a pub in France, hesitantly because it was not yet certain, it depended on – well, on various factors.

She didn't add that Mel was chief among them, but she kept her eye on Mel as she talked, waiting for some acknowledging look or smile or gesture. None came, because Mel was immersed in conversation with the assertive restaurateur and the nun, showing not the slightest hint of shyness or reserve, despite her youth. Showing no evidence, in fact, that she could not manage perfectly well without her mother at her side. Whatever Cathal had done, Mary could not dispute that he had given their daughter confidence – maybe even a bit too much, she thought, as she sat waiting in vain for Mel to turn to her, to refer to her in some way as her mother. But Mel didn't, and gradually she gave up with what she reluctantly recognised as relief. It was abundantly clear that Mel was well able to hold her own.

Although the atmosphere was sociable, and Mary was having fun meeting people with a common interest, it was the food itself that enchanted her. Virtually everything was fresh out of the earth or ocean, and as she held it, smelled it, she felt some pull in her blood, something quickening and reviving in her. Her ability to chop and slice soon attracted comment, envy from the restaurateur who marvelled at her dexterity, but it was when things were actually cooking, simmering and sizzling at their moment of perfection, that she felt most pleasure, most satisfaction, her spirit returning to those distant days when she had been so free and eager, her mind vaulting forward to a future she could now almost taste.

'Of course,' Jackie remarked one morning, 'food is a substitute for sex, you know.'

Sex! Mary laughed, hardly able to remember what sex was like at all, certainly unable to remember any great joy in it. But people raved about it, people who had evidently known something she had not; along with food it was one of the great driving forces of the universe. Could it really compare with this? As she sliced and stirred she began to wonder, to gaze speculatively at the daughter who was the product of it, would soon have a sex life of her own. Something jolted in her as she thought of it, a daughter outpacing her in terms of human relationships, learning things she never had, discovering vistas she had never seen. Her mind wandered and her vigour redoubled as she cooked, the ingredients seemed to dance in their pans, and she was much gratified to see each dish turning out better than the last, testimony that she could, at least, do this much. Do it well, and give pleasure to those who consumed what she produced.

They were into their fourth day of the week-long course before Mary got a chance to corner Mel and suggest that, tonight, they might eat together at a nearby pub for a change. Just the two of them, without any of the new people they had been meeting.

'OK,' Mel said offhandedly, 'if you don't mind not being surrounded by admirers for one night.'

Mary grinned, embarrassed even as she admitted the truth of it; people were constantly congratulating her on the dishes she was turning out, salivating over her spiced lamb, calf's liver with whiskey and tarragon, pheasant with celery and port, cod with cream and bayleaves. Darina Allen was an adventurous tutor, yet all her ingredients could be got within a radius of ten miles or less, and Mary was having a ball speculating how everything might be adapted in Aix. Mel was finding the recipes harder going, not as easy as they looked or sounded, but she was enjoying the course too for its social aspect, the chance to see how The Lantern's food might be jazzed up at a later date.

They drove to a pub about eight miles away, one with music and a belief, apparently, that it had to rise to the standard of the locally infamous Ms Allen. From a handwritten menu Mel picked beef-in-beer casserole with haricots, and Mary chose salted bass with olive oil and herbs, potatoes dauphinoise on the side. God, how Cathal and the customers would recoil at the sound of that! Indulgently, she let Mel have a glass of wine, telling herself that it was better than slugging cider with a bunch of yobs up some alleyway; if Mel got gradually used to alcohol under supervision, it might lose the allure of forbidden fruit.

'So. Are you enjoying the course, Mel?'

Mel sat back and crossed her legs, looking around her at the pub's rustic decor, half-listening to the music wafting from the bar area.

'Yeah. I am. But not as much as you are.'

'Me?'

'Yeah. You're really having a blast, aren't you?'

It wasn't exactly the word Mary would have used, but it was accurate; she was having what Mel called a blast. Food at last, proper decent food, and fun, and new friends . . . she couldn't remember when she had ever enjoyed herself so much. Only once, ever, that brief winter with Luc and Félix and Keeley.

'Yes. I am actually, since you put it that way.'

'Uh huh. You fit right in, Ma. I can see you were born for this.'

Mary gazed into the fire, and then looked candidly at her.

'Can you, Mel?'

'Yep. I never thought it in The Lantern's kitchen, but I can see it here – you're off the leash.'

Off the leash. That was exactly it, Mary thought, off the damn leash at last.

'Well – I just hope it's going to be some use, Mel. I could never cook or serve this kind of food at The Lantern. But I could in Aix.'

'Why couldn't you do it at The Lantern, Ma?'

'Because . . . because your father is very traditional, and so are the customers. The pub is not in what you'd call a foodie area. Tastes are traditional there, nobody wants anything new, anything different or unfamiliar – even if it's the same thing just cooked differently.'

'D'you think not?'

'I know not. I did try to experiment, years ago . . . but it was no use. I had to go back to what everyone recognised and wanted.'

'Huh. I bet I could change their tunes now, some of them anyway . . . the stuff you serve up is old hat, Ma. I reckon everyone is tired of it.'

'Do you? Well, then, when you're a bit older you can have my job! If you want it. I'd be delighted if you could pep things up . . . but Mel, I tried before, in vain, and I couldn't be bothered trying again. I want to start over from scratch.'

'Yes. I can see that.'

Mel looked thoughtful as their food arrived, hot, fresh and appealing this time, brought by a much perkier waitress than the one in the other pub. Here, the napkins were linen instead of paper, the dishes were all ceramic, there were flowers on the table and an aura of welcome, of efficient interest in the guests.

'God, I'm starving! And you're starving too, Ma . . . it's only now I realise it.'

'Sorry?' Mary wasn't sure she followed.

'You're starving. Really hungry, for – well, I'm not sure for what exactly. But it's something to do with cooking properly and having your own pub and doing your own thing. You're like a different person down here.'

Cautiously, Mary cut into her fish, pausing to savour the smell of it. 'Am I?'

'Yes! You know you are – you even look different, sound different. You're all chat with everyone and you talk as if – as if you know what you're talking about. Some of the people on the course are real amateurs, but you're not. You just love it, and understand it. All of it.'

'M'mm . . . I do love it, Mel, and understand it. Everything Luc taught me is coming back, after all these years.'

Mel didn't answer immediately, and for a while there was silence as they ate, interrupted only occasionally by comments on the casserole or the sea-bass. Mel was halfway through her meal before she spoke again.

'So you really want to do it, then?'

'Do – it? The pub in Aix, you mean?'

'Yeah. The pub in Aix, the whole thing . . . you really want to leave Dad and do it, don't you?'

'Yes, Mel. Yes. I do.'

Mel finished eating, and looked away from her, looked down into the burning logs.

'Then – then I guess that's what you're going to have to do, Ma. If it's what you really want.'

Mary swallowed, and also stopped eating, put down her cutlery to look at her daughter's flushed face.

'I only want it if – if you think you can handle it, Mel. Do you think there's any chance you could handle it?'

Mel sighed, and hesitated. 'Do you think there's any chance you could get back with Dad?'

Mary was aware of her tone becoming firmer, almost assertive.

'No. There's no chance of that. None whatever. I'm sorry, Mel, but I just couldn't . . . I will stay in the house if you want me to, for as long as you want me to, but Cathal and I are finished. Our relationship, whatever it was, is over.'

'Why, Ma? What went wrong?'

Mel was leaning forward now, her expression a mixture of curiosity and anxiety, her gaze level with her mother's.

'I – I can't tell you. I'm sorry. I would if I could, but – it really is too complicated to explain to you at your age, and besides Cathal isn't here to defend himself. You'll just have to believe me . . . please, Mel. I'm not making it up. We really are all wrong for each other, and very unhappy together.'

'But I never heard you having any rows.'

'No. I gave up having them when you were born, for the sake of peace . . . for your sake, I suppose. Maybe that was a mistake. Maybe rows are healthier . . . but it's too late for us even to fight now. I just want to end it and salvage what's left of my life while there's still time.'

Mel reflected, pushing her fork in and out of the last piece of beef on her plate.

'You – haven't – there isn't—'

'What? What are you trying to say, Mel?'

'Ma, you haven't met anyone else, have you? There isn't some other guy, in France?'

'Me? In France? Some other – oh, Mel! No, of course not! Don't be silly!'

'Why? What's so silly? I mean, you might have. That man with the five kids says his wife left him for some other man.'

'But I – oh, Mel, really! I'm thirty-five for God's sake, I'm worn out, I haven't time for—'

'You don't look worn out. And you're not *that* old. Not totally ancient.'

'Well, maybe not. But I'm certainly old enough to have sense, and to be realistic. All I want is to cook, and be my own boss, and be free. Answerable to nobody.'

'Really? You never, ever want to meet anyone else?'

'Mel, I haven't even thought about it. The thought has literally never crossed my mind.'

Mary knew she sounded adamant, and convincing, yet something niggled at her. How could Mel possibly know the things that haunted her in the night, the feelings of isolation, of having missed out somehow on life, on romance, on a real, decent relationship? Cathal was absolutely no advertisement for his gender, yet she sometimes wondered whether there might be somebody out there somewhere . . . somebody like Vincent, one of the worthwhile men she remembered Keeley insisting did exist, all those years ago after Erik had ditched her. That belief that kept Keeley going until finally she had met Vincent, and lived fifteen wonderful years with him. Whatever Keeley's wretched loss now, she had those memories, she had been loved, she was fulfilled as a woman. Whereas she, Mary, had never felt loved in her life.

'All right. If you say so. I just wondered.'

Mary forced a smile. 'No, Mel. I'm not planning to spring a new stepfather on you or anything like that. All I want for now is – is my freedom. Once bitten, as they say, twice shy.'

'I suppose . . . well, anyway, Ma, I've been thinking, like Keeley said. If you really, desperately want to live in France, and if you promise I can visit whenever I like and that you'll ring me every day and I can work in this pub in the summers if I want and you can sort things with Dad, then – then I guess it'll be all right. I don't want you to go, but I can see you'll be miserable if you don't.'

Hardly able to speak, filled with more guilt than she had ever known, Mary reached to her and took her hand.

'Oh, Mel. You don't have to do this, you know, if you don't want to. You really don't.'

Mel's eyes glimmered slightly in the firelight, but her voice stayed steady.

'I know. That's what Keeley said. But you – you can try it, anyway. I – I might come over at Easter, instead of going skiing. That's only three months away . . .'

'Oh, Mel. I wish I could just take you with me right away, for good. I will take you, if you want to come.'

'No, Ma. I've got school and my friends and Dad – Dad and I get on great, Ma, even though you and he don't.'

'I know. I know you do. He's mad about you, Mel.'

'Yeah – well, anyway, I don't want to leave him on his own. And there's the grandparents, too, they look after me . . . Granny Jameson is going to kill you, you know, she thinks you're nuts. So does Granny Sullivan.'

'Yes . . . that's part of the problem, Mel. I've spent too long trying to please them already, trying to be a dutiful daughter and daughter-in-law and all the rest of it. But I'm just not cut out for it. Not any more.'

Even more intently, Mel leaned forward.

'You only got married for me, didn't you, Ma? You only married Dad so I'd have two parents and a proper home?'

'Yes. That was why, Mel. I never loved your father. Nor he me.'

'That was stupid. I'd never marry anyone I didn't love.'

No, she thought. That's what I'd have said, when I was young. I could never understand why women married awful men, why they stayed with them . . . but I understand now.

'I hope you'll never have to, Mel. I hope you'll fall in love with somebody who loves you – and that you never have a child until you're sure about that, sure of each other.'

Wanly, Mel smiled. 'No way! You won't catch me getting into that kind of mess, it's not the dark ages now . . . but anyway, since you did get married for my sake, I reckon it's only fair to let you do whatever you want now in return. I wish I didn't have to – but I will do it, Ma.'

'Oh, Mel.'

Part of Mary felt euphoric, released like a bird into the sky; part of her felt weighted, wretched, laden with guilt and responsibility and sadness.

'What decided you? I haven't put any pressure on you, have I?'

'No. But I – I've made such a mess of Keeley's life, I don't want to make a mess of yours too.'

'Oh, Mel, it's not the same—'

'Yes, Ma. In a way it is. The minute I saw your face when you started cooking this week, real cooking, I saw – I don't know, I saw you looking the same way Keeley used to look when she was with Vincent. Really happy.'

Really happy. At this wrenching moment Mary had no idea what it meant, how anyone could ever be really happy. But Mel was giving her the chance to get as close to it as was possible. Wordlessly, she pulled her daughter to her, there over their empty plates, and held her to her, her tears soaking into the cool blonde hair.

They talked late into the night that night, and every night for the rest of the week, completing their course by day in a kind of harmony that was new to them both, an embryonic affinity that enabled them to laugh together, enjoy each other and draw close. Instead of exasperating her, Mary thought that Mel was now beginning to exasperate everyone else with her confident nonchalance, the way she had of sounding so authoritative for her age. Not yet fifteen, there were times when she sounded twice it. 'Get real!' she told the nun who wanted to make a coq-au-vin without any alcohol in it, and Mary heard the nun mutter under her breath in retort. 'Cheeky little bitch.'

Mel really was cheeky, even to the indomitable Darina Allen, but in Mary's eyes her daughter could do no wrong now, and she confided in her as if she were an adult, cherishing their time together because it was limited.

'It was all my mother's doing . . . she wanted me to marry Cathal because he was well off . . . she manoeuvered me into it when I was vulnerable.'

'You should have just said no, I won't! You should have made up your own mind – it's too late now to go blaming her for it!'

'I suppose it is. But she still likes Cathal, won't hear a bad word against him—'

'Such as?'

Such as that he's a stingy, domineering bastard, Mary thought, and a cross-dresser as well, Hitler in drag. God, I can't wait to get away from him, get shut of him!

'Oh, never mind. So long as he looks after you properly, I won't complain – and he does look after you properly, Mel, doesn't he?'

'Spoils me rotten,' Mel agreed cheerfully. Reassured, Mary sensed that there were no dark currents between father and daughter, that the pair genuinely got on well, had already weathered four months of her absence without trauma. If there were any shocks in store, Cathal would surely have sprung them by now, in desperation, in retaliation, whatever. But he had sprung nothing, done nothing wrong where Mel was concerned. The two might miss her domestic services, Mary thought, but she did not think either of them would sob themselves to sleep for very long after she left for good. Cathal's pride would throb, and Mel might pine for a week, but after that . . . they were survivors, both of them. Tough, hardy, resilient – just as Keeley had always been, until Vincent died, and was now trying to be again.

Keeley who, even in the midst of her own problems, had thought to talk to Mel, smooth this difficult path for her. It was because of Keeley's intervention, she felt sure, that Mel had given her a hearing, given her this chance. And, much as it grieved her to admit it, she knew that Mel was no martyr. If she thought she would be better off with her mother in France there was every chance that she would opt to go there with her; but Mel knew when she was well off. Mel was hard-headed, and although that was working in her favour at this moment, Mary felt a twinge; a gentler, sweeter daughter would be more rewarding, more endearing – and, also, much more difficult to leave. Admittedly Mel had mellowed a little since Vincent's death, seemed slightly more vulnerable and more affectionate than before; but she would never be a shrinking violet, much less any kind of victim. Yet she was a young girl, her only child, and Mary felt a shiver as she thought of the scenario awaiting her back in Dublin, when she told Cathal and the two sets of parents that yes, she was finally, irrevocably leaving. There were going to be endless recriminations, accusations, and it would take all her strength to hold steady, hold fast.

But she would hold fast. Freedom was so close now, so near she could feel it surging in every nerve, and she was going to get it, achieve it, possess it. Like a prisoner tunnelling out of jail she could feel the adrenalin pumping, the braced tautness, the terror of disaster and the thrill of the chase. Leesha would pursue her, Kevin would implore her, Cathal would decry her and his parents would disown her, but she was going to escape, and reinvent herself. In the eyes of today's youth culture she was all but an old woman, poised on the edge of middle age, but she was going to be a new woman. Still Mel's mother, but her own woman.

Chapter Seventeen

I'm home, Keeley thought. I am home, at last. Even without
Vincent, this is my home, this is where I belong. I will never
go back to Pearse Gardens again, I will probably never see
my parents again, but I know now for certain that I belong
here. I never thought I did until I got back, until I saw the
garden maturing and blooming, heard all the messages on the
answering machine from Félix, Luc, Francine, Sylvie, everyone who makes up the fabric of my life here. Vincent and
I built this house together, it's the product of the work we
did and the life we shared, it is us, it is ours, it is mine.
It is me.

From the kitchen window she could see Tony out in the
garden, talking to Alain Jou in some kind of tortured franglais,
and she waved to them as she prepared a tea tray, strolled out
to them with it; already the weather was mild enough to eat
outdoors provided you kept your sweater on. Spreading the
things on the table, she grinned curiously at them.

'What have you been talking about for so long?'

'Exhibitions,' Alain replied enthusiastically. 'Now that Tony
is here I can supervise him, organise his equipment and his time
professionally, double his output by the end of the year if he
takes my advice.'

For convenience Alain said this in French, and although he
didn't understand it Tony nodded and beamed. Mischievously,
Keeley grinned again.

'Alain's just saying what a dimwit you are, what a pain it
is having to communicate with a dummy who doesn't speak
French.'

'Yep,' Tony agreed heartily. 'It's a pain in the butt all right.
Not that I've ever been able to feel pain in my butt. But I'll
learn French. You can teach me.'

'You,' Keeley retorted, 'can go to the Chamber of Commerce like I did, and learn there.'

As she said it she thought it was a good idea; she could drive Tony into Aix and leave him to meet people, make friends as she had done. Even if he didn't learn anything he'd be happy to get out a bit, and besides the idea of being able to achieve something might boost his morale; for all his busy banter she sensed that he was uncertain on this new turf, conscious of how much help he needed. A nurse had been found, a strong brisk woman who was already bullying him, to his evident amusement, but she couldn't be there round the clock, and sometimes Keeley found herself having to do the most ridiculous, pathetic or peculiar things, down to holding a handkerchief while he blew his nose in it. On a larger scale, she was going to have to get rid of her beloved BMW and replace it with a space wagon, because getting him in and out of the car was a nightmare. But at least the wide, single-level house accommodated him with ease, she wasn't going to have to demolish walls or hack the place to pieces. And, somewhat to her surprise, she was enjoying his company; he could be very sardonic at times, very funny. God only knew what fist he'd make of French though, with a Dublin accent so thick that even she couldn't understand him sometimes.

He'd never manage the two-hour classes without help, without some kind of minder in case he needed any little thing done for him . . . they were only little things though, so maybe if he made friends with some kind souls he would be able to manage. Anyway, they could give it a lash and see what happened. She'd be driving into Aix anyway, to start her own classes in art history and literature – God almighty, Christy would have a brain haemorrhage if he could see the pair of them, studying! But she was delighted the university had admitted her, after much humming and hawing, could hardly believe that some day she, Keeley Butler, might even get a degree.

Alain Jou seemed delighted with life too, as he sat sipping tea at the beechwood table, without milk in the French manner.

'Your brother could never fulfil his potential before, Keeley, because he was cooped up in a small room, in the wrong climate, he had no peers to compare himself with . . . I will introduce him to some of my other protegés, I will introduce him to buyers and gallery owners . . . Serge will be here tomorrow . . . I will organise for Tony to have books and videos, see other painters' work, attend lectures . . . stimulus is very important, you know,

and if I understand correctly he's never had any. I had no idea
he was so mentally undernourished.'

Mentally undernourished? Alain, Keeley thought, it's a crying
shame I can't introduce you to our dear father, Mr Christy
Butler. You think Tony is undernourished, you'd want to meet
our oul fella. A rabbit would take more interest in its offspring
than Christy ever took in his. If you feel you can fill in the gaps,
now, feel free.

'And what of you, Keeley? How are you progressing, after
your – your terrible bereavement?'

The French were exquisitely polite, and Keeley knew that
the correct answer was to murmur discreetly to the effect that
she was managing quite well, *merci beaucoup*. But something
in Tony's candour, or in her brief return to Dublin perhaps,
seemed to have rubbed off on her.

'I'm pole-axed with pain, Alain. Absolutely banjaxed, on my
knees with it. Other than that I'm grand, thanks.'

Alain gaped, bewildered and blinking at them as they both
laughed, brother and sister, sharing some slang he didn't understand. Really there was no point in trying to speak English,
if they were only going to make fun of him ... coughing
discreetly, he reverted to French and left Keeley to interpret
for Tony. Trying to look contrite, Keeley asked him something
that had been on her mind, glad for Tony's sake of the language
barrier.

'Alain – if we do take Tony out, to exhibitions and to meet
people I mean – they – you – don't think they'll give him a hard
time, do you? I mean, he is in a wheelchair and it is an effort
to talk to him—'

Alain considered. 'Keeley, Tony's work will speak for itself.
For years already, it has done. People have always asked me
about the painter, and now they'll be delighted to meet him
for themselves. Besides, we'll keep an eye on him, between us.
He'll be fine.'

'Well, OK, if you think so. It's just that – I mean, I know these
soirées and *vernissages* can be a bit stiff, some of the guests are
very prim and proper, and Tony isn't exactly—'

Alain shrugged, and gestured eloquently.

'No. He isn't. But he is a very good painter, and I intend to
pull all his potential out of him, make him a great one. Genuine
art lovers won't care about anything else.'

'No. I suppose they won't.' Keeley smiled at Alain, thinking of their first meeting, of how she had been as raw and clumsy as Tony was now. But she had made progress, fulfilled her potential as Alain had fulfilled his: after quitting his 'day job' in the department store he had gone on to become the best-known art agent and critic in Aix. These days he was something of a celebrity, often heard on radio, writing a lively newspaper column that attracted much controversy. Tony would get off to great advantage under his protection, maybe even fulfil, some day, the potential that Vincent had been the very first to spot. Thinking of Vincent, exclaiming over those crude paintings in the hospital that distant day, she felt something click and lock into place in her mind; she was going to prove him right, nurture Tony's talent, bring out everything that lay dormant and frustrated in him. She was going to make him succeed, as she had succeeded, thanks to Vincent's faith and vision.

Later that evening, after Alain had left, she phoned her mother and held the phone for Tony so that he could speak to Gertie. Gertie worried and fretted, but he replied enthusiastically that he was fine, never better, loving every minute of his new life. Then he tried, they both tried yet again, to persuade their mother to join them, eyeing each other as they listened to her protests and excuses. In the background Keeley could hear the evening news bulletin on television, and was suddenly weary as she listened to the headline: 'A man was shot dead in Belfast . . .' Violence. The solution to everything. The same news, the same headline she had first heard when she was only nine or ten years old . . . it seemed to her that nothing ever changed in Ireland. Certainly Gertie hadn't changed, and would never change now; the conversation ended in mutual resignation, and neither Keeley nor Tony even bothered to ask how Christy was. As she put down the phone they eyed each other again, conscious of a guilty but tremendous sense of liberation.

It was more than a week later, when Keeley was sitting talking to Tony about his first day at his French class, that she heard a car coming up the drive, and frowned. Damn. She wanted to hear everything he had to tell her, especially about the other students whose help would be crucial to him, she really didn't want visitors just now.

But it was a taxi, and the moment it stopped Mary jumped out of it, flew to her and seized her in an engulfing embrace.

'Keeley! I made it! I'm here, I'm here!'

Thrilled, she grabbed her friend by the shoulders, held her and looked hard at her.

'You made it – you did it – you got away?'

'Yes!' All but dancing with delight, Mary bent briefly to kiss Tony, flung her bag and scarf on the grass and threw herself down on a garden chair, beaming.

Keeley gazed at the heap of suitcases by the door, a stack of them that really did seem to indicate that Mary was here, this time, to stay.

'I don't believe it! You seemed so uncertain, right up to the very last minute . . . but here you are! Tell me everything – did Cathal go mad, what about Mel, what did your parents—?'

Mary grinned from ear to ear.

'Cathal went bananas, absolutely berserk, when it finally sank in that I meant it, I was leaving him. Yelled and shouted and said I'd never set foot in his house again if I left it . . . it certainly wasn't what you'd call an amicable separation, in fact I think he would have hit me only he was afraid Mel might hear. But there was nothing he could do, and I think he got some consolation out of winning the battle for Mel, as he saw it. Since she's staying with him, people will assume I must be the guilty party, everyone will be on his side.'

'But he can't seriously have been thinking about his public image at a moment like that.'

'You bet your boots he can. I think it mattered more to him than anything, apart from Mel.'

'But what about Mel?'

'She – she was upset. Is upset. But that's the point, Keeley – it was Mel who urged me on, told Cathal to let me go. I don't know what exactly you said to her that night, but it worked wonders. Even though she didn't want her parents to split up she still took my side, said she understood and would be all right provided she can visit frequently and we talk all the time – we're going to have to work out something about the phone bill, because it'll be astronomical.'

'Yes, well, never mind – go on.'

'So the situation is that we're going to see how she gets on and she's coming over at Easter. And then, if the pub is open by summer, she's going to work with me in it . . . if it's OK with you for her to stay here?'

Anxiously, Mary looked at Keeley. But Keeley nodded.

'Yes. I told you that would be OK with me, and it is.'

'Oh, God, Keel, you are wonderful. Just wonderful. Anyway, the next thing was the parents. Cathal's and mine, the full set, all lined up like judge and jury . . . my mother was the worst of the lot, she said she was totally disgusted and disappointed in me, tried to get Dad to say mean things too only he wouldn't, he seemed to understand better. Then there were Carmel and Donal, going on and on about what kind of woman I was, a woman who could abandon their son and their granddaughter – but Mel stuck by me, said she wasn't being abandoned at all because we'd still be in daily contact, and that she didn't want to live with parents who weren't getting on anyway. That shook them all, I can tell you – not only to hear Mel taking my side but to hear the bit about us not getting on. It was like – as if – if nobody said it, it couldn't be true. But Mel said it, loud and clear. Cathal looked as if he was going to faint.'

Keeley sat down beside her, and took her hand.

'So you – you got away. You've escaped, you've really done it, at last.'

'Yes. At last, I have.'

'And how do you feel now?'

'I feel – oh, Keel, I feel wonderful, at this moment! I know that I might slide a bit later on, and there'll be moments when I'll miss Mel like hell . . . but in a funny way I wonder if I might actually be a better mother to her now that I've taken my own life in hand. More cheerful, less resentful, better able to communicate with her because I think she respects me now, sees me as a person instead of just a body running round after her . . . she was so strong, so good about it, I was amazed. If you want the truth, I really warmed to her, for the first time since she was a baby. We talked non-stop all the time we were at Ballymaloe, like friends instead of spoiled child and miserable mother. Even though we'll be apart a lot from now on, I felt we were drawing closer.'

Abruptly, Tony looked up. In their excitement, both Mary and Keeley had forgotten him.

'Good on you, Mary. I think you did the right thing.'

They gazed at him. 'Do you, Tony?'

'Yeah, I do. You've only got one life. Go for it.'

Suddenly, Keeley laughed. 'So here I am, with two refugees on my hands! God knows how we're all going to get along . . . but I hope we will. I'm really glad to have you both here with me.'

Mary beamed again, and squeezed her hand. 'I know things

are different now, Keel, but I'll do my best to make it fun for you, to have good times together like when we were young – and I'll help you with Tony too, I'm taller and stronger than you, I'll—'

Tony grinned. 'I know. You'll hit me a box if I get out of line. I know all about you, Miss Mary Jameson. You hit my oul fella a box once.'

'So I did, Tony. So I did.'

They looked at each other in wonder, and then all three of them laughed. At what in particular, none of them knew, but it felt like a good start to their new life together. They made an odd group, they supposed, with their various sorrows, problems and challenges, but they could help each other, and share whatever strengths they had.

It took some time, but gradually the new household got established, began to knit and blend together. Three days a week Keeley drove Tony to his French class in Aix and then went on to her own studies at the university, a project she found more difficult than she had anticipated. Tony made both friends and progress, knowing that he needed to learn the language and get acquainted with people who would sometimes take him off his sister's hands; but Keeley found the university daunting. Everybody was better qualified, better educated than herself, and keeping up to the standard, at lectures and seminars, was a real battle.

'But you don't have to do it,' Mary pointed out. 'It's not like school, it's voluntary.'

'I know. But I want to do it. I *will* do it. I'll probably fail some exams and take longer than everybody else, but I'll get there. I'll get a degree, you'll see.'

'If you say so! Just don't panic, don't get in a twist about it.'

Keeley had to smile at that. If Mary herself hadn't panicked, all those years ago, she wouldn't have married Cathal, wouldn't have inflicted all that endless misery on herself. Wouldn't have lost out on Luc either, and missed the boat to gastronomic stardom. But now Mary seemed reborn, with a kind of stately calm, not panicking or even worrying about anything.

'How's it going?' Keeley asked her one evening after Mary had spent a long time on the phone to Mel.

'As well as can be expected. She misses me, but she's looking forward to coming over . . . and to a disco at the tennis club on Saturday night. I said she was to be home by midnight, and she said her name wasn't Cinderella Sullivan – but Cathal's going to collect her, so she won't have much chance to get up to mischief.'

'Good,' Keeley replied, grudgingly thinking that she had to give Cathal that much: he was an attentive father, had never shirked his duties or attacked Mary through Mel. A prize shit, but not one whose daughter was ever going to get a reputation for hanging round street corners. The Sullivan name was too important for that.

'But it's not mine any more,' Mary told her a few days later. 'I've decided to go back to Jameson.'

And she did. While Keeley was busy at college, and Tony was painting at home or out with Alain Jou, she began the search for a pub premises, visiting estate agents and introducing herself as Mary Jameson. Keeley noticed one day that she had even taken off her wedding ring, and reflected on the difference between them; her own wedding ring and Vincent's were so precious to her. Nearly every day, she still visited his grave.

But Tony and college and the search for the pub were all very distracting, if she was not happy at least she was not lonely, during the day, or idle. Only at night, when she went alone to the bed she had shared . . . or with Francine, sometimes, she missed Vincent acutely. His mother was having a very hard time getting over his death, their mutual visits often ended in tears, and she cried herself to sleep afterwards.

'But that's only natural,' Mary told her one morning when she could not disguise her puffy face, her throbbing pain. 'It's only been six months. You're allowed to cry, Keel.'

But if Mary provided comfort and understanding it was Tony, surprisingly, who provided inspiration. Despite his severe and permanent handicap he was almost always in good form, revelling in every new experience, in the light, in the garden, in the new friends he was making. Not everybody was friendly to him, some people even seemed to dismiss him as mentally handicapped because he was physically handicapped; at an exhibition in Serge Rolland's gallery Keeley even saw people walking right by him as if he were invisible, excluding him from the conversation they were having only two metres away. But he just shrugged.

'C'est la vie.'

That was one of the first expressions he had learned, and he repeated it whenever anything went wrong, in atrocious French with a wry grin. As the days went by Keeley found herself becoming fond of him, and protective of him, inclined to worry if he appeared to be pushing himself too hard.

'Nonsense,' Alain Jou retorted when he heard that. 'Let him push himself as hard and far as he can. I want at least a dozen seriously good paintings out of him by next Christmas.'

Keeley and Mary both found it painful to see Tony painting with his brush in his mouth, but Alain was determined, unmerciful, a virtual slavedriver. 'Come on, Tony,' he would say over and over when he came to visit. 'What's keeping you?'

And Tony would beam. 'Dunno, Alain, it must be that game of squash I played earlier, has me worn out it has.'

And, eventually, there were results. Tony completed his first painting in early March – another ragged jagged business Keeley thought, only lighter, brighter than the dark work he had done in Ireland. Alain was delighted.

'Yes. Good. Very good. You can have tomorrow off, and start the next one on Thursday.'

Mary thought Alain was a bully, but Keeley began to see his strategy: Tony was to be given no pity, no quarter; he was to be treated exactly the same as Alain's other protegés, because that was what he wanted above all – to feel normal, a part of things, a painter like the rest of them. Alain had about ten, whose agent he was, and he took Tony to meet them all, see their work.

'They're your rivals,' he said. 'This is the standard you're up against. You can equal it, and better it, if you set your mind to it.'

'Right so,' Tony replied. 'If we're all fighting for exhibition space in a limited number of galleries, I suppose I better had set me mind to it.'

And, as the second painting began to take shape, Keeley was astonished. It was a picture of Mary, sitting out by the pool with the dog Cleo at her feet, and although it was still fairly abstract it was, for the first time, recognisably human. There was a quality of calm about it, a kind of peacefulness, and Mary posed for it every evening at the same time, casually, unselfconsciously. Tony winked at her.

'Don't worry, I won't ask you to strip – not when anyone else is around anyway, though I must say you're a goodlooking woman.'

Mary laughed, and was flattered. It was a long time since anyone had commented on her looks. Not that Tony was exactly what you'd call an eligible bachelor, she thought with a surprised smile, but he was observant, he had a good eye. Thereafter, as the picture progressed, Keeley was amused to sometimes see Mary putting on a bit of blusher before she sat for it, going out into the garden in a faintly perfumed haze.

But, during the day, Mary seriously set herself to the question of finding a pub. Visiting everything from derelict garages to deconsecrated churches, abandoned warehouses to customised brasseries, she scoured Aix with estate agents, with Luc and Félix, driving the BMW that Keeley had replaced, but could not bear to sell.

'I still love it,' Keeley said, 'but it's no use for Tony. I have to have a space wagon. So you may as well keep it, and use it.'

Delighted, Mary drove all over the city in it, but still could not find anything that remotely looked like having the makings of an Irish pub.

'Damn!' she cursed. 'I really wanted to find somewhere by Easter, to show Mel when she arrives. I don't want her going back to Cathal telling him I can't even get started.'

And, although she didn't say it, she wanted to get started for another reason. Already she had gone through over five thousand pounds of Cathal's stolen money, and the speedy expenditure frightened her. Air fares, phone bills, Ballymaloe – there had been a lot of expense, and although Keeley was very generous she didn't want to depend on her, she wanted to pay her own way. She needed to get her pub, and get cooking, as soon as possible. Already there was Mel's forthcoming plane fare to pay, because Cathal refused to cough up for the girl's visits to her mother, and then Mel's visit would doubtless eat another chunk out of the remaining money. Mel was what the magazines called 'a high-maintenance girl', who couldn't be let return to Ireland complaining of deprivation.

And then one day Luc came to call, looking tragic.

'What's wrong, Luc? You look like someone who lost a tenner and found a pound.'

Heavily, he lowered himself into a wicker chair on the terrace, and it creaked under his weight. With his bushy white hair, his thick dark eyebrows and his ever-increasing bulk, he looked intimidating, almost ferocious.

'Such horror. I have never heard the like.'

Mary poured him a beer and sat down beside him. 'The like of what?'

'The Moulin. The Vieux Moulin. My restaurant.'

'It's not your restaurant. You retired years ago.'

He frowned at her. 'I will always regard it as my restaurant. My beautiful restaurant. And now, what happens?'

'I don't know. What?'

'They sell it, that's what. The best, the most beautiful restaurant in all of Aix, all of Provence, and they sell it. They turn it into a *shop*!'

'A shop? Oh, no! Oh, Luc—'

'Oh, yes. I am driving by this morning, and I see a sign: property designated for commercial premises. The restaurant is closed. No lunch, no customers, nobody. Door closed. It is a tragedy, Mary, it is a *disgrace*!'

She was very saddened to hear it. The old Moulin, that they'd both loved so much, with its white kitchen and tiled floors, its thick walls and—

Oh, Jesus! Leaping to her feet, she grabbed his wrist and dragged him upright, out of his seat. 'Luc, come on – now, quick – we've got to find the owner!'

'But – Mary – it's no use, it is to become a shop—'

'Please, Luc, come on! Hurry!'

Spluttering, he lumbered after her as she ran to the car, and squeezed himself reluctantly into it, grabbing for his seat belt as she gunned the engine. Seconds later they were shooting down the drive, out onto the road to Aix in a cloud of dust.

'He *will* sell!' Mary repeated yet again a week later, like a dog with a bone. 'I'm going to get that place if it's the last thing I do. It's already got a kitchen, it's beautiful, it's perfect, it – it's home! Luc once said I belonged there, and he was right.'

'And how,' Keeley demanded for the twentieth time, 'are you going to get it?' Over the week they had tried everything, to no avail. First of all the Moulin's new owner refused to sell, then he wavered when Mary upped her offer. Not wanting to ask Keeley for more money than she had already offered to invest, Mary went to a bank which said certainly not, she had no collateral, no chance. In frustration she let off a lot of steam about it one night when Félix had come to visit, and was astonished when he said he would put up the difference; since Keeley had sold her business he had been thinking that it would be good to have a new interest, and he had every faith in her ability to make a flying success of the Moulin. Delirious with delight, Mary flung her arms around him as she had flung them that day years before, and next morning went running back to the man who owned the Moulin.

He would consider it, he said. And he did, for three agonising days, before saying no for the second time. In vain she pleaded, cajoled, argued and insisted; but his mind, he said, was made up. He wanted to open a shop, a ritzy shoe shop there on the square; it was a splendid location and he would make his fortune. Nothing she had said since, no amount of debate by phone or in person, had budged him one centimetre, and he was beginning to get irate, refusing even to take her calls any more.

'I don't know,' she repeated now, scowling at Keeley and at the kitchen wall by turns, 'but I want it and I tell you I'll get it.'

Keeley reflected, gazing into the dregs of the wine they had shared over dinner, a dinner cooked with passion and devoured with gusto. Mary's cooking was getting better and better – even Luc had raised an eyebrow one night on tasting her paper-fine lamb with minted potatoes.

'I don't think there's really any point,' she said at length, 'in approaching him again. You're banging your head on a stone wall.'

Mary sighed, recognising that Keeley was right; the proprietor was clamming up, turning hostile, refusing to negotiate at all.

'Well, if we can't get through the wall, there must be a way round it.'

'H'mm.'

In silence they sat mulling over it, staring into their wine, thinking. Mary felt almost hypnotised by the problem, could not stop worrying it, but for the first time since Vincent died Keeley felt wide awake, her mind running with the ball, enjoying the exercise. Over the years she and Vincent had confronted many business dilemmas, pondered and debated them here in this very kitchen. Sometimes the solution had taken ages to come to one or other of them, but it nearly always had come. They had shared a natural aptitude for this kind of thing.

Damn and bloody blast! What would Vincent think, what would he say or do? Gripping her glass Keeley racked her brains, trying to see the thing from some fresh angle, new perspective.

And then it hit her, with all the force of Christy Butler's fist.

'A shoe shop! A commercial premises!'

'Yeah. That's what the bastard says. Keeps saying, like a shagging parrot.'

'But Mary, the Moulin can't be a commercial premises! Not retail, anyway. It's a historic building. It's been a restaurant for years . . . they're so keen on preservation in Aix, they wouldn't give permission for a place like that to be turned into a shop.'

'But – he seems to have got permission already.'

'Yes . . . and how, I wonder? Is this some kind of deal, like the kind Cathal was involved in? Is this guy blackmailing or bribing someone?'

'Jesus, Keeley, we can't accuse him of that, he could sue us for libel—'

'Well then, we won't accuse him! We'll simply go to the *mairie* tomorrow and say we want to lodge a protest. We want this planning permission withdrawn . . . they're always withdrawing it, when people protest. I was once turned down for a salon myself, because the premises had traditionally been a pharmacy, and a herbalist's before that. You have to continue at least in the spirit of the place, keep the original façade – whereas this guy couldn't keep the Moulin's, not for a shoe shop!'

Mary began to rock back and forth on her chair, grasping her glass, clutching at the straw Keeley was holding out to her.

'God, we could protest! Or you could, because you're a long-established citizen, a respected member of the business community . . . they'd probably ignore me because I'm a foreigner and because they'll hear I want the place for myself – but you could lodge a protest. So could Luc, and Félix, and maybe Vincent's father would too!'

'I bet he would, if I asked him. Don't worry, Mary – just you leave this to me!'

Mary frowned, fiddled anxiously with her hair. 'But what if they find out you're planning to invest in my pub? They'll say you have a vested interest.'

'How would they find out? Huh? How?'

'Well, God knows, but they might—'

'Mary, wouldja give over worrying? They won't! I'm telling you, I can do this, I will do it! And just think, how sweet to beat Cathal at his own game. If for no other reason than that, you are going to get your pub. I'd swear it on a stack of bibles, if I had a stack!'

Slowly, Mary grinned at her, and Keeley grinned back. Airily, wickedly, resolutely, like the Keeley of old.

It was a week before the phone rang. Dashing to it Mary whipped it up, breathless as she was now every time it rang.

'Madame Jameson?'

'Yes?' Oh God, it was him, it was the man who owned the Moulin!

'Are you still interested in my premises? In the Vieux Moulin?'

She forced herself to sound nonchalant. 'Yes . . . well, I might be. Why do you ask?'

'I ask because I – I have run into some difficulties. With planning permission. Extremely annoying difficulties.'

'Oh?'

'It appears that someone has caused the building's history to be investigated. And now, the city fathers in their wisdom have decreed that my shoe shop is not suitable. I have consulted my lawyer, but she advises me that there is little hope of overturning their ruling.'

'Oh? Why is that?'

'It is because the Moulin, apparently, has been a hostelry of one kind or another for over two hundred years. A hostelry such as you inform me you wish to open yourself.'

The man's tone was pure acid, so bitter that she knew he was on to her, guessed that she was in some way behind the protest that had caused his trading licence to be revoked.

But if ever there was a moment for staying calm and standing firm, this was it. Virtually smelling the soups and sauces simmering in their pots, she struggled to sound normal, even sympathetic.

'I see. What a disappointment for you. But in that case, we may as well meet . . . my original offer still stands, and it is a fair one, I think.'

In fact it was more than fair; with Félix's money added to Keeley's, the man was not exactly going to be hard done by. In fact, he was going to turn a profit, get a good bit more for the premises than he had paid only six weeks earlier.

'Very well. Shall we say ten o'clock tomorrow morning?'

'Fine. I'll meet you there.'

As she hung up, her soul shot into orbit like a rocket off a launch pad. The Vieux Moulin! After all these years, she was going to cook there at last, come back as she had so fervently promised she would.

With a trembling hand and tears in her eyes, Mary signed the documents only two days later, and the Vieux Moulin was hers. All hers, officially, her pub, her property. As she wrote her name she recalled the last time she had signed 'Mary Jameson' on a formal agreement – her marriage certificate, binding her to Cathal Sullivan. And now, she felt, that long imprisonment was finally over, finished, done with. For the first time in her life, she had something of her own.

Deeming discretion the better part of valour, Keeley had said they'd better not be seen together in public at the moment, and refused her offer of a celebratory meal at a stupendous restaurant. Instead they were going to celebrate at home, tonight, with Luc and Félix and their wives, Lise and Annette. She was going to cook a banquet fit for the gods.

Then, tomorrow, an architect, a builder, a decorator. Kitchen staff, floor staff. Food and drink supplies, furniture, some kind of launch to let Aix know it now had an Irish pub. Her adrenalin level was such that she felt she could organise the whole thing overnight, have the pub open by dawn.

But first, the market. Ingredients for this feast she was going to cook up. Pocketing the documents and keys of the Moulin as carefully as if they were diamonds, she set off on foot, reached the market and was soon lost in it, lost in a daze of wonder and joy. What would Cathal say, when he heard she'd done it – or if he knew how she'd done it? Grimly she thought of him, of all the planning permissions she knew he had steered through deviant channels, or caused to be blocked. There wasn't much justice in the world, she thought, but by God there was justice in it today.

Choosing her fish and eggs and vegetables with as much care as pleasure, she lingered at the stalls, loitering with intent, chatting to the farmers and their families, the local growers whose quality could always be relied on. As ever the cheeses were fresh and firm, the onions pungent and silvery, the mackerel fragrant with kelp and ozone, all the salt tang of the sea . . . filling her basket was such a labour of love, she was almost sorry when eventually it was full to overflowing. But then there was yet another joy, the joy of driving home in Keeley's car, of being not only able to drive but confident now. If she lived to be a thousand, she felt she could never thank Keeley Butler adequately for all she had done for her. What a friend, *what* a friend.

When she got back to the house she found Tony out in the garden, painting with such concentration he didn't even notice her, but there was no sign of Keeley.

'Keel?! I'm home!'

I am too, she thought. Home and dry. As Keeley emerged from the lounge she dropped her basket and ran to hug her.

'I signed the papers! I've got it!'

'Whoopee!'

Keeley hugged her in turn, and they laughed together, thrilled.

'Pity you didn't get back two minutes earlier. Mel rang.'

'Oh? Anything urgent?'

'No. Just to say her school holidays start on the tenth and would you book her on a flight the next day.'

'Oh. Right.'

Whistling, Mary went into the kitchen to unload her basket of food, and Keeley followed her, her mind still half on the conversation she had had with Mel.

It had seemed like a perfectly ordinary conversation. As she ran over it in her mind she could pinpoint nothing specific in it, nothing unusual at all . . . only that Mel had sounded a little less chirpy than usual, very slightly reticent, as if debating whether to say something and then not saying it.

Or was it just her imagination? Maybe it was. She was still a fraction reticent herself with Mel, unsure how she felt about having the girl back in her house. Of course Mel was abjectly sorry for what she had done last August, would be on her best behaviour for the rest of her life, but still she simply could not warm to the idea of receiving her. In the eight months since Vincent's death she had tried hard to reconcile herself to the fact that her god-daughter would remain a fixture in her life, a frequent visitor, but it was not easy. Some day, she hoped, the rift would heal, she would be able to forgive – but not yet. Not yet.

As for Mary – Keeley knew that she, like her daughter, was consumed with guilt. But ever since the day she had implored her to stop apologising and feeling guilty Mary had struggled to do just that, to maintain their friendship in spite of the awful thing her daughter had done. Perhaps that was why she adopted such an airy attitude to Mel, not letting anyone see how she missed her daughter, as she surely must.

And maybe that was what was wrong with Mel, too. That was why she'd sounded a bit down on the phone. Naturally she must miss her mother. Letting Mary go to France could not have been easy, and Keeley was still a little surprised that the formerly selfish girl had been able to do it. Clearly Mel was trying to make amends, to do what was best for other people for a change, not think so much about herself. And if Mel could make an effort then so could she. She could grit her teeth at Easter and welcome the girl warmly, make absolutely no allusion to the accident, work at creating a harmonious atmosphere. Mary's mental welfare depended so much on Mel's, it was crucial that the atmosphere be positive, free of recrimination or sorrow.

As she helped Mary stash away the food for this evening's meal she was quiet, thinking about it. Mel would only be here for a week, mother and daughter would want to make the most of every moment together . . . all she had to do was be hospitable, and leave them to their own devices thereafter. She had plenty of studying to do, Tony to look after, some consultancy sessions at the hairdressing school, her in-laws to visit; there would be no shortage of distractions.

And still she thought of Vincent, of that other Easter so long ago, the one they'd spent honeymooning in Paris, planning their life and their work with such love, such wild optimism. That was the very first time Vincent had ever suggested having a child – not because he'd wanted one, then, but because he thought it might be a comfort to her while he was away on his travels around France.

But she had turned him down then, and she had turned him down every time after that, for years and years, long after it became clear that it was now what he wanted, longed for. If only she had done it, she would have something of him now, some fresh young life to help replace the old, lost one.

If only! But it was too late. She had not given Vincent the one thing he'd wanted so much, and now the gods were punishing her suitably, fitting Mel's crime to her own. Now she would never have any family, because something deep in her told her that she would never marry again, never love any man a second time. The first marriage had been so blessed, so perfect, it set a standard nobody could possibly attain twice. Although she was beginning to have her 'good days', on which she felt small stirrings of revival, her emotions still felt dead. It would be far better to settle for solitude, accept it with dignity, than ever go chasing after another such luminous rainbow. Meanwhile, she had company, which was as much as she needed; she had Mary and Tony, and soon she would briefly have Mel, for better or for worse.

Mel. So young, so lovely, so lively. As she stacked vegetables in a wire rack Keeley suddenly hurled the last one in, slammed the cupboard door and kicked it.

Mary jumped, and whirled round. 'Crikey, Keel, what's the matter?'

She forced a breezy smile, etched it onto her face.

'Nothing, Mary. Sorry. Nothing at all.'

Mary was visibly happy in the days before Mel's arrival, looking forward both to seeing her and to showing her the pub, even though it looked at the moment like a building site. Strict rules for renovation had to be adhered to, the façade preserved, exactly as Keeley had predicted, but inside it was starting to take shape. The architect recommended leaving the kitchen where it was, and turning the former dining area into the pub. Enthused with memories of Galway where he had spent several holidays, he understood what was required – comfortable simplicity, a rustic note combined with practicality and convenience. New slate tiles were being put down, the walls roughly washed in shades of butter and caramel, the woven and wooden furniture had yet to arrive. In the vaulted ceiling he put a galleried area, with a jumble of plants to tumble down and a couple of sofas for anyone who might want to retreat a little from the music and *craic*. A television was to be installed but shuttered behind louvred doors, for use only on major sporting occasions, books were to be scattered round, there was a corner for musicians to play in but under no circumstances, Mary insisted, was their music to be amplified. Finally, with much difficulty and muttering, a fireplace was being laboriously opened up, for the crackling blaze Mary said was indispensible on all but the warmest days.

'What'll we call it?' she mused one morning, showing Keeley round the clutter and chaos.

Keeley grinned, and gave it some thought.

'I dunno. The Gaulway Bay? The Irish Connection? Um . . . The Pret-à-Porter, with a glass of porter on the sign?'

'H'mm . . . could be. I'll have to let them all settle a while in my mind.'

'Right. And then give them a good stir, chuck them on the grill and see which one bursts into flames.'

Mary laughed, not minding that she was being teased for her constant preoccupation with cooking, so comprehensive now that Keeley said she was bubbling like a witch's cauldron. The side patch of lawn round the house had been dug and planted, and already spring shoots of basil, rocket, thyme and rosemary were showing through. Every morning she would pick them all fresh, add some edible nasturtiums in due course, dill, fennel, oregano, juniper, chervil . . . at The Lantern she had grown what she could in pots on the windowsill, but how they would thrive here, how many more varieties she could cultivate! Not that she knew much about gardening, but she knew what she wanted, and Keeley was good at it, would help her.

Absorbed in negotiations with fishmongers, butchers, breweries and endless other suppliers, she wished every day had at least fifty hours in it, and was astonished when suddenly Easter arrived, and Mel with it.

Keeley declined to go with her to the airport, and so Mary drove there alone, leaving a lively gathering at the house which included Luc, Alain Jou and four of Tony's new painter friends, a couple of people from his language class and Keeley's sister-in-law Sylvie. Briefly it crossed her mind to wonder whether Keeley was deliberately surrounding herself with people so that Mel would merge into them, be just one more; but then she thought not. It was Tony who had invited most of these guests, keen to demonstrate that he was getting to know people, depending as little as possible on his nurse or his sister. Thinking of his portrait of her, she smiled as she drove: it was bizarre, but she liked it, liked the sharp angles and strong colours.

Tony didn't go in for pastels, for anything sweet or wishy-washy, and she was as surprised as she was flattered that he had asked her to sit for him. Cathal had always seen her as a doormat, an acquiescent servant, but in Tony's eyes, apparently, she was somebody entirely different.

And she did feel different. Much stronger, nowadays, liberated and rejuvenated, capable and even happy . . . or as close to happiness as was possible with a daughter living a thousand miles away. Suddenly dying to see Mel, she sped on towards the airport.

And there was Mel, arrived early, waiting for her. Dashing to her, she consumed her in a long tight hug, savouring the surprise of having it returned. Mel even seemed a little emotional, genuinely glad to see her mother, brushing at her eyes and mumbling something unintelligible.

'Let me look at you!' Standing back, Mary surveyed her, but could find no cause for worry or guilt; Mel looked very healthy in stonewashed jeans and a lemon sweatshirt, her rucksack slung on her back, her hair cut in a new chin-length bob. She was made up, with a lot of lipstick and blusher, but she wasn't smoking or chewing gum. Reassured, Mary led her off to the car, firing questions as she went.

'Are you studying? Are your grandparents keeping a good eye on you? Did Cathal collect you on time from that disco? How are you getting on at The Lantern?'

Mel blew her fringe up in the way she had, and nodded impatiently.

'Yes, yes – I'm studying, I'm working, I'm fine – Jesus, Ma, don't get in such a stew!'

But she didn't say much more as she got into the car and they headed out onto the autoroute for Aix, and Mary wondered at that. Was it the car itself that was sobering her, the BMW in which she had driven off on that fatal night? Maybe she should persuade Keeley to sell it, after all . . . or maybe not. It was a salutary reminder and, like the accident itself, it was better for Mel to have to live with it than be helped to forget too easily.

But Mary was wound up, talking enough for both of them, and it seemed like no time before they were turning into the driveway of Keeley's house, snaking up the curved gravel path to the door that was now smothered in white clematis.

'God,' Mel whistled. 'I'd forgotten what a gorgeous house this is.'

'Yes – and a busy one, today. I left about a dozen people out by the pool drinking pastis. They're probably all pissed as newts by now.'

Pissed as newts? Mel eyed her mother, and giggled. The old Mary would have simply said 'drunk', rather primly at that. She couldn't remember her mother ever drinking – or wearing shorts as she was wearing them today, showing off long legs that weren't at all bad for her age. With her hair curling in a loose braid, and some kind of gypsy earrings dangling round her freckled face, she looked ten years younger than Mel knew her to be.

Grasping Mel by the arm, Mary led her to the group by the pool, some people lounging in beech or wicker chairs, others stretched on the grass amidst a muddle of dogs, drinks and painting equipment.

'Hello, everyone! Here we are!'

Instantly Keeley got up, went to Mel and embraced her.

'Mel. Welcome. It's good to see you.'

Nervously, Mel looked into her eyes, but there was no hint of sarcasm, nothing forced that she could detect. Awkwardly, she kissed Keeley on both cheeks.

'And you, Keeley. Thanks for having me.'

Pleased, Mary waved her arm at the others, making introductions.

'You remember Luc . . . this is Alain Jou . . . Keeley's brother Tony . . . Tony, introduce your friends!'

With a friendly grin he did introduce them, and Mel was glad that her mother had warned her about Tony, so she was prepared for what she saw. But for all his immobility he seemed lively enough, and popular, to judge by the number of people around him. And then there was Sylvie, Vincent's sister . . . flinching, Mel said hello quickly, and looked away.

After she was given a very watery pastis, and Mary had accepted a stronger one from Luc, the conversation resumed where it had left off, and for once Mel was glad not to be the centre of attention. With the exception of Mary, who kept smiling at her delightedly, and Sylvie who was consciously turned away from her, nobody seemed much interested in her at all. Instead they were discussing – as far as she could make out – which of them should do an oil portrait of the new pub to give Mary as a good-luck gift. Tony wasn't good at street scenes, he said; he wanted one of his friends to do it. Listening to his jumble of French and English, she smiled; it was like one of those Euro comedies on TV.

'We'll go to see the pub after lunch,' Mary told her, and she nodded eagerly – this after all was the whole reason why her mother now lived so far away, the reason why she'd had to let her go. And Mary looked so animated, so happy, it seemed to have been worth the wrench.

And Keeley . . . sneaking a glance at her, Mel thought that Keeley also looked well, certainly better than she had at Christmas. Was it just that the sun was shining today, or was she really getting a bit better, starting to recover? Certainly she seemed to be working at it, she was well dressed, wearing a bit of jewellery and make-up, even laughing as Luc said something about getting her a job as Mary's barmaid.

But Mel found herself unable to look at Keeley for very long, and turned away uncomfortably. So she did not see Keeley, a few minutes later, looking at her in turn, surveying her intently.

Letting the conversation float off around her, Keeley continued to look for several minutes, and wondered at what she saw.

Mel Sullivan, she thought, you're pretty as a picture. You get prettier every time I see you. You look well fed, well cared for, well able to hold your own. But, under all that eye shadow and blusher and what-not, you don't look *well*.

Why not? Are you nervous about staying here? Are you missing your mother, but not able to tell her? Are you finding The Lantern hard going, working every weekend? Are Cathal and your grandparents fussing over you, driving you crazy? Are your studies too hard, like mine, a daily battle?

I don't know what's wrong with you. But something is.

Mary was so glad to have Mel with her that, as the days of the Easter holiday went by, Keeley realised she was not seeing her daughter in any real, critical light at all. While Mary trekked Mel around to see the pub, to go shopping in Aix, to plunder the markets and eat in numerous restaurants, it was she, Keeley, who was surprised to find some almost maternal instinct stirring in her. Mel came back flushed and tanned from these expeditions, chatting about what she had seen and done and bought, but Keeley thought she detected the same reticence she had heard over the phone, something held back, or damped down, or smoothed over.

Yet on a day-to-day basis Mel seemed much as she had before, joining confidently in adult conversations, wheedling for goodies, eating everything around her. Half-child, half-woman, she was at an emotionally volatile stage, sometimes laughing at nothing, sometimes getting angry over less. Keeley saw that she had her mother wrapped around her little finger, and was not above profiting from the situation to phone Cathal occasionally, play the two parents off against each other if she looked like not getting whatever it was she wanted. As a result Mary spoiled her shamelessly, and smiled feebly when Keeley pointed out that she was doing it.

'What can I do, Keel? She's here for such a short time, I want her to enjoy every minute with me.'

Fair enough, Keeley conceded. Maybe next time, when Mel came for a longer stay in the summer, things would be more balanced. She'd help Mary in the pub which would be open by then, earn her keep, get to know some local kids instead of lounging around, as she was doing now, sunning by the pool.

'Fancy some gardening?' Keeley asked her sociably one morning.

'Oh, God, Keeley, I don't know anything about gardening, I've only just got up . . . isn't there some guy who helps you with it?'

Eventually, reluctantly, she weeded two herbaceous borders and pulled half the plants out of them. Then, saying she was exhausted, she went to take a nap before lunch. Gritting her teeth, Keeley said nothing.

Mary, meanwhile, seemed to have energy to burn. One of Tony's painter friends had volunteered to paint the picture of the pub, which she said she would hang in it, and again her thoughts turned to the question of a name for it. Félix, who'd put up a quarter of the money and therefore felt a proprietary interest, wanted to call it Le Coin Irlandais. But she wasn't sold on that.

'Too ordinary. I want a name that will stand out.'

Keeley suddenly giggled. 'Well, you want it to be good *craic*, don't you? Somewhere people will go to have lots of *craic*?'

'Yeah, but what—?'

'What about The Cracker? Just spell it so's everyone can pronounce it, and it's perfect!'

Taken aback by the unexpected ease of the answer, Mary laughed aloud. 'The Cracker – Keeley, that is perfect! Lots of *craic*!'

Giggling, they decided to try it out on the first French person to hand. It turned out to be Félix, when he dropped in later that afternoon for a drink, and to enquire about progress at Le Coin Irlandais. Mary was calling the pub that, wasn't she?

'Uh – well, get this round your tongue and see what you think of it.'

Blinking, looking slightly anxious as was his wont, he tried it cautiously.

'The – Crack – Cracker?'

Delighted, Mary clutched at Keeley. 'See, he can say it no problem!'

Looking somewhat affronted by his role of guinea pig, Félix frowned. 'But what does it mean, Mary?'

'It means fun. Craic is the Irish word for fun, Felix. But in this case it's also a bit of play on words, because a "cracker" is something explosive, or something very successful, as well as something you can eat. See?'

He didn't look as if he did, but by the time he left he was muttering it to himself over and over, leaving them laughing like a pair of banshees.

Mel grinned too when she heard the name, and approved it.

'Excellent, Ma. The very thing. I must tell Dad, it'll give him a laugh.'

'Well,' Mary retorted, 'whether it does or not, that's what I'm calling it. It's my pub and I can do as I like.'

A sign was duly painted, and she took Mel, Keeley, Félix and Luc with her to watch it being hung over the door, beaming with satisfaction.

'Now I am officially the owner of The Cracker. No doubt the French will puzzle over it, but the Irish visitors will explain it to them. Meanwhile, I haven't got any beer pumps yet, but I have some crates of Guinness, so come on in and have your first drink.'

It was Mel's last day in Provence, so she was included as the bottles were handed round. But Keeley noticed that she hardly touched her beer when it was opened and they all sat on upturned crates swigging it by the neck, even Félix, looking faintly aghast as he hitched up his trouser legs. The builders had gone to lunch, leaving their tools strewn everywhere, and he wrinkled his nose as he sat down amidst the mess. Keeley's attention, however, was fixed on Mel.

'What's the matter, Mel? Don't you like beer?'

Keeley knew she must have tasted it before, because she had once asked Vincent for some. But Mel grimaced.

'No. I don't. Not really.'

'Oh. Well, drink some anyway, to toast your mother's new venture. She's working her butt off to get this place open by summer, you know.'

'Yeah, I know.'

Mel slugged back a mouthful of the beer and raised the

bottle. 'Here's to you, Ma. I hope your new pub does really well.'

Mary beamed again, and moved closer so she could put her arm around her.

'Thanks, Mel. Thanks for your good wishes, and for letting me come to Aix to do it. I never could have, without your help and co-operation. You've been fantastic.'

Mel flushed, and shrugged. 'Oh – well – everything is working out fine. I've got two pubs to drink in now, one here and one in Ireland.'

'Yes. So long as you don't drink too much! But you'll be fifteen in the summer, old enough to help me in the kitchen if you'd still like to – or would it be too much like The Lantern? Maybe you should just have a holiday—'

'No. I mean yes. I mean – I like working in The Lantern, especially since that cookery course at Ballymaloe, and I'm sure I'll like working here too. It's just – it's only – that—'

Mary looked concerned. 'It's only that what, Mel? What do you mean?'

Abruptly, tears glistened in Mel's ice-blue eyes. 'Oh, nothing! Just that I – I'm not sure if I can come back in the summer—'

'What? Oh, but Mel, you must! I want you to, I'm looking forward to it—'

Mel's voice hardened. 'Yeah, well, just don't depend on it, OK? I might come or – or I might not. I don't know yet.'

Mary drew breath to protest, but then she saw Luc and Félix exchange glances, and realised it was neither the time nor place for a family squabble. Keeley, also, was looking anxious.

'All right. Whatever you want, Mel. I won't put any pressure on you, don't worry. We'll talk about it later, OK?'

'Yeah. All right. OK.'

But it was not all right. It was clear that, only hours before she was due to go home to Cathal, something was bothering Mel, distressing her. Swiftly, Mary made up her mind to find out what it was, right away.

'God, Keeley, what am I going to do? I know there's something wrong, but I can't get her to tell me what it is. Her plane leaves at seven – I've got to find out before then!'

'You've really tried?'

'Yes, of course! Tried everything I can think of, but she just keeps shrugging and saying she's tired, that's all. But how can she be tired? All she's done is eat and shop and sleep.'

'H'm. Where is she now?'

'In her room, packing. Keel, you – you wouldn't have a go for me, would you? I know it's a lot to ask, but if she's in any kind of trouble – maybe she's afraid to tell me, you'd be easier to talk to – Christ, if it's anything to do with Cathal, I – I'll—'

'All right, Mary. Don't panic. I'll go to her.'

But as Keeley made her way down the corridor to Mel's bedroom she felt a frisson, and considerable concern. This was a parent's job, not a godparent's, she had no idea how to handle a teenager – especially one with whom her relationship was so fragile, so fraught. Since Mel's arrival she had been studiously friendly to her, but had not recaptured any of the warm affection she had felt for Mel as a baby. Vincent's death – and now, dear God, what next?

Knocking on the door, she received no reply, so simply opened it and went in. Mel sat on the bed, desultorily folding a blouse, looking pale and mutinous. With a sigh, Keeley sat down beside her.

'So. What's the matter, Mel? Anything I can help with?'

She was surprised when Mel looked at her with sudden – sudden what? Some kind of eagerness, she thought, even fervour. But then she lowered her eyelids, turned down her lips sullenly.

'No, thanks. It's OK, Keeley. I know Ma sent you in here to cross-question me, but you needn't bother. I'm just – just a bit sorry to be leaving her, that's all.'

'Are you? Is that all that's wrong?'

'Yeah. That's all. I – I miss her sometimes, you know.'

Well, yes. Keeley supposed that she did, and felt a little pity for her. Mel really had made a sacrifice in letting go of Mary. And maybe now it was the sight of the pub that had upset her, the reality of her mother's dreams and ambitions taking shape. Mary was never going back to Ireland.

Surprising herself, Keeley edged closer to the girl, and took her hand. 'Well, you know, you could always come here if you wanted. To live, I mean. If you'd rather be with her, there's plenty of room . . .'

'Oh, Keeley! You can't mean that! Not after – after what happened. After what I did to you last summer.'

'Mel, I do mean it, if it would be the best thing for you and your mother – you're not having any kind of problems with Cathal, are you?'

'No. He's grand. We get on fine.'

Keeley searched her face as she said it, assessed the tone of her voice, but both seemed genuine. Whatever it was, it didn't seem to be Cathal.

'Well, that's good. But if you ever want to change your mind, you can. In the meantime, your Mum and I are a bit worried about you. You were nearly in tears earlier, and we don't want you to leave without knowing why. If it's anything that's hard for you to talk about – well, sometimes it's easier to talk to a friend than a parent, so why don't you tell me?'

'Because – because there's nothing wrong! I told you, I was just a bit upset. Maybe – maybe it's PMT.'

'Oh. Well, if that's all, you won't die this time! But if it is anything else, now's your chance to share it. Whatever it is, I won't go ballistic and I won't let Mary, either.'

Suddenly, out of the blue, Mel flung the blouse on the floor and stood up, began to pace the room.

'Keeley, when you and Ma were young, you – you used to write to each other, didn't you?'

'Yes. On and off, but all the time, for years. I think it helped your mother a lot, when she was having a few problems with – with your father.'

'Yeah. My grandmother says you were a terrible influence on her. But I think – Keeley, would you mind if I wrote to you once in a while?'

She was very surprised. Mel seemed to belong so very much to the phone and fax generation a net surfer.

'Of course I wouldn't. I'd be delighted.'

'And you – you wouldn't show anything I wrote to Mum?'

'Certainly not. Letters are private.'

'Then I – I might write, once in a while.'

'OK. If that's how you want to communicate, then that's how we'll do it. I always did like getting letters from Ireland.'

As suddenly as she had flung it, Mel picked up her blouse and packed it into her open suitcase, seeming to indicate that the conversation was over without actually looking at her. Bemused, Keeley stood up.

'So you're sure there's nothing you want to discuss now?'

'Yeah. I'm sure. But – thanks anyway, Keel.'

Nodding, Keeley left her, and went slowly back to Mary. As soon as she reached her, Mary looked up apprehensively.

'What did she say? Did you get anything out of her?'

'No. Not yet. But I think she does have some kind of problem, Mary. Nothing to do with Cathal. Something else.'

'Like *what*? Keeley, I'm her mother, I'm worried about her.'

'Yes, Mary. I know you are. But it seems to be something she's not ready to talk about yet. I think the best thing for the moment is to simply let her go home, let her go back to school and get on with her routine. She'll tell us in her own good time.'

'Us? You, or me?'

Faintly, Keeley smiled. 'Mary, when was it ever a question of one or other of us? Everything always seems to involve us both. And I suspect that this, whatever it is, isn't going to be any different.'

Chapter Eighteen

Mary redoubled her vigilant watch over Mel in the weeks after the girl's departure, phoning her as often as twice a day, persuading her own brothers Steve and Sean to drop in on her in addition to both sets of grandparents. Mel baulked, objecting that she felt stifled, she didn't need constant babysitting. So Mary reconsidered, persisted with less obvious tactics, and Keeley monitored the whole situation with some misgiving.

Had she expected too much of Mel, had Mary asked too much of her? After all the girl was only fourteen, and phone calls were not the same as having her mother around for all the little spontaneous things, the everyday exchanges of family life. Once or twice Mel wrote to Keeley, but her letters were short and trivial, revealing nothing of her real state of mind. Keeley prayed that Mel wouldn't burst into tears on the phone one day, beg her mother to come home, tell her that she couldn't cope with their separation after all. Mary would pack up everything and go, she knew, immediately. But what a waste if she did, after all she had achieved, was continuing to achieve!

Apart from this one thing, everything else was going great guns, the pub nearly ready, the launch party being planned with Luc, the air full of laughter and energy. And, once the pub was open, Mary would be nailed to it, unable to abandon it even if she wanted to, which she very definitely did not. Apart from a lot of money, her whole heart and soul were invested in it.

One day a painter friend of Tony's came to call, the one who had painted the sign and was now painting the picture to be hung inside, and Mary spent ages chatting with him, her rusty French making him grin from ear to ear even though she was improving daily. His name was Louis Crouzat, one of Alain's protegés and Tony's friendly rivals who, on turning thirty, had chucked his job as a label designer to paint full time.

He wasn't making much money at it, he admitted, but Alain promised he would, and meanwhile he was infinitely happier. Soup, detergent, chemical solvent, shoe polish . . . he'd have lost his marbles, he said, if he'd designed just one more label for one more product. Labels were tiny, tiny things he told them with thumb and forefinger curled a centimetre apart, whereas he wanted to paint big canvases – *big*! – and he threw his arms wide like a bragging fisherman, to show them what he meant.

Mary invited him to stay to lunch, and he accepted enthusiastically, wolfing the food she put before him, drinking three hearty glasses of beer, talking all the while. A big, cheerful guy with dark blond hair and lively brown eyes, he reminded Keeley very slightly of Vincent.

'I don't know why,' she mused after he had left. 'There's just something about him.'

Mary couldn't see any resemblance, but liked what she did see.

'He's fun, isn't he? I hope he'll come to the pub, he's just the kind of customer I want – he can have free drinks for painting the sign and picture.'

'No,' Keeley replied firmly, 'not free. Not for ever. What you'll do is give him the first one free whenever he comes in, and the rest at half price.'

'Why? I like him, he's doing me a favour and he won't take payment because he's Tony's friend . . .'

'No matter. The point is that nobody ever appreciates anything if it's free, Mary. They take it for granted – like Cathal took you for granted. Unless you want to become a doormat again, you'll listen to what I'm telling you.'

Reluctantly, Mary listened, and agreed to do as Keeley advised. After all, Keeley had a lot of business experience, she knew what she was talking about . . . still. It was a pity, in this instance, to have to be so businesslike.

'Why?' Keeley grinned. 'Have you your eye on him or what?'

'Don't be pathetic,' Mary retorted tartly. 'I'm a married woman, what you're suggesting would be adultery.'

'Adultery my granny! Don't give me that Mrs-Mary-Sullivan stuff, you'll divorce Cathal the day the courts open for business.'

'Yes,' Mary admitted. 'I will. The referendum result is a relief to me, but I'll only do it if Mel feels comfortable with it. She mightn't like the idea of formalising things at all.'

Keeley said nothing, deciding to cross that hurdle when they came to it. After all, Mary had only met Louis a few weeks ago, the two were merely pally – and uncomplicated friendship was just what Mary needed, if such a thing was possible with a man. For the moment, it seemed to be.

But Louis came to visit again a few days later, on some very flimsy protext, and after that he seemed to be around all the time, teasing Tony, eyeing Mary like a smitten spaniel. Keeley was surprised to feel a pang as she assessed the situation and conceded that there was a certain something in the air; not romantic, but definitely flirtatious, something that made Mary glow like a teenager. She was three years older than Louis, nearly four, but if she even noticed she apparently didn't care.

Keeley found herself struggling to stifle something close to jealousy. Mary was her friend, she needed her, didn't want her attention or emotions diverted at this still-vulnerable time . . . and there was a grain of irony in the thing that chafed like sand in an oyster. Here she was, widowed because of Mary's daughter; while there was Mary, grinning merrily, admired, flattered, delighted.

'He's not married, is he?' Keeley enquired one day, darkly, almost accusingly.

'Not any more. Apparently he was, briefly, in his early twenties. But his wife was ambitious, left him behind when her career took off, couldn't understand his waffle about wanting to paint. They divorced in '89.'

'Oh. So he's free, then, to remarry?'

'Yes. If he can find someone to marry. But it sure won't be me.'

Keeley was taken aback. 'Won't it?'

Vehemently, Mary shook her head, her eyes igniting with intense fervour.

'No way. I've tasted marriage once already, and I can assure you I'm not going back for second helpings.'

'Oh, cut it out!'

'I mean it, Keel. I swear it on a stack of Playboy magazines. You wouldn't get me onto an altar ever again with a forklift truck. You should understand that . . . I mean . . . you say you'll never marry again either.'

Keeley drew circles on the table with her forefinger.

'Yes, but I'm different. I've already had all I want out of marriage. You've never had anything out of it.'

'What I want can be got without benefit of priest nor paperwork.'

'Huh? What do you – you don't mean—'

'I do mean. A bloody great bonk, that's what I want, Keel. Dozens and dozens of them if possible. I want to discover sex before I'm a tottering old crone. The real McCoy this time, wild mad passion, stupid giggly romance – but as for yessir, no sir, three bags full sir, forget it. My pub will be my pub, his painting will be his painting, and never the twain shall meet. Not legally, not formally, not under any circumstances.'

'But what if he – what if Louis gets serious, Mary?'

'Then he can shag off. A burnt child dreads the fire, Keel. Anyway, he's been burnt too.'

Keeley said nothing, only continued to doodle on the table until Mary looked at her suddenly, candidly, forcing her to meet her eye.

'Keeley . . . Louis and I are just pals, for the moment. Nothing more. I'll drop him tomorrow if you want me to.'

'Why would I want you to?'

'Because you're widowed thanks to me and my stupid daughter, that's why. I won't be happy at your expense. If Louis is bothering you, then it's *au revoir*, Louis.'

Keeley reflected, was silent for some time.

'No, Mary. I don't want you to do that. You've been starved of all the things you've ever needed in a man . . . I don't want you to go on starving. Flirt with this guy, have fun with him, be friends, do whatever you want.'

'Are you sure, Keel?'

'Yes. I'm sure.'

As encouragingly as she could, Keeley smiled at her. But she did not feel sure. Not at all sure. She was trying to be happy for Mary, but every time she saw Louis she was reminded of what she had lost in Vincent – the energy, the laughter, the encouragement and the chemistry. Even if Mary and Louis were only friendly as yet, there were growing signs of all those things between them, and Keeley found the vision painful. It was the right moment for Mary, after so many miserable years, but it was the wrong moment for her, after only nine months.

She didn't want to ruin it. But she wondered whether she

could bear it. After some further thought, she looked at Mary again.

'Would you just do me one small favour?'

'Absolutely. What is it?'

'Would you – if – well – if things get anywhere, would you conduct them somewhere else? I presume he has a house or something?'

'He has an apartment in Aix.'

'Then I'd rather you slept with him there, or did whatever it is you plan to do. I don't mean to sound unwelcoming, but . . . it's just that . . .'

Immediately Mary was at her side, her arm around her shoulder, her voice low and soft. 'I know, Keel. I understand. I won't ask Louis here at all. If he comes to see Tony, well, I won't discourage that because it's good for Tony, but I won't encourage him to come to see me. In fact I'll tell him he's not to. I won't even talk about him, unless you specifically ask.'

Sadly Keeley smiled and sighed, simultaneously.

'Oh, I'll probably ask all right. But my moods are still a bit up and down at the moment . . . I'd rather have the choice, that's all.'

Biting her lip, Mary hugged her, reassuringly.

'Of course you'll have it. He's only a man, Keel. You're my friend. My dear friend . . . you matter far more to me, and so does my pub. You're my two priorities. Plus Mel, of course.'

Nodding, Keeley stood up, and changed the subject. But she wondered how long Mary's detachment might last.

Incredibly, the builders were only ten days behind schedule, and it looked as if The Cracker could be safely scheduled to open on June 8. Mary was fired with excitement, anxiety and demonic anticipation, and left with little time to see Louis much less worry about him.

'Smoked salmon, oysters, beef in Guinness casserole, a dozen kinds of potato, colcannon, champ, bacon and cabbage, farmhouse cheeses . . . look at the samples, Luc, and tell me what you think.'

Luc stood with her one morning in the old kitchen they both loved, sifting through the produce on the marble worktop as requested, squeezing, smelling, pulling leaves off things, frowning with concentration.

'I know this cabbage is the traditional Irish variety, Mary, and you've gone to trouble to get it – but I think it's too dark, too bitter. The French won't like it.'

'No?'

'No. I'd get a lighter local variety if I were you.'

'Why don't I try both for a few weeks and see which works better?'

He laughed. 'Because I am the boss! I taught you to cook, Mademoiselle!'

'And don't I ever forget it! But Luc, I'm Irish, this is an Irish pub, I do know what I'm doing, I promise you.'

'Pah. Then why do you ask my opinion?'

'Because if I don't flatter you you might not come to the launch. You might stamp your little foot and throw a tantrum.'

Dropping the cabbage as if it had bitten him, he grinned hugely.

'Don't worry, Mary. I'll come. I wouldn't miss it for the world. It may not be *haute cusine*, finally, but it is good honest food, and I am very proud of you.'

Proud of her. It struck her that nobody had ever said that to her before, except Keeley the day she rifled Cathal's bedroom. Nobody had ever said it once, about anything. She was very touched.

'Are you, Luc? Even though I'm not doing soufflés or flambés or—'

'Mary! Are you deaf?'

Hastily, she laughed, and subsided. Luc always meant exactly what he said, there was no need to fret or wonder or worry.

'OK, OK! But Luc – you will taste everything, won't you, and give me your real opinion?'

'I will, although of course you won't listen to it. You women always do exactly what you want in the end. You humour and flatter us men and then go right ahead with your original plan.'

Mary hoped that she would. She had had enough of compromise at The Lantern. This time, she was burning to do things her own way, and prayed that her best would please the customers. The French, for all their airs and graces, could be every bit as stubborn, as traditional as the Irish. No doubt some of them would complain on principle, send back dishes, give her grief just to show that they could. It would take a while to woo them . . . but meanwhile, they might enjoy the music and the *craic*, get into the spirit of the place. In summer, there should be plenty of Irish holidaymakers to jolly up the atmosphere, France being such a popular destination.

There *should* be – suddenly, she was seized with nerves.

'Oh God, Luc, what if nobody comes? What if it's a total failure, a disaster? Keeley and Félix have invested so much money, I've sunk my whole future—'

Luc straightened up from over the worktop, stretched his arms and rolled his eyes.

'That's right, Mary. Talk yourself out of it, talk yourself into a panic, just as you did before. Run home to Ireland, blow your life again.'

Run? Blow her life again? She flared up like oil on a flame. 'I will in the year 5000! The hell I will!' Smugly, he grinned at her, and she was incandescent. 'Don't tease me! Don't wind me up, Luc, I'm too tense!'

Maddeningly, he grinned even more broadly. 'Tense? When was a chef ever tense?'

She laughed then, but she really was tense. Not just because the pub was about to open, but because she had spoken to Mel last night. And Mel still didn't know whether she was coming to work in Aix for the summer, sounded very iffy and moody-adolescent about everything.

If only she knew what 'everything' was. If only Mel would revert to her usual cheeky upbeat self, and not be causing such worry at this horribly important moment. If only she could ask Cathal what he thought was wrong with her. But she and Cathal only spoke now when strictly necessary, icy frigid words to do with what debris of their joint life remained. Beyond that bare minimum, he delighted in giving her no information whatsoever, and she knew that to betray her anxiety would give him nothing but pleasure.

As Mary worked feverishly to put the finishing touches to the pub, Keeley studied for her summer exams, leaving Tony to the tender mercies of his nurse. But while she felt she would probably pass the exam in art history, thanks to all she had already learned haphazardly over the years, she knew she was doomed in the French literature department. She was going to fail, and would have to spend the summer revising and sit the exam again in August.

Still. Who'd ever have thought that Keeley Butler would even be let inside the door of a university, never mind enrol in one? Of course, she'd had to wangle her way in, pull a few strings, but still it gave her a kick. If anyone had ever told her it was possible, in the days when she used to sit on walls chewing gum with Mickser Sweeney, she'd have laughed herself crosseyed. The work was hard, now, but she was enjoying the sense of discovery, the accumulating knowledge; even if she didn't pass her exams on time like the 20-year olds, she'd get there eventually. Nobody was holding a stopwatch over her, she had – she had, she thought sadly, all the time in the world.

Idly, she wondered whether she should take a short break when the exams were sat and the pub was open. She hadn't been anywhere for nearly two years apart from Dublin, which was not her definition of a relaxing holiday. But Mary would be too busy to come with her, Tony couldn't travel without exhausting complications . . . maybe a weekend would be enough, on her own. She could drive down to Italy, perhaps? Sylvie or Francine might even come with her, or one of her hairdressing pals . . . except that they were all married, mostly with kids. Busy people.

Mulling over it, she wended her way out into the garden, where Tony sat eternally painting. Chatting to him usually cheered her up, because he was so optimistic and his problems put her own in perspective.

'Hi, Tone. Whatcha doing?'

'Just an old guy playing *boules*. I saw him one evening when I was out with Alain. Thought he had an interesting face.'

Unable to take photographs, Tony memorised things he saw very quickly, sealing them in his mind until he could revive them in oils. Peering at the canvas, Keeley could see no sign of any old man, but supposed that the thing would take shape eventually, in its weird way.

'Where's Mary?'

Keeley hadn't seen her all day, and wondered if she could still be at the pub. Tony grinned.

'She's on cloud nine.'

'Huh?'

'Cloud nine. Paradise. So is Louis. I reckon they'll be hitting the hay any day now.'

'Oh . . . do you?'

'Yep. Lustful as a pair of rabbits, they are – Louis fancies the socks off her.'

Yes. Keeley could see that he did, although Louis was around the house less than before, apparently warned away by Mary as agreed. But when he was there he grinned idiotically – and he was at the pub a lot, she heard, helping with bits of carpentry and things the builders were not doing quite to Mary's artistic direction. A mirror was hung wrong and Louis fixed it, a table was too high and Louis cut it down, a bench wouldn't fit through the door and Louis had to put his shoulder to it . . . Mary didn't tell her all this, directly, but the bits and pieces filtered through. Mary was very preoccupied, in more ways than one.

Keeley pulled at a straying strand of honeysuckle, and glanced sidelong at her brother.

'I'm thinking of going down to Italy for a weekend. Would you be able to manage on your own, d'you think? I mean, there'll be other people around, but—'

He dropped his brush and looked up at her, thoughtfully.

'Sure. Are you going on your own?'

'Probably. Unless I can find someone free to come with me. But I think it would be a bit much for you—'

'Yeah. It would. Anyway, I'm perfectly happy here. Which I think is more than can be said for you at the moment.'

'Oh . . . I'm all right. Most of the time, anyway. Vincent is gone and all the moping in the world isn't going to bring him back.'

'No. It isn't. C'est la vie.'

She smiled a little at his philosophical tone, as much as at his French. He'd learned, she supposed, that what couldn't be changed had to be accepted.

'Well, if you're going to Italy, Keeley, you may as well go now, before that young one arrives.'

'Young one? Huh?'

'That girl, Mary's kid – there's a letter from her in the house for you. Probably with her date of arrival. Wasn't she supposed to be coming for the summer?'

Keeley blinked. She hadn't seen any letter. But then she hadn't gone through the post yet today, too busy studying to bother. It rarely consisted of much more than bills and flyers.

Turning from Tony, she went into the house, to her study where Céline had left the mail stacked on her desk. Sure enough, there was a blue envelope from Ireland, with Mel's large adolescent script on it, all squiggles and green ink. Slitting it open, she carried it back out to the garden with her, reading as she went.

'Dear Keeley,

Don't leave this lying around, OK? Don't let Ma see it. Tear it up after you read it.

Keeley, I've something awful to tell you. Something really terrible, you're going to go ballistic – but I've got to tell you because I don't know what to do, I don't want Ma to know yet until after her pub opens. She's got enough on her plate and this is going to be the last straw. I can't tell Dad either, or anyone, they're going to kill me—

Keeley, I think I'm going to have a baby. I'm nearly sure I am. I haven't gone to the doctor but I'm getting sick in the mornings and my jeans don't fit and I haven't had a period since – I can't remember exactly, but ages. It was a boy I met in Dad's pub after work one Saturday, we went to a disco and he bought me loads of Ritz to drink, we went out to the park and – and it just happened, I don't know how, I must have been drunk although I didn't think I was, anyway I—

Keeley, what am I going to do? I'm petrified, I wish Ma was here, only she'll probably go spare when she hears, Dad might even throw me out, Granny Jameson and Nana Sullivan are going to lose their marbles for sure. I can't wait for school to be over in case any of the teachers notices, or my friends . . . I want to come over to you only I probably won't be let work in the new pub now, there's going to be terrible trouble – Keeley, what'll I do?

Does having a baby hurt? Does it take long? I looked up a book in our school library and it sounded gruesome. I don't want to have it all on my own but I'm afraid to tell anyone – Keeley, please write to me. But don't tell, will you swear it? Not until the pub's open and Ma is – if you could phone instead of write that'd be even better. Dad's playing golf next Sunday so you could call then, he won't know. I'm afraid to ring you in case you're angry, but I just hope you're not as angry as everyone else is going to be.

Please tell me what to do.

Love,
Mel.'

Keeley was faintly aware of the trees and vines blurring into a kind of Monet-like haze as she stood on the grass, still as a statue, gripping the letter, rigid with shock.

Mel. A child herself, Mel was going to have a child. Not quite fifteen, she had been legally raped, she was under age, she was pregnant. For nearly a full minute she could not absorb it, could not believe it, hardly heard Tony calling to her.

'So what does she say? When's the little brat coming over?'

Not answering, she sank onto one of the chairs by the pool and buried her head in her hands, blinking back the tears that leaped to her eyes. At eighteen Mary had become pregnant, her life had been diverted, ruined for years thereafter, and now her daughter . . . not that there was any question of marriage, this time, not at fifteen to some boy – oh, God. Oh, dear God.

'Keeley? What's the matter?'

Stuffing the letter into her pocket, she fought to compose herself. She mustn't let anyone know, not until she thought, figured out—

'Nothing, Tony. I'll be with you in a minute.'

She could hear her own breathing as she sat like a rag doll, her limbs limp with shock, her mind whirling with horror. In her mind she saw baby Mel, a couple of months old, lying on her back kicking her legs and shrieking while she struggled to change her nappy . . . the stuffed toys on the bed, the christening party in progress. It seemed like no more than a year ago, she could feel the silken infant skin, smell the baby powder . . . for a moment, thinking she was going to be sick, she leaned over the pool, her elbows on her knees, her fists clenched as she tried to absorb it, get some kind of grip.

Tony was staring at her. Suddenly aware of it, she forced herself to look up, get up, walk over to him on feet that felt like concrete.

He eyed her. 'So what is it? What's Miss Mel done now?'

'Oh – nothing. Just some bad behaviour at a disco.'

'Like what?'

'Oh, you know the kind of thing kids get up to . . . here, let me get your brush for you.'

Bending down, she tried to hide her face, knowing it must be white as ice. But her hands were shaking so much she dropped the brush, fumbled for it, and as she straightened up she felt his gaze on her like a laser beam.

'Come on, Keel. Out with it, whatever it is.'

'She – Tony, she doesn't want me to tell anyone.'

'For Chrissake. She doesn't know her own name, that one.

A total flake in my humble opinion. She hasn't been and gone and done it, has she?'

'D – done what?'

'Sex. Round the back of the bicycle shed or something, with some thick of a young fella?'

'A – uh – oh, Jesus, Tony, she has. That's exactly what she's done. How did you guess?'

He frowned. 'Well, for a start, she's ripe as a plum, jailbait if ever I saw it.'

Jailbait. She could see Vincent laughing as he said it, only yards from this very spot, last summer when he was stoking the barbecue. And now, he had been proven right.

'I hope you don't mean that it was her fault—'

'Just because she wears skirts up to her backside and bikini tops that Brigitte Bardot would be hard pressed to fill? No, I don't mean it was her fault, Keeley – it takes two to tango – but she'd pass for eighteen, with all that make-up and whatnot. How old is the young fella?'

'I – I don't know. She met him in The Lantern.'

'So maybe he's eighteen. With luck. At most. Ah, Christ, I could see it coming.'

'You – you what?'

'Keeley, a blind man could see it. A young one like that, her parents separating, just when she's dripping in guilt because she's killed a man – or caused his death, anyway. She's probably mixed up as a bag of broken biscuits. She might even think—'

'What?'

'Well, in some weird way, she might even think – be trying – to make it up to you, for Vincent. Might think you haven't got a baby, you're crucifying yourself for never having had one, so she'll get one for you . . . I know that sounds off the wall, but the things that go through teenagers' heads . . . she's not pregnant, is she?'

'Yes. She is.'

Slowly, dismally, he whistled. 'She is. Oh, Jaysus. That's lovely. That is bloody lovely, right enough.'

'Tony! Please, Tony, try to think – what am I going to do? What am I going to say to her? She wants me to call her – on Sunday, oh God, tomorrow is Sunday—'

He reflected. 'What about Mary? Mel's her daughter, not yours.'

'I know, but Mary's got the pub opening next weekend – I can't tell her yet, she'd fly home tonight and drop the whole thing!'

'H'm. Maybe that's exactly what she should do.'

'But – Tony, this pub is her lifeline! Everything depends on it, her entire future . . . somehow, I've got to hold the fort until it opens. I've got to.'

'Don't you ever wonder whether maybe you've done enough for Mary, Keel?'

Vehemently, she shook her head. 'Tony, look around you. Look at this garden, this house, that pool, that tennis court – even those dogs, for God's sake. I'd never have any of them if Mary Jameson hadn't brought me to France. I'd have nothing. I'd be Mrs Sweeney probably, mother-of-six, wondering whether Mickser was coming home with his dole money tonight or tomorrow or not at all.'

'Keeley, everything you have, you earned. You worked yourself brainless for it. Mary brought you here, but you did the rest yourself.'

'Oh, Tony – look, I don't want to argue about that now. I just want to think what's the best thing – the best way – Mary's going to hit the roof when she hears! And Cathal, he'll go insane—'

'Shouldn't Cathal have been looking after her, in the absence of her mother?'

'Yes, but – to be fair to him, Tony, he can't watch her every minute of every day and every night. She's nearly fifteen.'

'Old enough to have a bit of sense. That's what everyone said when I had me accident. I was twenty then – and, as we both know, I had about as much sense as a chimpanzee. Arguably less.'

'Yes. Oh, Tony, I don't want this to mess up Mel's life the way – the way yours got messed up, and Mary's got messed up, when you were both so young.'

'Face it, Keel. It is going to mess it up. Mess it up bigtime, if you ask me.'

She didn't answer. Instead, she plunged her hands into the pockets of her trousers and walked slowly away from him, round by the side of the house to where Mary's herbs and vegetables were growing. At first her mind went almost blank, not wanting to face the vision of Mel's suddenly stunted, arrested future – just when Mel was working at school, too, and showing aptitude for cooking like her mother. But then she began to visualise Mel, terrified, a baby growing inside her

. . . how long had it been there, when was it due? She must find that out first of all, tomorrow when she phoned, must see about a doctor, get a test done. Maybe Mel was mistaken. Maybe it was a ploy for attention.

Or maybe Tony was right. Tony, who had so much time to notice things and think about them, was such a good observer. Maybe, in some moment of insanity, Mel had actually thought that a baby might – might compensate, in some contorted way, for the loss of Vincent. She couldn't have thought that consciously, rationally, but she might have *felt* it, subliminally.

Could she have? Had she, Keeley, ever said or done anything to indicate that she regretted not having had Vincent's children? Desperately she ran over what conversations she could remember, but nothing rang a bell. On the contrary. She had been careful not to regret, not to refer to Vincent aloud; if Mel had picked up such a thought she had done so unconsciously, through some vibe, some unguarded expression.

And now, she was pregnant. In the muggy summer heat Keeley felt something squeezing and stifling in her, a crushing sense of oppression. No matter how she dealt with this terrible calamity, how they all dealt with it, it could never be anything other than a trauma and torture for Mel.

The child would never be a child again. She would be a mother, weighted down with worry and responsibility as Mary had been. Even if the baby was adopted she would never cease to think about it, to wonder and fret for the rest of her life. When the child grew up it might seek her out, claim the person Mel would be then. If she was married her marriage could be torn apart, the adoptive parents could be deeply hurt, the child itself could be bitter, accusing, endlessly haunting and wounding, or lost and pleading.

This is a nightmare, Keeley thought. This is infinitely worse than Mary's pregnancy. At least Mary was eighteen, nineteen when Mel was born, and she had me, she even had Cathal for whatever he was worth. He gave them a home at any rate, a roof over their heads. Whereas this youth, whoever he is – he might well be only fifteen or sixteen himself – there's hardly any chance of him taking any kind of responsibility.

France is an hour ahead of Irish time. I'll ring Mel the moment I get up tomorrow morning. But what am I going to say to her? And how in God's name am I going to break this to Mary?

She's going to be a *grandmother*! At thirty-six, with a new life

and a new man in it . . . somehow I'm going to have to work
it out so she doesn't panic completely, doesn't drop everything
and rush back to Ireland. Cathal would use the situation to
pin her down, nail her there if only so that he can show the
neighbours and family, hey, look, my wife is back here where
she belongs.

And yet, Mel needs her. Really needs her, urgently. If Mary
isn't to go flying back to Ireland, then Mel is going to have to
come here. Immediately.

Well, I needn't worry now about finding anyone to come
to Italy with me. That's the end of Italy. And the start of yet
another ghastly chapter in the hideous saga of the Sullivan
family. I swear to God they haven't a brain between the whole
bloody lot of them. They're a recipe for disaster.

Poor Mel. Straight from the frying pan into the fire. When it
comes to cooking up trouble, she really takes the biscuit.

Louis stood on a ladder, hammering a series of nails into a
wooden beam so that a collection of old plates could be hung
on it, and Mary watched him full of admiration. Unlike some
of Tony's painter friends, Louis did not take himself so seriously
that this handyman work was beneath his dignity; whistling and
grinning, he turned to her at intervals for affirmation.

'How's that? A little higher, a little lower?'

She squinted. 'A little further to the left . . . there . . . no, just
a tiny bit lower . . .'

Agreeably, he positioned everything to her exact instructions,
reaching all sorts of awkward angles so that the ladder wobbled,
his sweat-stained cotton teeshirt rode up his back to reveal
tanned smooth skin that made Mary's head swim with lust.

I'm losing it, she thought. I'm losing my grip, losing my
marbles.

But still she stood transfixed, admiring every muscle, every
contour until she began to feel like one of the nitwits in the
Diet Coke ad, and laughed at herself.

'What's so funny?'

'Nothing. Nothing at all.'

With an effort she composed herself and set about clearing
up the muddle of tools as, finally, Louis hammered in the last
nail and came down the ladder. Pushing back the hair that fell
over his forehead, he stood back and gazed up at the plates.

'Nice. Look like they grew there.'

'Mm. Thanks, Louis.'

She was surprised, but not remotely shocked, when he suddenly put his arm around her shoulder and kissed her on the cheek.

'Your pub is so different to all the brasseries with their cool glass and pinball machines. It will be a big success, Mary.'

'It had better be, or I'm toast.'

Nervously, she giggled, and he laughed with her, a wide easy laugh that warmed her heart.

'Relax! This time next week it will be open, everything will be fine.'

She grimaced. 'Easier said than done . . . right now I can't relax to save my life.'

Thoughtfully, he twisted a strand of her hair in his fingers, and looked at her.

'You can, you know.'

'How?'

'Come home with me. It's late. I will cook something for you, for a change – just scrambled eggs and a salad perhaps, some cheese – I'm not much of a cook, but we will open a bottle of wine and talk of other things, forget all about your pub for tonight.'

Go home with him? She had never been to his flat, for precisely the reasons she thought the invitation implied. And now, for those very same reasons, a smile spread across her face like melting butter.

'All right. That would be lovely.'

That, she thought, might be delicious. Although she had only known Louis for a few months, she was beginning to feel – out of nowhere, a vision of Lars leaped into her mind. Lars, Mel's father, her famous Swede in a field. Keeley still laughed at the joke. But there were going to be no jokes this time, no seeds planted in any field.

'Will you wait here a moment? I just want to pop out to the shops for a sec, if they're still open.'

But the pharmacy was a late-night one, she could see its coiled green snake winking in neon through the window; leaving Louis where he stood she grabbed her bag and ran out to it. Buying condoms was no big deal in France, and anyway she didn't care how blatant she looked, because she had had all the children she was going to have. One, as somebody had once famously said, was unfortunate; two was decidedly careless.

When she came back Louis was sitting on a beer barrel, waiting, smiling. Reaching out to her, he took her hand.

'Get what you wanted?'

'Yes.'

'Then let's go.'

The flat was only ten minutes' walk away, he told her as they set off into the milk-warm night, and as they sauntered through the dark cobbled streets she experienced a flash of nostalgia: these were the very same streets she had known and walked in her youth, going home every night to the flat she had shared with Keeley. Feeling as if things were somehow coming full circle, she walked slowly, savouring the happy memories as they mingled with a keen sense of anticipation.

This flat was in a narrow street full of squashed old buildings, its door lit only by a distant street lamp, and she watched bemused as Louis reached up to remove a curved stone from a niche.

'What's that for?'

'It's a secret hidey-hole. Look, the stone is carved in the shape of a bird . . . some frustrated builder must have had artistic leanings, about two hundred years ago.'

It was indeed carved; as she ran her fingers over it she could make out what looked like a sandpiper, some bird with a long bill, encircled with flowers and leaves. From the hole in the wall Louis removed a set of keys, and replaced the stone.

Inside, he snapped on the light, and looked at her with sudden shyness.

'It's not much of a place, Mary – nothing like Keeley's mansion, I'm afraid . . .'

'Louis. I don't care what it's like. Food and wine taste good anywhere when you're hungry, and I'm famished.'

Nodding, looking reassured, he led the way up three flights of wooden stairs indented with the feet of centuries, and unlocked another door. As Mary made her way cautiously into the shadows beyond, he turned on a lamp, revealing a dark room so cluttered she could hardly tell where it started or ended. All four walls were stacked with paintings, big landscapes and street scenes as high as herself; by the window there was an easel surrounded by jars, rags, brushes, and under an assortment of clothes, magazines, cushions and music albums she could discern two sofas, both draped in some kind of tapestry rug or throw. As homes went, it could not have been more different from Keeley's wide airy space, or from the neat suburban house she herself had once called home.

'What a magnificent mess!'

For a moment he looked thrown, uncertain, but then he saw her smiling, and smiled back as he cleared sitting space for her.

'Yes, well – bachelors are a bit messy, I suppose. Let me see what I can find in the fridge.'

He disappeared into what she supposed was a kitchen, and for the first time in her life she felt no curiosity to see it. She'd had all the kitchens she could take, for now.

'Riesling?' he called after a moment.

'Lovely,' she called back, uncaring. But she was surprised by the glass, when he handed it to her; a tall flute of cut crystal, it was weirdly out of place, and she murmured something complimentary. Drily, he smiled.

'Wedding present. I saved all six when Claudine was stripping my assets.'

'Claudine? Your wife?'

'My ex-wife. She even took the towels, the cutlery, the bread basket. I didn't really care. But I wanted to keep just one nice thing.'

'A relic of oul dacency,' she said in English, grinning, and he screwed up his face at her, trying to understand.

'Do you ever see her now?'

'No. She moved to Paris. We've both moved on.'

Good. That was all she wanted to know. Sipping the wine, she looked around her at the paintings – God, they were mammoth! She had no idea whether she liked them, or how good they might be from a professional point of view, but she was struck by their magnitude: nothing mean here, she thought, nothing small or crabbed or tight-fisted. Louis Crouzat appears to be a man who thinks big.

He came and sat beside her, balancing his glass on his knee, raising his free hand to touch behind her ear with his finger.

'You look a little tired, Mary.'

She supposed she was, after twelve hours of hard physical work, and it dawned on her that she must look a mess, needed a bath, was not a very appealing sight. But spiritually she didn't feel tired at all, she felt light and fresh and filled with freedom.

'I'm fine, for an old lady of ninety-four.'

He laughed aloud, and squeezed her to him in a way she found reassuring. 'Thirty-four, more likely! You're around the same age as me, aren't you?'

Well, yes. She wasn't going to quibble over a couple of years, especially if he didn't seem to see them. Anyway, what difference did they make? She felt at ease with him, on a level and a wavelength.

But . . . 'Louis, I have a teenaged daughter. And a husband.'

He looked puzzled. 'Yes. I know you have. I met her, remember?'

Yes. She did remember. But she wanted things to be clear.

'I just thought maybe I should mention it – in case—'

Oh, hell, what was she trying to say, why had she said it?

'In case what? Your husband bursts through the window in his Batman outfit?'

She laughed, a little hysterically. 'Oh, forget it. I don't know why I said it.'

He frowned into his wine, taking some time before looking up at her. 'I suppose you said it because we are here alone and, if I am lucky, you are going to spend the night with me. Or is that very presumptuous of me?'

She looked back at him, candidly. 'No. It's not presumptuous at all. I – I wouldn't be here unless I wanted to be, and had considered that possibility. But – it's just that – Louis, I'm very attracted to you, and I like you a lot. But I don't want to – to get into anything heavy. Anything serious.'

He sat back, and considered. 'No, I don't suppose you do, having only recently left your husband.'

'Yes. And – and – he – I – well, we weren't what you'd call sexually compatible. It's been a long time since—'

He sighed. 'It's true what they say. The Irish talk far too much. Mary, why don't you stop talking and worrying?'

Why didn't she? As he looked quizzically at her, she decided to do just that. Decided, in that instant, to take charge of herself, of this aspect of her life as well as the others. Putting down her glass on the floor, she turned to him without another word, took his face in her hands and kissed him.

Where his own glass went to she didn't know, but suddenly it vanished and his arms were around her, he was kissing her back, one of his callused painter's hands was inside her loose summer dress, its raw texture contrasting savagely with her own silky skin. Every nerve it touched leaped into life, her body bolted from her control, she was tearing his teeshirt over his head as they rolled to the rug on the floor, their bodies plaiting into one another.

Years, she thought as the last of their clothing fell away, years and years I have waited for this. For an ordinary man, a real man, a normal man. One who can make love to me, and make me laugh about it, maybe even nourish my soul a little.

My soul is another day's work. But let's just start with my body, because if it's not fed soon it will shrivel and starve to death. I'm not in love with Louis, but I like him more than anyone I've—

And then his lips were on her breast, and she was no longer thinking, at all.

'You had no business!' Keeley snapped. 'No business whatsoever to stay out all night, without even calling me! I was worried sick!'

Complacently, Mary grinned like a cat who'd swallowed the cream. But she'd better try to sound apologetic.

'Sorry, Keel. I really am sorry. I would have called, if I'd got a chance.'

'A chance? What do you mean – doesn't he have a phone? Surely to God—'

'I don't know. I suppose he does. I just never got to find out.'

Keeley snorted in disgust, as much at the speed with which things had happened, Mary suspected, as at her thoughtlessness. But try as she might she could not wipe the grin off her face; she felt as if she had spent the night floating in the slipstream of the stars. Louis Crouzat had the body of a tiger and the fingertips of an angel.

And then she thought of Vincent, and how Keeley must feel. Sobering a little, she sought to change the subject.

'Oh, you sound like my granny. Speaking of whom, did I tell you I had a letter from her? She's disgusted with me too. You certainly can't accuse me of doing things by halves.'

Granny, Keeley thought, Granny Jameson who is soon going to be great-Granny Jameson. If she's disgusted with you for leaving your husband, wait till she hears about your daughter – Granny. And wait until you hear. By golly, that'll put a stop to your gallop.

Mutinously, they eyed each other for a long moment. And then Mary burst out laughing.

'Oh, Keeley, stop looking at me like that! It was only a fling.'

'Was it?'

Well, no, actually. If she was honest Mary hoped that it wasn't. She couldn't wait to see Louis again, was ravenous for him. But when he'd asked her when he could, as he carried café-crème to her in bed this morning, she had held back a little. Maybe not tonight, maybe they'd better wait until after The Cracker was safely launched?

OK, he replied casually, whatever she liked. Did she want him to come to the launch then, or what?

Oh yes, she'd said hastily, she did. She'd love him to come, was counting on it. Him and all his painter friends, Friday night at eight o'clock. With a sunny smile he'd agreed to that, and they'd parted on the friendliest of terms. When she left she made a point of leaving the empty coffee cup on the bedside table, making no attempt to wash or clean up anything. Her duty days were over.

'Come on, Keel, don't be cross with me.'

Wearily, Keeley sighed. She really was cross with Mary. Not just because she hadn't phoned last night, or because she felt a variety of conflicting emotions, but because her nerves were stretched to breaking point.

While Mary was out gallivanting with Louis this morning, she had been on the phone to Mel. Assuming the role that was her friend's, she had tried to sound as motherly, as comforting, as supportive as possible. As Mel sobbed and babbled, she'd interjected all manner of consoling thoughts, trying all the while to elicit more information.

But Mel's stuttered answers indicated that she really was pregnant, would give birth in November if her calculations were correct. Taking charge of the situation as much as she could, Keeley repeated over and over that she wasn't to worry: when the school term ended next week Mel was to fly to France; a ticket would be booked for her and Cathal would think nothing unusual of it, since that was exactly the summer plan that had been arranged. Regaining some glimmer of assurance, Mel had stopped crying, thanked her profusely and then asked desperately – what did she think Mary would say?

Would she go spare, or what? Would she kill her, flay her alive, make her have the baby adopted or – or what?

Personally, Keeley thought Mary probably would go ballistic.

She would kill not only Mel but Cathal, her parents and brothers who were supposed to be keeping an eye on Mel, her in-laws, everybody. And then she would collapse in a heap of guilt, because at the end of the day it was all her fault, she had abandoned her daughter and now look what had come of her selfishness! In her mind's eye Keeley could envisage the whole gruesome scene, and had a momentary urge to flee to Italy after all.

But if ever she was needed, it was now. Somehow she had to keep Mel calm, keep her on an even keel until she got here, and try to shoulder some of the responsibility for her after that, because Mary would have a pub to run by then whether she still wanted it or not. Since putting down the phone nearly three hours ago, Keeley had been pacing the house like a caged cat, trying to think how best to cope.

But at least she wouldn't have to keep the secret to herself for very long. Just two more days and then she could tell Mary, break the news which was going to fall on her ears like a shower of splintering glass. Meanwhile, she had Tony to talk to, and she was very glad she had confided in him. Only six months removed from Pearse Gardens, he was remarkably pragmatic about it.

'Sure don't they all manage somehow, in the end?'

'Yes – but usually their mothers are left holding the baby! Mary can't hold this one, Tony, not with a new business to run, she'll be up to her ears—'

'She will,' he conceded, 'if everything works out safe and sound.'

'What do you mean?'

'I mean that Mel is only a young one, Keeley. Very young, to be having a baby. I know she looks mature, but . . .'

Trailing off enigmatically, he'd turned back to his easel, leaving her taut with fresh anxiety. Mel was indeed very young, even by Pearse Gardens standards, to give birth. Anything could happen, to her or to the child. Anything at all.

And now, here was her mother, grinning like the Cheshire cat, fresh out of her lover's bed. And maybe she was pregnant, too! Furiously, Keeley whirled back to her.

'Did you at least take precautions?'

Affronted, Mary blinked. 'God, Keeley, that's a very personal—'

'Did you or didn't you?'

'Well, yes, I – if you must know, I did. Why do you ask?'

'Because you didn't the last time!'

'Oh, Keeley! I know I didn't then, but that was sixteen years ago for heaven's sake—'

'Yes, and here we are to this day, still stuck with the consequences!'

Mary looked wounded. '*Stuck* with them? Oh, Keel, I wouldn't put it that way ... I know Mel has caused you terrible grief, but she's not a bad girl, she didn't do it on purpose. Can't you try to forgive her, just a little, like you said you would?'

Frostily, Keeley glared at her. 'Yes, Mary. I can try. And I hope you can too, if she ever causes you any grief.'

'Huh? What's that supposed to mean?'

You wait, Keeley thought. You just wait, Miss Mary, and you'll soon find out.

Everything was ready, as organised as it possibly could be, and as she dressed for her big night Mary felt a kind of regal calm.

Lots of music, lots of food and wine, lots of *craic*. That was what it boiled down to basically, this opening night; after that it was all in the lap of the gods. Naturally she would assist the gods as much as humanly possible, work herself to the bone, but the one vital ingredient she couldn't supply was luck.

Yet she felt that her luck was turning, this year. Since leaving Cathal in January everything had gone far better than she had hoped, right down to Félix's investment of extra money and the purchase of the perfect premises as a result. The renovations to it had been completed in time for tonight's party, she had had help from many wonderful friends, Luc was proud of her he said, Louis was – well, she didn't want to decide right now what Louis was exactly, but he was certainly very helpful apart from being the most brilliant lover in creation. As she put on her make-up she could see the sparkle in her eyes, the glow in her skin, the new Mary in the mirror. Like a snake sloughing off its old skin, she felt freed, reborn.

'Mary!'

Lipstick in hand, she stopped as she heard Keeley calling out to her from way down the corridor.

'Yes, Keel?'

'Mel is on the phone, wants to wish you luck.'

'Oh – thanks, I'm coming.'

Giving her hair a final fluff, she stood up and surveyed herself: not bad, for thirty-six next month. Although the French didn't get Coronation Street on television and probably had no idea what it was, she was conscious of wanting to avoid the Bet Lynch syndrome, and had dressed to look as unlike a pub landlady as possible. Besides, Louis liked the casual outdoorsy look she preferred herself: a long loose dress of cream cotton patterned with tawny leaves, wooden earrings and bracelet, summer sandals of cream leather – comfortable ones, because she'd be on her feet all night.

As she went to the phone she could hear Keeley having some final word with Mel, and was struck by the contained urgency in her voice, almost secretive, as if she were warning her about something. But then Keeley was a bit wound up about the launch herself, was probably telling Mel to be on her best behaviour and not whine about anything, or make any demands tonight.

Picking up the phone seconds after Keeley put it down, she greeted her daughter brightly.

'Hello, Mel! Aren't you a sweetie, to think of phoning!'

'I just wanted to wish you luck, Ma.'

'Thanks – I need it! But everything is ready, the place looks fabulous. I just wish you could be here.'

'I would be, if school was finished in time. But we don't get our hols till next week.'

'I know. Keeley told me she booked your flight for Saturday – why didn't you let me book it?'

'Oh, I just happened to be talking to her when you were out, and she said she'd do it.'

'Well, I can't wait to see you. I've given Keeley a cheque for the fare already – and I'll reimburse you too, if you'll bring over as many rashers as you can carry. Back bacon, no rind . . . the suppliers here haven't delivered half enough.'

'OK.'

OK? That sounded a bit flat, Mary thought. What on earth was eating Mel these days? Was her daughter really missing her, after all?

'Mel? Are you all right?'

'Yeah, sure, Ma, why?'

'Oh, I just thought you sounded a bit funny – how are your exams going?'

'Not great. I think I'm going to fail a few.'

'Oh, Mel! You told me you'd been studying hard!'

Abruptly Mel's tone changed, became defensive. 'I have been! It's not my fault!'

'Then what's wrong?'

'Nothing!'

Oh, great, Mary thought. She's a nervous wreck, doing her exams all by herself without me there at home for her. I wish I had time to talk to her about it. But I've got exactly fifteen minutes to get to the pub.

'Well, don't worry. Just do your best, and I'll see you next week. All right?'

'All right.'

On what sounded like a sulky note, Mel hung up, and Mary sighed, torn between concern for her daughter and nervousness about the night in store. Until now she hadn't been nervous at all, but suddenly she felt flustered. Putting down the phone, she went to find Keeley.

And didn't Keeley look glamorous, in her little black dress! That was her uniform, for glitzy events, but Mary had to say that it suited her, she looked very pretty and very – no, actually. She didn't look very well. She looked anxious and overwrought, agitated.

'Keeley? Are you feeling all right?'

'Yes. I'm fine.'

But instinctively Mary went to her, put a protective arm around her.

'Look, Keeley, I know you've invested a lot in this pub. But you needn't worry. I won't lose your last penny on you. On the contrary. I'm determined to make us both a fortune. You and Félix will see a handsome return on your money, don't you fret.'

'I'm not fretting.'

Suddenly, the penny dropped. Keeley was unhappy because she had no escort tonight, had to attend the launch alone except for Tony who, far from looking after her, would require care and supervision himself.

'It's Vincent, isn't it? You're missing him like hell.'

'Yes. As a matter of fact I am. But I'll try to cheer up.'

'Oh, Keel . . . Félix and Luc will be there, lots of your friends, and I promise I'll mind you.'

But Keeley thought of that other launch, of the first salon she had opened with Vincent, and could not halt the tears that rose to her eyes. Dipping her head, she tried to hide them.

'I'll be fine, Mary.'

'Well, if you're not, just let me know. But I'm counting on you to sing Dicey Reilly!'

Keeley thought she would strangle herself sooner than sing. Somehow she'd have to do it, she supposed; after all this was Mary's night, and it was important that a cheery atmosphere prevail.

'Are we ready to leave? Where's Louis?'

'Oh, I said I'd meet him there! I didn't want him coming here . . . Keeley?'

'Yes?'

'Give me a smile?'

Wanly, reluctantly, Keeley smiled. And then, with a huge effort, she turned it into a real one. After nearly seventeen years, Mary was going to get everything she wanted tonight, everything she'd been denied first time round – her own kitchen, her own menu, her own career. Her own life, at last . . . and probably Louis as well, later.

Let her enjoy it, Keeley thought. Let her enjoy it. It's going to be her last carefree night for a long time. A very long time, even assuming that her child and grandchild survive safely.

But then, she has survived herself, in spite of everything. Where there's life there's hope. And I'm still alive, even if Vincent isn't. I'm alive, and our friendship is alive. We're so lucky to have each other, as well as our health, our other friends . . . but she'll always be the most special one. I hardly even know why any more, that's just the way things are, we're like Darby and Joan.

Not that she'll be like Darby or Joan tomorrow. She'll be like a flaming antiChrist, when she hears what Mel Sullivan has been and gone and done.

Chapter Nineteen

It was a great night, and The Cracker opened with a bang. Cheered by the lively music and the many people who made sure she was never alone, Keeley sang Dicey Reilly after all, belting it out amidst much whooping and foot-stamping from the musicians and assorted Irish guests, who knew the words and joined in with her. The French guests looked somewhat bemused by the rowdy atmosphere, but after a quantity of Guinness had been poured into them they began to sing their own songs in chauvinistic retaliation, and it was well after two in the morning by the time the first of them began to think of leaving. Many of them complimented Mary on the food, and she saw in their faces that they would be back.

Louis made himself indispensible, helping with everything and promising to drop by again next day, because to everyone's surprise several of the paintings on the walls had been sold. Not that they were meant to be, but people simply enquired, and Mary saw no reason not to let them have what they wanted. Thrilled, Tony said he would paint more to replace them, as would Louis and the others, and Alain Jou turned an unexpected profit on the night. In the morning, Louis would hang up a temporary new batch to fill the empty spaces.

'Are you coming home with me?' he murmured to Mary some time after midnight, but she shook her head.

'Not tonight, Josephine.'

'Oh . . . why not?'

'Because I don't want Keeley to be alone tonight. Besides we'll want to hold a post-mortem after breakfast, have a chat about how things went.'

Disconsolate, he went home alone, but not until he'd helped to clear up the worst of the mess. It was nearly four by the time Mary and Keeley got to their beds, where they crashed out too tired to talk. But Mary fell asleep with a smile on her face, thinking of Félix who'd scandalised Lise by getting tipsy, and Luc who'd said her spinach and bacon quiche was 'a triumph, chérie, a triumph.'

After a bare four hours' sleep she was up again ready for action; there was a mountain of work to be done before The Cracker opened for lunch. By the time Keeley staggered into the kitchen looking groggy in her bathrobe, Mary was already dressed, whipping croissants out of the oven as coffee gurgled in the perker.

'Hi! And how are we this beautiful morning?'

'My head' said Keeley cautiously, 'feels as if someone had been using it for soccer practice.'

'Here. Fresh juice. Take an aspirin with it and you'll be grand.'

'Thanks. And congratulations. That was some party.'

Mary was all eager pleasure. 'Wasn't it great? I even enjoyed it myself. Especially the bit where you sang Monto.'

'Oh, no. I didn't, did I?'

'You did. Word perfect.'

'Well, I just hope Francine and Pierre didn't understand it, because otherwise they'll disown me – which would be a pity, they being my only family apart from Tony.'

'Don't worry. They were laughing. Hurry up and eat your breakfast now, we've got a lot of work to do.'

'We have?'

'Yes – you are going to come and help me straighten out the place, aren't you? It's all hands on deck today – if you'll hoover I'll wash, Louis will sort the tables and chairs, then you can help me do the vegetables for lunch—'

'Huh. I thought I was the backer, not the unpaid help.'

'I'll give you a free glass of champagne if you'll come. Nothing like a hair of the dog for hangovers.'

'Oh, all right. D'you reckon you'll have many for lunch?'

'Dunno. I've ordered supplies for about fifty, but maybe that's a bit optimistic.'

'I think you might run out. Last night was such *craic* word will have spread overnight.'

'Hopefully. Two of the musicians are coming in to play, anyway, and Luc has booked a table for himself and Annette, Félix and Lise – if Félix can face lunch, poor thing. He was forty-nine sheets to the wind last night.'

'*Félix?*'

'Yep, our Félix, drunk as a skunk. I'd say he has a hangover about the size of Mexico.'

Mary grinned merrily, and Keeley saw that she was in great form. But – but she *had* to tell her now, about Mel!

'Mary—'

'Just wear your jeans, Keel, because you're going to get filthy. Hey, wasn't it great about the paintings? Tony and Louis each sold three. Alain was like a hustler in an Arab bazaar, haggling over prices.'

'Yes. That was weird, all right, you'd think The Cracker was an art gallery.'

'But it isn't! It's my pub! Jesus, Keel, I feel like a million dollars this morning, I can't *believe* I've really got it, done it!'

Keeley winced, hating to burst Mary's balloon with such bad news. But there was no option. Drawing breath, she tried again.

'Mary, there's something I've got to—'

'And Louis, wasn't he great? He fetched and carried like a slave all night, even helped behind the bar.'

'Yes. But—'

'Oh my God, it's nearly eight thirty! Come on, shake a leg!'

Keeley gave up. Clearly Mary wasn't listening, was dying to get going. Swallowing her coffee, she went off to get dressed, thinking that maybe tonight after dinner would be a better time, when Mary wound down a bit. If she wound down. If she even came home for dinner.

But Mary was virtually married to her pub for the next several days, spending every waking hour in it, not coming home until after midnight and, one night, not coming home at all. With the holiday season just starting she was as busy as she could possibly hope to be, cooking lunches, dinners and snacks round the clock, getting to the markets by dawn. With Mel's arrival only four days away, Keeley began to grow frantic.

'Your friend is certainly industrious,' Sylvie remarked when she dropped in to visit on Wednesday morning, 'and a good cook, too. I had lunch at The Cracker yesterday. Mussel chowder with delicious brown bread, mackerel salad, fresh fruit compote – it was delicious.'

'I'm glad you enjoyed it. Was the pub busy?'

'Too busy! We had to wait ten minutes for a table.'

God, Keeley sighed to herself, I'll never get hold of her at this rate. What am I going to do? I'll have to make an appointment to see her – but this is ridiculous! There must be a lull sometimes . . . maybe if I call in this afternoon, around four, that's usually when pubs are slackest.

At four, steeling herself, she got into her car and drove to Aix. Parking across the square, she grimaced as she saw the number of people sitting outside the pub, drinking lazily in the sunshine, picking idly at snacks. But her mind was made up to nail Mary and have done with it, because she could not stand the tension a moment longer. Beating a path into The Cracker when she reached it, she elbowed her way to the kitchen.

'Mary!'

'Oh, hi, Keel!'

Mary spun round from the stove where she was stirring something and grinned, looking pleased to see her. 'Great timing. You could give me a hand with this—'

'Mary. Please. I have to talk to you. Right now.'

'Oh? What's up?'

'I can't tell you here. Would you just come with me to that café down the street, take a break for half an hour?'

'But I—'

'*Mary*! It's *urgent*!'

Looking puzzled and – suddenly – slightly alarmed, Mary handed her wooden spoon over to her assistant, an Irish girl from Louth called Nieve, and went to wash her hands.

'OK. Keep your shirt on. I'm coming.'

Minutes later they were sitting in a much quieter, calmer café with two mineral waters in front of them, into which Keeley stared miserably.

'Mary, I don't know how to tell you this. But I have to. Something awful has happened.'

'Oh, Christ. What has?'

'It's Mel.'

Mary gasped, looking terrified. 'Oh no – what – not another accident? Is she hurt, is she—?'

'No. She's not hurt. But she – Mary, brace yourself. She's pregnant.'

'*Pregnant*?' Shrieking it aloud, she repeated it twice, three times.

'But Keeley – she can't – how do you – oh my *God*—'

Biting her lip, Keeley sat back and waited for it to sink in before attempting to explain.

'She wrote to me nearly two weeks ago. She wanted me to ring her, was in a desperate state. So I rang her. And it sounded to me as if she really is pregnant. She hasn't seen a doctor, nor told anyone, but she – she had sex with some guy she met at The Lantern.'

Mary's face was frozen with horror.

'So I told her to sit tight until she gets here, on Saturday. And I promised to say nothing to you until after the pub opened, because she was worried that the launch would go wrong if you were upset. I've been trying to tell you since then, but you've been so busy . . . Mary, I'm so sorry. I know this is dreadful news and it couldn't come at a worse moment, but you're going to have to take things in hand the minute she gets here.'

It seemed an eternity before Mary spoke.

'Does – does Cathal know?'

'No. I thought it would probably be best if you told him yourself, after a test's been done. Mary, the girl is terrified. She thinks he's going to go mad and you're going to go mad. But I said I'd speak to you and make you see that anger isn't the answer. She's scarcely fifteen, Mary! She needs help. Right away.'

Mary didn't reply. For several minutes she sat in silence, staring fixedly at Keeley. And then, to Keeley's horror, she burst into tears, began to sob loudly with her head in her hands.

'My Mel, my little girl . . . she's only a baby herself . . . how could I have left her alone? How could I have done it? *How*, Keeley, how?'

'Mary, please . . . there's no point in crying over spilt milk. Or in blaming yourself. Or in crying, for that matter, although I can't blame you. But what you need to do is *think*. We both do. She reckons the baby is due in November—'

'November! You mean to say she's three, nearly four months pregnant? She's been keeping this to herself for weeks and weeks – she must be demented with worry!'

'Well, she's usually a fairly cool customer. But yes, I think she is pretty wound up. She's afraid Cathal or one of her grandparents will notice, a teacher maybe—'

'But all those people were supposed to be looking after her!

How can they have let this happen? I will kill Cathal with my bare hands—'

'Oh, Mary. Let's face it. She's old enough to be left on her own for five minutes – and five minutes is all it takes. It could well have happened even if you were there.'

'But I wasn't there. I wasn't there, Keeley.'

'Well, she'll be here, on Saturday. I know you're terribly busy, but you're going to have to take the day off – I'll come in and work in the kitchen, if that's any use, while you collect her and take her straight to a doctor. I think you should make an appointment right now.'

'Yes . . . oh, *Keeley*!'

Mary's face was bone white, her hands were trembling, and it dawned on Keeley that she was actually in shock. She summoned the waiter.

'Some brandy, please.'

Mary looked blankly at it when it came, and Keeley chafed her hand as she cajoled her to drink it.

'Come on, it'll help . . . look, Mary, don't panic. We've been through this before, remember? And we'll get through it again.'

'But she's only a child . . . only a . . . Keeley, who is this boy, this man, whoever did it? Have you any idea?'

'No, except that I suspect he's quite young, not much older than herself.'

'He raped her. He raped my daughter. She's under age.'

'I know. I know, Mary. That's why she needs medical attention as soon as possible. It's not going to be easy for her.'

Abruptly, Mary stiffened. 'I think – I think she should have an abortion. I'm sorry, Keeley, I know that must sound appalling. But I think she should. She can't have a baby, at her age.'

'Well – look, why don't we wait until she arrives and hear what the doctor has to say, what she wants to do herself?'

Looking suddenly drained, Mary sagged in her chair as the shock sank in along with the brandy.

'Keeley, her life is ruined. Destroyed. No matter what she does, she'll never get over this. Never.'

Privately, Keeley was inclined to agree. But for Mary's sake she forced calm, steadiness into her voice.

'Mary, she's a tough little cookie. If anyone has any chance of coping with something as terrible as this, it's your Mel. She's level-headed and resilient, physically she's well developed—'

'She's my little girl. And I left her alone. All alone, while I gadded off to France about my own business.'

'She understood, Mary, that you had to do it! Besides, you didn't leave her all alone, you left her with her father and grandparents and aunt and uncles, her teachers and friends, you spoke to her every single day, you did everything a mother—'

'I left her, Keeley. It's as simple as that.'

'Oh, God. If you are going to start on one of your guilt trips, I – I will wash my hands of you, of this whole thing! I helped you the last time, when you were in the same mess, but I swear to God that this time I will walk away from the whole bloody disaster.'

Mary gaped at her. 'No! Oh Keeley, no, please don't! I can't think straight, I need you – please, don't do that now.'

'All right. But then you'll have to give me your word that you won't panic, won't weep, won't upset the child more than she already is. You will be strong and sensible and you will see this through. Is that clear?'

Stricken, Mary nodded at her, her voice barely a whisper.

'Yes, Keeley. It is. It's clear. I'll do whatever you say.'

They looked at each other, and in Mary's eyes Keeley saw many things, but control was not one of them. Not yet. In the past year Mary had taken a greater degree of control than ever before, was far stronger than she had ever been, but it was going to take her a while to get her head around this.

And meanwhile she, Keeley, seemed to be in charge once again.

But it was Luc who stepped into the breach, out of a clear blue sky, when he heard the news that Mary distractedly imparted to him. She had no desire to tell anyone, not even this lifelong friend and supporter, but clearly she was going to have to take some time off, and wondered whether he might know any chef who could do Irish dishes.

'I will do them myself,' he said loudly, firmly. 'I will take charge of your pub while you take charge of your daughter. Just leave everything to me.'

His tone conveyed outrage, horror and disgust, but she almost wept with gratitude.

'Oh, Luc, I can never thank you enough for this.'

'Hmph,' he muttered. 'You'd better write down all of your

recipes for me, because it is vital that there be continuity in the food, that it taste exactly as if you were cooking it.'

At that moment she didn't care if it tasted like wet socks, but he was adamant. And very angry.

'So young – so silly – what on earth can she have been thinking of! As for the boy, I would make mincemeat of him if I got my hands on him!'

Neither Mary nor Keeley doubted it. But they speculated endlessly, on what Mel could, indeed, have been thinking of.

'She's not stupid, Keeley, nor ignorant either. I sat her down when she was twelve and explained the facts of life quite clearly.'

Yes. Mel had always struck Keeley as a young lady who was well aware, well clued in to the dangers of sex. So why, then, had she done it? Maybe she would tell them on Saturday, when she arrived. Meanwhile, her mind kept returning to Tony's theory: 'She might be trying to make it up to you, for Vincent . . . you're crucifying yourself for never having had his baby, so she'll get one for you . . .'

But it was insane! Completely preposterous – except that nobody could read the mind of a teenager whose parents had split up, whose mother had left the country, who had been the cause of a fatal accident. In her own grief, Keeley had never talked to Mel, had never wanted to, and now it dawned on her that nobody really had. Cathal simply refused to acknowledge Mel's part in Vincent's death, while Mary felt it was best to let the girl work out her own degree of responsibility. It was a reasonable, adult strategy, but perhaps Mel was too young to be treated like an adult. Under the glamorous, assured veneer, she was just a kid.

'I've got to ring her,' Mary said finally, desperately, when she felt she had got sufficient grip on the situation that she would not sound hysterical. But she felt hysterical; not just because Mel was pregnant but because she had been told this fact by Keeley, who in some curious way seemed to be on more intimate terms with her daughter than she was herself. Why had Mel not told her first, directly, in person? Because of the launch, she claimed . . . but it was demeaning, humiliating, worrying.

'If you think that's best,' Keeley responded. 'But are you sure you can talk to her calmly? I think you might be better off waiting until you see her in person. It's only another few days, and it'll be much easier than the phone.'

'But I want to know how she is! I have to know!'

'Then I'll ring her and ask her. You can listen in on the extension and break in if you want to – but, Mary, please don't fuss or shout or distress her. She's really pretty fragile.'

So Keeley rang, and chatted sympathetically, helpfully, while Mary listened. A dozen times she opened her mouth to interject, and a dozen times no word came out. Mel's voice sounded a million miles away.

'Keeley, what's wrong with me? I was aching to speak to her, and I couldn't!'

'Maybe you were afraid to say anything until you could be sure it was the right thing . . . but it will take a little while to find the right thing. Probably not being able to speak meant that you haven't decided what that is yet.'

At least Mel sounded relatively all right, was reassured to hear Keeley say that Mary was not going to murder her, that she would weather the news somehow 'when she gets it.'

With bated breath Keeley waited for her to arrive, now, while watching Mary go through the motions at the pub. Every enthusiasm for it seemed to have been crushed, within a week of its opening; Mary looked like someone who had walked into a brick wall.

'But you must concentrate. It's your – your—' She very nearly said 'baby', but stopped herself just in time. 'It's your livelihood, Mary. You need it. It's your independence, your future. When this crisis is over, it will still be there. You mustn't lose momentum.'

'I feel like locking it and throwing away the key,' Mary replied, dully.

'Well, *don't*! If Mel feels well enough she could even work with you for a while, and you could keep a constant eye on her. At the very least you'll need money to keep her. This pregnancy is going to be an expensive business no matter what way it works out, and besides you have staff to consider, salaries to pay. A lot of people are depending on you besides Mel.'

That roused her a bit, and Keeley saw that she was thinking of the hefty investment in the pub, hers and Félix's, that had now to be sustained and justified. Somehow she got through the rest of the week, forced herself to smile at all the customers, while wondering whether or not to tell Louis what had happened.

'Tell him,' Keeley advised briskly. 'Otherwise he'll think

you're ill or something. Besides, if he's any kind of a halfway decent chap, he'll be a shoulder for you to lean on.'

'But I didn't want to lean on him. That was the last thing I ever wanted to do. I wanted us to be completely independent of each other.'

'Yes, well, he doesn't have to get involved if he doesn't want to! But he might be supportive, might give a hand in the bar or even in the kitchen from time to time. Or he might simply listen to you, be a comfort.'

Eventually, reluctantly, Mary decided to tell him. And she was glad when she did, because he was horrified, insisted immediately that she must try not to worry, take as much time off as she needed, he would supervise things at the pub for her as best he could. With Luc and Nieve, they would manage somehow.

Gratefully, tenderly, Mary kissed him, thinking how incredibly lucky she was to have such friends. Everyone was rallying around wonderfully – except Cathal, of course, with whom she had yet to speak. That delight would have to wait until Sunday, and she quaked as she contemplated it; the fury, the bitterness, the accusations that would fly between them.

'Oh, for God's sake,' Keeley replied when she confided this fear to her. 'Why don't the two of you just forget about yourselves for once and think of your daughter? Just drop your bloody point-scoring and concentrate on Mel!'

Keeley sounded irritable, and it dawned on Mary that she was genuinely worried about the girl. Very genuinely, despite everything that had happened last August.

Mary sped away to the airport immediately after breakfast on Saturday, refusing to let Keeley come with her, insisting that she must, now, deal with her daughter herself. At the airport she found the flight delayed, and walked round in circles, willing it to arrive, to be safe, to *hurry*. It seemed like hours before she finally saw it flashed on the screen, and rushed to the arrival gates.

And then, as she saw her daughter coming to her, she knew why she had not been able to speak over the phone. No words were adequate to the emotion she felt, the love that welled up in her as she raced to gather Mel into her arms, to hold her, protect her, embrace her with every bone in her body.

'Mum, oh Mum . . .'

The tears flowed as they clung together, and only at that moment did Mary know for certain how much she loved Mel despite every factor that had held them at arm's length over the years: Mel's unlucky conception, the ruined career that had resulted, the disastrous marriage, the cheeky supercilious girl who had sided more and more with Cathal as time went by, perhaps sensing at the deepest, most unreachable level her mother's ambivalence to her. Now, it all seemed like water long gone under the bridge, and all she knew was the sweetness of her daughter's hair and skin, her tremulous voice, her pleading eyes.

'Mum, I – I – did Keeley tell you—?'

'Yes, love. She told me. It's all right. You're going to be all right. You're safe with me now, I'm going to look after you . . . oh, Mel, I'm so glad to see you! Come on, come with me, let's get you home where you can rest and talk.'

Wiping her eyes, she wiped Mel's in turn and they looked at each other, half crying, half smiling as Mary took the luggage in one hand and her daughter's own in the other, clutching it tight to her. Trying not to be too obvious about it, she sneaked a sidelong glance at Mel, but as yet the pregnancy did not show, perhaps because Mel was wearing a loose summer dress in place of her usual tight jeans and sprayed-on top.

They got into the car and Mary switched on the ignition; but suddenly her hands were shaking, she didn't feel she could drive. Letting the car idle in neutral, she turned to Mel.

'Mel . . . how do you feel?'

Mel mustered a flick of her fringe, a lift of her chin. 'Better, now that I'm here and you know about it – at least I don't have to worry any more about that. You're not going to eat me alive, are you?'

'No, of course not – where would that get us? But Mel, we have to talk. You must tell me how this happened. And then I'll have to talk to Cathal.'

Glumly, Mel nodded. 'I suppose so – oh, Mum, he's going to go nuts! He thinks I'm still his little girl, he – he's going to be disgusted with me. Absolutely disgusted.'

'Well, I imagine he'll be angry all right, but I hope not disgusted. Anyway, he's partly to blame, he should have kept a much closer eye on you.'

'He does – too close, sometimes. But it really had nothing to do with him. I did it all by myself.'

Mary looked closely at her. 'No. You didn't. Tell me – how old is the – father?'

'A – about sixteen, I think.'

About sixteen. She *thought*. Suppressing an impotent sigh, Mary put the car into gear and drove her home.

There was no sign of Keeley when they got there, and Mary realised that she had deliberately made herself scarce, refused to intrude on these first few hours between mother and daughter. Well then, she had better make the most of them, face up to what had to be faced. Making a pot of tea, she sat Mel down at the kitchen table and shut the door.

'OK. Let's get the details clear first. Who is the father of this child?'

Candidly, but with trepidation, Mel met her eye.

'His – his name is Ronan.'

'Ronan what?'

'I – I – Mum, I don't know!'

Suddenly Mary felt as if she were standing in a hall of mirrors, seeing her own teenaged self. But it couldn't have happened twice. It couldn't have.

'Mel, you must – surely to God—'

'Mum, I don't! I'm not trying to protect him or anything. I really don't know. I met him in The Lantern. He was gorgeous, I really fancied him. We had a couple of Cokes and – and then he asked me if I could get anything else. Something stronger.'

'The little—'

'So I said OK, I'd try, and when Bill wasn't looking I grabbed a bottle off the shelves. I didn't even look to see what it was. But it turned out to be gin. So we took it to the park and we drank it – well, he drank most, we got some lemon to mix it with on the way – and then we decided to go to the disco. Dad knew I was going to it anyway so I didn't have to call him or anything – he thought I was with Jane . . . and then when we got there I felt a bit sick, it was so crowded and hot, so Ronan said why didn't we go outside . . . we just kept walking until eventually we ended up back at the park and – and that's where it happened.'

Silently, Mary absorbed every word, gripping her mug and fighting the urge to hurl it across the room.

'So that's where it happened. That's how. A bottle of gin and a boy you met – didn't you even ask him his second name?'

'Yes. He told me, but I can't remember.'

Mary wrestled with herself in silence until such time as she could speak again.

'I see. And when did you discover you were pregnant?'

'About – about six or seven weeks ago – but I wasn't really sure, I just kept getting sick in the mornings and feeling really tired. I wanted to tell you, tell Dad, but I – I couldn't! I was scared of what you'd both say, and then you had the new pub opening, he had the election—'

'What election?'

'The county council, he's running for it.'

So. Councillor Cathal, finally, a pillar of the community. Mary dug her nails into her palms.

'So you haven't seen a doctor or anything?'

'No. I was too scared. I thought if I didn't think about it, maybe it wouldn't happen, maybe I was wrong.'

'Oh, Mel! You should have rung me immediately, you know I'd have—'

Tears rose in Mel's eyes then, tears she wiped angrily away.

'I couldn't! I couldn't say it over the phone, I – oh, Mum! What am I going to *do*?'

What, indeed? Wretchedly Mary contemplated the options, overwhelmed with anxiety and apprehension for her daughter.

'Well . . . first and foremost, you're going to see a doctor. Tell me, when did it happen exactly?'

'In February. The second weekend in February.'

Mary's mind flew through the calendar. It was now the second week in June. Four months. A baby, her grandchild, due in November. Her voice, as she spoke again, sounded strangled even to her own ears.

'Have – have you thought about it at all, Mel? About what you want to do?'

Mel gazed at the wall behind her. 'I've been trying not to think about it . . . I don't know anything about having a baby. I know you told me a few years ago, but I didn't really understand.'

No. Mary supposed that she couldn't have; at twelve it was hard to understand, even if you were precocious and cocky for your age. Biting her lip, hard, she studied Mel's face.

'It's not easy, Mel. Having a baby is no fun at all, at any age. Of course nearly everyone gets through it, because they're looking forward to the end result, but in fact that's only the start. Once the child is born, it's not a toy – it's a person, a human being for whom you are responsible for the next twenty years at least.'

'Twenty years.' Wide-eyed, Mel repeated it, looking faint.

'Yes. Even for someone twice your age, there are so many things to cope with . . . feeding, changing, minding round the clock, illness, education, money, more things than you can possibly imagine. Things which, in your case, you'd have no partner to help you with. Unless—?'

'No,' Mel whispered. 'I don't think so, Mum. I don't think he'd want to know.'

Anger coiled in Mary like a tornado. 'Well, he's going to know. I'm going to get Cathal to find out – to investigate—'

'Oh, no! Mum, please don't! He's only a kid, we're too young, I couldn't get married even if I – Mum, there's no point!'

Again Mary heard her own words, her own voice talking to her own parents: *There's no point . . . he's only a student . . . I don't know . . .*'

'But – but, Mel, how on earth are you going to bring up a child all by yourself? You can't, there's no way—'

In spite of herself Mel began to cry, quietly but desperately, choking back sobs.

'I don't know! Mum, I don't know *what* to do!'

As comfortingly as she could, Mary reached for her hand across the table, and held it.

'All right, Mel. Don't panic. We'll figure something out. But Mel, you must tell me – why did you do it? *Why?*'

Anguished, Mel struggled for words. 'Because – I – I felt – I felt lonely – you were gone and Dad was busy and Keeley was angry – I'd killed Vincent – I was confused, I didn't know it could happen so fast—'

Oh, yes, Mary thought. It can happen very fast. It happened to me, and I haven't a leg to stand on, there is nothing I can say.

'Don't worry, Mel. I'm not angry with you. I'm just trying to get the full picture, that's all, before we go to see the doctor.'

'Now? Are we going today, right away?'

'Yes. I've made an appointment for this afternoon. You probably don't understand all the implications yet, Mel, but there is no time to lose.'

*   *   *

Yes, Dr Bourry confirmed four hours later in a tone that made Mary's skin tighten, the young *demoiselle* was pregnant. The child was due in mid-November, and it was beyond her how such a thing could happen. Without much effort to disguise her opinion of the situation, she took Mary aside and spoke coldly.

'Your daughter is, of course, far too young. I strongly recommend a termination, as soon as possible.'

Swallowing, Mary nodded. Hating herself for it, it was what she thought too, no matter what Keeley said about waiting and thinking; she had thought about nothing else for a single sleepless moment since.

Frowning, Dr Bourry consulted a diary on her desk.

'I will telephone the clinic. In such an emergency, we might be able to arrange it for some day next week.'

Her mind whirling, Mary gripped the desk. 'Yes. Thank you. Only—'

'Only what?' The doctor's tone was impatient, her look chilling.

'Only I'd better talk to Mel first, to be sure it's what she wants herself.'

'What she wants? Madame, it is not a case of what the child wants! She is far too young to decide. Besides which it could well be dangerous for her to give birth, to continue this pregnancy – and she has been raped, she is not yet sixteen. The situation is quite clear-cut.'

The woman looked so angry Mary thought she might well be about to pick up the phone and report the case to the police. But it wasn't her business to do that. The crime had happened in Ireland. And Mel did have a right to decide – at least, to be made understand the danger and the lack of choice.

'Yes. But I must still discuss it with her.'

Dr Bourry pursed her lips. 'As you wish. But please do not delay.'

'No. I – I'll contact you on Monday.'

The consultation came to its frigid end, and Mary steered her white-faced daughter out to the car, where they both sat stunned and dizzy for several minutes, Mel weeping, Mary trying not to. Abruptly, she started the engine.

'Let's go somewhere – somewhere quiet, calm.'

The BMW seemed to steer itself as she pulled out and

headed away from the doctor's office in the centre of Aix, out towards the countryside. For some time they drove in silence, until amongst the signs she saw one for Simiane.

Simiane. It rang some distant bell in her mind, jogged some happy, peaceful memory. Why? She couldn't remember, but decided to head for it anyway. And then, as the road narrowed and began to twist through fields of poppies, it came to her. The abbey where the monks made the *calissons*, that sunny Sunday with Keeley and Vincent and Sylvie, so long ago.

Mel raised her head as they neared it, peered through her tears at the fields and flowers.

'Where are we going?'

'To an abbey where the monks keep bees, make honey and sweets.'

If it sounded obscure it didn't seem to bother Mel, who had been frightened by the doctor's stern demeanour and now seemed content, even eager, to put herself in her mother's hands. When they reached the ancient yellow building she simply got out of the car, put her hands in her pockets and waited to be told what to do.

'Come on, let's walk while we talk.'

Mary took her hand, which was given trustingly, as if Mel was almost reverting to childhood. Steeling herself, forcing her thoughts into some kind of order, Mary somehow got the words out.

'Mel, the doctor thinks you – thinks you should have an abortion.'

'Aah!'

Looking terrified, Mel gasped, stumbled against her and then groped for a low wall, onto which she slowly sank.

'Oh no, oh Mum – I can't do that, don't let her make me!'

In spite of herself Mary forced some kind of reassuring smile, tightened her grip on the girl.

'No, I won't let anyone make you. But Mel, this is a grown-up situation and you have to try to see it that way. You're far too young to have a baby, not only because motherhood is an adult undertaking, but because it is physically risky for you. You could be very ill, you – you could even die.'

'*Die?*'

Neither of them could speak as they looked at each other, and it was some time before Mary could go on.

'Mel, you won't be fifteen until next month. You're not fully grown yet. Your chances of carrying this baby to full term and giving birth safely are – are not good. And, even if you did manage it, the baby's chances of survival are—'

'But other teenagers have done it! I've heard about it, there was a girl in the newspaper, even younger than me—'

'Yes. It has been done. But Mel, the strain on you, physically and mentally . . . you can't imagine what it would be like.'

'But I – it's my baby! I can't kill it!'

No, Keeley. I couldn't. It's still a child. Like my kid brothers. I couldn't. The words welled up in Mary's mind like a river after rainfall, swirling through the mists of memory, carrying her back to that terrible day in their flat, sitting on an orange crate with her head between her knees. The day she had decided to have *her* child, to have Mel.

Mel, who sat now beside her, her cheeky, wilful, beautiful daughter. Her only child, because the next had died, and she had never again found the right conditions, the right man with whom to have another.

'But Mel – please, listen to me—'

'No!' Mel's voice rose sharply, something close to hysteria tautened in her. 'I can't! I can't!'

Her whole body was rigid as she sat upright and broke free of her mother, clenching her fists against the warm, old stone. Desperately, Mary tried to reason, tried to prise open her mind.

'Mel, it's too dangerous!'

'I don't care!'

'But you must care! You're only a child – you're my child, and I love you too much to let you do this!'

Jumping up, Mel whirled on her with a passion so unexpected she was stunned.

'You don't! You don't love me! You never even wanted me, because I messed up your career! Nobody loves me, only Dad!'

Jerking away from Mary, her eyes blazing, she looked at her mother with a fury fierce as fire, and ran away.

Mary had no idea how much time elapsed before she was able, finally, to get up and stumble to the abbey, the sun drying her tears into her face, blinding her as she scanned the fields and buildings.

An elderly monk walked past her, and she grabbed at him.

'Please – have you seen a girl – a young girl, in a mauve dress—?' He gazed at her before slowly shaking his head, and she ran on before he could articulate whatever he was about to say.

'Mel! Mel!'

She shouted as she ran, round by one side of the abbey, on down a long gravel path to some kind of chapel or oratory, through a lawn edged with flags of lavender, past the building she saw was still used as the sweet factory, a handful of visitors waiting outside it for the next guided tour to begin. Panting, she ran up to them, inspected them as they stared at her bewildered, but Mel was not amongst them.

And then she saw her, standing by the car in the parking lot, her arms folded, her stance hostile and repelling. The ground flew from under her as she raced to her.

'Mel! Oh, my God—'

Exuding anger, and some kind of challenge, Mel wrenched at the car door, but it was locked.

'Take me home! I want to go back to Keeley!'

But Mary grabbed her by both shoulders, and held her.

'No. We're not going anywhere. Not until we talk this out – Mel, how can you think I don't love you? How can you think such a thing?'

Mel refused to meet her eyes, but stood firm. 'Because – because you left me! You went off and left me, you didn't want to be with me—'

'Mel, I left Cathal, not you! I could not go on with the life we were living, and I told you I would explain why when you're older. But I thought you – you said—'

'I said what you wanted me to say. Go and open your pub in France, Mum, don't worry about me.'

'But, Mel, I've worried about you every day . . . I want you to come and live here with me, as soon as you finish school . . . don't you know that? You're my daughter, my only child!'

'And now you won't let me have mine!'

Mary felt as if the ground was melting from under her.

'I will let you, if you really want – if you feel able – Mel, I'm only worried about you because you're so young. Too young—'

'You were young, when you had me. You were only a teenager.'

For seconds that felt like eternity, they stared at each other. And then Mary felt her whole body go limp.

'Yes. I was. I was nineteen and I was terrified, I was away from home and alone except for Keeley ... but I went ahead and had you. Do you think I would have done that if I didn't love you even then, before you were born? If I didn't want you?'

Turning her face away, Mel gazed out across the fields. 'Well, I love my baby too. I want it.'

She said it quietly, distantly, and in that moment Mary saw why she wanted it: she wanted love. Someone to love, in the midst of the maelstrom between her parents, someone to whom her loyalty would not be divided. A new life to replace Vincent's, maybe even to ... she had never been told about her dead baby brother, but did she know? Could she possibly remember, possibly sense that loss which had closed the final door between her parents?

And something else came to Mary. She too wanted this new baby, this new life. Only not at the price of her daughter's.

'All right, Mel. It's all right. You can have this child ... we'll have it somehow, if the doctor thinks there's a reasonable chance of it being delivered in safety. I'll take you to an obstetrician and get an expert opinion, if you'll promise to listen ... Mel, I don't want to lose you, or to see you suffer.'

Still Mel seemed to be thinking, considering things she could only guess at. When she spoke next she still sounded defiant, but less so.

'And you won't – you won't make me give it away, have it adopted?'

'I won't make you do anything you don't want to do. You know, when I was expecting you, some – some people thought it would be best if I had you adopted. But I didn't. I wouldn't. Instead I married Cathal, to give you a home and family.'

She could see that Mel was reflecting now, starting to come round.

'Mum?'

'Yes?'

'Why do you always call him Cathal? Why do you never call him my Dad?'

The question was so unexpected, she very nearly fell headlong into the answer. But Cathal was the girl's father, in all but biology; the last thing she needed to hear now was the truth, on top of everything else. She hesitated only for the most fractional of seconds – but in that time, Mel saw it.

'He – he *is* my father, isn't he?'

No, Mel. Your father is some man in Sweden, probably with other children now, some man I had sex with in a field one night, out of sheer stupidity. Someone whose name I couldn't even remember next day, who got on his motorbike and went on to the next casual fling.

'Yes, Mel. Cathal is your father.'

For the first time since her arrival – God, was it really only this morning? – Mel seemed to relax the tiniest bit, seemed almost on the verge of a smile, of reassurance.

'Sorry. Stupid question. I – I'm just a bit mixed up at the moment.'

Mary let go of her shoulders, and put her arm around one of them.

'Yes, love. I know you are. Let's get you home, and decide what's to be done about it.'

As they drove up to Keeley's house both Mary and Mel were dismayed to see several people standing out on the lawn, talking and gesturing with hearty animation. It was hardly the moment for social chit-chat, but they were trapped, already spotted. As Mary pulled in to park Keeley waved urgently, beckoning to her to join the party.

It actually looked like some kind of party; there was a bottle of champagne circulating and another one, already empty, lying on the grass. Puzzled, Mary led Mel to the edge of the group, which was focused around Tony and included Alain Jou, Serge Rolland and, to her surprise, Louis. Evidently the gathering had something to do with art.

Keeley kissed Mel as greetings were exchanged, and then looked hard at her, as if to say they would talk later, privately. Then she flung out her arm and gestured, triumphantly, at her brother.

'You'll never guess what Tony has done!'

'What?' Mary murmured, trying to sound interested.

'He's sold a painting for four hundred thousand francs! To a Japanese collector – he was browsing in Serge's gallery and went wild when he saw it. Since there was no price tag on it, Serge just talked the price up and up, he could see the

man was both keen and wealthy. And Mary, it's the picture
of *you*!'

She was astonished. That portrait she had sat for so casually,
just to humour Tony? Four hundred thousand – but that was
over forty thousand pounds!

Beaming, Tony looked up at her. 'You've brought me luck,
Miss Mary.'

'No,' Keeley interrupted firmly. 'It was luck that brought the
Japanese guy to Serge's gallery, but it was talent that painted
the picture. Tony, you're a genius!'

As Keeley stooped to kiss his cheek, Mary watched her
face fill with pride, and belatedly the significance of the sale
dawned on her. It wasn't the money, it was what it represented:
vindication, at last, of all the faith Vincent had invested in Tony,
from that very first day at the hospital. Mary remembered it
clearly, walking round the grounds with Cathal and baby Mel,
waiting for her friends to emerge – and Vincent's enthusiasm
when he did, talking all the way to the airport about Tony's
potential. Today, his farsighted faith was justified, and Keeley
was wildly elated. Delighted for her despite the distracting
question of Mel, Mary hugged her and then turned to Tony.

'Congratulations, Tony!'

Not at all bashful, he grinned. 'Definitely, a nude next time.'

Louis intervened at this, putting his arm around Mary so
possessively that everyone laughed. Everyone, except Mel. In
a flash Mary saw the bewilderment in her gaze, the mixture
of puzzlement and dawning horror. Desperately, she strove to
make her voice sound steady, make light of Louis.

'Mel, you remember Louis, don't you? He's a painter too.
Not as good as Tony, though, he has to make ends meet by
giving me a hand in the pub!'

But it was useless. As Louis continued to clutch Mary to
him his affection for her was all too obvious, and Mel's face
froze icily over.

'Yes, I remember him. Mum, Keeley, will you excuse me if
I leave you grown-ups to it? I have a lot of luggage to unpack
. . . am I in my usual room, Keeley?'

Torn, realising that Mel felt as wretched as she felt ecstatic,
Keeley nodded, and Mel stalked away without another word.
Somewhat affronted, Alain Jou gazed after her.

'These moody kids – I don't know how or why anyone puts
up with them.'

But Tony looked at him, sharply. 'Leave it, Alain. That kid has a lot on her plate at the minute. God, I'd rather be in me wheelchair any day.'

Mary sought Mel out as soon as she could, and found her lying on her bed in floods of tears.

'Mel – please – Louis is only a friend—'

Mel jerked upright, and threw the bolster at her. 'He is not! He's your *boy*friend! You're going to divorce Dad and marry him!'

Oh, sweet Christ. This, as well as everything else.

'I'm not going to marry him! Mel, I'm not going to marry anyone. Come on, calm down—'

'I want Dad! I want to talk to Dad!'

'Then you can talk to him, there's no problem, you can ring him whenever you like. But I don't think this is—'

At that exact moment the phone rang, and with sudden fright Mary realised that it very likely actually was Cathal, calling to make sure that Mel had arrived safe and sound from Ireland. Quaking, she went out into the corridor and lifted the phone.

It was Cathal, and his tone was glacial.

'Mary. How are you. I'm calling to speak to Imelda, check that she got there and you picked her up.'

His tone somehow conveyed that she might not have picked Mel up, that she was the kind of mother who'd forget. But now that he was on the phone, she realised with a sinking heart, she was going to have to tell him the state in which Mel had arrived, the state in which she'd been for four months.

'Yes. She's here. But she's upset – Cathal, I have some very bad news for you. Mel is – isn't well.'

'What? What's the matter with her? She was fine when I—'

'Cathal, she's pregnant.'

There was a silence so total, so lengthy it felt like a journey through time, through space.

'What did you say?'

'I said Mel is pregnant. Expecting a baby. She's been raped by some youth called Ronan.'

Another silence, again so comprehensive that Mary almost felt sorry for him. But it had happened while the girl was with him, in his care!

'Is this some sort of sick joke? Mary, don't talk nonsense. I
drove her to the airport only this very morning and she was
perfectly well.'

'Cathal, she was afraid to tell you. Afraid to tell anyone.'

As she said it, Mary could well understand Mel's fear; both
sets of grandparents would be outraged, the whole milieu
in which she lived was one where people would gossip,
disapprove, drop her down a peg on the social ladder. In
fact, that might even be Cathal's first reaction: to wonder
what this was going to do to his chances of election.

But to his eternal credit, it was not.

'Afraid to tell me? But I'm her father! Mary, I can't believe
– this can't be true—'

'I'm afraid it is true, and you'd better believe it. She's
expecting a baby in November, and I am out of my mind
with worry.'

She could almost hear him thinking, digesting it. When he
spoke again his voice was different, filling with fury.

'She was *raped*, you say? By someone called Ronan?'

'Yes.' As concisely as she could, she told him what facts she
knew, listening to his breathing getting faster and heavier by
the minute.

'Jesus Christ. Jesus Christ almighty. And now she's over
there with you. Well, I'm coming straight over to see her for
myself – but first and foremost I am going to find this Ronan
person and tear him limb from fucking limb. He'll never father
another child, whoever he is.'

With that, he slammed down the phone. Faint with relief that
it was over, that she had broken the news, Mary hung up with
mixed emotions. Cathal storming over to France would only
make things worse, disrupt the whole household just when it
needed calm; but amidst her misgivings she felt some comfort,
too. Cathal sounded as if he would indeed locate the baby's
father, take charge of everything in his inimitable way.

She still cordially loathed, detested the man. But there was
no doubt that he was a good father, when the chips were
down, and that Mel needed him.

Belatedly, she remembered Louis, still out in the garden with
Keeley and the others. Fighting down an urge to go to him,
to run into his arms for support and solace, she turned back
instead to Mel's room.

'Mel? That was your – your father on the phone. He's coming

over to see you. He's terribly upset. But don't worry. He's not angry – not with you.'

Sitting up, Mel rubbed her eyes and looked at her with a variety of quavering emotions.

'Good. I'm glad he's coming. I want him. But I don't want you or your – your boyfriend.'

Suddenly drained, unable to take any more trauma or mood swings, Mary simply nodded, and left her alone.

It was more than an hour before Serge and Alain left, and Keeley wheeled Tony back into the house, escorted by an uneasy-looking Louis. The moment he saw Mary he went to her, and held her in a hug.

'Sorry to take so long. But I thought it would be better – your daughter—'

Wearily, but gratefully, she hugged him back. 'Yes. You were a shock to her. I wish I'd known you were going to be here.'

Thoughtfully, Keeley parked Tony in his favourite position by the window, and turned to them.

'Well, she had to know sometime.'

'Yes. But not right now.'

'How is she?'

'She's completely confused. The doctor confirmed the pregnancy and wants her to have an abortion. She says she won't, that she wants to have the baby. Oh, and Cathal is coming over. He happened to ring, so I told him the whole story, and he freaked. Says he'll be here as soon as he finds and disembowels the father.'

'Well,' Keeley said curtly, 'he's not staying here. Not in my house.'

'No. I suppose he can find a hotel in Aix. But Keeley . . . maybe he could just see Mel here, visit her? I don't want them having to talk in some public place.'

Keeley grimaced. 'All right. I suppose we'll have to put up with that much.'

With his hand still on Mary's forearm, Louis looked at her quizzically.

'Do you want me to disappear?'

'No, Louis. I don't want that at all. But I think it might be better, for the moment. I'll try to get to the pub at some stage over the next few days and see you there – how is it, by the way? Is Luc managing?'

'Luc's having a ball. Cooking up a storm, having great fun with the customers, bossing everyone around.'

In spite of everything Mary smiled, a little anxiously: what if the customers got a taste for Luc's food, preferred it to hers?

'Is the place busy?'

'Crammed.'

Well, that was something, she supposed – but God, what an awful wrench, to be away from The Cracker just when it was starting out, when she was longing to launch herself heart and soul into it! Thankfully she remembered Keeley's words: 'it will still be here when all this is over.'

With a last hug, Louis put on his jacket and left them. As he went, Mary put her hand to his face.

'Thanks, Louis. You're being great about all this.'

He flushed, and looked very pleased with himself. If the wretched husband was going to materialise, he seemed to be thinking, he would be more than a match for him. But in another way, Mary thought that maybe his pride was dented.

'And – and about Tony's painting, don't worry. Your turn will come too.' He grunted a laugh, and headed away to his ancient Citroen. Then Tony spoke up. 'If you girls want to be alone to talk about Mel, just shove me into the pool or something. I don't mind.'

Keeley looked enquiringly at Mary. But Mary shook her head, and smiled at him. Somehow Tony was the kind of man you could include in intimate conversation, indeed he might well help matters with his wry perception. Sometimes he could be quite astute, or lighten things with a joke.

'Well, as I was saying, that's the situation. Mel really is due in November, Cathal's on his way, the father's to be found and shot, my pub is being run by other people and Mel has decided I'm going to marry Louis in the morning.'

Tony guffawed. 'Ha! And apart from that, Mrs Lincoln, how are you enjoying the evening?'

She had to laugh, and so did Keeley. But then Keeley sighed, and threw herself down on a chair. 'So Mel really wants to have this baby, huh?'

'Yes. There was quite a scene over it.'

'And what do you want?'

Mary felt so distracted, she hardly knew. 'Jesus, Keeley, I want her to be safe. That's what I want, above all. With my head, I want her to have a termination . . . but with my heart, I – I – I'm going to take her to an expert, and find out exactly what her chances are.'

'Yes. And the child's, of course.'

'Y – yes. Of course.' As she said it, she saw that Keeley was thinking the same thing that she was, thinking back to the day she had found herself in the position Mel was in now. Only older – but even then, how she had needed her mother, gone running home to Leesha!

Leesha. The memory of Leesha, of the conversation they'd had when she returned to Ireland, jogged something in Mary, clicked some scenario into place.

'But, Keeley, even if she does manage to have this child, if they both come through unscathed, what's to happen then? Who will look after it? She's only a schoolgirl, she can't – and what about her cooking, her future? She's keen, and I think she has talent . . . a baby would ruin her life!'

'Mm. It certainly put a crimp in yours, right enough.'

'Yes. She thinks I don't love her, because of that, says I never wanted her . . . we had an awful confrontation over that too.'

'Mary, the child is a mess. She doesn't know what she's saying.'

'No. I suppose she doesn't. I tried to make her see that I never would have had her in the first place, nor kept her afterwards, if I didn't want her. But Keeley, you remember the state I was in, the fix – I just couldn't see any way to manage, except by marrying Cathal. She doesn't even have that option, at fifteen.'

'No. She's going to need a lot of help, Mary.'

Keeley said it warily, eyeing her, waiting to see her response. But Mary leaned heavily back in her chair, seemed to sag under the weight of it all.

'I know. I know what you must be thinking, and she's probably thinking too. The same thing I thought, I hoped . . . that Mum would dash into the breach, take over, mind the child. But Keeley, I've only just got my pub, my life, my own future! I'm up to my ears!'

Yes. There was no denying that, and still she imagined that both Tony and Keeley were listening to her disapproving, thinking her as selfish as she must sound. She faced them both.

'Go on. Say it. I'm useless, self-centered, hopeless.'

It was Tony who answered.

'No, Mary. We understand. You had a miserable life from the moment you married Cathal Sullivan. But you did your best, for him and for Mel, you slogged and slaved for fifteen years. You can't go right back to where you started.'

'No! I can't! And yet she doesn't want to give the child up for adoption. I promised her I wouldn't make her – but what's the alternative?'

Unexpectedly Tony sucked his teeth, like a plumber peering into a nastily twisted pipe.

'There is an alternative. There always is, even if it costs a lot, isn't perfect. Look at the three of us. We all found one, escaped from where we didn't want to be. We were trapped, but we tunnelled our way out somehow.'

That was true, and they nodded in somewhat surprised agreement. Tony and Keeley had ducked out from under Christy, Mary had got away from Cathal, they had all overcome lack of education and just about every other advantage and – this very day, Tony had sold a painting for four hundred thousand francs, launched himself on the trajectory to the status Vincent had anticipated. Even if he was never going to be Cézanne, he was going to be respected, accepted – and he was befriended now too, despite his physical isolation. In his dogged way, even he had succeeded.

Suddenly, Keeley stood up. 'You know what I think we should do?'

We? With immense affection Mary smiled at her, good old Keeley, still sharing every crisis, diamond-bright, rock solid.

'No, Keel. What should we do?'

'We should let Céline look after Mel for tonight, and go out to dinner. A whacking bloody good dinner at the pub, cooked for us by Luc, with gallons of champagne to celebrate Tony's achievement.'

At first Mary thought it sounded like a diversionary tactic, Keeley's way of cheering her up. But then she saw the way Tony was looking at his sister, the exchange of glances between them, and wondered whether the two were cooking something up.

God, if only they could! She was so desperate, she was prepared to listen to anything, consider the wildest of ideas. Not only because she wanted to help Mel, but because otherwise Cathal would come rushing over in a fury, gather up the girl who adored him and whisk her back to Ireland, where the serried ranks of grandparents would take command and ensure that she, Mary, never saw Mel again. They would not countenance any abortion, but they would almost certainly have the baby adopted despite Mel's protests, and Mel would blame her for the rest of her life for having been unable to prevent them.

No. Somehow she had to marshal her wits, marshal them *now*. Keeley had recently sat an exam she was sure she had failed, Tony had no formal qualifications whatsoever to his name, but neither of them was lacking in common sense or native wit. Mary was desperate for any suggestion they would come up with.

Chapter Twenty

Wandering through the garden, Keeley felt the soft warmth of the sun, the noonday stillness, the serene protection of the massed flowers and trees. It was where she always went when she sought comfort, quiet, solace.

But today there was none to be found. Walking slowly, aimlessly, she paused here and there to inspect a bud, untangle a vine, smell the delicate tendrils of sweet pea.

A fool, she thought. I was a fool to sell my business. Everyone was right about doing nothing rash after Vincent died. But I felt I couldn't bear to go on, at the time. Even now, I know it would be agony, I'd miss him every time I turned round. Now, I miss the business instead. I miss the people, the structured routine, the satisfaction of working hard and earning enough to support the kind of life I want to live. Now, I have Tony, I have my studies, but they're not enough. Something is missing. Something more than Vincent.

I think Mary knows that. She senses it. Even when we lived in different countries, we could always sense how the other was feeling. That's why she was looking at me the way she was last night, in the pub. She felt I might offer, I might come up with the solution.

Fair enough. I can see where's she's coming from. The way she looks at it, I have the time, I have the money, I might even have the inclination. I never wanted children, but I deeply regret never having had Vincent's. I love Mel even though there are times when I can't stand her, she's my god-daughter and Vincent's, and he'd want me to help her. She killed him, but I know he'd still want me to.

And Tony. Tony has no hope of having children either. He would love to see a child around this house, he probably thinks it would be good for me, a purpose, an interest, somebody to love. He'd tease it and spoil it and enjoy every minute of it. That's why he kept looking at me too, last night, waiting for me to say something.

And Mel. Mel wasn't there, wasn't involved, but she's at the centre of this. She wants her baby, but she knows she can't raise it, can't give it a home or anything else, by herself. She won't have it adopted, by anyone she doesn't know, but she understands that someone is going to have to take care of it, if it arrives safely. I have absolutely no idea why she got pregnant, but I can't stop thinking that Tony might be right, that it had something to do with Vincent, with having destroyed my marriage and whatever family we might have had.

But a child! Over the years I've done a lot for the Sullivans, I've helped Mary again and again because she's my friend, and because for all her faults I love her, I love the life that she got me started on. I don't feel I owe her anything any more, and yet ... she can't take the child herself, not with her work, Louis, her new life and love. After fifteen years she's just starting to taste real freedom, build something of her own, get the things I already have myself. Her own mother couldn't help her, couldn't raise her child for her, and now she can't raise Mel's.

What would happen, if I offered? How would it affect my life, affect all of us? How much control would I even have, would Mary and Mel forever be interfering, expecting me to perform all the duties of motherhood yet still feeling that they owned the child?

We'd have to discuss all that. We'd have to get things clear. If I take the responsibility then I have to take charge too, be the one who calls the shots. But I really don't know whether I want to, whether I'm suited to it.

Vincent thought I was. 'Oh, you're a hard woman,' he said. 'You'll make a great mother.' He had far more faith in me than I ever had in myself. But on the other hand, Cathal Sullivan has none at all, and he has to be involved in this decision too. I don't want him to be, but unfortunately he's got to be. He's the baby's grandfather, maybe not biologically but to all intents and purposes. And he certainly would drive me round the bend, constantly calling, checking, meddling – if he could ever bring himself to let his grandchild be reared by me, the little Butler bitch he hates. But at the end of the day he'll have to do whatever Mary tells him to, because she's got those photographs, that power over him.

And then, there's the baby itself. What would it make of the situation, as it grew up? Would it ever love me, or I it? Is it a girl or a boy, I wonder? Not that it matters . . . no doubt it'll get into all the messes and scrapes every other Sullivan has got into – being troublesome is a family tradition. If I took it on, I'd have years of hassle, my life would change radically.

But my life has already changed radically. It hasn't really been a life at all since Vincent died, it's just been an existence. It lacks a point. That's the first thing Vincent would notice, if he came back today, if he saw me wandering around this garden like a nomad in the wilderness.

He'd tell me to do it. He'd say: come on Keeley, get moving, get a life. This is a big house and there's plenty of room, one child won't kill you, it'll be fun, you'll cope.

That's what Vincent would say, if he was here. God, I wish he was. How I wish he was.

But he isn't. All I have is Mary, Tony, even Gertie in Ireland, all looking to me, depending on me in their various ways, for help and money and support. And now there's someone else, or will be in November if Mel makes it. Another little dependant, squalling, reaching out . . .

I don't need it, I'm not at all sure that I want it. And I won't be pressured into it. They'll all be looking to me, all waiting, but they'll just have to wait. I nearly offered last night, but I'm glad now that I didn't. This decision cannot be rushed.

Mary had no idea how it had happened, but somehow it had. Somehow Louis had managed to distract her, seduce her from all thought of Mel and of the pub, and get her into bed. Only for an hour, but what an hour!

Lying beside him, coming down from the highest high, the greatest sex she'd ever known, she ran her finger along the length of his neck and shoulders, caressing him with a mixture of tenderness and, she slowly realised, something much deeper. In the midst of all her problems, it hardly seemed possible, but she was afraid that she might be falling in love with Louis Crouzat.

Not merely afraid. Terrified. Because not only had she no idea whether he would welcome such a strong attachment, or reciprocate it, she could not envisage how it might affect the new life she was attempting to forge. Sex was heaven, romance was a fabulous new delight, but love implied commitment. Ties, knots, bonds, everything that had held her down before.

What if she told him, and he said yes, wonderful, let's get married?

No! Every bone clenched in her, recoiled from that word. She'd been married, she hated marriage, she was never going back there again, to where you were trapped and cornered, owned and controlled by somebody else.

But she felt trapped and cornered anyway. Not by him, yet, but by this baby Mel was expecting, was determined to have. Although nobody had said it, she knew everyone was looking to her, expecting her to do the decent thing, and take it. Take the burden from Mel, for Mel, love the infant, raise it, be responsible for it on top of a new business and all the responsibility that went with that. And now Cathal was on his way as well, to berate and hector her, tighten the screws yet further. Soon her parents would phone, his would phone, maybe they'd all descend on her, shrieking, shouting, demanding. Do your duty, woman, do your damned duty!

Feeling hot and cold all at once, stifled under the duvet, she let her finger trail away from Louis, and he exhaled a little sigh, rolled over to take her in his arms, brush her lip with a kiss and a smile.

'Happy?'

His eyes told her that he was, and she hadn't the heart to say no. In any case it wasn't entirely true; under all the pressure some little space lay cleared, a space for him, space for the love she had never believed she would find.

But what a muddle! Lying naked in bed with her lover one day, about to become a grandmother the next. It was so confusing, so ludicrous that she let out a little cry, halfway between a laugh and a sob. Concerned, he put his hand on her shoulder.

'Are you, Mary? Are you happy?'

Soberly, she looked at him, wondering how he really felt about her, how deeply? He'd been married too, maybe he didn't want another bond any more than she did.

'I'll tell you what I am, Louis. I am a thirty-six year old woman, four years older than you, with a pregnant daughter who will shortly present my first grandchild. I'm heavily in debt, I have virtually no money, only a business that will consume my every waking moment for the next ten years minimum. All I have is a fuming husband on his way over here to cause trouble, a child who has already made up her mind to hate you, and a bunch of friends to whom I have never been anything but a worry and a pest. I am, in a nutshell, bad news.'

She was amazed when he started to laugh. Utterly amazed.

'Well! Don't tell me Granny is feeling blue, after sex I thought would put a smile on her face for a month?'

Granny. She winced. 'Don't call me that! I won't be one, I won't do it!'

Grinning, he embraced her, full of affection – and strength, too, his body a wonder to her in the midst of it all. He was no more like Cathal than a truffle resembled a tin of peas. He was delicious.

'Mary, you don't have to do it. You don't have to do anything you don't want to.'

Above all, what she didn't want to do was involve him in her worries, the chaotic muddle of her life. But it was so hard to smile, to pretend, to behave like some airy bimbo. Why wasn't he with a bimbo, what did he see in her? For a moment she was still, silent, wondering, and he held her gently, wondering in turn.

'Mary?'

'Yes?'

'Do you feel anything of what I am starting to feel?'

'I – I don't know, Louis. What are you feeling?' Here, she thought, it comes. He's getting fed up with me, feeling ennui, groping for some easy way to say it.

'I am feeling . . . falling . . . I think perhaps I am falling in love with you.'

As sharply as if he had punched her, she gasped, drew back from him,

'In love? With me? Oh, Louis – oh, no!'

Hurt, his Frenchman's pride possibly wounded as well, he blinked at her.

'Yes. Well. I know it's probably the last thing you want to hear, that you've got some impoverished painter on your plate as well as everything else, but I just thought I would tell you. I – I had to tell you.'

She struggled half-upright, out of his grasp, grabbing at words.

'Louis – no – I – it's not that! I love it that you're a painter, that you're doing what you want to do! I don't care that you're broke! You're kind, and caring, affectionate – you're gorgeous, you make me feel like a million dollars! In fact you make me feel much more than that, I – I think you're making me fall in love with you—'

Putting his finger to her lips, he hushed her.

'Stop. Stop right there. Don't say any more.'

'But—'

'No. You have said the only thing I want to hear.'

For a moment, she was silent as he asked, looking at him, into his eyes.

'But . . . oh, Louis. I can love you, I want to love you. What I don't want is any of the other things that go with love. I've told you this before, or tried to . . . I can't marry you. Even though divorce has come now in Ireland, and I'm going to get one if I can, I will never marry again.'

He wound his fingers through her hair, and smiled at her. 'But I haven't asked you to.'

Puzzled, taken somewhat aback, she furrowed her brow, quizzically.

'But when people fall in love, they usually . . .'

'No, Mary. Not me. I have no further interest in marriage, in mortgages or dinner parties or three-piece suites. The only thing I want is plain, simple love. A warm friendship, a deep relationship. And freedom. Freedom for us both to be ourselves, to pursue our separate interests, simply to be there for each other at the end of the day.'

'Oh . . . oh. Do you, Louis? Do you really mean that?'

'Yes. You're not the only one who has suffered, Mary. I once had a spouse too. Now, all I want is a partner.'

'And you . . . don't you want . . . children?'

Again, incredibly, he laughed.

'Not if they want to play with my paints! I'm serious about painting, Mary. When I'm at it, I forget everything, everyone else. It's quite a selfish thing. That's why I'm concerned about this grandchild of yours. Are you going to take it, do you think? Have you decided?'

Biting her lip, she gazed at the picture on the opposite wall, a big oil in murky colours, a stormy seascape.

'Yes. I have decided. Only you must promise not to tell anyone, not to breathe a word yet . . . I have to tell Mel, tell them all in my own time.'

'Of course I won't. But please tell me.'

'I – Louis, I'm not going to do it. I can't. I know there will be many times when I will regret that decision, and be blamed for it, but I simply cannot take on another child.'

'I see. And I cannot say I am sorry, Mary. I want you all to myself, I want you to have your pub and your freedom. But what will you tell Mel?'

Stretching, sighing, she took his hand, but continued to stare at the wall.

'That's the thing, Louis. I don't know. I just don't know. I love her, I'll probably love the baby when it comes – but love is a trap, and I'm afraid of its power.'

Softly, he put her hand on his chest, and his own to her face.

'Yes. I'm afraid of it too, Mary. But don't worry. It won't trap either of us, this time. Our love will not trap us.'

She should leave now, she thought. Leave because people were waiting for her, leave before either of them said anything to damage this fragile moment, this tender new shoot. Instead, she slid back down into the bed, snuggling close, burying her body and her mind in his embrace.

Cathal got out of the taxi, paid the driver, looked around him and stopped short. Giggling like schoolgirls, Mary and Keeley watched him stagger as if punched as the view hit him: the beautiful house, the pool, the flowers and tennis court. Then, frowning, he spotted them, and came marching across the grass.

'Mary. Keeley. Where is Imelda?'

Deliberately ignoring his brusqueness, Mary smiled vaguely.

'She's out. With friends. She'll be back in an hour or two.'

In fact, Mel was with Félix and Lise, despatched out of the way until the adult conversations were dealt with. Sociably, Keeley grinned up at him from her beechwood deckchair.

'Hiya, Cathal. Welcome to my humble abode.'

'Hmph.'

'Would you care for something to drink? A glass of wine perhaps?'

'Drinks. This is no time for drinks. I want to see my daughter.'

Mary raised her hand, waved it soothingly at him. 'You will see her, I said she'll be here soon.'

He flung himself down on a chair at the garden table, looking hot and incongruous in his grey woollen suit, his solidly knotted tie.

'Well, I must say, you've done it this time, the pair of you.'

Mary raised an eyebrow. 'Done what?'

'Done this! This is all your fault! Imelda is pregnant because you weren't there, her mother left her high and dry, trouble was only to be expected—'

Keeley sat up. 'Trouble was indeed to be expected, Cathal, after she stole my car. Some fool taught her to drive, or to think she could drive. And trouble certainly happened.'

That pulled him back slightly, the death there was no denying. Evading the subject, he changed it.

'I've found the boy.'

Mary was all ears. 'The boy who – who did it? The father?'

'Yes. Ronan Burke is his name. Sixteen years of age, a swaggering little shit – only he wasn't swaggering any more, after I arrived on his parents' doorstep.'

'How did you find him?'

'I made enquiries. There are only two Ronans who drink regularly in my pub, and it wasn't hard to find out which of them had been seen at that disco with my daughter.'

'And – and what happened?'

'I went round to the house, got the truth out of him in no time.'

'He admitted it?'

'He certainly did. Not at first, but after I made it clear that the truth would be less painful for him than lies.'

'And – and then what?'

'The parents went nuts, of course. I told them I'd be having him charged with rape. There was one hell of a hullabaloo.'

'A court case? Oh, God, will Mel have to testify?'

'No. That was the only thing holding me back. I don't want her up in court, going through that.'

'But then – what—?'

'They offered compensation, which I accepted. Hush money, I suppose you'd call it. But I thought it might be more use to Imelda than any apology or prison sentence or anything else. The boy's only sixteen, as I say, good for nothing.'

Mary was relieved. It sounded as if Cathal had taken the

right course, the only one that would leave Mel any better off. If Cathal gave her the money.

'How much did they give you?'

'Seven thousand pounds.'

'Did you bring it with you?'

'Of course I brought it with me! It's here in my pocket!'

Seven thousand. Not a lot, but it would cover medical expenses at any rate, buy a pram and some baby things. Mary glanced at Keeley, who nodded, approvingly. And stayed firmly put, as Mary had asked her to, not wanting to be alone with Cathal for one moment. She could see that her presence irked him, but it was her house.

'Well, that's something. It sounds as if you handled it well.'

'Hmph. I'd have castrated the little bastard if I'd had my way.'

'Did he express any interest in the baby?'

'Not a whit. In fact I took such a dislike to him I made him sign an agreement, in exchange for accepting the money, that he'd never come next nor near the child.'

Good. Mary had to admire Cathal's presence of mind. She wanted this wretched boy out of the way, off the scene entirely.

'I see. And what about your parents, my parents? Have you told them yet?'

He looked at his former wife as if she were singularly stupid.

'Well, naturally I've had to tell them, we have to decide what's to be done. I can hardly look after the child, and frankly you're not fit to. So that only leaves them. But they – they're in a bit of a heap at the moment, as you can surely imagine. They don't know what to say or do.'

'Did any of them volunteer to help? Leesha, or Carmel?'

'They – well no, they didn't. Not yet. But I'm sure they will. I told them I'd be bringing Imelda straight back with me, and we'd work it out then.'

Mary stared at him. 'Back with you? But Cathal, she – she's staying here!'

Coldly, he glared at her. 'Oh, no, she is not. Not with you two.'

'Yes! She is! She wants to be with me, with us . . . and besides, it will be much easier for her. She doesn't know anyone here, doesn't have to face all the gossip and the inquisitions. She'll simply spend the summer here in France as arranged and then stay on until the baby is born, until Christmas. She'll miss one term of school, that's all, you can say she was ill or something and she'll catch up when she goes back.'

'What do you mean, she wants to be with you? She wants to be with *me*!'

'Oh, Cathal . . . please, let's not debate that now. We'll talk to her together about it. But for her sake, I think France is the best place. I've already taken her to a doctor, and obstetrician, they're in charge of her case. It will be very hard, but the obstetrician thinks she might be all right, if she rests and is properly nourished, looked after.'

'Mary, don't be ridiculous. You couldn't look after a cat.'

'I looked after you for long enough. And her. Both of you.'

'Hmph.'

They glared at each other. Mary had to clutch the slatted underside of her chair to stop herself from blurting out what she thought: that sixteen-year olds were not legally permitted to drink in The Lantern, or in any pub. If Cathal had paid more attention to that, paid less to making money, their daughter never would have met this Ronan Burke. *Her* daughter never would have met him.

But she couldn't afford to say it, couldn't afford to antagonise Cathal when his role in things was so crucial now, to Mel and maybe even to the baby. He was in a position to help and support them, in a way he had never helped or supported his own wife, because his bond with Mel was so tight and a baby would mean so much to him. A Sullivan baby, of sorts, to replace their dead son – *his* son, as he probably saw it. Something told Mary that this grandchild would be of interest, of concern to him. She could not see things in the way she knew he saw them, but she could see his involvement already, his resolution. Not that he would go so far as to take the infant, rear it himself; his pub and his council meant he was far too busy for that. But he wanted the child within reach, within proprietary radius. He would never let it go to a stranger.

There was an impasse, in which Keeley watched both parents stiffen their shoulders, square up to each other. In spite of all their failings, it was clear that they both wanted Mel, wanted her health and happiness above all. They would fight not only for her, but for that.

For a little while she looked at them, but then her mind drifted away, returned to the question she was still asking herself. Should she do it? Should she say *she* would take on the whole project, take the baby into her home and heart?

Cathal would go berserk. It was only a very minor consideration, on the tally of reasons why she should say yes, she would. But nonetheless, it was a pleasing thought.

Sitting together that evening on one of Keeley's bleached linen sofas, Mel and Cathal looked at Mary, and from her armchair she looked back at them in silence. After more than two heated, emotionally-charged hours, the family gathering was falling apart, degenerating into useless hostilities and blank spaces; nobody knew what to do, but everyone knew what she, Mary, should do.

She should say she would take the baby. It was as simple as that. Take it, love it, rear it. Mel could see it regularly then, visit and be involved, keep her son or daughter in sight and reach, without the everyday responsibilities for which she was, undeniably, not able.

But Mary had not offered, and she could see that both Mel and Cathal were starting to get angry with her – very angry, in Cathal's case. His face was flushed and rigid, his gestures impatient, his posture designed to intimidate as he leaned heavily forward, his hands clasped like a fist in front of him.

'It's the only way,' he said again, for at least the tenth time. 'It's the only solution, Mary.'

'No,' she replied as calmly as she could, 'it isn't. It isn't the solution at all. I've already explained that to you. There is simply no point in attempting to do something I know I cannot do. You both know I want to help, will do everything in my power to help, but—'

Mel winced, made some whimpering noise. 'But Mum, you and Keeley, there are two of you, surely between you—'

Mary sighed, and reflected. Somehow she had thought that Keeley might, yet again, help her. She knew she was concerned, even worried, thinking about the situation and wondering what to do for her god-daughter. But she had said nothing. Nothing definite, nothing tangible at all. She hadn't wanted children with Vincent and evidently that hadn't changed; she did not want this new baby in her house, nor any part in its future. It was so unlike her to hold back that Mary was baffled, even a little bit hurt, after all the crises they had shared together.

But Keeley had her own problems. She could not be eternally expected to pitch into other people's, no matter how close the friendship; bringing up a child was a major undertaking – a project which, by her own admission, she did not think she would be any good at. She was being as supportive as possible, but she clearly did not want to get involved.

She's done enough, Mary thought to herself; she really has done enough for me over the years. I can't turn to her again. For the first time, I'm going to have to think and act independently, figure things out without her. I wish I could turn to her, but it's not fair, I can't. She's already given me a home and Tony a home, she knows there would be endless complications with Cathal if she gave this child a home as well. That's why she hasn't offered, she doesn't want him constantly coming here to visit his grandchild . . . and I can't blame her. I don't want him anywhere near me either.

But, dear Jesus, what am I going to do? I can't leave my daughter in this terrible fix much longer, we've got to decide something. She's already upset about Louis, she'll end up hating me if I don't do something to prove I care, prove I love her.

Maybe I should speak to Keeley. Should I? But then, if I did, she'd think I was asking her outright, she'd feel obliged to say yes. I would be pushing our friendship to its limits, and maybe it would suffer, we'd all suffer in the end, even the child. Besides, I couldn't live in her house and let her rear my own grandchild . . . and I don't want to live here for ever anyway; I want to get a place of my own, even just a tiny one where I can be alone sometimes with Louis. Or simply alone.

I'd never be alone, if I did what Mel and Cathal are asking me to do. My new life would be wrenched away from me overnight, I couldn't work late at the pub, Louis might come to resent the baby. I might well resent it myself, and then Mel – oh, God!

What is the answer? Who could possibly look after this child? Someone young and unencumbered, because it's really too much to expect its great-grandparents to, even if they were the kind of people I liked and trusted, which apart from Kevin they're not. But they're getting old, they wouldn't be able to do it even if they wanted to, or I wanted them to.

Who, then? Is there anyone would could possibly take the thing on, someone close enough that Mel would be happy, be able to see the baby and yet get on with her own life?

There is. My God, there is. If they'll only say yes, agree to do it, understand why I can't do it myself. *If.*

'Mary?'

'Yes, Cathal?'

'You're daydreaming! Wake up and pay attention to what I'm saying to you! You're not putting your mind to this at all, you—'

Slowly, she stood up and went to him. 'Yes, Cathal, I am putting my mind to it. And I think I may have found the answer, if you'll just bear with me for a little while longer. Will you stay here with Mel while I make a phone call?'

'To whom? Who are you calling?'

'Someone who may be able to help. But I won't tell you who it is until I find out whether they can or not, because I don't want anyone blaming them if they have to refuse.'

Mel's head jerked up. '*Who*, Mum? Tell me! It's my baby, I want to know what you're going to do!'

As reassuringly as she could, Mary smiled at her, touched her cheek.

'It's all right, Mel. I know you do. Just trust me, OK? I can't promise you that what I'm thinking will work, but it's worth a try. Well worth a try, if you'll wait here with Cathal while I see what I can do for you.'

As she picked up the phone Mary remembered it vividly, indelibly – the morning of her marriage, the sudden fear, the cup of tea brought to her by her small brother Sean, so carefully carried in his pudgy little fingers. Sean had been only seven that day, as he cuddled up to tell her how he didn't want her to go away; but now, he was a grown man of twenty four. A newly qualified architect, he lived with his girlfriend Ruth, whom he was planning to marry in August. Since leaving Ireland Mary had kept in touch with him, much comforted by his support after she left Cathal, the way he visited and watched over Mel. Mel was fond of him too, was to have been a bridesmaid at his wedding in the autumn. Now it was unlikely that Mel would attend the wedding at all, but Mary felt that Sean would understand the whole predicament. Unlike their more extroverted brother Steve, Sean was easy-going, kind and affectionate, a decent guy embarking on what she thought would be a stable, cheerful life. To thrust his niece's child on him was quite a test of his warmhearted nature, but it was worth asking him at least, even if he said no or Ruth felt it would be too much. Sean loved Ruth deeply, and would obviously want to discuss it with her at length.

He worked with a Dublin firm of architects and was designing a home which, he said, he and Ruth intended to fill with children. Of course, he meant his own children, but – he might just do it. If Ruth agreed, if the house was ready by November, if Ruth really was planning to work only part-time as she said she was – if, if, if.

It was a long shot. But it was the only possibility that Mary could see, her hand shaking as she flicked through the diary with his phone number in it. He would be at work now, but he always interrupted his work when she called him from France, even if it was only for a friendly chat. As she punched in the numbers she could see his freckled face, his broad smile . . . but dear God, would he still be smiling when he heard what she had to say this time?!

At the very least, he would give her a hearing. She was sure of that. Of her two brothers he was the one who most closely resembled Kevin, concerned for his family, keen to help whenever he could. Even if he felt he could not do the enormous thing she was about to ask him, he would listen, without fuss, without accusation. He would be worried about Mel, try to think of other ideas if he could not accept the proposal himself. But as she listened to the phone begin to ring in Dublin, Mary prayed that he could and would accept it. He was her only hope, because Steve lived the erratic life of a bachelor and a pilot, did not have the same temperament at all. And there was nobody else; Cathal's family were an option she would not even contemplate.

At length, the phone was answered and she heard his voice.

'Mary! How are you, big sister?'

She sat down on the chair by the phone, and drew a deep breath.

'I'm in a mess, Sean. I'm in a truly terrible mess.'

*   *   *

It took nearly a week, finally, before it was all sorted out. Mary's nerves were shredded by the end of it, but it was worth it to see the huge smile on Mel's face when she told her that yes, uncle Sean was going to take her baby for her, and look after it with his soon-to-be-wife, Ruth.

'Oh, Mum! Thank you! Thank you!'

Weeping with relief, Mel flung herself at her mother and hugged her to her, and Mary held her with many conflicting emotions in her heart. Now that the infant was going to live in Ireland, she would be the outsider, the visitor, the one who had to fly back and forth to see it. She would not see the child's daily development, not be involved at close quarters – but she *would* still be involved, she promised Mel, she would drive them all crazy with her perpetual queries and silly presents and advice that everyone would laugh at. From France, she would do everything she could, and come over for every birthday, every milestone event. It was a compromise, but it was the best she could do.

'It's great! The baby will have a lovely home and I'll be able to see it every day, Sean says it'll have a brother or sister in a year or two, Dad's going to give him the money from Ronan to do up a nursery . . .'

Mel was wildly elated, and as she looked at her Mary thought that she had done something crucial: she had given Mel the incentive to get through this pregnancy, give birth safely and somehow survive the whole traumatic ordeal. It would not be easy for her, and she would be a very different person at the end of it, but now, with her glowing face and sparkling eyes, she looked as if she could do it.

Over the girl's shoulder, she caught sight of Cathal, and looked at him enquiringly. He was returning to Ireland tomorrow, so if he had any last-minute questions or quibbles, now was the time for him to air them. But even Cathal was looking satisfied.

'Not perfect, of course, but I suppose – hmph – since you won't do it yourself—'

No. She would never again do anything to tie herself to anyone or anything. She would not be a full-time grandmother, she would not marry Louis, she would not have any more children. She would do her best by the family she already had, but after that she would be her own woman. Was her own woman, at last.

Suddenly, she was longing to get back to the pub. Her mind

was back on it, her heart was back in it. Cathal would leave soon, but Mel would stay with her until the baby was born, and not return to Ireland until after Christmas. Then she would try to catch up the schoolwork she had missed, and take the first exam that would eventually lead her, she hoped, to the catering college at Cathal Brugha Street.

Meanwhile, she would be free to visit in the summers, to work in her mother's pub and get cooking experience, secure in the knowledge that her child was safe and well. Mary felt the deepest gratitude to Sean for what he had agreed to do, and to Ruth; if she had severed her links with home in one way, she had tightened them in another. Sean and Ruth would come often to France now, with the baby, for the holidays she could give them when she had a place of her own.

Mel disengaged herself, and looked at her.

'D'you think . . . is it all right to tell Keeley now?'

Mary had not wanted to tell Keeley about Sean until she was sure the plan could be brought to fruition, everything was agreed and finalised. But it was not Keeley herself who had decided her to hold off; it was Tony. Somehow she sensed something in Tony, some unspoken yearning that told her she had been right that first night: Tony would have liked Keeley to be the one to take the child. Would have very much liked her to, Mary thought.

But it was not to be. And although she felt sorry for Tony, if he had been cheated of something that might have meant much to him, she was nonetheless certain that what she had done was for the best. Sean was a blood relative, for one thing, and moreover she had succeeded in doing something, for the first time in her life, without having to depend on Keeley for help. She loved her friend dearly, but the sense of independence that this decision had brought was invigorating, exhilarating. In the midst of a terrible crisis she had stood firm, delved into her own resources and found a way. Now, she thought that she would never again lie down and want to die, never again despair or give up on anything.

'Yes, Mel. We'll tell Keeley tomorrow, after your father leaves and things settle down.'

Mary couldn't wait for Cathal to leave. But Mel looked at her curiously.

'I never knew you to keep a secret from Keeley before, Ma. Why didn't you want to tell her about Sean?'

It had been very hard not to tell her, not to let anything slip while negotiations were in progress, and Mary knew that Keeley was wondering. But she'd said nothing, left the family alone to work things out as best they could for themselves. Now, Mary felt the tension of having worked them out, and thought what a relief it would be to talk to Keeley, tell her what she had achieved without looking for help.

'I didn't want to put her under pressure, Mel. I didn't want her to feel she had to offer to do anything she didn't want to, if Sean didn't agree . . . it wouldn't have been fair to burden her with our family problems.'

As she looked at her daughter Mary searched her face, wondering the same thing she had wondered every day since first hearing of her pregnancy. Had Mel done it in some kind of misguided attempt to make things up to Keeley, compensate for what she had stolen? Or had she done it in an effort to lure her mother home, even force her home?

Perhaps. But the reality of the baby had been such a shock that now she seemed deeply relieved that some realistic solution had been found, any workable way at all. The next few years were not going to be any picnic, but hopefully everyone would get through them intact, and newer and stronger relationships would evolve. Maybe even some kind of truce with Cathal, in time, now that he had been forced to accept that their marriage was over.

I'm never going back to you, she thought as she looked at him across the room. Even now, you haven't asked to see my pub, asked about anything, taken the slightest interest in me beyond what I could do for you. But my pub exists, Louis exists, and I exist. I've got a life, and you no longer have a slave.

But Cathal was oblivious of her as he hovered close to Mel, and already Mel's attention had returned to him. Grudgingly, Mary had to admit that he had behaved well on this occasion, apart from his recriminations about it all being her fault. Was it her fault? Maybe some of it was. But she wasn't perfect, couldn't get everything perfect, as Keeley had been telling her for years. It was time to accept that. At least Mel still had two parents who loved her, even if they didn't love each other. As she grew up and matured, Mel might come to see that, compared to many teenagers, she was way ahead on all the counts that mattered.

*   *   *

It was early morning, the day following Cathal's return to Ireland after a loudly lamented parting from Mel and even louder warnings about keeping 'a close eye' on developments. As she went out onto the terrace with a cup of coffee in hand Mary felt the weight of him lifting from her shoulders, and paused to stand a moment in the rising sunshine.

Mel will be clingy now, she thought, but I won't take her to the pub with me today, it'll be too hot and tiring for her. She can hang out here with Tony and Keeley, cook lunch for them, that won't exhaust her. But I can't go anywhere until I talk to Keeley – God, I'm dying to talk to her, properly, without that damn man listening in on every word! Where is she? We have so much to catch up on . . . I never knew her to leave me to get on with things like this before, without even throwing in her tuppenceworth.

Sitting down with her coffee by the pool, she sipped it quietly for a few minutes, thinking about work, about Luc and Louis as well as Keeley, until eventually she heard the dogs barking. Good. Keeley must be up and somewhere about.

'Hiya, Mary!'

Turning, she saw her emerging from the house with a spring in her step, dressed but not yet made up, looking suddenly very young for her years. Small as she was, with her urchin haircut, there were times when Keeley still had an almost childlike aura about her, something both eager and vulnerable. Filling with affection for her, Mary smiled.

'Hi, Keel. Bring your coffee over here and sit down beside me.'

Obediently, Keeley came, looking refreshed after what had apparently been a good night's sleep. There was something strong about her this morning, Mary thought, something revived as if, for the first time, she was not starting her day with aching thoughts of Vincent.

'You look well.'

Keeley smiled, and nodded. 'Uh huh. I feel well. I've come to a decision about something I'd been pondering for quite a while.'

'Have you? What?'

'Oh, I'll tell you in a minute. But first I want you to tell me all your news . . . even though we're living in the same house, I feel as if I haven't seen you for ages.'

'Mm. Me too. I felt so inhibited when Cathal was here, I couldn't really talk freely – besides, everything was focused on Mel. We had an awful lot of talking to do, I didn't want to bore you with a blow-by-blow account of it all.'

'I know – and I didn't want to ask, in case Cathal accused me of snooping or interfering. I thought it was better to just let you get on with it.'

'Well, we did get on with it. And we made progress.'

'Did you? What kind of progress? Mary, I hope he didn't talk you into doing anything you don't want to do – or Mel into having an abortion because that doctor said she should?'

Keeley looked alarmed, and Mary hastened to reassure her.

'Oh, no. He didn't get me to do anything. Or Mel, either. In fact I think he's secretly a bit chuffed about this baby . . . he'll be able to show it off to everyone when they get over the shock of Mel being such a young mum, it'll probably suit him fine to be seen as a doting grand-dad when he gets over the shock himself, at barely forty!'

'Well, I'm not interested in what suits him. I want you to suit yourself, and do whatever is best for Mel.'

'Yes.' Suddenly, Mary felt a surge of elation. 'Keeley, I think I have. I actually have.'

'You have what?'

'Done what's best for both Mel and for me.'

Looking rather taken aback, Keeley frowned. 'But, Mary, I thought you were only discussing the various possibilities – I didn't realise you were actually doing anything, so soon – it's going to take a while to decide what's the best thing for this baby and its mother, you mustn't rush it.'

'No, well, but – Keeley, Mel and Cathal were both looking to me to do something. Looking to me to offer to take the child and raise it myself, in fact, which is something I did not feel able to offer.'

'No. I didn't think you could, not with your work and Louis and so much on your plate. That's what I've been thinking about, all the time you were talking with them. Thinking that you've got a new life and you mustn't let go of it, you have to hang onto it if there's any possible way—'

'There is a way. I've found one.'

'You – you what? But Mary, how can you have, so soon? Without – without a word to me?'

Surprised by her anxiety, Mary put down her cup and tried to explain why she had not consulted her.

'Keeley, I'm sorry, of course I was going to talk to you about it. I just didn't want to have to ask you for help, if there was any way out of asking. You've done so much for me, not just this summer but for years and years, but now – now it's time I stood on my own two feet and ran my own life. It's time I took less from you and started giving more.'

'Oh, Mary! You have given – given me so much. You gave me a start in life, which is the greatest thing anyone ever could have. You took me to France with you and I—'

'You did everything since! Every little thing, for me when I was in trouble. I wouldn't be here today, if it wasn't for you.'

'Well, snap!'

They both laughed, then, the frown fading from Keeley's face. And then Mary pressed on with her news, dying to divulge it.

'Keeley, I rang Sean. My brother, you know, he's engaged to Ruth. They're getting married in the autumn. I rang him and told him all about Mel, the whole thing, how I didn't want – *couldn't* become a grandmother, in any practical sense. About how Mel wanted to have the baby and not let it be adopted – so, to cut a long story short, Sean said he was willing to help out. He and Ruth are going to take the child, and Mel will have full access to it.'

Beaming, she paused, waiting for Keeley's delighted response. What an ideal solution, and she had worked it out all by herself, hadn't needed to come begging for anything this time!

But Keeley sat immobile, her cup in her hand, her whole body frozen.

'You asked Sean – and he – you never—'

Puzzled, Mary gazed at her. 'I never what?'

'You never asked *me*!'

'You? To take Mel's baby? Keeley, I couldn't possibly do such a thing! It's a huge responsibility! And it's mine, not yours!'

'But Mel is my god-daughter, I'm responsible too – Mary, how could you do this? How can you have done this to me?'

Throwing down her cup, clenching her fists furiously, Keeley looked as if she was going to burst into tears. Bewildered, Mary struggled for words.

'Keeley, what have I done to you?'

'You've given away Mel's child! The child *I* was going to take!'

'You – you were going to? Oh, my God, Keeley, surely you weren't?'

'Yes, I was! I just didn't offer immediately, that's all, because I needed time to think, to be sure – but I've made up my mind, and now I am sure! Vincent always wanted a child in this house, now Tony wants one too, and – and I want one myself! I have virtually no family, I have the time and the means – I had it all worked out, all planned, I only finally decided it last night!'

Strangled, Keeley stopped with a gasp, looking anguished. Horrified, Mary stared at her, overwhelmed as much by her generosity as much as by the tortured expression on her face.

'You – you would have done this, for me, for Mel?'

'Yes! I would! My studies leave me plenty of time at home, and it's your home too even if you're not here very often, we'd have managed—'

Almost in slow motion, Mary sat back and considered, saying nothing until she composed and controlled the things that flooded her mind. It took some time, but it was too important to be rushed even by the tears that threatened in Keeley's dangerously dark eyes.

Finally, she reached forward and took her hand. 'Keeley. I can't tell you how much I appreciate this. It's wonderful of you beyond belief. But Keel . . . first and foremost, Mel will see her child far more often in Dublin than she could in France, during these first fraught years. By the time she comes to live here, if she does, the child will be established and things will have calmed down, worked out.

'And – and for another thing – Keeley, I won't always be here. I can't go on sharing your house, accepting your hospitality indefinitely.'

Aghast, Keeley gazed at her. 'W – what?'

'Keeley, look. Let's try to be reasonable about this, and work it out together. I love living here, but I – I need some independence.'

No answer. Reluctantly, but firmly, Mary forced herself to go on.

'And you need your independence too. Maybe not at the moment – it's good for you to have me and Tony, even Mel, to distract you – but some day you're going to look at me and my daughter and say, God, will they never go? Obviously, Tony is different, he's your blood relative and a long-term commitment, but I – Keel, I'm going to look for a place of my own. Somewhere small, near you, I'll still come to stay for weekends and we'll see each other all the time . . . but I have to establish myself, set up my own adult life, the same way you set yours up years ago. Keel, do you understand that?'

Blankly, Keeley looked at her, saying nothing. Feeling as if she were somehow wresting something away from her, some precious lifeline, Mary met her eyes.

'Keeley, there is nothing I'd have loved more than for you to do this tremendous thing, to take my grandchild, if I thought it was right for you, for all of us. But – but Keel, do you think it was the baby you really wanted?'

Keeley looked stunned. 'I've just told you I wanted it!'

'I know. But was it that particular baby, Keel? Or was it *a* baby, of some kind?'

'*A* baby – Mary, what do you mean?'

'I mean that I'm wondering whether the time hasn't come for you to get your teeth into some new project, some lifelong interest that will engross and challenge you the way your salons did. I know you have your studies, for now, but what will you do with your degree when you get it? What about maybe meeting some new man, some day? Keeley, please don't misunderstand, but I think it's time for you to stop visiting the cemetery every day. Your love of Vincent will only hold you back, which is the last thing he'd want.'

'I'll always visit his grave! I'll always love him!'

'Yes. I know you will. I just mean that – that maybe you'll eventually love someone else as well, if you give yourself the chance. Keeley, you're too young to stop loving, to stop working, to cut yourself off from the chance of having a child of your own if that's what you want. I know it's scarcely a year since Vincent died, you're still raw and grieving and hurting . . . but you have a lot of life ahead of you, a very long life I hope, you could make so much of it and I don't want to get in your way when you're doing that. I want to help you, which is why I'm taking myself and my family off your hands at long last. Not out of your life, but off your hands.'

Looking close to tears, Keeley struggled to master herself, and Mary waited, letting her words sink in.

'I know, Keel. I know it's hard, and it takes time. But if

I'm to help you rebuild the life my daughter stole from you, I
have to say what you need to hear. And if Mel was trying to
compensate you in some way by getting pregnant, she went the
wrong way about it, she's too young to understand that what
you need is your own life, your own child, not hers. I've got
a new one and I want you to have one too, when you're ready
for it. The timing and the decision have to be yours. But Keeley
– Vincent died, not you. You are still very much alive.'

Slowly, almost wonderingly, Keeley nodded. 'Yes. I am,
aren't I? I felt as if I'd died when he did. But I didn't.'

'No. And now it's my turn to get you on your feet, up and
running again. Have you any idea what direction you want
to take?'

'No, Mary. Not yet. All I know is that I want to break free
of the misery somehow, find some purpose, someone to share
my home and my life.'

'Then that's what we're going to set about doing. To start
with, I'd like you to get to know Louis . . . not just for my sake
or for his, but because he has so many friends. They're young,
interesting, energetic guys, so even if you never marry again
you could have some kind of relationship, have fun, maybe a
child some day – a little boy, called Vincent!'

'Oh, Mary. That sounds so distant, so unlikely . . .'

'Maybe it is. But who knows? It's a possibility! And that's
what I want for you – the chances, the openings you gave me.
I'll give you all the support and help I can – dammit, I'll be the
godmother this time, bake you a cake the height of the Empire
State Building!'

And then, finally, she heard what she wanted to hear: Keeley
laughing.

'Oh, Mary! I'd have thought you, above all people, would
know that men aren't the answer to everything.'

'You can say that again. They're a nightmare, a disaster, a
joke, and that's why I'll never be calling upon your services
as bridesmaid again. But Keel, as you once said yourself, there
are some good ones too . . . you could have warmth at least,
a companion to share things with. When you get your degree
you could do so many things – start a new career, meet an art
dealer or lecturer or maybe a gardener, someone who shares
your interests.'

'But I have Tony to—'

'Yes. You have Tony. And look at him, look at how far he's

got, because he took the initiative, was open to it. That's all I'm asking, Keeley – that you be open to the future, to whatever chances come your way. That's not too much to ask, is it?'

Keeley sat up, and gazed deep into the garden, into the masses of vivid summer foliage.

'No, Mary. It's not.'

'There you are. See, I'm getting less demanding already.'

'Of me, maybe! I'm sure you'll soon have Louis worn out instead.'

'No, Keeley. I won't, because the one thing I've learned is that everyone has to make their own happiness. Other people can help you do it, but they can't do it for you. All they can do is share it. I want you to share mine, and find some of your own to share in turn.'

The sun was getting warmer, rising higher and brighter in the azure sky, twinkling in tiny points on the water of the pool. As if stretching awake after a long sleep, Keeley uncurled and stood up, reached out to finger a creamy yellow rose.

'They do bloom, finally, don't they? In winter they die, vanish completely, in spring they're plagued with pests and disease, you think they'll never make it . . . but they do make it. I often wonder how.'

'Willpower, Keeley. Your willpower, and your care. You nourish them, and they survive.'

'Yes. They survive, get stronger every year . . . I love this garden so much, Mary. I always wanted it, couldn't believe it when I got it. But I did, and I remember the day we planted these roses, they were so small and fragile. Now, look at them.'

'Yes. Look at them, Keeley. Will you do that today, while I'm working at the pub? Just look at them, and think about them?'

Keeley hesitated a moment before inclining her head to inhale the flower's lovely scent, and nodded.

'I will. I'll keep one eye on your daughter for you and the other on my roses. Will you be home for lunch?'

'No. But I'll be home for dinner. Tell that young one of mine it had better be good.'

Keeley straightened up, and snapped a mock salute.

'Very good, madam. I'll see to it. We'll all eat together – you, me, Mel and Tony. Even Louis, if you'd like to bring him with you. There will be roses on the table, and we will eat out here, in the garden.'

Getting up, Mary smiled, and put her arm around her friend.

'That sounds wonderful. That sounds like it might be the best meal any of us has ever tasted yet.'

Thoughtfully, Keeley considered. And then she grinned. 'It will be. Even if you're not cooking it yourself.'

'Keeley Butler,' Mary replied, 'that is where you are entirely wrong. We might not have all the ingredients yet, but it will be done according to my recipe. I've tested it, and I can tell you for a fact that it works.'